ROAR OF THE REALM

ROAR OF THE REALM BOOK ONE
MEAGHAN RAUSCHER

For Oma,
give Jesus a hug for me.

BOOKS BY MEAGHAN RAUSCHER

Droplets

Ripples

Torrents

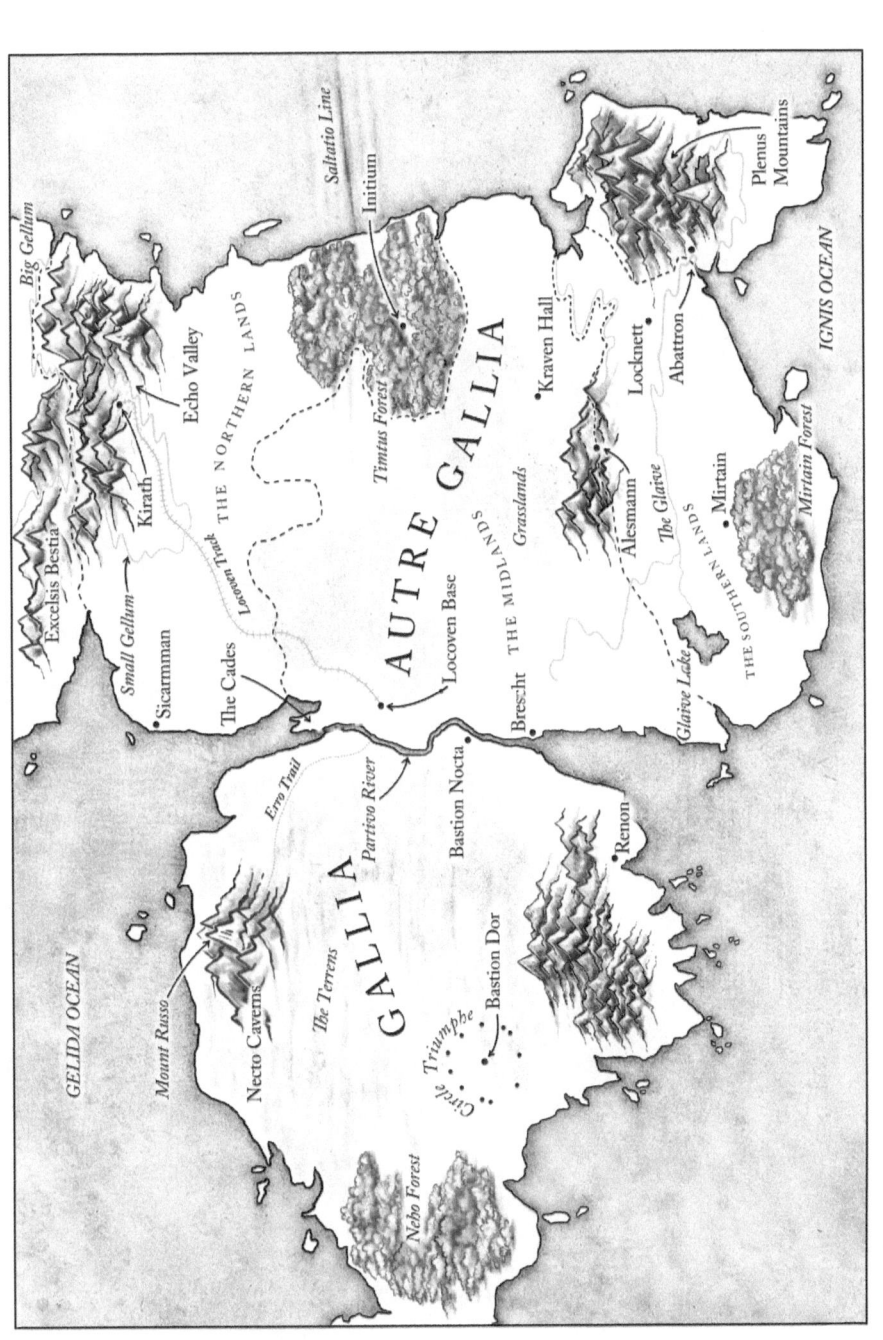

PROLOGUE I

Initium

I was born by fire, and unto fire, I shall return.

The words he had repeated all night sprung forth as death stalked his pounding footsteps. The light of both moons was secreted behind the clouds hiding him in the smoke-filled pitch of darkness. The swift padding of heavy paws tracked his every move across the silent grounds.

Scaling through a window, he landed in a rolling crouch and straightened just in time to see the shadow of the *panthier* leap upon the windowsill. The gleam of golden eyes lit the darkened shadow of the enormous cat's body.

It was nearly time.

He fingered the hilt of the sword across his back, knowing it would still shine red when pulled from its scabbard. A dark pink tongue licked the upper jaw of the *panthier*, its tail snapping back and forth nearly invisible in the smoke shrouding them. It was silent for now, but they were coming. Release was coming.

Spinning, he ran down the hall. He was a shadow, shifting across the stone floors and through wooden doorways. It wouldn't be long before everything was overrun.

He edged around a corner, his destination in sight. The *panthier* surged toward him, taking her place at his side, her favorite spot. Her head almost reached his shoulder and she walked on powerful legs. Legs strong enough to carry him across the realm when necessary. But that had been before they were overrun by legions.

She pressed up against his side, her head almost reaching his shoulder. He resisted the urge to scratch behind her ears. It would only make things worse.

Shuddering to a halt, just before the doorway, he braced himself for what he would meet inside. A cold nose nudged against his arm, touching his skin where his shirt had been torn. Her tongue flicked out, licking the wound clean. He flinched—it was one of the many wounds he carried.

By the Espiritu, he would make it through. He would fight long enough for hope to remain.

Beside him, the *panthier's* ears suddenly pricked and she whipped her head in the direction they had come. It wasn't long before he heard their approach.

They shot through the shadows like lightning, gold cracking across a dark sky, moving faster than he could ever hope to. A pale-faced young woman, her golden hair plaited and her mouth set in a grim line, ran toward him, a *cheeterah* by her side. The bounding cat's head hardly moved as she kept pace with her warrior, her legs gliding in rhythmic elegance.

He caught the girl's eye as they slowed to a walk—a weak smile lifted the corner of her too-pale lips. His chest tightened.

It's nearly time.

The *panthier* shouldered him again, knowing where his thoughts had turned. Unconsciously, he scratched her behind the ears and her head rolled to the side.

"They're almost here," the warrior said, her voice a little breathless. He nodded, he had seen them when he left the barracks. They had come for the others, but there was nothing left.

The *panthier* shifted, turning back to the still closed doors. She was more ready for what was to come. He swallowed heavily, fighting the knot in his throat.

"How much longer?" he asked, already knowing the answer. The night had been full of horrors, but the worst was still to come. He turned around to face the room again, the sight of it making the muscles in his stomach tighten with unrepressed regret.

The woman's small frame sidled up to him, her cream skin seeming to glow. She was in every way his opposite and when her pale, warm fingers interlaced with his own, he found himself staring at the mixed colors.

"Together?" she whispered and he could only nod, his eyes fixated on the stray wisps of hair which had fallen from her braids. They created a halo around her head. It was only fitting she would look this way when death was near. Her inner spirit fighting off the dark.

With her *cheeterah* on her right and his *panthier* on his left, they entered the wooden chamber. A roaring fire scorched his eyes, the flames stretching nearly to the roof, the smoke streaming through the once domed glass, now shattered and broken. It had, at one time, been beautiful.

Shuffling feet passed them, the brute shape of a *simian* walking on hind legs, one furry, black arm filled with books and scrolls, the other helping him walk. A few of the ancient texts dropped to the ground and he used his hand-shaped feet to chuck them into the fire along with the rest. The shelves all around them were nearly empty, the gleam of the fire all the brighter on the dust-covered wood.

The silhouette of a hunched-over man passed through the smoke. A silver beard graced his cheeks with simple dignity, his robes billowing in the air from the swirling breeze, revealing a glimpse of the two daggers hanging around his husky middle.

"Is it done?" The instructor's voice betrayed no emotion.

"Yes," he said, swallowing around the bile in his throat. He didn't want to remember the blood or the eyes of those who had fought back.

There had been a moment as he swung his sword off his back that he had almost relented, but as he summoned the Espiritu he watched the fear grow in their eyes. They cried out, their souls ready to defend, but they were no longer able to take up the power of the light. Darkness reigned.

His soul had cried out as he plunged through the barracks, each slice of his sword bringing down those he knew. The darkness had led them astray, they no longer believed.

What the rest of the realm thought was magic, was a power unlike any other. And it had been sold by those he called his brothers and sisters. They had trained with him, laughed with him, helped him, and in the end, they forgot the true Espiritu. They gave it up for the price of greed, wanting to conquer Gallia. They forgot to protect that which they had sworn to die for.

Turning to darkness, they were welcomed by demons like old friends. The Animle were no more. Where they once protected and saved they now stalked and destroyed. Only three Animle remained, and not for long.

Before him, his instructor nodded, and when he turned away his shoulders seemed to hunch as he stared into the gleaming flames. The *simian* threw another load of books onto the licking orange tongues, and the fire roared. From up above, another chunk of glass broke free and shattered to the floor near their feet.

"How did it come to this?" the old man mumbled to himself and shook his head as though in disbelief. He didn't need an answer, they all knew how it had begun.

And they knew how it would end.

"I remember when I first saw this room," the instructor's voice, always so strong, broke. He puffed out his thick chest, the girth of his belly enhanced by the belt tied around his waist. "I was only a lad then." The old man waved a hand as though to dispel the thought and watched his *simian* crawl along the top shelves, the long arms stretching to lengths a man could never hope to reach.

The creature was bred for battle and protection. He had seen those powerful arms throw a Nexen across a battlefield. Those men who had turned to the darkness of demons and called upon the powers of Nex were no match for the power of the Espiritu. He'd heard the roar of the *simian*, and seen those heavy fists beat the broad chest, terrifying any who dared to cross him.

The creature now carried the final load to the flames. Turning back to his owner, the *simian* listened to a silent command, nodded, his hands empty as all in the room looked to the shelves. Nothing but blank expanse met their eyes.

The instructor turned to them once more and dabbed at the sweat along his brow, his fingers trembling. "You left none alive? Everyone was accounted for?"

They both nodded. The traitors could no longer betray the Animle. It was true, the demons had turned them to Nexen—the darkness had won a battle but not the war. The light would go out for some time, but it would return, and when it did it would blaze all the brighter. Rolin had promised him.

"Oh, how did it come to this?" Their instructor shook his head again and the *simian* stepped closer as though sensing the old man's need for his presence. The silverback placed a heavy hand on the man's shoulder, if his frame hadn't been hardened by years of grueling training, it would have made him collapse.

"They'll be here soon," the young Animle warrior beside him spoke with calm assurance. The *cheeterah* paced the room and promptly sat before her owner in diligent patience, a smiling pant making her bloodied-lips twitch.

"Then we shall finish what we started." The instructor moved beside the flames until he was facing the *simian*.

The creature's head dipped, the large empty palms falling to the floor. Each finger was longer than his master's hand. How many Nexen had faced their deaths in the grips of his strong grasp? He was a legend in battle, a beast who had kept the realm safe for years, only to watch what he had fought so hard for come to ruin.

The creature let out a sigh of the soul—a deep yearning.

The instructor pulled a dagger from the scabbard about his waist, the blade shaking in his grasp. The simian breathed before him, waiting, his chest ready to receive the steel.

The flames crackled and the old man's hand lowered, "I can't." He rasped and turned to them, the shame filling him. "I can't do it."

Tears filled the warrior's eyes and he almost went to him. He had taken so many lives tonight, he could do this—it was part of the plan. A dark hand reached toward the old man, the simian's large fingers pulling another blade from its scabbard. It looked like a toy in the hands of so large a creature. The instructor and the simian shared a look, man communicating with beast—a deep growl rumbled through the ancient chest.

The young woman's hand was slick beneath his own, he squeezed her fingers wishing he could do more. Wishing they had one more moment together.

"You were to save this realm," their instructor turned to them, his eyes pooled with sacred tears, "to fulfill the prophecy of *unum ad mortem*." He waved a hand in the air as though to dispel the thought. "I wanted you both to know." They nodded, he had told them before.

The older man turned back to the *simian*. "Forgive me, I cannot kill them with my own hand." The warrior knew of those he spoke. There were Nexen who used to be called Animle, students of this dying man before him. The warrior looked away.

A storm was raging across Anglas, Gallian forces rising and conquering all in its wake. From their lands, the Nexen had risen, and one by one they had captured, tortured, and killed those Animle who would not turn. Those who had were stripped of their creatures and given a wolf instead.

The warrior shook his head, trying to block out the howls he heard in the distance. It wouldn't be long now.

The instructor placed his hand on the neck of his *simian*, bending forward until their foreheads touched. The large skull of the creature trumped the old man's and as they looked into each other's eyes an unspoken bond passed between them. They never looked away from one another when at the same moment they drove the blades of the daggers into the other's chest.

The instructor's knuckles whitened and his head fell into the chest of the *simian*, his blood blossoming across his breast. The creature scooped the man into his arms and cradled him like a mother holding her child. But with a final breath, he too fell to the ground before the roaring flames.

"It's over," the young woman, he had come to know so well, said. He couldn't help and wonder if she could feel the sweat sliding between their fingers. He wanted to look down, but he was afraid to see the blood still clinging to his skin—blood that wasn't his own.

The smoke stung his eyes as he nodded and tried to speak around the lump in his throat. He never could have imagined this was how it would all end. He had come here before the uprisings tore the land apart. Before what had once been a trusted and revered practice had been cast into the dust and dirt of disgust by all who lived.

He cleared his throat and pulled the woman to his chest. She placed a kiss on his lips and turned before he could wipe away the tears caressing her cheeks. How could this be the last time he would hold her?

With lithe moves, she unsheathed a dagger from the harness at her elbow. The blade gleamed in the firelight, smeared blood still gracing the sharp edges.

She sat before the *cheeterah*, her hands feverishly petting the ears of the smiling cat. Without hesitation, her shaking hand shoved the blade into the white underbelly of the beast, the whimper from the cat making her cringe. A cry tore through her throat as she clung to the animal. The warrior turning from woman to girl.

It had to be done. They had seen too many Animle be taken and tortured until their bodies were exhausted. An Animle warrior was only at their most powerful when bonded by *simul ad mortem*—a joining of souls between Animle beast and warrior.

He moved closer to her, and she placed the dagger in his grasp. His hand was trembling as she stared at him, tears pooling over and running down her ashen face. "Be strong," she said and kissed his bloodied hand.

He swallowed, stepping closer to the window. They had concocted this plan, but he didn't think it would be like this. They would fight until death, and death was certain.

Give me strength.

Always a shadow, he moved to the window taking in the swarming camp. Silhouettes of shifting bodies with lit torches shoved the scorching flames into the barracks in anger. They had found none of the traitors alive—they were too late. No one would take the spirit of an Animle tonight. No one.

The treachery of it all almost made him shake with anger. At least those who weren't Animle, those who still believed in the power of the Espiritu would be safe. Rolin would see to it, he had promised to keep the Praelia safe. To lead them. The thought gave him some courage as he tried to drown out the muffled sobs behind him.

His *panthier* nudged his arm with her nose once more, and he leaned in to rest his head against her large skull.

We've had some times, haven't we? He asked, directing his thoughts to her. Their bond allowed her to understand. Her head bowed and lifted, making his shoulder shift. She paced back to the fire, her paws caressing the worn stone floor.

Do you remember our first day together? Her lips lifted to bare her teeth into an otherwise terrifying grin. He choked out a laugh through his tears. He couldn't help the way his heart lifted at the sight. There had been too much killing tonight.

The shouting on the grounds below grew louder. The Nexen would be here soon.

He stepped away from the window and reached the *panthier*. She was sitting on her haunches, her yellow eyes watching his every move. He knew he only had to ask and she would let him onto her back, let him force her to charge out into the fray of the slewing masses until they were taken and tortured, or worse, turned into Nexen.

He knew she would stand beside him if he asked, fighting as she always had to keep him safe, but there was nothing she could do tonight. He had made a promise, and he would not see her suffer. The Nexen would use her against him to find the others, to eliminate all who believed in the Espiritu. They had taken a vow to protect and they would see it done to their dying breath.

A rumbling purr stirred in her chest. Though he hadn't directed his thoughts to her, she knew him better than he knew himself.

We could at least try, he proposed, letting the thought hang in the smoke-filled air between them.

She purred again, reminding him of what was most important. A log fell in the fire, the snap causing sparks to rise into the air. He shivered.

You're right of course, he conceded and swallowed, hating the way her ears perked as the rhythm of pounding of feet hitting the stone floors drew near.

Shouts from the floors below echoed through the halls. Swallowing heavily, he pulled on the long sword from the sheath along his back. The blade flashed, stained with the blood of the Animle traitors he had slain that night. The young and grown alike were now burning beside the remains of their creatures. Most had accepted their fate, knowing their treachery had cost them their lives. But it was the young who had tried to escape.

Squeezing his eyes shut, he cast aside the memories of what he had been forced to do. The *panthier* bumped his chin with her snout. It was time.

You know I have to, he said to her in thought and she closed her golden eyes, her back straightening as she sat on her haunches. She offered her chest to him completely. Tears pressed from his eyes and rolled off his chin.

A hand rested on his back, the young warrior offering her strength to him. He glanced down. A strand of her hair was stuck to her cheek, sticky from the salted tears. She squeezed his shoulder and he stared back into his *panthier's* eyes, fear making him pause for a moment.

A cry rang out from just outside the hall as he drove the long sword through the cat's body. He felt the sting of the blade in his own chest, as her eyes widened with a yellow gleam that soon faded like the setting of the sun. She fell forward, her large paws sliding along the ground and her head landing in his lap. The weight of it nearly knocked him backward.

Stumbling, he rose to his feet and took up his sword. Side by side they waited, weapons drawn and lips muttering as they began to call upon the Espiritu. Without their *anima reflecta*, their beasts, they were weakened, but this wasn't a battle to be won.

Clambering and grasping claws strangled through the hallways, bursting into the room and taking in the sight of the fallen Animle creatures.

They were the Nexen, dark cloaks billowing about their bodies, hoods covering their heads, but he knew what lay underneath. He had seen the black eyes of the ones who had turned to darkness. Once the demons lay their hands upon a soul it left its mark.

Beside the soldiers were the enormous wolves. Their heads were narrow and the white fur along their shoulder blades stood on end. Each paw was the size of a man's hand, their heads reaching shoulder level and their eyes seemingly redder by the light of the fire.

He should have been terrified, frightened at their presence. But the weight of his *panthier's* death was nearly too much for his heart. He nearly laughed at the irony of it all. He had given all of himself to this, and now he would give his last breath.

Brandishing his sword before him, he called upon the Espiritu. A warmth filled his chest and his right hand glowed with translucent, blue light. For one more battle, he would fight. He would take down as many as he could before the end came. A wolf snapped and another howled, hackles raised and frothing at the mouth.

Beside him, the young warrior smiled, she felt the warmth too, her hand glowing blue. Oh, how he wished he could kiss her one last time.

Upon some silent command, the wolves charged and the battle began. He hit the first with a force from his hand, the Espiritu guiding and protecting, but the onslaught was too much for his depleted strength. Steel met steel as the Nexen charged forward. He refused to look into the eyes of the one he knew had betrayed them all.

"Take them alive!" Was the commanding shout, that voice so familiar, but it wasn't to be. They had made sure the Nexen wouldn't succeed.

Darkness and light collided above them, the clang of steel and snapping of jaws filled the chamber. From somewhere beside him he heard a gasp and knew she had fallen. His heart was too heavy to know more pain.

The jaws and steel were closing in, pushing him further and further back. He was nearly to a broken window when the sharp swish of cutting air reached him.

A surge of pain shot through his back and then through his heart, the tip of a bloodied arrow poking through his chest. All stilled and he fell to his knees on the stone floor. His eyes focused on the shaft. It was mercy.

From somewhere outside of Initium, Rolin had saved him. The Regent of Gallia might command the Legions of Nexen, but he couldn't have the souls of those who believed in the Espiritu.

He cast his thanks up to the sky above as his sword clattered to the ground. The traitor cried out realizing their final chance was destroyed.

He smiled, to himself. Even in death, the Animle had won. The Rising would happen—it would blaze across the realm with a fire of spirit.

A command was given to the feral dogs and the frothing mouths surged toward him, their teeth snapping. His eyes stared into the flames—unto love he would return. Something inside his chest glowed warmer than ever before.

He breathed his last before the wolves reached his body.

Long after the smoke had cleared, Rolin stepped into the sacred wing of Initium. There, upon the ground were the last of the living Animle. The fire had burnt itself out, and he moved closer searching among the charred remains.

Dipping low, he struggled to push a few of the logs aside. Beneath the soot was the labeled stone. If only the Nexen had stopped to look, they would have what they had been searching for.

He shook his head, Gallia would destroy all that Anglas held dear. Darkness was coming.

As he lifted the stone slab, he reached in and drew out the book that contained all they needed to know. The Praelia would live on. He would see to it.

Tucking the ancient text beneath his arm, he drew his hood around his head. His daughter stood in the shadows waiting, her eyes wide at the sight of the blood covering the floors. This was a place of death.

But the light would continue on. Together they dipped into the tunnel, sealing the entrance behind them. The heart of the mountain awaited.

812 YEARS LATER

PROLOGUE II

"Order 51667: hereby signed by His Royal Sire, the Regent Trinian I
All Chroniclers, those harboring Chroniclers, or those presumed to be hiding
Chroniclers, will be brought before a local magistrate. If so judged to be
members of the Praelia the accused will be taken into custody and executed.
Gallia and Autre Gallia can only exist in harmony if all yield to the true power
of His Sire. If any man, woman or child refuses to bow before..."

Trinian grumbled and crossed his arms as he listened to the official crier through the cracked window of his chambers. There, just outside the gates of his palace were his people—Gallians, and they claimed him as their Regent. As did the gods. He took a deep breath. If only all of Autre Gallia were as easy to rule as Bastion Nocta, the capital city bordering both lands. One realm, two names, and a multitude of discord.

He picked at the cuticle of a nail, his thoughts drowning out the murmurs below. His blood still boiled, news having reached him yesterday of a raid in the north. The Renegades were mounting their numbers, and though his officials worked to quell the rumors, word still got out. He cursed and turned away from the cracked window. His valet hurried to shut it.

"What would you have me do, my Sire?"

Trinian stared at the map of his lands, his eyes roving over the northern lands and Beastly Mountains of the Maereo tribes. He shook his head, they were too far north to be his concern. Moving along the worn paper, he perused the mountains and Echo Valley, the Renegades had to be hiding somewhere in the mountains. But they weren't his target. Not yet.

He needed to find the Chroniclers, the priests and scribes of the legends of old. No one knew which two he sought. Two brothers, believers of an old faith and members of the Praelia. The Renegades wanted their land returned, the Praelia clung to the belief of the Animle and their power. They dethroned any king, Regent, or heir, claiming all gods false—aside from some hidden power they held dear.

His hand tightened on the corner of the recently polished wood. He inhaled allowing the sweat from his ride across the spanning gardens to cool his rising anger.

"My Sire? Should we look to the southern lands?"

Near his hand were the southernmost portions of Autre Gallia. The people there were normally forgotten, the lords in residence easy to control. Only once in his seventeen years as Regent had there been any discord. The fact that it happened last year was of little consequence, though his counselors told him otherwise.

His gut told him the root of this evil was elsewhere. Pursing his lips he felt as though the answer was staring him directly in the face.

"They can't be in the Plenus mountains," he muttered, passing a thumb over the southeast portion of the map. Plenus was its own territory, a peaceful people who wanted nothing but to live unhindered. They wouldn't harbor Chroniclers, especially if they were members of the Praelia. "The south will not come against me, it has to be toward the north." He tapped a finger over the small speck on the map. It rested not far from the eastern border, the faded dot of little significance if it weren't for the scrawled word beside it. *Initium.*

He knew his history, he knew where the Animle had taken their final stand. Rumors had reached him of strange beasts and creatures beginning to walk the forests of Autre Gallia. He wouldn't let it happen. Anglas was long since conquered and he would not see it fall apart.

The Animle were gone, forever. His father had silenced any man or woman who dared to claim they were a warrior. And any creature of size or strength was eliminated in the games. They tore one another apart so no one could reach them.

He rubbed a calloused hand across the stubble still residing on his chin. He needed a shave—his normal routine having been altered. The silence in the room stretched, those watching him waited and seemed to hold their breath.

"Take your men north, through Echo Valley and beyond. Root out the location of the Renegades. If they are with the Maereo I want to know." A commander knocked off a salute and left the room. One of the counselors shifted, if he so much as uttered a word Trinian would see he never spoke again. "I want three regiments sent out here, here, and here," he pointed. A few of the men leaned forward as commanders saluted and left.

"You are dismissed," he waved a hand and turned back to the window.

Outside the people cheered as the trumpets and fanfare announced the power of Gallia. Within the walls of Bastion Nocta all was well, but out amongst the Anglans unrest filled his lands. "Maybe you're right," he proposed, knowing one of his commanders had remained behind. He always did. "Perhaps it's time we look into these rumors from last year. Something must have caused the skirmish."

"I agree, my Sire." The jangle of a sword in scabbard reached Trinian. "Do you want me to go directly there? Or stop by Fort Jontru first?"

"Go to the fort." Trinian exhaled, his thoughts on the coded report his men had intercepted. Only three men knew of its contents. Somehow it was all connected, but how? The southern lands, the Renegades, the two Chroniclers—all of it. "If the girl is still alive, bring her to me," he ran a hand through his hair.

"Yes, my Sire." Boots snapped together and thudded across the wooden floors.

"Jolson," Trinian turned. "Search Initium first."

The commander nodded, though his eyes widen slightly. Only the strangest of creatures lived in Timtus Forest. "Yes, my Sire."

Trinian turned to Jolson, his thoughts on the two Chroniclers who had defied him. Their executions had been set before they disappeared into the night.

"Those men thwarted me once at Wollmorn, don't let it happen again." Trinian knew Jolson understood the weight of what was needed. This was no small task—it was the key to quelling a rebellion. First, the Chroniclers would fall, then the Renegades, then the Praelia. By this time next year, he would see it through. The Animle would never rise again and a golden age would be restored.

Jolson reached the door and placed his hand along the knob, he knocked off a salute. Trinian straightened and nodded back.

"Find them."

CHAPTER 1

Mirtain, Autre Gallia

The seventeenth year of Regent Trinian I

The branch beneath Willem's hand snapped. He cursed.

"Steady, Willem."

He bit his tongue to hold back a retort. Despite his age, Jep didn't know what he was talking about.

Another twig snapped, this time from across the wood. Willem shifted again, the pine needles upon the ground sticking to the elbows of his jacket. Between the gap of the bush, he spotted the beast.

A tree bent and snapped backward as the needles and cones gave way to the mouth of the enormous grinspur. The front legs of the beast grasped for balance over halfway up the tree, the thick trunk wide enough to hide four grown men on one side. Only the very top of the tree retained its pine cones.

Near the feet of the beast, a body shifted. Willem nearly cursed out loud again. They were all such fools.

The grinspur's forked tongue strained for the top branches, the two prongs reaching to opposite sides and moving as grasping fingers to pull the bark clean in one fell swoop. A boorish moan rumbled in its scale covered chest—rippling through the throat, as the beast pushed away from the tree. The focus of every man heightened.

Round hooves, the size of wagon wheels, crashed to the forest floor in a cloud of powdered dust, the scaled body trembling.

Willem shot from his hiding spot. He raced forward, like a cat on the prowl, the shouts of the other men filling the sky. He joined his voice with theirs.

The grinspur startled, retreating, his hooves nearly killing three men at once.

They closed the back of the circle, their spears and knives pointed at the beast as it reared on its hind legs, only to bring them down to the ground with a mighty thunder which shook the floor beneath Willem's feet. Again the beast reared.

"Close the circle!" he yelled. The others scrambled to trap the beast. Intimidation and surprise, their greatest allies. "Close it! Close it!"

He saw it happening a moment before the grinspur's eyes widened. Its brute of a head was swinging back and forth looking for an escape when it spotted the small opening, Willem had only a split second to react.

He darted to the right just as the grinspur reared, this time gathering its strength before plunging ahead.

Shuffling, Willem darted toward the broken circle. The last of the men were just making it to their stations, unaware of what was about to bear down upon them. Willem knocked one aside as the thunder-like hooves hit the ground and sounded into a charge heading directly for him.

The boorish growl split the air as one of the men was trampled underfoot. Willem cursed, this was exactly what he had tried to prevent.

Behind him, Jep yelled his name.

The beast was by his side in a matter of steps and he pushed himself harder to keep up. Trees swayed and snapped as the heaving sides of the creature knocked them aside, no longer caring to follow a path, but making its own. Pine needles rained down upon his head, catching in his too-long hair. Ansie said it looked better long, but all it did was get in the way.

Darting around trees and over fallen logs, Willem kept to the side of the beast, moving quicker in the closely packed trunks. The grinspur was outmatched for this sort of travel.

Keeping abreast with the knees of the creature, he watched the neck of the beast, high above him; The throat thrusting back and forth in an attempt to pump more power into its sinewy legs. Each hoof beating the floor rendered the wood silent for an instant, before the snap of the branches above collided in a complete cacophony.

His spear in one hand, he poked at the beast's legs directing it. The grinspur roared its disapproval. Willem darted beneath a falling tree too weak to stand up to the turmoil wrought upon its being. He surged on ahead, a hill he knew well in sight.

The grinspur saw it too, slowing as the ground sloped beneath its heavy hooves. Each step had to be taken carefully or the beast would tumble to its death. Willem nearly grinned as he closed in.

Leaping onto a fallen tree trunk, he ran up its length. The slope reached higher as he neared the roots, bringing him within shoulder height of the descending grinspur. The beast's eye widened in fear. For an instant, Willem saw himself reflected in the bright blue orb and drew his sword from the hilt along his back. He launched into the air.

In mid-flight, he let the spear clatter to the ground, tossing the knife into his left hand. He swooped before the creature, the sword slicing in a giant arc along the neck of the grinspur. The forest floor came toward him fast, he tucked into a roll, letting the sword fall from his fingers.

The moan of the beast was cut off as its legs stumbled and it fell headlong into the ground with a tremendous crash. The jolt shattered the forest and the straining trees steadied as the chest of the beast heaved beneath its own weight.

Gathering to his feet, Willem took up his sword once more and hurried to put the creature out of its misery. When the final breath passed through its lips, he finally heard the shouts of the other men coming down the hill. He took care to wipe away the splattered blood from his face.

"Willem!" Jep called from the top of the slope.

"We got it!" he yelled back. Cries of victory and raised arms surrounded him. They would all eat well tonight, more than the meager rations from the village.

He held back a smile, not wanting the others to see. They would no doubt accuse him of it, as they did so many other things.

The men scrambled down the hill and joined him around the carcass of the enormous beast. Like hawks tearing apart their prey, they began to slice the scales and leathered skin away.

"I wish you wouldn't do that." Jep came up beside him and pulled out a dagger to help Willem cut open the skin.

Willem grunted in response. They had had this conversation many times before.

"Just because we don't trap the beast, doesn't give you the right to go after it."

"My right?"

"Yes, your right," Jep grumbled and tugged on the leather flesh, revealing the meat beneath—a soft swirl of steam rose into the cool air around them. "I know you. Doesn't matter if there's danger, you want the glory."

Willem chuckled, pleased with his friend's idea of him. "And here I am thinking I was helping everyone eat."

"Don't fool yourself, you did it for your own stomach." Jep breathed heavily, as they pulled back the carcass together. Jep was getting closer to the truth. The last thing Willem wanted was recognition. He had enough of that as it was—though they would never admit it, they watched his every move.

Being Lord Hernan's favorite was far from appeasable.

"Regardless, this should fetch a good price," Willem said, talking more to himself than to Jep.

"Aye," the older man said, "I have to agree with that."

It made it easier to do Lord Hernan's biding if he knew others would benefit. It had been a sparse season and more than one person had already died of starvation. With the temperatures dropping by the day, more would starve unless Hernan decided to ease the portion control.

If they were lucky, enough of the usual traders would be willing to pay a high price for grinspur meat. It was said to be a delicacy and favorite of the Regent in Bastion Nocta. Willem shook his head as he handled a hunk of grinspur, it looked tough and gamey to him. He idly wondered if the meat would travel on the locoven—a sort of wagon that was on a track. Anise had just been telling him about it yesterday.

Supposedly it was faster than riding a horse, and slaves used a sort of lever to turn the wheels while up above sails caught the wind for extra power. The rumors said that tracks were going to be built all along Autre Gallia, but Willem doubted they would ever reach the southern lands. They were lucky if the rest of the realm even remembered they existed. If it weren't for the mystery of the grinspurs, they would be entirely forgotten.

Hours later after the carcass was dismantled and both wagons filled to the brim, they left the forest. Chunks of the meat had been portioned off and wrapped into tweed bags. Long strips of the leather skin were carefully folded, lying in wait to be tanned and dried. Every part of the beast would be used, nothing would go to waste, and for that Willem was thankful. Even the scales would fetch a price on the market; their sharp edges were perfect for whetting a blade.

Willem picked up his sword, accustomed to the familiar ache in his shoulders after the many hours of pulling apart the beast. At least this time he was satisfied with the load they were bringing back to Mirtain.

"Willem," a voice called and he turned. It was Skurn standing with a raised hand in greeting from across the clearing. Willem nearly cursed—all day he had been trying to avoid him.

He watched as Skurn walked toward him and rested his hand on the dagger at his waist. Skurn always walked with a sort of rocking thump in his step, as though he used all of his foot, even to the tips of his toes to propel him forward. With golden hair and broad shoulders, many in the Mirtain had thought them brothers when they were young, but now there was a defining difference.

Willem scrunched his nose and felt the pang of the recently broken bone. Though it had been set back into place, he knew it would remain slightly crooked. He could only wonder what Skurn thought of the black bruises beneath his eyes. When he had seen his own reflection in the water bucket earlier that morning, he'd been surprised by the darkness of the half circles.

"This is for you." Skurn held out his hand. The extension seeming to be a truce between them. One Willem was unwilling to accept.

In his palm, lay the glistening horn of the grinspur—the most coveted part of the beast. By tradition, it was given to the man who proved his worth when felling the creature. Normally, bringing down a grinspur was a group effort, but it had been a long time since Willem had done anything the way it was expected to be done.

He snatched the horn out of Skurn's palm. The other hunter straightened, his narrowed eyes studying him.

Willem ignored him and stuffed the horn into his pocket. It rested in a bulge against his outer thigh as he began to walk away.

"It wasn't my fault." Skurn hurried to catch up to him.

Willem bit his tongue, he wouldn't be baited like this. Instead, he focused on the crunch of his boots across the needle-padded, forest floor.

"We could have been more discreet." Skurn shrugged and Willem fought off the urge to hit him.

If Skurn had shown any sort of remorse for what he'd done, then he might have been able to release his anger. But it was the way Skurn refused to back down from what had happened that kept Willem's blood boiling. The least Skurn could do was appear apologetic.

"As I said before, I don't care." He walked faster, annoyed with how easily Skurn matched his every step. A problem which accompanied being the same height.

"Would it have been better if I had come to you first?"

He nearly scoffed. The man was relentless. "Of course," he rolled his eyes. "You come to me and ask for Ansie's hand, I would then say Lord Hernan will never give his permission. You then go to Hernan and he says no. Then you go behind my back anyways and spend time with Ansie after curfew."

"So...same result?" Skurn admitted, but the lightness in his voice made Willem clench his fist. It didn't matter that he could see the bruise his well-landed punch had left on Skurn's chin.

Willem strode forward pretending he was alone, following the wagons as they rattled out of the woods and onto the dirt road between the parted grass of a deserted meadow. To their left were the ruins of Shirnway Castle. Bits of the roof had caved in hundreds of years ago. Legend had it the town was named after the powerful man who used to live there. Willem no longer cared nor understood why it mattered. Some people simply needed a reason to understand where they belonged.

You used to be that way, Willem shook the thought away.

"What are your plans for the horn?" Skurn asked, still walking beside him, forcing conversation.

Willem sighed. Every man here knew the price of a grinspur horn was high, just what Willem would do with it he hadn't decided. Similar to the last time, it had taken a while for him to figure out what should be done. Part of the money would go to Lord Hernan of course, but Hernan always gifted him with some coin. His mouth began to water thinking of some of the food he would be able to purchase.

"Hernan will be pleased," Skurn snorted.

"Don't talk to me as though nothing has changed."

"Why?" Skurn leered at him, his chin lifted high, the drawl of his voice rolling off his tongue. "Not up to the task?"

"Leave it alone," he warned.

"It's not as if you're ever going to give her the life she wants."

"Are you still here?" Willem halted, whipping around to look him directly in the eye with a baleful glare. At least Skurn had the decency not to cower.

"You know as well as I do that as long as Hernan has you as his favorite, he will hold Ansie over you." All lightness had retreated, Skurn stood facing him now with the anger Willem had seen last night. Didn't Skurn realize that half the reason Willem was so mad was that he was mad at himself?

Skurn's words had hit their mark, better than the punch which had broken his nose. "Get out of my way," he grumbled.

"I'm not stopping you," Skurn called to him and Willem refused to shake his head. It was enough that he had let his anger break through again. "And you can be certain this isn't over."

He ground his teeth once more and fought the urge to pull on the sword resting across his back.

Skurn was right, it wasn't over. But when he got home, he would see to it that it would be.

CHAPTER 2

One of Ansie's nails split as she dug into the dirt. It was the third one to crack that week.

She clicked her tongue and shook her head until the pain dissipated. She didn't want Riffnen to see her stop in her work. At least the sun had long since begun its descent toward the ridge at the end of the field.

"Did you hear what I said?" Safron asked, pulling Ansie from her thoughts. Her friend had a knack for making her feel as though she had ruined the day by not paying attention.

"Sorry," she mumbled, not really meaning it.

"As I was saying," Safron continued, her dull brown hair matching the color of the dirt their fingers worked tirelessly to overturn, "I overheard one of the Gallians telling Shorn that the Regent called a meeting with some of the Chroniclers. Apparently, they were brought before him and he had every third man executed. The rest he put in prison."

"Really?" Ansie couldn't help the dullness of her voice. They were constantly hearing bits and pieces of stories like this. Various atrocities committed by the Regent and his soldiers. Just last week Safron had told her that a Nexen soldier was spotted near the border of the Plenus Mountains. She cast it off as falsehood, there was no reason for one of the Nexen to be in the most peaceful part of the realm. The Nexen were rumored to be men of the dark, and they fought with special powers and white wolves by their sides. It was all ancient history to Ansie.

There had been a time she was more interested, but all of that had changed. Instead of thinking of death, rebellion or war, she preferred to wonder about the niceties and finery of the Gallians. They were a different kind of people, the women dressing in tight corseted dresses and crisp skirts while the men went about in shiny boots and tailored overcoats. Even here in little Mirtain, those who were Gallian dressed differently.

For good reason. She thought, looking down at the worn brown pants that had seen too many days, and the once-white shirt that billowed about her arms.

Safron breathed deeply as she grabbed another seed from the bag at her waist and dropped it into the hole. One hand worked in a blur to cover the seedling, as the other began to dig a hole beside it. Ansie's hands worked in a similar manner, only the tinge of pain in her newly cracked nail slowed her.

"Suppose none of it's true," Ansie suggested, and received an exasperated sigh.

"You know it has to have some foundation," Safron shook her head. Ansie looked up from the row of seeds between them for only a moment, before returning her eyes to the loose dirt. "People don't just go about making stuff up. Not anymore at least."

"Why do you always do that?"

"Do what?"

"Bring up the old days, as though we could even remember them." Ansie smiled, hiding the weight that rested in her chest. At one time she had wanted to see the old days, now she wanted nothing to do with any of it.

"Because it gives me something to think about." Safron shrugged, as though it was the only plausible answer, but Ansie knew better.

An odd lull fell between them for the next few minutes as they pressed on with their work. Every now and then, they shuffled to the side on their knees, digging and planting seeds. Ansie detested this method of planting. She had even been so bold as to tell Riffnen of her ideas for making the process faster. His answer had been a crack of laughter, and the restriction of her ration for the day.

"Do you think they caught anything today?" Safron asked, breaking the silence between them.

"I certainly hope so." Ansie's stomach gave a mindful grumble in agreement, and they both smiled. "Willem said Jep spotted the tracks of a grinspur near the wire fence."

"Chet told me, it's why I can't think straight. I don't know why he thinks it's necessary to risk his life that way."

"He's just doing the best he can. You know Lord Hernan loves it when they bring in a good catch. Especially since the last caravan of supplies never reached us."

"Yes, but it's a grinspur." Safron waved a hand. They shifted along their aching knees to make new holes in the row of dirt "They're so dangerous."

They were ahead of the women in the row directly beside them, but not so far ahead from the rest that they would be called upon to do more work. It was all about timing.

"That's why it's so rare to spot one alone."

"But one wrong move and you're dead." Safron snapped her fingers in the air, somehow making the action fluid, as though it was part of their job. "I just don't like thinking about how Chet's life could be over in an instant. It's not worth it."

Ansie didn't know what to say. She normally prided herself on being able to say something in nearly every situation, but in this case, her fears matched Safron's. They weren't the only women in the field thinking about the many men, who had been given leave to hunt for the afternoon. Every single one of the women working along the seemingly endless rows had someone out in the woods.

The sun dipped lower in the sky and Ansie ached for the end of the day's work.

She was gazing toward the tops of the trees, along the end of the field, as though expecting Willem, Skurn, and the rest of the men to suddenly appear. Riffnen glanced her way and she immediately returned to her work.

"What else did you hear?"

"Oh, nothing to bore you with," Safron shrugged.

"Look at me," Ansie paused, holding up her dirt-caked hands, a small grin lifting one side of her mouth. She knew half of her braid had fallen out of the kerchief she had covered it with earlier that morning, strands of her wavy, red hair billowing about her cheeks. "Does it look like my life is exciting?"

Safron laughed, the worry in her eyes disappearing as she began to tell Ansie another rumor. This one had nothing to do with the Regent, but instead focused on some lord they had never heard of and a rather interesting set of events which took place around his wedding. It seemed the man was under some confusion upon the wedding day when he realized he would not be allowed to continue his pursuit of the chambermaid.

It wasn't long before they were both laughing and thoroughly enjoying themselves, the work of their hands long forgotten as they moved closer and closer to the end of their row.

"That'll do it," Safron said, standing and placing her hands along the base of her spine. Ansie remained on the ground, knowing what aches and pains awaited her knees when she stood.

"Done already?" Riffnen's voice drifted over to them and Ansie hurried to her feet. Though she stood next to her, her head barely reached Safron's shoulder.

Along with her dull, red hair which hung in flat waves, and her easily sunburned skin, her height was just another thing which made her wonder how she had been spurned even before birth. More than once she had made Willem laugh as she tried to get her hair to knot on the back of her head and away from her face. The curses she admitted once made him choke on a too-dry biscuit.

At least her one favorite feature was often commented on. Beneath her right eye were six freckles. Willem had told her once that they reminded him of a crescent moon, but it was when Skurn had called them stars that she had melted into him.

Riffnen cleared his throat, drawing Ansie's eyes up from his poorly polished boots. He always had a disgusting way of smiling, his bottom lip jutting out in a slobbery bulge. She had often thought if he worked to keep his lips closed he would be much easier on the eyes.

Safron stood in his presence like a soldier at attention. "Yes, sir," she said quietly, never meeting the overseer's gaze.

"You know you don't have to call me that."

"But I'd rather."

He took a step closer, whispering as though his words were meant only for Safron. "And I'd rather you call me by my name."

"It's a term of respect, sir." Ansie butted in, and he turned to look at her. Where he could look Safron directly in the face, he had to tilt his chin down to meet her gaze. "I think Safron wants to do justice to your high position, being from a Gallian family and an overseer and all."

"Oh," the man's protruding lips puckered once more. He seemed to be on the verge of saying something more, but after a long glance at Safron, he turned and left.

Ansie let out a breath.

She had figured Riffnen out a long time ago. A fool could see how easily pleased he was with his position as overseer, but it didn't mean his ego was easily ignited. Only sometimes was she able to fan the fire of his pride and get him to step back.

Beside her, Safron's shoulders relaxed. Ansie shot a small smile up at her.

The other women were finishing their work and beginning to gather the bags and coats they had discarded upon their arrival early that morning. Some grabbed the coats of their husbands and sons, as well. Though warm in the sun, the cool of night would soon be upon them.

Safron gracefully folded Chet's leather coat over the crook of her arm as Ansie shoved her arms into her own. She knew Willem's must be lying nearby. Finding the black worn piece of clothing against the shed where their few personal items were kept during the day, she threw it over her shoulder and strode toward the barn to return her seed bag in the ration line.

The line shifted slowly, and Ansie found herself teetering on the tips of her toes, trying to see over the heads of the women to the front. How many hours of her life had been wasted in this line?

And how many more would she waste?

As the thought drifted across her mind, the line shifted forward two steps. She followed.

The rain started long before Willem arrived home. Ansie had already set buckets and various pots all along the dirt floor to help keep the rain from turning the interior of the cottage to mud.

Smoke billowed about the room, as the meat over the fire caught flame and she rushed to put it out. It was just as she slammed the too-small chunk of charred mutton onto the table, an ensuing hiss filling the room, that Willem stepped through the crooked, latched door.

He didn't speak as his fingers fumbled with the buckle on his harness, which held his sword across his back. She sighed, knowing what that meant. Hernan must have some plan in mind—most likely the Black Market. That sword was a sign of Hernan's hold over Willem, no one was allowed a weapon unless there was a hunt. And then, if you were Lord Hernan's favorite sometimes you had the privilege of being able to defend your hearth and home.

Willem left the harness hanging beside the door, over the peg which also held his coat. She eyed him as he shuffled about with practiced moves.

Rolling her eyes, she knew exactly what he was doing. She had worried about him all day, but in her gut, she had known he was fine. But it wasn't fine between them—he had avoided her since the encounter last night. "How'd it go?" she asked, her voice softer than usual.

He remained silent and instead reached into his pocket and threw its contents on the table. She stared at the golden horn, her mouth hanging open.

It was the second one he had brought back this season. Her heart lifted, thinking of the price it would fetch.

Lord Hernan was certain to be pleased. Perhaps he would go easier on Willem, not threaten him so much. But she doubted it.

"Another one?" she asked, trying to hide her blatant awe. She didn't want to be the first one to give in.

"Yes," he grumbled and dropped the dagger he wore about his waist onto the table beside the meat. Without being asked, he began to carve the mutton into thin strips—she wished for larger pieces, but thinner meant it would last longer. She would salt what they didn't eat tonight and allow it to dry, there was no reason to let any go to waste.

He offered a thin, steaming strip and she took it in her fingers knowing what it was—a peace offering.

"Thank you."

"Is this the last of it?" he asked, his eyes never leaving the meat.

She nodded. "I thought you wouldn't mind."

"If we hadn't killed the grinspur, I would have." There it was, the recent disapproval of her every action.

"We?" she asked, trying not to sound too interested.

She hastened to the worn out cupboard in the corner where the thick-tasteless bread from yesterday was kept. At least it was better than the potato mash they had eaten this morning.

"Everyone did their part." The knife hit the table with each slice in a rhythmic thud. "Only one death, so it could have been worse."

"Who?" she asked, her heart in her throat.

He named the man and she welcomed the relief. At least Safron and herself had been spared. She hated to think of the woman who was now a widow, but it was the way things were. Maybe she could take some of the dried mutton to the fields with her tomorrow. She was almost certain she knew the woman who had lost her husband.

"Did the boys come along with Jep?"

"No," he said quickly. The knife continued to slice with practiced ease, the strained silence building between them. Suddenly he let the dagger clatter to the table. "I won't talk about what happened last night."

There it was, finally.

She had out-waited him, a part of her smiled even though she knew there was nothing to laugh about. The hours of waiting for him to say something had nearly been torture. She wasn't one to hold her tongue, while Willem could take ages to say anything he really meant. One time she had called him a stew pot, he liked to process things before he gave them a voice. He only spoke quickly if he was certain, or angry—which he was now. And he had been last night too.

"Then there's no need to bring it up." She shrugged, tearing the bread into two chunks and placing them on the crudely carved boards which served as plates.

"What were you thinking?" He snapped.

She wanted to feel sorry, truly she did, but when she saw the dark bruises beneath his eyes and the way his nose now humped, she couldn't help the small smile which tried to tug at her lips. She had honestly never seen him so angry when he had found her with Skurn, and yet he now looked ridiculous.

"I thought you said we weren't going to talk about it."

"I just don't understand how you could be so careless?"

"It's not like we did anything."

"Really?" He quirked an eyebrow. The expression only managed to set off his nose even more. "I found you with him. Do you really think what I saw was nothing?"

"Yes," she said and crossed her arms.

"I stand by what I said. You won't see him again."

"What makes you think you're in charge of me? You don't own me."

"You're right, I don't, but Lord Hernan does and if he saw what I did, you wouldn't be standing here." He had a point. She broke their glare and stared down at the table. "You don't want that do you?" he asked, his voice gruff.

"No," she admitted, tears beginning to build behind her eyes.

"Don't you remember Kata?" He said her name with a painful twinge to his voice.

Her head shot up. "Of course," she ground out the words.

It had been nearly a year since it happened, but the horrors of it lived in her memory. For a month afterward, she had startled awake every night, drenched in sweat on her pallet. She would then lie for hours, gazing at the ceiling of the cottage, trying to still the erratic beating of her heart.

Willem sighed and ran a dirty hand through his golden hair. "I don't want to see you end up like that. It's bad enough with Chet and Safron."

"Not all of us can be like you," she spit. "Some of us would like to spend our lives with someone. We all aren't dooming ourselves to a lifetime of loneliness."

"I hardly consider living on your own until you're twenty-two a lifetime of loneliness," he said. Due to a population control law Hernan had instated, no Anglan was allowed to marry before they reached their twenty-second year.

"That's not the point," she raised an eyebrow, challenging him.

"I'm not getting into this with you again."

"Why not? You brought it up." She put her hands on her hips. "You know as well as I do that it doesn't matter what age I am. Five years from now when I turn twenty-two, I still won't be allowed to marry because Hernan won't allow it. He has to have some hold over you, and," she stuck her arms out to the side, "I'm his choice of weapon. So while you continue to bow to his will, allow me to carve out some tiny bit of happiness for myself, and stay out of my business."

"You are my business!" He slammed a hand down on the table and she nearly jumped back.

When he turned to her, she had the sudden wondering at the pain in his eyes which he covered all too quickly. It had been a long time since she'd seen him like that. He took a few breaths to calm himself. "If you were caught with him, then Lord Hernan would have taken you. Whether or not you intend to marry Skurn, you cannot be found that way again."

"It was only a kiss," she admitted quietly. "And he asked me to marry him—to run away with him." Her lip trembled as her anger dissipated.

"I know." Willem sighed. "But do you really think Skurn thought it through?" She hated the way his logic was making her fearful for what she had done. "Did you?"

The laws in their village had been in place for years—ever since Hernan realized the Anglans were beginning to outnumber the Gallians residing in Mirtain. It was only recently the marriage age had been pushed back even farther. There were plenty in the village who had done the same as she, but it was the ones who were caught who became a lesson for the rest. Thinking of Kata again, she shivered.

"I guess neither of us did," she said softly.

He returned to cutting the meat. "Can you promise me it won't happen again?"

"Yes," she whispered, feeling as though her heart was lodged in her throat. It was over.

She had nothing more to say on the subject. She hated the way she was trapped in a corner, the walls were pressing in, forcing her to live a life she had never wanted. It wasn't her fault, it wasn't Willem's fault. It was simply the way things were here. She wanted to scream, to run away, but she couldn't.

She had once had a dream of living away from all the rules, the restrictions and the work. She wanted everything she did with her hands to be hers—no more Riffnen, nor more rations, nor more Lord Hernan. She wanted to work with a man by her side and have children too. But there was nothing about this land which afforded her that dream.

"Ans," Willem sighed, the pet name softening her. He laid the knife down on the table again. She turned away from him, not wanting to see the care in his eyes. He always did this. Ever since he had found her in the woods that horrible day nine years ago, he had tried to protect her from the darkness surrounding this realm. Stars help her, she couldn't deny him. "I only want you to be safe."

But she saw what he really meant. He was sorry, sorry for being the reason she couldn't be with Skurn. She shrugged and smiled as tears filled her eyes, wishing things were different.

"I know," was all she could manage to say.

"I wanted to kill him for putting you at risk. If he's what you want, then maybe there will be a way someday soon."

She almost choked out a laugh. They both knew what he said would never be possible.

"Just...be safe," he urged.

"I will," she promised. Her voice was soft, even to her own ears.

"Here," he said, offering her more mutton and his stomach gave a loud grumble. She smiled when he held a hand to his middle and grimaced.

"So," she said, popping a chunk of the meat into her mouth. The juice ran down her throat and she nearly groaned. "How did you kill this grinspur?"

"I never said I did," he mumbled and pulled up a second chair to the table.

She rolled her eyes. "And they gave you the horn as a gift for standing on the side watching? Did you clap your hands and cheer them on as they brought it down?"

He smirked. "We tracked it to the south edge of the forest, it had left a trail which cut through..." and on the story went.

Ansie soon found herself lost in his velvet voice. It was the one sound in the world she knew she would always remember. He had a way of spinning stories, telling her all about his adventures in the woods in such a way that made her feel as though she had been right beside him all day.

In some way, she felt like she had.

CHAPTER 3

Damn, it's cold.

Larn was used to it and liked to pride himself on not really noticing anymore, but tonight was different.

He trudged across the frozen grass, the blades snapping like broken fingers. Each crunch irked him. He was no closer to getting the answers the Renegades needed.

The ground beneath his feet turned to stone and before he really knew where he was headed, the warm light of a tavern on the outskirts of the town pooled before him. Shrugging in his cloak, he braced his face against the whipping wind.

Damn, it's cold, he thought again.

A shout rang out from farther down the empty street, and his hand shifted closer to the dagger at his waist. A drunkard stepped out of the shadows, staggering on his feet and nearly falling on a patch of ice. The man spit out some foul language, his breath drifting beneath the light of the two nearly obscured moons.

Pushing open the door to the tavern, Larn was rewarded with the welcoming murmur of voices and clinking mugs. Laughter spilled from many a mouth and when a serving wench passed him, she sent a wink in his direction—her peering eyes trying to see his face beneath his hood. He smiled back knowing she could only see his mouth, and her cheeks colored. At least she would serve him promptly.

Striding through the room, he tried to ignore the stares of some of the men as he passed. In his leather coat and dark pants, he fit in, except for the swords strapped around his waist. Little did these people know he had weapons all along the lining of his boots and braces along his forearms. At least with his hood over his head, no one would guess who he was. If he removed the hood there would be more staring and whispers.

The north was fraught with controversy, the Gallian soldiers from the surrounding ruling lords were on the hunt for any hint of the Renegades. He smirked to himself. If the right whispers were placed in the right ears, it was hard to define truth from a lie. They were chasing ghosts all throughout the northern lands.

Just last night a strike by the Renegades in a neighboring village had angered the Gallian soldiers. Larn laughed, at least they had had the right date, but it just so happened their snatched missive told them the wrong rendezvous spot. Too bad that very missive had been penned by his own hand and dropped discretely where it would be found.

Larn had nearly laughed out loud as he watched them all stand in confusion last night, their spears and swords ready to take on those they thought were traitors to the realm. But the Gallians were the traitors—they had turned everything Anglas once stood for into dust. At least that is what Girshon, the leader of the Renegades, said.

Moving toward the back of the tavern, he reached into his pocket and pulled out some coins. Laying them on a table along the back wall, he took a seat facing the door.

"Hello there," a scantily clad woman purred, walking in his direction. He watched her long legs as they expertly sidestepped wandering hands. "Is that for me?"

He smiled at her and saw the way she tried to hide her approval. She wouldn't want him thinking he was better looking than her. Most likely he was better, younger, company than she was used to.

Her painted fingers landed on the sercs. He placed his hand on top of hers. "I'm sorry, that's not for you." He was careful to keep his face in shadow— lest she see his eyes.

"Oh," her mouth made a perfect little pout and she shimmied closer to him. He ducked his head.

"I'm only here to drink," he said and she made another pout as she suggestively slid her hand out from under his. He ignored the blatant action and focused on the scars surrounding her wrists. They were burn marks, brands permanently marking her as property of the realm. A thin red line encircled her wrists and he knew if he flipped over her hand he would see the swirling letter 'R', the emblem of the Regent.

There was a time when he first joined the Renegades that he had pitied women like her, but this life had made him hard. He was ashamed to admit that he couldn't do anything about it, at least not right now. It was one of the many reasons the Renegades fought. They sought liberation from Gallia and the many laws it placed upon them.

The woman before him straightened, her scars disappearing behind her back. "Be sure to call me over when you change your mind," she whispered. He could smell the faint smell of drink clinging to her skin.

He smiled back, indulging in her good graces for a moment longer than necessary before saying, "Don't hold your breath."

His words had the desired effect. Her face fell, though she tried to hide it, and when she turned to leave he watched as she spotted her next victim. She had no sooner left the table when the barmaid swept over and plunked a mug of ale before him.

He nodded in thanks and took a small sip, it was bitter but helped to warm the cold which seemed to have seeped into his skin. The door opened and closed with a defined pop and though no one turned to look in the direction of the newcomer, Larn's attention was focused solely on the man beneath the hood.

The dim gleam of blue eyes spotted him from across the way and he shifted through the room avoiding anyone who dared to look at him. In the way Larn attracted attention for his looks, Pike had a way of keeping them at a distance. Maybe it was his hulking figure or the way he kept his head ducked and his long blonde hair swinging along the sides of his face—back and forth it swayed with each step. Whatever it was, it worked.

Pike threw back his hood and made a motion to the barmaid, pointing to where Larn sat. She nodded and appeared just as his husky form took the seat across from Larn. He pushed the strands of blonde hair forcefully out of the way before taking a long drag from his mug. It was half-gone before he set it down again.

"So?" Larn waved a hand as he leaned back against the wall, planting one foot on the bench beside him. He wouldn't have anyone thinking their conversation was anything but casual. No reason to stop the raucous noise coming from the bar.

"It's gone." The man huffed, and Larn nearly smashed the table with his hand.

"How can it be gone?"

"Just is." Another long pull from the ale.

"But the lead was clear. You told me you heard him say it."

"And I spoke true then, and I'm speaking true now." Blue eyes glared at him. "We searched everywhere. Someone got there first."

Larn heaved an agitated sigh, he hadn't been this upset in weeks. He had been so sure it would be found tonight. Grinding his teeth together, he gazed back at Pike from beneath his hood. "I knew I should have done it myself." *Damn it all.*

"You think I'm lying?"

"No, but I could have gotten there quicker." There was no denying Larn had stealth on his side. He liked to think himself more skilled than any of the others in the Renegades. Of course, his position as Head of Intelligence had only been given to him when he had proven his worth.

"Then who would have entertained Lord Duggard?"

Larn snorted. While the rest of Girshon's men had been infiltrating the Lord's house, he'd been playing the role of a most becoming guest. A task he had only agreed to because he'd been certain the slip of paper was there. He inwardly groaned—he'd been so sure they would find out the names of the two Chroniclers who had escaped the Regent at Wollmorn.

"What do we do now?" he asked.

"Track it down." Pike leaned back and motioned to the waitress for another ale. She nodded in his direction, though many other men were calling after her.

"But where to start?" Larn said, more to himself than to Pike. They had spent months skirting Gallian patrols and the Nexen to try and find out something about these men. The tip they received was either false or they were simply too late.

"Did Duggard's men give you anything?"

"Nothing new." Larn snapped. It was always a risk to show his face, to not have gotten anything for it was a waste of time. Somehow all of it was connected, the Chroniclers, the regiment of Gallian soldiers sent from Bastion Nocta, the Nexen, the rumors about the strange animals spotted, not to mention the one he had seen with his own eyes—Larn shook his head and cursed. Something big was coming, but he didn't know what it was.

In many ways it felt as though the realm itself was holding its breath, ready to plunge into the midst of a war. But who would come out on top?

He tapped his thumb on his raised knee, wondering, not for the first time what the Regent was thinking. At times it seemed as though it was his mind pitted against the Regent's. And this was only the beginning. His grand Sire had no idea Larn even existed, someday he would. Larn would make certain of that.

"I keep thinking there has to be a way to get these Gallians to talk more, besides the obvious."

Thinking back on the wiry blue-coated Gallian soldier he'd met earlier that evening, he gritted his teeth. He had met his match in wits, he knew the soldier had more information than he was willing to give. No matter how drunk Larn had acted, the soldier hadn't given him anything.

"We should go back then."

Larn shook his head, he didn't want to think about returning to camp without the Chroniclers' names. Names had power. He swallowed an overflowing mouthful of ale and sucked in a breath through his teeth. "Where's Heben?"

"Outside," Pike grunted and then squinted to his left. Larn wondered what bet Pike had lost to have to come into the bar. It was well known the man hated any form of social gathering.

The table nearest them was packed with a rowdy group of men, ice cutters by the looks of them. Their thick, patched coats lay on the benches, some strewn on the floors—their hands red with raw, cracked skin. The woman from earlier was prowling around them, her eyes flicking to Larn with annoying consistency.

The group cheered as the barmaid returned with a tray laden with mugs, but when one of the men grabbed for her waist, the drinks shifted, teetering for a moment before they were flung into the air.

A few of the lost drinks smashed on the table, but Larn was able to avoid the worst of it, though his cloak and pants were splattered. Pike wasn't so lucky.

There was a moment of complete silence, after the terrific shattering of glass, before Pike stood and threw a punch at the drunkard still holding onto the barmaid's arm. The man crumpled like a leaf and hit the floor with a surprisingly graceful thump. The barmaid fell by the wayside, Larn caught her before she could hit the ground.

So much for obscurity.

Larn eyed the other men in the tavern.

Everyone stared in their direction, looking at Pike, looking at him. Only now were they beginning to take more of an interest in their appearance. They were both dressed as travelers to the casual bystander, but if one cared to really look at the weaponry strapped along their waists, they would be able to see through the disguise.

A man across the room whispered to his friend and pointed at Larn. It was time to leave.

One of the companions of the fallen man, bent over to feel the pulse of his friend. Seemingly satisfied, he stood up and looked Pike in the face.

"What ya' do tha' for?" The man bristled, his face red from drinking. He had an odd way of speaking, the sound of the common language awkward on his tongue. "I think ya' need to be lesson taught." He pushed Pike's shoulder. Though the broad chest didn't budge, there was enough drink in the smaller man's blood to make him think he could take the skilled fighter on.

With his band of buddies behind him, the drunkard rolled up his sleeves.

"Leave it." The words were out of Larn's mouth before he could stop them. He let go of the barmaid, who hurried away.

As though they only just now noticed his presence, the men looked to his corner. The one at the front turned away, waving a hand in his direction as he made a sound of dismissal.

Larn's blood began to boil. "I said, leave it." He repeated, straightening to his full height and moving out of the shadows. He tossed back the hood of his cloak.

It was normal for him to be the tallest man in the room, but it wasn't the size of him which had the men staring. Their reaction was something he was accustomed to, he had seen it on the faces of anyone he had met since leaving his people.

With deep-set slightly, slanted eyes, which left him looking as though he had no eyelids, he appeared more foreign than the men before him. With his dark hair hanging down around his ears, he could only imagine their thoughts turning to the stories of the tribes from the Beastly Mountains. A few people gasped and one uttered the foul word like a curse, nothing he hadn't heard before.

"As I was saying," Larn leaned forward, placing one boot on the bench while he pulled a dagger from the belt around his waist, "it'd be best if you left it alone." Normally, his foreignness and weapons were enough to discourage others. As long as they stayed focused on him, maybe they wouldn't make the connection they belonged to the Renegades.

Two of the icemen backed away, but the drunkard wasn't about to. He was trying to focus his eyes on Larn when the foul name came from his lips. "*Maeri*"

It was a crude word for the damned—all who looked like him were thought to be spawns of the darkness. There had been a time when the word had hurt.

Pike's fist shot out, knocking the man unconscious by his friend. That was all it took.

Glass shattered as a wooden chair was broken against Pike's shoulders. Larn swung into action beside his companion.

Punches and well-placed kicks kept them from falling beneath the onslaught of the entire tavern. They had been singled out as not belonging. All traces of raucous laughter had disappeared.

Through the mayhem, Larn found a smile forming on his lips as he spun through the moves which kept his body from harm. After the many hours he had spent cooped up in Lord Duggard's manor playing guest, he needed this. The thrum of his blood coursing through his veins, his heart beating heavily in his chest, moving on instinct—it was intoxicating. Glass shattered all around them and men from all angles tried to fight their way closer.

"The door?" Pike called, just before head-butting a man. Another decoration for the floor.

"Window!" Larn shouted back, and between punches hoisted a chair through the back window. The glass shattered, scattering over the tables where they had so recently been sitting.

"Go!" he called, ducking a punch.

Pike fled. After one more kick, Larn was right behind him. He teetered on the windowsill, an idea forming. He grasped at the discarded coats and found purchase—when a kick to his shoulder sent him in a tumble down the frostbitten hill. He rolled with perfect ease until he came to a stop. When he looked up, Pike's hand was extended in his direction.

He took it without a word, noting Pike's grin, a rare sight. He hadn't been the only one to enjoy the scuffle.

Knuckles bleeding, they began to jog down the hill blending into the shadows of the night. He was certain they would get in trouble for this, another risk for nearly exposing the Renegades, but for the moment Larn didn't care. They would get the information they needed. He was certain of it.

Too many lives depended upon it.

With a chuckle, he threw the stolen iceman's coat over his shoulder and tossed the other one to Pike. The blonde warrior fingered the coat with his stubby fingers.

"I think it's time we stopped looking for answers from the Gallians, don't you?"

Pike's smile grew and he held the coat to his chest, as they dodged off the frozen road and onto the dirt pathway out of town—Heben joining them before the next bend.

CHAPTER 4

The chains cut into her wrists, biting the already torn flesh. Each movement of the jolting carriage sent a shock through her arms and spine. If it wasn't for the steady breeze passing through the bars, she would certainly have been sick again—not that there was anything left in her stomach.

Soft sunshine filtered into her dreary cage, making her revel in its gentle warmth. She closed her eyes, forgetting all of it for a moment. She was tired. So very tired.

She didn't see the spear hilt before it cracked into her jaw. The pain lanced through her mouth and she spit out blood onto her worn shift. She had moved too close to the bars again.

Tears leaked from the corners of her eyes and the Gallian soldier's laughter made them come all the faster. Tasting the iron in her mouth, she curled in on herself, trying to hold her body without allowing the rock of the carriage to send her reeling back in pain.

For too many miles they had been trudging through the realm like this. They were chained together, the other women in the cage with her. She had learned their names, but only at night when the role was called, and they were allowed to rest on the stiff grass beside the rutted road.

Sometimes, at night, she stared at the stars. It had been years since she had been able to look at them. Darkness had been something she longed for, but now she hated it. She lived in it every moment of her day, breathing in the clouded hopelessness of those around her. She had tried to keep it at bay, to keep it from closing in, but the fight had long since burned out.

They had turned her into nothing. She was no more than the dust covering her body.

There was nothing left of the woman she used to be. She was a mere shadow in the midst of a scorching flame—consumed at the slightest touch. And though she wanted to cast away the darkness, she knew she was drowning and there was no one who would save her. No one who could.

Hours later the carriage came to a halt, and the sigh of relief which escaped her lips didn't go unnoticed by the sneering soldier outside the cage. As they were dragged out of the wagon and staked to the hard ground, she cast her eyes about. There were once two hundred women, ten to a carriage, she had counted the first day. From what she had overheard the previous night, this was the largest haul any of the Gallian soldiers had seen—though their numbers were lower now.

She winced as her stake was shoved into the dirt and she stumbled forward, her hands locked before her.

"Easy now," the Gallian soldier grumbled, her voice surprisingly deep for a woman's, there was laughter beneath the words. Just like the day she'd first met her.

"What do they call you?" the female soldier had asked her that very first day in the caged wagon.

"Umbris," the name had sounded odd on her swollen tongue. Her mouth was sore and it had taken days before she felt as though she could truly speak again.

Brute. That was the name Umbris had given the Gallian soldier upon meeting her. The woman was far from ugly, but it had only taken moments for Umbris to realize what would happen in her hands. She ruled with iron and spears, anyone who dared to cross the rules she had set received a blow they would long remember.

Brute shoved Umbris to the ground and her knees met the grass, mercilessly. She refused to let any other sound escape as she sank to her side.

All throughout the valley, groans and wails filled the air, but Umbris hardly noticed. After so many months, they were as familiar to her as breathing. All around her was pain and death. They numbered one hundred and forty-seven now, but the cries of pain still came.

Night fell upon the prisoners, but Umbris still couldn't close her eyes. This was the only time she had to herself, the only time she felt a glimmer of her past.

Looking up at the stars, her heart stretched in her chest, pulling as though tearing her skin apart as it yearned for her home. Tears leaked out of her eyes, leaving trails as they dripped off her cheeks and onto the ground. Her only comfort was the life they would give to the dry grass beneath her.

She had once believed all things worked in harmony, and life was a gift. But she had seen the truth and there was no going back.

Curling her knees to her chest, she turned away from the open sky and stared at the boots of the passing Gallians on patrol. Ten feet away lay Neen, already lost in the relief of sleep. She knew the names of the rest of the girls around her. She had heard them speak quietly to one another when the Gallians were distracted, but they had never heard her voice.

Sometimes she wondered if her voice was completely gone. Her father used to say she had the prettiest singing voice in the land, but that was before it all fell away.

She hadn't said a word since that first day when Brute had asked her name, and she didn't plan on speaking any time soon. There was an empty pit inside.

She was afraid if she ever opened her mouth, then her soul would come pouring out; tearing her heart and everything she was, until there was nothing left—until she was only the shadow she had become.

She told herself it was better to pretend, better to forget.

When she closed her eyes, the images of the past danced before her, but she locked them away, refusing to open them ever again.

CHAPTER 5

Willem covered her mouth with his hand. The bright brown eyes flew open, but she relaxed quickly upon seeing him. Sleep still clouded her, and he wanted to smile at the way her brow soon furrowed into a disapproving frown.

"Here," he whispered, handing over his dagger. Her tiny hand wrapped around the hilt.

"Why?" Ansie asked, the word cutting him.

He balanced on the ladder which led to her lofted bed. He always felt guilty for leaving her alone in the cottage so early in the morning. She always hated being left behind, her old fears of abandonment creeping upon her.

She had asked him to stop going to the Black Market. But her heart hadn't been in it. They both knew Lord Hernan would never allow it, and their survival depended upon it.

"You know why," he murmured. "Bolt the door after I leave."

"It's not worth it."

He shook his head, he wasn't getting into this again. "I have to go."

"Please, just leave it." In the dim light, her skin glowed like a ghost.

He opened his mouth to say more, when a twig snapped outside the cottage. They both froze, holding their breath for an instant. No other sounds permeated the darkness.

"Remember what you told me?" she asked. "You said to 'Be safe.'"

"It's not the same thing, this is reckless for a purpose." He grinned and shifted down the ladder, internally cursing the creaks from the wood.

"Take your coat," she whispered, her voice drifting from her pillow, down to him.

He shrugged into the leather, throwing his hands into the pockets for momentary warmth. Making sure the grinspur horn was securely sequestered in the pocket of his pants, he strapped his sword over his back.

Stepping into the night air, he glanced to his right and left, peering into the shadows of the trees across the small pathway before the cottage. If he were anyone but himself, and he was spotted, a Gallian soldier could have him whipped and thrown into prison for breaking curfew. As it was, every Gallian soldier under Hernan's control knew he had permission to go to the market. Being a respectable Gallian, Hernan could hardly allow a trail to trace back to him if his secret was found out.

Willem shook his head, knowing that if the Regent ever dared to look at Hernan's misdeeds, his own life would be forfeit. It would mean death, or worse being sent to a labor camp. Even in the southern lands, they had heard the horrors of those places.

Another twig snapped, and he ran. He moved softly through the underbrush and into the trees where shadows hid him from sight. Up ahead was the barb-wire fence lining the land of Mirtain. A sneaky addition Hernan had instated over fifteen years ago—the first of many.

Plucking two rags from his back pocket, he got to work moving through the wire. There was a simple trick to the task of moving through the fence without getting pricked, but it afforded no lack of concentration. With three rows of intertwining wire, he had to take his time getting through.

Once free, he dodged through the swaying shadows and fell into a rhythm for the next hour. His breath clouded before him and the tang of iron in his lungs gave his tongue an odd taste.

In all his visits to the Black Market, he had never once used the same path through the forest. *Never let them know where you've been.* It was a motto he often lived by.

The sky was lightening, but not enough to see farther than twenty feet in front of him. The tree trunks gave him a wide berth, easier for running, but making him feel more exposed to whatever might be watching him move through the forest. There was a reason Hernan didn't send his own men to the Black Market.

The groan of some beast split the air, most likely a porcun or a verral. He would prefer the first rather than the later. A porcun could be easily tricked, the low walking hoofed creatures only became violent when startled, if brought to violence they would charge, their horns glowing red. Easy to handle in the dark.

Verrals, on the other hand, hunted in small groups and attacked their prey through trickery. They had paws, but each was armed with a six-inch claw that could tear through flesh.

Slowing to a walk, Willem knew he was nearly there. Winding beside a well-trodden path, he kept the padded dirt in sight as he shifted through the trees. Making one last turn over the needle padded ground, the sight of the camp opened up before him.

It was a simply made structure, wooden planks and thin pegs driven into the ground to create a large circle around the entire market. Four guards were stationed at the only opening and before Willem had even passed around the final curve, he knew they had known of his presence. Each guard was skilled and trained at a special school since birth. Its name, Sicarmman, was an ancient school for assassins.

He waited patiently for them to give him a once over, their dark hoods covering their features. Aside from their height, he couldn't tell one of them apart from the other. With gloved hands, they waved him forward.

Smoke from low ember fires billowed in swirls, drifting like the steam from a pile of mulch on the fields he would work later that day. Simply thinking of the mind-numbing job he would endure, Willem pressed ahead, knowing there was nothing else he could do but enjoy his time here while he could.

Travelers from nearby villages passed in milling crowds around him. There was a blacksmith off to his right, his sign worn with cracks from the dew in the forest after years of hanging on the outside of the hut.

Mud squished beneath his boots as he trudged on, keeping his eyes down, though his back was straight. The market was more crowded than usual, he had presumed as much. With word spreading about the grinspur, more men were willing to risk the forest and see what they could trade for the skin of the large beast. How word traveled so quickly, he would never understand.

Striding across the muddied ground, a few men looked his way, though none dared to call out to him. On either side were huts of wares, goods, and food gathered by merchants from all over the land. The drifting scent of spices passed by Willem, and he pushed by a scantily clad woman, where a group of men drank around a barrel of ale. They had obviously spent the night in the hut to their backs, and Willem looked away in disgust. There was nothing but trouble in those places.

The woman he had passed earlier, entered the hut, not before one of the men could swat her on her backside. She didn't seem to care, and Willem turned away bile building in his throat. He focused on the brute who paused mid-drink to stare back at him. The man's eyes shifted to Willem's pocket where the grinspur horn rested.

Not now, he told himself. He had one job to do and he would see it done. He hurried by, glaring at the man as he did. If the ruffian even dared to take what wasn't his, he would meet the blade of Lord Hernan's hunter.

Brushing past them, Willem shifted on his feet and pushed through the crowd, bumping into shoulders on his way. Various languages reached his ears, some similar enough he could understand their meaning. He passed a merchant and a Gallian arguing about the price of a jeweled necklace, and he had to grit his teeth.

A hand suddenly clapped on his shoulder and he whipped around, ready to gut the man.

"Whoa!" Chet held up his hands, in mock surrender. Willem slid the dagger back into his belt, though he kept his hand on the hilt. "Just me."

"What are you doing here?" Willem glanced around. Not only was Chet breaking curfew, but he was also far from Mirtain land.

"To trade of course," Chet winked. At least that explained how word had gotten out. If Willem had to take a guess, Chet had probably never gone home from the hunt and had instead come straight here. It wouldn't have been the first time.

"Is Sarnon here?"

"Back there," Chet jerked his head in the direction behind him, his chestnut hair falling into his eyes.

"Right, well I'll see you later. Do try and be at least a little careful." Willem didn't wait for Chet's response before making his way through the crowd. He quickly located Sarnon's banner, the half-moon with six stars and a thistle branch, hanging from his hut. The deep red fabric embossed with silver thread seemed to wink at him as he approached.

Sarnon was working with another customer as Willem stepped into the enclosure. The merchant held up his finger, but Willem knew he would be with him soon. Anything for Lord Hernan's best. He rolled his eyes at the thought.

Biding time, Willem rifled through some of the trinkets and frosted glass bottles of aged wine along the counter and shelves. Another container had a strange language written across the top of the wooden lid, inside were vials of herbs with little pictures depicting what they cured. After picking up one with a sketched label of a man dying from oozing wounds, a hand suddenly reached out and grasped the vial.

"Willem," Sarnon said, "what brings you to my hut?" There was a gleam in the thin man's eyes. His beard hung in wispy strands from his chin, making him look even more as though the life had been sucked out of him.

"Shall we?" Willem gestured toward the private section of the hut.

There was a curtained off area at the back of the wide circle to hide them from prying eyes. He couldn't help feeling as though someone was watching him.

Sarnon swiped his hand before him, his tan shirt was tucked into the pants that were nearly pulled up to his nipples. The result left him looking even taller than he was—his legs seeming to make up three-quarters of his body.

Willem stepped behind the curtain, having to duck beneath hanging spices drying until they could be bottled. Hardly any light reached the other side of the division.

Once Sarnon joined him in the dark, the merchant fumbled about, lighting a candle. Willem snuffed it out quickly with his hand.

"I have another one," he whispered, trying to keep his voice down from the idle villagers surely trying to listen.

"Another? My stars, I never expected…" the merchant's voice trailed off, Willem knew he had already heard the tale. He wasn't unaware of the greed in the older man's eyes.

Willem produced the horn, the golden gleam seeming to catch what little light there was and reflecting it along the back curtain. Sarnon inhaled sharply, though he tried to hide his surprise.

Willem nodded. "It's larger than the last," he said as though the merchant couldn't see the obvious difference. "This time it was a bull."

Again the inhalation. "You have a gift." The man murmured and took the horn from Willem's palm. "I will give you forty sercs for it."

Willem shook his head and reached to grab it back. The merchant hissed, but let it go all the same. "You'll give me sixty."

"That is too much."

"Last time you gave me thirty-five, and this is more than twice the size."

"It is still too much."

"Well then," Willem straightened his broad shoulders, "I will have to take it elsewhere. You know I come to you first, I can always go somewhere else." He made a move to leave.

"No, no, no." Sarnon shook his head. "I will pay." The man readjusted the wire rims hanging on the bridge of his nose. Willem could only imagine how much the horn would fetch at other markets, or even Bastion Nocta.

"Come with me." Sarnon murmured.

They stepped back to the lighter side of the curtain. Sure enough, a few of the men who had been drinking outside the whore house, suddenly appeared very interested in the trinkets on the merchant's table. For the first time since it had happened, Willem was thankful for the bruises beneath his eyes. He knew it gave him a more intimidating appearance in this soft gloom before dawn.

Sarnon came gliding back, one hand holding a small coin purse, marked with his symbol. He handed the bag to Willem and the grinspur horn was fished out of his pocket once more. One of the men behind him took a deep breath. Sarnon's slave guards stepped further out of the shadows along the walls—their intent clear. With spears in hand and crossbows along their backs, they were enough to make any man think twice.

The merchant's eyes lit up as he fingered the horn and hurried to place it in his chest at the back of the hut. A masked slave girl stood beside it. She had never spoken a word in all the times Willem had seen her, but by the size of her spear and the thick muscular legs encased in black pants, he had never dared to ask her a question. He always felt her glare on him and any who took one step toward the chest. It unnerved him that he couldn't see any other weapons aside from the spear. He hoped to never find out what blades she had hidden beneath her garb, for no merchant as popular as Sarnon would allow his wealth to go unprotected.

"Thank you," Willem said dragging his attention back to the task at hand. Shaking the small bag, he weighed it in his hands.

"Always nice doing business with you." The merchant smiled, a truly terrifying sight. "Always remember, Sarnon works to give you the best."

"Of course," he replied, though he had to work to not roll his eyes.

He stepped away from the hut and passed through the crowd keeping one hand on the bag in his pocket and the other on his dagger. He had learned his lesson the wrong way once, and he would never make that mistake again.

The men followed him as he shifted from stand to stand and hut to hut. He pretended he was unaware of their presence. There was only one way to really deter them, and as the money dwindled, becoming simple items for the cottage, the men slowly drifted away. Hard cheese, two sacks of yeast, supplies for the cottage's leaking roof and a hammer, were not the coveted items of those looking for prosperity. He knew they thought he was wasting his sercs, but he would rather have something concrete.

He had been twelve the first time he had been jumped, to which the older men had *relieved* him of all the money he had made after hunting. Their word, not his. He had only needed to learn the lesson once.

It was rare they ever caught wind of something worthwhile to hunt—let alone a grinspur on its own. All of this had started one day when he was eight, and angry at the loss of his mother. He had hidden in the woods for days and Mirtain had thought him dead. He had turned up one morning with the skin of a dead bear to trade.

That was when it had all began. The bearskin had been sold at a high price and Hernan pounced on the wealth. Not on the bearskin, but on Willem. In Willem, he saw his road to prosperity.

Even as Willem spent some of the sercs now, he knew that most would go to Hernan. It would always be that way.

He often wondered if he would be the same if he hadn't found Ansie that day nine years ago. Ever since then, she had been his sole reason for working as hard as he did. He couldn't stand to see her hurt by Hernan, and the man knew it. She was Hernan's bidding chip and the price of breaking free was too high—Willem would never betray her.

Stuffing most of the sercs into the inside pocket of his coat, he glanced around. The men were no longer watching. Sure enough, they had presumed he had spent most of it. He shook his head. *Idiots.*

Swinging goods onto his back, he adjusted their weight. There were two sacks, one to help him and Ansie, the other was for Jep. With six mouths to feed, the food wouldn't last long, but he knew it would be appreciated. He always left the bag in the dilapidated barn near their cottage, in a hidden spot where no one but the family would find it—never the same place.

They had never spoken about it, and Willem never wanted to. He refused to let the older man think he was indebted to him. Not after all he had done for Willem when he was younger.

One of the men still watched him as he moved, but he was no longer worried about their presence. He had been certain to mention, to more than one of the merchants he purchased supplies from, that the money came from taking down a bull grinspur. Not something often heard in these parts.

It was a warning. One of the greatest lessons Willem had learned over the past few years, was the power of intimidation. As long as he made others think he was more capable than he was, they would think it. People believed what they feared, and planting doubts in their minds was as easy as a few spoken words.

Passing along through the smoke-filled air, the sharp tang of the gray fog stung his nostrils. He was about to leave when the roar of an animal caught his attention and he stopped in his tracks, turning toward the sound. He had told himself all the way here, he wasn't going to see them again—it never did any good. But even as he chided himself, he found his feet carrying him to the south wall where the cages and deep pit were located.

He came upon the tiger first, its black and orange coloring standing out in the dim light of morning. It hissed as he came closer to the cage. A hyena rested in the cage beside it, and beneath the tiger's domain was a wild fox, its legs were bleeding and it scooted backward when he knelt to look inside. He wouldn't dare to put his hand through the bars. The small dog-like creature shuddered in the corner. It wouldn't last long in the pit.

To the left was a bufalus, an ancient creature with a heavy head and massive shoulders. Its fur had been used by the old kings as rugs and cloaks, but when the Gallians took over they found the coats to be unfashionable. Willem shook his head, looking at the gleaming coat of the mutilated creature. Even the wings which folded along its back were clipped, preventing flight.

Willem took a step away from the bufalus. This was why he hated coming here. He would be unable to think of anything else for days on end, his thoughts on those trapped and caged in by the decrees of some Regent who lived far from Mirtain.

As though confirming his thoughts, a roar from one of the animals sounded again. The solid snap of a whip cracked through the woods, and Willem stood to walk toward the pit.

Behind the cages and crates of animals awaiting their doom, was a gathering of men in a circle. They leaned against the railings, waving their hands and shouting for the mayhem below.

No one protested as he pushed his way into the crowd, and leaned over the railing, making sure to keep his bags before him.

Down in the wide pit was a gorilla, its fists pounding on the ground, its arm bleeding and scars were violently torn across his chest. The animal was large, huge compared to the animals Willem normally saw there. Before the beast was a crocodile, its leathery legs ready to swerve and its gaping mouth smiling even as it hissed in a violent show of aggression. Willem bit down on the anger rising in him.

The reptile slid forward, striking like a snake and the gorilla darted out of the way, his heavy fists trying to strike the head. The silver-back missed and pounded the ground once more, allowing the crocodile to clip him on the arm. Another roar and the gorilla darted back, huffing and groaning as he went. He looked up toward the men silently cheering for his blood—the many arms waving in approval and excited spittle clinging to lips. There was urgency in his gaze, a frantic searching as he looked at each man in turn.

Willem's heart lurched at the desperation. He had told himself not to come here.

Some of the men who had bet on the crocodile were hugging one another across the pit. It was the way things were, fights between exotic animals and beasts that roamed the lands were idolized.

It disgusted Willem and at the same time, he was enthralled by the pure animalistic nature of the creatures. He couldn't help wondering where they had come from. It was shameful to see them used in such a way. But he always came back—something about them called to him.

The gorilla was still searching the crowd when his eyes settled on Willem. Even from so great a distance, Willem knew the creature saw him clearly. One instant he was staring back, and the next the gorilla had turned away, his focus returning to the pit.

The crocodile lunged once more, this time the gorilla was ready and jumped over the log-shaped body. The vicious smiling head swung to follow the gorilla, but he was behind as the beast lunged across the pit where he somehow found a foothold. With strength that was beyond the means of any man, the gorilla climbed up the side of the wall, dirt raining down on the hissing reptile.

No animal had dared to escape before.

When the enormous, black hands of the beast reached the top, the men stared in astonishment. The gorilla roared, his head coming into view and the men stepped back-shouting. The bars around the pit suddenly seemed feeble.

The beast huffed, his chest trembling in rage as dark blood oozed from his wounds. Willem had been wrong, the creature wasn't just large, he was massive, nearly twice the height of the men around him.

No one dared to move, and for a moment, all was silent. For some reason, Willem found himself thankful for the quiet, it was one of reverence, not the eerie screams of blood lust by men gambling what little money they had on the deaths of these animals.

The crack of the whip shattered the silence. The handler clicked his tongue and hissed at the gorilla who remained just on the edge of the pit, his powerful hand clinging to the wooden railing. The large, oblong head swung back and forth, taking in the men, daring them to come closer when suddenly he locked eyes on Willem.

The heart-shaped nostrils flared and retracted, the breathing of the creature steadying with every passing moment. In. Out. In.Out.

Willem stared back, enthralled. Light brown pupils stood out from the black face, flecked with silver hairs. He saw something there he had never seen before. It was intelligence, acknowledgment for the life around him, but more than anything else, there was sadness. A deep mourning in the beast's soul.

The whip of the handler cracked once more and snapped against the shoulder of the gorilla, but he never looked away from Willem. In some way, they seemed to understand one another. The whip slashed forward again, and this time, the beast was ready. He lifted his arm into the air, letting the whip curl around his arm and he jerked the handler forward. The man's mouth opened in a scream, but it was cut off all too quickly when a black hand wrapped around the man's throat.

Some of the men shifted back as if only now realizing what stood before them. One of the men near Willem wet himself in fear and ran away, his money forgotten in the mud.

A sharp tug was all it took. The handler was flung into the pit and the ensuing screams and hissing from the reptile below were enough to tell them all what had happened. It was silent a moment later.

The gorilla gave another huff, before climbing over the fence and into the crowd. The men shuffled back further, their silence long since broken. The mournful gaze swept the crowd, landing on Willem once more. His heart seemed to pulse in his throat as the beast fell to all fours and began to walk toward him. Their eyes were locked, and the beast stopped directly in front of him. A large hand reached up, and the gorilla lay his palm against Willem's pale head for a moment.

Willem's heart thundered in his chest. He never moved but remained like a statue as the beast sniffed toward his face, then suddenly, the hand slid down his head to his shoulder. The brown, warm eyes seemed to harden, the brow furrowed and Willem had the sudden feeling the beast was disappointed in him.

61

With two pats, the gorilla turned away, a groan seeming to come from the large chest. He walked to the fencing on the other side of the pit, and with lithe moves, swung his enormous body up the wall. Without a backward glance, the beast disappeared into the morning light. Willem almost fancied he could hear the creature exulting in his freedom at last—but not another sound was made.

The wind stirred Willem's hair, the smoke from the fires billowing around him as he continued to stare where the beast had so suddenly disappeared. It was only when one of the men touched him on the shoulder, that he flinched in response.

He tried to move, but looking at his feet, his boots had been forced down into the ground, twelve inches deep in mud.

He struggled to pull his feet free and left the animal pit without a backward glance. The many stares on his back left him shaken.

Had they all noticed the way the creature had looked at him? Looked at him as though he understood him?

He had always liked animals, but this was something different. Something he didn't want to understand.

Picking up his pace, he sped through the gates and set off in a jog through the forest, the sacks bouncing against his back. Around trees and over roots he moved, like a cat on the prowl, and only once he had climbed back through the wire fence did he let himself breathe and think about what he had seen.

The strength the gorilla had withheld was something he had never encountered before. The sheer size and intelligence were unlike anything he had ever known. As far as he knew, gorillas were said to be under six feet. This one had rivaled ten.

Letting the shiver pass down his spine once more, he hurried toward the cottage, still wary for any extra sounds in the forest. He told himself he was listening for verrals, but he knew he was really waiting to hear the heavy breathing of the beast.

What worried him most, as the cottage came into view, was the disappointment he felt at still being alone as he broke through the last of the trees.

CHAPTER 6

A knock sounded on the wooden door about an hour after Willem left. Ansie hadn't fallen back asleep, her worries keeping her awake. Sighing, and internally cursing whoever dared to make her leave the perfect warmth of her bed, she threw back the covers.

Climbing down the shaky ladder from her loft, she nearly tripped on the blankets from Willem's bed. He was always leaving the rough blanket in complete disarray, and she cursed him for it too.

Outside, dawn was slowly approaching. Curfew was nearly over, but there was nothing within her that wished to greet the day.

The ground seemed frozen as she stumbled to the door, her worries mounting. If Willem was back, he would have slipped inside on his own. She held the dagger to her chest as she unhooked the latch. Opening the hatch, she was surprised by the face on the other side.

"Skurn?" she said, her mouth suddenly going dry, and her heart hammering at the sight of him.

"Hey," he whispered, his voice gentle and warming her. She fought against the feeling. He placed his hand on the door and pushed it open so he could slide inside. A blast of cool wind wrapped around her, and she was suddenly very aware of how thin her nightshirt was.

"What are you doing here?"

"I thought I might walk you to the fields."

"It's a bit early for that," she muttered, suddenly uncomfortable. He strode across the small space, avoiding the half-filled buckets of rainwater. His hands slid over the worn chairs at the table, as though he needed to touch everything.

For some reason, the action felt too intimate and she crossed her arms over her chest.

"Where's Willem?" he asked.

When she didn't answer, he looked her way. She knew his eyes better than her own, there beneath the surface was the same fear she had curled in her gut. "As if you'd be here if he was."

He smirked, masking the pain. "True." He bit his bottom lip and turned away again, his eyes drifting to her loft. Her makeshift pallet mattress was crumpled, she was certain it had lost all of its warmth by now.

Heart thundering, she dreaded the words she was going to have to say, the very words she had been mulling over long into the night. "You need to go."

He turned. "Why?" She hated the way his voice broke. She pushed back the crack forming in her chest.

Her argument with Willem ran through her mind. Although she didn't want him to be right, she knew he was.

"You know why."

Skurn sighed, and she closed her eyes to the sound. He wasn't going to let her do this easily. She struggled against the tears forming, knowing she was going to have to sever whatever bond they shared. Her lips started to tremble.

He had been the one to help her when the rest of the village turned away. That horrible day Kata was taken, he was her only comfort—Willem had been lost to her. She blinked back the tears and hugged herself tighter. She would miss the feel of his arms around her.

Skurn glanced up at her after looking under the cloth covering the mutton from last night's meal. "Willem's too afraid to do anything against Lord Hernan." He was stalling, skirting around the pain they both knew was coming.

"Maybe," Ansie shrugged. "Or maybe he sees things more clearly than we do."

Skurn sniffed, bracing his hands on his hips. The movement somehow made him look more boyish—vulnerable. She swallowed.

"Look, I only came here to tell you I'm sorry. What happened was a mistake. Not one I wouldn't do again, but I should have proposed in a different way. I should have asked Willem, and maybe gone to Lord Hernan, or we could, maybe, ..." he ran a hand through his hair as he drifted off.

She nodded, that was exactly the problem, there was no answer. Well, there was an answer, but until last night she hadn't wanted to face it.

"I can't," she admitted—the whisper like an arrow shot through the darkness. A crack of morning light fell across his face. Her words had met their mark.

"No, Ansie, don't do this." He sniffed again and strode closer to her. She backed away, not wanting him to touch her if she was going to get through this.

"I have to."

He was already shaking his head. "No, you don't. We can continue on, I'm willing. We can keep it hidden."

She choked out a laugh. "We never could—it's impossible!"

"Run away with me," he reached for her in desperation and drew her to him. She inhaled the sweet smell of the lye soap she knew he used. So many memories flashed through her mind, but she steeled herself against them. She couldn't endanger his life. If they were found out, he would be sent to a labor camp—and she couldn't live with herself if that happened.

"I can't," she whispered again. "You have the chance to move on without me." He squeezed her tighter and laid his cheek on the top of her head. "I don't. Hernan will never let me marry, he has to have a hold over Willem."

"Please, don't do this," he kissed her forehead. He reached for her chin and turned her face toward him. Bending down he brushed his lips against hers as if wanting to force her to reconsider. But you can't hold water in a broken jar. All you can do is hang onto the few drops that remain.

Cupping her face, he wiped a tear away with his thumb. "Ansie, you know I lo—"

"Don't," she placed her fingers over his mouth.

"So that's it?" He stepped away and the cool air swirled around her. She hung onto his arms, looking into his eyes. There had been a time when his gaze reminded her of the emerald fields of spring.

"It has to be."

He shook his head. "No it doesn't," his chest began to heave and she knew he was fighting back tears. "You made your choice."

She didn't respond, knowing all had been said. She wanted to shout, "I choose you!" But she couldn't because he would never understand. How could she explain to him the pain she had been wrestling with, the guilt that had rested in her chest ever since they had fallen in love? All along she had known this decision would have to be made, and yet, she had carried on. She had allowed herself to dream and to believe that somehow, someway they would be able to be together—but she had lied to herself. She had lied to him.

He ducked his head and she wondered if he was contemplating the same choices she had dealt with. For hours she had lain awake, looking at the ceiling as she tried to dig through what Willem had said, but the truth was right before her. She could choose safety, or the road Kata had been forced to walk. And she wouldn't see Skurn beaten and sold like Jethron.

She might not like it, but there was no other choice.

"So you'll take his side?" Skurn's voice broke, the betrayal clear on his face.

"There isn't a side," she explained, running her hands up his arms, feeling the worn sleeves of his shirt rippling beneath her fingers. Tears pooled in the bottoms of her eyes. "I'm choosing safety. For both of us."

"No," he shook his head and stepped back. "You're choosing a side. You told me you wanted to be with me, but what it really comes down to is what Willem thinks."

"Leave him out of this."

"Why?" His voice broke again, "You were perfectly fine with what we were doing before he saw us."

"I was a fool. I didn't stop and think about what it could really mean." The tears spilled over.

He shook his head and looked away. "I can't believe how he gets to you," anger laced his words.

"What's that supposed to mean?"

His eyes flashed and he chuckled. "You've been with him since he found you. You've let him control your life ever since. I've seen it. He won't let you be who you really are."

"Is it so wrong that he's protective of me?" Her heart ached and she found relief in the spike of anger. Was that all this was? A tourniquet for the hole in her chest?

"You know exactly what I mean."

"I actually have no idea what you're talking about. I've never let anyone control my life—least of all Willem."

"It's more than that," he said, stepping away from her, the ripping in her chest continued. "There's something going on here and it isn't right."

"You're horrible," she spit.

That he would even hint at the dreadful rumors some whispered about in the village, she couldn't forgive. He knew how much it hurt her when someone whispered behind her back.

For the last nine years, she and Willem had lived like brother and sister. She didn't remember much of that day, but she could recall Willem asking for permission to keep her—demanding it was more like it. Lord Hernan had granted his request, instating Willem as her ward and he, her guardian. For nine years they had lived in such a way, but three years ago the rumors had started. Some thought it odd for them to live together.

"How dare you say that to me." She glared.

"I can't help but wonder."

"Well then," she said, biting the words. "You'll just have to keep wondering." She strode to the door and flung it open. "Get out."

He sighed, and she found herself wanting to break his nose the way he had Willem's. She would love to leave him with some mark on that perfect face of his, something to make him feel as awful as she did right then. Her lip trembled.

"Stop, Ansie." He took a deep breath, though his hurt pride still filled his eyes. She wanted to feel sorry for him, truly she did. "You always do this. You get upset and say things you don't mean."

The breeze brushed past her, raising her flesh in little bumps. "I'm sorry, maybe next time I can call you a whore and see how you take it."

They stared at one another, their gazes like swords drawn in battle. He lowered his defenses first and stepped through the door without another word. She should have felt like she had won, but winning didn't leave an ache in your heart.

And he was right, the words she had spoken weren't meant to be said. She covered her mouth with her hand and slammed the door shut. If a Gallian soldier heard she could be questioned, but at this point, she no longer cared.

Aching, she climbed up the rickety-ladder, skipping the broken rung and huddled beneath the blankets. She watched the door through tear-filled eyes, hoping he would come back. But he wouldn't.

If she had learned anything in this life it was that she always ended up forgotten and left behind.

Her tears had long since dried when the latch on the door moved again.

"Hey," was all she said, her voice thick, as Willem slid through the door, a pack slung over his shoulder. At least his presence eased her fears. She always breathed easier with him nearby.

He didn't say anything, but strode to the table and began to unpack the bag with quick movements. The load surprised her, he'd done well.

"Did you drop some of it off at Jep's?"

He paused, glancing toward her bunk. "I didn't know you knew about that."

"I only assumed." She shrugged and climbed down to help him. She would put Skurn behind her. "I've heard the going rate for grinspur horns, somehow this never seemed like enough."

"Maybe I'm just bad at haggling."

"I wouldn't believe that for a second." She scooped up the jars of yeast. Maybe the bread wouldn't be so tacky for the next few months. "But I'm glad you do it."

A grunt was the only response he gave. "How come you're up already? I expected you to still be asleep."

She sighed and pushed her hair behind her ears. She would move on, she had to. "You know I worry," the excuse came easily.

Turning back to him, he was no longer watching her. The dark circles beneath his eyes were all the more pronounced, his face having grown pale. When he looked up, she suddenly realized he hadn't even heard her.

Something wasn't quite right about his expression. His pupils were wider than usual. She had been so caught up in her own thoughts, she hadn't even noticed before.

"Are you all right?"

"Yeah," he gave a shrug.

"Don't lie to me."

"I'm not lying."

"Yes, you are," she shook her head. "I can always tell when you do that."

"Do what?"

She shrugged her shoulders in perfect imitation of him, perhaps a bit over the top, but it worked to make him smile all the same.

He shook his head and leaned on his hands along the table. For a moment he stared down, the silence beginning to unnerve her.

"I think I might have done something I wasn't supposed to."

"Did you steal?" she asked, her mind jumping to conclusions. She could grab the knife under her pillow in an instant, and the packs for an emergency escape were hidden beneath his bed. They could be out the door and into the woods in less than five minutes if needed.

"No," he shook his head. "Nothing like that. I—I went to the pits."

"Why?" she asked, knowing he had a hard time resisting.

He always came back in a fog, a dazed look in his eyes after seeing the animals and the horrors they were put through to meet the demands of their handlers. The more violent the death, the more money the handlers made. Legends told that right after Gallia conquered Anglas, calling it Autre Gallia, they used the casualties of the war to fight in battles to the death for entertainment. When the land ran out of prisoners, the Gallians began to use animals as a supplement for their blood lust.

It always disgusted her to hear the stories, but for some reason, Willem always told her about them. Stepping toward the table, she plopped into a chair. The wood protested with a few creaks when she leaned back.

"What happened?" She knew he wouldn't tell her unless she asked.

"I—I'm not sure."

"Start at the beginning," she said around a yawn. It really was too chilly in this cottage. How she wished they could light a fire during the night, but that was against the rules.

He began, his eyes unfocused. "I was going to avoid it, but I heard this roar, and for some reason, it felt like it was calling me. I know that doesn't make any sense, but I felt it. In here." He placed a hand over his heart as though she could feel it too. "It was a gorilla, pitted against a crocodile, but it wasn't winning. It was faster and stronger, but it kept letting the reptile cut it, bite it. It looked up from the pit at all the men watching and then it looked at me." He shivered. His voice dipped so low, she could barely hear it. "It climbed out of the pit."

"How?" she asked, quickly. No animal had ever escaped—at least not that they knew of.

"I don't know," he shook his head. "But before any of us could really move, he was at the top, and he kept looking at me." He shook his head again, as though trying to clear the image from his mind. "I've seen gorilla's there before, but this one was different. He was huge, nearly twice the normal size."

"What did it do?"

"He threw his handler into the pit." Willem waved a hand, and Ansie found herself staring in surprise.

You are what you reap, she thought idly. And then backed away, knowing how her own actions would be regarded by many. The raw wound of Skurn threatened to tear again in her chest.

"He stared at me," Willem lifted his gaze once more and she wanted to smile, but it was the seriousness in his tone which kept her steady.

Willem was always levelheaded, steadfast even in the direst of situations, but this was different. Something was stirring inside her, reminding her of stories she had heard long ago. The stories she had lost hope in.

"He looked at me like he understood—like he was a person. His eyes—" Willem broke off and ran a hand through his golden hair. "It doesn't make any sense."

"What happened then?" she whispered.

"It left," he looked toward the door. "It just turned and climbed over the fence."

A long silence passed between them, and she tried to imagine what he was telling her. Somewhere, out there in the woods not far from their door was a creature of myth. She shook her head, refusing to believe it. Willem was right, it didn't make any sense.

They had been told over and over again that having, and or, caring for any animal was forbidden. They were to see them as food and nothing more. For years she would have believed it all if she wasn't able to still remember her father's stories—stories of the warriors that used to walk the realm.

She looked up at Willem. His back was still to her, his hands braced on his hips as though he was waiting for something. The sword he carried across his back gleamed.

"There's something else, isn't there?" she asked.

"No," he said and shrugged. She shook her head, he never could lie to her.

He would tell her when the time was right.

A gong from the village suddenly sounded and it was all she could do to contain her sigh. Another day in the fields awaited. She moved to get ready when his voice stalled her.

"Don't say anything about this to Safron. There are enough rumors about me as it is."

She couldn't agree more. Thinking back on the false rumors which had been directed her way, she moved to the other side of the room where her clothes and boots waited.

"Don't worry," she said softly. "I won't."

CHAPTER 7

It was unusually chilly, the wind whipping through the fields and changing direction every few minutes. The breeze swirled again, bending the wheat in the opposite direction.

Shifting his position, Willem swung the scythe, slicing through the stalks with ease. An apparatus of prongs gripped the pole, working to gather the trimmed stalks as he swung, casting the wheat to the ground in neat piles.

Beside him were the other men, all working at the same pace, their blades zinging through the shorn crop. Behind them came the women, gathering the wheat together with braided twine. Only when Riffnen was distracted, did Willem risk looking over his shoulder. Thankfully, the auburn of Ansie's hair made her easy to spot in the pack of women. Though she wore the faded brown bandana around her head, it did little to keep strands of her hair from blowing all around her in the wind.

He kept his thoughts on her and her safety, not wanting to think about what had happened last night. Every time he remembered the eyes of the gorilla, he felt a sudden chill crawl up his spine. More than once Jep had had to cover his tracks for him. The older man had muttered to him, asking what was wrong, but Willem refused to answer. He would say nothing with so many ears close by.

The end of the field was in sight and as the hour drew to an end, Willem felt the muscles in his back protesting against the weight of the scythe—the day's work catching up to him. Normally working in the fields numbed his mind, but each swing of the scythe brought the gorilla back to mind. Each sharp wisp of the metal cutting through the stalks turned into the creature's roar.

"Now will you tell me?" Jep murmured when they reached the end of the field, the other men farther back than they had been all day.

"You wouldn't believe me if I did."

One of the overseeing Gallians strode toward them, snatching the scythes from their hands before they had the chance to step off the field. The calluses on Willem's hands throbbed and he cracked his knuckles as he watched the rest of the men finish and relinquish their tools. To his right were more fields, stretching as far as he could see, the wheat waving and winking at him in the wind.

"Try me," Jep offered as soon as the soldier was out of earshot.

"I can't, not here."

Jep only nodded and set his mouth in a grim line as he watched his sons labor their way closer to where they now stood. After all the work they had done today, Willem was thankful he was able to give this family a little something to help them get by.

The men pushed the laden wagon of scythes toward the barn while the women were finishing in the field. It was a group effort to get the wheat gathered and into the barn before the sun dropped too low in the sky. As a whole, everyone was quiet and exhausted when the bell from the tower rang out the departure from work, and a communal sigh seemed to pass through them all. Only the realization of working on another field tomorrow kept Willem from truly feeling satisfied.

Ansie sidled up to him as he strode toward the barn to gather their day's rations. Her head barely reached his shoulder and though she was tiny, he knew better than anyone she could hold her own ground. She looked up at him, a smile in her eyes and he winked. She was trying to cheer him up.

It was a gift of hers—and a curse. He had told her more than once that she tried to hide pain by caring for others. As always she had ignored him, but he knew she was aware of her plight. She hated to be vulnerable, and that meant never letting others see she was hurt. She wore her happiness like a protective suit of armor. Someday she would let someone inside, and when she did she would have to make the decision on whether or not to trust them to never leave her.

He was lucky enough to know that she trusted him. She had allowed him to see the vulnerable parts of her soul, but not everything.

He had noticed the downturn of her mouth this morning as they made their way to the fields. But it was how she began to walk with a lightness in her step the closer they got that made him realize something was off.

"We need to refill the water-skins tonight," she muttered, never speaking too loud. Other conversations drifted on the breeze. "There was dirt in the water buckets from the rain."

He nodded, having assumed as much. "I can hurry back to the cottage and grab the skins if you get my ration. I'll meet you at the Split."

She nodded and opened her mouth, but then shut it quickly, the color in her already pale cheeks draining. The six freckles which curved in a half-moon beneath her eye stood out all the more. She turned back to face the barn.

Willem glanced and spotted Skurn standing not far off. He loathed to leave her in line with Skurn not far away, but he would have to hurry if they were going to use the well before curfew.

Jogging down the road to the cottage, Willem passed a few others hurrying to gather what belongings or necessities they needed to trade in the village.

"What took you so long?" Ansie called when he later rounded the curve in the dirt road. She stood at the Split. It was a fork in the road, trees lining both sides of the dirt pathways. One trail split to the left, leading toward the village. The other led to the ruins of Shirnway Castle, which stood on the grounds near the forest's edge.

"I went as fast as I could," he muttered, shifting the empty bags on his shoulder. She reached up to take the two smaller skins from him.

"Maybe you should try getting sleep, sometime. I hear it's a good thing to do." As always, her eyes were twinkling as she teased him, but there was something about the way she looked away quickly that left him wondering what she was hiding.

"Maybe I will."

"You're still thinking about the gorilla aren't you?" she asked in a hushed whisper, their boots crunching on the rocky, dirt road.

"What makes you think that?"

"You've been off all day."

"I'm just tired." He shrugged and she shook her head in amusement. He preferred to think he was avoiding the situation, rather than lying to her. The gorilla was all he really thought about.

"Safron told me Chet heard a roar near his parent's place last night. Maybe it was your gorilla friend."

He stopped walking, glancing up and down the path, though he knew no one was there. For some reason, he had the innate feeling of being watched, the same feeling he'd been having all day. After a moment of silence, he dared to speak.

"First off, the gorilla was a mere coincidence," he said, and she scoffed standing in front of him. "Secondly, don't say that again, I don't want others hearing."

"I didn't say anything to—"

"I don't care, the fact people are already talking about it has me worried. One mention of it and Mirtain won't be the same."

"Maybe that's a good thing."

"Trust me, it isn't." His hunter instincts were on high alert. Staring into the trees, he thought he saw a shadow, but it must have been a trick of the light. "Besides, I've felt like something has been watching me all day."

Ansie glanced around them, she must have just now realized how quiet it was. A shiver ran along her spine. "Right," she nodded and started to walk. "We had better hurry. The line is going to be long."

They reached the outskirts of the village and only then did his hand no longer itch to grab the dagger hidden in his boot. It was illegal to carry a weapon, but he didn't care. They lived too close to the forest for him to count on the Gallian soldiers to save them. All it would take was one stray verral to cross the wire fence and break into their cottage. Without a weapon, they would be long dead before word could reach the barracks.

Those very barracks stood not far from the village—simple in construction and close enough to a discarded field for the soldiers to train. Along the main road to the village were a few stone buildings. Before them, a sewage clogged gutter ran down the side of the street and the stench hit Willem like a punch to his nose. It never mattered how many times he smelled it, he would never get used to the overwhelming putrid air.

Ansie ducked her head, wrinkling her nose like a rabbit as they pushed their way through the crowd toward the plaza. Houses and little shops stretched before them, all leading to the main square, where on occasion the village would gather for announcements from Lord Hernan. The plaza stretched for nearly a hundred yards in width and length, the lord's manor wrapping around one end with a balcony on the third floor, where he would make announcements to them.

In the center of the plaza was a fountain, a bare statue of a man with his arms around a woman holding a baby. Water dripped from his outstretched hand, falling off his fingertips and into the pool below, in his other hand, the one wrapped around the woman's body, was a sword. Its tip pointed toward whoever stood before the fountain. The eyes of both gazed into the sky, the smooth faces seeming to search and not find what they were so desperately looking for.

The constant trickle of the water was lost in the din of the many voices as they hawked and traded their rations for goods and necessities. Each table or little storehouse was run by a villager contracted by Lord Hernan. Prices were triple what Willem typically saw on the black market. But that was no surprise. Lord Hernan always pushed toward squeezing as much money out of every Anglan on his land.

Just as Ansie had predicted, the line for the well was long. They waited behind the shifting forms, each shuffle forward seeming to take longer and longer in between. Willem rolled his shoulders, stretching out the stiff muscles.

Some of the villagers called to Ansie and she waved back to them, Safron passed by with her family and they spoke for a moment in hushed tones. No matter how many times Willem had met them, the children in the family gave him a wide berth. He knew it was because of Safron's mother, the woman had beetle black eyes, her gaze never leaving him as though she was waiting for him to pounce on her children.

It wasn't uncommon for him to be ignored. He had the ear of Lord Hernan, and that labeled him as one of "them." Ansie had tried for years to get others to see him differently, but he had given up long ago. The others knew that Hernan held Ansie over him as a threat. The last thing they wanted to be was another bargaining chip—and he agreed.

Willem shouldered Ansie's bags until she was done speaking. When she finally caught up, he was nearly to the well.

"Next!" The Gallian soldier bellowed and a little man shuffled forward with his family.

"I think she likes you," Ansie said, nodding in the direction of Safron's mother. She squinted up at him and he nearly laughed, his eyes continuing to search the crowd.

"She seemed to only want to kill me this time, not dismember me."

That got a giggle out of Ansie, but she silenced it quickly when a passing soldier looked her way, his sharp blue coat standing out in the crowd.

"She doesn't know the real you," she whispered and he nodded, it wasn't worth arguing over again.

He had considered her words at one point in time, but the sacrifice was too much. He wouldn't risk others, he couldn't. Let them say what they wanted, it didn't really matter to him. As long as he obeyed Hernan's rules, then he could live in peace—and Ansie with him.

"Next!"

They shuffled forward and it was at that precise moment he felt eyes on him again. It was distinct, crawling up his spine and making the hairs on the back of his neck stand on end. He had spent most of his life being watched, but this was different. These eyes weren't waiting, they wanted something.

Ansie continued to jabber beside him, chatting about the things she had heard in the fields, but he hardly listened. His palms began to sweat.

"Next!"

He took a step forward, his eyes searching all around the plaza. There were too many windows and people for him to find the source. His gaze darted all around the stone enclosure, searching windows and over heads.

"Next!" A shadow moved in the corner near one of the stands. "Next!" He glimpsed a body, shifting back into the shadows of the crowd. He strained to see more when he felt a tug on his hand.

"Willem!" Ansie pulled again. The Gallian soldier behind her had a hand resting on his sword, his head cocked to the side, watching and waiting.

Not wanting to attract any more attention than he already had, Willem hurried forward and attached Ansie's sacks to the two ropes. With practiced movements, he lowered them toward the water and moments later pulled back, his arms feeling the difference in the weight. Grumbles came from behind him as he handed the bags to Ansie and attached his own to the ropes. One man voiced his displeasure loudly enough that his curses made Ansie turn around and stare at him with her hands on her hips.

He hurried with the final two bags and they stepped out of the way. Ansie reached forward to help him, her small fingers working to seal the leather sack with its lid quickly. He followed her movements, holding the bag as best he could, when quite suddenly a wild call rang through the air.

He froze.

The bellowing moan bounced off the walls, echoing all around the villagers until the sound drifted into the air. Only once before had he heard the plaza become so quiet, but he wouldn't think about that horrible day.

Soldiers darted and spread out around the plaza, word had reached them about the gorilla, just as Willem had feared it would. Heads were turning, trying to find the source of the sound, the faces twisting this way and that. He couldn't move, he couldn't think. How could the beast be here?

"Willem," Ansie made a clicking sound with her tongue, "your hands must be tired from the fields. Let me help you." He snapped out of his reverie and looked down. He had foolishly spilled nearly half of the water from his sack, the stones beneath his feet were colored dark. The soldier beside the well was watching him, his eyes narrowed.

Ansie worked quickly, helping him get both bags onto his shoulders, hers already hung across her back.

"Shall we?" she asked, as though no one was watching. Every eye seemed to be upon them as they stepped away and pushed into the crowd. The murmurs began all too soon.

He half expected to see the gorilla pushing his way into the plaza, those strong arms shoving the villagers aside and challenging the Gallians as they ran at him with their swords drawn. A part of him longed to see it, he wanted to feel the gaze of the beast on him, to feel the draw once more. The mere thought was enough to make him tremble inside.

"Come on," Ansie said through parted lips, as casual as could be.

He shifted the bags on his shoulder, carrying his head high as they neared the end of the square. It wasn't until they rounded the curve in the road leading toward the Split, that he heard Ansie let out her breath.

"What was that?" She asked.

"The gorilla."

She shook her head, "That was no gorilla."

"It sounded similar to what I heard last night."

She was quiet for a moment, letting their boots do the talking between them. "But it didn't seem animal."

He quirked an eyebrow her way, but decided to remain silent. She was right about one thing, the sound was a little different than what he had heard last night. The gorilla's roar had been filled with a heart-wrenching moan, despair mingled with pride, but this had been a call, more of a warning. But what did it mean? And why had the sound been so much softer?

Giving into temptation, he glanced behind him, relieved to find the path empty. But it didn't mean something wasn't lurking in the shadows. He wished he had his sword with him.

Birds took off in a flock from the trees on their left and his hand twitched by his side. Instinct took over and without breaking stride, he shifted around Ansie, placing himself between her and the side of the road.

"Keep walking and don't look to the left." He muttered under his breath and she nodded. "Why don't you sing one of those songs from the fields?"

She lifted her chin a little, the only sign she gave of her heightened awareness and began to sing. It was simple, the dips and falls of it perfect for working hands, the rhythm encouraging movement. He soon found his steps falling into the perfect cadence of her voice.

A twig snapped and by the way her voice didn't even falter, he found himself proud. If it wasn't for the white around her knuckles as she held onto the straps of the water bags, he would have thought she'd missed the sound. The crack came from his left, and not far behind.

His hand twitched in anticipation as they continued forward.

Another twig snapped and this time he was ready. Dropping the bags in a swift movement, he raced for the woods, tearing into the underbrush directly where the sound had broken through the trees.

Feet bounded backward in the shadows, scrambling ahead of him. The sound was lighter than he expected.

He heard a grunt and kept pace. Leaping over a fallen tree, a small dip cleaved the side of the hill and led toward a stagnant creek. Shooting forward, he dodged around a tree, catching his stalker unawares as he pounced on him from behind.

They tumbled to the ground together, as Willem reached into his boot and whipped out a dagger. The blade was pressed against the pale white throat before he heard the soft chuckle.

"Jethron?" The color drained from Willem's face. Gleaming white teeth leered up at him.

Though Jethron's face was scarred, marred with a line from his right temple, across his eye and mouth to his jaw, the smile still was nearly the same. Ansie had once said that Jethron was considered the best looking man in the village, a fact Willem had never noticed, but one Kata certainly had.

"Get off me, will you?" Jethron was huffing, his ribs protruding into Willem's legs. Willem pulled the dagger back, moving away as Jethron sat up. "If the Gallians find you carrying that, you could be punished."

"Hasn't stopped me before," Willem grumbled, still grappling with who stood before him.

"Of course not," his friend's expression went dark for a moment and Willem knew he was seeing and hearing the same things which lived in his every nightmare.

"How?" Willem asked, still gawking at him. That day when Kata and Jethron had been found out, he'd been taken. Soldiers beat him and dragged him off. The last Willem had heard Jethron was headed for a labor camp. But no one left those camps alive.

"I escaped," another flash of the gleaming teeth.

"Not on your own, I assume." They both knew Jethron wasn't the most skilled when it came to using his hands. Better than some, but he could easily be defeated by a trained soldier, or even an Anglan with moderate training.

"That's a long story and not one you're going to hear right now." A few dead leaves clung to Jethron's chestnut-hair and he hastened to pull them out. "I'm here for you."

Willem waited for him to make more sense of his words, but when it seemed none was forthcoming he made a move to stand. Jethron pulled him back down. He glanced to either side before whispering, "I've been sent for you."

Willem drew back as though seeing Jethron for the first time. His clothes were in good condition, and for being an escaped prisoner he was nowhere near starving. It could only mean one thing. The Renegades.

Willem's face turned to stone. "I don't want to hear it."

"You have to," Jethron grasped for his arm, this time in desperation. "*They* want you."

"No." Willem stood this time, ready to leave. He was foolish to have put the dagger away so quickly. "How many are with you?"

"I'm alone."

"How many?" Willem demanded, keeping his voice low. "Don't make me force you."

Something hard formed in Jethron's eyes, a look Willem had never seen before. They had spent years growing up together—all three of them. Kata had been the glue that held them all together. Willem shook his head, not wanting to think of her.

"You think you can break me?" Jethron challenged. "I'm alone. They're miles off." It was a lie and Willem knew it. "I told them you would only speak to me."

"Not even you," he muttered. Thinking about Ansie alone on the road, he made a move back toward the path cutting through the forest.

"Wait," Jethron held up a hand. "Just listen to what I have to say."

"I don't think so." He took two steps before Jethron's voice called him back.

"Not even to find out what happened to the gorilla?" When Willem turned back to the friend he used to know, he could see the fire in his eyes. The hardness had turned to a spark.

"What did you say?" Willem asked.

"I was there last night. I saw what happened and so did my companions. That creature looked right at you, that means something, and you know it. I can't explain everything unless you decide to come with me." Willem should have known it would come to this. "You want to know, I can see it. Why else would you have been so startled when you heard the roar?" Jethron asked, pushing further.

Willem suddenly wished he could hurt him. "That was you?"

Jethron shrugged, he always had been a proficient imitator. "Of course. Did you really think that beast would come so close to the village? Even you should know better than that." He took a step closer to Willem, his crisp, blue eyes seeming to burn into him. "You've heard the stories, and they're all true. Join us."

"No," Willem shook his head quickly. To even think of what Jethron was asking was enough to have him killed, enslaved, or worse it would come down on Ansie's head. "You need to leave."

"You used to say you wanted to change things."

"I learned my lesson. Nothing will ever change."

Jethron's scarred face lifted in a crooked smirk. "Then why am I still standing here?" He spread his arms wide. "Don't you remember going to Shirnway Castle? We used to have dreams, we used to have plans for something better than this. You said it yourself, we shouldn't be made to live like this." There was a far off gleam in Jethron's eyes that Willem didn't want to see.

How long had it been since his own light had burned out? Deep down, he knew exactly when he had lost all hope. He knew the date, the hour, the second it had all crumbled to dust.

"Don't—" Willem said, shaking his head, unable to say anything more.

Jethron stepped closer again, he was nearly an arm's length away. The scar seemed to fade beneath the glow in his eyes. "You need this. Ansie needs this. All of Anglas needs this. Join us." He extended his hand.

"No." Willem said the word more forcefully this time, and Jethron met him straight on. For a long moment, they watched one another. If it was another time, another place, maybe he could have said yes—but the past had scarred him. He would never be able to live the way he had.

Willem cleared his throat. "Do you need anything before you go? Food? Water?"

The glow in Jethron's eyes dimmed. "I have what I need," he sighed and looked into the forest. "You know, I never really thought this could happen. It was all childish dreams, hoping for something more. A game, really." He turned back to Willem, his voice dipping as though into a pool of ice. "But it's real now. And we need you."

Willem refused to answer, no matter how hard his heart was hammering in his chest. He backed away. "We're done here."

"So you think," Jethron said. "I'll be waiting. The next time you need to speak with me, head to the Black Market. Look for me in the last place they would expect to find you."

The trees swallowed Jethron's final words, refusing to give them the birth they needed to echo throughout the forest.

The world was closing in on Willem and though he raced through the underbrush and toward the road, he had the feeling he was still being watched. Only this time, he knew the eyes threatened more than he'd ever dared to comprehend.

CHAPTER 8

"What now?"

It was Heben who spoke, but Larn ignored him as he continued to look for a safe place to cross the frozen river. The stolen iceman's coat still covered his shoulders, the extra warmth helping against the stinging wind.

His horse trod carefully over the sloping loose stones, sparse patches of tall grass bending in the air whipping around them. The ground slowly leveled out, the sun glaring off the ice in a way which made Larn feel as though his skin was freezing and burning at the same time.

His horse snorted, puffs of hot air forming into clouds around his frothing mouth. "Easy, Tympmor." The large black head, swiveled from side to side, the coarse hairs of the mount's dark mane shaking.

The river's edge spanned before them, the loose stones leading to the treacherous ice. Sliding to the ground, Larn gathered his feet beneath him; after so long in the saddle, he was hard-pressed to walk steadily.

Reaching the edge, he placed a foot against the ice, testing its weight. It groaned, but the ice was always moaning, protesting, while far beneath water still coursed in strong currents. The question was how deep, and how strong the bond was on the surface.

Glancing back at Tympmor, he beckoned to him with his hand and the beast obeyed without question. Stepping gingerly, the hooves pressed onto the ice, first one hoof and then the other. The rest soon followed and beast and man were balancing on the ice, hoping for it to hold.

Larn refused to glance behind him as he picked his way across the river. Heben and Pike weren't far behind, their horses seeming to distrust the ice more than Tympmor. Pike was muttering to his mount, urging the beast forward one hoof at a time.

The pebbles on the opposite bank soon crunched beneath Larn's feet. As he turned back to the other scouts, a crack shattered the air. A split in the ice erupted knocking both men to the ground and the horses whinnied, their hooves scrambling for purchase.

"Easy!" Pike called, trying to keep his voice as quiet as possible.

The silence was no matter now, what little stealth they had accomplished over the past few hours was already destroyed. The men were getting to their feet as Larn rushed to the edge, leaving Tympmor to munch a frozen patch of grass.

"Come on," Heben urged his mount forward, pulling on the reins, his thin arms not up to the task. The sunlight reflecting off the ice cast his head in a sort of halo when his hood fell back. The wind had chapped his lips and pieces of dried skin hung off his nose.

The chestnut sides of the mount heaved, but the horse stumbled forward, its eyes wide and ready to panic at any moment. Larn darted out of the way as he crooned to him.

The language was old, from the Maereo tribes. Before he was sold to a passing caravan, his grandmother had taught him how to soothe the horses with a word, a soft chant of ancient mutterings that connected man with beast. The song drifted off his lips, the words lost with meaning, but the beast responded, its head steadying and reaching the stones.

Pike's mount wasn't so lucky. It was stumbling from side to side, the whites of its eyes shining. Any moment now, it would lose control.

Not daring to step any farther onto the river, Larn raised his voice. On the breeze, the words traveled to the creature. Pike yanked on the reins, the brutish man tugging the horse forward by sheer will. The back legs strained beneath the weight of its own body, not wanting to give in.

It was nearly sitting, when its ears pricked, as the ancient language reached him.

"Give him some slack," Larn called, breaking the song for only a moment.

Pike obeyed, cursing the creature all the while. Larn shook his head, knowing it wouldn't be long now before they would be overrun.

He chanted gently, the simple tune reaching the startled horse and slowly, the muscles loosened and the beast took a step forward. Pike's echoing curses were silenced when beast and man finally reached the shore. There was only a moment to take a breath.

"Let's ride," Heben muttered.

All three men swung into their saddles just as a howl split the air. It was one piercing cry, raised into the wind, but was soon joined by the forces of a pack. The Nexen.

Cursing all the stars above, Larn kicked his heels into Tympmor's sides and they were off. Pike's mount charged ahead, the beast wide in the mouth and eyes, ready to whinny any moment.

They weren't going to outrun them, not this way. Not with their every move being echoed into eternity in this cursed valley.

Larn reined Tympmor down to a trot, his companions slowing and looking over their shoulders. Agitated, Pike's mount pranced around as he tried to maintain control of him.

"Tympmor," Larn gestured toward the horse, "his leg is lame." The excuse rolled off his tongue easily.

Pike nearly growled but refused to speak. Any words they now said could be carried on the wind to listening ears. Over the howls of the white wolves, Larn gestured toward the path before them.

"We'll have to walk from here. Follow my lead." He didn't give his scouts a chance to disagree. Tympmor walked forward, his head bobbing with each step, the reins in Larn's hands strained. The beast was waiting for the chance to bolt. He crooned to him softly and the black nostril's flared.

The howls echoed all around, coming closer by the second. Soon the steady beat of hooves thundered through the valley. Against his better judgment, Larn pulled Tympmor to a stop and turned to watch the Nexen cross the river.

These mounts moved with practiced ease across the ice, never faltering on their spike-tipped hooves.

Fear flooded his veins, trained as he was to fear these dark-cloaked men. As a child, they had terrorized his tribe and the urge to flee was just as strong. He raised his eyes to the sky. Help him, he couldn't fight these men—not if they called upon their powers of darkness.

He shook his head. Yet another reason they needed to find the Chroniclers. Only those men could explain what the Renegades were truly going up against.

Pike's mount swiveled and Larn crooned to no avail. He turned fully to face the oncoming soldiers—his eyes roving over them, as they surged over the frosted ground in perfect formation, their black cloaks billowing out behind them. It was almost show time.

He could play this two ways, friendly or confused. As he watched them approach, he breathed out his last easy breath, knowing from that moment on he would have to weigh every word he spoke.

White shapes danced across the hills in the distance, the howling stopping for a moment as the beasts bolted toward the valley's center. If not for the snarls ringing off the mountaintops, Larn would have watched them in wonder. Their speed was incredible, bolts of white darting down the mountainside, their hackles raised and jaws snapping as they communicated with one another. Red eyes gleamed at him in the sunlight as they came closer, their fur ruffling in the constant wind.

He held up his hand in greeting. "Ho!" he called, the blood pounding in his head. Every childhood fear of attacking white beats seemed to flood him. He drew a deep breath, carefully constructing his face—he'd been trained to never reveal his thoughts.

Tympmor danced to the side as the wolves came closer, their teeth bared. Their heads rested at the perfect height to rip a horse's throat from its neck, their paws as large as the hooves walking beside them.

He raised his hand again as the soldiers came to a stop twenty feet away, their horses heaving great puffs of hot air. There were ten Nexen in total—a disheveled bunch. Thick jackets lined with fur peeked out beneath the cloaks. Every inch of skin covered and prepared for this weather, if Larn dared to guess, he figured these men knew every inch of Echo Valley. Across their breast was a mark he knew all too well. Two arched bows curved in the same direction, a line running through their middle. It had once been a sign of peace.

The Nexen crest. As if the wolves weren't proof enough of who they were, the red emblazoned marking signified their ranking in the realm. They were the elite soldiers of the Regent's armies.

"Dismount." The barking order came from the man in the center of the line. His jaw was covered in a sparse, whiskery beard. Blond hair sprouting at odd angles, his eyes as crisp and clear as the ice all around them.

Larn kept his hand up, "I would, but I'm afraid my mount is going to charge off if I don't keep a strong hold of him."

"I said, dismount." The hackles on one of the wolves raised higher, lips trembling as spittle dripped to the stones beneath the giant paws. The Nexen were rumored to be able to control their wolves with the merest of commands. Larn eyed them now and saw nothing unnatural. Were the stories untrue? Surely it must be more than simple training.

He remembered all too clearly how those beasts had terrorized his village. Haunting his nightmares, making him wake up in a cold sweat most nights. Even now, as a grown man, he was ashamed to admit the howl of the wolf often made him shake inside.

Heben dismounted first, his mount skittering. He kept a firm hand on the reins, straining to still the horse. Pike and Larn followed, both mounts shifting, their sides heaving. Larn didn't dare croon to them again.

"What brings you to Echo Valley?" The leader asked and Larn smiled up at him, blocking the sun from his eyes with a gloved hand.

"Is that where we are?" He looked to his companions, feigning surprise. "We've been trying to figure that out for the last two days. I'm quite sure we've gone in a circle more than once." His eyes crinkled with a smile, but the leader didn't give way.

"Search their packs." The command was given and nine Nexen dropped to the ground. Hands on hilts, they approached, patting down the scouts as though they were animals being sold at the market. The men searching through Larn's things, spilled most of the contents on the ground. His weapons hit the frozen dirt with solid thuds. He held up his hands to help them in their pursuit.

The leader's eyes never left him and though his heart was hammering in his chest, Larn refused to let the smile fade from his lips.

"Careful with that," he said, furthering his role, as one of the Nexen fingered a dagger. "My father gave me that dagger. You know what he told me when I left? He told me not to let it come to harm. He said, 'As long as this is 'round your waist it'll keep you safe, boy'. And he sure was right. I've had it with me for ten years and not a drop of my blood has been spilt by a blade." The man before him grunted, continuing to pat him down. "There's not many who can say such a thing, but I can. I'm sure you soldiers know all about killing and that sort of thing. You must have adventures every day."

A grunt from Pike off to the side, made Larn shift. *Not now.* The scout's temper had gotten them into more than a few close scrapes in the past, but Larn knew when they were outmatched.

"Careful, friend." Larn called to the Nexen going through Pike's things. "His horse is skittish. Poor man can't speak to calm the beast down."

"Can't speak?" the soldier paused and gave Pike a once over, the object of his perusal looking just as astonished. "What's wrong with him?"

"Don't know?" Larn shrugged. "He can't tell me now can he?"

A few of the men grunted in approval.

"It got us into a bit of trouble a couple of days ago," he leaned against Tympmor's neck. "We were in a pub, back in uh, Joth," he called to Heben, the alias rolling off his tongue, "what was the name of that town?"

"Kirath?" Heben shrugged, as though he couldn't quite remember. The Nexen leader shifted, but Larn didn't give him a second glance as he focused on the soldier still looking through his things.

"Right, Kirath. We were in the pub, nice little place tucked back on the edge of the town. Nice ladies there." He winked at one of the Nexen and gave another chuckle. "These men walked in, two of 'em, both brutes. They sat in a corner talking in whispers and just when my friend here was about to get his way with the serving wench," he gestured toward Pike, "one of 'em stood up and knocked him to the ground. Well, I started fighting," he knew he still had the bruises on his chin to prove it, "but they overwhelmed us. Like they were trained or something."

He gave the soldier before him a meaningful look and the Nexen returned his dagger and other weapons to him.

"Did they say anything?" The leader asked, an urgency in his gaze that Larn didn't want to understand. He focused on stoking that spark.

"Not so much as I could hear." The words rolled off his tongue awkwardly. Speaking like a commoner was always an interesting task.

"They spoke real secret-like," Heben added, and Pike gave a grunt. The men turned to him. Pike gestured with his meaty hands, crumbling and turning his fingers, beating his chest every now and again, using the spy-language they often used to silently communicate with one another. Each grew gesture cruder than the next. Larn shot him a warning look—as he tried to fight back a laugh. Only Pike would attempt to suggest such vile proclivities about the Nexen.

"What'd he say?" a soldier asked, looking to Larn, and then back to Pike.

He clucked his tongue, "He said, they robbed him of a good time. You've got to understand, he doesn't get much coming his way in his condition. He was close to having a bed with the wench for the night when those men started in on him."

One of the Nexen shook his head as though it was the most mournful thing he'd heard in a long time.

"They did say one thing, far as I can remember." Larn held a hand up to his forehead as though trying to pluck the words from some far off place in his mind. "They said they needed to head south, something about following a map...or finding one...I can't remember exactly."

The only reaction the leader gave was a stiffening of his jaw, but Larn knew he had played his cards right. It would only be a matter of time now, all soldiers, in his experience, were the same.

"South?" The leader lifted his head. "What else can you remember about these men?"

"Not much, I was pretty far into my cups as it was. You know how it is, after long days in this freezing wind, a man needs somewhere to drink away the cold." A Nexen soldier gave him a nod of agreement.

The leader snapped his fingers in the air and the growling stopped in an instant. All ten wolves pulled back and sat on their haunches, though their red eyes remained fixed on Larn.

"Return their things. It's time these men were on their way."

Larn lowered his head in a sort of bow. "Thank you, sir. All the same, might I ask if we can join you until the end of the valley? My father might have given me that dagger, but it doesn't mean I'm any good with it."

"How nice," the lines around the man's eyes crinkled, but his lips remained in a firm line. Larn wondered if he had ever smiled. Like the frozen ground beneath the horse's hooves, he was unmoving. "We have duties to perform, nothing to concern men such as yourselves with." The steely eyes shifted to Heben and Pike.

"We'll stay out of your way," Larn held up his hands. "We just want to follow behind. We came through with a caravan last year and we numbered near to one hundred men and were still ambushed. I'm certain we would be dead if our numbers hadn't been so great. But with your men and those dogs," one of the wolves growled out a warning, "we'd feel much better."

The leader looked him up and down, clearly not trusting anything he said. It was a normal occurrence, his eyes and skin marked him as one of the

Maereo—the untrusted, the damned. Larn held his tongue. If there was one thing he knew how to do, it was when to speak and when to remain silent.

"Put thirty paces between my men and yours. We ride hard and directly for the southern exit of the valley. If you fail to keep up, I won't wait."

"Yes, sir." Larn gave a deeper bow this time.

"Saddle up. We've got a long ride."

Without another glance, Larn stepped into the saddle. Swinging his leg over the leather, he caught a glimpse of Pike on his right. The man gave away nothing, no inkling of his delight, but he knew both of his companions felt it all the same.

The tidbit of information they had procured from the icemen had proven true. If the Regent's men were hunting in the south, then they were certainly getting closer to their goal. Maybe they would get lucky and stumble across a village that had spotted the escaped Chroniclers, or perhaps the slip of paper with their names would turn up. Either would be enough to call their mission a success.

Larn took a deep breath and steadied Tympmor beneath him. They would need all the luck they could get over the next few days. Rumors of the Renegades movements had made the Nexen more vigilant in their efforts. Though it made moving without notice more difficult, Larn was more than willing to take the challenge.

Clicking his tongue, Tympmor began to race after the Nexen. The wolves streaked ahead, blending into the snow with perfect transcendence. Only as they hastened forward did Larn allow himself to smile and glance at his companions.

They were in the mouth of the lion. Who would ever think to look for them there?

CHAPTER 9

Umbris must have been foolish to think the past would stay away. With every jolt of the carriage, she felt as though her memories were winking at her, tempting her to turn to them.

Over the past weeks, they had continued their journey on the deeply rutted roads. Sometimes the wagon wheels got stuck and it took hours for the Gallian soldiers to get them free again. Brute had cursed them all to the underworld and back when their carriage was stuck in the mud after a rainstorm. Umbris had secretly smiled, watching the woman slide in the filth as she worked with the other soldiers to free the wheels.

It seemed as though one day stretched into the next, with hardly a change. It wasn't until after the rains that she began to notice the change in temperature. The wind now whipped by them, lifting her shift to press it tight against her body, making her shiver and the chains around her wrists rattle.

Their caravan moved north, or so she had heard one soldier say. He had said after passing the Glaive River they would move west and what those lands might bring, she had no idea. After leaving the fort, they had crossed through lands she had never seen before, plains and working fields—the villagers stopping to point at them as they rolled by. She had averted her eyes, not wanting to see their gazes. She didn't need their pitying stares or the solemn shakes of their heads. She'd done this to herself.

When they'd first reached the Glaive, as the river was simply called, she'd stared in awe while watching the frothing foam. She'd never seen so much water in all her life. More than anything, she liked the way it drowned out the sounds of the other women talking amongst themselves. She could lose herself in the sound of the water, always rushing by with an energy and freedom she envied.

They seemed to be following the river's edge for some time as though it was a road. One of the girls in Umbris's cage said she had seen a map once and the river cut a safe path across the southernlands. The other night, another one of the girls had said they were heading for Bastion Nocta. Umbris shivered, not from the wind, but from remembering the stories of the capital city. Her mother used to tell her tales of the immoral center of the realm.

The other women wondered aloud what it would be like, but she didn't join in. Her fear mounted with each step the horses took, dragging them closer to the capital and whatever dangers awaited them there. But even on the road, they were not safe. Only two nights ago, they had been attacked by a pack of verrals. Sticking with routine, all the women had been staked to the ground in preparation for the night, but no one had slept after the screams of one of the women woke them. The verrals had taken her, a girl close to Umbris's age, and dragged her into the woods.

The soldiers had followed the screams, but they were too late. The girl was dead long before they reached her.

Since then, the soldiers had kept them in the cages through the night. Oh, how she longed to get up and stretch her body. Her spine felt as though it was curving in on itself. She idly wondered if she would be like those old women she used to see in the village, their backs permanently curved from their life of labor.

"Halt!" A soldier's voice rang out in the night. The jolting cage came to a stop.

Umbris looked ahead, though there was little she could see in the pitch of night. Neither moon could shine through the thick ominous clouds. Neen had wondered aloud if it would rain.

"What's going on?" One of the women asked.

In the last week, there had been more speaking in the cage than before. With the death of the girl by the pack of verrals, it seemed the soldiers were more worried about safety than what the prisoners said to one another.

There was a gleam in their eyes which unsettled Umbris. She knew there must be a large reward for these soldiers when they delivered the women safely to the capital. The way they glared at all the women made her wonder what they would receive.

Looking to her left, she spotted Brute. The woman was in charge of their wagon and made sure they all received at least one blow a day. Usually, Neen was hit for speaking, but Umbris was hit for remaining silent.

Umbris wished it was all some nightmare she had yet to wake up from.

"What is it?" Brute barked, looking forward.

Umbris shook her head. If there was any chance of going unnoticed, it was now gone.

"A commander, from the Regent."

Brute spit on the ground in disgust as some of the girls pressed closer to the bars trying to spot him. A commander? What could he possibly be doing in a place like this? It was well-known commanders had the direct ear of the Regent and were in charge of his most skilled regiments—aside from the Nexen of course. But the Nexen were something else entirely, or so she'd heard.

A few of the prisoners wondered aloud what he must look like—but their curiosity was soon quenched as a horse trotted into sight. The straight-backed personage of the commander was young and handsome, even in the dark. With a wide strong jaw that was cleanly shaven, his face betrayed refinement—his dark hair pulled back at the nape of his neck. He wore a hat with three points and his deep-blue cape was made of the finest fabric.

He settled his horse and took a moment to look at each soldier in turn. Umbris noted the way he eyed Brute a bit longer than the others.

"On behalf of the Regent, I am taking over command of this caravan." He spoke eloquently, a nearly infinitesimal pause between each word. "There are some bandits up ahead, pass by on the left, do nothing to disrupt them." The soldiers knocked off their salutes, knuckles pressed to foreheads.

A few mumbles from the women in the cage were passed around, their chains clinking. Umbris found herself wondering just what these bandits must look like. Ever since she was a child she had heard of them—they were a violent people, living outside of the rules of all society.

"You are not to harm or provoke them in any way." The commander eyed them all again and pulled on the reins to leave. Just then, Brute grumbled under her breath and the commander's horse was brought about once more. He glared down at the woman from above, one hand resting on his thigh, the other grasping his reins.

"Is there something you wish to share with us?"

Everything about this man screamed refinement. With his cloak slung over his shoulders, Umbris could just make out the shiny gold buttons of his uniform. Against the deep blue of his coat, she had never seen a button so bright, like a star against a cloudless night.

"No, Commander," Brute said, even to Umbris the title seemed mocking.

The commander's horse skittered to the side, he calmly turned it back around, never taking his eyes off Brute.

"Might I remind you," he spoke harshly, his voice carrying over the din of the rushing water behind him, "your payment only comes when we reach Bastion Nocta. If you care to make the rest of the journey, then you should hold your tongue."

"Yes, Commander." This time Brute ground out the words.

The horse pranced to the side again as the commander stared down at the soldier. "Lift your torch." He beckoned to one of the other soldiers who often walked at the back of the wagon.

The man obeyed without question.

The light from the torch flashed into the cage. Umbris had to blink quickly, the glow hurting her eyes. It seemed the light from the ground was not enough to meet the commander's demands. He snatched the torch from the soldier and held it up himself.

Umbris shrunk away from the light and felt Neen do the same beside her. For the first time since she had been flung into the caged wagon, she was relieved to have the bars around her.

The commander leaned in closer. The shadows of his face seemed to play tricks on her, he was at once both handsome and dangerous. The muscles in his neck flexed as his gaze roved over each of them, taking them in one by one. Ten women in all.

"How many weeks have you been traveling?" he asked calmly, but Umbris had the feeling something dangerous loomed beneath the surface.

"Three, Commander." Maybe the other soldiers could sense it too.

"Three," he clicked his tongue, leaning back into his saddle, torch still held high. "Then tell me, if these women have been chained inside this cage for the last three weeks, how is it they have so many bruises?"

Not one of the women dared move.

Umbris raised her eyes to the commander, but he was no longer looking at them. His glare was focused on Brute.

"Maybe you misunderstood your orders. You will only get paid if these women are delivered in worthy condition. From the looks of them, they won't sell for more than five sercs." If looks could kill, the commander would have been dead. Brute was glaring at him with a hatred Umbris feared would turn on them. "Do I make myself clear?"

"Yes, *Commander*," Brute spit out.

"Good," he shoved the torch back at the soldier. "If any of you provoke the bandits up ahead, I will strip these prisoners from you and leave you to fend for yourself. Am I understood?"

All the soldiers mumbled their agreement.

The chestnut stallion began to move forward, but was reined in one final time. "I will check on their condition in two days. If I don't see an improvement, you will want to make plans for the trip back to Bastion Nocta alone. I highly doubt verrals will allow you to finish the journey." His glare was solely focused on Brute, the threat clear.

He finally gave the prancing beast rein, and they took off in a cloud of dust. The raised dirt drifted toward them. Umbris inhaled some of it, but refused to cough for fear of Brute's wrath. It didn't matter what the commander said, she didn't put it past the woman to beat one of them out of spite. At the back of the caravan, she could get away with anything.

A call rang out and the carriage lurched forward with painful familiarity. Her mind was still reeling with all the commander had said when the light from the bandit camp beside the Glaive caught her attention. The men and women were huddled into groups, their wagons laden with provisions and wares. She had heard of these people, how they traded and moved through the realm, selling their wares to those who risked speaking to them. They often frequented the black market network, or so she had been told.

She noticed a small flag blowing in the soft breeze. It depicted a half-moon, and six stars—there was something else, on the flag, but she couldn't make out what it was.

From behind the bars of the cage, Umbris somehow felt as though her world had become a little bigger. The old part of her wanted to meet them, ask a question, but as they rattled by, within throwing distance, she shrunk back.

The men had the same look in their eyes as those who had seen them over the past weeks. They knew where they were headed, and what their purpose was for. It didn't matter she was covered in dirt and bruises. It didn't matter her hair was matted around her face, or that the mud from previous rainfalls stained her shift, all they saw was her beauty.

There had been a time when it was her crowning glory, but no more. She shrank as far back from the bars as she dared, refusing to look up again. She could feel the men's eyes on her and she shuddered as she recalled the words of the commander.

He had said they would fetch a price. Just how much, depended upon their appearance.

Staring at her chaffed wrists, she wondered, not for the first time, what she could do to her face to make a change. What sort of blunt force would scar her so she would no longer be seen, so she might disappear? It would certainly be a benefit to see Brute punished for her appearance.

But even as the thought furled around her, she knew there was nothing she could do. She wouldn't be able to do the deed. No matter how much she wished, she couldn't do it.

There had been a time when Umbris thought herself brave, but she knew the past was something she could no longer touch. It would be wrong, and she could hear her mother telling her so. But to face what was coming as she was would take more courage, something she no longer had.

Oh, Mother, she thought, remembering her face. Shaking her head, she knew she would never have the strength to do it. She looked like her mother, and a part of her would never let that go. They could never take that away from her.

Her thoughts kept her awake all night until they stopped beside the Glaive to wash. She refused to look at her face in the reflection of the pool. The water was like ice, rippling over her skin, but the coolness was refreshing after spending so many days in her own filth.

Some of the women smiled, letting the water run down their arms, caressing their chaffed wrists. Umbris sank to her knees in the water and ducked her head beneath the surface. She wondered if a cloud of dirt swirled around her. In the silence of the underwater world, she could finally hear herself think.

Echoes of her past pulled at her, like the water tugging on her shift.

Only when she reemerged did the voices of her fellow prisoners reach her. They stared at her in wonder, gaping at her dripping head. She had been foolish to let herself feel so free.

It wasn't common to know how to swim, to even be in the water waist deep was pushing it farther than most. Realizing her mistake, she copied the movements of the other women, bending over to scrub out her hair and splash water on her face, but the damage was already done.

As she stepped out onto the banks of the river, she felt Brute's eyes upon her. She knew the gleam she would see in them. As her prisoners, these women were prizes to the soldier, the commander had made that clear the night before. Her ability to swim would only make her a more prized sell when the time came in the capital city. They would tout her as a witch, a mysterious creature.

As the water trickled down her back beneath her shift, she hastened to pull the cloth away from her body. It clung close to her starving frame, too close for comfort, and her dark hair did little to hide her porcelain skin. If she had been smart, she would have remained on the bank, covered in dirt. But the water had been too inviting.

The soldiers herded them back into the carriages, with shoves and pushes, eyes always wandering. Even though she was freezing, the wind pulling at her, she felt the least bit comfortable for the first time in weeks.

Neen sighed beside her as the carriage jolted forward, and she took comfort in the sound.

As the wagon rattled over the rocks and back onto the rutted road, they passed by the commander and his attendants. In the light of day, he was better able to see them. He nodded his head in approval, though Umbris knew their bruises stood out all the brighter now that dirt no longer clung to them.

Her only guess was the road to Bastion Nocta was long, and there would be time to heal.

The chestnut stallion skittered forward again, and this time when she raised her eyes to the commander, he was looking back at her, his gold buttons gleaming. He straightened in his saddle, only meeting her eyes once before kicking the horse toward the front of the wagon train.

All too soon, the cloud of dust from the other carriages swept upon them. She ducked her head, letting her hair take the brunt of it. It seemed the washing had only served to let the dirt stick all the more.

Leaning back against the bars, she settled into the rocking of the wagon, her mind focused on the look the commander had given her. She had seen something similar to it once before. A look that went deeper than her appearance, beyond what most saw in a prisoner. He had looked at her as if he could see her soul.

She shook her head, remembering how *he* used to look at her. The memories she had so long held at bay crept up and made the tears well in her eyes.

You're so weak. The little voice in her head chided. *One look, and you remember him.*

The shame covered her like a blanket, nearly suffocating her.

Shaking her head from side to side, she tried to close the memories back into the little box she had put them in. Only after hours of focusing on the rattling of the wagon wheels was she able to let them go.

Holding her arms around her waist, she let the tears fall. She had become a master at crying silent tears.

CHAPTER 10

The flickering flames from the bonfire danced in the middle of the Plaza. Shapes and shifting bodies twirled around in a circle, as the twisting tunes of the fiddles cut through the air, making Ansie's feet tap beneath her woolen skirt.

It was Festis Luna, "The Festival of the Moons," as it had been called. What had once been a celebration of harvest, a time when families would gather together with their neighbors, gifting one another with their presence and provisions, had turned into the simple scene before her. There were pictures in her mind formed from stories and her own fantasies about this night.

Images of the carousing and dancing filled her thoughts, the blindfolding of all the young men and women until they found one another on the dance floor, spinning around the flames until morning light dawned. There were songs, long forgotten, families used to sing, their voices drifting into the sky with the sparks from the flames. Chants of celebration and thankfulness for life.

But what had once been was no more. Instead, when Anglas was overrun by the Gallians, the old traditions died. Now the Regent allowed the festival to take place only to calm any resistance. It was far from what it had once been. With soldiers stationed around the plaza, the atmosphere was more tense than usual. She saw more than one person glancing at the soldiers before attempting to take part in some revelry.

"Ansie!" Safron called to her from across the dancing couples and made her way around the edges of the crowd. Only the unmarried men and women danced, some traditions still held.

Ansie raised her glass in greeting. Mrs. Cobert had outdone herself, this year's mulled wine was better than any she had ever tasted.

"Come dance!" Safron exclaimed, her eyes bright and cheeks flushed with exertion. Her merriment couldn't be contained, regardless of the hesitations of others.

"I'm fine right here," Ansie declined with a shake of her head.

"You are not," her friend grabbed her hand and began to pull. "You've been swaying to the music for over an hour. No need to waste your dress."

Ansie let Safron drag her closer to the swarm of bodies. Safron had a point, Ansie shouldn't let her outfit go to waste even if it had been made with the intent of pleasing Skurn. She'd debated for hours on whether or not to wear it.

A thick leather belt trimmed her thin waist, holding up the long plaid skirt stretching to the ground. The billowing fabric gave the impression of long legs, with her hair left hanging down around her shoulders, the shades of auburn and red seemed heightened in the light of the flames. If she had really cared about how she looked tonight, she would have put more effort into weaving flowers into her hair, as it was, she was the only woman in sight without the jewels of the ground adorning her locks.

Pulling her into the fray of the dancing bodies, Chet grabbed her hand, the other in Safron's and they shuffled in a circle, stepping back to clap and grasp each other's hands once more. Ansie's bare feet padded over the stones in perfect rhythm with the beat of the hand drum.

As they danced, the thump of the drum collided with her heart. She felt it in her veins, pounding through her flesh. Around the fire they danced, the circle of villagers growing wider with each clap and stomp. Ansie allowed her broken heart to ease away, her thoughts turning to those of the past. Oh, what it must have been like.

The music ended, and other sounds seemed to crush her. The constant murmur of voices and careful conversations of those too frightened to lose themselves in the music overcame her. Sweat trickled beneath her white, loose blouse.

She gave Safron's hand a squeeze and pressed her way to the edge of the crowd, over to the table with the mulled wine. Mrs. Cobert ladled another glass for her, the woman's cheeks flushed with the many compliments she was receiving.

"Thank you," she said when Ansie told her the drink was better than last year's.

All the villagers knew the wine took the woman nearly a year to make. Her only allowance to make it was because Lord Hernan enjoyed the drink himself. Such a drink was outlawed to Anglans, but about this, Hernan turned a blind eye. One of so many things he did that made himself king over Mirtain, rather than a lord to the Regent. Bastion Nocta was too far away and too regal to be concerned with the petty annoyances of a village like Mirtain.

"Has his lordship had any?"

"Of course," the woman clucked, puffing her chest up in pride. For such a thin woman, she certainly knew how to make an impressive figure. "He tried it this afternoon and said the same as you." She blushed again.

One of her helpers nearly stumbled into her and Mrs. Cobert's expression softened for a moment. She reached out a hand and helped steady the woman's tray. Ansie tried not to look at the woman, knowing who she was and what she had lost. She didn't want to think about it.

"Poor thing," Mrs. Cobert said when they were alone again.

"Yes," Ansie said and cleared her throat, pressure building behind her eyes.

"Today's news nearly killed her." Mrs. Cobert sighed her thoughts seemingly on similar things. "Well," she huffed, "why are you still standing here talking to me, dear? You ought to be dancing."

"Not when I can drink this," Ansie replied quickly.

All night people had been urging her to dance. She was considered one of the best in the village, and some of the older folk took pleasure in watching her dance her way around, but her heart wasn't in it this year. Her heart was lost to a future she could never have.

She used to dance around the cabin when she was alone. It was her way to be free from prying eyes, to allow the thrum of her heart to move. Often times it was when she felt the weight of the world crashing down on her that she danced. She dreamed and she danced of times long gone—of the places where no one could find her.

"Come now," Mrs. Cobert tutted, "I see many young men looking to dance. All you have to do is stand near them and I'm sure you'll be asked."

"You're more certain than I am," she laughed, making sure to keep her tone light.

"Or you might wait for Skurn to finish this song." Luckily, the older woman was watching the swaying bodies and didn't see Ansie's wince.

"You never know," she wiggled her shoulders, and stepped away from the table, giving her thanks again. Mrs. Cobert laughed, thinking she had parted some wisdom to her.

Ansie had noticed the way Skurn's eyes drifted her way every now and again, even while he was dancing with the other girls, but she refused to let it bother her. She didn't have the freedom to let it bother her.

Instead, she wondered about where Willem had gone. For the last few days, he had refused to tell her what had happened on the road back from the village. Her heart had hammered the entire time he was in the forest—his excuse was to say it was a false alarm, but she knew him better than that. It angered her to have him keep something from her. At times she felt as though when he looked at her, all he saw was the little girl he had found by the river.

Ansie sighed, as she sipped the wine. She wasn't paying attention to where she was going and nearly stumbled into the chest of a Gallian soldier. Looking up, her blood turned cold.

"Ansie," Riffnen pursed his lips, looking her up and down. She swallowed the sweet wine, all too aware of how he watched her throat bob.

"Sir," she said, forcing her tone to be light. "Are you enjoying the festival?"

"A tad," he said, and took a large gulp from the mug in his hand. There was something about his eyes that seemed off—something she had only seen once before. She shivered to think of what had happened the last time. Riffnen took another slurp, his eyes roving over the dancers who laughed and sang along to the songs. "You should be dancing."

Another drop of sweat ran down her back. "I was."

"I saw," his eyes flicked to her face and away again. "Where's Willem? He doesn't enjoy dancing?" There was a viciousness in his smile which made her stomach tighten.

"I believe he was talking to Mrs. Cobert earlier, but I seem to have lost track of him." She spoke with cheer, though every part of her was on alert. This was exactly why she had told Willem to stay in sight of the festival, even with the news which had arrived earlier that day. She silently cursed him.

The soldiers were waiting for Willem's response to the news. There were simply too many eyes—she had noticed it when she first arrived. Too many Gallians watching. Normally Hernan only had a few of his men monitor the festival.

"Maybe I've had too much to drink," Ansie said, looking down into her mug. She gave a small giggle before letting the now empty cup twirl in her hands.

Riffnen turned to her, "When you do see him, come and find—"

"Ansie!" Skurn swung up beside her. Her heart pinched painfully. "Come dance with me!" His voice was cheerful, overly so, but she took his arm, tossing her cup aside with abandon. She didn't dare look behind.

They swung into the dancing crowd with perfect ease, her small frame matching his long strides as the tune wove around them. She tried not to think of the way she fit so perfectly into his arms, or how much she had missed talking to him.

Only when they were on the other side of the fire did she dare to whisper. "Thank you."

He didn't say anything and he didn't need to. She wouldn't allow herself to think what he had done was specific to her. She had seen many do the same for other girls. Riffnen was notorious for his prowling, though Lord Hernan kept him on a short leash.

The music slowed, the pace of their feet settling into a gentle sway as Skurn twirled her around the crackling flames. She dared to look up at him, the sparks from the fire dancing above his head.

"I mean it," she said even more quietly.

He glanced down at her, a small tug at the corner of his mouth. "I know."

They remained silent, letting the music speak for them. She wanted to lean her head against his chest, but knew she never would again. "You look beautiful," he said.

She blushed, ducking her chin and watched their feet step over the carefully laid stones. Her pale toes next to his boots seemed out of place somehow. It was a tradition for the women to go barefoot and the men to wear boots. There was a myth that if the man could forego stepping on a woman's toes the entire evening, then he was a good lover. The first time an older woman had spoken the tall-tale to Ansie, she had snorted mulled wine out of her nose.

The music changed, picking up the pace again and she was lost for words as they spun. Apart and back together, he twirled her around him until they were both out of breath. Her hair lifted in the breeze as she moved in perfect rhythm with him. There was a mournful note to their dance, the simple movements taking on new power. Though he touched her hands, her arms, her back, she hardly felt him, the distance between them was too great.

Dipping forward and back, they passed along the outer edges and she felt the tears burn the back of her eyes. After the news which had reached Mirtain today, she couldn't take any more. She just couldn't.

She stepped back in the midst of a song, drifting into the crowd and moving to where it was quieter.

Skurn followed her, keeping their bodies apart, a safe distance for anyone who might be watching.

In dancing, she could let herself go, but she wasn't foolish enough to forget all that had happened. Lord Hernan had used Kata to serve as a reminder, and the lesson was well remembered by all who gathered. Especially upon the news of Kata's fate.

A royal missive had arrived today—Kata had died in prison. Ansie's throat swelled simply thinking of it. What had been a constant wondering in the back of her mind for a year was now confirmed. Kata had not made it.

"So where is he?" Skurn asked with such perfect ease, pulling her from her thoughts.

"I really don't know," she shrugged, though she had been wondering the same thing all night.

She couldn't help scanning the crowd for Willem's head, which usually stood above the others. Her worry for him was growing by the minute. She couldn't let him return to the dark places he had turned to when they first took Kata away.

"He came, though," Skurn said, leaning his back up against one of the shop doors. Everything had closed earlier than usual in preparation for the festival.

"I would know since I walked here with him." If this had been a more normal time, she would have nudged him. But to even touch him now felt like drifting into the forbidden past. She was silent for a moment, the atmosphere between them dipping, growing more serious by the second. "I'm sorry for everything I said." She murmured the words, still watching the revelry before her.

The music sounded as though a horde of fiddlers stood in the plaza. The notes echoed off the walls, turning the tune over again.

"Maybe it had to be said," he whispered back. Something about his tone made her look up at him. His eyes remained fixed on the flames, the shadows from the dancers passing over his face, casting it from light into dark and back again.

"Maybe, but I could have been nicer about it."

"True," he acquiesced and then looked down at her. "But when have you ever taken the high road?" The subtle attempt to lighten the situation had her thanking him more than he could ever know. "I'm sorry too. I never should have said anything against Willem. He has every right to protect you the way he does."

"Someone has done a lot of thinking," she whispered.

"There isn't much else to do in the fields."

She nodded.

It was endless, the mind-numbing work they went through every day. If it was worth something, she would feel driven to do it, but there was hardly any purpose. Aside from her small ration at the end of the day, there was no reason for her to even work.

She was trapped, stuck here forever and all she wanted was to leave. But news of Kata reminded her that any dream came at a high price—one she was unwilling to pay.

"I do wish we could get away from all of this," she breathed aloud. "If it were a different time, a different place—I would go with you." She glanced up at him.

His mouth was set in a firm line. He gave a short nod to let her know he'd heard her. "Please, don't," he held up a hand.

She dipped her head, knowing his heart was as hurt as hers. She wanted to feel better about it, but she didn't. They would need time—for time could heal all wounds.

They stood in silence, shifting awkwardly until he cleared his throat and left her to stand on her own. She watched him as he made his way through the crowd and over to Mrs. Cobert's table.

He downed a glass of mulled wine, and then another.

―――――――――――――――――――――

The notes of the fiddles faded behind her and soon turned to the symphony of crickets and nocturs—birds of prey that hunted blind, their impeccable hearing providing more than enough skill to feed their bellies. They were beautiful creatures by day, their colorful plumed feathers catching the light like the glow of stars. But at night they were dangerous, and when they grew hungry were known to pick on larger prey than crickets and small animals.

Sighing, Ansie lifted the woolen skirt in her hands, she wasn't used to the extra fabric. Her pants usually clung to her legs throughout the day, and in the summer made the sweat cling to her skin. It was nice to be free, at least for a little while.

The plaid of the skirt was barely visible so far away from the flames. Here in the shadows of the trees, she was a mere passing thought in the nature whisperling all around her. Up above, the moons shone with a brilliance she hadn't seen in a long time. One red, the other, white.

Tears pricked her eyes, the words which had been passed around so quickly that day filling her mind. It wasn't right. *Oh, Kata.*

Turning down the Split, she pulled herself from her thoughts and remained on alert. She didn't think anyone had followed her off the main road from the village but it never hurt to be cautious. If there was one thing she had learned from Willem, it was to "Never let anyone know where you've been."

Following the overgrown path, Shirnway Castle soon came into view through the last copse of trees. She darted forward, making sure to keep an eye out for any movement, or any sound behind her. If Willem was here, he had most likely spotted her approach already.

She scaled a small wall, crawling in through one of the windows into what used to be the kitchen. The familiar dank musk of wet leaves and dripping walls met her nose. Sliding her fingers along the stone, she envisioned the trails her fingers left, as she dashed up the stairs leading to the main entryway.

Moving with practiced ease, she scaled the stairs, careful to keep her footsteps soft. She almost wanted this place to remain empty. There were too many memories here, ones she didn't want to face, especially tonight. Too many moments of adolescent joy taunting her with the horrors of what had become.

He was standing with a shoulder against a wall, looking out one of the broken windows lining the room. A light breeze lifted his hair, making the golden strands flicker for a moment; a glow from the rose moon pouring down on him.

She wanted to say his name, should have, but there was something about the way he stood that made her freeze. She felt as though she had stepped in on something private, something she and the rest of the realm weren't allowed to see.

His shoulders slumped in defeat, an action she had only seen once before. His head was bowed low, and the sorrow in each breath brought a hand to her chest. Only one side of his face was visible to her, but the lines pulling at the corners of his mouth told her where his thoughts remained. Just where she knew they would be.

He straightened and turned to her. His expression was one she knew well.

"Don't," was all she said holding up a hand. He shut his mouth, whatever words he had planned to speak lost upon his tongue. "Don't tell me you're fine."

He turned away again, looking back over the grasses which stretched toward the forest, the border of the Mirtain's land. "Can you imagine what this place must have been like?" He asked, resting a firm hand against the stone. "The people, the balls." He shook his pale head, clearly distracting himself. It hurt her to see him this way, he was so dangerously close to where he had lost himself.

"Of course I can," she said, delighted to see the small tug at the corner of his mouth. They both knew her imagination could run rampant without prodding.

"Must have been something to see."

"I'm sure it was." She took another hesitant step into the room. "I can imagine the music, the way these halls would echo with harps and trumpets blaring, the smells coming up from the kitchen, and the dresses of all the ladies glistening with diamonds."

He turned back to her, and she spread her arms wide.

"My guess is they danced with straight backs, very rigid. Like this," she mimicked dancing with a man but made her back extra straight as she moved with stiff halting steps. "One step here, then another there, and no twirls mind you," she glanced at him, pleased to see he was following her movements, "because that would be improper. Then when the music stopped, a curtsy, the ladies' noses nearly grazing the floor." She dipped as low as she dared without falling flat on her face.

When she rose, Willem brought his hands together and gave two mocking claps, before folding his arms over his chest. She rolled her eyes, pleased to see some lightness return to his gaze.

She met him near the window, looking out over the land before the castle. There was something peaceful about it, this quiet stillness, seeing the world as it should be.

By her side, he leaned against the stone again. She had the feeling he wasn't really seeing anything in front of them.

"What is it?" she asked. "You've been off since you took the grinspur horn to the market." She wouldn't mention the news about Kata.

"I already told you about that."

"Then what really happened when you left me on the road the other night?" She asked, this time bolder. In this place where memories lingered, she was more herself.

He sighed, "It doesn't matter."

"Tell me," she urged. He gave her a side-long glance, his gaze at once inviting and pushing her away.

"How long has it been since you've come here?" He turned away from the window, beginning to mindlessly walk through the room. His back was to her, but she felt as though her answer was important to him.

"This is the first time," she said quietly, "since it happened."

Hands on hips, he stopped in the middle of the room. "Me too."

If it hadn't been so quiet, she would've never heard his admission. Heart aching, she stepped forward thinking to touch him—to give him some sign of comfort for what he had been through. Something stopped her short.

He huffed loudly and looked up at the arched ceiling high above them. "She loved this room."

Tears pricked Ansie's eyes. The pain lacing his voice was something she didn't want to face. Even after it had happened, she couldn't bring herself to really understand what he had been through. And now to know the end had come.

He turned to her, his eyes haunted with the past. "She was always free here." His voice broke on the last word.

Ansie nodded. "We all were."

He looked away quickly, the torment of the past alive in his every movement. She forgot, all too easily, how much he had to ignore, how much he had to pretend.

As though she already knew what she was supposed to do, she sat down in the center of the room and patted the ground beside her. Little puffs of dust rose with each pat. "Come here."

Surprising both of them, he sat beside her and she leaned her shoulder up against his. Broken slats from above filtered the rose light of the moons into the room; a natural panel of stained color.

They called it the *luna amatorbi*, or the Lover's Moon. Only on Festis Luna would the light of the moons join together—the rose-colored moon shining brighter than the white. Ansie knew the story, the lover's tale of Neho and Cadna, and their tragic love.

Legend had it Neho fell in love with Cadna, a maiden with flaming red hair. He was called away to battle and she pleaded for him to stay behind, to be with her, but he went anyway. On the battlefield, he met with glory, and as he returned, his skin shining white from the gifts the gods had given him for his success, he found Cadna's health fading. Her hair, which had once been fiery red, had dulled, and when he took her into his arms, he tried to give her his strength. Her hair glowed with soft rose lights, accepting his love, but it wasn't enough. She breathed her last. Upon her breast, Neho rested his head and asked the gods to keep him with her. Taking pity on them both, the gods took his breath and placed them both among the stars, letting them shine together. On the last night of autumn, their lights crossed one another. In the small patches where the glow of the white moon met the rose, the light shone with a vibrant red brilliancy—Cadna's life breathing once more.

It was a beautiful story, but not one Willem needed to hear. Ansie knew in his heart, Willem felt what Neho had so long ago. There were some things you couldn't protect people from.

"It was Jethron," Willem said suddenly.

If he had slapped her across the face, she wouldn't have been more surprised. "What?"

"He was following us, I spoke to him." Her mind reeled as she tried to understand what he was telling her. It was impossible. "He saw me at the market when the gorilla escaped. And he was the one who made the sound we heard."

"You spoke to him?" She stared in disbelief. They had all thought Jethron dead—or worse.

Willem nodded, not looking at her. "He said he escaped. He thinks what happened with the gorilla is important. He wants to see me again."

Her mouth was hanging open as she looked at him. "Why didn't you tell me?" She wanted to hit him for keeping something so great from her.

"I couldn't believe it myself." He shook his head as though he was still trying to understand. "He's with the Renegades." He spoke softly, if anyone overheard him even speak that name, he could be whipped, tortured for information, and then hanged.

"Why would he risk coming to you? Coming here?"

"I don't know." Willem's eyes looked haunted again, and he shrugged. "But he seems all right."

"Why didn't he see me?" she whispered, it stung to think she had been robbed of the chance.

"Risk? He might not have wanted more than one person to know where he was." He heaved another breath and squinted up into the rose moonlight, his thoughts lost to her. Ansie's shoulder leaned into his, even as her thoughts ran in circles.

"We should head back," Willem said the words, but neither of them moved.

"What did he want from you?" she asked.

"He said *they* need me."

His words made her heart jump into her throat as the blood drained from her face. Here in this place, they had once let their thoughts wander, their minds expanding and dreaming of a world that was better than they lived in. Willem had been adamant about changing it all, about escaping Mirtain to join the Renegades, but he had paid a price. A price, she knew, he wouldn't pay again if he could change the past.

"What are you going to do?"

He glanced her way, his head high above her own. He had to tilt his chin to look her in the eye. "I don't know. I've been running through it the past few days, and I don't think I can make myself believe again. Especially now."

She nodded, she felt the same way, though his hurt went deeper than hers. She had lost a dear friend, he had lost so much more.

"I understand." She reached for his hand and patted it before pulling away. They were silent for a few minutes more.

"Shall we?" he quirked an eyebrow.

She nodded and they stood together, drifting away from the castle and the memories the old building held. The rose light of Cadna's moon followed them all the way back to the cottage, and only when they stepped inside did she feel as though she could really breathe.

Back in what they knew, she felt normalcy sweep around her in a gentle embrace. Crashing back into the mindlessness of their world, a part of her dared to dream, but as Willem said, she had a hard time believing anymore. The stories of the past were simply that, stories.

Everything had changed nearly a year ago, and today the news had confirmed their worst fears.

Kata was dead.

CHAPTER 11

"...to all those willing, their family shall receive an extra ration each week."

The murmurs began almost immediately. The entire village had been called from the fields to the plaza after work was completed. Announcements were often made, but none like this before.

"In seven days' time, all those willing shall report to the Registrar's office, whereupon said man or woman will be outfitted and trained. Only those who have passed into their thirteenth year are eligible." Mumbles stirred around Willem again, many of these families had children under the age of thirteen and to get an extra ration would help immensely. But something was off, he could feel it.

"...only those eligible to work in the fields will be allowed to participate." More grumbles. A trumpet sounded and the caller left the balcony.

Almost immediately the villagers began to push and press one another, startled into the reality of what had been spoken. As far back as Willem could remember, nothing like this had ever been done.

"What do you think?" Ansie's voice broke into his thoughts. Standing near his arm, she had dirt smudged over her nose, strands of her red hair sticking out in all sorts of directions.

"I don't." He folded his arms over his chest, his eyes alighting on Jep and his family. The older man had a hand to his forehead and his boys were already surrounding him. With two children old enough to work in the fields, the extra rations would be essential for his family. For some reason, Willem felt his own mouth was set in a hard line.

"Something's wrong." Ansie hardly said the words, but he heard them all the same. He nodded, refusing to look at her and attract attention. Something had Lord Hernan worried.

Why after all this time would Hernan arm his villagers? In other places weapons were allowed, but never in Mirtain. Something had changed, and if Willem knew anything it wasn't for the better. Could it simply be rumors about the Renegades that had Hernan worried?

First Jethron, and now this.

He grimaced and pushed his way through the crowd, knowing Ansie would follow. He didn't even want to know what she was thinking. Aside from her shared suspicions, the words the crier had spoken sent a tremor through him. If she was able to work in the fields, then she was able to be trained as a soldier.

As though confirming his suspicions, Ansie gave a little hop step beside him as she skirted around a young family looking disappointed, the announcement wouldn't include them.

"...give me a moment's peace, son. I will think about it."

Jep's oldest son, Bishawn, was close to baring his teeth when Willem and Ansie approached. Nelna, Jep's wife, turned to them and ran a weary hand over her brow, leaving smeared trails of dirt across her skin.

"Ansie, Willem," she said, acknowledging their presence. The other children turned to look at them, two of the younger ones were holding their mother's hand, one hiding behind her leg. Ansie leaned down to ask her a question, but she disappeared even more.

"Bunch of nonsense," Jep shook his head and glanced at the people around him.

"It does seem odd," Ansie agreed, quietly. Though it would be hard for the soldiers surrounding the plaza to hear them, there were those who wouldn't mind whispering secrets to Hernan for a pretty serc.

Willem nudged her with his shoulder to keep quiet. She shot him a glare and he had the distinct feeling of knowing what Jep was going through.

Bishawn caught onto the moment as well, the boy always too smart for his own good. "Will you join the ranks, Ansie?"

"I don't know," she shrugged, watching Jep's young daughter hiding behind Nelna. "It sounds rather exciting, and the extra food would be nice." Bishawn and Issak pointedly looked at their father. "But, I'm worried about what it all means."

Issak frowned. "How so?"

Willem gave her a side-long glance.

"Oh," Ansie sighed for dramatic effect, tossing a chunk of her hair over her shoulder, "I'm sure both of you understand, being so smart and all, but it probably wouldn't be worth it. I mean working in the fields, and then adding on more hours of work each day. Well, it should be worth much more than just one extra ration a week. Why not seven?"

Her words were treacherous and Willem wanted to cover her mouth with his hand without attracting attention. Jep was staring at her, jaw hanging open as though his mouth had gone dry.

"Oh," was all Issak said, some of the light dimming in his eyes.

Willem glanced down at Ansie again. She appeared simple, yet he knew there were many secrets hidden behind that smile.

Bishawn scratched his head and looked between his father and Willem as though wanting a second opinion. "It doesn't matter. I'll still be signing up."

"Suit yourself," Ansie shrugged her shoulders as though it was of little importance. "But you might want to think about it before you do." Smiling brightly, she nodded to the parents and excused herself into the crowd.

"Tomorrow then," was all Willem grumbled before following her.

In the past, they had laughed because she found him easy to spot in a large gathering. She said with his broad shoulders and height, he stood out like a bolting star across a night sky. What she refused to comprehend was her immediate presence wherever she moved. Her hair glowed like a beacon, its length often rippling in the wind. He would be hard pressed to lose sight of her in a crowd.

He came abreast of her quickly, and they shoved their way through the masses until they reached the exit from the plaza, the dirt road opening before them. One of the soldier's eyes slid up and down both of them as they passed. Willem recognized the face. He was one of the soldiers who had aided in taking Jethron and Kata away.

Willem shook the thoughts from his head, refusing to fall back into the horrors he had been a part of. He remained focused on the feeling which was slowly creeping over him. They were being followed.

Beside him, Ansie was muttering to herself. When they rounded the bend in the road, she opened her mouth to speak, but he grasped her hand and squeezed, hard. Her eyes opened wide and he shook his head quickly, his inkling growing all the stronger.

"How was work today?" He asked, cautioning her with his eyes. Only when she nodded did he pull his hand away.

"It went by quickly," she said as they began to pass along the path.

Sure enough, he heard footsteps behind them. He listened for more, none of it making sense. If Hernan needed something, all he had to do was summon him.

Ansie's bag jangled with each step she took as she prattled on about the field and how the wheat stalks were making her hands raw. Her words were lost to both of them, and they came to a halt when a hooded group of men rounded a curve in the road up ahead.

They were clad in black, their uniforms differing from the deep blue of Gallian soldiers. They strode with a sense of arrogance, with knee-high boots and crossbows strapped across their backs. More than likely, they had more weapons hidden along the thick coats beneath their cloaks. "Keep walking," Willem mumbled and Ansie nodded as though this was something they did every day. The soldiers came closer and he nodded to them, looking to pass.

A hand shot out and pushed against his chest. "Where are you headed?"

Willem didn't recognize any of the faces surrounding them. The one who stopped him had a mark on his chest that he had never seen before. A red line with two arching curves pointed in the same direction. He wondered what it meant—though he had a feeling it meant power. Was it possible these were the men Jethron had been talking about?

"Home." Willem nodded his head in the direction of the road behind the soldier. He didn't dare raise his hand.

"That so?" The man looked him up and down, the grey sparse whiskers making his already sun-scarred skin appear mottled. He had an odd way of puckering his lips after he spoke.

Willem chanced a glance behind them. Just as he suspected, two of Lord Hernan's soldiers were lying in wait, having followed them from the village. The way they lingered, hands on swords, told Willem they were as surprised by this seemingly foreign group of soldiers as he was. Never a good sign.

"Yes, sir," Ansie spoke up and the man's gaze shifted. "We live just down the road." She too kept her arms by her sides.

One of the soldier's grey eyebrows lifted, his companions shifted as though finding prey. Willem knew what was coming before the man said the words.

"I don't see a ring there, boy."

"We aren't married."

A short laugh escaped the man. "Well, how about that. Here I thought the Regent had written a law for all of Autre Gallia. But in Mirtain it's just a suggestion."

The soldier folded his arms across his chest as he looked between the two of them. "Now," he stepped closer to Willem, his fingers ground into fists, and lips pursed, "let's go talk to Lord Hernan and see what he thinks about all this, shall we?"

"Yes, sir," Willem nodded, not giving a thought to the ice in his words.

"Yes," Ansie spoke up, "I'm sure Lord Hernan would appreciate having us pulled into his presence once again to disrupt his day unnecessarily."

"You can't mean he knows about this?" He looked on the verge of laughter, but when no one corrected him, his eyes turned hard.

"I'm her guardian." Willem couldn't help the way his chest seemed to swell when he said the words. He would glare down any man, no matter what station, who dared to think he could lay a finger on Ansie.

The soldier spit on the ground near Willem's feet, missing his boots by a few inches. It was obvious his intent was to hit them. "Guardian?"

"Yes, my guardian." Ansie's voice was strong, though her head came up to about the middle of each man's chest. "He was awarded guardianship of me nine years ago."

"That's a long time." The soldier clicked his tongue. Willem wanted nothing more than to knock him to the ground, he settled for keeping his gaze focused on the cold, grey eyes. "What are your names? You can be sure I will be speaking with Lord Hernan about this."

"Willem, son of—"

"I don't care about what poor bastard you came from, or the whore who carried you." He glanced down at Ansie, "And you are?"

"Ansie."

"Very good." The grey eyes glanced between the two of them. Willem was certain his knuckles were turning white with restraint. "The *guardian* and his ward."

One of the soldier's gloved hands shot forward and before Willem could do anything, two of them had Ansie by the arms. They pulled her in front of Willem and she cautioned him with her eyes. Hernan's men behind them shifted, uncertain of what to do. He knew no help would come.

The past taunted him, blinking at him as the soldiers mocked him with their power. Somehow they all knew. They knew what he had done, what he had managed to do the day Kata and Jethron were taken. He had to maintain control.

The lead soldier stepped closer, cutting off Willem's sight of her.

Willem's heart pounded in his ears and his knuckles tightened from restraint. He focused on quelling the hatred thrumming in his veins. For a moment, his mind flashed to the gorilla and the way it must have felt to be trapped with no escape. He needed to escape this, to break free and use all of himself to protect her. He wanted to use his arms, his legs, anything to break away from the bondage coursing through him.

He hadn't felt this alive in months.

The head soldier spun on his heel and aimed two punches directly into Ansie's gut. Her breath shot out of her lungs on the first, and when the second hit, her legs buckled. The soldiers dropped her and she wheezed on the ground, struggling for air. Dirt turned to dust as she gasped for breath.

Willem watched it all from where he stood, the familiar feelings of his own inadequacy creeping over him. He had been here before, he knew what this was like, and he welcomed the darkness like an old friend.

"Guardian?" The soldier puckered his lips, giving Willem a skeptical glance. With a small smile, he flicked his wrist to his men. They passed by without a further look toward Ansie wheezing on the ground.

Willem didn't dare move toward her until the soldiers were completely out of sight, taking Hernan's men with them. Their backs disappeared around the bend, and he knelt down to touch her shoulder. She was breathing now, more easily, but the way the air hitched in her lungs made him want to hit something.

Ansie struggled for a few moments longer, and when he offered her his hand, she took it. She winced upon straightening, and he knew she was going to carry the bruises from the encounter for the next few weeks. She patted his hand, and he wanted to shake it off, knowing he didn't deserve her unwavering faith.

They reached the cottage in seemingly record time. As soon as the door was closed, she turned to him and pointed to the hook where he kept his sword. Hernan had given it to him—wanting him to hunt tonight.

"Soon," she wheezed, resting her hands on her hips. Her eyes were wide with fear and her lips trembled, but it was the set of her jaw that conveyed her determination.

He had lived with Ansie long enough to know what she meant when she pointed at the weapon. There had been a time when he thought it was possible for the realm to change.

"You," she pointed at him, "or me. But soon."

If there had been a light in her eyes when he told her about the gorilla, it was nothing compared to now. Those men had struck a spark inside her—a spark that used to burn bright. It had been over a year since he'd seen it.

She was right—though he didn't think anything would change. Something would have to. "Soon," he agreed, wanting to believe it as much as she did.

One act of rebellion would solve nothing.

But even as he thought the words, he knew one act had the power to rip apart worlds.

His one act already had.

CHAPTER 12

The fire popped and crackled with delightful pleasantness in the bitter winds around them. One minute the tongues of fire curled toward Larn, the next, unfurling in the other direction.

Across the flames, the soldiers shifted and stirred, their fingers grasping, pulling at the meat of the wandering elk they had shot hours ago. Larn took a bite of his own portion, it was tough and gamey but better than anything he had eaten in the past days with the Nexen and their wolves.

"How about a tale, boy?" One of the Nexen, the men called him Riv, asked from across the way, his eyes on Larn. Ever since the first day, Larn had been speaking more words than he had in a long time. His tongue weaving webs of tales and stories as though he had few cares in the world.

He had told them his name was Epen, but they were adamant in dubbing him, Teller. The leader, which the men simply called Captain, at times appeared annoyed by his constant talking.

Not as annoyed as I am, he thought.

For as long as Larn had been talking, Pike had remained silent. Every now and then, Larn wondered if he was going to explode. Just yesterday, Pike's horse had skittered and stepped on his boot. The stream of expletives which normally would have fallen from the man's mouth, was silenced—though his glares spoke volumes.

"Not tonight," Larn said over the flames, making sure to wear an easy grin. Riv threw a bone at him and the other men laughed.

One of the horses stirred and everyone grew silent for a moment. It wasn't the first time they had stopped in their jovial teasing of one another. Although the meat gave them merriment for the evening, there was a general

128

nervousness around the meager fire which did little to tame the bite of the wind.

The wolves were on edge, their ears perked, red eyes glaring through the pitch of night. Not for the first time, Larn wondered what all they could see and hear.

Captain paced back into the makeshift camp, kneeling to grab a piece of meat. The grease dripped from his fingers, sizzling on the frozen ground.

"No story tonight, Teller?"

Again the silly grin was in place, "I have to keep some of my tales." The men chuckled, and one protested, but the general amusement was good for cover. Larn shifted on the hard stone he sat upon.

"I have one," one of the Nexen, named Cardon, lifted his hand. Behind him, a wolf passed by with a soldier in tow; keeping the perimeter.

"Ahh," Larn smiled wider, "I knew someone else had stories. I can't be the only one." As always, chortles followed his words. It seemed the men were in such a desperate need for some form of mirth in this frozen wasteland, that they took everything he said to be a joke. *All for the better.*

"My da' told me this one," Cardon began, his voice soft but drifting on the wind. If Larn had been alone with Pike and Heben, he would have cursed the sound. But the Nexen's voice only added to what the flames were already accomplishing. "The wind wasn't so loud as it is now, not so strong, but that didn't matter to my da' when he got to the village."

Two of the soldiers shifted forward as one of the wolves on duty snapped at them. Always unruly, the beasts could never be trusted unless the captain kept them at bay. In their short time with the Nexen, Larn had learned the power of the captain. Not only was he in charge of his men, but the wolves responded to him. He had heard it once that these wild dogs had an alpha—and only to him would they respond.

If only there was a way to overthrow the alpha.

"There were all sorts of people there, but mostly villagers." Cardon kept talking and Larn wondered if the man had ever told a story in his life. Pike

129

caught his eye and rolled them to the stars above. If they had been alone, Larn would have laughed.

"And then," Cardon continued, "my da' came upon the fighting ring."

The mood shifted, like the flames bending in the wind—like the snap of a strained rope. *How could this man speak of such things here?*

Larn chanced a glance at the captain, his mouth was set in a grim line, but he didn't stop Cardon.

"It was set up real simple." Cardon used his hands as he described it. "The pit was the largest one my da' had ever seen. There had to be close to a thousand people there. All of them, watching." A collective breath was taken. "They started with the smaller ones, the foxes and small cats, but my da' knew they were going to bring out the real beasts soon. He waited in the cold and it paid off because they brought out a bear."

Despite the lack of skill in storytelling, Larn found himself leaning into the words, waiting, holding his breath.

"She was near twelve feet tall, standing on her back legs, her head the size of a wagon wheel. She was white, her fur bristling as she stood and roared out her war cry. They pitted her against a tiger."

Larn could see it now, the elimination of these ancient creatures by throwing them into fighting rings. Forced to fight to the death. His stomach lurched. If only these men knew the real crime they had committed. The real creatures there were killing, but that was the underlying fear of it all. Gallians feared anything that had to do with the Animle.

Cardon continued, "They eyed one another, and then the bear sat down." One of the soldiers gasped. "She wasn't going to fight. The handlers poked her and whipped her, but she never moved. The tiger kept prowling around, waiting to charge. It was starved, its ribs standing out within the stripes. The bear never moved, until they brought out a girl."

Another collective breath. Cardon's lips lifted slightly, seemingly lost in the moment. Larn's heart thundered in his chest and his hands balled into fists.

He was no longer smiling. This story was the reason they needed to find the Chroniclers. It was time for an awakening.

"It was the bloodiest fight my da' had ever seen." Cardon sniffed, running his hand beneath his nose. "The tiger charged at the girl, but the bear was faster. Swiping with mighty paws which could crack a man's skull in one fell swoop." He demonstrated; the men hooked on the story. "Each time the tiger got close to the girl, the bear would pound the cat back, never letting the claws get too close. But then the tiger pounced on the bear's back, claws latching into the fur.

"The bear's fury rang through the ring and she stumbled on her hind legs, her eyes never leaving the unconscious girl. The tiger prepared to make its final leap at the girl when suddenly, the bear reached behind and held the tiger in place. Blood oozed across the bear's white chest and the tiger roared, finding itself stuck. Then with a mighty crash, the bear toppled backward, the tiger screeching its last breath as it was crushed beneath the weight of the beast."

Larn's palms began to sweat, his breath unfurling in clouds. Heben placed a hand on his shoulder, drawing him back to reality.

It was silent, each man lost in the conjured image of bear and tiger entangled in mortal combat.

"Then what happened?" Riv asked, his voice nearly breathless.

"The girl woke up."

Larn closed his eyes, not wanting to hear the rest. He knew what was coming.

"A soldier prodded her awake. She stood, the crowd cheering as the bear rolled off the tiger, the cat's body crushed beneath the weight of the beast. The girl tried to reach the bear, only stopping when the chain around her ankle held her back.

"The bear called to her, its lumbering body dripping with blood and yet the girl could not reach the beast. She urged her closer, though she never said a word."

Larn turned away to look out over the open land, the cloud-covered sky afforded no light. The only shapes he could see were those of the Nexen and the wolves on patrol. Two wolves stood facing to the west, their backs hunched as growls rippled through their lips.

"The bear reached the girl," Cardon continued. "It rested its great white forehead against hers until the Regent appeared."

Larn didn't want to hear the rest of the story. There was only one way it would end.

"He's that old?" Riv asked, his jaw hanging open.

"No," Cardon cursed Riv with a foul name. "Our Regent is not yet twenty-five. It was his father, our Sire Regent Ferth." His voice dropped, returning to the story. "Regent Ferth held his hand out over the crowd beckoning for silence, but it was already quiet enough to hear the bear's every breath. He commanded the girl to fight the bear."

More gasps. If Larn had a weapon handy, he would have drawn it. But what was the threat of steel against a story? Words had the power to change things—when speaking of truth no weapon could withstand their strength.

"She wouldn't do it." Cardon looked around at his fellow Nexen. When his gaze landed on Larn, he paused, his eyes narrowing. "She told Regent Ferth he would have to kill her before she would ever harm an *Animle*."

An audible gasp, some mutterings and prayers were said. One man beat his chest, three times and tapped his nose before looking to the stars. Cardon's words were those of old, the words of things long forbidden. Warriors the Gallians had wiped from Anglas. Only the Chroniclers could know of such things.

And the Renegades, Larn thought idly.

"That's enough." The captain stood up as silence fell. He focused on Larn "It appears Teller didn't care for that story."

Larn glared at the captain. Beside him, Heben coughed and shifted, making sure to jostle Larn's shoulder. The captain smiled.

Ever since they had followed the Nexen a few days ago, the captain had been keeping a close watch on Larn; and well he should. It had made it harder for Larn to leave markers, but all the same, he'd been able to get the job done. Who would suspect the friendly storyteller, the one with the silly grin? All eyes were on Pike and Heben when he left the little pieces of fabric or dropped objects to mark their trail.

"No," Larn mumbled, slowly gathering his feet beneath him. He rose to his full height, tossing back his hood. Let them look at him and really see what they had been missing all this time. They had known he was of the Maereo—that couldn't be missed, but with humor, he'd been able to force them to see past it all. Gallians hated a serious Maereo. Serious was dangerous.

The truth now stared them in the face.

Larn's eyes narrowed, and his mouth set into a grim line as he faced the captain. The man nearly matched him in height and his hand shifted to the sword strapped at his waist.

"I didn't find the story amusing." As though Larn had declared war, the other men rose—Heben and Pike standing on either side of him. His words, no longer muddled with simpleton phrases declared their betrayal, but it no longer mattered.

The captain was drawing his sword when one of the wolves growled, the fur standing on end and a Nexen shouted out a warning. An arrow hit Cardon in the chest and men cried out as fear took hold. They scrambled for swords, in fury and fear, but they were too late. Out of the darkness men charged the camp—the Renegades had arrived.

Larn cut down three Nexen with the hidden small dagger he pulled from his boot. A heavy hand grasped the back of his cloak and threw him to the ground as the clamor of battle echoed through the valley—steel against steel. The wolves were tearing into flesh and charging at those who dared attack.

The captain raised his sword, bringing it down toward Larn's face. He rolled to the side, the blade missing. Reaching quickly, Larn stabbed him in the thigh. A cry of pain issued from the man's mouth as he crumpled to the ground. Larn kicked him in the back, but a large hand clutched his legs and pulled him forward. The dagger fell from his grasp.

The captain was above him, hands punching and pounding any area he could reach. Balling his legs beneath him, Larn pushed back. Fighting for some distance, he struggled when the captain fell on top of him, his hands wrapping around Larn's throat. Larn gargled, the wind becoming suddenly stagnant.

He kicked and prodded, but the fingers on his throat only tightened. The captain's lip curled and without further thought, Larn whipped his head to the side. There at the edge of the man's glove was bare skin. He sunk his teeth into the flesh with all the strength he could muster.

The Nexen cried out in shock, releasing his throat. Larn lifted his leg and pushed it against the captain's stomach, knocking him to the side. It took only one more move for him to remove a dagger from the captain's boot and thrust it into his side. And one more to kill him.

Breathing heavily, Larn stood, ready for the onslaught, but all around him was death.

The skirmish was over.

Wolves lay scattered around the ground, their white coats matted with dirt and blood. Two horses had fallen near him, their throats ripped out by a wolf. Their riders hadn't fared much better. The culprit lay with an arrow through his chest, the snarling jaws still quivering.

The wolf glared up at him, red eyes promising pain if he came any closer. Even on the brink of death, these beasts promised to destroy whatever came near. For some reason, Larn thought of the bear in Cardon's story.

He shook his head and plunged the dagger into the white chest, waiting to retract the blade until the last breath had shuddered from the wolf's body.

Larn frantically searched around the destruction for Tympmor and spotted the steed standing not far from the men, eyes wide, but otherwise unscathed. He exhaled, thankful for one blessing.

"Larn!" A gruff beckon called and he whipped around. Girshon, the leader of the Renegades, strode across the ground, picking his way through the dead.

"Girshon," Larn said in greeting and lifted a knuckle to his forehead in salute.

The leader was a man of thick stature—tall, but not overwhelmingly so. He was one of those men who seemed large due to the great expanse of his chest, the squared off jaw, and the rounded bulges of his arms. He was a man of darkened skin, making him nearly a shadow in the night. Only when he smiled was he easily spotted.

Girshon heaved a clouded breath and looked at the discarded corpses. "We thought we'd never catch up."

"Took you long enough." Larn greeted between heavy breaths, a smile returning to his lips. For the first time in days, it was genuine. The older man grinned back, his stature was only extenuated by the fur cloak he wore. "Pike was going crazy."

"Isn't he always?" He gave a harsh, bark laugh.

"I wouldn't know," Larn shrugged. "He hasn't spoken since they found us."

"Smart move on your part."

The object of their discussion spit on the ground and lumbered toward them. Pushing three men aside, Pike pointed at Larn with his sword. "If you ever do that again, you can be sure I'll cut out your tongue."

Larn laughed and wiped at the blood clinging to his hands. His hair whipped in the wind, the dark strands tickling his neck. He pushed it out of his eyes. "You would have had us killed within an hour."

Pike shrugged. "I didn't say it was a bad plan, I only said I didn't like it." The rough lines of his face lifted into a grin. The sight was always a bit terrifying, but Larn always appreciated it.

Heben made his way over to the men. "Are we done standing around like a bunch of fools? We have a lead to follow."

"Men," Girshon hardly had to lift his voice to the band of fifty rebels. Most had come in on foot, but Larn knew runners had already sprinted toward the rest of the Renegades to get more horses. Their hideout numbered over five thousand men strong. "I've asked for half of our number to join us. We will meet in two days. Prepare to leave."

Heads nodded, and the scavenging began. The men rifled through the dead's belongings, pocketing anything of worth.

"A word," Girshon jerked his head toward the expanse of darkness surrounding them. Stepping outside the ring of light from the crackling flames, Larn allowed the cold to surround him.

"The names?"

Larn sighed. "Lord Duggard didn't give us anything new."

"As I suspected," Girshon said, driving a thorn of disapproval into Larn's side.

"We heard a lead from some icemen in Kirath. They gave me the name of a trader who might know something about the missing Chroniclers. He often travels to the southerlands, though they hadn't seen him in nearly a year."

"His name?"

"Sarnon," Larn smiled.

"Lucky you already know him."

"Exactly," Larn nodded. Maybe, just maybe, this would lead toward something. After so many years of guessing and maneuvering it was time their plans grew into fruition.

Girshon nodded. "The best lead we've had in months." A grim smile lifted the corner of his mouth, dark whiskers decorating his chin. When he scratched his face, it made a harsh, prickly sound. "There's something more. We received word, there's been a Rising."

"Where?" Larn's heart skipped a beat.

"South. One of your contacts, a..." he thought for a moment, trying to recall the name, "Calig sent word."

Larn nodded, knowing exactly where his spy, Calig, was located—anticipation began building in his gut. For so many years they had been waiting to hear these words. It would soon be time, time for them to move on to something greater than themselves.

Then, freedom.

He could almost taste the word in his mouth, see the wide open plains and feel the wind swirling around him. The idea taunted him, the looming promise of getting what he had always wanted.

"Get your things ready, we're riding ahead of the rest. There's no time to seek out the Chroniclers now, this takes precedence."

"Yes, sir." If there had been a Rising, it was better to secure the warriors and find out more from the Chroniclers later.

"Calig says they have a prospect. He was spotted releasing a *gorilla*," he gave Larn a meaningful look. "Apparently the boy needs a little convincing."

Larn nodded. Another moment, another mission. "Convincing?" he quirked an eyebrow.

"Nothing you haven't done before, just a little persuasion."

The commander strode away and Larn heaved. Staring into the darkness he felt the thrum of the land. Something was changing—the very air awakening. Once he had stood on a cliff and watched as rocks gave way beneath his feet, it was the very same feeling. A crumbling of all that held this realm together. But rather than death, it would bring life.

Thinking of the bear from the story, he strode toward Tympmor. The story had awakened hope within him. At long last, maybe they had found the one who would bring the Animle back.

The Renegades carefully extinguished the flames, the hissing simmers turning the cracklings to silence. Darkness enveloped them, but Larn wasn't fazed. He turned Tympmor to the south, ready for what was to come.

CHAPTER 13

"Where are you from?" Neen's voice rose over the din of the rain hounding them from above. With the splatter of water masking their voices, more of the girls felt the freedom to speak, though Neen was the only who dared when the soldiers were so close.

Umbris shook her head, trying to communicate she would not speak. She knew Brute was somewhere nearby.

"I come from a big family, ten kids." Neen continued on, unfazed. "My father always said he didn't know what to do with so many mouths to feed," she grinned.

There was something about Neen's smile which seemed a little off. It wasn't the first time Umbris had wondered if the girl really knew what she was saying. There had been times like that back in the fort when girls would start speaking without thinking—as though in a daze, their eyes glazed over.

"We all worked really hard, but there were so many of us we hardly had any food." She shrugged, her chains clanking. "But, what family isn't starving." She gave a maniacal laugh. Another one of the girls shook her head. Umbris had forgotten her name now that they no longer called out role each night. Ever since the new commander had taken control, they remained in the cage.

"It was just me and my mum," the other girl said, the corners of her eyes crinkling. "I don't know what she's doin' now that I'm gone."

It was the same story Umbris had heard a hundred times over. At first, the need for a companion had overwhelmed her. After they took her from her home, she had been forced into a cell at Fort Jontru. Days there were spent in complete darkness, no chains, simply caged walls surrounding her.

She had lost track of time in that dank group, too many weeks and months without fresh air had erased all she was. There had been a few girls there whom she had spoken to, but the fever which wiped out half the group took them away. It was then when she stopped speaking.

Even now she wanted to silence Neen, they had all heard these stories more than once. They were the memories of what used to be, and what would have been. She had listened to her own thoughts running through the memories—the hopes that were never to be.

Her memories had a gold light to them, treasured moments of the past which were at once crisp and clear, and dulled as though life had never been so beautiful. It couldn't have been. But deep down, she knew it had.

She would never return to such a life. Never.

"Do you think they miss us?" Another girl asked from the other side of the cage. They all sat with their backs braced against the bars, no longer threatened by Brute or her spear.

"Of course they do," Neen spoke with such confidence. "What happened isn't our fault."

"How come?" the first girl asked, the one who had worried about her mother—she was younger than most.

Neen shrugged and took a deep breath, the rain running down her face. At least in the caged wagon, they had fresh air. In Fort Jontru they had been careful to breathe, as though afraid they would run out of oxygen.

"I got caught in the wrong place at the wrong time." Neen's voice turned mournful, gazing at the river rolling past. They watched her. "It was simple really, he was walking me home and I tripped. He caught me before I hit the ground." Neen had a sort of musical voice, Umbris could only imagine what she must sound like if she could sing.

"You shouldn't have let him walk you home," one of the girls pointed out. Umbris wanted to agree, but deep down she knew the injustice of it all. At least Neen wasn't at fault, her own shame was like a cloak around her.

139

"I couldn't say no, I loved him." She sniffed. "I don't know what they did to him."

Umbris shook her head, blocking the images from her mind. They had taken her away before she knew what happened, but she could guess. If she found out they had killed him, she was certain her heart would stop beating. In some way, she felt as though he was still alive.

The rain coursed down her face, her eyes welling with tears. There was more than one runny nose in the cage.

The girls continued to speak, their voices just low enough so the soldiers couldn't hear, but Umbris turned away from it all. She didn't want the memories to come back, to hear the crack of the whip as they dragged her away—his cries of agony ringing in her ears. He had cried out her name, as they dragged her away.

She sucked in a clogged breath and turned from the past.

If she pressed her cheek against the bars, she could see the horses' hooves sinking into the muddied path. The steady resilience of those hooves became her lifeline as the voices swirled around her. She ignored them, watching each hoof rise and fall, and rise and fall. She clung to them, holding on in hopes of never returning to those memories.

A new set of hooves entered her vision. Her eyes lifted quite suddenly to the stout figure of the commander riding toward them.

The girls grew silent beside her as he turned to pull up beside the wagon. Another rider, not far behind, did the same. He seemed to be shielding something beneath a cloak made of some creature's skin. The water rolled off it with ease.

"How many here?" the commander asked, his eyes roving over the carriage. Neen was about to answer when he gave the number to the man beside him. "Ten in this one. Take those numbers and report to me when you have the total."

The Gallian soldier knocked off a salute and spurred his horse forward, leaving the commander behind. Even in the pouring rain, he appeared immaculate and unfettered.

His horse's head bobbed with grace and Umbris had the sudden notion the mount was putting on airs. She glanced up to find the commander watching her.

His gaze dropped for only a moment, but it was enough to tell her what he'd seen. Her dark shift was clinging to her body and there was no way to hide it. At least he had the decency to avert his gaze.

No one had dared to look at her like that before, at least no one who wasn't discouraged. The sudden memory of watching one of the men in her village get punched in the stomach for an inappropriate comment flashed through her mind.

She almost smiled, but all too soon remembered there would be no one here to help her now. Unwanted words were the best she could hope for.

Steeling herself for what she might see, she raised her gaze back to the commander's but he was already turning away. His horse kicked up mud as it darted back to the front of the line. For some reason, she felt as though she had missed something. In her moment of quiet reverie, she hadn't seen what the commander thought of her.

Same as always, she thought, knowing it was more than likely the truth.

She settled back against the bars, once more listening to the girls speak, a part of her wishing she could no longer hear. She turned to the mindlessness of the rain.

CHAPTER 14

"Hold!" Riffnen's voice boomed over the field. All the men stopped, scythes frozen in mid-swing. "Those enlisted, depart!"

Many of the men hurried off the field. Even some of the women left their stations, rushing down the road to the village where the training fields rested near the soldiers' barracks. There they would begin another day of training. Ansie gritted her teeth against the dread rising within her.

It had been the same every day since they started allowing the villagers to be trained as soldiers. She had revisited her decision hundreds of times, looking at it from every angle, but she couldn't reason why she should join their ranks. Even as the logical thoughts reassured her, the nagging need for something different bit.

"Continue!" The call came, and work resumed as though nothing had changed.

In the light of the setting sun, the men were silhouetted against the horizon. Only Willem's steady swings brought a stillness to the unease inside her.

"I can't take it anymore," Safron mumbled beside her. Ansie didn't look up from the bundle of wheat she tied. "Every time he leaves, I worry." Safron had said much the same thing over the past week. Ever since the training started, she had been worrying about Chet. She fretted for his safety and had threatened to enlist more than once.

"I know," Ansie mumbled back. Dropping the bundled wheat to the ground, she shifted forward. One of the older women grasped the bundle she had dropped and took it to the wagon. Always so efficient.

"You're lucky, you don't have to worry about Skurn anymore."

"It doesn't mean I stopped caring." Ansie gritted her teeth.

"But it's not the same," Safron shook her head.

Ansie worked quickly on another bundle, hurrying to drop it to the ground. The aching in her back seemed to heighten in her annoyance. "Maybe you should enlist," she called over her shoulder as she moved forward.

Safron caught up with her, eyes wide. "What?"

"If you're so worried, then maybe you should join them. Then you won't worry as much. It's better than listening to you mope."

"Keep moving," one of the Gallian soldiers grumbled as he passed by Safron. She started forward immediately, not wanting to feel the sting of the whip he carried.

"I can't believe you."

Ansie sighed, she didn't have the patience for this. "Then why don't we leave it alone?'

"No." Safron set her mouth in a firm line. "Maybe I will enlist, Ansie. Then when we get attacked, I can die in a battle."

Ansie had to bite her tongue to keep from laughing. Everyone always said she was dramatic, but when it came to drama Safron took the lead. "That's only if you make it through training. You might not even make it that far."

Safron glared, her mouth gaping. When Ansie waggled her eyebrows at her, her friend refused to smile.

"One of these days," Safron spit, as she bent to pick up another handful of the wheat stalks. "Your tongue is going to get you in trouble."

"I was only trying to make light of the situation."

"It's not something for you to joke about," Safron spoke sharply through her teeth, her words just loud enough for Ansie's ears. "Not now."

"Fine." Ansie shrugged. Safron didn't make a further sound, for once, and Ansie was glad for the silence. It gave her a chance to think.

The rumors she had heard this morning made the hairs on her arms stand on end. Rumors she was too afraid to believe.

It began last night, the word traveling from cottage to cottage, spreading like wildfire through the night—whispers of the Renegades, men banding together and making their way South. The rumor claimed they were headed for Bastion Nocta.

What would happen when they reached the Regent, she didn't know. She had asked Willem what he thought and his answer was what she had come to expect in the last month. He said it wouldn't change anything.

There was a part of her which agreed. After all the years of oppression since the Gallians took over Anglas, nothing had ever really changed.

When Gallia had first taken over Anglas, they had rid the realm of anything that wasn't deemed "Gallian." A dichotomy had been put in place. The Gallian families were given portions of land by the first Regent of the joined realms, and all the Anglans of said land were to serve that family.

Ansie shook her head, wondering what Lord Hernan's ancestors had done to receive Mirtain as their portion. Nothing good no doubt.

It was because of the Gallians that she worked in the fields—the system demanded it. Every lord had subjects beneath him, workers to till the fields and create a surplus of food which was then distributed in rations. Their reward for their work was protection—though from what she didn't know.

Some trade, she thought handing her latest bundle to the woman behind her. They were more likely in need of being protected from Gallians than Anglans. The gong which signaled the end of another day's work sounded over the fields.

She left without a backward glance at Safron. No doubt her friend was still fuming.

The sky dipped into the dark brushes of maroon strokes along the horizon. The deepening color only made her skin feel hotter from the sunburn she had received. She was certain to have a few more freckles—though none stood out as much as the six brown dots curving around her right eye.

The gravel crunched under her boots as she swung her coat on and waited in line for both rations. Willem had said he had some things to do at the cottage and she had told him to go ahead and get started without her.

She was only halfway to the front when Riffnen called her name. Back straight, she stepped out of line. A week ago, standing straight had been difficult, but as the bruises on her abdomen slowly healed she was able to stand without wincing.

She had seen the new Captain a few times since his arrival. His name was Captain Fergin, and what he was doing in Mirtain remained a mystery. Though Safron had overheard someone mention the word Nexen. Ever since hearing that word, Ansie had kept a sharp eye on the lookout for wolves. She could have sworn she'd heard a howl just last night.

Why, when she wanted so badly to be free, was she so fearful? Those two punches to her gut had been enough to make her want to run away—but she was too afraid to try.

Keeping her eyes on the ground until she reached Riffnen, she snapped to attention before him. "Yes, sir?" It felt informal to look him in the eye, though she had done it many times before. In a different world, if she was Gallian and lived in Bastion Nocta, she would be wearing a dress of immaculate design and would have curtsied before Riffnen. But here, she merely dipped her head and then looked up at the man who controlled most of her days.

"I won't waste your time," Riffnen smiled, a sickening sight. She never could get over the way his skin always appeared slippery, as though he hadn't washed in days. "I was going over enlistments and didn't see your name on the list. Tomorrow is the last day to sign."

"I know," she said, then quickly added, "sir."

"You don't intend to enlist?"

"No, sir."

"Hmmm," the sound came from the back of his throat, as his eyes rolled over her. She wondered if her skin looked as oily as his. With the way the dirt was caked on her shirt, she feared it looked worse. "Might I ask why?"

"No reason, sir."

"I also noticed Willem's name is missing." If he had been casual before, his manner was anything but now. His eyes bored into hers, parts of his greasy hair hanging lank on his forehead.

"He doesn't want to be a soldier." She said the words softly, after choosing them carefully.

Riffnen gave a fake smile of amusement. "He would rather work in the fields the rest of his life."

"What else could we wish for?" If she could slap herself in his presence, she would have just then. Safron was right, her tongue was going to get her into trouble. "What I mean is, we're happy with what we have."

"Your allegiance astounds me," Riffnen snorted.

"Sir?" she asked, confused.

His voice suddenly dropped. "Don't think I'm oblivious to the looks you give the soldiers, or the things you say when you think no one is listening. You want more, something other than working in these damned fields."

Ansie swallowed heavily and his eyes gleamed, knowing he had guessed correctly. She felt her skin crawl as his gaze wandered. She had been foolish to think he wouldn't notice, foolish to think he was simple-minded.

"All the same," she said, a little breathless, "I'm fine where I am. I wouldn't know what to do with a sword."

He opened his mouth but was cut off when a hand landed on his shoulder.

Ansie's stomach tightened as Captain Fergin stepped into view. The sparse whiskers had turned into a full beard, giving the man a more commanding appearance than he'd had before. It was varying shades of grey. She swallowed and dipped her head.

"Ansie, we meet again."

She didn't speak. The bruises where his soldiers hit her were just beginning to fade away. She still felt them every time she bent over in the fields.

"You've met Captain Fergin?" Riffnen asked.

"Yes. I had a bit of a run-in with her and her *guardian*." The captain's face twitched on the last word.

"Willem." Riffnen seemed determined to establish his knowledge.

"Yes," Captain Fergin replied, his eyes still fixed on Ansie. "Where is Willem?"

"At the cottage," she ground out, "sir."

"I was just telling her how interesting it is to find neither of them enlisted."

Captain Fergin only nodded at Riffnen's words. She shifted beneath his grey gaze, feeling colder than she had all day.

"I have a feeling he'll be enlisted soon enough." The way he said the words with such determination, gave Ansie a queasy pinch in her gut.

"How?" Riffnen questioned the captain, so quickly making himself subservient to the man.

"Recruitment rates have been low," Captain Fergin's grey eyes burned into hers, as though she was to blame. "But we expect a change soon. Willem will present himself for enlistment later today, that, I can guarantee."

If it wasn't for the way his attention drifted over her shoulder to the line standing near the ration window, she would have thought his threats empty.

Without looking her way again, he dismissed her with a wave of his hand. She didn't dare to linger and hurried back to the line where the woman, who had been behind her earlier, was saving her spot. She thanked her quickly and rushed to the counter to gather her rations and hustled away from the murmuring crowd. Her conversation with Riffnen and Captain Fergin had not gone unnoticed.

Just as she turned to head down the road to the cottage, Jep's wife, Nelna, called to her. "Have you seen Issak?"

"No," Ansie shook her head quickly and turned around on the spot, taking in the fields, the ration house, and the quickly dispersing line. "Was he working today?"

It was common knowledge the oldest son, Bishawn, had enlisted, but Jep had put his foot down when it came to Issak. He refused to let the younger of the two join.

"I saw him around the time we finished, he was supposed to be in line, but I don't see him now." Nelna's voice was growing more panicked by the second. Her eyes darted over the moving forms, but she patted Ansie's hand quickly. "Not to worry, I'm sure he's here somewhere." She sounded as though she was trying to convince herself.

Ansie could only nod as the woman left to search around the other side of the ration house. She was turning to leave when she saw Captain Fergin. His eyes never left Nelna and as he tightened the dark gloves over his hands, a sneer pulled at one corner of his mouth.

They know.

The thought shot like a beacon across her mind and she took off running for the cottage. It didn't matter if they followed, she had to get to Willem.

There was only one reason why the soldiers had been asking her about Willem all day. She had foolishly thought it was to get a rise out of her—but it wasn't. They wanted to see him lose control again, just like he had the day they took Kata and Jethron. They wanted to see the warrior beneath the calm façade he forced upon himself daily. He had only slipped once before, and if what she thought was happening was true, it was bound to happen again.

She cursed her short legs and ran faster.

The cottage came into sight and she surged ahead, slamming the door open. It bounced on its hinges and Willem shot up from his work at the table.

"They have Issak."

His face never changed, but he moved quicker than she expected. Without a word, he was out the door and taking off down the road toward the village.

She followed as fast as her legs could carry her, the distance between them growing with every step. All the way, she could only send up cries to the stars that she was wrong—but with every beat of her heart, she knew she was right.

CHAPTER 15

Willem heard the crowd before he reached the plaza—shouts and protests ringing off the walls.

He ran through the entrance, the soldiers sneering at him. The heat of the crowd hit him with a powerful strength, and he slowed to a walk. He couldn't break control, not this time. He had been warned what would happen if he ever acted in such a way again.

Mutterings began behind him as he shifted through the gathered villagers. They watched him, wondering what he would do in light of this injustice. The fountain blocked his view of the platform beneath the balcony of Hernan's house. The closer he got, the more it took up his view, but the crack of the cane told him enough. A cry of pain set his blood to boiling.

Finally, the platform came into view. He had braced himself for the sight.

Issak clung to a pole, his arms chained. A blow cracked down on the young boy's back and his knees buckled. Disapproval marked the faces of all who stood near, some shaking their heads, but no one moved to action. Near the platform stood Jep and Nelna, their eyes filled with tears as they watched their son be punished. Willem had to look away before he saw the silent tear roll down Jep's cheek.

Beside the boy was Captain Fergin. He kept a hand on the post, watching as his soldier delivered another blow. If it hadn't been for the way his eyes shifted to the crowd and back, Willem would have thought him bored.

Glancing to his right and left, he noted more of Hernan's men than usual in the crowd. They stood casually, but their hands rested on the hilts of their swords. The last time, Willem had barged in empty-handed, and still, he had defeated eight of them before they took him down. He wouldn't dare to try again—not with Hernan's threats that day, and not with the Nexen standing nearby. Ansie wasn't the only one who had heard the howl of a wolf in the midst of the night.

Suddenly, Fergin's eyes landed on him. For a breath Willem held his gaze before the captain pulled away from the post, halting his soldier mid-swing. Silence reigned. Everything held in the balance.

"That's not his," Willem said, pointing to the bag of evidence resting on the platform. The contents spilled out on the wood revealing various food and goods—a portion of what he had purchased at the Black Market. "It's mine."

"Then how," Fergin bent over to pick up the bag, "did Issak have it?" He mocked him, putting on a show for those watching.

The boy shifted, wide eyes filled with tears, blinking at Willem. His gut tightened and he pushed back the memories threatening to overcome him.

"I hid it, he must have found it."

Fergin's face scrunched as though he was working hard to put some pieces together. "So this boy was unlucky. Is that what you're saying?"

"Right. Wrong place, wrong time," Willem agreed. His nostrils flared in anger, but he maintained control, they wouldn't break him. "He isn't to blame."

"Ahh, I see." The man spoke with such arrogance. "What you mean is, this is everything you received in payment for the grinspur horn? I must say, Willem, though Lord Hernan brags of your tracking and hunting abilities, you fail miserably when it comes to bargaining."

Fergin was baiting him, Willem could feel it. He gave a wry smile. "I'm better with my hands."

"Your *ward* must be disappointed."

"If she knew anything about it, she probably would be." He shrugged and the captain's eyes hardened. He had been baited this way before, too many times. Ever since Hernan had noticed his skills, threats and warnings had been Willem's entire existence.

Fergin turned back to the post. "Cut him loose."

The soldiers worked quickly, forcing Issak to clamber off the stage on his own strength. Some of the tightness in Willem's chest lightened as the boy reached his crying mother. Jep eyed Willem and gave a slight shake of his head.

"Would you like me at the post, *sir*?" Willem asked. Two could play this game.

Now that Isaak was out of the soldiers' clutches for the moment, he was able to give some fire to his voice. He hoped Ansie was smart enough to keep herself hidden in the crowd. The last thing he needed to witness was her getting hit by Fergin's men again.

Fergin's jaw tightened and motioned him up. Willem held his hands in front of him as he climbed the stairs. Memories of the last time he had ascended the platform tried to break free. He struggled to stay in the moment.

Stepping up to the post, the captain's hand was suddenly on his chest, pushing him back. "No."

One word was all he received before he was spun around to face Hernan's manor. A sharp shove in the middle of his spin sent him stumbling forward. As the metal doors swung toward him, the dark confines of the lord's chambers were anything but welcoming.

"This way." Fergin passed him, leading him into the main entryway and down the hall where Willem knew Lord Hernan's study was located. Four Nexen flanked his sides, the doors slamming behind them.

It looked the same as it always did. A worn, imposing desk took up most of the space. Chairs with cushions lined the room, a few scattered in front of the empty hearth. Papers and documents covered every surface available, a sweet stench reaching his nose. It had a pungent tingling to it, as though someone had desperately tried to get rid of an unpleasant odor. The result was an overpowering, sweet aroma with an underlying bitter tinge which always unsettled his stomach.

Lord Hernan sat behind the desk, focused on the papers before him. The mere sight of him made Willem's hands ball into fists.

Hernan was young, younger than one expected when told of his twenty years of lordship over Mirtain. Robed in a dressing gown made of fine silk, Lord Hernan was always a sight. Though Mirtain rested far from the reach of the capital, the lord was always dressed as though he was a member of the court in Bastion Nocta. He had long blonde hair, parted directly down the middle revealing a shockingly white scalp. His hair brushed against his shoulders and he had an odd manner of pushing strands of hair away from his face without bending his fingers, but never past the edge of his clean-shaven jaw. All the more to show off his pristine skin and perfectly cared for nails.

Sighing and looking up from the stack of papers, Hernan's sharp blue eyes focused. "Ahh, Willem!" The man stood and moved his parted hair along the sides of his face with perfectly manicured hands. "I was wondering when you would show up."

Willem refused to answer. He hated these games. If he spoke, he was afraid what he really thought would come pouring out of his mouth.

A Gallian soldier entered the room and placed the bag of food on the table. Enough evidence to have Willem whipped.

"He confessed, your Lordship." Fergin gestured toward the bag.

"And well he should," Lord Hernan said, looking Willem up and down. He spoke in a high pitch, one which could never command presence in a room full of men, but was dangerous all the same. Each word laced with precision and poison. "Willem, you know how I detest the Black Market. I'm very disappointed. When my soldiers reported your attendance, I thought you would never do such a thing, and yet," he pointed to the bag, "here we are."

Another game. In a different time, Willem would have laughed, but there was nothing funny about this. Hernan's rule was absolute—Fergin and his men had no idea that Hernan allowed Willem to barter at the Black Market. Not only did he allow it, but he also insisted that Willem be the one to carry out the deed. It was harder to follow the trail if the case was an Anglan's word against a Gallian lord's.

"I needed food." Willem refused to look toward Fergin or any of the other soldiers. His sole focus was on Hernan—the one he knew how to handle.

"According to the log, you haven't missed a ration." The blue eyes pierced him. The manicured hands gently pushed the hair back again, always so perfect, not one strand out of place. "Why then would you need more?"

"I eat a lot."

Hernan gave one of his high-pitched laughs. "Watch yourself." He stepped out from behind his desk, the long dressing gown dragging across the floor with a swift whisper. The sleeves dipped into wide cones at his wrists, making him appear smaller than he was. He stopped near one of the windows looking out over a private garden.

"What you've done is punishable by a severe beating, five days in the stocks, a restriction of all rations for a week following your release, along with confiscation of any food you now have."

Willem caught his breath. He knew he would suffer the consequences for helping others—Hernan had warned him of it. Sucking in a breath, he waited. Hernan clearly didn't want Fergin knowing that he permitted an Anglan to visit the Black Market, but he would have to be punished to save face. Everything had a price for Hernan.

"However," Hernan said, the clean fingers waving in the dismissal of his earlier words. "I would be willing to let some of those stipulations go if you do something for me."

There it was, the threat so easily drawn as a request. Year after year, Willem had stood in front of this desk and heeded every request. Some were degrading, but most were simple. Keep Hernan happy, and Mirtain was better for it. Hernan didn't think he shirked the law, he was the law. He saw no crime in what he had done—but every time Willem saw him he had to lock down all emotion.

He'd heard Kata's screams when they took her away. Most likely, Hernan had brought her into this very room. The law of the Regent was for any unmarried man or woman who was caught in an act of indecency to be punished. The man was to be beaten and sent to a labor camp—the woman was to be beaten and sent to a working house where she would spend the rest of her days trading her body for survival.

But Hernan had seen fit to change the law that day. He'd taken Kata for his own before sending her away. Willem bit the inside of his lip to force back the echoing screams in his mind.

If there was any way to strangle the man without the soldiers interfering, he would have done it already. He wanted to feel the smaller man struggle beneath him, to watch as the light left his eyes. More than anything, he wanted Hernan to scream, the way she had screamed when he took her away.

But he had a role to play, and he would do it. Ansie's safety depended on it. "Why would I ever do anything for you?"

Willem never saw the blow from Fergin, but the crack on his recently healed nose split again. Pain exploded along his face and for a moment he lost sight before the images came back together. Blood dripped down his chin and onto his shirt.

"Captain Fergin," his lordship sighed, "that won't be necessary."

"Yes, my lord."

Lord Hernan focused his gaze back out the window. "I know we've had our differences," he muttered, "but you must consider my offer. What happened with *that* girl was a shame."

His hands curled into fists.

"Kata," Willem said, no longer playing the game. Lord Hernan turned to him, his brow furrowed in confusion. "Her name was Kata."

"Oh, yes, of course." Hernan waved his hand again and went to take his seat. "We've been over this Willem. She was caught and needed to set an example for the rest of the village. It wasn't *my* ruling. The punishment was signed by the Regent, himself." He put a hand to his chest, the pale white fingers seeming to absolve the man of all guilt. "I only did my duty to the realm."

Willem took a deep breath, as Hernan eyed him. He knew what he was doing, tightening his hold on Willem while he flaunted his crime before him. Fergin didn't know what Hernan had done, and he wouldn't, for it was treason to go against the Regent's edict. The room remained quiet, and Willem refused to be the first one to break the silence—the blood in his veins throbbed.

"Now," Hernan's fingers created a little tent on the desk, "that is not why we're here. What I want to know is why you didn't enlist?"

"I believe the announcement said it was voluntary."

"True, but I have need of you." The man gave a quick flash of too-white teeth. "You will oversee the training of your fellow Anglans, teach them how to handle a sword. With all these rumors about, I need my land protected."

It was in the lines of Hernan's mouth that Willem found his answer. The downturn of his lips held the seriousness of the rumors crossing the realm. The Renegades were on the move. Thinking of Jethron, Willem wondered if Hernan knew how close some of the Renegades were.

Willem pondered his words for a moment, knowing Hernan meant what he said. Until now, Willem hadn't truly believed the rumors of the Renegades, but even a fool could confirm what others believed.

"You will also be given a special mission which upon completion will wipe you of these charges," Hernan waved a robe-clad hand at the bag on his desk.

"Yes, sir."

"You see Captain, I told you he would agree. It's only a matter of persuasion," Hernan said, and picked up a cherry and ate it before continuing on. "That being the case," he shifted a few of the papers around, "I have here a decree from the Regent, that any and all animal fights are to be stopped and the beasts executed."

Willem froze.

"You're aware of the pit at the Black Market?" His lordship didn't wait for him to clarify. "It just so happens one of my soldiers saw you there the night a gorilla escaped. A rather interesting story, I would ask him to tell you, if you hadn't been there yourself, but no matter, no matter. What I want, is for you to track down that beast and kill it. The others have already been taken care of."

Willem's heart pounded heavily in his chest, as Fergin turned, eyeing him. Just what the Nexen captain thought was too much to consider at the moment.

"And if I refuse?" Willem asked, his voice sounded hoarse even to his own ears. Hernan met his gaze and whatever pretense had been formed had long disappeared. In its place was the man Willem had come to know over the years. The cold, heartless man who would use anyone or anything to cater to his whims.

It was all a test of allegiance. Obey Hernan, obey the Regent, or obey his own heart? Each led in a different direction, but only one offered the slightest chance of freedom.

"For the last ten years, I have granted you permission to take care of that *girl*. Do I need to bring it to the attention of the Regent? All it takes is one messenger from me." He held up a finger. "Her punishment would be very similar to, what was her name again, Kata?" He glared—his blue eyes gleaming in a sneer. "Do I make myself clear?"

"Yes, your lordship," he said quickly. His heart was hammering faster than he thought possible. For all the threats Hernan had given him over Ansie through the years, he had never said anything like this. A door slammed on any hopes he had at rebellion—the shackles of death and destruction to all he held dear tightening around him. "When would you like me to begin?"

He knew he probably looked foolish, standing in a room surrounded by soldiers, his nose dripping blood. There was no doubt Captain Fergin was enjoying himself.

"Tomorrow." Hernan's voice turned sweet again.

Fergin gave Willem a nudge toward the door. He turned to leave, wiping beneath his nose with a hand. It came away with a smear of red.

"Oh, and Willem?" The sweet voice said from behind him, and he turned back to the desk. Lord Hernan's eyes were on the papers once more. "Ansie will receive her rations for her work in the fields, but it will only be one ration." Suddenly the blue eyes were on his. "You can keep what food you have, and no time in the stocks. Be quick about it." The last words were directed to Fergin, and Willem knew what was coming before the first blow landed.

They released him roughly twenty minutes later, tossing his body onto the platform outside of Lord Hernan's manor. The stairs nearly gave way beneath him as he tried to stand.

Gentle hands were suddenly on his shoulders, helping him sit up. "Here," Ansie said softly, giving him a skin of water.

The light was nearly extinguished from the sky, the moons beginning to shine as the night took its course.

"Get going," one of the Nexen who'd beat him yelled from the balcony above.

It wasn't enough for them to humiliate him inside. They wanted to watch their handiwork hobble out of the plaza.

"In a minute," Ansie called back up cheerfully with a smile, and then muttered under her breath, "shut your mouth or I'll give you a swift kick in the crotch that'll do you some good."

Despite his pain, Willem hid a laugh. She always knew how to make him smile.

"Come on," he grumbled, his voice rougher than it was an hour ago.

She sidled up to him, her small frame doing more pain than help as she tried to use her strength to assist him standing. He nearly lost his balance, his head rushing, but gathered himself.

The remaining villagers watched as they passed, Ansie holding tightly to him. If it wasn't for Lord Hernan's threats he would have been comforted by her presence.

They reached the exit to the plaza, passing through it with little acknowledgment of the soldiers. Only one of them dared to meet his eye as he limped by.

He stumbled on, wondering how he had never realized how many bones and muscles were in his body. It seemed they were all crying out to him, wanting him to know they were present. As far as he saw it, they could go back to being invisible at any moment.

"What did Lord Hernan say?" Ansie asked when they were out of earshot.

"How do you know I saw him?" When she didn't answer he groaned. "You watched didn't you?"

"Not the beating," she said softly. "But the other stuff, yes."

"Ans," he shook his head.

"I wanted to know what was happening. There was a pipe, I climbed it. What's the big deal?"

"The big deal is I don't want you getting caught."

"I know what I'm doing."

He sighed, feeling it all along his ribs. "Let's not do this. Not now."

"Why not now?" She stopped walking, placing her hands on her hips. "I want to know what was said and why you got off with only a beating. You tell me now Willem, or so help me I will—"

"Kick me in the crotch?" he asked.

She bit her lip to stop a smile—she always had the hardest time staying serious. "This isn't the time for joking."

"They want me to track down the gorilla and kill it."

He watched as she gaped at him, but he didn't give her a chance to recover. He began limping down the road toward the cottage. She caught up soon enough.

"Are you going to?" she asked, sidling under his arm, allowing him to use her body as a crutch.

"I don't have much of a choice." Even as he spoke, he could feel the constraints of Lord Hernan's words. "He threatened you, Ans."

"What else is new?"

"No, not like this. He means to hurt you." He couldn't say the words.

She was silent for a moment, and then softly spoke. "Thank you." Her anger ebbed away like a passing wind. "But you can't protect everyone forever."

"I know." He grit his teeth. He'd already failed once, he wasn't going to let it happen again.

"So, what are you going to do? About the gorilla, I mean."

What was he going to do? Was there an answer to his problem? Lord Hernan had only given him one option. The solution was to do what was asked of him and everything would move along as expected.

"Will you kill it?" She asked, her thoughts following along the same path as his own.

It was simple enough, really. How many other beasts had he tracked down and hunted?

His skills in the forest were the main reason Lord Hernan allowed him to keep Ansie as his ward. Lord Hernan liked fine things, which was a difficult way to live in obscure lands. Willem had often wondered if the Regent even knew Mirtain existed.

Fine things were the way to Hernan's heart. Willem knew he could always appease him if needed, for he had tested the strength of Hernan's will to give up his life of luxury. On the day Kata and Jethron were taken, he should have died for his actions, but instead, he'd been pardoned.

Thinking of the new task he had been given, he knew it was simple enough. In comparison to the grinspur, the gorilla would be easy, but a part of him pulled back from the thought of even touching the creature. The brown eyes of the beast seemed to dance before his own as he hobbled down the road. The cottage came into view and he hurried toward it, Ansie keeping pace beside him.

He needed answers, and there was only one way he knew how to get what he wanted. He needed to know just what kind of creature this was, and he had a hunch.

"Get your things ready," he muttered under his breath, knowing she could hear him. "As soon as I get the chance, I'm going to see Jethron, and you're coming with me."

CHAPTER 16

The burning began at dawn.

Umbris had awakened to the clanging of Brute's spear against the bars lining the cage. They were hustled onto the ground and into a line with soldiers standing on either side. Some of the women had started crying, but after the minutes dragged on, forcing them to shuffle forward every now and again, the tears stopped. Instead, they were replaced with exhalations of sadness and pleas for mercy.

Umbris didn't understand what it was all about. She had known this was coming ever since they had taken her. They all had. Maybe it was the finality of it all.

As the line shifted closer and closer, she began to smell the rancid stench of burning flesh. Only then did she begin to really feel the fear creep upon her, her stomach flipping on itself.

They were beside the Glaive again. This time, within a hundred yards from the bank. Women were scattered about the edge, dipping their arms into the cool embrace for relief.

The trees rustled up above as another woman's muffled scream rose into the air. It had only taken the first prisoner to scream as they branded her skin, for the soldiers to find a gag.

There seemed to be three different reactions to the process ahead. One was screaming, though it seemed to do nothing to help the pain. The second was wailing, something Umbris couldn't stand to hear. It reminded her of the way the women in the village used to cry when burying their husbands or children.

The last was better than the other options, a path taken by the strongest women. There were only two so far who had accomplished it. They had been silent, their eyes dry as they glared at the soldiers branding their skin with the mark of the Regent.

Umbris swallowed heavily, unsure of what kind of strength she would have to muster to get through what was ahead. For the past few weeks, she had stared at the chaffed scars around her wrists, where the manacles rubbed her flesh raw. Some part of her was looking forward to the freedom of having the chains removed, though it came at a price.

Only three more to go, she thought, her nerves getting the best of her. Brute gave her a nudge with the butt of the spear, but she wouldn't dare to hit her—not when the commander stood nearby.

Neen was before her, for once the girl was no longer smiling. Even in the worst of times, the girl had found a way to see the best in things, but there was nothing good about this. Her screams were muffled into the rag as the soldiers held her, one behind her back and another securing her wrist. The branding stick wrapped around the pale flesh and the sizzling made Umbris wince and look away. Neen cried out in pain as they pressed the mark to her other wrist before letting her stumble to the water.

"Name?" A stumpy soldier grumbled. On his lap was a scroll of parchment with inked scratches carefully marked in columns. The commander stood behind him, his eyes on her as she parted her lips to speak.

"Umbris," she said softly. Her throat felt raw. It had been weeks, maybe months, since she last spoke.

The soldier checked her name off the list, writing some words she couldn't read beside it. When he looked up again, he gestured toward the soldiers to proceed.

Arms wrapped around her stomach and instinct told her to struggle. She was at war within herself, her body urging to flee, her mind telling her it was no use. Her chains dropped to her feet and for one single breath, she felt the relief of the weight before her arm was pulled forward, the pale chaffed skin facing upward. A gag was shoved into her mouth.

She squirmed as they brought the branding iron closer; instinct taking over.

The soldier behind held her steady, her head pressing into his chest. Her eyes searched frantically, her mind screaming at her to break free. It was then her gaze alighted on the commander, his blue eyes always watching, his jaw tight.

The iron encircled her skin. The pain was immediate, nothing like she had ever felt before. Fire, so acute and powerful she had the sudden sensation of losing all sight. She burned, inside and out, her flesh alive with knives of slicing fire along her wrist. Her entire body pushed away from it, her head whipping from side to side.

Tears escaped, trailing down her cheeks as the iron clamp was pulled away. The soldier behind her remained in place as the one holding her newly-scarred arm, switched to her other wrist.

This time, she was ready, though she shrunk back internally as the second iron came closer. Her gaze landed on the commander, and this time, she didn't look away. The tears dripped out of the corners of her eyes, trailing down her cheeks as the fire burned. The rancid stench of her own flesh burning made her stomach turn over.

Not now, she chided herself.

The pain receded and the soldier held her up a moment longer, waiting for her to gather her wits before letting her stumble down to the river's edge.

The water seared, as much as the fire and she gave a small yelp as she shoved both of her arms into the passing water. The cry was lost in the sighs and tears of those around her. She let more tears fall, mixing into the fresh water and disappearing forever.

Her senses were strangely heightened, as though the burning of her flesh had made her more aware of the world. Some part of her, she had buried, was beginning to climb back to the surface. Her fate was before her, it had loomed ahead, but now the deed was done, and there was no turning back. She was forever marked.

Her body continued to tremble, her hands shaking as she watched the sunlight ripple across the water. Her heart seemed to vibrate in her chest—it was all too familiar a feeling.

Heavy boots crunched behind her and she turned slightly. She moved to jump to her feet, when the commander raised his hand, beckoning her to stay where she was.

"Is there anything I can do for the pain?" His words were smooth, eloquent even.

Her cheeks warmed at the thought of someone trying to help her. How many days had gone by without a kind word? Some of the other women were watching them.

She shook her head, glancing up only for a moment. His hair looked different today, not so carefully groomed.

"There is a salve for you to rub on when the flesh has cooled." He pointed in the direction of another line. She had watched the process over the past hour, she knew what to expect. While standing in line, she had contemplated what was worse, experiencing the pain first, or having to watch nearly every prisoner go through the torment before testing your own strength.

"Does it feel any better?" he asked, and she didn't speak.

Her lack of response seemed to bother him as he sank down until he squatted at her level. His eyes focused on her wrists just beneath the surface of the water, the bright red of the ravished skin glared at them. She wanted to pull them out of his sight. In some way, it felt as though he could see her past, see what they had done to her.

She turned to look at him and his eyes lifted from her wrists. Something behind her back caught his attention and he looked away for a moment, his lips dropping into a frown. "Is Private Carine still giving you trouble?" Her brow furrowed. He waited expectantly.

"Who?" she asked, her voice still cracked from disuse.

A ghost of a smile pulled at the corner of his mouth in satisfaction. "Private Carine. Your wagon leader."

"Oh," she said, "I—I didn't know her name."

"Then what do you call her?"

She shook her head, refusing to say the word out loud. The commander was crazy if he thought she would be honest with him. Her shift was dripping, her back aching as she continued to lean over the water's edge. Every now and then, she flexed her wrist, the tug making her wince.

"You won't tell me?" His voice dropped lower.

She shook her head again.

"Shall I get some salve for you?" He left without giving her a chance to refuse.

When he returned, she pulled her arms out of the water, the passing breeze kindling the scars. Bright red markings scarred her wrists, with matching symbols. She had seen the mark every day since she could remember, the simple band encircling the wrist to where the regal curved 'R' rested just beneath her palm. It was the mark of the Regent, a mark proclaiming her to be property of the realm.

She expected the commander to inhale, maybe catch his breath at the sight of her wounds, but he did no such thing. Perhaps he had seen too many wounds as asoldier, or maybe it was the simplicity of their differences. She was an Anglan, and her pain meant nothing to him. Instead of saying anything, he handed her the salve and she rubbed it on her smarting skin, the sting making her bite her lip.

She needed something to distract her from the pain. Other moans were beginning to lift into the air all around her. She spotted Neen farther down along the bank, staring at her wrists as though she couldn't believe they were attached to her arms.

"Brute," she mumbled.

"Excuse me?"

"I think of her as Brute." Her eyes were closed as she spoke, trying to block out the pain. When she opened them, the ghost of a smile was hovering around the commander's lips.

"You should probably keep that to yourself."

She nodded.

"Why are you here?" he asked, his eyes roving over her, but in a different way than most men. Her brow furrowed again, and she had the sudden desire to be left alone. "I mean I know why, I just don't understand how." He stumbled over his words.

She pressed her lips together, she wouldn't let him bring back the memories she had locked away.

"Is it why you don't speak? You have a beautiful voice."

Beauty. She thought with ire. It always came down to that.

When she didn't answer he cleared his throat. "What do you do in the wagon? I'm told by *Private Carine*," he raised an eyebrow as though he wanted to use a different name, "that you never speak to the other girls."

"I don't," she admitted softly, the salve finally rubbed into her flesh. The pain was ebbing, slowing with each pulse in her wrists. "I watch, I listen."

"Ahh," the commander nodded. "Then you know all the secrets."

"No," she shook her head quickly. He didn't understand her at all. "I read people."

"What do you mean?" He looked mildly curious, and ducked his head, trying to meet her gaze.

"Pick a soldier," she said meekly. She wasn't sure why she was playing along, maybe it was the relief she needed in this moment of extreme discomfort—a distraction to reduce the swells pulsating through her flesh.

"There," he nodded his head in the direction of the Gallian soldier, who had held each woman during their branding.

He had a sparse beard, the hairs coming in patches along his jaw. The sides of his mouth were turned down in a frown and he took a swig of something from a proffered skin, wincing as he swallowed.

"He's young," she whispered. The commander watched, seemingly unimpressed. "One would think this is his first journey with prisoners, but it isn't." Now she had his attention. "You can tell by the way he held us. He knew exactly how to keep each woman from squirming. He's stronger than he looks. His family is poor. You can tell by his hands. Those are working hands, see the calluses? My guess is he took this position to help his family, or to get out of some village, not knowing what he would have to do. That's why he drinks." She finished speaking in a quiet huff, it was the most words she had said since she had been taken, the most since she last saw...*Stop!*

"Impressive," the commander cocked his head to the side and looked away again. "What about him?" He pointed to another soldier and she took a short moment to evaluate him. Maybe the commander didn't realize this was one of the soldiers who patrolled her wagon.

She had named him Cower for the way he bent to Brute's, or rather Carine's, demands. After she finished her evaluation of him, he tested her on three more soldiers, each of them different and yet similar in manner. They all carried themselves with arrogance, making her believe they knew nothing of the world outside of their profession as soldiers. They bragged constantly, even now as they looked over the wounded women, one of the men adjusted his pants, making a rude gesture. She turned away in disgust.

"What about her?" The commander asked, pointing to a woman beside Neen.

She heaved a breath, "She's weary. Do you see her back, her shoulders, the way she hides? She's trying to block it all out. Everything she believed in, hoped for, is gone. She used to think there was good, but now it's all gone. She..." her voice trailed off as she realized the mistake she'd made. It wasn't the girl she was speaking about, but herself.

The tears prickled but didn't fall. When she had them under control, she glanced up at the commander; there was an understanding in his eyes she hadn't expected.

"What about me?" he asked quietly.

"I can't say," she said in a whisper, though she had already made out what she thought of him. The bright gold buttons told her everything she needed to know.

"Won't you?"

She shook her head and he looked away. He straightened, his knees cracking as he rose to his full height. She had entertained his musings long enough.

His boots snapped together and he surveyed the soldiers and prisoners scattered along the banks. "Move out!" he bellowed.

Women, still crying over their wounds, were pulled to their feet and shoved in the direction of the wagons. Umbris staggered to her own feet, glancing at the commander before shuffling away.

"Umbris," he said her name with eloquent prose. She turned. "My name is Commander Jolson, I wouldn't want you calling me otherwise."

Without another word, he strode away and she had the sudden wondering if he had been making a joke. Her mind ran over his words, dissecting them as she was loaded into the carriage.

For hours, she played with the words, turning them over and inside out. Whether or not they had meant anything, the future was more real to her than she ever realized. Glancing down at her wrists, she traced the raw marks with her eyes.

It didn't matter whether Commander Jolson had been kind. Her fate was set—she was property of the Regent now. There would be nothing kind about what awaited.

CHAPTER 17

He was fastening the sword to his back when Ansie jumped down from her bunk, fully clothed.

Willem nodded, "Ready?"

"Yes," she nodded, tightening the belt around her waist. She'd hardly slept a wink after they'd discussed their plans. For the first time, Willem was going against orders. What exactly had happened in Lord Hernan's study was a mystery to her, all she knew was that it had changed him. There was a set to his jaw that hadn't been there in a long time.

At least he had his sword. Hernan had allowed him to keep it in order to train the villagers. He took a deep breath and rested his hand against the wooden door frame. "I've never done this." He cracked a smile.

"You think I have?" She winked.

"Well, no sense standing around."

He peeked outside the door as though trying to see through the pitch of night. She swallowed down her fear and tightened her belt again. It was now or never.

Securing the hood in place, she made sure to tuck her hair out of sight. Together they crossed the wire fence and moved toward the forest where the lingering shadows enveloped them in darkness. She kept her hand resting on the dagger at her hip. Willem had taught her everything he knew about self-defense over the years, she only hoped if the time came she would remember it.

Glancing up, Willem eyed her—the bits of gold in his brown eyes seemed to gleam. What little light broke through the clouds above, dashed shadows across the land, trees stirring and branches crackling.

She remembered when they used to steal away to Shirnway Castle. In those moments he had been freer—more himself. Beside her, Willem took a deep breath and straightened his shoulders.

"Try and keep up," he challenged and took off into the shadows.

She shot after him, straining to match his pace. The wind whipped against her cheeks, tugging at her cloak as they bounded over fallen trees and up pine-covered hills. Her feet padded more loudly than his, he was a silent cat darting beside her in the night. Their breaths began to fall into a rhythm and she felt a surge of freedom all the way down to her soul.

This, this was living. She nearly laughed.

To be out of the confines of the cottage, away from the rules of the soldiers, it was almost too much to take in one moment. She wanted to laugh, to sing, to dance.

One glance at Willem silenced her delight.

As if the dark circles under his eyes and the scab across his nose, didn't spell out the story, his wounds were more vital beneath his shirt. Over the past four days, she'd been dressing them and rubbing in a soothing balm to help them heal faster. He hadn't complained, but she saw the way he moved each morning before reporting to the soldiers' barracks to conduct the training.

She had bombarded him with questions the first night when he returned from training, but he had been too tired to say much of anything. Each following day he grew quieter. When she'd seen the storm clouds gathering in the late afternoon, she'd known tonight would be the night. A sharp crack echoed through the trees and she swallowed, wondering what sort of creature could have made such a noise.

"Stay close, keep your eyes down." He slowed to a brisk walk and she edged closer to him.

The ground was dry beneath her boots as they strode into the circular fortress. Keeping her head down, the hood casting her face in shadow, she tried to see as much of the market as she could. The scene was vastly different than the one in the village, a distinct lack of rigidity in the movements of the people she saw.

Willem shifted behind a building where scantily clad women were leaning out of doors and lighted windows. A few of them glanced at Willem, before turning to other men passing by. Ansie's throat tightened when she took in the markings on their wrists—the red band of scarred flesh and the mark of the Regent.

She stepped closer to Willem, expecting him to draw away but he didn't. "This way," he mumbled and they ducked into a hastily perched structure. The sides leaned at an angle, as though a big gust of wind had made it tip to one side, but it had yet to fully give in.

Inside, the air was smoky, pipes emitting small puffs of smoke with the sharp twinge of burning leaf. Ansie wrinkled her nose to keep away from the sting.

There were five other men in the makeshift tavern, including the keeper, who eyed them as they strode across the dirt floor. They moved to the back corner, Willem motioning her to sit on the far side of the table with her back against the wall. Rather than sit across from her, he sank into the seat beside her, his eyes on the door leading from the brothel.

"When he comes in, let me do the talking," Willem whispered, and she nodded.

The minutes ticked by. The longer they waited, the harder her heart began to pound in her chest. So much had changed since she'd last seen Jethron.

"There he is." The new shadow had hardly ducked into the room before Willem spoke the words.

She watched, fingers trembling. It was Jethron, all right. She could tell by the way he sauntered across the room—the slight sway in his hips with each step he took. His shoulders were slumped at the slightest angle, his eyes shifting to all four corners before he managed to make it to their table.

"You came," his voice reached them from beneath his hood. Her eyes welled at the sound, it was like hearing him come back from the dead. Never had she hoped to hear his voice again.

"I didn't have a choice." Willem nearly grunted, still quiet. The other murmurings in the room seemed to pick up in strength as Jethron took his seat.

"There's always a choice, Willem." Jethron's head turned one way and then the next. "For instance, why did you choose to bring her?" He pushed back the hood slightly so they could see his face. Ansie nearly gasped.

The scar running from his temple, over his eye and down to the corner of his mouth, was more gruesome than she'd expected. Both eyes still worked, or so it seemed, though his lips were almost permanently twisted into a side grin. He had been handsome once, was still handsome now—the scar giving him an edge that he'd never had before.

She'd seen him just after it happened, the blood gushing from his face when they'd taken both of them. Ghost-like screams rang in her ears, tormenting her. She had to look down at her hands before her true feelings gave way.

"She wanted to see you for herself," Willem said.

"No doubt mad when you didn't tell her I was nearby, huh?" Jethron smiled, the corner of his scarred mouth pulling back. He winked at her. She swallowed, he'd guessed right. "It doesn't hurt as bad as it looks." He motioned to his face, and she realized she'd been staring. Warmth spread over her cheeks.

"Enough of that." Willem cut across him. "I'm here, so you know my decision. What do I do next?"

"You really haven't changed," he laughed and looked to Ansie, waiting for her to smile. It had worked in the past, but seeing the reality of what the Gallians could do was enough to dampen any lightness she carried with her. He sighed and turned back to Willem. "It's quite simple, really. We want you to train the villagers, something I'm sure Lord Hernan demanded when you were taken to his study."

Ansie shifted uncomfortably.

"Don't worry about how I know," Jethron leaned back in his chair, waving a dismissive hand. "We want the villagers trained and prepared, as best as you can get them, in the shortest amount of time."

"Rumors of Renegades have reached us," Willem mumbled. "Hernan's afraid."

"He always has been," Jethron leaned close. "And that's where we lay the trap. Right now he's moving outside of the Regent's decrees. That's where his weakness lies. You must see the men and women trained."

Willem shook his head and looked away from the table. There was something they weren't saying, she could feel it.

"What is it?" She barely spoke.

Jethron leaned forward. "He's realizing how much work he has cut out for him."

"Why do they need training?" Willem asked.

"We have our reasons."

Willem snapped back to attention. "If you want information from me, then this has to go both ways. I'm not going to do all of this unless you tell me what's really going on. I've spent the last four days training boys, men and women the basics of swordsmanship. It's gotten worse each day, they'll never hold their own in a fight, so tell me why I should even get their hopes up."

Jethron eyed him for a moment, the casual air disappearing in a flash. Unblinking, he spoke, "The rebellion will begin in Mirtain. There's to be an ambush."

Ansie gasped and clamped a hand over her mouth. Willem was already shaking his head—this was treason.

"It will be the beginning," Jethron said with such finality, she felt as though it was already done. "It will send a message to the Regent himself."

"You can't mean that," Willem had gone pale beneath his hood. "Those men and women won't survive an attack. You're leading them to slaughter."

"They won't be fighting against the ambush."

Slowly, the words replayed in Ansie's mind. *If they weren't fighting against the ambush, then...*

It dawned on her and she stared. "That's not possible."

"It's already set in motion. The villagers will fight, they'll have to choose a side. Our men are ready to attack."

"I'm not listening to this."

"Then why are you here?" Jethron challenged, leaning over the edge of the table, his eyes shining. His words surged with a passion Ansie dully remembered, as if he was reminding her of something she had once held dear. "You're here because Issak was beaten for something you did. You're here because as much as you want to deny everything I'm saying, you believe as much as I do. I know you, Willem. I listened to you say these things for years. You want this. The time for standing in the middle has come to an end. Our numbers are growing—it's time we send the Regent and his people back where they came from."

Silence fell between them—Ansie shifted uncomfortably along the wooden bench.

"Say I do this," Willem said. Jethron grinned as though he'd already won, "who's going to protect her?" When their friend leaned back in confusion, Willem hooked a thumb in Ansie's direction. "You know Hernan spoke with me, but not what he said. He threatened her. If I don't do as he wishes, her future will be the same as Kata's."

So that's what it was—the lingering anger in Willem over the last few days. She inhaled a deep breath. This was a first. Hernan had threatened her bodily harm more than once, but nothing like this. She bit her lip, beginning to realize the gravity of what was happening in Mirtain. Someone had placed their hand upon the wheels of fate and pulled it. Now it was loose and spinning but without course or direction.

The light in Jethron's eyes dimmed at the mention of Kata. "That won't happen again."

"Really?" Willem countered. "Can you guarantee it?"

"We've been over this." The bravado Jethron had maintained upon entering the worn out tavern was slowly slipping away. "What happened to Kata hurt me as much as it hurt you."

"You put her in danger."

"Don't you think I know that?" Jethron was glaring at Willem now. Ansie reached out a hand to touch his fingers. The contact seemed to draw Jethron back, he took a steadying breath. "I know how you felt about her, but there's nothing we can do about it now. It's over."

Ansie's eyes stung with unshed tears. "Let's not talk about it," she whispered and watched them lean away from one another.

One bore the pain of what he had experienced in the scar along his face, the other carried a scar in his heart.

"This, this rebellion is real. It's all we have." Jethron tugged the hood down, casting his face in shadow. "You used to wonder about the past, and we have answers. It's going to happen with or without you, but you'll have to choose a side. I chose freedom, but you have the chance to become something more than the rest of us."

Jethron was looking at Willem when he spoke, his words pulling at an old memory. They had been dreamers, all four of them—meeting in Shirnway Castle and pondering the past. More than once Kata had told them about the warriors who used to protect the realm. Ansie's very hopes had thrived on those stories.

"That's not why I'm here."

"Then why?" Jethron challenged Willem, his spine straightening. There was something different about the way he carried himself, she wasn't sure what it was, but she didn't like it. He had always been determined before, but this was more than determination.

"Why Mirtain?" she asked. Jethron turned his attention to her.

"I told you, Hernan is weak and we need to start somewhere."

"No, why?" Willem said, his voice dipping lower.

Jethron explained further. "It's better to start in a place outside of the Regent's reach. That way we don't have to worry about an immediate counter-attack." Ansie had the distinct feeling he was hiding something.

"What are you not saying?" She prodded.

Jethron glanced at Willem. "He can tell you."

"Not if I complete the other task Hernan gave me, or don't you already know about that?"

"What task?" Jethron asked, seeming to not care.

"Yes. He wants me to track the gorilla. Track it, and kill it."

Jethron paled beneath his hood. "You can't." The words came out in a whisper.

The stories Kata had once told them came back to life. It seemed impossible—the stories were treason. *The Animle.*

"I haven't been given much choice."

"You can't." Jethron gripped the table. "This is more important than preparing the village, more important than anything. You must keep the creature alive, at all costs. Do I have your word?"

Silence held on the brink of cracking. It rarely snowed in Mirtain, but one time when the creek froze over, Ansie had tried to step onto the solid water. It had held for a moment before she stumbled as the ice cracked beneath her boots.

Listening to Jethron now, reminded her of that ice. Something flowed beneath the surface, it was cool and alive and ready to crack the ice that held it back.

"I'll do what I can," Willem said and held up a finger, "to an extent." He glanced at her, his meaning clear.

"What can I do?" she asked, her voice timid.

"Ans," Willem said.

"This is her fight too." Jethron leaned toward her. "I have contacts in the village, but no one in the fields. Keep your ears open. Any rumor, anything to do with caravans or soldier movement is important."

She nodded.

"She shouldn't be spying," Willem interjected, "not with Fergin and his Nexen around. Do you know why they're here?"

"Don't worry about that." When Willem opened his mouth to object, Jethron waved a hand. "Fine, they are under direct orders to find the gorilla. As Nexen, they are subject to the Master of the Legion of Nex, and therefore, they come directly from the Regent himself."

"So the Regent controls them?" Ansie asked.

"In a sense. Their leader resides in Gallia, but like the rest of us they take their orders from his grand majesty," Jethron rolled his eyes. "They are just highly trained." He shrugged. "You haven't seen their wolves have you?"

She knew she'd heard a wolf howl the other night! A shiver ran down her spine.

"No," Willem shook his head.

"I suspect Captain Fergin has kept them locked up." Jethron mused.

The tavern keeper gave a loud grunt, clearing his throat and Jethron whipped around. "I have to go. I'll contact you when next to meet. Don't do anything rash." The last words were meant for Willem, and they shared a look before Jethron disappeared through the front door.

Together Ansie and Willem sat in silence before he nudged her shoulder. She stood without further beckoning and as they passed the bar, the keeper looked up, waving to them subtly.

"Might be best if you go through the back door." He flashed a piece of cloth at them; it had a crescent moon crudely stitched onto it. Without a word, Willem pulled her behind the counter and they hurried into the tavern keeper's room. A small bed stood in the corner, rumpled sheets hanging off the edge.

The front door to the brothel slammed open. A few short cries of surprise made Ansie's pulse quicken, then came the heavy pounding of boots.

"Interesting guests tonight," Fergin's voice boomed throughout the small enclosure. Ansie covered her mouth with a hand—eyes wide. "Three men entered your bar, where are they? I won't ask..."

Willem didn't wait for Fergin finish as he grabbed her hand, yanking her out the back door. They walked quickly, Ansie ducking beneath her hood as they hurried from shadow to shadow.

Circling around the outskirts of the market, the gate loomed ahead. Bangs and shouts rang out from the tavern behind them, but she didn't dare look back. One of the masked guards at the entrance waved them forward. They hurried and dipped into the shadows just outside the walls.

Willem turned to the guard who had motioned to them. "Tell him to pick someplace different next time."

The hood nodded and Ansie thought she caught the ghost of a smile hidden in shadow. How Willem had known the guard was part of Jethron's group, she couldn't say. She had little time to think as they sprinted into the forest.

They were moving faster this time, leaping over roots and brambles. More than once she nearly lost her footing, but her breaths heaved in her chest as she tried to keep up with Willem.

Just as she settled into a rhythm, the piercing howl of a wolf shattered the night. Her heart skipped a beat. They were being hunted.

She ran faster than she ever had before. The howling followed them, ringing through the woods over and over again. Her hood flung back and she pumped her arms all the harder.

They were reaching the hill toward Shirnway Castle and she wanted to breathe a sigh of relief, they were almost back when Willem grabbed her arm and pulled her to the left. She didn't have enough breath to ask what he was doing.

All thought fled, as another course of howling rained upon them. The wolves were getting closer. She scrambled over the dry pine needles, darting around bushes and under a fallen log.

"Almost there," Willem breathed just loud enough for her to hear. His words gave her some relief and she pushed harder, knowing she had to keep moving.

A heavy pound shook the ground beneath her feet and she stumbled. Willem caught her before she could lose all footing.

"Keep going, Ans," he urged.

She darted forward. Willem drew his sword from across his back, the blade cutting through the darkness with an ethereal glow.

Another beat shook the forest floor and pine needles rained down on them from above. She shook them from her hair, wondering how the trees swayed though there was little wind. It wasn't until the hulking shadow formed that she nearly lost all feeling in her body.

A new roar lit the woods, a moaning scream from the mouth of a beast twice the size she had ever imagined. *How had he killed these?*

Willem ran straight for the grinspur, the gold horn gleaming in the night. The beast reared on its back legs and shot toward them. Her heart was in her throat when Willem grabbed her arm and pulled her to the right, at the last second. The beast came to a halt, its head swiveling back and forth as it tried to find them. Willem held her against a tree trunk, the size of it nearly enveloping them.

The beast's head snapped in their direction, its gaze fixating on them. It dug its thick legs into the ground ready to spring forward, hooves straining. Her breath caught.

"Come on, come on, come on," Willem muttered.

His sword gleamed, ready to do what must be done when the howls of the wolves split the air once more. It wouldn't be long now. The grinspur's sides shifted as it looked around, the whites of its eyes were visible even in the darkness surrounding them.

"Get ready to run," Willem whispered, she was already grinding her boots into the dirt, ready to take off at a moment's notice—the plan unfolding before her. He shot toward the beast, one slice of the blade along the back leg of the grinspur sent it into a panic. It charged away from them, heading straight toward the howling wolves.

Willem didn't have to grab her, she was already sprinting in the opposite direction before he turned around. They shot over the hill and ran in what must be the direction of the cottage. Behind them, she heard the wolves snarling growls and the moaning of the grinspur. The cries of both beasts were nearly overwhelming, but what terrified her more were the shouts of men's voices. The muffled curses made her tremble, but she gave them no further thought as they began the painstaking process of climbing through the barbed wire fence without getting pricked. Cursing each wire to the underworld, they made it through and broke out of the last of the trees.

She was looking behind her when Willem grasped the back of her cloak and threw her to the ground. The wind was knocked from her lungs.

He leaned over her ear. "Soldiers."

Sure enough, there were Gallian soldiers posted outside their cottage. She counted quickly, only four of them—all looking toward the forest and the commotion there.

"What do we do?" she breathed.

His hand flicked toward the sword along his back, but she shook her head quickly. If he killed any of them, his life would be forfeit.

The barking continued behind them, a far off cry from the grinspur passed on the wind. It would only be a matter of time before the wolves were back on their trail, maybe the wire fence would stall them for a moment. Willem had told her about the poison lacing each prick; it was enough to incapacitate a grown man. It could certainly affect the wolves—though if they were as large as she had heard, they could clear the fence in one jump.

Searching the scene. Ansie bit her lip when an idea came to her.

"The roof," she whispered. He nodded, following her lead.

"On my count." His face set with grim determination and she prepared herself for the race across the chilled ground.

"One." She held her body up, hovering.

"Two." He shifted beside her, grasping a rock in his palm.

"Three."

The rock took flight, landing in the forest before the soldiers, with a resounding crack. The Gallians looked to one another, then back again, before drawing their swords and moving toward the trees.

She was off.

Like an arrow from a bow, she shot forward moving as quietly as she could. For the first time tonight, she was thankful for the cloud-filled sky. Not a shadow betrayed their movement as she scaled the back wall of the cottage.

Willem was right behind her when she found the small latch in the roof and slipped onto the mattress of her top bunk. He came in with a soft thud beside her and scrambled from the bed.

"Hurry," she whispered and he nodded frantically, kicking off his boots. She tossed hers to him, her cloak following. He placed them beside the door before jumping into bed, all signs of their travels gone.

"Try and relax," he whispered.

Her harsh breaths and pounding heart refused to cooperate. From the sounds of it, Willem was having a similar problem. He cursed under his breath and rose from the bed, bare feet padding on the ground as he grasped his sword.

The wolves were out of the forest by now and she shivered to think what trails they might pick up. Willem took a seat at the table, cleaning the blade, his eyes on the door as she wrapped the blankets tighter around her knees. She quickly plucked away stray pine needles from her hair.

A howl split the night and she covered her ears. They were right outside. A man shouted as the barking began. *How many wolves are there?*

The door burst open and she screamed. Willem jumped to his feet, sword at the ready.

Red eyes glared through the darkness, hovering in the face of white fury. The lips of the beast were curled back in a snarl, the head higher than she could have imagined. It would be able to look her directly in the eye.

Captain Fergin stepped into the cottage beside the wolf, his cloak billowing around him as his gaze swept the room, landing on the boots near the door. A twitch tugged at his mouth as he looked back to Willem. The wolf beside him snarling.

The captain muttered something in an odd language to the overly-large dog and the beast drew back, sitting on its haunches. The red eyes never leaving Willem. Ansie didn't want to contemplate the other sets of eyes she could see just outside their door.

"Who were you meeting?" Fergin demanded.

"Meeting?" Willem blinked in confusion.

"Don't play games with me, *boy*." Fergin had a way of speaking where his bottom teeth were nearly always visible, making him appear permanently irritated.

"I don't know about any meeting," Willem shook his head. "I've been here since nightfall. I wouldn't break curfew, not again." His voice was so innocent, Ansie nearly believed him.

"Then why are you out of bed?" The man's eyes alighted on the sword.

"The curfew only restricts me to my house."

Fergin fumed. "You won't wriggle your way out of this one."

"There's nothing to wriggle out of." Willem gestured with his hands, having laid the sword down on the table. "I heard the wolves and got up in case something happened. You've no idea how thankful I was to hear your men's voices. I thought they were wild."

Captain Fergin slammed a fist on the table. A command, in some language, passed through his lips and the wolf shot forward, knocking Willem to the ground. Ansie screamed. The beast's claws dug into Willem's chest, jaws inches from his throat.

Like a shadow, the captain moved beside the beast and placed his hand along its side. "Who were you meeting?"

Willem's eyes were wide as his gaze shifted from beast to man and back again. "I don't know what you're talking about!"

Fergin's hand shot out and jabbed Willem in the side. Ansie winced, knowing it was one of the places he was badly bruised from the beating.

"Tell me," the man growled, and the wolf joined him.

"I don't know!"

He hit him again. This time Willem didn't even groan but shut his eyes. She couldn't watch this, not again.

"There were two sets of tracks in the forest, two sets leading us right back to this cottage. I see one," he held up a finger and turned to her, "two people."

"You're insane!" Willem's voice nearly cracked as another blow hit his side. "You really think we could outrun your men and your wolves?"

The wolf seemed to understand the insult more than Fergin, and the beast snapped its jaws in Willem's face. A splotch of slobber landed on his cheek.

Ansie leaned forward, the boards beneath her mattress groaning. She tried to make herself look as small as possible in the dim light, the blanket across her shoulders helping to frame her face with her hair.

Fergin looked up, and she watched as understanding filled him. There was no part of him which could accredit her with being able to outrun his best men and wolves. It was a thought many Gallians had. In Gallia, the women were delicate and not to undergo any physical strain. As Fergin's eyes roved over her once more, Ansie shrunk beneath the blanket, her heart hammering as she played her part.

The muttered command turned the wolf away from Willem. The beast left the cottage without another glance, the white fur still standing on end as it disappeared. Fergin followed without a word, slamming the door behind him.

Only then, was she able to breathe. On the floor, Willem sighed, holding his hands to his forehead.

She leaned over the mattress and meeting his eyes gave him a small smile. He returned it and struggled into bed.

In the darkness, his voice reached her from below, "At least we know one thing."

"What's that?"

"Fergin's too proud to believe a girl can outsmart him," he gave a small chuckle that was silenced quickly. She had to place a hand over her mouth to cover her own laugh. Maybe it was a release of the tension, but they couldn't stop. Over and over again she tried to silence her laughter, but it broke through in half-breathed chuckles. Willem snorted below her and it sent them both into another round of hilarity.

"Thank you, Willem." She whispered, finally gathering herself, and wiping the tears from her eyes. She stuck her hand out over the edge of the cot, her fingers hanging in the darkness.

As always, he reached up and gave them two small squeezes. "Goodnight, Ans."

She smiled, and rolled onto her side, knowing sleep would elude her for hours.

"Goodnight, Willem."

CHAPTER 18

The dust passed Larn in a furling cloud, like smoke filtering from a pyre. Scouts had been sent to determine what sort of caravan traveled in the valley below. It had been nearly an hour since they left.

Larn wondered what was taking so long. He slid his finger along the edge of his sword, somehow knowing Pike was the one to have gotten them in trouble. Larn had hastened to join them, but Girshon had refused.

He grit his teeth, his ears straining for any sign of what lay below. All he could make out was the scuffing of boots along the dirt road. Hidden as they were in the trees, this caravan had no idea that a band of Renegades was encased on the high ground. It was difficult to hear above the murmurings of the men and the soft nickers of the horses, but every now and then he could make out the rattling wagon wheels. His back was braced against a tree trunk, his legs bent and his sword across his lap.

They had been traveling for what seemed like weeks, though it was only a handful of days. They were days spent almost entirely in the saddle, and nights of careful walking over uneven ground. The temperature had heightened as they moved toward the southern lands, the winds continuing to stir the air. It was chilling, but nothing like the frigid bite of the north.

Thinking of how far they had come, he fought off a yawn.

A birdcall, from one of the scouts, alerted all the men of their approach. Larn hastened to his feet. The clouded expanse above them left a dull gray gleam in the forest where the tree branches rattled as the wind brushed by. More than a few leaves were beginning to fall to the sloping earthen floor.

Pike and two other scouts were climbing the hill, leaves and bracken clinging to their cloaks. Tympmor shook his mane as though the smell of the men was too much for him.

"It's a prisoner caravan," Pike heaved. As though of one mind, the Renegades returned their eyes to the cloud of dust.

"Men or women?" Girshon asked.

"Couldn't tell. There are twenty-one wagons, six soldiers to each. Twenty are caged, one is a supply wagon."

It had been quite some time since they'd had fresh supplies. Luck seemed to be on their side. They weren't known to ambush, but when it was a Gallian patrol or supply train, they would take their pick. Larn hastened to sheath his sword and grabbed Tympmor's reins.

"Make this quick, Bastion Nocta is twenty miles to the west." Girshon clicked his tongue. "To your saddles."

"Sir?" Larn fell in beside the Renegade leader. "We can take that supply wagon with only a few of us. No need to alert the entire caravan. All we have to do is wait for the cover of night—"

"We all go."

"But sir—"

"We have the time now." Girshon cut him off again. "Twenty miles is a lot of space."

"But enough to count," Larn grumbled though he hoisted himself into the saddle. The last thing he needed was for the one goal they had fought so hard for over the past two years to be destroyed.

Girshon sighed, still standing near Tympmor. He squinted up at Larn. "Do your part. I won't pass up the chance to garner supplies."

Larn nodded, he'd known the Renegade leader since he was a young boy and it didn't matter what facts were placed before him, if Girshon had made a decision, then it would be carried out.

The creak of leather and skittering hooves lifted beneath the trees as the men swung into their saddles. Larn patted Tympmor's side. The loyal steed braced his legs, the other men bustling into position.

"Ready?" Heben asked.

"Not even a little bit," Larn muttered under his breath. His gut told him this was wrong, there was something down there they weren't expecting.

Girshon rode to the front of the group, the horses darted forward and back into line, the men holding the reins tight in their hands.

"Go for the supplies. If you have the chance, release some prisoners." The leader's black stallion held still, waiting for the charge. Together, both rider and steed were a shadow. "Move light, move fast."

"Or we could simply move," Larn mumbled and Heben chuckled, his thin lips puckering and cheekbones protruding. Girshon shot him a sharp glance.

"Now!" Girshon's fist punched forward and every man kicked his mount's side. Whinnies from the beasts rose in the woods, but it was nothing compared to the thundering of the hooves as they charged down the hill.

They shot through the last of the trees, breaking through the dust cloud like a mortal wave. Cries from the scrambling Gallian soldiers reached Larn's ears, but he hardly noticed as he launched into combat.

He killed a soldier, then another, Tympmor taking vengeance on anything which moved before him. Larn reined in the beast, his sword clanging against the spear of a soldier. He parried two blows before cutting the man down. Blood spattered and a sword cut along his left shoulder from a Gallian he hadn't seen. Tympmor seemed to understand his pain and kicked the man back with a hoof to the head.

"Good boy," he patted the beast's neck. Larn's ears seemed clouded in the cacophony. He swung his head from side to side, picking his next victim, but there was no one beside him. The Renegades had already overtaken the men.

So much for a skirmish, he thought, his lust for action going unquenched.

Girshon rode near the front, pointing to the horizon where three men were charging away. Larn gritted his teeth, one of the Regent soldiers appeared to be the leader, his cloak more dignified than the others. Pike and another took off after the cowards.

All around them, the skirmish was over, the soldiers dead or dying. Tympmor shook his head, prancing in pride at their win.

"That's right," Larn patted his side again and slid out of the saddle. Pain radiated from his left arm, shooting up to his shoulder. He caught Heben's eye and nodded as he rested his sword against his legs to wipe the blood from his hands. Blinking the sweat from his eyes, he readied himself for what he would see in these wagons—he'd never witnessed a prisoner caravan before.

Just then a shrill scream rang from the back of the caravan line. He was running before he had time to think—his sword discarded to the ground behind him.

A soldier stood beside a tipped over wagon, her spear aiming between the bars as she jabbed it over and over again at the prisoners inside. Another scream tore at him as he ran. The first had been a cry of fear, this was a cry of pain.

He reached the soldier and tackled her to the ground. Blood was already pouring from a cut on her head, her face half covered in smeared red. She grabbed his injured arm and squeezed. He cried out and scrambled back.

The soldier gave a bark of maniacal laughter as she pulled a dagger from her belt. He was on his feet before she could take a step closer. Ducking beneath her first jab, he braced a kick into her chest, she went sprawling, only to roll over her back and onto her feet again. She darted to the side and he let her set the pace, keeping her blade just out of reach.

She taunted him and he smiled back as he eluded each of her traps. On the third, he caught her arm and bent the blade back toward her own body. Her eyes widened seeing the end was near. She spit, her other hand clawing at his neck, but he refused to relinquish his hold until the blade found purchase. Her body fell to the ground lifeless.

He was breathing heavily when he looked up, Heben sprinting in his direction.

"About time," he grumbled, favoring his shoulder.

"You didn't need my help." Heben clapped him on the back.

Larn shook his head and eyed the body of the woman. She was stronger than he had expected. His gaze landed on her discarded spear and he suddenly remembered the wagon behind him.

Wide eyes met him when he spun around. *Women.*

The wagon had keeled over onto its side—the prisoners were standing, their legs awkwardly finding ground between the bars of the cage. Two of the women held hands over arms and legs, their limbs pulsing with blood from where the spear had caught them. But it was the girl in the front who stole his attention. On her shift was a deepening dark red stain, it grew with continued strength as the girl weakened in the arms of the one who held her.

"Get them out," he muttered. The cage was locked and it took only a moment for Heben to find the keys on the dead soldier. As soon as the latch swung open, two of the girls pushed forward, bowling him over. He struggled to his feet watching them take off in the direction of the forest. He hesitated, Tympmor not far away.

"Leave them," Girshon said, approaching. "Maybe they can find some bit of life elsewhere." Larn highly doubted it.

Heben was helping the other ladies crawl out of the cage, each one moving with caution, refusing to take his hand. *How long had it been since they had been offered a helping hand?*

Only the wounded were left when he knelt down to look into the cage. The two prisoners with their shoulders and legs bleeding limped out with his and Heben's assistance, leaving behind the girl with the wound to her stomach.

The spread of blood had increased—it wouldn't be long now. Trembling hands held the girl, and he looked up, finding wide blue eyes staring at him.

"Here," he said softly, reaching forward. His shoulder smarted, but it was nothing he hadn't been through before.

She offered the wounded girl but kept her eyes on his face. A groan passed from the wounded prisoner's lips as he lifted her into his arms, pulling her from the cage. He straightened, surprised to find his legs trembling. The past few days of exertion had taken more of a toll on him than he realized.

The girl in his arms hardly weighed anything at all, her thin frame bony beneath his hands. Searching around the destruction of bodies, he found Tympmor and the rest of the men setting up camp about fifty yards away. The men would be up most of the night, discarding the bodies of the Gallians off the road, and raiding the supply wagon.

He reached Tympmor's side and attempted to remove the roll from the back of the saddle—it proved too much for him with the load in his arms. Bloodied hands pushed his out of the way and undid the clasps.

It was the prisoner from the caged wagon, her blue eyes wide with something he didn't want to see. It reminded him too much of his reflection those first weeks at Sicarmman.

As a small child, the rigourous training had stolen his innocence—or what was left of it. Ther ein the middle of the school he'd spotted his reflection in the fountain—that haunted face staring back at him. He'd sat there wondering how his mother could have sold him, terrified by how his life had been destroyed so quickly. It was only by luck that the cobbler he worked with had given him to Girshon, a trainer at Sicarmman.

Looking into the girl's eyes, he saw the weariness that came with the loss of hope. It was like a veil that covered the heart, choking its beat until all that was left was an endless expanse. He blinked quickly and watched the girl's bloodied hands unroll the rough blanket along the ground. When he knelt to lay his burden on it, the wounded prisoner groaned.

"Neen?" the blue-eyed prisoner whispered. "Can you hear me?" She had a soft voice, nearly musical. Her eyes turned to him, blue orbs piercing. "I need a needle and thread."

He grimaced. "You should let her rest in peace."

"No."

He wasn't going to argue. It took only a moment for him to find the requested materials in his pack. He handed them to her without looking at the prisoner. *Neen*, he thought, correcting himself, *her name was Neen*.

The blue-eyed girl tore Neen's dress where the hole was already made, opening the front to reveal the depth of the wound. The soldier had done her job well. Larn had seen worse wounds in battle, but many men had suffered less than this and still perished. If he had to guess, the spear had nearly impaled her. How she was still breathing was a mystery.

The girl's bloodied hands froze, perhaps realizing the depth the spear had reached. She shook her head back and forth, placing her hands along Neen's face. He watched them tremble, catching a glimpse of the mark around her wrist. The girl was whispering to Neen, as he stood to find Girshon.

"What is it?" the leader asked, seeing Larn's approach.

"We can't free them." Larn motioned to the prisoners standing in huddles consoling one another. Now that he had noticed the mark, it was all he could see. "They've already been branded."

Girshon spun on his feet and approached the nearest women. He pulled their arms forward, the newly healed marks of the Regent glaring up at them. When he cursed, some of the women drew back in terror.

"What should we do?" Larn asked his commander, knowing the answer was not something they would come by easily.

"We'll think of something." Girshon walked off before Larn could object.

He breathed a sigh, uncertain where to turn. Usually, he was ready for moments like this. He hated the way his mind worked, the way it noted how much easier everything would be if the prisoners had run away, or been dead when they arrived. It was easier to deal with the dead, but having to face the realities of what these people were forced to live through left him breathless. He never liked to be unsure of himself—but deep down he knew he was afraid. Afraid of not being able to help.

Stepping back to the blue-eyed girl, he listened to her murmuring. Neen's eyes were closed, a soft smile on her lips. At his approach, the anxious, blue gaze reached him.

He held his hands up, the wound along his shoulder smarting. As he sank to the ground beside the blanket, she looked away.

"Do you need anything else?" he asked. She shook her head, brushing her fingertips along Neen's tangled hair. The needle and thread were discarded, unused.

The end was coming. The girl's back shivered and tears fell along her cheeks, making clean trails over her dirtied skin. When she looked back up at him, his breath caught. She was beautiful and he hated that he even noticed it in her moment of pain.

"I hardly knew her," she said softly, the emptiness in her voice pulling at him. "She always tried to be happy." She breathed a sigh.

"Those are the best kinds of people," he said, wanting to ease her pain somehow.

Neen gasped, her eyes opening. The girl leaned forward, her hand cupping around her friend's face. "I'm here, I'm here."

"Mama?" Neen gasped, her lungs sounded flooded.

"That's right," the girl crooned and Larn watched her as she held her dying friend's hand. This wasn't the first death the blue-eyed beauty had seen, she knew what she was doing. Neen gasped for air, her breath rattling with each painful inhalation.

"Let go, you can sleep now."

"Sleep?" Neen asked, and Larn had to look away from the desperate hope in her eyes. His gaze landed on the men dragging the female soldier's body away from the overturned carriage.

"Yes, sleep, sleep Neen." The girl crooned over and over again, until a final rattling breath told him it was over. He turned back to the prisoner, finding her gaze still on the lifeless form. He knelt before the body, folding the rest of the blanket over Neen, as though sheltering her from the world and all the sorrow it had brought her.

"Thank you," the blue-eyed gaze was on him again. "You saved us."

"I would hardly say that." He was squatting, his eyes nearly at her level. She shifted beneath his gaze, her hand moving to her hair, in the middle of pushing the brown locks behind her ear, she hesitated, and let it fall back around her face, keeping part of her in shadow. He wondered at the motion.

"Hey!" Heben yelled from across the way, "We need you over here!"

He nodded and stood to leave. "Wait," the girl said, "your shoulder."

"I'll manage," he said softly and strode off before she could say anything more.

It took over an hour to get all of the bodies off the road and hidden beneath the trees. A passerby wouldn't even know of their existence and the verrals would take care of removing any more evidence. By this time the following day, the skirmish would be just a memory.

The sky grew darker, the deep brushes of orange turning to the dull glow of gray, then to the dark blue of oncoming night. A gentle breeze had begun to rustle through the leaves. The silent chill was just enough to raise the hairs on the back of Larn's neck as he dug a grave for Neen. He worked silently, and the blue-eyed girl helped him cover Neen's body with dirt and rocks before they moved on by Girshon's command.

The whole company of Renegades moved through the trees, the new female companions taking care to huddle together. Many of them rubbed at their wrists as they moved, a motion of discomfort after spending so long in chains.

After another hour's walk, they came to an opening in the forest and marched into the underbrush, maneuvering their horses into the dark depths. Some of the women muttered to one another, but none seemed brave enough to leave the men behind. He searched the group, the blue-eyed girl was lost in their midst.

Girshon called for a halt when they were sufficiently huddled within the trees. The location was tight enough against the sharp rise of the mountain that they wouldn't be attacked from behind.

Words from his training came back to him. *Keep your enemies where you can see them.*

The group settled and hard biscuits were passed around with a designed efficiency. Each man offered some of his provisions to the women. Larn took Tympmor toward the front of the group, nearly twenty feet away. Just far enough for the horse's black coat to blend into the shadows.

He heard her approach before she reached him. He turned to her, laying the unfastened saddle on the ground. Even in the dark, her blue eyes stood out from the rest of her heart-shaped face. Her brown hair was in more of a mess than before, and the trails made from tears along her cheeks left ghosts of what had been.

"I—I—wanted to thank you," she said, her voice soft, hands twitching together.

Larn gave her a grim smile before pulling the blanket off Tympmor's back. The steed gave a snort. He wrapped a cloth around his hand and ran it along the black hair until it shined.

"You didn't have to be so gentle with her." She seemed to think he didn't accept her gratitude.

"It was nothing," he shrugged. He was slowly returning to himself after the events of the skirmish. Though the evidence of the prisoners had shaken his world, he was unable to return to the comfort of what he knew. It would never be the same, but he preferred the familiarity of a soldier's world. Hearing about the hardships of the Anglans, and actually seeing them, were two very different things.

"What's his name?" The girl, or rather woman, asked, her voice light in the din of the masculine voices behind her.

"Tympmor," he said over his shoulder, a smile coming to his lips.

"Tymp—" she hesitated.

"Mor," he finished for her, ducking beneath Tympmor's head to rub down his other side. She watched his every move, and he paused to rest his good arm across the back of the horse—laying it perfectly in the dip along Tympmor's spine.

She was thin, incredibly so, but longer in her frame than he had realized as she sat hunched over her friend. She was beautiful to be sure, as a soft breeze blew by, the shift tightened around her body. He averted his eyes, remembering the way she had hid her face from him. Her future was bleak, and they both knew it. The markings on her wrists would make sure she would be looked at, desired and used. He nearly shook his head—the insanity of it all.

"Do you want to know what it means?" he asked, somehow keeping his tone light. Maybe if he ignored her glaring reality, for just the moment, she could too. She tilted her head in confusion. "His name," he patted the horse and Tympmor gave a snicker.

She stepped closer, "Yes."

"Drums of Death," he whispered and her eyes widened. He cupped a hand around the left side of his mouth to whisper. "But he's a complete coward most of the time." He winked and her eyes lightened as she took another tentative step closer.

"Then why did you name him that?"

"It sounds better than, 'Likes to eat flowers'."

She bit her lip, and Larn had the sudden wonderful feeling of almost having made her smile. He had a notion it would make her breathtaking in the darkness. He could only imagine what she must look like when she was clean, no longer garbed as a prisoner, and had eaten food on a regular basis. It was no wonder the soldier had tried to kill her in the carriage, the girl would fetch an incredible price in any market. Only one look at that vile Gallian soldier had told him enough. If she couldn't sell the girl, then no one would.

"May I?" the girl asked, her hand reaching out toward Tympmor. There was an emptiness to her that left a void between them. It was as though she had once been full of life, but had long since lost any will to live.

"Let me ask. Tympmor, would it be all right with you if Miss..." he paused for her name.

"Umbris," she said softly.

What an ugly name.

"Right, Tympmor, would it be all right if Miss Umbris pets you?" He looked to the beast's head. Sure enough, the horse was ignoring him, too focused on the grass. He turned back to her. "He seems fine with it," he shrugged.

She reached out a bony hand. He caught another flash of the curling 'R' scarred on her wrist. Tympmor's flesh twitched when she touched him, but he held steady all the same. Larn knew if needed, he could speak in the language of his people to calm him, but he would prefer to not use that language in front of Umbris. Not when her eyes seemed to see straight through his pretenses.

Her hand paused along the sleek black coat for a moment before she spoke again. "What will happen to us?"

"I don't know," he admitted.

"But you must have some idea," she looked up, blue eyes shining. "Some plan before you attacked."

How did she disarm him so quickly? "We did, but we didn't expect so many of you."

"Prisoners?"

"Women."

Her head dropped at the word and he wanted to chide himself, but he knew it was the truth. They both knew what she was bound for, and he could guess what had most likely happened to her before she was thrown into that cage. She had been beaten and imprisoned, that was at least certain.

"You won't do anything because we're branded," Umbris said softly, her voice merely a whisper. If his hearing wasn't so acute, he wouldn't have heard her.

"That's not true," he shook his head and she looked up. Within an instant, she was aware he was lying.

"If we weren't branded, you wouldn't hesitate to help."

"It's not that simple," he breathed and was suddenly wondering if he should say anything at all. As he spoke, she took a step closer; he had to lean over Tympmor's back to see her whole face. "Before we thought each of you could return to where you're from, or at least find someplace new to live, but now there are many things to consider. You could always join the Renegades of course, but they're too far away, and we don't have enough time as it is." His excuses left him feeling helpless, even if they were true. They wanted to help, truly, but sometimes there was no easy way.

"We aren't far from Bastion Nocta," she said, accepting her fate like a sheep being led to slaughter.

"I don't think Girshon will take you there." He had been around the man long enough to know he would never deliver them into slavery. They fought to disrupt the Regent, it made no sense to allow what had happened to these women to continue.

"There's no sense fighting it," she breathed. "It doesn't matter where I go." She held both hands out, wrists facing up for him to see the twisting 'R'. The ridged skin glowed with the mark of the Regent. By all accounts, she was considered the Regent's property now. It didn't matter where she went, she would be forever labeled as a worker of men.

Larn opened his mouth to say something but the signal call of a bird reached them, he made the sound back. A moment later Pike and Yulit, another of his scouts, came into view, their horses' heads hanging low.

"Did you—" Larn asked, but was cut off by Girshon's approach.

Both men knocked off a salute, knuckles to foreheads. "We lost them," Yulit said, his face contorted in a snarl.

Girshon sighed, "Two soldiers, and the commander?"

Yulit nodded as Umbris breathed a name. Larn watched as she stared at the ground, her lips now pressed together. The other men seemed not to have heard her.

"I'm afraid we'll have to move out sooner than planned." Girshon shook his head, bracing his hands on his hips. "If they reach Bastion Nocta, we could have an army on our tail." He turned, "Now tell me..." his voice drifted off as the men moved closer to the camp.

Larn watched them walk away, not bothering to listen as his own thoughts took precedence. It was necessary for them to leave. The spy in Mirtain had given them hope and they would be hard-pressed to let anything stop them from reaching it. Without a word, Larn finished rubbing down Tympmor's back before ducking around to the other side. Umbris was still there, her eyes on Tympmor's coat.

"Jolson?" Larn asked, saying the name she had whispered under her breath.

Umbris grimaced and took a step back toward the camp.

"I won't tell," he said quickly. He knew well enough who the men were that had run off. The commander and the two men under his command, but what Larn didn't know were names.

"He was the leader, he took over our caravan a while ago," she said softly. "He spoke to me once." She seemed to shrink in on herself and he knew he would have killed Commander Jolson if he was standing before him right then. To think any man would do what had been done to this woman disgusted him.

"He's a dead man," he said.

"No," her eyes widened.

"What do you mean, 'No'?"

"He doesn't deserve death," her fingers twisted as she spoke.

"Didn't he harm you?" he asked, his eyes drifting to her hands. She looked down, taking in the scars, and then back up at him. He watched as her expression changed, from confusion to understanding, then to anger.

"Just because I wear these marks, doesn't mean I would stoop to that level." It was the first time she had ever spoken above a whisper—a spark of passion in her voice.

"I didn't mean you had a choice."

"He didn't force me," she said quickly. "I said he spoke to me, nothing more." She heaved a breath.

"I'm sorry for the confusion," Larn muttered. "I've—I've heard stories of these caravans. But seeing this," he waved a hand toward the other women, "it makes it all too real."

She looked up, "You aren't from around here are you?"

"I think both you and I know that." He said candidly, she had obviously made conclusions about him. He winked, and this time she let the corners of her mouth lift, if only a little. "Maybe you can forgive my judgment?"

"Maybe," she shrugged. "If you can excuse mine?"

"What do you mean?"

"I've heard stories too."

He sighed. She really was much more intelligent than she let on. No wonder the so-called Commander Jolson had sought her out for company. She had a way of making you want to know more about her, maybe it was those soulful eyes which seemed to see everything.

An idea began to form. He had seen a bit of her passion, could he fan the flames? "What do you want to know?" he asked.

"Whatever you'll tell me, but you need to get your shoulder looked at." She missed nothing.

"It's fine."

"It needs to be cleaned."

He grit his teeth. There was only one way he was going to say something about his past, and it wasn't going to be within earshot of the other men.

Normally he took care of his own wounds. As it turned out, this one wasn't in the easiest of places to reach. Along his left shoulder, he would be hard pressed to get the needle to go in and out of his skin without creating more damage. He knew he could always ask Pike, but the scout had the canny ability to stick him much harder than was necessary. On more than one occasion, Larn had thought Pike was taking out a personal vengeance against him.

"Do you have experience with a needle?" he asked.

She nodded.

"I hope you're better than Pike," he gave a small grunt. "Do you still have that needle and thread?" When she nodded again, he shifted to give her a better view of his shoulder. "We're going to need it."

CHAPTER 19

The man was charming. Umbris had realized that about him almost immediately. He had a way with words that piqued her curiosity.

He was a conundrum, intelligent and sensible when around her, but jovial around the men. They seemed to look to him for answers and quick wit, something he had in abundance. For the first time in a long time, she found herself focusing on someone outside of herself.

She hadn't planned on breaking her silence when the attack had begun. But Neen's death had hurt her in places she had thought were long dead.

It had taken them all by surprise. Commander Jolson's warning yell had roused them from their bored stupor. The Gallian soldiers had barely moved into position before the swarm of men rode down upon them. She had watched the whole scene from inside the cage, her eyes following Jolson as he swung his sword at the oncoming force.

It didn't surprise her that he had abandoned them. The gold buttons had told his tale clear enough. A prison caravan didn't fit him, he belonged somewhere fine, where riches were abundant. She had yet to figure out why he was traveling with them.

As the rebels rushed down the hill, it hadn't taken long for Brute to realize the battle was over and she would lose everything. Neen had been leaning against the bars, watching the skirmish with awe when Brute's spear struck her in the stomach. Umbris wasn't foolish enough to not realize the soldier had been aiming for her—a misguided thrust had met the bars and deflected the blow.

Umbris shook her head, knowing she would never be able to forget those few horrible seconds when there was no escape from the spear and the maniacal gleam in Brute's eyes. She never thought she would say she was happy someone was dead, but the past two months had made her wish for many deaths. So many.

"This may sting," Umbris warned quietly.

"I'm counting on it," the man sighed, and braced himself. She poured the spirits over his wound, the alcohol cleaning the slice in his flesh. He inhaled sharply but made no other sound.

"You know my name," she said, rubbing the wound free of dirt, "but I don't know yours."

He raised an eyebrow. "Larn."

She nodded, somehow the name fit him—if it was even his real name. He would have been smarter to have lied.

The name was simple and yet different enough to give her pause. A common name simply wouldn't do—he was anything but simple. She had noted it almost immediately, his intelligence coupled with his appearance, made him an intriguing figure. The stories of the Maereo tribes ran through her mind, as she stitched his shoulder.

It was her mother who had taught her how to sew, something they had done to make extra provisions for the family. She could hear her mother instructing her to keep her hands steady, to keep calm as the needle moved in and out. It didn't matter if the needle was passing through skin rather than fabric.

"I thought you were going to tell me a story," she prodded, dabbing the edges of the wound with the cleanest rag she could find.

"Ahh, that," Larn muttered, leaning forward. His hair fell around his face, the ebony strands shimmering. She had the sudden idea of it matching Tympmor's coat. He glanced up at her, his angled eyes pulling her in again. "Maybe it would be better if you told me what you know?"

She didn't reply. She wasn't a fool, she wouldn't give away her secrets if he wouldn't share his.

He glanced up when she didn't respond, she kept her eyes on her work. There was something about him which made her uncomfortable. She had the innate feeling he was able to see right through her. After so many days spent as nothing more than a prisoner, she felt naked beneath his gaze.

"We're the Renegades," he said. Even though she had known who they were, her hands still froze at the word. It was treason to even think such things. "The rumors are true, we're on the move."

He didn't speak for a moment and seemed to settle into the rhythm of her needle moving in and out of his skin. He no longer flinched whenever she touched him. Four stitches and then five more and he didn't say a word but turned to look up at her.

"But that wasn't what you were referring to, was it?" He asked and she shook her head. She chanced a glance and shifted when his eyes narrowed. "You have probably guessed, I'm from the north, from *Excelsis Bestia*, or as you have probably heard it called, the Beastly Mountains." This time she didn't try to hide her shock, her hands were frozen on his skin. "It's true, the beasts walk there, animals larger than those you would see here. Smarter too."

"No," she whispered and a hand came to her mouth. She had heard the stories, had wanted to believe at one time, but she had never truly believed in them. It couldn't be true, it just couldn't. They were just stories, legends of when man and beast had worked together to protect Anglas.

Larn was looking up at her again. "I'm proof enough that they exist." He winked.

What he said was true, she had never met anyone with his color skin before. It was a form of tan, the skin beneath his shirt pale but his hands darkened to the color of faded leather, but smooth and unhindered by any imperfection. When she had first looked at him, she could hardly believe her eyes.

"They call us *maeri*," he leaned in and gave a smirk.

She looked away quickly, hoping he couldn't see her blush at the terrible word. It meant damned—cursed. Dreadful horrors were encompassed into one simple word. Those of the Maereo were seen as tormented souls who could see into the future. Their unnatural abilities making them creatures of death and destruction.

"Don't worry, they work much the same as yours." Larn tapped the corner of one of his eyes, teasing her.

"I'm not afraid of you."

"You don't think I'll start seeing spirits and or begin dancing with animals in the forest?" He asked in mock offense. All too soon his tone changed, growing serious. "Then you really don't believe the legends. They have some foundation, all stories do—it's just a matter of how far they've grown." He took a deep breath. "My story began when I was a little boy. My mother was a seer," she paused and he glanced up again, before continuing. "She was nothing special in the way of visions, but she had more of a gift than I do. To this day, I've never predicted a single thing, although it can be fun to pretend."

She nearly smiled. "That's horrible."

"How so? People believe what they want to believe. I can't help it if they expect me to fill in their futures. I might as well give them something to think about." He shrugged and then winced when she pricked him.

"Hold still."

"Sorry. Where was I? Oh, right, well like I said, my *people* are considered to have special gifts. We live in huts up in the Beastly Mountains, but only those with the ability to see the future are allowed to stay. I didn't have the gift and was sent to Sicarmman to train as a soldier. I was only a boy at the time, five years old, it's been nearly seventeen years since I left."

She inhaled. "Do you miss it?" Why did her voice always sound so small?

He looked up—he really was quite handsome when he tried to see through her words. "At times, but it's been so long now I can hardly remember my life any other way. Do you see those men?" He nodded in the direction of the group. She had nearly forgotten they weren't alone. "They're my home. The Renegades are my place. But someday, when I've done my duty, I'll leave. I don't know where I'll go, but it will be away from all this."

His voice drifted toward the end and she wondered if he had forgotten whom he was speaking to. Hidden beneath the words was a longing for something she could understand, or at least, she used to. Now she was only trying to come to terms with her fate and knowing she could never go back home. Home was no longer a part of her, it was the reason she was here.

She finished the last few stitches on his shoulder and tied off the knot. When she pulled her hands away, he glanced up and adjusted the fabric to hide his pale skin.

"I seem to have rambled."

She let her mouth lift on one side. It felt wonderful to not be afraid, if only for a moment.

"So tell me," he said, patting the ground beside him. "What kind of stories have you heard about my kind?"

She took her seat beside him, wrapping her arms around her legs. "I'm sure it's nothing you haven't heard before."

"Tell me," he urged and she shook her head. She was too embarrassed to admit she had believed most of the stories. "We have nothing else to do."

"Fine," she sighed, keeping her eyes away. "They say you're a violent people. You foresee the future, communicate with beasts, live in herds like animals, and only when a male has killed a pale man from the Regent's lands is he considered notable within his herd."

Larn choked out a laugh, his shoulders shaking. Her cheeks flamed.

"Your people actually believe those stories?" he asked, his shoulders still shaking though he had quieted the sounds coming from his mouth when the Renegade leader sent him a look from the middle of the camp.

"We didn't have any reason not to." She had decided truth was the best course of action.

He sobered quickly. "I suppose not." He turned to look down at her. "Which ones do you believe? I want to see if you're right."

"Some of them are true?"

"One," he held up a finger.

"Oh, then the last one." She ducked her head.

"Not that one," he rolled his eyes. "Although I have killed men, it has nothing to do with becoming a part of the, what did you call it, herd? They are called tribes, and my mother was part of a large one. Really, the best way to be seen as a man was to predict the future. As I said, I showed no talent at an early age and haven't since. I was lucky enough to have the Renegades take me in."

"I guess they lied to us." Umbris thought back to the many times she had listened to the stories about the northern people, men and women, who looked and lived differently from them. They were feared because they were not understood, but all Umbris saw before her was a man. A person.

"They probably lied, although, as I said, it has some foundation. They wanted to keep you out of the Beastly Mountains, and what better way than to say the strange people who lived there would hunt men down? There's nothing as terrifying as a creature who can hunt and is as smart as a man."

She shivered, he spoke as though he knew this to be true. "Which one is real?"

"No more guesses?" He winked at her again. "The animals. You people are very uncreative with your names. Beastly Mountains? I could have come up with something better than that."

"It's true? You can communicate with animals?"

He shrugged, "Not the way you think I can. I have sway over them, a way of speaking to them which they understand. If I wanted to, I could make Tympmor charge through the trees right now, but I think I'll let him rest."

She glanced behind them at the still form of the black beast. "No one needs the drums of death right now."

He smiled, perfectly straight teeth gleaming, "Exactly."

"Can you do it to all animals?"

"That's the thing, actually." He hesitated, his eyes searching over the shapes and forms now resting on the ground. Aside from a few guards paroling the edges, everyone was settling into sleep. "Have you heard of the Animle?"

She nodded, her throat suddenly going dry. These were the warriors of legend.

"When the Animle disappeared, there were years of silence. No beast disturbed the realm, until stories of strange sightings in *Excelsis Bestia* were reported. I lived there with the Renegades for years, and I never saw anything which resembled what the legends used to speak of until three years ago.

"I was on a scouting mission, following the tracks of some soldiers scouring the forest for Animle, when I came across the tracks of a mountain lion, but the paw prints were twice the size of any I had ever seen before. My men and I followed the trail, searching for the beast for three days when we came across a frozen massacre. Nexen, nearly twenty of them lay dead upon the ground and at least eight wolves were slaughtered beside them. I had never known of anything to kill the wolves before, they are too fast, too smart. We were scouring over the tracks when I felt hot breath behind me."

Umbris's eyes widened as she seemed to see it all happening.

"I dropped to the ground right there, my men following my lead. We played dead, but I knew the beast was aware of our warm bodies. It hopped down from the tree, slowly pacing through the snow. It didn't even smell me, but stood for a moment above us, before moving on. I'll never forget the way the snow crunched beneath its paws, as though the very snow itself knew it was an unnatural creature."

He paused, seemingly lost in thought. Umbris was certain he was seeing it all again before him. A part of her wanted to reach him, to force him to tell her what had happened.

Larn turned to her, his eyes slowly refocusing. "He left," he shrugged. "The cat left us lying there in the snow."

"Were you right? Was it a mountain lion?"

He nodded. "Biggest one I've ever seen." When he caught her curious gaze, he shifted. "I couldn't resist, I had to see how big it was. As it walked away, I glanced up. It could have rested its chin on my shoulder."

She shook her head. "I never believed it." Even after all the stories and the reasons behind them, she had never truly believed it was possible. *If the Animle exist, then I—*

She stopped her thoughts before they could get too far. There was nothing she could do about it now. Maybe before she would have been able to do something, but the tingling in her wrists where her scars resided was enough of a reminder of what she had become. There was nothing for her now.

"Does the Regent know?" She asked suddenly, trying to take her mind off her future.

"He must." Larn sighed. "There's a new decree we intercepted a week ago. The Regent wants all animal fights stopped."

"Why now?"

"There has been a sighting." If his eyes had looked light, it was nothing compared to how they were now. A deep desire glowed in them—passion for a journey Umbris wished she could be a part of. "We've heard rumors of a beast going free from one of the black markets."

She gasped. "How? Did it escape?" she asked. From what she had heard, it seemed impossible for a beast to break free, especially with the crowd and the owners controlling the animals with chains and spears.

"We've heard the beast had help."

This time she covered a hand over her mouth. If the animal had help from any man or woman, that person was surely dead by now. No lord in the realm would allow something so treasonous to happen beneath his watch. He would be known as a traitor to the Regent.

"Are you hunting the beast?" she asked.

"Hunting? No." He shook his head quickly. "But searching? Yes. If we're lucky, we'll find the man responsible for releasing the beast."

"He's still alive?"

"As far as we've heard, but we don't have much time."

"Then why are you waiting here tonight?"

He gave her a wry grin and she nearly blushed. For only a moment she had forgotten who she was. She had forgotten all the protection the Renegades provided to them in their time of need.

"We'll move on in the morning." He sounded a bit disgruntled.

"But you'll go with them," she said, not a question but a fact. She knew enough about men and how when they got an idea in their heads, they would carry it through to the end.

"Yes," he said quietly.

"Can you promise me something?" she asked, her voice all the smaller.

"What's that?"

"When you find this man and the beast, when you return the Animle to their rightful place," she watched his eyebrows rise in surprise, "will you come find me? Not because I'll need to be saved, but because I have to believe in something greater than what's ahead." She blinked back tears.

"Yes," he said in a hoarse whisper. "It might be years."

"I don't care," she said, quietly.

She wanted to say more, but her future was understood to both of them. The only decisions before her were what kind of house she would end up in. She had heard the other women speak of the horrifying conditions of those houses near the outer wall surrounding Bastion Nocta. She hoped above all else she was away from that place.

"Umbris," he said her name softly, barely reaching her ears. "Would you be willing to be part of this, part of the rebellion?"

"What?"

"I'm serious," he said.

"I don't know how to use a sword," she explained. She didn't know how to do much of anything.

"No," he shook his head quickly. "Girshon is going to give you a decision tomorrow, to go off on your own, or to be escorted to Brescht, it's a small village about fifteen miles from here, close to Bastion Nocta. Your fate there will be much the same as it would be in Bastion Nocta, but I want you to consider my offer. I need eyes, and ears inside the capitol. Someone to tell me the secrets of the Gallian soldiers and their movements."

She shifted, realizing what he was suggesting. They both knew she would be in the most intimate of places with the men, though the thought still made her tremble with fear.

"I'm only one woman," she whispered.

"Yes," he agreed, "but one is worth so much."

"I—I—don't know."

He took her hand. "I only want you to think about it. There's the chance you will end up somewhere of very little influence, but if I had to guess, you'll be exactly where you need to be."

She turned away, knowing he was referring to her beauty. It was something she hadn't wanted to face over the past few weeks, though from the talk of the other women, her looks might save her from living in a house near the outer wall where starvation was certain.

She felt his hand on her shoulder and he turned her to him. "I didn't mean that," he said softly and she wondered how he had known where her thoughts had turned. "I meant, you've already proven you're able to draw the attention of those in important positions. Commander Jolson included. If you can get his attention, then I'm certain other men will follow in his wake. You saw right through me, and I've watched you judge each man here. I wouldn't doubt you know more about them in one glance than they could ever realize."

She shivered, uncertain how he saw so much of her. The feeling of being naked again passed over her. She wrapped her arms around her shoulders and held all she was inside. If someone believed in her again, it would bring her past to light. It would make her face it all again.

"You don't have to make a decision now."

"I'm not," she said simply, eyes downcast.

"Good," he sounded pleased and she suddenly realized her misstep. If she was going to refuse, she would have done so already. She bit her lip as he leaned forward and grabbed a spare saddle blanket from the ground. He handed it to her.

She took it, but he didn't let go until she looked up. She met his brown gaze with a look of her own and it wasn't until he left her to fall asleep next to Tympmor, that she was able to understand what had been in his eyes.

It was something she hadn't seen in a long time. Something so pure she could hardly let her heart contain her memories.

It was hope. Wrapped in the grace of it, she drifted off to sleep. For the first time since they'd taken her, tears didn't accompany her dreams.

CHAPTER 20

Mist hovered over the ground, the forest damp after the morning's rainfall. The soft glow from the sun lit the trees with an ethereal light, the mist silencing the sounds of creatures moving through the forest. Willem couldn't have asked for a better time for fresh rain to erase all tracks.

As duty called, he had been forced to track the gorilla for the last few days—Fergin following his every move. On the first morning, Fergin and his men had escorted him to the Black Market where all the animals near the ring were slaughtered. Then the hunt had begun. Though it had been weeks since the gorilla had disappeared into the forest, Willem could still find the tracks.

They weren't hard to miss—enourmous footprints, mimicking hands, created an odd impression across the forest floor. Only a creature of that size could be counted on to leave such a clear trail.

Once when he was a young boy he had watched a rodent run across the upper branches of one of the trees, with each step the branch grew thinner, turning to twigs and leaves. The little paws had clung on, grasping and balancing. He laughed at himself to think of it now. He was the rodent balancing on a twig that could snap at any moment.

Stalling the Nexen was becoming more difficult each day. He was proclaimed to be a skilled hunter and had to act as one while holding up the hunt long enough for the Renegades to arrive. Every night, upon his return, he asked Ansie if she had heard anything from Jethron or the Renegades. Her negative response was enough to keep him uneasy and scrambling.

It had only taken him but a few hours to figure out where the gorilla was hiding. Why the creature was resting in a cave near the old spring he used to visit, he didn't know, but it remained all the same. It didn't help that Fergin was a skilled tracker as well.

Glancing to his left, the man gave Willem a quick glare from his saddle. After another day spent on the back of a horse and nothing to show for it, they traipsed back to the Black Market. Willem held his breath, waiting for the questions to begin.

After each day in the forest, Fergin had spent close to an hour interrogating Willem about each decision he had made while tracking. The intent was to trip him up, but Willem was ahead of the game.

The rugged expanse of the Black Market walls came into view. His horse gave an extra trot forward, hooves squishing in the mud. Willem's only hope for tomorrow was for the gorilla to stay put. The rain had washed away all remnants of old trails, but if the beast moved, he would be hard pressed to keep the hunt from heading straight into the cave.

They entered the marketplace, men shifting out of the way and dodging into the corners of the houses and small buildings—the Nexen making them nervous.

It was eerily quiet without the hisses and growls of the animals in the pit. Willem wasn't sure if he missed the sound. Until now, he had never wondered why he was always so drawn to it.

Men littered the market, standing beneath the overhang of various taverns, as they watched Willem enter, the Nexen with him. There was hardly a sound aside from their own horses' hooves sucking in the mud.

Fergin pulled his mount to a halt. "Wait here," he muttered to his men and dismounted. Without hesitation, he strode toward Sarnon's tent, the elderly merchant's eyes flicked to Willem. He hadn't seen the trader since he last bartered for the grinspur horn. The slight downturn of Sarnon's mouth gave him a distinct look of displeasure. Nexen captain or not, Sarnon would bow to no one's will.

Spectacles dangling on the tip of his nose, Sarnon welcomed Fergin to his tent. Willem watched their quick exchange with a sense of dread. Fergin's silence today had seemed odd to him, and he gritted his teeth. The captain knew he was stalling.

All too soon, Fergin bowed his head and returned to his horse. Willem hid his surprise and led the way out of the marketplace. There would be no questions tonight, only assumptions, and he could only guess where the captain's thoughts had gone.

The horses trotted along the ill-picked trail of the forest. Breaking through the last of the trees, Fergin called his men to a halt. Willem dismounted.

"Tomorrow, then." Fergin's voice came from the saddle of the grey steed, his cold eyes on the cottage.

Willem looked up, the man's hand was extended for the reins. A sense of foreboding suddenly came upon him.

"Yes, sir." Willem knocked off a quick salute, knuckles to the forehead, and handed over the reins. The soldiers were gone in an instant, the mud from the hooves of their horses splattering him. He grimaced, uncertain of what to make of the encounter.

Shoving open the cottage door with more force than necessary, he grumbled under his breath. Ansie was working over the stove and didn't jolt at the entrance, no doubt she'd heard them approach.

"Success?" She turned to him, her glowing from the pulsing light of the flames behind her.

"I don't know why it's still there," he muttered, slamming the door behind him.

"It still hasn't left the cave?"

"Not as far as I can tell. And with the rain, I would have been able to see it."

She returned to her work over the stove. "Maybe you were wrong, maybe it doesn't understand. Maybe Jethron is wrong too."

Willem could hear the doubt in her voice, but he knew intelligence when he saw it. That creature had looked at him—stared him directly in the eye and for the breath of a moment, Willem had somehow known it had thoughts, a soul, something not of this realm.

Ansie twisted her hands together. "Does Fergin suspect anything?"

Willem gave a short laugh, his temper getting the better of him after spending the entire day controlling every single facet of his being. "Of course he does."

"But he hasn't figured out where it is yet."

He gritted his teeth, moving to the cupboard to look for something to eat. Ansie always had a way of making light of any situation, taking the worst of something and seeing the best in it. At times like this, he wanted her to sink to his level, to wish each of those Nexen dead and Lord Hernan along with them.

If he had learned anything in the past few days, it was the patience of Captain Fergin. The man was more cunning and ruthless than he had suspected. A foolish tyrant was still a tyrant, but a controlled aggressor could strike without warning. Willem would take the former any day. He knew how to appease Lord Hernan, but Fergin was a mystery.

Everything he had tried so far had yet to trip the man up. He was running out of tactics, out of tactics and out of time.

He slammed the cupboard door shut, the last of his patience disappearing. This time Ansie jumped. "I don't know, I don't know how to stall them any longer, and I don't know what that damned animal is going to do next."

He glanced up and saw the white around her brown eyes, she blinked once and then turned away. He glanced at the door he had slammed shut, some of the wood had splintered. With a guilty realization, he noticed the way she stared into the fire. She had never been one to tell him when he needed to shut his mouth, to chide him for an outburst. To see her timidly looking away now gave him pause.

She returned to stirring some lump in a pot. It would be another night of meager rations. His only regret was Ansie having to share in the loss for his actions in the plaza. But as she had said, it was better they be a little hungry than Jep's family starving.

He sighed, his shoulders slumping. "I'm sorry." How many times had he used that phrase in the past few days when speaking to her?

"I should spit in your gruel." She said without turning, and he smiled.

His chest lightened, if only a bit. "You really should."

She glanced over her shoulder and gave him a once over. "So Fergin is catching on?" She knew him too well, with one look she was able to understand what he'd been through.

"He seems to be." He sighed, spreading his hands out on the table. "It would be really great if you had some news today."

She shook her head, the lines along her brow creasing. He curbed his irritation. Jethron had told him to distract the Nexen and do what he could to equip the villagers in fighting, but he hadn't given them a timeline for the arrival of the Renegades. What could possibly be keeping them?

Jethron was determined that there would be a battle for Mirtain. The very idea set his teeth on edge, he didn't want Ansie anywhere near the fight, though he was certain she would be.

The girl in question glanced up as she set the steaming pot on the table. The gruel looked as unappetizing as it had last night, but his stomach grumbled in hopes of gaining some form of nourishment. Ever since Lord Hernan had restricted their food, Willem had been hard pressed to have enough energy to continue through the day. Between dealing with Fergin and helping to oversee the training of the villagers, he felt as though his only few moments of peace were at night when he fell asleep. But even then, his dreams were littered with nightmares of Kata.

Ansie cleared her throat, breaking into his thoughts. "Before I tell you something, I need you to promise me you won't run out that door as soon as you hear it." She pointed and he stilled himself, waiting. "I went looking for nuts on my way back from the village today and walked past Shirnway Castle. There was a rose in the upper window."

His heart, what was left of it, skipped a beat, and all the warmth from his face drained. "That's not possible," he whispered.

"I saw it." She shrugged as though it was the simplest thing in the world, but it was everything.

"How—how—do you even know about that?" Was his voice always so soft?

She waved a hand, "I knew about that ages ago. I saw you take a rose there once, I was curious. But it must be Jethron."

He grimaced. "He knows?"

"I suppose so," she whispered. "Maybe she told him."

He brought a hand to his mouth, rubbing against the whiskers starting to appear. "I thought it was a secret." Willem felt as though his heart was bared to the world, humiliation sucking him under a wave of shame.

"I'm sorry I followed you. I shouldn't have, but I wondered where you were going."

He nodded, wordlessly accepting her apology. She wasn't the one he was angry with. Of all the ways to get his attention, why Jethron would pick this was beyond him. It was always the same with Jethron, though they had been friends since youth, he was always trying to prove himself. He was weak when it came to swordplay, but he had more cunning than Willem cared to admit. Wits were a game Willem hated to play, and Jethron knew it.

The rose was another one of his jabs, or rather the twisting of the blade in Willem's heart. As always, Jethron was marking his territory when it came to Kata—drawing the lines of battle. But it didn't matter anymore. Willem had his memories and they were enough to allow him to remember her as she was, when she had been partly his. No one could take that from him.

He sucked in a breath, barely containing the ache in his heart.

"She always told me roses were her favorite," Ansie said after the ensuing silence.

With the simplest of comments, she disarmed him. A lump formed in his throat and he turned to look into the firelight, the memories of Kata dancing behind his eyes.

"They were," he said simply. The gruel had even less taste now. There had been a time when he and Kata were inseparable. He had loved her and given her a rose each time he came back from the woods. But that had been before she fell in love with Jethron. Back before she had told Willem she loved him like a brother.

He could still remember the way his heart sank as she said those words. He had been teaching her how to skip rocks on the stream they often visited. She had patted his arm and he'd never said another word about it, but for all those years he'd continued to love her.

Roses used to bring a smile to his face. Now, they were thorns in his side.

It was silent in the cottage for a few minutes. Willem refused to look into the brown eyes that always saw too much—he was holding on, but barely.

"She loved you, you know."

He dropped his spoon with a clatter on the table, bringing his hands to his head. Ansie's chair scraped back and her hands were on him in an instant.

"I'm sorry, I'm sorry," she muttered over and over again, but it was her closeness that made it worse.

Maybe it was the heightened emotions of the day, the expectations resting on him, but somehow the mere mention of Kata was enough to shatter what was left of his heart. Tears burned behind his eyes, but he gritted his teeth against it all, refusing to let the weakness run through him.

Kata was never even his, she never had been and never would be.

"Try and remember something good," Ansie whispered. He nodded and she sank to her knees beside him. "I'm such a dolt, I never should have said anything."

For one breath longer, he kept his head bowed. The pain thrummed through his dead heart, stirring things he hadn't felt since he'd heard of Kata's death. "You're right, she did love roses. She always had."

Ansie watched him, the warmth in her gaze shining with tears. "I'm sure Jethron meant nothing by it."

If Willem had been in his right mind, he would have laughed. "I'm sure he did. He was always jealous of the way she looked to me for protection. Jethron had wanted her and got her, but it didn't take away our past." He sighed. "But it doesn't matter now."

"No," Ansie said, though she didn't seem to agree. "I guess not." When it came to Jethron, Ansie had a softer spot for him. The parts of him that were rough and at times ruthless, she would see as passion and conviction. What she often didn't see was his ability to stir up trouble between others. Willem had long given up arguing about Jethron with her.

"I'm starved," he decided to say, "let's eat first, then we'll go."

He hid all traces of his pain and tucked it away deep inside. He hadn't always been this way. He used to be able to control himself in any situation, but Kata had been his ultimate weakness. Not many had known, but Jethron had.

And for that, Willem could never forgive him.

Shirnway Castle loomed in the shadow-filled night.

He could have at least taken down the damned rose. Willem bit into the thought—Jethron would be in rare form tonight.

Ansie trudged beside him, nearly concealed in her dark cloak. After their last venture to the Black Market, she didn't seem as keen to leave the cottage at night, something he was thankful for. Their race back to the cottage had given her a healthy respect for the Nexen. If he had known what it could do, he would have taken her with him years ago.

They passed by the castle and crept toward the creek that ran along the bottom of the sloping hill. The familiar rocks and brambles shrouded the pathway, but they both moved with ease. As they crept forward a crack of thunder resounded up above.

Willem held out his hand, cautioning Ansie to stop. She looked up confused. How trusting she was.

He held a finger to his lips and pulled a dagger from his belt. It didn't hurt to take precautions. He peeked through a break in the branches, sure enough, Jethron's shadow passed by them and then again. He was pacing.

Nothing else moved and Willem slid the dagger back into its sheath before stepping through the shadows. The dim glow of the moons shined in jagged bands across the waters behind Jethron. Willem knew that if he dared to swim in the cool night, the creek would reach well past his head. He had learned as a young boy that the water was deceptively deep.

Jethron spun to face them, his hair mussed and sticking out at odd angles. There was something in his eyes that made Willem shift uncomfortably.

"What took you so long?"

"Oh, just a little thing called curfew, and having to dodge the Nexen," Ansie answered with just enough sass to make Willem thankful he had brought her along. After the day he was having, he didn't expect to keep his temper in check.

Jethron gave a soft laugh and Ansie hurried to give him a hug. The clear blue eyes shifted to Willem, one eye shadowed by the scar running across his face.

"Here," she said and handed Jethron a parcel. "It isn't much, but I thought you might be hungry." What little they had, Ansie still offered.

Jethron dug in quickly, after a short thank you. "You always make the best food. What did you put in this?"

Ansie opened her mouth to answer, but Willem beat her to it. "Perhaps instead, we can talk about what you came here for?"

"Always business," Jethron shook his head and rolled his eyes at Ansie.

"Don't tempt me."

"Willem," Ansie chided, but he ignored her. This was between Jethron and himself.

The man in question sighed dramatically. "The Renegades will be here in two days."

Willem sucked in a breath. It was too long, too much time. Each minute was a risk, sooner or later Fergin was going to snap, and when he did, blood would be shed. Willem could feel it, sense it. For years he'd been trained to hunt, he knew weakness and attack when he saw it. Fergin was hedging his options, but the attack would come soon.

"So soon?" Ansie asked, not knowing his thoughts. It was anything but soon. "What should we do?"

"Nothing," Jethron shrugged and a grin spread across his lips. "As long as Willem has kept the Nexen from finding the gorilla, then we can deal with the rest. I'm assuming you've been training the villagers?" He glanced at Willem, seeming to size him up. Was it just Willem's imagination, or did the scar actually make his friend seem more confident?

No, it was something else. Something about the way Jethron now carried himself.

Willem shrugged and turned away. "I've kept the Nexen busy, the Gallians are satisfied and Hernan suspects nothing." He couldn't help the sharp edge in his voice.

His eyes roved over to the creek, remembering the rose Jethron had placed in the windowsill. He refused to focus on it, though the knot in his chest wouldn't budge. He was falling apart these days, he had never meant to let Ansie see so much of him.

"That'll do…for now," Jethron nodded, eating the last of the cracked bread.

A roll of thunder rumbled in the distance, it wouldn't be long before the clouds swept over the moons and poured forth their sorrows.

"Do you have any parchment?" Willem asked. Jethron and Ansie turned at his seemingly odd request. "I have the names of the men most ready."

"No parchment, but you can still tell me. Like I said I have contacts."

"Of course." Willem began ticking off names, listing the ablest villagers. Surprisingly, many of the men had improved a great deal in the last few days, though they wouldn't hold long against Gallian soldiers, not to mention the Nexen and their wolves.

"Skurn?" Jethron asked when Willem said his name. "I didn't think he would be interested. He always seemed more preoccupied with other pursuits," his eyes drifted toward Ansie. "Aren't you fond of him, Ansie?"

"I was," she shrugged. "We've since parted ways."

Had they? Now that Willem really focused, he realized Ansie had been around the cottage more than usual, something she hadn't done in a long time. How had he missed that?

"Shame," Jethron shrugged. "I always liked him. But he's a ready fighter?"

"You know he is," Willem said quickly. "He can beat me in hand to hand combat any day, but he has a lot to learn with a sword. The men look to him as a leader of sorts, he catches on quick and is a good instructor."

Jethron nodded, seeming to take his words to heart. "Don't look so surprised Ansie, Willem can be quite pleasant when he isn't angry at everything that moves."

Ansie shook her head, did Jethron notice the way her shoulders seemed to droop? Willem had seen it before, but Kata had always been there to lift her up. Sometimes he was so selfish, thinking he was the only one to truly miss her, but Ansie had lost a friend in this, they all had.

"You haven't asked me about the rumors," she said softly. "The soldiers were talking about a caravan of goods coming in tomorrow. I don't know what that means in light of the number of soldiers in Mirtain, but I thought you would like to know."

Jethron nodded, "I'll let my men know. Anything else?"

She shook her head, the red mane rustling, and then paused, squaring her shoulders. "I want to know why the gorilla is still here."

Willem sucked in a breath. It was the same question that had been running through his mind over the past few days.

"Really?" Jethron raised an eyebrow, the scar making the lines of his face harsher. His eyes flicked back and forth between the two of them. "I thought it was quite obvious."

Willem shifted. Somewhere in the back of his mind, he knew this was what Jethron had been leading up to. He'd been waiting for the right moment to tell them all of this. The gorilla, the searching, the rose, all of it led to this.

But you already knew that, the thought slipped by.

"It seems you've forgotten the stories."

"Not forgotten," Willem shook his head, "I simply don't believe they're true."

"What more proof do you need?" Jethron opened his arms as though the very air around them was evidence. "You saw the gorilla with your own eyes, he's an Animle warrior and you know it!"

"It's nothing."

"Nothing?" Jethron scoffed, shaking his head.

"It's not nothing, Willem." Ansie turned to him, her eyes shining with something he hadn't seen in a long time. It was hope, hope for something more than what they had.

He shook his head and paced closer to the creek, the soft glow of white reflecting like cream. Over the trees, a small flash illuminated the sky, a moment later thunder rumbled in the distance.

"It's the Animle, Willem. Remember the Rising? Kata told us about it."

Didn't they realize what they were asking him to believe? What they were asking him to accept? He used to want this, he'd had an innate desire to rebel against Lord Hernan and against the Regent, but when Kata's life was forfeit, he had been thrust back into his place and his dreams of ever changing this world were shattered. He'd believed he could be the difference, but he now knew things would never change. To make himself believe again would be accepting the past as part of something bigger than himself, and he couldn't do that.

"The gorilla, the wolves, the Renegades, all of it's connected," Ansie said and turned to Jethron. How could a voice so soft affect him so much?

"I know what you want from me," Willem looked to Jethron this time, he couldn't see the disappointment in Ansie's eyes, "but you won't get it here."

Jethron's jaw tightened. "The Rising is happening, with or without you it's happening."

Willem shifted and continued to stare over the creek. The Rising, even the word was bitter in his mouth. It was said the Animle would return and a new kingdom would be born when the warrior of the Blood Moon was found. He had never believed in the prophecy and he wouldn't now.

His mother had told him about it when he was a child, but the night he had been born was dark. Both moons sequestered behind the clouds, but still shining. The Blood Moon had happened years before he was born, the red moon hiding the white behind it, the night the prophesied Animle warrior was said to be born.

Willem shook his head, it was all ridiculousness. Yet, he couldn't deny the gorilla, that was his only hindrance. "I know the prophecy well enough."

"Then you also recall what Kata told us about the beginnings of this realm?"

"No, I remember Kata telling a story and that's all it was." He shot a look at Jethron and watched the blood drain from his face. "I don't care about the five founding rulers who landed on the shores of the realm, I don't care about the Deceiver or the Truth-Bringer," he rolled his eyes, "what I care about is the breath I'm taking now and the one that follows." Ansie turned away from him, crossing her arms as she did. "I wish things were different, but that's all it is, a wish."

Jethron was already shaking his head. "You're wrong. It's so much more than that."

"The Animle are gone," Willem nearly shouted.

"They were," Jethron eyed him refusing to back down.

"It doesn't mean anything will change," he countered.

"Things are already changing." It was Ansie who spoke, surprising him. He turned to face her. "Look at the facts Willem. You want to know why that gorilla is hanging around, it's waiting for you." She heaved a breath, "You. It looked at you, somehow it knows."

He was shaking his head before she finished speaking, though her words confirmed every thought he'd had this past week. He'd given up his hopes, the fight inside him long buried after that horrible day, but there had always been a part which held onto the truth his mother had spoken before she died.

"I can't afford to believe anymore."

"Can't or won't?" Jethron asked. "I know you still believe. It's because you still believe, he looked to you." For a moment, Jethron's face became illuminated as a flash of lightning lit the sky around them. "He will find you, Willem."

Thunder rumbled.

Willem closed his eyes, pressing a finger and thumb to his now crooked nose.

"You say you don't believe in this, but for the past few days, you've been leading Captain Fergin's men on a fruitless hunt in the hopes of keeping that creature alive. You believe in this more than you think." Jethron gave him a knowing look and strode toward the sequestered path. "Be ready, two days and the Renegades will be here, then you'll have to decide."

Jethron disappeared without another glance. Somehow it felt as though the creek bank was more crowded after he left, as though the memories Jethron had brought to light took on a life of their own.

Refusing to give them thought, Willem focused on what had been. As always, the tear in his chest pulled and he focused on the pain, allowing it to wrap around him, eating him from the inside out.

CHAPTER 21

He was silent for nearly ten minutes before she couldn't take it any longer. The way he shut her out was causing her more pain than she cared to admit.

"Talk to me," Ansie said, her voice softer than usual.

He remained with his back to her, no doubt remembering all the hours they had spent as a group splashing around in the creek. Why Jethron had decided to use the rose to get Willem's attention, she had no idea, it only brought to light that which was gone.

The two had always been at odds with one another, not as though they hated each other, but as though they were two ends to the same sword. One was the hilt, the other the blade. Where Jethron was ready to fight, Willem was cautious, when Jethron wanted to hold back, Willem was ready to charge in, blade slashing. They had always been that way, one ahead of the other, always tugging back and forth.

It had been Kata who was able to keep them in line. She'd had a way of making them see eye to eye. As it happened, the past two meetings between Jethron and Willem, when Ansie was present proved she wasn't up to the task.

"What do you think I should do?" Willem sighed and turned around to face her. She braced herself for the pain she knew she would see in his eyes.

"About Kata?"

His face hardened. "The gorilla."

"I thought we already established that." She sighed and ran a hand through the auburn strands of her hair. Surprisingly, she was able to get her fingers out with little difficulty. Though it wasn't curly, it was unruly and often tangled at the ends.

"I'm still not sure what to do about it."

"You know what you're going to do." He grimaced at her words. Everything Jethron had said was only a confirmation of what Willem had used to hope for. Though he would fight it every step of the way, she needed him to see what could be. The time for living in the past was over—Fergin and his men had shown her that. Nothing would change if they refused to move.

"Right," he said and glanced at her. "Shall we leave?"

She braced her hands on her hips and looked him straight in the face. He was living in pain, and had been for quite some time. She had tried everything she could think of to get him to talk to her, anything to ease the pain he held so close, pushing everyone else away.

"No." The one word offered no flexibility. This had been a long time coming.

There was a poison inside him which festered and grew with each day he held it back. She had tried consoling him, making him laugh, reminding him of good times, but it all went deeper than that.

"What is your favorite memory of Kata?" she asked, her voice no longer soft.

"Ans, no."

"Tell me," she demanded.

"We aren't doing this again."

Lightning flashed, illuminating them for a moment. "I say we are."

"No," he cut her off, "we aren't."

"Why?" She folded her arms across her chest.

"I'm leaving."

She stepped in front of him. He could knock her out of the way in an instant if he wanted to, but he never would.

"Move."

"Why won't you talk about it? Why?" She pushed and he looked around frantically, running a hand through his hair. All of it came crashing back to her. The hours spent trying to nurse Willm back to health after he'd been beaten to within an inch of his life. Only Skurn had helped get Willem back to the cottage, and Skurn had been there as soon as curfew broke in the morning. But she had faced the night alone—fearing Willem would breathe his last and leave her forever. She had never told Willem what that night had done to her, and she never would. All her anger surged into her voice, strangling her with the need to understand why she'd had to go through the torment of watching him suffer.

"Why?" She shouted.

"Move," he nearly growled at her, and she lost all feeling.

"Dammit, Willem! I'm trying to help you! I've tried everything over the past year, but I can only go so far. If you want to wrap yourself up in pity, then go ahead. But if you're actually going to accept the fact that Kata is gone, I'm here for you. But so help me, I will throttle you if you try to push me away again." Her voice was louder than she intended, but the rumbling thunder only made it more threatening.

Willem stared at her as though she had sprouted horns from her head. She was well aware of how she must look, her face flaming with color, her eyes glaring at him, hands braced on hips. She was a sight to be reckoned with if only she wasn't so short.

"I might not survive if you throttle me."

"I didn't say you would," she muttered. Slowly, the tension eased. Her lips were already turning up at the edges. She never was able to stay mad at him for long.

"When did you get so confident?"

"I got old."

"Old?" he scoffed, playing along, though pain still lingered in his eyes. "If you're old, that makes me—"

"Ancient," she finished for him and he chuckled.

"You've gone and grown up on me."

"You always sound old when you say that," she pointed out. It was something he had always done. Though he was only four years older than her seventeen years, he acted as though it was a lifetime.

"That's why I do it, it confuses people. Just like your height makes everyone think you're younger than you are."

She grimaced. "Don't remind me. Although most kids don't have tree trunks for legs." She gave a breathless laugh and saw him smile in return.

Her legs were one of her greatest complaints and he knew it. She was small in stature, petite even, but her legs were muscular. Where Kata had been slender, she was thick with toned muscle.

"You always say that," he chided.

"And you always say I'm wrong."

He gave a chuckle before turning to stare out the window again. The silence stretched between them, a sudden stillness in the quaking of the storm still miles off. Within the shrouded embrace of the creek, she felt as though they couldn't be touched.

"What do you want to know?" he asked. His voice was hardly above a whisper, as though he already regretted speaking.

"Whatever you'll tell me," she said and tried to keep her mouth from hanging open.

"That could take some time," he sighed and sat to rest his back against a thick, moss-coated tree. She hurried to sit beside him. Sidling next to him, she bumped his shoulder.

"I don't have anywhere to go." She shrugged. "Although, we can head back to the cottage, you could tell me along the way."

"I thought you said I couldn't leave?" he quirked an eyebrow.

"Only when you were misbehaving," she shrugged.

He chuckled and then sobered quickly, all signs of humor fading away. "It's easier here."

His words bespoke of a longing she couldn't fully understand. Even after nearly a year, he still hung on.

"All right." She said and wrapped her arms around her knees. Was he aware of how hard her heart was pounding? She could only imagine what he was feeling. She had come upon the scene too late to see it all, but there was something eating at him, something had happened before she got there, on that horrible day. She had asked around, desperately wanting to know the answer in the days that followed, but no one had known.

He leaned his head back against the trunk of the tree, his eyes closed and she wondered what he was seeing as he opened his mouth to speak.

"It was after we came back from a hunt," he sucked in a breath. "I have another thing to apologize for. I killed a grinspur that day, but I was going to give the horn to her family. Of course, Hernan took it before I could give it to them."

His eyes were still closed so he couldn't see her nod, she had already known about the grinspur. She'd simply thought he had forgotten to mention it in light of everything that happened. Skurn had told her not long after, when she was trying to put the pieces of the story together.

"I went to her house," Willem continued, "but didn't find her. So I went looking." He grimaced, this time the turn in his lips was split from pain. "I should have been paying more attention. I didn't know I was being followed when I spotted them here." His breath caught, and she stilled. "I turned to leave, but Riffnen was already right behind me."

Ansie's eyes watered. She hadn't known Riffnen was the reason everything had turned to death in a moment.

"I yelled for them to run, but he'd already seen them. And then it—it happened. I froze, Ans." The admission seemed to take every part of him, his voice cracking. "I didn't know what to do, and I froze. She screamed when they caught her, yelling for Jethron to run. He made it into the woods, two of Riffnen's men going after him, but Riffnen brought Kata back in my direction and she looked at me." He shook his head, seeming to relive the memory. "She knew I was the reason her whole world had been torn apart, I could see it in her eyes."

Ansie wasn't sure when the tears had started, but they rolled down her cheeks and onto her worn shirt with abandon. His pain mingled with her own. She had been stuck in the fields that day, finishing extra rows of planting because she had let her tongue run again. She had returned to the shattered remains of what life she knew. If only she had been there.

"She didn't blame you," her voice was thick with tears.

He turned to her, his eyes so filled with guilt, she could hardly stand to look at him. "She's gone because of me," he whispered. He hung his head, his shoulders sagging as though he could no longer carry the weight of those words.

Ansie wrapped her arm over his shoulders, her tears soaking into the fabric over his arm. He didn't cry, nor lose his breath, but the way his head hung told her all she needed to know.

"You tried to save her," she offered.

"After it was too late. I ran up those stairs to try and keep them, *him*, from hurting her, but I couldn't. They took her Ans, Hernan raped her, and now she's gone."

Ansie leaned into him, hoping in some small way this was helping release the pain he had carried with him for far too long. The ruling of the Regent was absolute. Any unwed couple found in physical intimacy was to be punished. The penalty was a beating and labor for the rest of their lives. But it was Hernan who had decided to assault Kata before sending her away.

Willem continued, his words pulling at her heart. "I know she wasn't mine, and I never asked her to be. She chose Jethron, and I knew she would be with him until the end of time, but I thought I would at least get to see her. Talk to her. Laugh with her. But because of me, it's over." He grew silent, breathing in and out slowly.

She now knew what had hung over him for the past year, keeping him trapped in the depths of sorrow. Only now did it fall over her as well. He was the one who had seen Kata and Jethron in a forbidden embrace by the creek. He was the reason they were found out, the reason for Kata being taken, the reason Jethron now bore a scar along his face.

She had been there for the rest of it, showing up late to the village square as the soldiers dragged Jethron by, his face cut and bleeding. She had watched as they whipped him and then threw him into the dungeon. The next day they transported him to a labor camp, but somehow he'd escaped.

She had been there to hear the screams coming from inside Lord Hernan's manor, knowing who they belonged to, and she had stood still. Willem had charged forward, using nothing but his own strength to try and get past them— to save Kata, but there was no way to get inside. They beat him then, nearly to death, and she had screamed for them to stop, but he hadn't even put up an arm to shield himself. Now she knew why.

In some way, Willem had wished to join Kata.

"You're right," Ansie said softly, squeezing his shoulder. "You were too late." He nodded, his head hanging lower. "You were too late because this started months before when Kata chose to be with Jethron." Willem stilled beneath her arm. "It was their decision to be together. Regardless of how Hernan acted, they both knew the risk."

It was silent a moment longer before he lifted his head. There were no signs of tears on his face, no outward expression of what he had been through, but she knew where the bruises and breaks had been on his body.

"I think you've punished yourself enough," she whispered.

He shrugged and turned to look at her. "It doesn't really matter does it?"

"Of course it does," she said, letting her arms slide back around her knees. "You may not have been able to save Kata, but you saved me."

Thinking about how foolish she had been with Skurn, she wanted to hit herself. What kind of person saw the pain Willem had gone through, the pain her friends had endured, and then carelessly discarded it in a moment of heady passion? They had only been kisses, but it had been enough, if not more than what Kata and Jethron had done—it could have been the end.

"I could have killed him," Willem admitted, and she knew he was talking about Skurn.

"I know," she said softly. She had never seen Willem as angry as he was at that moment. For the first time since knowing him, she'd been afraid of him. "I'm glad you didn't."

"Me too," he chuckled, knowing the punishment for murder was more severe than any other. A flash of that moment returned to her, Willem had looked behind him as soon as he found her with Skurn. Now she knew why. Guilt twisted in her stomach. It had been fear which had inflamed his anger that night.

"I still remember all of their faces," Willem said, pulling her from the memory. "The soldiers—Riffnen's men. I know each one that was there, that day. And someday, they're going to pay."

Ansie swallowed heavily. In the months following that dreadful day, Willem had seemed to cope with it as best he could. As his injuries had healed, she had struggled to work and barter enough food for them to survive. More than once, she had skipped a meal to feed him. Slowly, he had walked out of the land of the dead and back to the living, but there had always been something off. Now she knew it was the role he had played in their downfall.

It wasn't until Festis Luna, that the solemnness returned and the guilt he carried had doubled. The simple letter sent to Kata's family was a reminder to all the men and women in the village of what the repercussions for disobedience were.

"It no longer matters," Willem said beside her, his voice calmer than it had been all evening. "She's gone."

Ansie could only nod.

Gone. It was the word he had always used, as though she might come back.

"She's at rest," Ansie said softly and squeezed his arm. Willem nodded, his eyes closed. She hoped in some way his pain had eased.

After a moment of quiet, she stood and he looked up at her. "Shall we?" she asked and stuck out her hand to him.

One side of his mouth lifted, no doubt amused at her offer. She couldn't pull him to his feet if she tried, but he took it all the same.

Together they walked away from the creek and past Shirnway Castle, the haunting memories floating behind them. Just as they were passing into the shadows of the trees, she peeked back at the ancient stone window.

The rose was nowhere to be seen.

CHAPTER 22

Hooves thundered all around Larn as the Renegades raced onward. The cold wind whipped his hair behind his ears, his cloak billowing.

The saddle creaked and his legs ached from the hours of hard riding across the cool earth. Tympmor was waning, his strength beginning to lessen with each passing hour. The other horses were straining too, their endurance long since tested.

The land stretched before them, open sections of lush grass and rolling mounds. Nothing so dangerous as the land he was used to, no sharp descents or icy patches which forced riders to be more than wary. After many hours without sleep, Larn knew if there had been dangers, more than one Renegade would have fallen prey to the land's traps.

Two days had passed since they left the group of female prisoners behind. In that span of time, Larn had continued to go over the words he spoke to Umbris and everything she had told him in return.

They had left early in the morning before the clouded breath of the horses had dissipated. Fog was rolling across the open ground when he mounted Tympmor, and Umbris woke from her sleep in time to see them off. He'd been captivated by her ability to notice everything around her, yet she remained a mystery to him.

She had stitched up his shoulder quite well. It certainly wasn't the first time she had ever held a needle, and he wondered whether she had stitched skin before. She hadn't turned away from the sight of his gaping wound, which led him to believe she had known what she was doing. Coupled with her calm words to Neen as she died, Larn knew Umbris had seen death and destruction before.

"Be safe," he told her before he left. Thinking back on it now, he wondered if he should have said more. He had left enough hints of his desire for her to become a spy in Bastion Nocta, but she had never given him an answer.

Girshon had left eight men behind to protect the women with the intention of reaching a small village near Bastion Nocta, called Brescht. Whether or not the former prisoners would be able to make something of their lives there was up to them.

Once more, Larn regretted not coming across the prison caravan sooner. If only they had reached them a week earlier, those women wouldn't have been scarred and marked for the rest of their lives. Of course, they could cover up their wrists, but even such a gesture was deemed curious, and many often viewed those who covered their wrists as hiding their true shame. Women like Umbris were seen as the lowest of the low.

Idly, Larn wondered what Umbris was doing at that moment. It was nearing night and the men were tiring, but the women had a much shorter path to Brescht—they would most likely reach the village before sunset. It wouldn't be long before Pike and the men could leave the women to their own fate. It seemed cruel, but there wasn't much else to be done.

Larn attempted to ease his guilt with the idea the women had a chance to make something of themselves, instead of being sold in the capital to work for a house. Maybe, when the rebellion was over and won, they could go back and free them. Umbris had asked to know about the Animle, and he would do right by her.

Digging his heels into Tympmor's sides, he leaned forward in the stirrups nudging the horse on. If only there was some way to give Tympmor his own strength.

Larn's guilt followed him, chasing him over the ground as he worried about the last words he had given to Pike. He wanted his comrade to give more hints to Umbris about joining the Renegades. He needed eyes and ears inside Bastion Nocta, and she would be more than sufficient.

He prided himself on using those no one noticed. As for himself, he was a conundrum in his obvious difference by appearance. It made it harder to blend in—not impossible, but harder. But it was easy to play upon wonderings, rumors, and fears. As one of the Maereo, he was seen as something "other" and that was just fine by him.

Umbris had seen through it all, she had stood there listening to him talk as she stitched his shoulder. *And long after*, he thought idly.

There was something about her which drew others in. It wasn't simply her beauty, though she was breathtaking, especially when he had seen her in the morning light, but it was something about her large blue eyes—like crisp water, flowing on the banks of the northern rivers. Her face was one of calm assurance and because of it, he had found himself saying too many things.

More than anything, that experience of his own openness with her was enough to make him want her as one of his spies. She would get more information due to her position and abilities than any contact he had in the realm.

"Slow down there," Heben's breathless voice broke into his thoughts, as the makings of a forest loomed on the horizon. They were nearly there.

"Whoa, Tympmor," he said softly, pulling back before giving the horse more rein. The wind around him settled, as the hooves resorted to a trot.

"You were riding as though death was chasing you," Heben heaved beside him.

"I'm ready to make camp," Larn flashed a quick smile.

They rode in silence the rest of the way to the copse of trees, immediately covered in stretching shadows from the setting sun. The crimson bands stretched across the sky, nearly turning black where the deep blue of night began to appear. Larn's breath clouded once more, as the chilling air enveloped them in the shade of the forest. Trees stretched high above their heads, needles hanging off the limbs, and thick trunks which could hide a horse, stood to either side.

The other men pulled into the shadows making more noise than necessary. The forest seemed to shudder as they came to a halt, the leaves trembling above them before the breathing wind pushed past.

"Make camp," Girshon grumbled to the men and hastened his way over to where Larn rested on Tympmor's back. He no longer wore his fur cloak in the warmer atmosphere of the southern lands. His stature was lessened by it, but he was nonetheless intimidating. "When will Calig make contact?"

Larn quirked an eyebrow, "Sometime in the night."

"Good, tell the men to keep quiet. We aren't far from Mirtain."

Larn glanced around the camp, their numbers stretching to nearly eighty men, all highly skilled and trained. Calig, his contact's alias, had told him clearly the numbers would be enough, but he still worried how many villagers would join their ranks.

Hours passed with the general movements of the men. They were so accustomed to one another's duties that hardly a word was spoken. It was past midnight as Larn was rubbing down Tympmor's back when a whipper bird call echoed in the trees. A few birds took flight, only their wings making a sound, though he couldn't see them in the darkness. Girshon answered back.

Larn stepped toward the other men, all of them waiting and watching for Calig to appear. After an uncommonly long time, Larn began to finger his sword.

"No need for that," an assured voice said from behind.

Larn whipped around. A young man, about his own age, was standing on the edge of their camp, his hands free of any weapons. With a quick move, he dropped the hood of his cloak, what little light was available revealed the scar etched across the spy's face.

Calig.

Larn shoved his sword back into its sheath along his hip. His other spies had told him how Calig could be recognized.

Larn stepped forward, his hand extended in greeting and Calig took it. Upon closer look, the spy was more than likely a year or two younger.

"Come, Calig," Girshon patted the spy on the shoulder as though he knew him, something he always did. "Have something to eat and tell us what we can expect in Mirtain."

A smile lifted the corner of Calig's mouth, the scar, which stretched from his right temple to the left side of his mouth, shifted awkwardly. He took a bite of offered bread and then turned it aside. Larn shifted, at least this spy was well-fed. Sometimes his other men had hardly enough to receive a meal each day. Again, he wondered about Umbris.

They stepped into a small alcove, skirting around the lumps of sleeping Renegades. They would need their strength for the battle tomorrow. Larn inhaled sharply, not liking the feeling in his gut. He was used to deception and cunning, but this was an outright attack. An explosion of lightning in the midst of the realm.

Aside from the scar, Calig had a dignified air about him. His clear blue eyes and shaggy brown hair gave him an almost innocent look, something necessary for the job he had decided to take on.

Unknown to the ruling Lord of Mirtain, four of his Gallian soldiers weren't Gallians at all. They were Renegades, having been dispatched by Larn nearly three years ago, to help him get a feel for the morale in the southern villages. What had started out as a simple job, turned into a fortuitous circumstance when Calig had volunteered to join the Renegades.

Even now, the sharp eyes of the spy watched Larn carefully. He could almost see the silent wonderment in the spy's gaze. Larn couldn't help wondering about the scar across the man's face, it was a miracle both of his eyes still worked.

"Come now, soldier," Girshon looked Calig straight in the face, "tell us about this village of yours."

"Where to start," the spy clicked his tongue, Larn never took his eyes away from him, all the while wondering what his real name was. "Mirtain rests but a three hours ride from here." By their looks of surprise, the spy spoke faster. "The soldiers don't patrol this far."

Larn wasn't so easily assured. The men were tired and rightly so, it made them vulnerable in light of what they wanted to accomplish tomorrow. However, only three hours of riding would render the men better rested when they reached the village and the fighting began.

"One of our contacts tells me there are thirty-two men who are able-bodied and skilled with a sword. They should join our forces when given the chance."

Should, that word ate at Larn. All of this was a guessing game, a matter of allegiance and whether or not the men of the village would take the chance to overthrow this Lord Hernan, who presided over the area. Mirtain was meant to be the first of many, but if they failed here, then everything they had tried to achieve in the last few years would be over before it had really even begun. The rest of their forces waited in the north, hiding in the Beastly Mountains the Renegades had grown, waiting for the moment when they could rise again.

"Good, good," Girshon nodded as Calig continued to tell them of the skills the enlisted villagers had. His words wove a web of reasons why the time was just right, even pointing to the cold front which had swept through the southern villages as a means to make the Gallians lazy.

This is considered cold? Larn mused.

There was a lull in the information as the spy continued to put forth his arguments. But there was something the spy wasn't saying.

"What of the Rising, who is the man you wrote to me about?" Larn interjected.

"Ahh," Calig straightened his back, looking him full in the face. "That has been an interesting situation and I have had to work on him."

"He isn't ready?" Girshon growled.

"No, no," Calig shook his head quickly, denying the claim. "He has agreed, but he's...resistant."

Larn swore internally, this was the last thing they needed. "I thought you said he would be ready to take the chance, the creature had looked to him."

"I did, and all of that is still true." Calig sighed, rubbing a hand over his brow. "He is, well, I've known him since we were boys. We grew up in Mirtain together. His dreams for this realm nearly surpass our own."

"Then what changed?" Larn didn't like the direction this was heading. Calig hesitated before going on.

"About a year ago, a girl was taken on the basis of *vox prima*. She was found with me," Calig spoke quickly, a look entering his eyes which made Larn wonder about the depths of the man's hatred toward Lord Hernan. The scar across his face bore new meaning. "She was taken, but not before Hernan raped her. He claimed he only did what he was supposed to do by law."

Larn clamped his jaw tight, no such thing was stated in the law. His spies had been right, Hernan was a domineering lord of a tiny little kingdom. He waited for Calig to continue.

"Word recently reached her family," Calig continued, "the girl, she died, waiting in a cell for transportation to Bastion Nocta."

Larn sucked in a breath, no doubt she would have been in a caravan similar to the one they had left only two days prior. His thoughts returned to Umbris again, wondering if she had known this girl from Mirtain. She too had been a victim of *vox prima*. Though she had said nothing of her past, he had seen the way she averted his gaze, as though she was already a worker of men. She had known her fate, it would be the same as this girl who had died in Mirtain.

"His name is Willem," the spy looked at Larn pointedly, drawing him from his thoughts. "He's still messed up from her death. He's lost hope."

Larn ran a hand over his face, this was all much more than he had expected to hear. "Then how can we trust him?"

The corner of Calig's mouth lifted again. "No reason to worry there. If anyone hates Lord Hernan more than I do, it'd be him. Which brings me to another matter, Willem has already proven his allegiance."

Girshon straightened as though ready to receive a blow. Larn gritted his teeth, knowing this was what Calig had been avoiding. He certainly had a way with words, a way of skirting around until the right moment—like a fighter darting around his opponent. The feeling left Larn uneasy.

"The *simian* looked to him and escaped the pit at the Black Market." The same excitement built in Larn as it had the first time he had read Calig's message. How it was all really happening was beyond him. Years of waiting, finally coming to fruition.

"And we're certain it's a *simian* and not some gorilla."

Calig was already nodding, "And it hasn't left."

Larn's head shot up, "What?"

"It's been waiting, for what I'm not sure, but it hasn't left this forest."

Girshon shifted, glancing around at the shadows, as though expecting to see the creature of legends walk into the camp.

Simian, an actual Animle was in this very forest. Larn could scarcely contain his wonder.

"Willem is in a tight spot. Lord Hernan received the missive from the Regent about the outlawing of animal fights, he hired Willem to track down the *simian* and kill it."

Within an instant, Larn was ready to jump back into the saddle and find this beast in the dark. There was time to sort out the other issues tomorrow, the only thing that really mattered was keeping the creature safe.

"Hold on," Calig placed a hand on Larn's arm. "Willem has been leading the men on. They haven't found the *simian* yet, though he knows exactly where it is."

"Is he aware of what he's hiding?"

"To some degree," Calig nodded. "But he only refers to the beast as a gorilla."

Degrading at best, Larn thought. No creature as revered as an Animle deserved to be called such a name.

"Why hasn't he met with the *simian*?" Larn asked, again having the distinct feeling Calig was leaving bits of his story out.

"He's in a tight spot."

"As you've already said," Larn stated.

"Is it because Lord Hernan hired him?" Girshon asked, as though already knowing the answer.

"Yes, but it's how he hired him. Willem's hand was forced to train the villagers and find the *simian*. The Regent sent Nexen soldiers here." Calig took a deep breath, as Girshon cursed. "They're here because of the *simian*. Word has spread. But Lord Hernan has delayed the investigation, to arm his villagers to protect himself. He knows the Renegades are on the move and fears for his life."

Larn sighed, running a hand through his hair. Lord Hernan had more reason to be afraid than he realized.

"They have wolves with them," Calig said softly.

Though Larn had assumed as much, having it confirmed made him suck in a deep breath. They would be facing wolves tomorrow, and not the kind they had seen in the north, though they would look the same. Only the weakest of Nexen were sent to the north, due to the lack of restraint needed in those areas. An oversight Larn was thankful for, without it, they could never have expected to gather allegiance from so many men, and train soldiers from childhood.

"Wolves," Girshon grumbled, realizing their plan for an attack was going to be more difficult than they previously thought.

Calig nodded, "At least ten, as far as I can tell."

"What are our numbers?"

Larn ran them off, "We have seventy-eight men, four Regent soldiers, thirty-two villagers, and a *simian*."

Calig made a face.

"What now?" Larn asked. The more Calig said, the less he wanted to listen.

"Well," it was the first time the spy looked uncomfortable. "We don't have the *simian*, yet."

"How so?" Girshon asked, his breath clouding.

"Willem has been leading the Nexen around the forest each day, and the *simian* has yet to leave the cave, but the captain is catching on. Willem is considered the best hunter and tracker in the southern lands, for him to take so long to find the creature is quite obvious. He's been stalling."

"Why not take the beast and leave these lands?" A part of Larn had expected Calig to show up with Willem in hand, the creature beside them.

"Spit it out." Girshon ground his teeth.

"Willem has," Calig searched for a word, "responsibilities here." He shifted. "He has a ward, a girl, in his caretaking. Lord Hernan gave him leave to be her guardian ten years ago, and they have lived together ever since, like brother and sister."

Taken aback, Larn watched the man's face for any hint of distrust. He had never heard of any such thing happening in the whole realm—only a village as small as Mirtain could keep something so large from the Regent.

No doubt seeing Larn's surprise, Calig explained further. "Lord Hernan saw Willem's value at a young age and wanted a way of controlling him. As a boy, he was more skilled than any man in the village. By giving Ansie to him for protection, Hernan has a way of controlling Willem."

"So he's threatened the girl?"

"Yes, to do to her what happened to Kata." He glanced up.

Larn was shaking his head before the spy even finished talking. A part of him wanted to see this Lord Hernan and deliver a message personally. Rules didn't apply to this man, even edicts from the Regent were taken with little regard. But rules didn't apply to Larn either—he'd been breaking them since birth.

"That's everything I have to report."

Larn nodded and Calig knocked off a salute, knuckle to forehead.

"How early have they been leaving to track the *simian*?" Girshon asked.

"Before the break of dawn, one of your soldiers reached me before I left to find you. He overheard the Nexen, they're taking the wolves with them today, to hunt the *simian*."

Larn swore, this time letting the word pass through his lips. There wouldn't be enough time to overcome the Nexen, save Willem, the *simian* and then attack Mirtain.

"Do you know where the *simian* is hiding?" he asked, already moving to where Tympmor was munching on oats.

"Yes," Calig's eyes shifted from Larn to Girshon and back.

"Take me there."

Again, the spy looked uncomfortable.

"Do it," Girshon nodded. "Larn has a way with animals, he'll know what to do."

His commander's words gave him too much credit. Animals he knew, but Animle were a mystery to him. Thinking of the mountain lion, a shiver ran down his spine. It wasn't the size of the beast that had rattled him, it was the peace surrounding the creature. It was not of this realm, of that he was certain.

"What about the wolves?" Calig asked, the first trace of fear entering his eyes.

"I know about those too, although these ones are probably larger than I've seen."

Calig nodded, "Their heads almost reach my shoulder."

Much larger, Larn conceded.

"Here," he tossed a dagger to the spy, who caught it with ease. At least, he was now comfortable with a weapon. The spies he'd planted in Mirtain had told him of the progress Calig had made in handling a blade.

"Take men with you," Grishon commanded. "Protect the creature and get to Mirtain as quick as you can. We attack at dawn."

Larn nodded and swung into the saddle. Heben was on the back of his horse moments later, two others joining their ranks.

Shaking his head at the low numbers, Larn looked to Calig. "Lead on, and let's hope this *simian* is willing to stay put."

Calig nodded and hopped onto a borrowed horse. Without another word, he kicked the mount into a run, his form immediately enveloped in the shadows of the creaking trees.

With a click and a nudge, Tympmor took after the silent spy, somehow the horse seemed to sense the urgency with which Larn needed to move. He tried not to think about how their hopes depended on what happened at the break of day, but with each beat of the horses' hooves his fears were confirmed.

Their only hope was to reach Mirtain before it was too late. Three hours distance seemed much too long.

CHAPTER 23

It was still dark when the pounding on the door began. Willem was already dressed and ready, his coat hiding the two daggers he had tucked into a harness around his waist. He secured the sword, he was given leave to carry, across his back as more pounding began.

"Good luck," Ansie whispered, still sequestered in her cot. After two days spent training the villagers, Fergin had told him to prepare to track the simian. Willem's gut clenched as it had all night, the Nexen captain had something dangerous in mind.

Willem pulled on the cottage door and it flew open, the chilling wind seeming to nip into his bones—it had grown cold in the past few days. The weather setting him even more on edge. Within an instant, he heard the tell-tale sound of a growl.

Excellent, the word ran through his mind with a sharp bitterness.

Red eyes followed him as he approached the horse with an empty saddle, the hairs on the back of his neck standing on end. Captain Fergin held the reins, and only when Willem was seated did he toss the leather to him.

"Are you ready?" Fergin asked, his voice dipping low. It was too dark to see the man's gray eyes.

One of the wolves snapped in his direction, clearly ready to be let off the chain. There was a distinct pause in the air, as though everything, the forest, the creatures, even the birds, were silent, as though holding their breath before the plunge.

Willem glanced around, taking a moment to recognize Riffnen sitting astride a dappled stallion, a few Gallian soldiers with him. As the warm, stale breath of a wolf brushed by him, he looked to Fergin. "Shall we?" he asked, grasping the reins tighter in his hands.

Why the overseer was riding with them didn't sit well. Maybe Fergin knew how much Willem despised the man for the way he looked at Ansie. As if he could read Willem's thoughts, Riffnen gave a sly smile, his always-wet lips jutting out.

His heart raced as he tried to understand the meaning behind Riffnen being there. Just yesterday the villagers had been issued a modified Gallian soldier's uniform. Instead of blue, they would be clad in black pants, high boots, coats, and shirts. Not much unlike what the Nexen wore.

"Hold on, boy." Captain Fergin pulled back on the reins of his own horse which danced to the side, the horse's agitation making the rest of the mounts uneasy. A wolf growled.

Fergin snapped his fingers, the sound muffled by the thick gloves he wore. Immediately, two Nexen dismounted and headed for the cottage.

"Hey!" Willem shouted, making a move to follow.

"Hold it!" a crossbow was pointed directly at his chest, Fergin smiling on the other end of it. Like glass shattering, the pleasant silence of the morning was broken.

A curse from inside was soon followed by Ansie being dragged out of the cottage. She resisted as much as she could, bracing her feet, but her small frame was no match for the men pulling her. Dressed in nothing but a loose shirt and pants, she was certain to freeze in the cold air whipping around them. Her bare feet dug into the dirt.

At a signal, they held her steady beside Riffnen's horse. Willem cursed the stars above as his heart thrummed to a steady hum, his stomach turning over. His hands trembled on the reins.

"Now," Captain Fergin turned to Willem, his gaze nearing black with crazed delight. "I know you've been making us traipse through the forest like damned fools, and I refuse to do it again. You take us to where the beast is hiding and she wot be harmed."

"But I don't—"

Fergin raised the crossbow higher, cutting off the rest of Willem's words.

"If you don't, then I will give her to Riffnen. I don't think I have to tell you what that means, do I?"

Willem's fingers curled around the reins until the leather seemed to cut into his palm. He knew if he let go his hands would shake.

How long would he be trapped? Ever since his youth, he had been used. Beaten, abused, tormented, and threatened into submission. No more. But Fergin had him cornered, and he knew it.

"No," Willem admitted.

"Good," Fergin said and made a motion to the soldiers holding Ansie. She shifted awkwardly as they handed her up to Riffnen.

She met Willem's eyes for a moment as Riffnen reached around her to grab the reins. Her fear was palpable, but there was a determination in that quick look which gave Willem a sense of hope. She would fight for all she was worth, he could always count on her. Before he looked away, she shifted her head, right then left. It was nearly imperceptible, but to him the message was clear. He only wondered if he had the strength to endure what he knew would happen if he failed.

"When you're ready," Fergin waved a cordial, gloved hand toward the forest. The challenge was set. Willem kicked the horse's sides and moved forward.

They entered the forest, hooves and padded feet making nary a sound on the soft pine-covered ground. There would be no getting out of this, not in any way he could see. Willem's only hope was to figure out a way to distract the men before Fergin's patience wore out.

Saddle creaking, he let the air of the forest give him strength, he was more himself in these woods than anywhere else. He shifted forward, the dappled mount's ears twitching as they paced down a sloping hill and deeper into the thick trees, where shadows lengthened and even the trees seemed to groan with longing.

Scrambling for a plan, he searched the forest floor knowing the gorilla was to his right, the trail leading toward the caves was nearly ten minutes on horseback. He could only pray to the stars above the creature had remained in the cave over the past two days. Even a hint of the creature's scent would be enough for the wolves to track.

Fergin's eyes were on him, watching his every move and decision. Willem adjusted in the saddle, leaning forward as though peering at the ground more deeply. Without a word, he kicked the horse toward the left.

The padding of the wolves set his nerves on edge, but he kept his back straight and face calm as they rounded down the winding path, the rocking of the horse making him bounce. He didn't dare to glance behind him, though he could feel Ansie's gaze following him.

The night sky was growing lighter by the moment, the dark blue turning to a dull grey. Steam filtered up from the dips and swells in the ground, dirt clinging to the last of its heat.

It was only a few minutes later, just as they descended onto a flat terrain of the forest Willem knew well, that a crossbow clicked behind him. He immediately put his hands in the air, internally cursing.

Fergin sighed as he came around to the front of Willem's horse, his eyes never leaving him. "I thought I made myself clear."

"You did, I'm doing what I can." Even Fergin didn't realize he spoke true. They were closer to the cave than any of the Nexen realized. Close enough for the creature to hear, but not for the wolves to pick up its scent. He had seen the gorilla in action once before, and if the creature could be coaxed to battle, maybe some of the wolves would meet their end. Animle be damned, Jethron be damned, Renegades be damned, it was Ansie he was worried about and would save until his dying breath escaped his lips.

Fergin shook his head and his eyes flitted toward Ansie, somewhere behind him. "I see you're going to need more motivation."

His heart leapt into his throat. *Not again, not again.* His mind scrambled for anything to save her.

"Now," Fergin slid closer, his eyes gleaming in a way Willem had never seen before, "I'm going to give you one chance to tell me where that beast is. I wasn't sent here by the Regent to be thwarted by some Anglan bastard."

One chance. He had one chance to draw the gorilla, or whatever the creature was, from its cave. Willem breathed, the cloud gathering around his face. Ansie had given him his answer before they left. "If we follow this trail, then we'll find it."

The captain's eyes widened for only a moment before they hardened. Without another look at Willem, he passed to Riffnen's horse. Willem stiffened in his saddle as the crossbow was lowered.

"Come Ansie," the captain held a hand out to her. She didn't take it. He wrapped his gloved hand around her arm and threw her to the ground. She hit with a huff and the wolves were in her face immediately.

Willem's horse skittered. His heart in his throat, he whipped his sword out from its sheath along his back. Crossbows and swords were pointed at him in an instant.

"You'd best think before you use that!" Fergin shouted, his voice echoing. He turned to Ansie. "It seems, your *guardian* is unwilling to protect you. I know he told you where the beast is hiding. I'm going to give you one chance to live. You have three minutes to run, and I suggest you run toward the beast, because if my wolves catch you before you reach the creature, then they will have an early meal."

Ansie's eyes widened, her face paling and making the freckles beneath her right eye stand out. Her gaze flicked to Willem and when he shifted forward one inch, a warning arrow shot past his shoulder.

"Whoa!" Willem yelled holding up his other hand, squeezing his legs to stay put on his nervous horse.

"Is this really necessary?" Riffnen was staring at Fergin in shock, his normally greasy countenance paler than usual.

"This boy has led us around like traipsing idiots for too long. Is it the hunt you're afraid of missing, or is it disappointment that you won't be able to have her before she meets her end?"

"She doesn't deserve death," Riffnen countered.

"You're right," Fergin shrugged, and laid the crossbow across his mount's back, "but by the Regent, I have the power to do what is necessary to carry out his will. Perhaps you need to be taught that lesson?"

Riffnen shook his head frantically, and the captain smiled once more. Ansie remained on the ground, one of the wolves breathing beside her, a red strand of hair wafting near her cheek. Willem's horse danced to the side, nervously.

"Enough of this!" Fergin spit, "You have five minutes—"

"No!" Riffnen cried out, shaking his head. "This is ridiculous, treasonous!" Ansie glanced at Willem and he motioned for her to remain on the ground. Her eyes shifted between the men.

"Treasonous?" Fergin's smile faded. "Perhaps she needs a demonstration? Varne!" The wolf beside Ansie whipped his head in the direction of the captain, hackles raised. "*Imcaedo!*"

No sooner had the foreign command left Fergin's mouth than the wolf leapt in a blur of white fur. Ansie screamed as Riffnen's body fell at her feet, the wolf's jaws around the man's throat. All the horses skittered nervously, Riffnen's beginning to dance around, the reins hanging down.

Ansie's wide eyes met Willem's and fear was replaced with determination. She was going to run. He brought the side of his sword down on the haunches of his horse. The beast reared and Fergin turned to look at him.

Ansie darted for the empty saddle of Riffnen's horse.

"Put your sword away!" he bellowed, his eyes filled with blood lust.

Hooves thundered through the air, Ansie was heading straight into the forest, her red hair streaming behind her.

Go! Willem screamed after her in his mind.

The other soldiers looked to the captain who watched Ansie's retreating form. Riffnen's blood soaked into the dirt, his eyes staring blankly up at the lightening sky. Willem kicked his horse again, but a sword tip was suddenly placed against the back of his neck. One of the soldiers grasped the reins of his horse.

"I promised three minutes, and I'm a man of my word," Fergin shook his head, his eyes never leaving where Ansie had disappeared. The wolves all stood at attention, their noses pointed in the direction she had taken. Two of them paced back and forth, their eyes darting from the woods to Fergin and back.

Willem swallowed, praying in desperation for some force to keep her alive. As if knowing which direction his thoughts were headed, the wolf called Varne glared up at him, blood dripping from his quivering jaws.

He heard the zing right before it happened, the subtle swish of air, a singing arrow just before it plunged into the shoulder of the soldier with his sword to Willem's neck. The blade removed, as a cry rang out.

Dark shadows on horses were pounding across the forest floor, bows aimed at the wolves. Two hit the ground before Fergin had his mount turned. The wolves hackles rose, noses turned to the shadows riding toward them. The soldier nearest Willem aimed to take a shot, but he disrupted the path with a swing of his sword.

Varne, dug his claws into the ground, ready to pounce as the thundering hooves came closer. Willem recognized Jethron the moment the shadows broke through the fog, three others riding with him.

"*Confu* Varne!" The wolf looked up at Fergin's command. His hand pointed in the direction Ansie had taken. "*Imcaedo!*"

"No!" Willem's strangled cry rang through the air, his sword clanging with a soldier's before he could reach Fergin. But the wolves had already shot off into the woods, moving faster than he could have imagined, their captain within their midst.

Willem sliced the blade of his sword along the chest of the Nexen before him, he fell to the ground. Another soldier came toward him, his mount charging, he blocked the first blow, and shoved the sword deep within the man's gut.

Jethron knocked a Nexen soldier to the ground, his only weapon a small dagger. Shifting back and forth in his saddle, Willem fought to clear a path. The soldiers were falling one by one, each driven back by the new arrivals.

Without a further glance, Willem kicked his horse into a sprint, following the howling of the wolves. A curse echoed behind him and more hooves joined his race after Ansie.

He urged the mount on, his heart in his throat, his terror threatening to tear him apart. The howls seemed to grow longer between intervals. *Was that good or bad?*

The horse thundered over the ground, hooves beating behind him and getting closer. He glanced back only a moment, taking in the dark hair and clothing of one of the strangers.

The dappled mount Willem had been given seemed to tire quickly under the pace, the stranger's horse catching up easily. The black steed stretched its legs, neck pumping forward as its rider ducked low over the back. Willem didn't give them a further glance as the howling picked up again. They weren't far ahead.

A horse screamed and Willem let a string of curses run from his mouth. The stranger shot him a look.

Please not her, not her, not her, Willem pleaded over and over again. The prayer desperately pouring from his soul.

The wolves howling turned to barking and they thundered on, they were within hearing range of the cave. How Ansie had known exactly which way to go, he would never know.

They broke through the last of the trees, the black rider moving quicker than him. White shadows danced around an enormous tree. They lunged for the trunk, attempting to climb, before falling down to the ground. Riffnen's horse lay dead upon the ground.

A zing from a crossbow cut the air, Willem instinctively ducked. Looking up a moment later, he spotted Fergin on the other side, his bow directed up at the tree. Following his gaze, he spotted Ansie clinging to a branch, her hair making her a blatant target. Willem charged forward, riding straight for the captain when an arm from the stranger shot out and knocked him to the ground. All air fled his lungs.

The stranger leapt to his side, angled eyes narrowing. "Fight them from the ground."

No sooner had he said the words then two of the wolves charged in their direction. They moved at the same moment, swords flashing in the dim light of morn. The wolves paced, one feigning right, then left before shooting toward them. One lunged toward the stranger, but a sword was in its chest before it hit the ground. The other charged for Willem.

He dodged out of the way, moving faster than he had in a long time, the wolf recovered and recounted its steps. It lunged, danced to the side and then charged. This time Willem was more than ready, he darted out of the way, his sword slicing along the beast's shoulder. It growled at him, but was soon silenced as he plunged the blade into the back of the beast.

"Varne!" Fergin yelled as he let another arrow go. Ansie gave a small cry from above.

Willem didn't have time to help her as the head wolf attacked. Red eyes glared at him, teeth snapping. He reached for the dagger in his boot and brandished the weapon, ready to throw it if needed. The wolf growled and leapt into the air, Willem ducked and rolled beneath the wolf and returned to his feet. The wolf had already recovered and was charging again. This time, Willem clipped the beast along the leg, but claws dug into his shoulders. He winced in pain and came up standing, the wolf pacing before him.

Hackles raised, the wolf continued to growl when three more joined him. Willem shifted, his back nearing the tree Ansie had climbed. Four sets of red eyes stared at him, teeth bared. Fergin rode up behind them, his crossbow set on Willem's heart.

Off to the side, the stranger was fighting three of the wolves, holding his ground in a way Willem couldn't understand. From somewhere, the murmurings of some language—similar to the words Fergin had used to command the wolves— were filtering around the woods. Two of the wolves before Willem shook their heads, as though trying not to hear the sound.

"Give up, *boy*!" Fergin yelled.

Willem shook his head, his eyes focused on Varne. The attack would be swift and deadly, but Fergin wouldn't shoot. His lust for blood would allow Varne to tear Willem limb from limb.

The red eyes gleamed. Frozen as the beast snarled, Willem waited until all of a sudden something shifted, a tightening of the eyes, and the creature leapt. Willem darted to the side, plunging his sword into the wolf at his left as Varne ran into the tree.

From up above, needles rained down upon them all. Surely the wolf wasn't large enough to sway the trunk? Ansie called out Willem's name from above, a strangled scream.

He jumped to the side as another wolf attacked and he felt the claws dig into his coat. Varne was waiting. He plunged a dagger into the dog's chest, then rolled over onto his stomach and saw the leader of the pack standing before him, hackles raised. Two wolves appeared on either side. Fergin started laughing.

A familiar roar pierced the air.

Willem's heart skipped a beat.

The ground shook, as a black beast landed on the forest floor. Pine needles raining down around him, the gorilla raised himself to his full height, fists beating his chest as a new roar broke through the trembling lips.

The wolves quickly changed direction and ran for the gorilla, one was hardly within reach before the white body was flung against a tree, spine snapping. The others pulled up, waiting for a command.

Varne paced before the gorilla, looking for an opening. Willem hid behind the creature, ready to see the battle won, when he caught a flash of movement off to the side.

Fergin's bow was raised at the beating chest of the gorilla, it would take only a moment.

A streak of red came down from above, Ansie's small body colliding with Fergin's and knocking him out of the saddle—the arrow missing its mark. Willem was running for her as she tucked and rolled away. The captain pulled two blades from his belt and threw one, just missing Ansie's head.

Willem knocked the second one aside in midair with his sword, as he ran for the man. Fergin blocked two blows before knocking Willem's feet out from under him. Both men scrambled to standing, coming up with swords poised for attack. Fergin feigned forward and Willem countered, attacking with a speed he had honed over years of practice.

He charged, blow after blow raining down on the Nexen captain, the roars and growls from the beasts behind them ringing through the woods. With a twist of his wrist, the sword Fergin held flew from his grasp. Fergin produced another dagger and threw it at him, but Willem dove beneath the dagger's path and hit the captain headlong in the chest.

Hands wrapped around Willem's throat and he struggled, as Fergin rolled over him. With a tightened fist, he punched him in the side, but the captain's hands only tightened. Willem's vision was going dark, his air completely cut off. Bringing his knees up, he kicked Fergin in the chest. With a sucking breath, Fergin released him.

Air mercifully filled Willem's lungs. He scrambled for his sword and it was back in his hand before the captain had a chance to recover. Fergin charged, but Willem's sword prevented any further attack, the blade going all the way through the captain's body. Fergin's eyes widened before he fell to the ground.

"So much for that, *boy*," Willem muttered. Ansie was still on the ground, her eyes wide, watching him.

The gorilla and stranger stood between her and the wolves, fists and blades slicing as the last of the beasts attempted to break through their defenses. Willem spotted Varne pacing behind the three other wolves—the alpha locked eyes with him. He knew his master was dead.

The shoulders hunched before he raced in his direction. Willem grasped his sword, ready to take on the wolf, when a large black arm grasped the wolf beneath the chest and threw it against the cave wall.

A small yelp was the last sound from the white monster.

CHAPTER 24

Ansie wasn't sure if she was breathing, or if she was even alive.

Every heartbeat rang in her head, clanging inside her body, her senses on high alert. Her eyes were fixed, unable to move from the dark beast before her. Mud stained her clothes and the moist dirt squishing beneath her fingers was her only connection to reality.

She heard her name from somewhere seemingly far off and saw Willem. He was asking her something, but she could hardly understand the words. She only nodded, her eyes never leaving the gorilla. It stood as tall as the strange man when on all four limbs, the large arms bracing his chest. His back gleaming with silver fur. She idly wondered what it would look like in the sun, probably like light streaming across a still creek. Patches of fur stuck out in odd angles, scars running along the gray, worn skin. Remembering what Willem had told her about the animal pits, she shuddered.

The pounding of horse hooves reached them just before three riders appeared between a break in the trees. The gorilla stepped back, his body blocking her from sight, his feet digging into the ground—ready to battle. The dark stranger sheathed his weapons, and the muscles in the gorilla's back eased. Ansie let go a breath she didn't realize she'd been holding. Peering around the gorilla, she watched as a familiar face swept off the back of his horse. It was Jethron, a bloodied dagger in his hand.

The new arrivals looked at the carnage of wolves all around them, their eyes lingering on the gorilla, before turning to her. Jethron's mouth hung open in awe.

"Took you long enough," the dark-haired stranger who had arrived with Willem said, a hint of amusement in his voice.

"We were a bit preoccupied." Jethron took a deep breath and exhaled while wiping the bloodied blade across his pants.

"Did any get away?" the stranger asked.

"No," one of the other men spoke, he was thin with high cheekbones.

"Good." With his back to her, all she could see of this dark stranger were his broad shoulders and long legs. His hair nearly reached his shoulders, and thin fingers remained wrapped around the hilt of his sword. Ansie could have sworn at one point in the fight she had seen him smile, as though he was enjoying himself, but there was now a steady calmness surrounding him. She eyed him further. He was different, in a curious way. Willem had a hard time remaining still, but she had the distinct feeling this man could remain steady and calm, and in an instant be stirred into action with a speed unlike any other.

Willem took a step forward. "Tell me there are others."

Jethron shifted. "They're headed for the village."

Willem was already shaking his head before Jethron had finished speaking. "How many?"

"We have close to a hundred men," Jethron said quietly.

"A hundred!" Willem's voice rose, the break was coming soon. "Jethron, that's hardly enough to—"

"You don't think we're capable?" The dark-haired stranger turned to Willem, his tanned face becoming visible. Ansie shifted, noting the shape of his angled eyes. *A Maereo.*

"Calig here, or Jethron, is actually lying. We have seventy-eight men including myself. Four of Hernan's Gallian soldiers are ours and with the villagers turning to our side, we should have sufficient forces. Now, what exactly is it about this plan you seem to dislike."

"They aren't ready," Willem glanced between the two men.

"Regardless, they are preparing to attack as we speak. Our men inside will communicate our message to the villagers."

Willem shook his head. "They won't listen to Gallians. They'll think it's a trap."

"Willem, listen," Jethron reached for his arm, but Willem slapped his hand away.

"No, you listen! I said I wanted her protected, at all cost. I told you they threatened her and she nearly died!"

Ansie flinched at his words, knowing he was right. She had never seen Willem as afraid as he had been when Fergin threw her to the ground. She had known in that moment something was going to snap. She had seen his face while they beat him for trying to reach Kata, she had seen the blood, the ripped flesh, but nothing had prepared her for the look on his face as he feared he might lose her too.

Ansie never wanted to see him look like that again, and knew she would in her nightmares. Along with the howls of wolves, she wouldn't be sleeping much the next few nights. Only by some miracle, had she been able to get on the horse without one of those wolves tearing her to pieces.

"She looks fine to me," the dark stranger glanced her way, their eyes locking for a moment. His were subtly slanted, the pupils a dark brown, nearly black. He had a sharp jaw that was almost square, and lines around his mouth that hinted at the ghost of a smile even when relaxed—perhaps he was kind.

With a rather long neck, he peered down at her, giving her a once over before looking away. She immediately felt dismissed—a nuisance.

So much for kind, she thought.

The large head of the gorilla turned back to look at her with a huff that almost sounded like a laugh. She stared back, eyes wide. *He doesn't understand, does he?*

"The name's Larn," the stranger stuck his hand out to Willem, breaking through the tension radiating from Jethron and Willem.

"Willem," he grumbled.

Jethron waved a hand. "We came as fast as we could, alright?" He looked down to where she remained on the ground.

"No, it's not alright. She very nearly died and…" Willem continued talking but his words were lost to her as the gorilla turned, his foot shaped like a giant hand moved along the dirt. As he came closer, she glanced up into the wide face of the creature. He had a heart shaped nose, pouting lips, and scars running along his chest. He huffed a few times and reached out to her.

She now understood what Willem had meant when he said the creature was intelligent. She could sense it too. There was something different about this creature. It wasn't simply an animal—there was something more. She had seen those hands grab the wolves and snap their spines, she had watched him throw the alpha wolf into the cave wall, and yet, when she looked into those large brown eyes she saw nothing but kindness. He was waiting, his eyes searching her face. She was drawn to him as he stared back, desperation lingering in intensity.

He gave a soft huff, almost disappointed, and extended his arm further. She reached for him and placed her hand in the overwhelming palm. Leathery skin met her own. He hastily pulled her to her feet, towering above her. She could only imagine how small she must look next to him; she would appear to be a child if he stood to his full height.

"Relax, Willem," Jethron said, talking to him as though he was a horse. Didn't he know he was only going to make matters worse? If there was one person who could get under Willem's skin, it was Jethron.

"Shut it, Jethron," she snapped. The dark stranger, she'd already forgotten his name, was apparently amused.

"Stay out of this," Jethron muttered.

"Wait," the dark stranger looked at each of them in turn. "Do you all know each other?"

"Yes," she confirmed, before the boys could get involved, meeting the man's gaze head-on. "We've known each other since we were kids."

"Wonderful," he mumbled, though the word sounded like a curse. He rested his hands on the hilt of his sword still sheathed at his waist, and stood with feet spread wide. With his shoulders set back, he had the very presence of a soldier, and yet, there was a fluidity to him that was almost unnatural. It was as though the soldier's posture was forced.

He glanced her way once more, and she averted her eyes. She had been staring. From the corner of her eye, she saw his smirk grow and her cheeks warmed. He knew she had been watching him.

Perfect.

"Look," Jethron held up his hands. "We did what we could, but he had to be protected." Jethron motioned to the gorilla. As one they all turned to look at the creature. The heavy head gave a slight dip, was it respect?

He does understand, Ansie realized.

"As pleasant as all this is," the laugh was clear in the dark stranger's voice, "I wonder if we might leave for Mirtain. Girshon is expecting us."

Jethron agreed, turning to leave when Willem grasped his arm. His eyes were wide, a sudden look of horror taking hold of him as he stared in the direction of the village.

"What time were they planning to attack?" Willem asked. Jethron stuttered and Willem grabbed him more firmly. "What time?"

"Dawn."

Willem cursed and ran to the nearest horse, the black mount skittered to the side as he jumped into the saddle and took off through the trees. The dark stranger yelled after him and then swore—the word so foul it almost made Ansie laugh.

Jethron turned to her and she tried to make sense of what Willem had done. The others were moving to the horses when it suddenly hit her, all of Willem's words falling into place. Just that morning he had told her of the new uniforms the villagers would wear. They would look like Nexen, Hernan was using them as bait for the Renegades. She gasped.

"It's a trap!"

"What?" the stranger said, pulling the grey steed around.

"The villagers, they were being outfitted as soldiers today. It's a trap!"

She didn't have the chance to say another word, all four men were already racing toward Mirtain, leaving her behind. They disappeared through the ever-lightening fog within seconds.

"Don't mind me," she mumbled. *Idiots.*

If Willem was right, the Gallians knew about the attack and the Renegades would be fighting the wrong men. Her mind reeled, Skurn's face flashing before her.

Skurn, Chet, Safron, Jep, Bishawn...all of them.

The thought of Skurn fighting was enough to make her stomach flip. She began running then, her shaking legs stumbling over the muddied forest floor—her frozen barefeet slipping. She knew she would never reach the village in time, but she had to try. There was no part of her which could stay behind with the dead bodies of the soldiers and wolves.

A huff sounded behind her and before she could even turn, a massive, heavy hand grabbed her shoulder. She stumbled and fell to the ground, dirt getting in her mouth and down the front of her shirt. She came up sputtering, the gorilla's face right in her own. Wiping at the dirt, he stared at her and then at her feet. With a simple jerk of his head, he beckoned her to him. His lips parted as he gave small grunts, the sounds from his mouth were almost childlike, setting her at ease. His eyes grew soft and she grinned. When he gave a short huffing laugh, she smiled wider.

As soon as she placed her hand in his, he tightened his grip and threw her bodily onto his back. She clung to his shoulders, the incredibly thick muscles twitching beneath her hands. Digging deeper into the surprisingly soft fur, the raised humps of scars, long since healed, rubbed against her fingers.

The gorilla began to move, his body shifting awkwardly as he ran, shoulders and feet seemingly out of sync. She clung to him, the woodsy smell of pine surrounding her as it wafted from his fur. Her every hope was pinned on him keeping his balance.

A huffing laugh passed through the creature's lips and she found herself smiling, even though she knew what they were headed for. She cursed herself for not grabbing a weapon of some sort.

They raced toward the break in the trees over the wired fence, surging out of the forest near the cottage. She nearly shook her head at the absurdity of it all. Had she really been in her bed only a few hours ago?

They were moving faster now, the gorilla seeming to grow more focused beneath her.

"Almost there," she muttered and he grunted, this time she knew he understood her. "Take the road."

The great head swung back and forth, ignoring her as he ran straight for the trees. A squeal passed through her lips when he jumped into the air, grasping a low hanging, sturdy branch. Somehow it held their weight and she clung all the tighter, attempting to wrap her hands around his too thick neck. He swung forward, arms alternating as they grasped from branch to branch, the ground falling away beneath them.

An extra-long jump brought them into a freefall for a moment and she squeezed her eyes shut. They landed against a trunk with a jolt. A big hand patted her head and the creature laughed again, this time she had to join him. Something about his innate joy was filling her as well.

He swung to another tree, his arms reaching heights she could scarcely comprehend. The branches dipped with his weight when he paused, hanging in the air looking toward the village. Shouts rang out over the early dawn, the clanging of swords reaching her ears.

"Go, go," she urged and the beast growled. This time the sound was deep and serious, a rumble in his chest. She licked her lips, not sure if she was ready for what they would see.

He landed beside the road and ran faster than before, toward the village walls. The last of the trees parted behind them and Ansie gasped as they came to a skidding stop.

The fields outside the village were covered with men, their swords flashing as volleys of arrows were aimed at the Renegade cavalry. The rebels were pushing their way through the Gallians. She knew Willem must be somewhere in the mayhem, and she searched for him frantically.

All of a sudden, the gorilla took two menacing steps forward, the battle only a stone's throw away. He braced himself and raised to his full height on hind legs, a mighty roar splitting the air. For a moment, the battle was silenced as the creature beat his chest, attracting all eyes to him. When he slammed back down to the ground, another roar passed through his mouth and any who had been wavering in bravery turned and ran.

The gorilla beneath her needed no further encouragement; he shot into the midst of the battle without fear. Those closest retreated.

He grasped a spear—throwing the weapon and the Gallian soldier holding the other end, into the air. Another came at them from behind, brandishing a sword. The gorilla smacked the man aside with a flick of his wrist. An arrow shot past Ansie's head as she searched the battle frantically.

"A bow, a sword, I need something," she muttered, hoping he would understand.

He continued to swing his fists, the large hands doing more damage than any other weapon she had seen. A sword cut his arm and he let out a groan of frustration before throwing the soldier twenty feet across the field.

Ansie spotted a Gallian soldier with the bow at the same time as the gorilla. He charged into the fray, somewhere between the lines where Gallians met the Renegades. The man screamed when the enormous black fist grasped his ankle. The bow fell to the ground and Ansie slipped down the silver back to grab it.

She hit the frozen dirt and gathered the bow and quiver. She swung into position, an arrow at the ready when a soldier ran in their direction. Shooting, she missed, but the gorilla knocked the man aside. He towered above her, keeping her safe as she searched for Willem.

They were in the center of the field, both sides clashing, when she heard shouts from the Renegade side. The call to arms came from a large dark-skinned man who rode by on horseback, his eyes piercing those uncomfortable with their weapons. The more she looked, the easier it was to tell which were Gallian soldiers and which were villagers newly trained. The leader was calling the Anglan villagers, her own people, to join the Renegades.

Slowly the tide turned, the Anglans rising up against the Gallians. She watched with pride, when a bowman centered in her vision. She hastened to string the bow, taking aim. Willem had only given her the basics. She pulled back and shot, the arrow clipping the man's leg when he let go of his own.

"No!" she shouted, but it was too late. The arrow hit the gorilla's arm. He hardly seemed to notice as he snapped off the end and continued in his battle. The bowman lined the string with another arrow and she aimed again, this time hitting his shoulder. He cried out in pain but continued to take aim.

"Move!" she nudged the gorilla, and his head whipped in the direction of the shooter.

He stood on his back legs and beat his chest. The arrow took flight, but the creature dodged it, ducking beneath its path before charging toward the bowman. The soldier screamed before he was knocked aside, the blow snapping his spine.

Standing in the middle of the fray, she ducked beneath the sword of a soldier, suddenly feeling desperate and alone. She ran after the gorilla knowing he would protect her. A cry sounded behind her, but she didn't look back.

It was then she spotted villagers, dressed in their field hand clothes, running for the edge of the forest. She wanted to cry out, to rally them to the fight, when a sudden flash of metal caught her eye.

She came to a stop, everything slowing around her. Each breath seeming to last a lifetime.

Those weren't villagers, they were Hernan's soldiers. They would take the Renegades from behind.

"Wait!" She ran for the gorilla, and he stopped. Smacking a man aside, he pulled her onto his back again and she pointed to the disguised men creeping around the edges of the battle. He grunted and rose to his full height.

His roar pierced the air and she waved her bow, hoping she didn't seem as helpless as she was. He hit the ground running and she searched for Willem, not finding him. As they flew over the ground, she spotted the dark stranger from the forest.

"Hey!" she called to him, not remembering his name. He came to a stop and looked in the direction she was pointing. "Those are Hernan's men!" She didn't know if he heard her, but he at least understood her meaning. He shouted a command to the rebels nearest him and they took off together.

Her hair clung to her damp skin as they thundered across the ground, headed directly for the disguised Gallians. The soldiers realized all too late their surprise was ruined. Swords were whipped out from sheaths and a volley of arrows flew through the air.

She attempted to string an arrow along the bow, but doing so with one hand and legs gripping the gorilla's side was proving more than difficult. She bit her lip, waiting for when she could hit the ground.

The first line of men charged forward, unafraid of the rebels and beast. The gorilla slowed, readying for the first swings of his arms, and she was able to get an arrow in place before the first soldier reached them. The man was knocked aside, and another came in behind him, two swinging around to the back of the gorilla. A sword was stabbed into his back leg, he let out a growl, and she shot an arrow at the man. He fell to the ground.

The stranger from the forest passed by, his sword cutting off the arm of a man who had been aiming for her. Ansie heard the soldier's cry of anguish and turned away.

Lacing another arrow, she waited for the right moment to shoot. No sooner had she let the arrow go than the gorilla shifted backward, his injured leg giving way. He stumbled, falling to his haunches and crumpling.

She climbed over his shoulders, flipping away from his back before he could crush her beneath his weight. The hard ground reverberated through her knees. When she raised her head, four armed men stood before her.

CHAPTER 25

Larn heard the cry of the *simian* and watched the girl tumble to the ground with surprising agility. She came up facing four disguised Gallians with nothing but a bow in her hands. He headed for her, jerking on the reins of the strange dappled mount beneath him, he had lost sight of Willem and Tympmor in the midst of the battle.

One of the soldiers swung his sword at the girl, and she dodged beneath the blow. Thundering across the field, Larn urged the horse on and cut down three soldiers as he neared them. Two Gallians were pressing in on her sides as the gorilla struggled to regain his footing. She held her ground, swinging her bow back and forth, ready to fire at a moment's notice.

He grimaced as the mount neared the men and braced himself for the jump. At the last moment, he leapt from the saddle onto the back of one soldier, he hit the ground as the girl let one of her arrows fly. The man was screaming on the ground, an arrow through his calf.

Larn moved with the practiced ease perfected during his years of training. He cut down the rest of the men, dipping beneath their swords, as his own found its way into their flesh. When the last man fell, he straightened, inhaling deeply through his nose. His lungs filled with the crisp morning air.

The girl was watching him, much like she had in the forest. He wondered at her stare, knowing it was for the way he looked, and yet, she regarded him differently. He had noted it in the forest. She knew what he was, but there was no judgment in her gaze, no wariness—just simpl curiosity.

Her eyes shifted and the whiz of an arrow reached his ear. He ducked on instinct, feeling the arrow stir his hair. The flying weapon found its purchase in the *simian*'s arm and the beast growled. With a mighty roar, the creature slammed his fists to the ground and shot toward the Gallian soldier who had aimed the arrow.

The girl dashed into the fray. Larn caught up to her easily, knocking a soldier aside.

When the girl stumbled as a man swung his sword out toward her, Larn's own blade protected her from the blow. The man was dead within seconds.

"Here!" he shouted, handing her the sword of the fallen man.

She took the weapon without comment but struggled to lift it. He swapped the sword from her hands, replacing it with his own. The lighter metal would help her.

Her startled look made him smirk as he picked up the crude weapon of the fallen Gallian. The weight of it was tremendous compared to his own blade. He would have to adjust, calculate the greater strength and timing it would take to use the blade, but it was nothing he hadn't done before.

The *simian* stumbled to the side, taking down one of the men, he fell to the ground with a heavy thump and the girl ran to him. Larn cut down two more soldiers and continued to circle around the *simian*, keeping the Gallians at bay.

From somewhere behind them on the field, a cry rang out; one of surrender. Larn smiled—they had won the day.

He cut down the last man before him, the steady ache that had been building in his shoulders only heightened with the weight of the new sword. Silence met his last swing and he glanced around, his eyes meeting Heben's across the field. His men were the only ones standing. He smiled, Heben giving him a mock salute, though blood trickled down the side of his face.

He turned back toward the *simian*. The girl was standing, his sword held before her as she searched for any who dared to come near the creature. He had the quick passing thought of a mother wolf protecting its pup. He dropped the sword he held and walked toward her, his cloak seeming too heavy on his shoulders.

The girl looked his way, her frame appearing much smaller than in the midst of battle—strands of thick, red hair stirring in the breeze. It was a vibrant color, though it hung in gentle waves past her shoulders. She pushed back some of the strands as he walked toward her, though they continued to drift in the breeze. Beside the *simian*, she looked no more than a child, yet he had seen her come flying down from the tree in the forest to knock the Nexen captain to the ground. Then, she had appeared on the battlefield on the back of a *simian* of all things.

He shook his head, knowing he would never forget that sight. Something inside him had surged with pride when the roar of the Animle warrior had rung out over the bedlam of the battle. The creature had beat its chest with those powerful fists and over his shoulder was the billowing hair of this fiery, red-fairy.

Maybe if Larn had been paying attention, he would have seen the Gallian soldier rise to his knees and throw the dagger. But he hadn't been. He had been wondering why the girl was barefoot when the blade buried into the chest of the *simian*.

Time stopped. Held.

The creature roared in pain, falling more to its side.

Heben killed the Gallian, but it was too late. The blade had done its job. Larn blinked, not quite sure it had really happened. The girl dropped his sword and fell to her knees beside the powerful head of the creature.

"No, no, no," she crooned, her hands fluttering as though she wanted to touch him, but didn't know where.

Blood was oozing from various wounds, but the warrior had eyes only for the girl. He was groaning, deep breaths turning to grunts.

"What do I do? What do I do?" The girl was muttering to herself. She reached for the hilt of the dagger sticking out from its chest. As soon as she grasped it, the *simian* moaned.

Something in Larn's gut dropped as he saw the pain in those eyes, and the dark wetness covering its chest. The Animle, all their hopes...gone. He had been waiting for this moment for years. Why now? Why? He scrambled to make sense of it all, knowing it was of no use.

"Leave it," Larn said, his hand snatching hers away from the mortal blade.

She turned to him then, her eyes brimming with tears.

"I can't just leave him."

"You don't have a choice." He spoke with more conviction than he expected, his words making one of the tears she was holding at bay run over and down her cheek. "He deserves a warrior's death."

She nodded and looked back at the creature. His chest was heaving, each breath labored.

"Ansie!" a desperate voice called.

Ansie, he would have to remember her name.

Larn turned, watching Willem run toward them. His eyes were wider than they had been in the forest, his relief palpable as he saw Ansie kneeling next to the creature. He stopped short as the eyes of the *simian* reached him.

All three set there gaze upon the warrior and watched as each breath become shallower than the one before. The heart-shaped nose flared, the eyes wide as he shifted his gaze from Ansie to Willem and back. There was such desperation in its eyes, Larn had to look away.

Girshon had told him once of a legend of the Animle. They chose their warrior partners—two souls joined together, empowering one another. It was mystical, magical, and there was only one creature for one warrior. Glancing back, he could feel the desperation in the *simian's* gaze. The creature was almost frantic, wanting to find his warrior partner in either Willem or Ansie, but it wasn't to be.

The crushing weight of it all came down on Larn. Even if the creature had lived, they wouldn't have been any closer to seeing a bond made and the Animle rise. He wanted to hit something, fix it all somehow, but there was nothing he could do.

"What does he want?" Ansie asked, her voice filled with tears.

"He's looking to either of you," Larn interjected. Both heads rose as though suddenly remembering he was there. *"Simul ad mortem."*

If they had been confused before, they were more confused now. Larn sighed, they had so much to learn.

"He's one of the Animle." When he said the word, the *simian's* eyes settled on him, searching. He shook his head, knowing it to only be a desperate hope. "He is a *simian*, a descendant of warriors, searching for his *anima reflecta*, or his reflection." Still blank stares. "Animle partner with a human, becoming more than blood brothers, they reflect one another in a bond that is unrivaled. He's looking to you, waiting for the connection."

Ansie just stared at the *simian*. Larn wondered if she understood the meaning behind the *simian* allowing her to ride on his back. Not just anyone would have been able to accomplish such a feat.

The *simian* gave another mournful groan and laid back, its breaths shortening to mere gasps. It wouldn't be long now.

"Is there anything I can do?" Ansie leaned forward, hesitantly reaching out to touch the side of the black face. The *simian's* eyes locked on hers and held. Each breath became desperate as the *simian* searched her face, clinging to the hope of finally finding his match. Until, with a heaving gust, a final breath passed through his lips.

Larn looked away, staring across the fields and to the clouded horizon. He cried out from his soul, cursing whatever god was listening to the depths of the earth. This was exactly why he couldn't believe in some god. Some said the stars ruled, some said it was the Regent who was a god, there were those who were Wielders and believed in the old ways, and the Chroniclers had gods, but all he saw was man and woman, both forces of destruction and death. And he was a weapon in their hands.

A piece of the little hope he carried, shattered.

Red hair swung forward, touching the dark fur, as Ansie leaned in to close its eyes and kiss its head. Willem watched her, a solemn downturn to his mouth.

Larn moved to the other side. Men and women were beginning to filter off of the field, walking in their direction. He grasped the dagger in the *simian's* chest and pulled. It came out as Ansie's tears fell on the dark fur. Their eyes met over the large body and Willem pulled her to him, tucking her beneath his arm.

"What can we do?" the hunter, Larn had heard so much about, asked.

"Put him to rest, the way he deserves." Disappointment radiated through every part of him. Years of work had been crushed in a single battle. He should have seen the signs when they were in the forest. He should have left Willem and Ansie behind. The *simian* had been looking to both of them, his great head swinging back and forth. Now that Larn recalled the moment, he couldn't believe he had been so blind.

Swallowing, he hid his disappointment behind a carefree look—the mask he often wore.

"A loss to be sure," Girshon said, coming up behind them. His normally gruff voice was soft. Some of the villagers were gathering around the fallen creature, the rest of the Renegades maintaining a perimeter in case more Gallians attacked from the walls.

One young man stepped forward, moving closer to Ansie and Willem. He was dressed in the garb of a soldier, but everything about him proclaimed his unease in the uniform. Upon closer evaluation, the uniform was black instead of the deep blue of the Gallians. He must be an Anglan.

The same worry which had been running through Larn's mind for weeks took precedence. These Anglans had no idea what they had just joined. The rallying cries of the Renegades had been enough to turn them in battle, but the next few days would prove their worth. A rebellion had started here, but that didn't mean it couldn't end here if they weren't careful.

The flames of rebellion would ignite across the realm. More Renegades were on their way, and the north was teaming with rebels. Now they could only hope the other villages in the southernlands would follow in Mirtain's wake.

"What you see here, is a fallen Animle, one of the ancient warriors from when man and beast walked together to protect this land." Girshon's voice rose over the gathered rebels and villagers who stood in awed silence. "The Regent and Lord Hernan have lied to you, claiming these creatures no longer exist. But here before you is the proof of their lies! My name is Girshon, and I am the leader of the Renegades. What you have done today is the beginning of a new era—the beginning of rebellion. For Anglas!" Girshon raised his bloodied sword.

"Here, here!" A middle-aged man, standing beside two boys, raised his fist in the air with a smile grazed his face. Somehow, the simple gesture was enough to break the tension. Others raised their fists in the air, and a chant began. "For Anglas!" echoed across the field.

One worry down, Larn thought idly. He shrugged toward Girshon and his leader nodded back.

Jethron edged into the group, his mouth set in a grim line. The scar running along his face made him appear more dangerous than Larn knew him to be. Four soldiers stood behind him, the loyal insiders who had been Larn's sources for three years.

"Deagan," he greeted, the one spy he had worked closely with stepped forward. They spoke for a moment, Jethron standing off to the side, his gaze focused on Willem and Ansie.

There was something going on between these two men which he couldn't quite understand. A trust set upon an old relationship, but fraught with a rift because of a girl who had died. Yet another reason why love was often worthless. He would have to get them to find common ground. Maybe Ansie was the key. He shook his head, wondering if the blow he'd received from the butt end of a spear had addled his brain.

"Hernan?" Jethron asked, scanning the fallen men.

"You think he'd be out here?" Willem sounded as though he was on the verge of laughter.

"Leave him be for now," Girshon shook his head and motioned to the men gathering around them. "It's time to rest and gather riders for delivering our proclamation to the realm."

"But first, Hernan dies," Jethron said eyes focused on the village walls, he began to stride across the field.

"Halt soldier!" Girshon shouted. Willem rose quickly to his feet, leaving Ansie on the ground. She watched the men, her brown eyes wide, her tears forgotten.

Jethron turned, his hand holding a bloodied dagger. Deagan and his men passed through the walls of the village and out of sight.

"There will be time for Lord Hernan later." Girshon motioned to a group of men. Larn irked at the calm proposal, always balancing, always controlling. Just once, he would like Girshon to move without thought or feeling.

"Heben," the Renegade leader continued, "follow Deagan and his men, make sure Lord Hernan is safe. Sequester him in his chambers and I will meet with him later. No one, *no one*," he gazed pointedly at Jethron, "is to touch him."

Several heads nodded, Jethron's included. Larn eyed Willem, who didn't nod and remained like a statue. As the men began to disperse, Willem turned to the middle-aged man who'd raised a fist in triumph. For only a moment longer did Larn watch them, something about Willem's expression was off.

When nothing changed, Larn turned away, commissioning his men to move the body of the *simian*. There would be a ritual burning that evening.

As the men heaved the body between them, twelve men lifting with what was left of their strength, his eyes fell on Ansie. She watched, still seated on the ground, her hand brushing against the large fingers of the creature before they took him away.

"It's alright Ans," the young man, whom Larn had noticed earlier, knelt beside her. For some reason, Larn didn't like the way the man shortened her name. He waited for her response, keeping a safe distance from them as though disinterested.

"I told you not to call me that," she replied, the words barely a whisper. Larn found himself watching her, as he did all people, wondering why she said such a thing.

277

"You did, but I thought it would be the best way to get you to talk." The intruder chuckled and she gave a small laugh. The young man reached out and wiped a tear from her cheek, his thumb lingering on her skin.

"I don't believe we've met," Larn stepped forward quite suddenly, watching with satisfaction as the man straightened and knocked off a salute. He could certainly tell the young man a salute wasn't necessary, but where was the fun in that? "I'm Larn, Renegade Commander and Head of Intelligence. You are?"

"Skurn." The Anglan swallowed, his eyes staring over Larn's left shoulder, as he had been taught.

"No need to treat me like a Gallian soldier," Larn gave Skurn a light clap on the shoulder and saw him smile in return. Unlike Jethron, the smile improved the villager's appearance. "Was this your first battle?"

"Yes, s-sir." The second word came out with a shake. "We weren't expecting to fight so soon."

"To be sure," Larn nodded, ever aware of the way Skurn tried not to stare at him. As always, his appearance was something to be ogled at. He grit his teeth, at least Willem had spent very little time looking at him. "It's probably best if you follow the rest of the men. Most likely they're getting provisions."

Skurn nodded and knocked off another salute. He was gone without another glance in Ansie's direction.

Larn turned to her. She was still seated upon the ground, mud and blood staining her clothes, and her bare feet were turning a light sort of purple. He wondered if she even felt the cold, and pondered again why she was so poorly dressed.

"Here," he said, offering his hand. She looked up, her brow furrowed in confusion. When she didn't take it, he egged her on. "Do I have to call you Ans as well to get a response?"

Her cheeks colored, but she still didn't take his hand. "That's not necessary."

"What is? The hand, or the name?"

"Both." She had some gumption, he liked that. Even after hearing his title, she wasn't complacent to let him have his way. Something, about the way her eyes sparked with intelligence, gave him leave to squat down to her level.

"If I'm not allowed to call you Ans, then what should I call you?"

"Ansie would work," her voice had a bit of bite to it.

"Ansie," he said, rolling the name on his tongue. "I'd give you my name, but you already know it. Although you were only recently reminded," he amended.

"You said it in the forest."

"But you forgot," he pointed out.

"I did not," she crossed her arms, looking every bit the stubborn child, though the hint of a blush tinged her cheeks. He had the sudden notion of Willem's job as her guardian not being an easy one.

"You did," he spoke with conviction, he'd seen the way she panicked to get his attention during the battle. "If you had remembered my name, you would've yelled it to get my attention. It's a very lucky thing I have keen hearing." He tapped his ear with a finger, his smirk growing wider.

She rolled her eyes, clearly ignoring him. "Should I call you Larn or do you prefer Renegade Commander and Head of Intelligence?" She straightened as she spoke, her voice dripping with a refined Gallian accent. The kind of accent that was common in Bastion Nocta, not that she knew it. It had a soft cadence and various rollings of the tongue.

He found a chuckle escaping his lips before he could stop it. Her eyes lightened, and she smiled at him. It was the kind of smile that was more in the eyes than in the lips. The kind of mirth that came from an inner joy. All too soon the corners of her mouth fell.

"I wish there was something we could have done."

Knowing she was referring to the *simian*, he nodded. If anything, he wished either Willem or Ansie had been the creature's *anima reflecta*. He had never seen such pure desperation in the eyes of a creature—human or animal.

"Looks like someone's hungry," he said, changing the subject—diverting from lost hopes. He pointed at Tympmor who was wandering toward them, eyeing the ground as he went. Ansie shifted and glanced at the black steed.

"That's the horse Willem took."

"That's *my* horse," Larn said with emphasis. There was a part of him which was a tad jealous of the steed's allowance for another to ride him. He had at one time or another fancied himself as the only human the horse would listen to. So much for allegiance.

"Really?" she asked. "What's his name?"

"Tympmor," he smiled.

The horse in question raised its head and trod lazily across the grass to Ansie. She stood quickly, resting her hands against the thick, muscled neck. As Larn straightened, he became all the more aware of how small she was. Not dainty, but certainly short. Her fingers glided along the dips of Tympmor's neck and Larn watched her, suddenly realizing he was staring. Clearing his throat, he averted his gaze.

"Do you want to know what his name means?"

She shook her head quickly, her eyes almost amber, reminding him of warmed cider. "Let me guess."

"Really?" he challenged.

"Yes," she tilted her chin.

"What's your first guess?"

"I'll let you know when he tells me." She patted the horse's neck for emphasis.

He nearly laughed, "It's been quite some time since he last spoke."

"Maybe you should call him Ans," she suggested and gave him a wink. His breath caught in a chuckle, her quick wit surprising him.

"Ans!" Willem called, they both turned quickly.

"Coming," she yelled back and gave Tympmor one more pat along his neck.

"He can call you Ans?" Larn asked before she turned away. "Do you have trouble speaking to him too?" He tried to hide his curiosity behind humor—something he often did.

She shook her head. "Willem's always called me that." Her eyes softened and Larn suddenly realized what she meant.

I thought I told you not to call me that, she had said to Skurn. He had thought she hated the pet name, but now, he saw it for what it really was. Willem had the right to call her by something different.

In an instant, Larn realized the shortened form of her name was cherished by the one closest to her. She was loyal, that much was certain. The question was, how hard was it to earn her loyalty?

He watched as Ansie strode toward Willem and placed her hand along his arm, her head only coming up to the middle of his chest. The hunter glanced back in his direction and gave him a nod, before leading the way toward the village walls.

Larn watched them leave until Tympmor butted him in the chin. "Yes, you're in trouble," he said. The horse shook his mane. "What were you thinking, riding off with Willem? I'm thoroughly betrayed."

The horse shook his mane again, as always, seeming to understand his banter. He gave him a playful smack on his thick neck before rubbing his nose and beginning the process of taking care of the steed.

With each rub of the wiry coat, he kept seeing those warm amber eyes of Ansie's winking up at him. It was his turn to shake his head, and he returned to his work, refusing to think of her anymore.

CHAPTER 26

The group of women hid in the bushes, their eyes focused on the scant village of Brescht. Curfew had long since passed, the two moons shining brightly against the pitch of black spread above them.

Umbris shifted on the ground, the leaves just above her head snagging strands of her hair and forcing her to hold still. Cackles of laughter poured out from various wooden houses, dim candlelight illuminating the windows. She had never seen anything like it before, none of them had.

Two days had passed since the Renegades had left them. Girshon had given the women a choice, either flee and try to make it on their own, or be escorted to Brescht. All had chosen the escort. The threat of verrals and other creatures were powerful forces of conviction.

They had walked long miles the past two days, their weak limbs nearly succumbing to exhaustion after so many months of degrading chains and little movement. She was sore from head to toe, but for the first time in nearly a year, she felt the least bit alive—more than a shadow.

They had been hiding in the recesses of the forest for a few hours on Pike's command. He refused to let them march into the village while the sun still shined. But now the moons rose above and the clouds scattered the ground with patches of shadows as they swept across the sky.

Brescht rested near an inlet to the Partivo River, a canal of sorts that divided Gallia and Autre Gallia—at least that was what Pike had told them. The red and white light of the moons seemed to pulse, winking across the surface, as the water dipped and wove its way along the bank.

For longer than she cared to admit, Umbris stared at the water. Her eyes focused on the opposing bank. For years she had heard the stories, practically since she could first talk, the stories of the mighty land of Gallia. This river had at one time, been the partition between Anglas and Gallia, but now it ran in the middle of the land. Idly, she wondered just where the first Gallian soldiers had crossed into Anglas to take over the realm.

Another crack of thunderous laughter and ribald singing carried on the wind as the door to a tavern opened. Umbris cringed as the music drifted up to them where they lay along a hill, high above the village.

"How much longer are we waitin'?" a woman asked. She was from one of the carriages that had been at the front of the caravan line. Umbris didn't know her name, but it hadn't taken long for her to dislike the woman.

"When I say so," Pike grumbled.

They were upwind from the village, a situation Pike had insisted upon even though some of the women had cursed him to the depths as a result of climbing the steep hill. Umbris had glared at them but didn't get involved. The last thing she wanted was a fight. She'd seen enough fights in Fort Jontru to last her a lifetime.

"I say we go now," the same woman rebutted. There was an eagerness about her that set Umbris on edge. As soon as they had arrived, the woman had been badgering Pike to let them go into Brescht. There was something about the way her eyes gleamed, each time a door to one of the many taverns along the water opened, that made Umbris's stomach flip on itself.

She wants money. Umbris shook her head, the reality of her situation staring her in the face.

How many times over the past months had she been dreading this moment? In truth, it was part of her ever-waking thoughts. There was no moment of release, no relief from what she knew she was destined for. Glancing down at her wrists, she could just make out the scars of the Regent's emblem.

"All right," the woman stood up, no longer whispering. "I 'bout had enough lying here like a twit. I'm goin to get down there and start making somethin' of myself."

Pike looked ready to strangle her, but didn't say a word as she passed by, eight of the other women with her.

It took a moment or two, but the mutterings began not long after. The rest of the women were whispering amongst themselves, wondering if they should follow. As much as Umbris hated to think about what she must face, she couldn't help wondering if she should join them.

"If you want to go, then leave!" Pike shouted, his apparent control slipping. Two women scurried past him and a few others dared to do the same. Umbris shivered beneath the bush she still lay under. She needed to move, in her heart she knew she must, it was her fate, her burden to bear. But she couldn't get her body to work.

She watched as the women, who'd suffered alongside her left, their silhouetted forms like walking corpses, the shadows stretching out behind them like their souls were resisting the walk to their doom. Her throat became dry as she watched the first women reach the taverns. She could hardly make out their movements until a tavern door opened, the first prisoner had reached her destination. A man grabbed at her almost immediately.

Umbris wasn't sure when the tears had started, but her limbs were shaking, trembling. It was as though her body was preparing her for what would happen, and it was trying to keep her safe. She wanted to curl in on herself, but there was nowhere to go.

"Would you be willing to be part of this, part of the rebellion?" Larn's words shot through her mind for the thousandth time. A small beacon of hope.

Ever since he had left, she had been running through what he said. He had told her to be safe two mornings ago when he left with the rest of the Renegades. His words had stirred something in her chest. After a year of no one caring, his words had nearly brought tears to her eyes.

The tavern door opened again. This time a woman stepped out the door on the arm of a man, both were dressed in finer clothes than any she had seen so far. The orange light from inside cut a sharp strip across the sloping ground, as the last of the women approached. In a way, they looked like a dead army, their frames appearing all the more skeletal next to healthy bodies.

The pristinely dressed man and the woman on his arm, waved the former prisoners forward, taking them around to the back of the tavern. When they had all disappeared, Umbris remained in her spot afraid to move. She simply couldn't make herself get up and walk down the hill. She couldn't.

Maybe I can make it on my own? She shook the idea away, it was absurd to even think it.

If she wasn't alone, if she had *him* with her, she could do it. This time new tears welled in the bottoms of her eyes. They always did, when she thought of him. It seemed so long since she had last seen him. They had torn him from her, he was lost to her.

"What are you still doing here?"

Umbris whipped around, rolling onto her side from beneath the bush. Her hair was still stuck on a grasping branch. Pike was crouching down, just close enough that she could see the crinkled lines around his eyes in the dim light of the moons.

"I-I c-c-can't," her voice drifted, speaking so softly, she wondered if he could even hear her. He gave a grunt, so she assumed he had.

He stuck his hand into the bush and untangled her hair. When she looked back up, his hand was extended to her, palm facing up in open invitation. She forced herself to reach out, to not shrink back. Larn had trusted him.

The skin of his palm was coarse, toughened by calluses and dirt. His hand enveloped her own in a way which made her feel all more the helpless in light of her current situation.

She was pulled to her feet. Suddenly feeling naked in the night, she wrapped her arms around her body. A shiver ran down her spine as the blue eyes in the creased, worn face of Pike reached hers. His gaze narrowed, but for some reason, she didn't find it disconcerting, instead, she warmed.

"Why didn't you go with them?"

It was something Larn would have asked. She had only spoken to him once, but in that one shared moment, she had been able to understand the depth of Larn's character. He was someone who asked, rather than told. A listener. He understood people, how they worked and what made them move. He had so easily been able to read her, to understand her past without exploring it.

But there was something more to him. He had been able to guess at her ability to read people as well—maybe it took one to know one. She knew she was a shell of what she used to be, had noticed the way he looked at her eyes in curiosity. If he had thought she was dead inside, he was right. And yet, he had seen something in her, which made him offer a chance to change her course.

Pike was staring, the piercing gaze seemingly out of place with the caked dirt along his forehead. He had seen hard times, it was written in every wrinkle and scar along his brow.

"I...can't," she whispered again. He nodded as though he had suspected as much all along, but how could he? She hadn't spoken a word to him over the past two days, though she had often caught him looking her way.

"What is it that you want?" His voice was gentler than she had ever heard it, his head dipping low as though trying to coax her to hold her head high.

"Would you be willing to be part of this, part of the rebellion?" Larn's words ran through her mind again, as clearly as if he had been standing right in front of her, speaking them now. She inhaled, the cool air of night filling her lungs, the pungent stench of fish and rotten sewage nearly gagging her.

What did she want?

She wanted to matter again, to have a purpose of her own. She wanted to be something more than what the rest of the realm saw. Be more than the scars she bore upon her wrists.

"I want to help," she said the words softly—nearly a mumble, but she lifted her chin a bit higher.

Pike's eyes narrowed again, this time with something close to approval. If she had to guess, she would say he was fighting back a smile, the very thought helped lighten the weight of her words.

"All right," he grumbled. "It won't be easy. We need all the information we can get. You'll have to keep your eyes and ears open in the capital, even the smallest of things can be of the greatest significance. One spark is all it takes to begin the fire in the hearts of an Anglan, the fire to burn away the destruction of Gallia."

Umbris nodded, following his words with more concentration than she had shown in weeks. She never would have guessed he could be so poetic, but his words stirred something within her own chest. Was it possible she could still serve a purpose even though her fate had been sealed?

"We have a day's journey ahead, I will teach you the basics along the way." He turned as he spoke, and she followed him toward the tethered horses. She wondered if this time she would be allowed to ride, and idly thought of Tympmor. The black stallion had some sort of spirit within it which she couldn't quite understand. A flicker of the types of creatures she had once heard about.

Pike halted beside his horse, his broad shoulders blocking out the light of the moons behind him. "Before we go, I need to know why you're doing this."

She wanted to worry her hands, to twist them until she no longer had to answer, but instead, she found herself looking directly at him. "If they're going to force me into this life, then I might as well fight them." He gave a swift nod, neither confirming nor denying her words. He was about to swing into the saddle when she spoke again. "How will I know who to watch or what to listen for? How will I get in touch with you?"

Hands resting on the saddle, he paused and looked down at her over his shoulder. This time a crooked smile cracked his face. "If I knew, I'd tell you. All I can say is do what you can, it's the best hope we have in this world." He looked away, the wind blowing strands of his thin blonde hair across his face. "You've been put here for a purpose, know that. You and only you can do this, perhaps fate has given you a second chance?" His words stirred something deep within her chest and she thought of the stars above. "And don't you worry about making contact, when I get back to Larn we'll find you."

She nodded, letting his words warm her and settle the fears, if only for a moment. Pike swung into the saddle, the leather creaking beneath his weight as he settled his muscular frame onto the uneasy beast. The creature didn't seem as docile as Tympmor was with his owner.

She glanced over her shoulder, the dim glow of the tavern windows winking at her as bodies passed by the source of light. Raucous laughter drifted up to her, the sounds haunting and empty; laughter that was drowning in hopelessness.

There was nothing for her here, only emptiness. She'd had enough of emptiness.

Swallowing around the lump in her throat, she thought of her family, and the man she'd left behind. She would never see them again, she had known it the day they took her away, but this was different. She once again had—a purpose.

Tears welled but didn't fall. She looked up to the stars above and cast a prayer unto the heavens, the first one she had said in ages—a plea for help.

Pike's hand extended toward her again as the other men swung into their saddles. Once more a palm was openly waiting, an offering, and one she had the choice to take or leave. Without further thought to what she was leaving behind, she grasped the coarse fingers and was hoisted off the ground until she came to rest before Pike on the saddle. His arms wound around her body, reaching for the reins, and he threw his cloak over her shoulders.

"Ready?" he asked.

She swallowed. "Take me to Bastion Nocta."

They thundered across the ground and into the night.

CHAPTER 27

The flames stretched, reaching for the stars as the dark form of the *simian* charred, flesh turning to ash and smoke. Each dance of the flames made Willem drift deeper into a trance. The moons cast the flames in a tint of red, much like the blood still lingering on the *simian*'s chest.

Simian. Willem thought the word again, nearly casting it aside. How many years had he spent running away from what he feared awaited him?

"He's one of the Animle...searching for his anima reflecta, or his reflection...He is looking to you, waiting for the connection."

Larn's words had brought a sudden stirring of childhood memories. How long had it been since he last thought of his mother? He'd spent years avoiding thoughts of her, not wanting to remember how she died, but tonight he couldn't cast her from his mind. Her stories about the Praelia, those who believed in a powerful spirit, had enchanted him as a boy. She wove tales and prophecies before him of the old faith and those who believed. She had told him stories of Anglas and the Animle warriors who protected the lands— protected the Praelia.

It was as though his past was winking at him, staring at him with open eyes until he would acknowledge its presence. His mother had whispered to him at night, as she tucked him into bed, her callused, hard-working hands gripping his as she knelt beside his cot. She had told him of the Animle and the *anima reflecta*, of how the bond between man and beast was something gifted to those who believed and were part of the Praelia.

She had told him he was special, more than anyone thought he was. She died trying to provide for him, and it had cost her life. Willem shook his head, not wanting to remember those final days. It was then that he had sunk into the forest and learned the ways of the woods.

He skirted the outer edges of Mirtain, climbing upon the backs of grinspurs, learning how animals moved and hunted. He had watched verrals, porcuns, and bufaluses—he was drawn to them. Only now did he realize what he had been searching for. He always looked into an animal's eyes before he moved in for the kill, never finding what he was looking for. It was only animal instinct which flared in their gaze.

It wasn't until he had seen the *simian* in the pit that he had understood what he had been looking for all along. But he had refused to acknowledge the truth, and now the *simian* was gone.

Willem shook his head, his eyes clearing as the light of the deep red flames stretched in flickering tongues. Somehow the moons seemed duller as though mourning the death of the creature as much as he was—standing in reverence.

Ansie stood across the pit, tears gracing her cheeks. His chest tightened, the image of her riding on the back of the *simian* came into being before him. In his twenty-one years, he'd seen and experienced his fair share of panic and complete fear for those he cared for, but that one moment had been unlike any other. With one glance, he had been terrified, and yet, prouder of her than he'd ever been before. How well he knew, she was something to be reckoned with.

Beside her stood the stranger, Larn, his dark eyes watching the flames and his hands wrapped around the hilt of his sword. He was tall, broad in the shoulders—muscular in a way that declared the skills he had wielded during the fight. His clothes were worn, dust-covered and weary. Yet, he stood without slouch but not as straight-backed as some of the other men. There was a sense of wildness to him that Willem didn't understand.

When they were fighting in the woods against the wolves, Larn had dealt with them tactfully. It only made sense to presume Larn was tactful in all other areas. Even now, he seemed relaxed, but as his eyes remained transfixed on the flames, Willem would bet he was very much aware of all going on around him.

There were rumors about the Maereo tribes in the north. Stories of how their people could foresee the future, and legends of their murderess provocations against Anglans. Yet, Larn didn't seem to pose a threat—at least when he wasn't wielding a sword.

From across the flames, Larn's mouth moved and Ansie looked up at him. She seemed surprised and replied. It was Larn's turn to look confused, and after he spoke again, Ansie shrugged, returning her gaze to the flames.

The crowd jostled slightly to Willem's left, stealing his attention as Jethron came up to stand beside him. "All of it gone," Jethron gestured with a mug toward the flames. "Something so ancient lost. All our work, lost. All of it, gone to waste. We've been searching markets and forests for years, and now that the Rising finally happened, he's gone." Jethron remained still, the slump in his shoulders saying more than his slighty slurred words.

"Years?" Willem asked.

"Yes," Jethron took a swig from his mug. "I have been communicating with the Renegades for almost three years now."

Willem turned, certain he heard wrong. Slowly the pieces began to fall into place. "You were working with them before it happened?"

"With Kata?" Jethron nodded, answering his own question. "We worked together trying to reach them. We sent out messages through black market tradesman for nearly a year. Eventually, one made it into Larn's hands."

Willem's hands balled into fists, something about Jethron's words irked him. "Why didn't you tell us?" So many times they had spoken of rebellion, of finding the Renegades, but they had never acted upon it. At times, Willem had fancied they were going to do something one day, but in the back of his mind, he had known that nothing would ever change. Yet, it had.

Jethron gave him his full attention, the flickering light from the flames making his scar appear all the more jagged. One side of his mouth twitched and he seemed to be struggling for words. "I wasn't sure if I could trust you to keep it quiet."

"After everything you couldn't trust me? I told all of you I would leave Mirtain and find the Renegades myself if I had to."

"That's just it," Jethron's lips set in a grim line, the jaw nearly locked, as his voice dipped low. "You talked, but you didn't *do* anything. None of you did. After my grandparents died, I had nothing." Willem tried to interrupt, but Jethron held up a hand. "No. I lost everything. I know you lost your mother years ago, but I lost my family. You still had Ansie, I had nothing."

"You had Kata," Willem spoke around the anger mounting inside him, even saying her name stung his throat. His next words came out in a grumble. "You had me, you had Ansie. We were there for you. How can you even think I wouldn't have followed you?"

"For the same reason you won't now." If there had been any lightness in Jethron's voice before, it had disappeared completely into the night. He glared at Willem. "Hernan has his claws in you, he always has. I could never fully trust you, which is why everything went all wrong." He gulped the last of his drink. "You won't do anything to risk Ansie, to risk anyone, but sometimes risks must be taken. Sometimes, there have to be risks in order to make way for the greater good."

"I'm not going to listen to this."

"As always," Jethron shrugged, turning back to the flames. "And you wonder why I never told you?"

"Nothing is worth risking innocent people."

"But allowing the same innocent people to suffer because you're afraid to act? That's a type of punishment I can't understand." The mug dropped to the caked dirt at their feet. "You know you're powerful, you know that creature was looking to you. You can be the key to unlocking the Rise of the Animle and yet you stand here and do nothing because you're afraid to take a risk."

Willem shook his head at the accusations, knowing Jethron was baiting him. Deep down he knew he wanted to agree, that he had to understand the sort of sacrifice it would take to change the realm. *But haven't I already paid the price?*

Two years ago he had been a different person, he had dared to dream of the stories his mother had told him and had prayed the Animle would return. He had asked without answer as a boy, and after years of nothing, his heart had turned bitter. He had drifted along, losing himself in hunting and fieldwork, but it was only when Kata and Jethron had been taken, that he lost all hope.

"When will you be leaving?" Jethron asked, his hair hanging into his eyes.

"Leaving?" Willem said softly.

"Larn hasn't spoken to you yet?" he raised one eyebrow, the scar stretching. Willem could almost remember him before the scar. He'd had a winning smile, one that always made Kata light up. "I guess he's waiting until after the ceremony." He waved a hand toward the pyre. "Girshon wants you to leave with some of the Renegades to search of another Animle, somewhere in this realm is your *anima reflecta.* Most likely up North."

His mother's words seemed to dance like the flames before him. It couldn't be true. It just couldn't.

"If I agree," he held up a hand when Jethron quickly turned to him, "*if* I agree, what happens to Ansie?"

Jethron licked his lips, the scar momentarily stretched. "She'll go with you."

He was shaking his head before Jethron finished. "No."

"It's not your decision. She already said she would go."

"Still making moves behind my back, I see." Willem quirked an eyebrow, attempting to keep his voice calm. As far as he was concerned, Ansie wouldn't be going anywhere. If they couldn't figure out a way to keep her safe in Mirtain, he wouldn't leave.

"Not at all," Jethron dipped his head, a mock bow he had often given Willem in the past. The gesture always irked him. "The choice is no longer yours, the *simian* made sure of that."

Willem froze.

"Didn't think of that, did you? It was no small feat for her to ride on the back of an Animle, let alone have him look to her. He was trying to connect with *both* of you. Either of you. She has just as much right to find her *anima reflecta* as you do."

Willem waited for some thought, some form of logic to stop the worry mounting inside him, but there was nothing to counter the words. He knew what his friend said was true—he'd known it since the first moment he saw Ansie riding on the back of the *simian*, but hadn't wanted to acknowledge it.

Any fight at this point would be futile on his part. There was nothing he could do to stop the inevitable from becoming his reality.

"Fine," he muttered, and Jethron chuckled.

"I knew you could be persuaded to see reason."

"It's nothing you said, it's fact. She does have a right."

Jethron sighed, the sound almost disappointed. "One of these days Willem, you're going to realize she's much more capable than you give her credit for."

"I believe she's proved that already."

Jethron nodded, "She did. I don't know if I've ever seen something more fearsome than when they came bursting through the trees."

An unhindered smile crept over Willem's mouth, his pride for her blossoming again.

"Excuse me," Jethron said, suddenly. "I see Deagan and his men waiting to speak with me. How funny, he got a few Gallians to sympathize with our cause, and Hernan has no idea." He chuckled and walked away.

Willem ducked his head as a farewell, breathing in the stillness around him.

"Where is he?" He heard Jethron ask from behind him, the response too low for Willem to make out. "Still in his study? Has anyone been in or out of that room?"

Willem leaned back a little, his head cocked as he tried to make out the reply. Anything that had to do with Lord Hernan was his concern. The man had been a hound on Willem's back since the day his mother died, his frustrations mounted. He knew Jethron had the right to kill Hernan, but he couldn't help feeling it was somehow also his.

"Girshon hasn't seen him yet?" Jethron's voice rose into an angered whisper. If he wasn't careful, the rest of the Renegades would hear him.

Willem glanced over at Larn, but the northern man was still staring into the flames. Again, Willem had the distinct feeling Larn could hear more than he let on.

Jethron spoke again, this time too low for Willem to hear. He turned, ready to eavesdrop, when he recognized the face of the soldier speaking to Jethron. He froze.

All thought left, as he stared at these men. Gallian soldiers, supposedly turned by Deagan to join their cause. He had seen their faces every night before he fell asleep for the last year. He had seen them in the village, their eyes always watching him in the plaza, and at the black market too. They had haunted him.

Somehow he'd missed it after the battle. He'd seen Girshon say something to him, but it hadn't really clicked until now.

His heart thrummed, coursing with pain as he remembered those men the day they dragged Kata away—the day they spotted Kata and Jethron. The screams began to echo in his ears.

"Willem?" Jethron was staring at him. Willem swallowed, breathing heavily, never taking his eyes off the soldiers. All four of them were watching him, their hands braced on the swords at their hips.

"They were there," his words came out in a soft, nearly unintelligible whisper.

When Jethron didn't say anything, Willem let his gaze drift toward him. He was suddenly aware of someone touching his arm, a delicate hand and a voice he knew well saying his name. But everything had gone dark, the world falling away as he looked into Jethron's face. He had called him friend, had sacrificed his own happiness for him, and now he stood looking back with guilt lining every feature of his scarred face. Suddenly it clicked. All of it.

Jethron held up his hands. "It wasn't supposed to end the way it did. She was meant to live."

Willem's breaths were too loud, his head rushing with the sound of his heart beating heavily in his chest.

"We needed to unite Mirtain against the Gallians. We had to show that Mirtain was a worthy place to begin the rebellion. We were able to test our strength and see where its weaknesses were, you being one of them. What you did that day should have gotten you killed, yet here you are." Jethron licked his scarred lips. "It was a turning point against Lord Hernan. We did it together, sacrificing ourselves for the cause."

"She knew what would happen?" he gasped.

The guilt was as plain on Jethron's face as the words he had spoken earlier. "Neither of us thought Hernan would rape her, we just..." tears filled his eyes as he searched for the words, shaking his head. "We were going to endure the beatings and then Deagan and the others," he waved a hand at the spies, "we're going to raid our wagons and break us free. Only, Hernan must have caught wind of something. They sent out two caravans and I picked the wrong one. We pursued them but lost track. I spent nearly a year visiting forts and brothels trying to find her. When we finally figured out where she was, it was too late. Tears rolled down his cheeks, the scar etched in pain. "I was too late."

Willem didn't have to hear anymore, and turned to leave, but stopped. "Is this the kind of sacrifice you were talking about?" He shouted and moved closer to Jethron, staring down at him. "I hope you're happy, because of you, Kata is dead."

"That wasn't supposed—"

"I don't care about what was supposed to happen, what I care about is that you lied to me. You lied and you killed her. We're done here."

He took two steps before Jethron spoke again. "Kata was the one who planned it all." It was like a punch to his gut. Willem turned back. "She was the one willing to sacrifice her life for all of this. The Renegades needed somewhere to begin the rebellion, together we decided to do this to join them and test the strength of Mirtain."

"Enough of your lies," Willem silenced him.

"You think you knew Kata, but you didn't know the half of her."

"Watch it," he warned.

"It still burns you up that she chose me. She chose me because she knew I would act. She wanted freedom and decided to risk everything for it. It was her plan, her risk, and her demand that you and Ansie remain in the dark about it. She knew that if you found out, you would do everything in your power to stop the fires of rebellion."

Willem's fist struck Jethron across the chin, silencing the words. Jethron held his lip for a moment before launching himself at Willem. Together they tumbled to the ground and as their grunts filled the night air, grappling hands struggled to pull them apart. There were shouts all around them, but he heard nothing more as he drove his fist into Jethron's face. Blood splattered, but he saw nothing else until strong arms pulled at him, dragging him backward. He screamed in rage, completely lost in the pain of those words.

His own memories betrayed him. All this time he had thought Kata had been afraid as they dragged her away, but it was for him. She had feared for his life, knowing what he would do. And yet, her screams from Hernan's manor had been real. That had not been part of the plan. Her betrayal to them all had become a reality when faced with Hernan.

"You killed her!" he yelled, wanting to blame someone, anyone for all of the pain he felt in his heart. But the one responsible was now dead.

Jethron still lay on the ground, a hand to his jaw where Willem had landed more than one blow. The scar seemed to twitch with pain. "She wasn't supposed to die," Jethron said, weakly.

Willem tried to break free from the arms restraining him.

"She was going to join the Renegades with me, we had agreed to it. We were simply too late. By the time we figured out where she was and worked our way into the fort, they told us she died of lung disease. We didn't mean for it to happen."

Willem's blood was boiling, his cheeks flamed. Ansie suddenly laid her hand on Willem's chest, pulling him from himself. He drew his eyes away to look down at her, but her gaze was focused on Jethron. "Kata's dead because neither of you trusted us," her voice broke. "You're no better than the rest of them, you might as well have slit her throat yourself."

Jethron flinched and moved to stand, Willem finding satisfaction in the way his hands shook.

"What's going on here?" Girshon entered into the small circle which had formed around them. The leader glanced back and forth between the two, assessing the situation. "Larn?" the man asked looking toward Willem.

"It seems," said a voice, right behind Willem's ear, "Willem has just discovered what really happened to his friend, Kata."

Realization dawned on the leader's face which soon turned to a grimace of anger. "What happened to her was terrible, Lord Hernan didn't have a right to do what he did."

Larn's grip loosened on Willem's arms. "It's more than that, sir. Jethron has just revealed the whole ordeal was planned, the discovery, the capture, and then imprisonment. But not the rape and imprisonment, that was where the plan got off course, isn't that right? It was all a matter of aligning the village against the Gallians and a way for Jethron and Kata to escape Mirtain without being hunted." Larn took a deep breath. "However, the death of the girl wasn't planned either. Am I leaving anything out?"

"Is that all?" Girshon said, his dark lips growing tighter by the moment. "Who was involved?"

"These men, and this one." Larn even removed his hand to point at Jethron. Willem tensed, ready to pounce again.

Jethron held up his hands again. "It wasn't supposed to happen that way, but I blame myself. We should have planned better, but we didn't know."

"Of course not," Larn removed his hands, stepping in front of Willem, his dark hair stirring in the soft breeze. Others began to mutter as he moved, his foreignness taking all of their attention. "Did you get to see the prisons where they kept the women? Walk inside the cells and see the utter hopelessness in their eyes?" Jethron didn't answer. "I thought not. No, you waited for the commander of the prison to tell you she had died."

Tears pooled in Jethron's eyes. "I loved her, they gave me a lock of her hair."

He pulled it out of his pocket, a small gathering of beautiful chestnut hair was held together with a dirty strip of rag. The mere sight of it sent Willem's heart racing again. How this man had ever been his friend, he couldn't understand. He had lied to him. Over and over again, Jethron had lied without one mention of what those consequences might be. They both had.

"You claim to have loved this woman," Larn continued. "I'm Maereo and I'm sure you've heard the stories. As vile as we may be, when we love someone, we don't throw them to the dogs."

The crowd shifted, seeming to really look at Larn for the first time. Maybe it was just Willem's imagination, but it seemed as though the whole gathering was holding its breath.

"Shall I tell you what we found only two days ago?" Larn was like a hunter stalking his prey. "We came across a caravan of women, victims of *vox prima*, nearly a hundred of them, headed for Bastion Nocta. If you can even think her sacrifice was worth it, whether she planned it or not, then you're wrong. Those women were shells of what they used to be, destroyed and discarded in the worst manner possible by all that is evil in this world. For you to stand there and say it was for the greater good, to say—"

"That's enough!" Girshon butted in, glaring at Larn.

Willem couldn't help but feel thankful for the interruption. His heart was pounding heavier than it had before. He knew he would never be able to forget those words. His worst nightmares of what Kata had been through were confirmed. The knife which had been living in his heart for the last year, twisted, gutting him.

"You will all be questioned, we will have order here." Girshon's voice boomed. "Since these actions did lead to our victory here, I will remain hopeful that we can put this behind us. As for Kata, we thank her for her sacrifice, though it was in the end unwillingly given." He rubbed a hand across his brow. "Lock them in the dungeon to cool off," some of the Renegades moved, "and take him with you." He pointed toward Willem.

Ansie argued in outrage, making a move toward Girshon—one of the rebels grabbed her arm. Willem stepped forward to knock the man down when the hilt of a sword hit the side of his head with a loud clap.

As he slumped to the ground, his last sight was of Larn's boots and the man leaning over him. He welcomed the darkness with open arms.

CHAPTER 28

Ansie's footfalls were silenced by the plush rug as she passed back and forth along the hallway. It seemed like hours since they had taken Willem to the dungeon. Not wanting to push the matter farther than needed, she had sought to find a moment with Girshon, to plead Willem's innocence. After spending an hour, pacing up and down the hall, she wondered if her efforts would be futile.

Keep it together, Ans, she thought, running her fingers through her tangled hair—most likely making her look even more disheveled and forlorn. She had caught a glimpse of her reflection in the window at the end of the hall earlier, a sight she was startled to admit was her own. Her hair stuck out in all directions, the dirt on her clothes making her appear as though she had rolled in mud. Sighing, she attempted to comb her hair with her fingers.

The distraction did little to ease her mind in regards to what she had learned. She'd been grappling with the past ever since Larn had told them about the Animle. Her eyes prickled with tears again, thinking of the *simian*. She hoped it was from exhaustion, but knew it had more to do with the desperate look the mythical creature had given her before he breathed his last. How she wished she could have given him some peace.

Everything that had happened in the forest that morning seemed like a nightmare. It all swirled before her, as did the words Jethron had spoken. All along Kata and Jethron had planned to try and escape Mirtain, to join the Renegades. But they had been doomed from the beginning.

"Oh, Kata," she sighed, turning to walk back along the hall again.

Wrapping her arms around her body, she paused near the door to see if she could make out the voices inside. As before a dull, indecipherable murmur reached her ears. After passing the length of the hall two more times, the door finally opened.

"Ansie?" Larn's face came into view. "What are you doing here?"

She straightened, raising herself to her full height, little though it was. "I need to speak with your leader."

"*My* leader?" he quirked an eyebrow, testing her. "Not our's?"

"I suppose." She shook the importance of the thought away. "I need to speak with him about Willem. It wasn't his fault. You see, there was more going on with Kata than..." her voice drifted off when Larn held up a hand.

"It's already been taken care of." His dark eyes watched her carefully. "He'll be released in the morning. I think we can both agree some time alone will do him good."

"True," she agreed, if only a little. "Thank you."

He waved the words away. "Thank Girshon, not me." His hands began to fumble with the collar of his shirt. "Is it always so hot here?"

"Only always," she laughed. It was a bit stuffy in the hall, but outside she knew the wind would chill her. Until now, she hadn't really thought about how cold it must be in the northernlands. If this was hot, what must winter there be like?

Removing his cloak, he began to roll up his sleeves, revealing thick forearms. She had never seen skin like his before. It was darkened, as though he had spent time in the sun, and yet he didn't have any spots which marked him. While she had six dots cresting around her right eye—from the sun, no doubt.

Realizing she was staring, she turned her gaze on the sword sheathed at his waist. "Thank you for giving me your sword, earlier."

"I was surprised you knew how to use it. All the restrictions down here."

She shrugged. "Willem taught me how to spar with a broom handle. He thought it would be a good skill for me to have—just in case." She grinned.

"Seems he was right."

"He usually is," she smiled up at him, suddenly wishing she had taken the time to clean herself up before attempting to meet Girshon. Meanwhile, Larn had that distinct ability to look both unkempt and yet presentable. She always wondered how some people could do that.

"Well, at least he's right about some things." Larn stepped to the side and took a seat with his back leaning against the wall. He looked so relaxed, his knees bent, arms looped over them. His hands broke apart and he patted the rug next to him. "You look like you could use some rest."

"I could say the same about you," she replied but moved beside him. There was something about Larn that put her at ease. A calm assurance coursed through him, a relaxing peace that drew her in and made her feel comfortable.

"It seems like ages since I've been inside," he gave a wide-mouth yawn. "I might as well enjoy it while I can."

The thought made Ansie smile. Larn leaned his head back against the wall, the quiet in the hallway enveloping them. Ansie felt as though she could hear everything and nothing at once, as though they were the only two people in the realm still awake. It was a silly thought, but one she enjoyed. Maybe if the world was asleep, it couldn't hurt itself.

"Where is he?" she asked, her voice timider than before.

"Who, Willem? In the cells beneath us." He spoke without opening his eyes.

"No," she whispered, "Hernan."

"Ahh," he ran a hand through his hair again. She wondered if he did that a lot. "He's being held in his study. Girshon hasn't decided what to do with him yet."

"Willem wants him dead."

"Willem wants to change the past." Larn opened his eyes and stared at the wall opposite them. The ornate tables seemed out of place compared to the rustic cottages lining the village.

"Can you blame him?" she said under her breath, not thinking he would hear.

"Not entirely," he responded. She looked at him, surprised he had heard her. He glanced down. "I'm exceptional in a lot of areas," he tapped his ear and winked.

She rolled her eyes and returned her gaze to the wall across from them. "Normally Willem's calmer, steadier, but when it comes to Kata, well, there's a lot of pain."

"For good reason," he shook his head. "I still can't believe what they planned and what that," he broke off, looking as though he had wanted to say something vile, "man did to her."

She couldn't come up with a reply. While she had been pacing, she had tried to come up with some explanation for why Jethron and Kata hadn't told them what they were doing.

She wondered if Kata had lived, if she would have made the same choices again. Jethron had claimed Kata would sacrifice anything for freedom and Ansie believed it. But dreaming and doing were two very different things.

Ansie cleared her throat, for some reason wanting Larn to understand what they had been through.

"We used to tell each other everything, all four of us" she admitted, feeling his gaze on her. "There's an old ruin outside the village, Shirnway Castle, where we used to meet after working in the fields. Or the creek just behind it. We broke curfew, thinking we were rebels and never got caught." She shook her head. "Willem told us stories of the Animle, stories his mother had whispered to him in his childhood. Down here, the Animle are myths, legends of untruth, but we wanted them to be real. We all dreamed, or at least Kata and I did."

"What do you mean by that?" His voice was gentle, probing.

She sighed, beginning to use her hands as she talked. "Kata and I talked about the stories as just that, stories. But it was always different for Willem and Jethron. It nearly became an obsession for them. Willem wanted to leave Mirtain, but he couldn't because of me, and Jethron wanted to do the same."

"So that's why he joined us," Larn said more to himself than her.

"I guess so, although I don't know when he did."

"I've been in contact with him for two years, although he mentioned he joined three years ago," he gave her a half smile. "I overheard him talking to Willem. Impeccable hearing, remember?"

"Right," she nodded, just now realizing how much he was able to discern from a distance. They had been all the way across the pyre, the crowd talking around them. It seemed impossible he was able to hear Willem and Jethron's private conversation.

It made sense now, there had been a moment while she was speaking with him by the pyre that she thought he wasn't paying attention. She had mentioned the legend of the Neho and Cadna moons. Of course, he had looked at her as though she had sprouted another head and told her there was another reason for the light. She had asked him to tell her, his only response was, "I'll tell you sometime."

Looking at him now, there was no doubt in her mind he had a different idea of the moons' origins. Everything about him was different. From his skin to his hair, to the way he carried himself. He even fought differently. She had seen the way he ran, determined and hostile toward his enemies, taking them down one by one with fell swoops of his sword. He had kicked, punched and dodged each attack with lithe speed and graceful precision, using every part of his body to his advantage.

"As much as it hurts me to admit it, you now know Jethron is loyal to the Renegades. Kata was too." Ansie sighed and Larn gave her an odd look. "Jethron talked of little else after he lost his grandparents."

"He's shown he's capable of keeping a secret."

She glanced up, he was watching her. "I don't think I can understand what they did. I know it was risky, but they lied to us. For so long. I don't know if I can trust him again," she admitted.

"Only time will tell," Larn shrugged. "But he's right to keep his movements close. You don't know what it's like out there. One word can be the difference between life or death. You can't trust anyone."

She stared at him, hearing the bleakness in his voice. Was there no one he trusted?

"What do we do now?" she asked.

"We wait until morning, then I can talk to Willem."

"About our leaving?"

He nodded slowly, his eyes unfocused as though his mind was elsewhere.

"What will you tell him?"

"Same thing I told you," he shrugged. "You can no longer remain hidden in Mirtain. Either the Regent will come here and find out about you both, or an Animle will reach Mirtain. Neither can happen, we have to leave. And of course, there are the rogue Chroniclers to worry about too." He seemed to add that last bit on for his own benefit.

"The what?"

"You haven't heard? Oh, two Chroniclers escaped a meeting with the Regent. They've been missing for, well, quite a while now. Before I heard about Willem, I was actually searching for them."

"Why?" she asked. She had heard of Chroniclers, the students of the old religions.

"Not long after they went missing, the Regent issued a decree that any person harboring these men would be found guilty and executed. He was trying to smoke them out." Larn ran a hand through his hair again. "If the Regent wants them, then so do I."

Ansie smiled at his logic. "Do they have something to do with the Animle?"

He nodded. "Yes, they probably know more than all of the realm combined." He glanced down at her, "It makes sense why the Regent would want to know too, huh? There are forces at work in this land, forces much larger and stronger than we could dare to comprehend." He had a way of staring at the opposite wall, his eyes seemingly focused on something she couldn't see. "There's the good, and the bad, both always at war with one another—or so I've always been told."

She felt a stirring inside her chest, much in the same way when the *simian* had first looked to her.

"I'm told the good always wins." Larn glanced down at her, a smile in his eyes.

"But you don't really believe that?"

"Can you?"

"No, I can't," she shook her head. It was maybe the first time she had admitted it to herself. "I've seen too many things happen here for me to ever believe good always wins."

"A man I once knew told me that good has already won," he smiled, though it didn't reach his eyes. "Do you remember what I said about the moons?"

"Yes," she breathed.

"It has to do with that. And the Praelia—" She opened her mouth to ask, but he explained before she could, "—a religion. The Chroniclers, the Animle, the Praelia, they're all connected."

"So you'll tell me about the moons sometime?" she asked.

He winked. "You can count on that."

"I'll hold you to it."

"Good," he gave a gentle, weary sigh. "Now what can you tell me about your past?"

"What do you mean?"

"How you came to be in Mirtain." She froze at his words, wondering how he'd known. He didn't meet her gaze, but she felt as though he was looking into her soul. "I know you're Willem's ward, but what I'd like to know is what part of the realm you're from."

"Oh," she said, looking down at her hands in her lap. "That's kind of a long story." Much longer than she was willing to tell.

"Really?" he quirked an eyebrow.

"Maybe too long for this hallway at least," she gave a small laugh, attempting to disperse the more tense atmosphere. "All you need to know for now is Willem is like a brother to me. He kept me safe when I had nowhere else to go."

"And how old were you?"

"It's been around ten years."

"That doesn't exactly answer my question," he pointed out.

"Just trying to keep it interesting," she shrugged and gave a small laugh, fidgeting beneath his gaze.

"Fine then, keep your secrets" he ran a hand through his hair—the dark strands making his fingers disappear for only a moment. "What I don't understand is the relationship between all four of you."

Ansie sighed, he really was asking too many questions. Leaning back against the wall, she straightened her legs, crossing her muddy boots at the ankles. At least her toes weren't frozen anymore, like they had been on the battlefield. Again, she wondered why she hadn't taken the time to comb her hair when she returned to the cottage.

"Willem, Jethron, and Kata were friends before I arrived. Particularly, Kata and Willem. They grew up together, and as they got older Willem fell in love with her." She shifted. "You know, I'm really not comfortable telling you all this."

Larn held his hands up in a sign of surrender. "I won't tell anyone. I just need to understand what we're dealing with."

She took a deep breath debating, then plunged forward. "Willem never talked to me about how he felt, at least while Kata was still alive. I could tell, but he never said anything." Her fingers idly twirled one of her strands of hair into a curl. "Willem's a very private person." Her mind flashed back to his admission of guilt about being the one to find Jethron and Kata. But now it no longer mattered, it had all been planned.

"Willem and Jethron are opposites," she said quickly, "they always have been. They don't think the same way and yet, they were somehow friends, but that was mainly because of Kata. She was able to get them to see eye to eye." Ansie glanced to her side, Larn was watching her, the dark angled eyes giving away his interest.

"Sorry," she said, "I'm not making much sense."

"You're making perfect sense, actually." He looked away. "So Kata had a way of keeping the peace between them?"

Ansie nodded. "She was able to make them see the other's point of view, to make them understand what they were really thinking. It's something I can't do."

"Not many people have that ability. Did you know her well?"

Tears sprung to her eyes. She turned her head to look down the hall toward the open window. "Yes, she was like a sister to me."

Larn didn't speak for a long time, letting her sit in the silence as she replayed the last moments she had seen Kata. It had been a simple moment. Kata had given her a cheery wave, leaving Ansie to finish the extra work she had received as punishment. Kata had been smiling, her face bright, as it always was. It was how Ansie wanted to remember her, but instead the images Larn had conjured up came to mind. Starving women, shackled and chained together. She shivered.

"Did you really see them?" she asked, her voice thick.

"Yes," he said quietly. Somehow he understood just who she was referring to.

"Was it really as bad as you said?"

"Yes," this time the word was hardly audible. "When we got to them, they had already been branded." Larn made a gesture to his wrists and her stomach flipped. To think of the pain was too much.

"Then I'm glad Kata died before that happened. She died as herself, and not as some property of the Regent's." Ansie hated the way her memories taunted her.

Larn nodded. "The truth is, many of those women still had strength, though they hid it well. One, in particular, was very strong." He glanced down at her.

"I guess we don't know our true strength until it's tested. That's when we get to see who we really are."

"Prophetic," she teased. Larn chuckled.

"So the question is," Larn said, turning serious once more, "Do you think Kata had the strength in her to not give up?"

Ansie was nodding before he had finished talking. One tear ran down her cheek and she stopped the others from falling, wiping at her eyes. "Yes, she was brave, braver than I ever knew." She took a shaky breath. "Thank you."

"No need," he shrugged, as though his words were of little importance, but they were everything. They gave her a way of remembering Kata as when she had been alive. "Now, I suggest we get out of here and find some rest. We have a long day ahead of us tomorrow."

"We?" she asked, a little surprised.

He pushed to standing and adjusted his cloak. "I'm going with you and Willem."

He extended his hand toward her. Calloused palms met her own, his hand nearly engulfing hers. She was pulled to her feet in one quick motion and when he let go, her hand fell to her side, the warmth of his skin still lingering.

"Get some rest," he nodded, "we leave at dawn."

"Okay," she murmured, and then he was gone.

She replayed the moment in her head more than once, her breaths clouding before her as she walked back to the cottage. It was eerily quiet, the only sound, her worn boots padding over the dust-caked road.

Tomorrow she would leave this place. Tomorrow, she would say goodbye to all that held her back. And yet, she feared what she would leave behind. Skurn's face came to mind, but she pushed it aside. Her heart had taken enough of a beating for the day. She could wait to think about him, and what this new-found freedom might mean.

She ran the rest of the way to the cottage, only lying down to sleep when all the provisions she could think of were packed. Only when the wind began to howl outside the cottage did she drift off to sleep.

CHAPTER 29

The clanging of the keys, in the newly-appointed dungeon master's hand, was almost deafening. Both men strode more forcefully than necessary in the midst of the cells passing on either side. Only a few of the metal-barred cages remained empty—most having more than one Gallian soldier within.

"How far back did you put him?" Larn asked.

"Girshon didn't want him speaking to the other prisoners," was the response.

It was understandable. Before Willem had been knocked out by the hilt of Larn's own sword, he'd been fuming, and ready to attack anyone in his way.

"Is he awake?" he asked, having to speak louder than he would like over the steady clink of the keys and their boots pounding the stone floor.

"You tell me," the jailer replied. Girshon had told Larn the man was trustworthy, a villager who'd proved his allegiance. He wasn't one to mince words, that was certain.

The man stopped beside a door with a small square of bars grooved into the wood. They were at the right height for the jailer, but a little too low for Larn.

The hinges voiced their disapproval as the door swung open and Larn stepped inside. His eyes adjusted quickly to the dim light, something he'd learned others had difficulty with. Willem sat opposite him, his back resting against the wall, watching him, waiting. Molded, brown straw was scattered around the floor giving the dank space the musty stench of rotting wood. Larn wondered how long it had been since the cell had been cleaned.

"Leave us," he said over his shoulder. The jailer pulled the squealing door shut behind him, his footsteps fading quick enough.

"Where's Ansie?" Willem asked.

Larn braced a hand on the hilt of his sword hanging off his hips. "She's fine." He shrugged, always aloof. At least, he always tried to remain aloof, but his words by the pyre had poured out of him before he could stop them. He had thought of those women from the caravan, thought of Umbris. Now he wished he'd never spoken the words. He'd painted a picture of horrors that would live in their memories. Maybe, Willem wouldn't remember what he had said. He had hit him pretty hard.

"I'll disagree with that," Willem said softly, his eyes never leaving Larn's face. "She was in a lot of danger."

"True," Larn nodded, "but she's safe now." Some of the things Ansie had told him in the hall were falling into place.

He nearly smiled to himself thinking of the way she had tried to explain Willem and Jethron's cantankerous relationship. It wasn't as much what she said, but the meaning behind her words. In his short dealings with both Jethron and Willem, he'd begun to build a profile of their character, her words had confirmed his suspicions.

Willem was the kind of person who gave all of himself, not for the better of his own life but for the better of others. Jethron was the exact opposite. He cloaked himself in the impression of helping others, but his true goal was to seek glory—he lived off it, thrived off of it. But even while he sought glory, he wanted others to share in it as well. He was a leader, at times dangerous and risky, but a leader all the same.

"Let me guess," the temporary prisoner broke through Larn's thoughts again, his voice mocking, "you're here to set me free and send me on some mission."

"Yes, and no." Larn crossed his arms. "I'm not so much sending you, as I am telling you to come with us."

"Us?"

Larn nodded. "Myself and Ansie."

"You're wasting your breath. Ansie and I aren't going anywhere."

"That's not what she told me," he rebutted, countering Willem's move.

"She isn't of age."

"True, but she has her own mind." An unexpected smile pulled at the corner of his mouth. The fact Heben had to hold her back earlier was enough to tell Larn she was courageous and fiercely protective of Willem.

Willem sighed. "She does, but it doesn't mean we're leaving."

"Fine," Larn shrugged, wincing a bit. The exertion of the battle had not helped his recently stitched shoulder. "I wonder what we should do when the Regent arrives? Personally, I hope to kiss his pristine boots before they hang me or, better yet, cut off my head. And then, of course, there's the Animle to be concerned with too. Maybe if we're lucky, the Regent will arrive here at the same moment an Animle walks out of that woods again."

Willem stared at him, the curiosity and anger mingling. "They'll come here?" he asked.

"More Gallians? Of course, not to mention the Regent could send more Nexen. This rebellion isn't going to go unnoticed."

"I know they'll come, I meant the Animle," Willem whispered, his fingers laced together.

"Yes."

"So it's either go find them, or they find us."

"Yes," Larn said again. "The way I see it, there's a better chance of keeping this quiet until we find your *anima reflecta* than waiting for the creature to arrive here in the midst of a Gallian army."

The brown eyes watched him, piercing the darkness. Larn shifted beneath his gaze, something he never did. Willem had a depth to him that was different than most people, something Larn hadn't quite understood until now. After his actions in the forest and next to the pyre, Larn had drawn conclusions about the hunter—thinking him the type of man to take action without regard for consequences. But what he saw now was the direct opposite. Perhaps he had been wrong in judging Willem. It was an odd feeling, not being right.

"Then I guess you've left me no choice." Willem sighed.

"Perhaps," Larn shrugged.

"What will happen to Jethron and the others?"

"Ahh, that." Larn took two steps to the side wall and leaned against it, his shoulder seeming to stick to the grime coating the stones. "Girshon will give them some form of punishment. Night shifts on watch, that sort of thing." He sighed, "Then we will be back to normal. Regardless of what happened, we will have to trust them."

Willem looked away from him, hiding his face in the darkness, Larn could only guess what he was thinking.

"The truth is," he continued, "without Jethron this rebellion wouldn't have started."

"And without Kata," Willem winced at her name, swallowing before moving on. "You've probably guessed as much, but she meant a lot to me, and I'm trying to work through it all, to understand why they lied."

"But it's not enough," Larn said softly, and the hunter looked up. He nodded again, his brow furrowed. "There's no sense justifying it." Silence fell between them for a moment.

"Thank you, for what you did, in the forest, protecting Ansie."

Larn held still, not wanting to disrupt whatever thoughts were running through Willem's mind. Battles often had that effect on people. After staring death in the face, a person found himself either shocked into silence or spilling his deepest secrets.

"How many will be accompanying us?" Willem asked after a long moment of silence.

The change in the question surprised Larn. "None, it will just be the three of us."

Willem nodded. "And when will we be leaving?"

"Now, if you're ready."

"There's nothing holding me here." The hunter sighed again, this time moving to stand. When he straightened, Larn noticed they were nearly the same height. "I do have some conditions though."

"Name them," Larn crossed his arms over his chest, tensing. One of the many reasons he wanted to live on his own once the realm was overtaken, was to avoid taking orders from anyone.

"You will help me protect Ansie at all costs, and, you will see both of us as equals, not lording your training and skills over us. I've had enough of lords."

"Done," Larn said quickly, trying not to sound too relieved. At least he was reasonable. "And I have one for you."

"Yes?"

"Think before you act."

The blonde head dipped for just a moment, though the brown eyes never left his. "That won't happen again. I'll put it behind me."

"Good," Larn gave him a small smile. "We can make this work. It's easier for three to move undetected than having the entire Renegade company go with us, which actually brings me to one more condition."

"What's that?"

"If you steal my horse again, I will have to beat on you a little bit."

Willem snorted. "You sound like Ansie."

Larn chuckled, moving to the door and opening it with a resounding whine. "She does have a bit of fire in her."

"You have no idea," Willem shook his head back and forth, speaking with the same affection his ward had earlier. Larn never had a brother or sister, but he wondered if this was what it was like.

Together, they walked along the halls of the dungeon. Willem's eyes were focused straight ahead when a familiar voice called out to him by name. The hunter stopped, his eyes closing. Larn tensed, ready to move if needed.

Jethron's face was visible through the hole in the door. His fingers wrapped around the bars.

"We never should have done it," he gasped, the scar along his face made his guilt all the more apparent. "I knew the plan was dangerous, but we were willing to risk it. Had I known, I never would've done it."

Willem glanced his way, eyeing Jethron for a moment. "Never speak of her to me again. I could've helped keep her safe, but—" he broke off. "Leave it in the past." Without another word, he strode forward, leaving the spy behind bars.

Larn gave Jethron one final nod before following Willem down the hall and up the stairs to the main floor of Lord Hernan's manor.

His companion seemed to know the way outside, and Larn wondered how often Willem had walked these halls. According to some of the villagers whom Larn had questioned, Hernan had paid Willem uncharacteristic attention, often threatening him and Ansie in turn.

Willem shoved open the door leading into the main square and hurried down the stairs. When Larn caught up with him, he gave him a sidelong glance.

"That was well handled."

"Part of me still wants to throttle him," the hunter grumbled.

"Let's go find Ansie."

The sky was turning lighter by the moment, the dark pitch of midnight black slowly turning to the hints of deep blue, leading to dawn.

"Will she be ready?" Larn asked.

Willem chuckled, "You might as well ask me if the sun is going to rise."

It seemed mere moments later they roused Ansie from her bunk. She had jumped down fully dressed and handed them packs and water skins to throw over their shoulders. As her eyes brightened in the lightening sky, she mounted one of the horses they had brought along. Willem gave Larn a sidelong look and he nearly laughed—she was more than ready. The quiet girl he'd spoken to in the hall was gone, replaced by this fiery sprite.

Without a word, Larn pulled out the long sword from beneath a roll on Tympmor's back and handed it to Willem. The hunter took it in his hand, holding it comfortably as a practiced swordsman. In a swift movement, he had the weapon strapped across his back—a token of freedom in a land that had taken so much from him.

"Shall we?" Larn asked.

Two sets of wide eyes met his, but it was Ansie who spoke—the corner of her mouth lifting into a toothy grin. "Let's find the Animle."

As though he needed no further encouragement, Willem gave his horse a kick and they took off into the dawn.

CHAPTER 30

The steam from the iron tub scorched Umbris's hands, her back aching from lifting the water-laden sheets with nothing but a wooden paddle to help her. Carefully twisting, she slapped the heavy fabric onto the table where it would cool before she would be able to press out the excess water and then hang it to dry. She returned to the steaming tub, fishing for another lump of sheets swirling in the deep recesses of the boiling water.

Back nearly breaking beneath the weight of the water-laden cloth, she dropped the last of them onto the table, making sure to keep her feet well away from the water draining off the edges. She had been burned before, both her feet and her hands.

She set about taking down the previous days linens from the thick line of wire running through the small courtyard. It hadn't taken her long to realize this would become the only place she knew in Bastion Nocta, a thought which both pleased and worried her at the same time.

Nearly a month had passed since Pike left her near the road just outside the capital city. She had moved in the crowds, keeping to the shadows, as those around her pushed by. It hadn't taken long for her to witness how the poorer classes were treated, a passing lord nearly trampled a small child and his mother with his horse. Anyone not dressed in the most refined clothing of the upper classes was hardly noticed by those above her station. They seemed to ignore the poor, as though they were mere flies or cats prowling the streets.

Maybe it wasn't so much the poor, as it was Anglans. In her home village, the Gallians had certainly drawn a distinction between themselves and Anglans, but this was different. Here in the hub of the realm, all Anglans were seen as less-than, as nothing more than servants to Gallians.

After spending a few hours wandering the mind-twisting alleyways and roads, she had found a women's house, *Le Jupon Rouge*. It was a leaning, wooden building with ivy crawling up one side. A popular alleyway ran right in front of the building, allowing for a steady stream of customers to enter the brothel. That first day she had sat in the shadows across the alley, watching as well-dressed Gallians entered the house, while dusk crept upon the city.

It had taken more courage than she realized to make herself move from her hiding spot and walk up to the front door of the building, the scrolling red letters boldly gleaming above her head. She had knocked and was greeted by the heavily powdered face of Madame. She had flashed her wrists and was pulled inside, as the older woman glanced up and down the streets.

Umbris shook her head as she began to wring out the water from the steaming linens. It seemed like ages since she had begun working in the house.

At first, Madame had declared her a gift from the stars. Her good humor had too soon turned to anger. For ten nights, Madame had dressed Umbris in the finest clothes the brothel had to offer. She had coated her face in makeup, styled her hair, and spritzed her with perfumes that had choked Umbris's lungs. But none of it worked.

Each night the men came in and took their pick of women. Umbris had stood with the rest of the girls, shaking as she waited to be chosen. But she never was. So often the men would look at her, their eyes roving over her body, but when they reached her face, they stopped. She had wondered, that first night as the men lounged around and the women were presented, if there was something wrong with her. But night after night, she had received enough attention, until the gong rang leaving her alone in the welcoming chamber. It didn't matter how much makeup and fine clothes adorned her body, it did nothing to entice the men.

It hadn't taken long for Madame to decide she was worthless as one of her girls and put her to work as the scullery maid.

The relief, which came over her that day, was something she couldn't quite describe. To not be made into what her wrists proclaimed her to be, was a stroke of luck Umbris never could have hoped for. Even now, she wondered what it was about her which made the men turn away. She had looked up at the stars in thanks that night, and every night since, knowing it had to be a gift from somewhere.

"Girl? Are you finished?" Madame's tight high-pitched address reached her. It was always sharp when speaking to the girls, but could turn into the softest drip of foolishness when she fawned over the men who came to her house.

"Almost, Madame," Umbris replied, keeping her eyes on her work.

In her small courtyard, she was normally left alone, unless there were a few garment requests from the working girls. Umbris preferred it that way.

She was considered the lowest in the house, her food less than the others and her clothes that of someone of the streets, but she didn't mind. At night she had a chance to rest, while the others in the house were awake, the sounds making her hands tremble. She preferred her little world.

"The third floor needs to be taken care of," Madame said, before leaving with a swish of her stiff ruby red skirts.

"Yes, Madame," she whispered to her retreating form.

The sun was beginning to drop, long shadows stretching across the worn stones of the small courtyard. The space was only a little wider than an alleyway and stretched only half of the length of the building. But it was better than spending hours in chains, riding in a carriage with nine other women.

Working faster than before, Umbris squeezed and twisted the cream-colored sheets on the table. Her hands had grown red and raw from dealing with the hot water, making the markings on her wrists stand out all the more, but in a place like this, the markings were as ordinary as another curl in one's hair. Even Madame was branded.

Umbris hurried through the rest of her chores, hanging the freshly cleaned linens on the line before taking the dry ones up to the third floor. As she moved from room to room, some of the girls passed by, ignoring her presence. As soon as the men had refused to have anything to do with her, the other women had adopted the same practice and saw her as nothing worth their time—she was invisible and liked it that way.

Umbris shrugged the new load of dirty bedding into her basket and hurried down the stairs. Passing by the dining hall, her stomach gave a small rumble, but she would have to wait to eat. Madame never let her have dinner until after the guests arrived, and the gong was rung. But she had steady meals and was slowly gaining back her figure—she could only count a few of her ribs now.

Throwing the new load of bedding into the water, she tended to the fire and began on the pile of clothes waiting to be mended. Inside, the women were moving about, calls and last minute shouts to one another as they prepared for the evening. Her tiny courtyard was almost entirely covered in shadow, and she welcomed it gladly. Only in the dark did she finally feel at peace, as though the rest of the realm couldn't see her.

Pushing a lock of her dark hair out of the way, she looked up at the stars, her mind wandering to the forest. The guilt she often tried to keep at bay swept over her.

She had decided to come here with aspirations of doing something with her situation—to help the Renegades. *Instead, you're mending clothes.*

In the past weeks of hard labor, she had listened to everything she possibly could, even creeping into the halls to listen to conversations. But the truth of the matter was she couldn't hear anything and what she did hear made her stomach turn over. As much as she wanted to help, and give Pike some piece of information to take back to Larn, she couldn't figure out how she could change her situation.

"Because you don't want it to change," she mumbled under her breath. Even as she said the words, she knew they were true. As much as she disliked working with the bedding and the steaming water, it beat having to do anything inside. Somehow, she had been lucky enough to get passed by. Madame said it was because there was only death inside her, and men wanted someone who would make them happy.

Umbris hadn't corrected the woman. Madame was closer to the truth than she realized.

Regardless of the death inside her, the reality was her failure as a spy. Just yesterday, Pike had slipped into her courtyard while the women were entertaining the guests. She had nearly screamed.

She had felt horrible telling him she was merely a scullery maid, and his disappointment had been palpable, though he tried to hide it. Her own guilt was doubled as she wondered what Larn would say when he heard the news. He had hoped she would serve a greater purpose, had complimented her on her ability to read people and draw them out.

Not here, she sighed, wishing there was some way she could still help. But here it was easy to forget the realm. The courtyard was her own little realm, and she liked it just fine.

Laughter peeled from inside, high shrills raking on her nerves. They were too fake, too careless. She often thought she could hear the sadness beneath the laughter, the death beneath the attempt at life and wondered if anyone else heard it.

A window opened directly above her head, some of the light spreading into the courtyard. "Stars above, that's better!"

Whoever had opened the window had pulled back the curtains as well. Madame wouldn't like that.

It was a man who spoke, and his voice drew nearer as he must have leaned over the window sill. Umbris kept her body pressed back against the wall as much as possible, not wanting to be seen.

"Why they use so much perfume, I'll never understand," the same voice spoke again, the sound slightly muffled, as though something was obstructing his mouth.

There came a mumbled reply which made the first speaker chuckle. Something about the sound was heartening, deep and musical as though the person was used to refined things. If that was the case, she couldn't understand why he would be in a place like this. *Le Jupon Rouge* wasn't the worst of the brothels she'd seen, and it certainly had clients of great wealth, but it was far enough away from the palace to not be considered a house of excellence. From the various conversations she'd overheard, she knew many of the women wished to work closer to the palace where the best clientele would be found.

The man above her took in another deep breath. "Come, smell this."

Movement shifted above her, and another man took a deep breath. "Smells like rubbish."

Umbris's brow furrowed. The second voice was familiar somehow, not the pitch but the way each word was formed carefully, with almost a pause in-between each word. There was something about it which had her on edge. She pressed further into the wall, hoping neither man would dare to look down, while preparing to feign sleep if needed.

"No," the first speaker said, this time his voice dipping low, "beneath the general smell of sewage, it smells clean."

The second man took a deep breath and then coughed. "It's repulsive." Again, the man's voice sounded familiar.

The one who enjoyed the smell gave a sigh. "You never were one to enjoy anything beneath your strict standards."

"I like my comfort."

"Comfort?" the first speaker mumbled, sounding as though he was talking to himself. Umbris wondered what it was, obstructing his mouth. Was he wearing a mask? A scarf over his face? She desperately wanted to look up. "I like my comfort too, but sometimes it's good to see the underside of this wretched city."

"Underside?" the familiar voice asked, clearly having heard his friend. "This is nothing compared to what's really out there."

"I know." The first voice spoke softly, the drawl almost charming. "I've left these walls before, regardless of what everyone thinks." The familiar voice didn't reply. "Did you receive your missive from the Liege?"

Umbris' attention perked. The Liege was a title she had heard plenty, the man was supposedly still in Gallia, though the Regent often used him for military strategy. The Liege was rumored to be a hardened warrior with hundreds of wolves at his command. The Master of the Liege of Nex.

"Yes," the familiar voice said. Umbris grew frustrated, she couldn't place it. If only the man would remove whatever was covering his mouth, then she would be able to discern his voice better.

"And?" the first voice prodded, almost urgent.

"He suggests finding them, and interrogating each one individually."

"Ahh," the man sounded a bit disinterested. "As I thought. One of them has to know." He sighed in frustration. "I can't believe we are even having to deal with this."

Umbris straightened, continuing to hide in the shadows beneath the sill. Her heart hammered inside her chest.

"And you're certain they were Renegades? Do you think they know?" the first voice asked. There was a tinge to his words, as though he stood on the edge of anger.

"That, I'm unsure of," the other cleared his throat. "They were aware of us, but they seemed surprised to see—"

"Gentlemen!" Madame's high-pitched call carried through the window, halting whatever words the man was about to say. "One can gaze at the stars any night, but what about the dazzling stars I have in here?"

"Ahh, Madame," the unfamiliar voice said, all signs of seriousness drawn away, and in its place a delicate charm. "You are too kind." His Gallian accent dripped with veiled pleasure.

"Come, sirs," she simpered to them, "come and we will find you some company."

"As you wish, Madame."

Movement sounded above Umbris's head, but she didn't dare to breathe until the window clicked shut and the light from inside was extinguished by the curtains. A gust of air left her.

It seemed *Le Jupon Rouge* had more interesting visitors than she had previously thought. She twirled a section of her hair around her finger, something she often did without thinking.

Just what had the familiar voice been about to say? She felt as though he had been ready to give away something of importance. And why was his voice so familiar? He didn't remind her of any of the soldiers from her village.

She really couldn't say what it was that made her want to know more, but there was something going on between those two men. They knew things, at least knew the Liege and had correspondence with him. After weeks of trying to hear anything important and listening to nothing but nonsense, Umbris felt herself waking up, as though she had been asleep all this time.

Fingering the mending in her hand, an idea came to her. She would have to wait an hour, but if she timed it right, she just might catch a glimpse of these men. If she at least had a description of them, maybe she would have some bit of information to give Pike when he next visited.

Time passed, at once slow and then quite suddenly when the gong rang. The sounds of laughter quieted and the house grew solemn behind her back. Her heart rate seemed to accelerate as each second passed.

Hearing a voice inside, she drew herself up, her aching knees groaning beneath her meager weight. As her spine straightened she took a large breath, feeling it as though her whole chest was filled with the smoggy air coming from the steaming bed sheets.

The back door opened silently into the dark hall and she slipped along the wooden planks to the lone staircase at the back of the house. Three flights of stairs brought her to the ornate hallway, deep red carpets covered the floors, and dimly lit candles flickered behind stained glass. Shuffles behind each door left her wondering what to do. She hadn't really thought what might help her to see the men. If she dared to barge into one of the rooms, Madame would throw her out before she could say a word in rebuttal. But perhaps there was another way.

Near the end of the hall, leading to the main staircase was a table draped in rich, red silk that was more than likely fake. Swallowing hard, Umbris skittered down the hall, hoping her shift wasn't leaving a trail of dirt behind.

Hidden within the confines of the silk, she hastened to the corner of the table. It rested near the staircase with just enough space for her to push back the cloth and view the stairs without being seen. From this vantage point, if she was lucky, she just might catch a glimpse of a face.

A door opened, and not a moment too soon, for she had begun to worry the company had already left. Footsteps wandered their way down the hall, a man humming to himself in a drunken stupor. His voice was unfamiliar to her and she didn't bother pushing the silk out of the way.

After the same thing happened a third time, she began to wonder if she had already missed the men. She was just about to crawl out from her spot when another door opened, this time a female voice drifted along the hall.

"You can't be leaving already."

"Oh, but I have to."

Umbris sat up a little straighter, nearly hitting her head. It was the charming voice, the one she had first heard downstairs. Her heart skipped a beat as she waited for him to walk down the hall. He seemed to be lingering at the door for a moment, and a sigh from the girl told her a parting kiss was in order. She waited, stomach clenched.

"Until next time," the man whispered and the girl giggled.

Umbris edged to the corner, hoping she just might be able to see his face. The man cleared his throat as he passed along the hall, each footstep bringing him closer. Her heart was thundering as his shadow stretched across the floor, bending along each stair.

He was tall, surprisingly so, his legs lean and reaching to a trim waist which stretched to broad shoulders and long arms. His hands fumbled with a jacket and tri-pointed hat, the coat made of dark, but expensive looking fabric. Shifting a little closer, she caught a glimpse of his light brown hair which he smoothed back with a free hand.

Another door opened and the man turned to look behind him, one foot resting on the first step. In the dim light, Umbris couldn't see the color of his eyes, but she was able to make out the uneven dent of a dimple along the right side of his cheek. His nose was rather large, but thin and had a ridge in it. He peered back in the direction he had come and raised a hand in greeting to another man as he approached. A smile pulled at his mouth, making lines appear along his cheeks and the dimple deepen.

"Are you ready yet?" he asked, his voice again refined as he mocked his companion. There was something elegant about his mouth when he spoke, a perfect delicacy to the way he formed his words. The other man didn't answer, but his shadow crept across the first man's face. "Perhaps you need another round?"

"I could certainly go for another."

Umbris nearly shot to her feet at the sound of the now unmuffled voice. It was Commander Jolson, she would have recognized his voice anywhere.

Heart hammering, she watched as he came into her line of sight, not wanting to believe it was true. Sure enough, she caught the gleam of his buttons as he tightened his waistcoat.

She didn't need to see anymore, as both men began to descend the stairs, their ribald jests putting her on edge. Each breath came in a short gasp, and it wasn't until her own stomach grumbled, she realized Madame might be looking for her soon.

Checking to make sure the hallway was empty, she darted out from under the table and ran down the back stairway, her mind still reeling with what she had seen.

It all made sense now. What Jolson had been saying about the Renegades before Madame interrupted. They had been speaking about something that was missing, and she knew exactly what had been lost beneath Jolson's watch.

Jolson had left them behind in the midst of the Renegade attack. She had often wondered why he had left them in the midst of the skirmish, but it seemed now part of the reason was to get word to Bastion Nocta, the other was selfish gain.

She nearly grumbled to herself as she fled down the stairs. She wasn't looking where she was going when she ran into one of the working girls.

"What are you doing in here?" the girl cried out, her chest showing more skin than it should.

"I'm sorry," she said quietly and hurried around her before the girl could raise even more of a fuss.

Nearly running down the hall, she heard the voice of Madame up ahead and hurried to make it back to her courtyard before the woman could see it was empty. She passed by the corner at the same time a man stepped into view, and she ran straight into his shoulder, tripped on the hem of her shift and crashed to the floor.

Madame rounded the corner and cried out, "I'm so sorry!" She fawned over the man, the elegant one from the stairs. Umbris swallowed, hoping most of her hair hid her face. Crying out to the stars above, she hoped Jolson wasn't with his friend.

The matron of the house turned to glare down at Umbris. "What are you doing, *girl*?"

She shrunk back, hoping it shadowed her face from what little light came in from the door. "I'm sorry, Madame."

"Get outside," she pointed to the door, her tone sharp. Another body stepped up next to the first man's.

Jolson. She didn't dare look at him, not saying a word as she hastened to her feet, she felt the eyes of both men upon her.

"I am deeply sorry," Madame was simpering, "Do believe me when I say it will not happen again. Allow me to have your coat washed and pressed, dear."

"That is quite all right," the charming voice, muffled once more, filled the hall, somehow easing the nerves of the matron. It had an odd effect upon Umbris as well. "Shall we?"

The man must have been speaking to Jolson, but there was a lack of response. Umbris had just reached the door when his voice called to her, the sound slightly muffled again. "Wait, girl!"

She froze, her hand holding onto the edge of the door. She was trembling inside as she turned back, keeping her head as low as she dared, praying her hair would be enough to hide her.

Jolson stepped forward, his boots shining until his hand curled and reached toward her chin.

"Sir, I have plenty of other girls if needed..." Madame rambled on, something about her only being a chambermaid.

He raised her chin until her eyes finally met his. He looked the same as he had on the road, dark hair parted down the center and tied back at the nape of his neck, though a scarf of sorts covered the bottom half of his face. "I thought so," there was a smile in his voice, though she couldn't see it.

"What is it?" his companion asked, a black scarf now covering the bottom half of his face as well.

"We might not need to send out a search party after all." Umbris's stomach dropped.

His companion stepped closer, his eyes moving from Jolson and back to Umbris again. He was much taller than she had realized. There was a decisive sense of force beneath his calmness, as though he could easily be roused to anger, to action.

"What do you mean?" All charm was gone.

Jolson was still holding her chin, turning her face back and forth as though looking for marks and bruises. "It seems fate is going to be kind to us. This is one of the women from the caravan."

"The caravan?" Madame asked, her voice breathless, "The one attacked by the Renegades. Stars! If I had known, I would have hawked her before every man who came through my door."

Jolson's companion turned to the woman, his eyes going a little tight along the sides. "Madame," he said, the sound at once charming and dangerous. "You never laid eyes upon this girl."

Jolson finally let go of her chin and Umbris ducked her head once more. She fought every urge not to retreat toward her courtyard. She felt the walls of a cage closing in on her.

"I'm sorry, sir," Madame shook her head quickly, not hearing the threat in the man's voice, or choosing to ignore it. "I cannot let a girl as well-known as her to leave my house. She is nearly exotic, used by Renegades. Many men will pay to conquer—"

Used by the Renegades? Umbris nearly lost the contents of her stomach at the thought. The Renegades had been nothing but kind to her.

The elegant man held up his hand. "I wasn't asking. You will say nothing about this." Something in his voice had changed. Gone was the charm and in its place was a man of authority. A quick flash of a gold ring before the matron was enough to make the older woman's eyes widen. She stared at them and swallowed, the aged skin along her throat bobbing. The large bauble along her chest rose and fell, casting an odd light on her haggard face.

"Yes, sir." She gave the man a small curtsy, though it seemed to pain her.

"For your trouble," he fished into his pocket and tossed a small bag to her. The woman's eyes gleamed as she looked at the contents. Umbris wondered how many sercs rested inside, how much was she even worth?

"Shall we?" the man asked, looking to Jolson. The commander nodded and wrapped his hand around Umbris's elbow, leading her toward the back door before she could think. In a rush, they were out the door and standing beside a carriage with dark wheels and a driver sitting in a hooded cloak.

Jolson hurried inside, soon disappearing into the dark but Umbris remained behind. Her pulse thrumming in her neck, every nerve on high alert.

"Come now," the dangerous man said, his voice charming again. He extended a long-fingered hand in invitation as the light from the moons reached them. Cast in the dim pink glow, his eyes were a deep blue with a hint of green, the depths of them drawing her in. "No need to worry," he said, and she had the sudden wondering if his lips were parted in that pleasant way she had seen before.

He took her hand in his, the skin as soft as she had suspected. He was certainly well-born and within high standing, if he was in correspondence with the Liege of Nex. Without a word, he urged her forward.

She felt as though her body moved without her command—her feet leading her into the covered carriage, to the back where she sat against velvet cushions. A musky scent of wood and pine filled her nostrils as she settled into the shadows, the elegant man taking his place beside her. His arm was warm against hers and she fought every urge to pull away.

Jolson, who had taken off the scarf, was watching from across the space, and hit the roof with his fist. The carriage gave a small jolt forward and they took off.

"How are you, Umbris?" he asked, his voice as gentle as she had remembered. Simply hearing it brought back the pain of the journey. She cast her eyes down to her wrists where her scars stared blatantly back up at her, the swirling 'R' of the Regent claiming her to be his property. She didn't hasten to give Jolson an answer.

"Umbris?" the man beside her said, his voice no longer muffled. The way he pronounced it was different than any other. He made the name seem prettier, more feminine by rolling the 'r' with his tongue and turning the 'i' into a sharp 'e' sound.

"Yes," Jolson answered for her. "She spent time in Fort Jontru."

"Then she might know her."

"Exactly," Jolson's buttons and eyes gleamed. Umbris had the sudden feeling she wasn't fully understanding what was transpiring between the men. "And she was in the tenth carriage."

The elegant man beside her smiled, the lines growing around his mouth again. He turned his full attention on Umbris, and she shrank into the cushions, well aware it was the most comfortable thing her body had ever touched.

"So tell me Umbris," the elegant man's eyes seemed to smile at her as he spoke gently, "did you know any of the women in your cell?"

"Some," she said softly, her voice sounding like gravel next to his refined speech. She didn't want to think of those days in Fort Jontru, or the other women in the carriage. She didn't want to think of Neen.

"What about a prisoner named Kata?" Her eyes widened before she could tamper her response. "I thought so," the elegant man said and gave a small chuckle.

She looked to Jolson, wondering how he knew so much of what had transpired in the fort. How did he know Kata's name? A lump formed in her throat, as memories she had long since buried began to creep up. She could hear the moans of the prisoners in the fort, of the women wailing each night as they huddled together for warmth. *Oh, Kata.*

She was certain she looked like a startled deer, a terrified child being caught with no way to escape. Casting her eyes between both men, she searched them, her mind whirling with what was to come.

Jolson gave her a small smile. "I'm sorry, where are my manners. Umbris," he cleared his throat, "might I introduce you to His Sire, the Regent."

If her heart had been hammering in her chest before, it was nothing compared to the way it thundered now. She glanced to her side and the man gave her another smile.

"Have you ever seen my home?" he asked, the elegant drawl passing through his perfect mouth. She shook her head quickly. "Then onward to *Chateau de Plaisance.*" He smiled and she turned away.

The royal palace? She was headed to the royal palace, sitting beside the Regent himself.

Her thoughts muddled, rolling over and over again until she could no longer think clearly. It was hot in the carriage, too hot, and as her stomach rumbled she realized she hadn't eaten all day. A cold sweat broke out across her brow and she wiped it away with trembling fingers.

She was only slightly aware of Jolson asking if she was all right before her vision turned to stars and she dipped forward into darkness.

CHAPTER 31

The steady tilt and lope of the horse beneath Willem had long since lulled him into a stupor. He knew he should be more aware of his surroundings, especially as they descended the winding path toward the town resting in the recesses of a flattened mountain ridge.

Pine trees reached high above their heads, the branches too far up to help cover the rain coming down at a slant. Willem tugged his coat tighter around his waist and pulled the hood farther over his head. What little sounds he could hear over the rain, were those of the hooves beneath him sliding in the mud. From so high up, it would be hard to discern anything other than their own movements.

Ansie rode in front of him on her mount, Larn leading the group. As they had begun their journey, Willem had left the navigation to Larn, having been no farther than a day's walk outside Mirtain. His senses had been on high alert for the first few days, until he settled into a general routine of continuous hours of travel, followed by a brief respite. They all took turns at watch, each of them forcing their eyes to remain open as the others slept. As Ansie said, fear was an excellent stimulant. After hearing the sharp barks of verrals in the mountains a few nights ago, they all remained vigilant.

They had long since used up the dried jerky Ansie had brought from the house. The crusty bread had lasted a day or so longer. In the midst of travel, they had added hunting to their list of daily duties. At least this was one area where Willem was proficient.

Up ahead, Ansie's back was hunched forward to shield herself from the wind and the rain. They had been traveling for hours in the torrential downpour, the water soaking through their clothes until they could feel the chill in their bones.

Larn raised his hand into the air, the fist halting both of them at once. Willem straightened searching for any sound or sight which would give away a foe. So far, they had only had two run-ins with Gallian soldiers. In both cases, they had been able to sneak around the soldiers before they were aware of their presence.

In part, the credit was due to Larn's horse, Tympmor. The creature had an odd way of responding and listening to Larn's commands. It seemed to understand the man, as though he spoke the same language as him, the horse's innate calm and quiet nature in times of extreme caution had a similar effect on the other mounts.

Willem shifted in his saddle, looking ahead. The rain was a dark grey curtain all around him, he felt the trails of the water rolling off his nose and along his cheeks. Ansie shifted in her saddle, her hair was a dark brown from the rain and clung to her pale skin. She was shivering, her small frame trembling each time the cold wind blew the rain into their faces.

Larn twisted to look back in their direction. His hand wrapped around the hilt of the sword on his waist. Willem itched to grab his own from his back.

"What is it?" he asked, barely speaking above the rain. It hadn't taken long for him to realize how keen Larn's hearing was.

"I thought I heard wolves," Larn held still, his eyes shifting from one side to the other. "I must be hearing things."

"Let's get to the village," Ansie breathed.

Willem nodded. There was no part of him that wished to face off against the wolves again. After his battle with Fergin's head wolf, Varne, he'd had enough of those creatures. At night when he wasn't on watch, he often had nightmares where red eyes watched him and snarls filled the air. Ansie, too, was having trouble sleeping.

"Agreed," Larn looked down the steep hill, along the winding path to the town resting in a nook along the mountain. He'd called the place Alesmann the other night. A trading center of sorts and a stopping point in the mountains when traveling to the southern lands.

"Stay close," Larn said, looking at them both in turn.

They moved through the rain with painstaking slowness, the last of the journey seeming to take hours as the trail dipped steeper. Their caution was of utmost importance, but left them drained when each step could lead to their deaths. As the hill continued to deepen in its plunge toward the valley below, the mounts' haunches began to slide. Willem leaned back in the saddle, hoping the horse's strength was enough to keep him steady.

When they reached the last of the pathway leading to Alesmann, Ansie's shoulders began to drop farther, the ground leveling out as well. Before them stretched an expanse of wooden cottages, their structures scattered about the flat stretch of land which served as a conjoining point between two mountains. Further down, off the edge of the cliff, was a valley, or so Larn said. Through the thick curtain of rain, it was impossible to see. The sheer drop of the cliff had Willem leaning back as though he could feel the ground slipping beneath him. Even the buildings had a similar sense of dread and leaned away from the edge, as though the valley beneath was trying to steal them away.

A sharp wind tugged on Willem's cloak, temporarily removing the hood from his head. He yanked it back in place, the sodden fabric causing as much damage as their surroundings.

"Whoa," he murmured to his horse, the brown steed skittering in the mud beneath him. Larn dismounted with a resulting slide. Ansie followed and landed with an ungraceful lurch, which turned into her stumbling and sliding in the mud until she landed with a solid splat on her backside. A curse came out of her mouth, which she soon covered. Larn offered his hand to her, a soft laugh coming from him that made her curse again.

"Can you tend to the horses?" Larn asked, and Willem nodded, grabbing the reins of all three tired steeds.

"We'll be in the Caw's Nest."

Again, Willem nodded and led the horses off, watching Ansie as she walked beside Larn into the nearby tavern. Stepping into the leaning shelter which served as a barn of sorts, Willem gave the stable hand a serc and hurried to remove the worn, wet saddles from their backs. The man grumbled as he hurried about his work, something about the fog and rain eating away at his weathered bones, but Willem didn't answer.

It seemed as though months had passed since the battle in Mirtain. Ever since leaving, he had felt at odds with everything around him. Ansie teased him, saying he was out of his element here, as much a stranger to the realm as she was. He was afraid to admit she was right.

Willem entered the Caw's Nest drawing as little notice as possible. The building was larger than any other standing in the village, a perfect place to stay inconspicuous for the night. A long room stretched before him, lined with poorly constructed tables and chairs. It was the sort of room that could host a grand gathering of drinkers and revelers, but tonight most of the tables stood empty.

At the end of the room was an enormous fire roaring in a stone hearth. The glow was nearly blinding with warmth after the damp dark he had been riding through for the past few hours.

Keeping his sodden hood over his head, he was well aware of the puddle he was making at the door. A barmaid of sorts was walking toward him when he spotted Larn's hulking form near the hearth. Why the man had chosen a seat in the most obvious of places, he couldn't say. At least Ansie appeared to be getting warmed by the breathing air of the flames. It was the first time they'd been under a roof since leaving Mirtain behind, and Willem intended to enjoy it.

He swung into a seat beside Ansie, feeling a little more comfortable to have only one table behind him and the front door in his sights. They had noticed all too quickly that hearing gave Larn a greater advantage than sight, and he often hid in the shadows where others weren't inclined to look.

"Here," Larn slid an ale toward Willem and he took a gulp without prodding—the tang warming his belly.

Ansie had tossed back her hood and strands of her hair were slowly turning back to the burnished amber as the heat of the fire dried them. The rest of her hair remained dark and damp against her shoulders—a few soft curls clinging to her cheeks. She was distracted for a moment, as she attempted to pull them from her face. Larn watched her with amusement.

"What news?" Willem asked, taking another gulp of the ale. This time it seemed to burn his throat on the way down, as a grumble rolled in his stomach. How soon they would get food, depended on how much the tavern cook appreciated the kill they had brought with them. Willem had tracked and hunted the stag yesterday, the freshly killed beast had come along for the ride with them as payment for wherever they might stay.

"We have lodging for the night," Larn said, rubbing his thumb up and down the handle of his mug, "and word may not have reached here yet, can't tell."

Willem grunted back in acknowledgment. Larn claimed that word of the battle in Mirtain would spread like wildfire through the realm. Then it would be time for villages to choose a side. It wouldn't be long before those who wanted to remain on the outside would have to choose. Not for the first time, Willem wondered if he had done the right thing in listening to the Renegades.

"You don't think they've heard?" Ansie asked, her hands wrapped around a steaming mug, her eyes on a group of men near the bar. They appeared to be hunters, traders maybe, by the looks of their slight builds and hastily patched clothing.

"Possibly," Larn nodded, his head still slightly cocked to the side. Willem wondered which conversation he was listening to.

Closer to the door were a couple of men, a few women with them, their table was loud with raucous laughter and the barmaid seemed to be serving them faster than others. One woman caught Willem's eye and gave him a wink, before turning back to the man beside her. His cheeks warmed as he studied the room, taking larger and larger gulps of the heartening ale.

"Are you really so cold?" Ansie asked, leaning closer to him.

"What?" He pulled his eyes away from the room and looked down at her.

"If you stare any harder, the room might burst into flame."

Larn audibly choked on his drink and pounded his chest. "She's got a point, you know?"

Willem shrugged, not allowing Larn to get to him. It hadn't taken him long to realize Larn and Ansie could match one another for wit, and they both knew it. Often times it seemed they were trying to outdo the other.

Just what he needed, another sharp-tongued, observant know-it-all.

He grumbled under his breath, nothing audible, and Larn gave another sly smile before taking a healthy swig. The door to the tavern opened and closed behind Larn's back, Willem had to lean at an angle to catch a glimpse of the three, hooded men who stepped into the door. He tensed immediately.

After years of tracking, he was able to discern people for who they really were in an instant, the slightest details giving away a person's true motives. One glance at the men's sodden clothes revealed a small hump across the breast where an emblem lay beneath their cloaks. If he had to guess, he feared it was the mark of the Nexen. There was a chance it was a trader's mark, something like the stars and half-moon of Sarnon's camp, but he doubted it.

"Easy," Larn said, turning back to the table, after casually glancing over his shoulder. The northern man called the barmaid over with a gesture of practiced normalcy. "Don't say anything out of place, talk amongst yourselves, I want to hear what they have to say." He smiled brightly, one side of his face visible to the three new strangers.

Willem tried to relax and took a swig of his drink. Beside him, Ansie kept her head down. After their first attempt in an obscure village to pass her off as a boy had failed before they even made it to the outer gate, they had all agreed it wasn't necessary. Willem wondered if the precaution would have helped them now.

They had yet to run directly into any soldiers, but if the men noticed she was a woman traveling with two men, there could be dire consequences. He had hoped being her guardian was enough, but outside of Lord Hernan's influence, the title would have no meaning.

"Safron told me something odd a while back," Ansie's voice reached him, her finger running along the rim of her mug. He watched as it trembled.

"Anything interesting?" he asked more for the sake of keeping up Larn's charade, though by the glances of the three strangers, Willem knew their chances of going unnoticed were already gone. The men were speaking to one another, their voices too low and lips hardly moving, but their eyes shifted in their direction more than once.

"She said there was a rumor going around about the Regent, something about him calling a meeting with all the Chroniclers in the realm. They came under the impression of advising the Regent, but instead, he threatened them and lined each man up against a wall. He then had every third man killed."

Willem shrugged, after years of hearing horrors and rumors about the Regent, this one didn't surprise him. If he knew anything about rumors, it was most likely less gruesome than it seemed, though the story had some merit.

"What?" Ansie asked, and he almost answered when he realized the question wasn't directed toward him.

Larn was staring at her, his eyes narrowed more than usual, there was an intensity in his voice which Willem hadn't heard since Mirtain. "What else do you know?"

"Nothing." Ansie shrugged, "What do you know?" Ansie had told Willem about Larn's other mission—his intent to find two Chroniclers who had gone missing. Was it possible these men had been summoned by the Regent that day?

The northern man shook his head. "Not here."

"Can they hear us?"

Willem glanced toward the men, they were still speaking to one another, their bodies hunched over their mugs. If Willem hadn't seen them arrive, he would've hardly noticed their presence.

"No," Larn shook his head, "But they're talking about us."

"Anything good?" Willem asked.

"They didn't compliment me on my looks," Larn shifted, "which is rather rude. I was born this way for a reason. Might as well take notice."

Willem shook his head. If there was one thing predictable about Larn, it was his way of behaving as though he hadn't a care in the world. A façade held to hide his true purpose.

"We should move on," Willem grumbled, Ansie shifted beneath her slowly drying clothes.

"No," Larn said.

"There's no sense pushing our luck."

"The horses need rest, and so do you," Larn said, adamantly. Willem understood the words for what Larn really meant. There was no part of Larn which wished to get back on his horse, but he could if needed. Ansie, however, was fading fast. She would never admit it to either of them, but she was worn and weary, the past days of endless travel stealing her energy.

"I still think we should leave," Willem pushed, knowing she would be able to push through. She always had. Lard didn't realize how strong she was. His worries left a bitter taste in his mouth. Hadn't Larn said he heard wolves?

"So do I," Ansie said glancing between the both of them. "Why stay?"

Larn sighed, his front of calm cracking for only a moment. "We have to remain here, until tomorrow." Ansie shifted beside him. "I have my reasons."

"Oh, as long as you have your reasons," Ansie rolled her eyes. "By all means keep them to yourself, it's not as if we aren't reb—ow!" she exclaimed after a well-placed kick from Larn jolted their table. She leaned down to rub at her shin.

Larn eyed them, his eyes flicking quickly back and forth. All signs of the carefree man had disappeared in an instant, replaced by the one they had glimpsed in Mirtain, the one who was Head of Intelligence for the Renegades.

"I'm waiting to make contact with someone." He said the words off hand as though they were of little importance, but it was more than Willem wanted to fully comprehend. Sometimes, it was easier to believe what they were doing would only affect them. He didn't like to dwell on the powers working throughout the realm. The arm of the Regent, the force of the Renegades, and the strange spirit the Praelia claimed lived among them. Yes, he knew about that spirit...but he refused to believe in it.

"Who are you meeting with?" Willem asked, making sure to keep the three strangers in sight. They remained at the bar.

"One of my men," Larn shrugged. "I'm waiting to find out if he was able to get a contact inside Bastion Nocta."

Ansie inhaled sharply, as Willem stared at the man before him. To think Larn was actually playing so dangerously close to the Regent was hard to understand. He was certain the stories of spies and what the Regent did to them was not unknown to Larn. The horrors of tortured remains and dismembered bodies had left him with nightmares as a child. He pushed the thoughts aside, knowing what they were doing now would merit the same death.

"What do you know about these missing Chroniclers?" Willem asked, and Larn leaned back. If anyone chanced to glance at their table, they would see a casual traveler sitting upon a bench with two companions. But the disguise only went so far, from the glances of the strangers at the bar.

"I said not now."

"You've said that a lot. I think it's about time we get some answers," Willem spoke quickly and Ansie nodded beside him. He could only wonder how rampant her avid imagination was running, as they waited.

"Fine," Larn's short jagged fingernails picked at a snag on the wooden table. "Your friend was right. The Regent called the Chroniclers to a meeting in Wollmorn under the pretense of needing advice and instruction. He focused on the Praelia and found our two missing Chroniclers to be well versed in their understanding of the Animle. They escaped before he could question them further, or about the Rising. The rest he had killed, and now there is a decree that anyone harboring a member of the Praelia is to turn them in."

"That's horrible," Ansie breathed.

"As I told you, I was actually looking for them before Calig's, I mean Jethron's, message reached me about the *simian*." He looked pointedly at Willem.

"Where do you think they are?" Willem asked.

"Ahh, that," Larn nodded, looking over Ansie's shoulder and into the flames. "No idea. My guess is they're smarter than the rest of us. They'd have to be to stay out of all of this, right?" Larn took a deep breath and ran a hand through his hair. "We need them, need their information, on our side. I spent months tracking them, but I haven't heard anything until now." He waved a hand. "But now, you know the story too." The dark pupils shifted to Ansie.

Ansie shrugged, "I don't know where Safron heard it."

"I do," Willem said, the thought coming to him. "It's most likely from the Black Market, the traders, well one in particular. Chet often visited him too."

"It's a shame we didn't get a chance to speak with him." Larn pursed his lips, seemingly distracted in thought. "Any chance you might know where this man is?"

He shook his head. "I never really asked questions. I simply traded for the grinspur horns and left."

"Grinspurs?" It was the first time Larn looked truly surprised. "You've seen them?"

"He's killed three of them," Ansie mentioned offhand, a mischievous smile reaching her lips.

Willem shifted when Larn looked his way. He had the sudden feeling Larn was sizing him up, just like the men in Mirtain often had. Seeing a grinspur and killing one were two entirely different things; to have killed three was unheard of. Willem was the stuff of legends, and it never sat well with him.

"Well, that is very—" Larn's face hardened in an instant and there was only the slightest hitch in his speech, "—impressive. They're coming over here, keep talking."

Willem's pulse quickened in his throat, even as he let a smile pass over his lips. Sure enough, the men were pushing away from the bar, moving with practiced ease.

"That late?" Larn asked, continuing a conversation no one was having. "I think that might work, I know the horses are tired. But shouldn't we leave earlier in the morning?"

The strangers were upon them as Willem answered. "Most likely."

"Can we help you?" Larn looked up, the three men taking in all of them at once. Willem couldn't help noticing how they stared at Larn, the northern man's appearance proclaiming him as something foreign. He could see the wariness in their eyes as they watched Larn—*maeri* might as well have fallen from their lips. Willem wondered if Larn even noticed.

"Not at all," the first one grumbled, his gaze lingering on Ansie. Willem forced himself to remain calm. They were all in danger if they realized Ansie was unwed. He would claim her to be his wife if he had papers to prove it. Any traveler had to carry proof of their marriage with them, and it seemed smarter to risk being seen than to present a fraud license. Only the rarest paper was used for marriage licenses, and to present a fraud was certain death. As Larn had said once, they simply had to keep their heads low and hope no one asked.

"Just looking for a place to sit," the man grumbled.

There were many empty tables around them, but Larn waved a hand and slid down along the bench, the lines around his eyes crinkling with a form of amusement drawn from somewhere. Ansie tensed beside Willem as she scooted closer to him.

All three men seated themselves around the table, two on Larn's bench, with the man who spoke first drawing up a chair from a nearby table to sit at the end. All three men were bearded, the two along Larn's side of the table appearing about the same age as Willem, but it was the speaker who had him on edge. A dark beard grazed the edges of his chin, hair surrounding his mouth in a thin perfect line. He had precision with a blade.

Willem shifted and took another gulp of his ale.

"Whereabouts are you boys from?" Larn asked, seemingly casual.

"The south. So many interesting stories are coming out of that part of the realm." The man in the chair had an easy smile, the words laced with meaning. "Where do you hail from?"

"Is that really a question?" Larn chuckled, pointing toward his face. The others began to laugh with him, the sound stinted and tight. Willem's stomach clenched.

They know, the warning ran through his mind. Not just about Ansie, but about Mirtain, the *simian*, everything.

"A Maereo," the dark-eyed man wagged his finger. "I told my companions you were one of them, but they didn't want to believe me. That's why I simply had to introduce myself and prove the truth." He spread his hands in simplicity.

"Of course," Larn smiled brightly and waved for more ale. When the barmaid set it down on the table, Larn swayed a bit on the bench. "What else could I be? From Gallia? Or the woodlands? Or the Plenus mountians?" That gave the strangers a chuckle—most of the people from the southeast mountains were pale skinned.

Larn tapped the nearest one on the shoulder, turning to them more fully. "Go ahead, ask away." His gestures were broader, less inhibited, than before.

"No questions?" Larn asked, looking at each man in turn. "All right then, I'm from the Beastly Mountains, and it's true what they say, we're dangerous." He let go a maniacal smile and then took a swig of his ale. "I was just telling my friend here how hard it is to travel in these southern lands. We hate this star-forsaken rain."

Ansie nodded and huddled around her steaming cup of cider.

"You don't find it too warm here?" The man spread his hands again, flashing a too-bright smile.

"Not when it's wet," Larn laughed, and the strangers joined him.

"How long have you been traveling?"

Larn pursed his lips looking at both of them in question, "What's it been, two, three months?"

Willem nodded, lying right along with him.

"How nice," the soldier said, his voice dipping lower. He inhaled deeply through his nose. "Then you must have heard the stories?"

"Stories?" Larn leaned in, glancing over his shoulder, as though checking to make sure no one was eavesdropping.

"Oh, you know," the stranger shrugged, leaning back and crossing his legs. The barmaid placed three mugs of ale on the table. "Stories of strange creatures, and people," he glanced at Willem and Ansie, "about the land."

"Really?" Larn appeared vastly interested. "This is the first place we've stopped in nearly a week, we've heard nothing."

The man flashed a dim smile, his eyes going hard. "I wouldn't think so. The Regent is trying to keep it all hushed up."

"But you won't."

"What's the Regent to me?" The man shrugged, his smile broadening.

"You dare to say such things?" Larn swayed on the bench. If Willem didn't know better he would think him severely intoxicated. "The Regent is, well, everything."

"Really?" the man shrugged again, leaning forward to grasp his mug. "I would think a *maeri* wouldn't agree." The slur hung in the silence between them, Ansie's hand tightened around her mug, and Willem shifted uncomfortably at the word. It meant damned, a creature that was not quite human. And there were all kinds of horrible stories that proved the Maereo ways were less than pleasant.

"But I'm not in the north, am I?" Larn asked and narrowed his angled eyes, the slur seeming to have no effect on him as he broke into a cackling laugh. The men joined in.

"You have me there, we're certainly not in the north."

"No sir," Larn took a swig of his drink, slamming it back down on the table so the remnants spilled.

A short glance between the soldier and one of his men drew Willem's attention. In the woods, he had a way of knowing, an almost instinct when it came to hunting. A man had to take his time, become one with the forest around him, follow the trail, watch for drifts in the wind and dips in the ground, and slowly, ever so slowly, he would spot his prey, watch his every move, his every breath, his every flinch, and then move in for the kill.

As he eyed the stranger at the end of the table, Willem slid his hand up his leg to where his dagger rested in his belt. The sword across his back could be drawn in a mere moment's notice if needed, but he would have to knock Ansie out of the way first.

"Now," the stranger leaned forward and flashed a grim smile, all pretense shattered. "I know what you really are, I know what has been done and where we're going to take you." The gaze flashed to each of them in turn, the perfectly trimmed beard seeming to make the lines of his face all the harsher. The man beside Larn shifted, his hand reaching toward his belt. Willem had the distinct feeling more than one blade was drawn beneath the table.

Larn smiled, licking his bottom lip, the drunken disguise slipping away like the smoke of an extinguished campfire. "What is it you suggest then, Captain?" The soldier's eyes widened slightly. "Perhaps, you shouldn't think you're the only one watching. I know what lies beneath your cloak," Larn's right hand appeared on the table, a dagger pointing toward the stranger's breast. "The mark of a Nexen is an important one to carry. We heard your wolves as we were coming in."

All three men straightened, their postures going stiff like ice over a suddenly stilled creek. Dark eyes shifted, and knuckles tightened. Willem adjusted the dagger in his left hand, ready to throw Ansie out of the way on a moment's notice.

"I know things, too," an accent laced the Nexen's words, a harsh elegance that seemed used to speaking in the higher rungs of society. "This girl cannot be of marrying age, and there are stories of a hunter from the southernlands." He glared at Willem.

"Stories," Larn shook his head, "what is it with this realm and stories? I deal in facts." He leaned in closer, his voice dipping deeper by the moment. "The fact is you're outnumbered, this village will side with us in an instant. What your dull ears cannot hear is what's happening behind us. Do you see those men?" As one they all seemed to glance at the table near the front door, where the men were laughing and yelling loudly at one another. "Do you see how their laughter is forced, do you hear the way they talk in code?"

The dark eyes narrowed as though the captain was trying to make out what the men were really saying.

"No, our story isn't one you'll get to hear. " Larn said, his voice no louder than a whisper—the threat imminent. "Don't you find it odd that your wolves have stopped howling?" All three men shifted. "We know where you left them, in the outcropping at the edge of the mountain. You followed our scent here, but didn't want to raise suspicion."

The dark-haired stranger appeared unconcerned and Willem gripped the dagger in his hand, his damp palm nearly slipping on the hilt.

"So you have another man? It's of no concern." The flickering flames cast the Nexen captain's face in shadow.

"I would at least check," Larn suggested, keeping the tip of the dagger pointed toward the end of the table. "It would be a shame to return to Bastion Nocta without your wolves. What might the Regent think? Or the Liege?"

"A shame I'll have to endure it seems," the man shrugged. "So tell me, since you're so fond of facts. What happens next?"

Breath held—Willem waited. No one moved.

"Two things, two paths which can be taken, but they all depend on you. One," Larn held up a finger, "you can take your men and leave this tavern and these people behind and go see if your wolves have been slaughtered as I lay claim. Or two," the other finger joined the first, "we can test your skills with a blade."

The man tilted back, his arrogance disconcerting. "Neither are good choices," the man rubbed his chin. "Might I suggest a third option?"

Larn waved a hand for him to continue.

"I have more men with the wolves, and more surrounding this entire tavern at this moment. You think you're the only one who can play a game, well I have been at this longer than you, and here's what will happen. My men will take you, and you, and you into custody." He turned to each of them, his eyes roving over their faces as though memorizing them. "We'll visit Bastion Nocta and after you have met with His Sire, the Regent, you will be publicly tortured, hanged, and dismembered."

Larn gave a snort of laughter and turned to Willem and Ansie, there was something in his eyes which Willem had never seen before—a beckoning and warning for what was about to come. "I don't think I like that option. I've always been quite fond of my neck."

Larn laughed again and the captain flashed a smile before turning serious once more. The silence pulled between them like a rope tightening around a prisoner's neck. Something had to be done. Willem chose his words carefully, ready to displace the anger in the soldier's eyes.

"I'm a hunter," Willem said softly, all but condemning himself. All eyes turned to him—this was where he struggled. Words were lost to him in moments of negotiation. Lord Hernan had always played him for a simpleton. But Ansie had always believed Willem had a way with words, especially when it came to stories. Kata had too.

"Do you know how to hunt?" Willem asked, and the soldiers blinked in astonishment.

The captain nodded, amused. Willem nudged Ansie's leg, beckoning her help.

"Then you'll know the intricacies of tracking, of waiting for the opportune time, drawing it out until the moment appears. The small blink of an eye, the twitch of muscle before the beast takes off into the night."

"Of course," the captain threw back the rest of his drink. "Distraction, which leads to death."

As though in slow motion, Ansie lifted her drink to her lips. As soon as the liquid touched her mouth, she spit, and splashed the rest of the drink into the captain's face. Larn had both of the man's companions on the ground as Willem launched himself at the sputtering captain. His dagger was pressed against the Nexen's throat as the tavern fell silent.

"Take it outside." The tavern owner pulled a crossbow from beneath the bar. "There'll be no fights in here." He had a deep booming voice, like thunder.

"Well said," Larn jumped to his feet, leaving the two men on the ground looking up at him. One was unconscious.

The captain beneath Willem was still frozen, his hands up in surrender.

"These men are from Bastion Nocta after all," Larn said and grumbles rolled through the tavern. It seemed Larn had picked the right village.

The tavern owner slipped out from behind the bar and walked toward them. He flicked open one of the Nexen's cloaks with his crossbow, revealing the emblem underneath. "You're the slime that tore down my sister's house. Get out of my tavern."

The captain sputtered beneath Willem but stopped as the blade pressed harder against the man's throat.

"Get out," the tavern owner bellowed, the muscles in his neck straining.

Willem shoved off the captain, letting him linger on the floor a moment longer. The soldiers rose to their feet with a new scene around them. Every man and woman in the bar had a weapon of some sort pointed in their direction.

"Let them go," Larn said softly, though his voice seemed to echo in the now silent room. "Send them back to the Regent so he'll know we no longer care for his reign."

A cheer went up as soon as the men scooped their companion off the floor and left the tavern, four others escorting them out to their horses. Willem's heart was only settling in his chest when the tavern owner turned to them.

"You have a room for the night?"

"Yes," Willem said, quickly.

"I'll take it you need two. A separate one for the girl?" The tavern owner rubbed a large hand over his bald head. A young boy, long in the leg, came up beside him. Standing next to the tavern owner, Willem noted the similarities in the way they stood, feet braced apart and their lean arms hanging well past their hips. Father and son, no doubt.

"One will do," Willem said.

"You'll take two." The man spoke without any room for rebuttal. "I might not stand for what the Regent is, but I'll be damned if a patrol comes by and a girl is found in a room with two men. It'll not be on my head. It's been a year since a girl and boy were taken from Alesmann under *vox prima*, but I'll not soon forget it. Two rooms it is."

Willem nearly grumbled, wondering if the man realized what he'd just done was more of a sentence of death.

"We'll take them," Larn assured the owner before anything more could be said. The owner told his son to show them to their rooms.

As they were gathering their things and heading up the creaking stairs, Willem whispered to Larn. "About the allegiance of this town...?"

"Was it a guess?" Larn quirked an eyebrow at him as Ansie passed by and into the bedroom furthest from the stairs. "Yes, yes it was."

CHAPTER 32

The rain became a cloak around Larn as he stood just outside the outcropping of trees leaning away from the cliff face. Somewhere in the night was Pike.

A yawn passed through Larn's lips, even as the water trickled down the back of his shirt making him shiver. The last thing he had wanted to do after dealing with the Nexen was return to the rain. Tympmor snickered, his head poking out from the small window in the decrepit barn. Larn gave the steed a rub along his leathery nose.

"Shouldn't be too much longer," Larn muttered.

Peeking around the barn, he caught a glimpse of the candlelight flickering in the tavern. The fireplace had long since been extinguished and only those who were too intoxicated to return to their homes or rooms remained at the bar.

He had, after leaving Willem and Ansie upstairs, thought about staying within the tavern, but the owner's request for safety was something Larn wouldn't deny. After all, it was only by luck he was able to guess the villagers' allegiance. If the people had swayed in the other direction, Pike would have arrived to see three bodies strung from a tree branch on the outskirts of Alesmann.

A sharp wind whipped over the edge of the cliff and pushed the already wet fabric of his shirt against his body—he inhaled sharply, the gentle downpour turning to sharp pelting. Not for the first time, Larn wondered where the Nexen had run off to. He hadn't been lying when he told them their wolves were most likely dead. He hadn't heard a howl since they'd arrived. It was because of their silence, he assumed Pike was nearby.

Upon departing, he made plans to meet Pike at the Caw's Nest. Or at least in the general vicinity of it.

A crack in the woods had him turning toward the sound, Tympmor's muzzle nudging his shoulder. Another snap and he smiled, Pike never was one to mask his approach. Try as he might.

"You made it?" Larn smiled.

Out of the shadows stepped the hulking form of Pike, the pale hair hanging in lank strips along the sides of his face and water dripping off his bulbous nose. He swayed forward, the broad sword glinting over his back and raised his hand in greeting.

"How'd it go?" Larn asked, hoping against hope.

He needed eyes inside Bastion Nocta, he needed Umbris there more than he cared to admit. Looking as he did, Larn needed others who were more inconspicuous to get information. He had weaknesses in his chain of contacts, but he wasn't sure where the information was slipping out. But he knew with Umbris, he wouldn't have to worry. One look, in those sapphire eyes of hers, told him once her allegiance was won, it was won for good.

Pike grumbled, rubbing a hand along his scruff-covered chin. "She's in."

"Really?"

"Yes."

"How close to the palace?"

Pike made a face. "She isn't exactly where we hoped she'd be."

"How so?" Larn crossed his arms, some of the excitement dissipating. Sometimes it took Pike ages to spit out what needed to be said.

"She started working at a brothel, but she's a—" he paused for breath, "—a scullery maid now."

"Oh," was all Larn could say. All the plans he had made over the past weeks began to fade. "But she can still pick up on some things, hear things, can't she?"

"Not really. When I last saw her, she didn't have any information."

He wanted to curse, needed to. Umbris had been a major focal point for the changes he wanted to make. The information she might have been able to procure would have been invaluable. It was useless hoping for anything else, and...

He stopped his thoughts from going any further; his sudden realization of what he was doing almost making him sick.

When he had seen those women and met Umbris, he had been torn apart by their fate. Umbris had known there was nothing else for her in this land but working in a brothel. She had been terrified, that he had been sure of, so how could he deny her one little glimpse of being something other than what the realm had made her? He'd let his own worries overcome the reality she lived in. He was no better than the Regent himself.

"Was she happy?" he asked, the guilt taking over for not having wondered sooner.

"She talked more," Pike grumbled.

Then no, Larn thought. But how could he expect her to be happy when her family and life had been torn away from her. Not for the first time, he wondered where she was from.

"When will you see her again?"

"In a few weeks," Pike focused on the mud coating his boots, the rain dripping down the side of his face making him appear all the more tired, pale. "She wants to help."

Larn nodded, knowing anything he might say at this moment he would regret. His need for information was tantamount, especially in light of what he heard in the tavern earlier. Ansie and Willem hadn't realized what those men and women had been saying. A traveling lord and his entire household were murdered in their beds, blood written on the walls saying "Remember Abattron." It was enough to make anyone think.

Abattron had been a peaceful village on the edge of the Plenus Mountians. They were a quiet people and refused to pick a side when the Gallians began their conquest of Anglas. For hundreds of years, the people of the Plenus

Mountains welcomed fleeing Anglans into their mountain lands, but that was before they offered shelter to a man who claimed to be descended from the Animle. With him was an ancient winged-beast who breathed fire. One night, death struck Abattron. Every living creature was slaughtered, no one escaped, but the fire-breathing beast had disappeared. All that was left of the village was the charred remains of some Nexen soldiers and their wolves, the rest were dead. Men, women, children, both rich and poor were all slaughtered by either blade or teeth.

And now, someone had thought to strike back against the Nexen for what they had done. Was it possible someone had escaped from Abattron? And why strike now? Larn couldn't remember exactly when it had happened, but it was at least over ten years since Abattron had fallen—probably closer to eleven, if he was thinking straight.

Running a hand through his wet hair, he knew he would have to look elsewhere to find someone to get closer to the palace. If only he could know what the Regent thought of all this.

"Next time, tell her to keep her eyes and ears open as much as she can."

Pike nodded. "I think she already is."

"Good," Larn said and sighed. "If she gives you anything, take it to Girshon. No telling where I'll be in the coming months. I left Heben in charge."

"Fair enough," the man said and without another word stepped into the shadows once more. "There are Nexen nearby, and we passed a Gallian patrol headed this way."

Larn nodded. "Thanks for getting rid of their wolves."

Though he couldn't quite see Pike's smile, he could feel it in the darkness as the man slipped into the night. Larn followed the sounds of him traipsing through the mud to where the horses and Renegades awaited. All too soon, the only sound was the rain splattering on the rooftop behind him.

Tympmor nudged Larn's shoulder and he rubbed the side of the black steed's face. "I know, I know. I was hoping for more too." The large head shook back and forth.

With a final pat, he left the barn and returned to the tavern, his thoughts on Umbris. He only hoped she would overhear something, see something. At least, he knew her life was better than it would have been.

Climbing the stairs, he found Willem waiting for him on the second landing of the tavern.

"What is it?" Larn asked, his mind elsewhere.

"The owner, he got me thinking." Willem took a deep breath. "I've been wondering how we should explain Ansie's presence. I think it's best if we have a story."

"We already do, she's your ward."

"But that won't be enough, not out here."

"It's fine," Larn shrugged and moved to step around him toward the room he would be sharing with Willem. He pushed open the door, glancing back toward the stairs. Who knew how far their voices carried. "In here."

Willem followed him inside, though he stood annoyingly close to the door.

"I don't think it's that big an issue. We'll hardly come within reach of any villages on our way to the Beastly Mountains, and when we do, we can only send one of us into town to get provisions. As far as Ansie is concerned, she can stay hidden." He removed his jacket, the sodden fabric hitting the floor with a wet thump.

Distracted, he poured himself a glass of whatever offered drink sat on the table just inside the door. It had quite a bite to it, making him suck in a harsh breath as the liquid burned his throat. He wondered if the drink would be enough to stop his mind from swirling through the implication of those words, *Remember Abattron.*

"I still don't feel right about it," Willem said from somewhere behind him.

"About what?"

"Ansie. Out here, her being my ward won't mean anything."

"So say she's your sister." Of all Larn's problems, this wasn't one he really felt needed solving.

"That won't work," Willem was shaking his head, arms crossed over his chest, the hilt of his sword still poking over his shoulder. It suddenly occurred to Larn that Willem hadn't rested since leaving them both in their rooms hours ago.

"Why not?"

"You saw those soldiers. They knew who we were. Not to mention after you left some of the other villagers were talking about Mirtain and what happened there. And if they know that, they might know Ansie isn't related to either one of us."

"It's not going to make much of a difference either way. I told you we can protect her, and we will." Larn waved a hand, he was hearing more than he wanted to in the hunter's words. It was admirable the care and concern Willem had for his ward, he was a brother to her.

Willem took a deep breath. "I just, I have a weird feeling about this place."

"That's because you've never been anywhere," Larn threw back another glass of the burning drink, the bite seeming to warm his stomach and take away the hunger.

"Is that why you're refusing to get any sleep?"

"Maybe," Willem said, looking toward the window. "I told her to bolt the door, but I'm not above sleeping outside her door."

"Why not just sleep in her room?"

"The owner would know, you can see her door from the balcony."

He had a point there, Larn ran a hand through his hair. "The window?" he asked, it would be simple to climb outside and slide into her room.

"Already tried, the lock is jammed."

"We'll just have to leave it. Tomorrow, we'll leave this place and not look back."

"Agreed," Willem grumbled and poured himself a glass, dark circles dipping beneath his eyes.

"I don't think those Nexen will return."

"You can't know that, and your hearing is impaired with this rain."

Larn had to admit Willem had a point. "True," he grumbled.

"I don't think they are going to tuck their tails and run."

"Nice choice of words," Larn quirked an eyebrow at him. "Then sleep in the hall if that makes you feel better."

Willem sighed, "It's more than that. I don't trust any of them."

"Really? I thought you were standing by that door because it was comfortable." There was more bite in Larn's tone than was necessary—Willem nearly glared at him.

"If you cared about her at all, you'd be worried too."

"Worried?" Larn shook his head, stooping to pick up his jacket again. "Concerned, maybe, but not worried. I never worry."

"What are you doing?"

Larn sighed. "The way I see it, I have better hearing than you do, regardless of the rain. If you stay inside, you can protect her from anyone in here, and if I'm outside, I can warn you of anyone coming."

"I can go outside," Willem said, and Larn appreciated the offer though he knew it was half-hearted.

"No sense in both of us being miserable." He shrugged the already-wet coat over his shoulders and took a deep breath, preparing himself for the onslaught of rain once more.

"Are you going to sleep on the roof?"

"We both need sleep and the way I see it, this solves our problem."

Willem nodded, "Let me know if you need to switch."

"No need. It's not my first time sleeping on a roof."

"In the rain?"

"Oh, this?" Larn waved a hand as he opened the window and the wind whipped inside, chilling him. "Remind me to tell you what sleet feels like."

"All the same, wake me if you need to switch."

"Noted," Larn said and climbed out the window into the pounding rain. Was it possible the skies were dumping even more upon the land than before? He supposed it was. Sometimes being wet made him wonder if he would ever know what it was like to be dry again.

The shingles were a little slippery beneath his hands and boot-covered feet, as he moved into position above Ansie's room. His still-wet hood clung to his head, helping to shield the rain from his face. Lacing his fingers around his knees, he became one with the wind and water, allowing it to pull at him until there was nothing. He could make out the far off sounds of herds of deer stirring in the sparse trees along the mountainside, but nothing moved toward them. They were alone here.

Alone. It was a word he knew all too well and cherished above any other.

For how many years had he been fighting toward his own freedom? He'd worked harder than any of the children training in Sicarmman. He'd sacrificed all of himself to become the best warrior he could be. And for what? For Girshon to share his secret with him—the secret of the Renegades. Even then, the words had stirred a picture of freedom. He'd joined without so much as a hesitation.

Doubt filled Larn, as it always did when he thought about the task ahead. It wasn't the process he feared, but what came after. People had a way of letting him down, their humanity getting the better of them.

There has to be something more than this, he thought.

The wind stirred around him as chills ran up his arms and down his spine. He knew the stories of the Animle and what they represented. Their power was pulled from a spirit, some force that had long been forgotten, or so the realm was told.

Shivering, he cast the thought aside. Maybe if he ever got the chance to talk to the two missing Chroniclers, he could ask them what it all meant. But he doubted they would ever be found. Just like the fire-breathing beast in Abattron, all that was mythical had disappeared into the night.

Shrugging deeper into his coat, Larn became a small lump on the roof, and as he slipped into long-awaited sleep, he had the sudden feeling he wasn't alone. Something was stirring inside him.

But being alone was all he had ever wanted, and he would keep it that way.

CHAPTER 33

Ansie was drifting, lost somewhere between unconsciousness and awake. Her dreams dwindled on a string of eternity, twisting and morphing into shapes of her past. Skurn danced before her, his emerald gaze seeing the deepest parts of her, until she couldn't breathe, couldn't think. She reached for him and his hands tightened around her waist, pulling her with him over the cobblestones. There was a distance between them, but a longing for what had been and what she still hoped would be. He leaned in toward her, his eyes closing, their breath mingling…

A soft bump sounded behind her head, startling her awake—visions of Skurn and Mirtain disappeared. She searched the room, the shadows seeming to stretch as though teasing her imagination. Chills ran up her arms. Something wasn't right.

She scrambled beneath the ragged blanket, reaching for the dagger beneath her pillow when a coarse hand wrapped around her wrist. She froze, a scream building in her throat, but he slammed his hand down onto her mouth.

"Don't even think about it." She recognized the voice of the Nexen soldier who'd threatened them downstairs. "Your man killed my wolves. Now, who are you? And I want a real answer this time."

He raised a dagger into the air and she struggled against his hand, as he pushed her whole body into the hard mattress. She froze beneath him as he leaned down, his face slowly coming into sight. The stench of ale and wet dirt nearly overwhelmed her. His skin was clammy and cold, she tried to roll away from him when he brought the knife closer. The dagger she had been reaching for fell off the back end of the mattress.

He shook his head back and forth slowly, taunting her. When she bit his hand, he drew back for a fraction of a second and she aimed a kick at his groin. The man cursed under his breath and grabbed for her as she tried to scramble off the bed and toward the door.

A heavy thump and crash sounded on the other side of the wall. *Willem!*

She kicked again and was rewarded with a gust of hot air blown in her face, as the man struggled to maintain control. With all that she was, she squirmed, slapped, and kicked, his hand continuing to cover her mouth until the blade was pressed against her throat.

She stilled in an instant. The blood in her veins going cold.

A crash came from the other room and she nearly screamed when the window near her bed shattered into a million pieces, a new body flying into the darkness. The shadowed figure's dagger was drawn, a dark hood still covering his head.

Her attacker hardly had time to register the shadow before he was knocked aside by the new arrival and thrown to the floor. The shadow's hood fell back, Larn standing in its place. He pulled another dagger from his belt as the soldier leapt to his feet. The vile man was dressed in new clothes, disguising him as a villager.

They danced around one another for only a moment before Larn dipped beneath a blow and shoved his dagger into the soldier's gut. His body crumpled forward, blood spilling onto the scratched, worn floor.

Ansie wasn't sure if she screamed, but she was aware of sliding off the bed and onto the floor. Her hands were shaking as she cast her mind about, trying to make sense of the sights before her. She hoped, crying out to the stars above, that it was all just a nightmare, but as she stared into the whites of the dead man's eyes, she knew it wasn't.

She was visibly trembling when Larn knelt down to her level.

"Willem," was all she could say, and he nodded, about to leave her when Willem burst through her door, sword drawn. She watched him take one look at the dead man on the floor, his eyes growing wider by the second.

"Is she?" he whispered.

Larn looked her over, "Are you hurt?" She shook her head. "She's fine," Larn breathed, still kneeling before her. From this close, she could see how smooth his skin was, how easily his mouth moved when he spoke.

"What happened?" Willem asked, as he continued to stare at the dead Nexen soldier on the floor.

"I fell asleep," Larn said, his voice low and nearly a growl—traces of guilt lining his words.

"Me too."

Larn nodded. "Did you…?" He waved a hand in the direction of the other room.

"Yes," Willem nodded and pushed the door to a close. "Both of them." Ansie couldn't help staring at the blood on his sword.

"Two?"

"I think they thought both of us were in there."

"Disguised?"

"Yes," Willem admitted. "I didn't recognize them until after."

"Good," Larn nodded again, turning to look at her more fully. He dipped his head, the dark, angled eyes pulling at her. "You're sure you're all right?"

It took a moment for Ansie to find her own voice. "I—I think so."

"Good," he said once more and gave her a small smile. "Let's get your things, and get—" he broke off, looking to Willem.

"What is it?"

"The patrol." He spit a foul word. "They rolled in about an hour ago. I heard them, but didn't think they would know about us."

"Gallian soldiers," Willem muttered under his breath, his jaw tightening.

Larn ran a hand through his damp hair. The rain must have stopped, though how he had come in through the window she couldn't understand. Unless he had already been on the roof. Her thoughts distracted her as Larn searched frantically around them. "They're coming."

Willem cursed, his hands twitching at his sides. "What do we do? There's no way we can get out of this," he whispered quickly. Killing one man was enough to see them all hanged, killing three, well, they were done for.

Larn stared at the door, eyes wide. He pursed his lips in deliberation. "I have an idea. It's a long shot, and neither of you will like it." Ansie nodded. "Open the door, and keep your sword drawn."

Willem did both as silently as possible and stood staring down at them. Larn leaned in closer to Ansie, his hands wrapping around her waist and drawing her to him. Though his hands were damp from the rain, they were warm, as warm as if he had offered them to her after resting by the fire. She wondered how that was even possible.

Course yelling sounded outside the tavern and solid banging on the front door seemed to shake the rafters. There were shouted curses from the other overnight travelers waking in their rooms.

"They set us up," Willem said, doing little to soothe her nerves. She had just come to the same conclusion. How else would the patrol have known to come to the tavern so late, and at just the right moment?

Larn's threats had not been taken lightly. And the now dead capatain had said something about his wolves.

The thumping of feet and the loud voice of the tavern owner began to move toward the stairs, echoing along the hallway.

"Hold," Larn said, glancing toward Willem, and then he leaned in closer to her. "Keep as quiet as you can. Follow my lead. We have to be close. Come here."

He pulled her further into his arms and she leaned into his chest. She had the slightest recognition of the faint scent of hay and rain fresh upon his skin before the men burst through the door.

She jolted.

The shouts and exclamations seemed to ring about the room as they took in the sight of the dead man on the floor. Four Gallians, armed to the teeth in weapons, stood near the door with the tavern owner in their midst. Even more threatening, were the looks they shot in Larn's direction, seeing him huddled over Ansie, hugging her to his chest.

Fear mounted as she watched their acknowledgment of the situation, in some way she knew they weren't getting out of this unscathed. They would take her away, enslave Larn and Willem, and brand her wrists with the mark of the Regent. She'd die before they did anything like that to her.

"Explain yourself!" A Gallian soldier shouted, his blonde mustache drooping down over his bottom lip. His chin quivered, the sight before him seemingly too much.

"Sir," Larn spoke with more calm than she would have ever been able to muster, "that is my dagger and I killed this man." He took his hand away to point at the body still staring blankly in their direction. "He broke into our room through the window, and attacked us."

"You have killed three Nexen!"

"But, they attacked us and he tried to assault my wife."

If Ansie had been breathing before the moment Larn said that word, she wasn't now. His hand rubbed along her back, a gentle reminder for her to follow his lead.

The word hung in the air, swirling around each of them as though testing their thoughts, giving them a moment to adjust to the seriousness of the word.

"Wife?" The Gallian soldier asked, his gaze never leaving Larn's. The now dead Nexen must have told him of their suspicions.

"Yes," Larn nodded, his head brushing against the top of hers. "We were recently married."

From her vantage point, she chanced a look at Willem. He was avoiding looking at her directly, his face seemingly carved of stone. He was anything but calm, his anger brewing near the surface.

"Follow my lead."

Larn's words ran through her mind again and she leaned into him a bit more, tucking her head into the crook beneath his chin. He tightened his hold on her, his calm only unseated by the erratic beat of his heart beneath her ear.

"Names?"

"My name is Lial, his name is Wint and this is Arna." He smiled down at her, rubbing the top of her hair with his hand. The movement sent a jolt down her spine.

Arna, she would have to remember the alias. *Arna, Arna, Arna.*

The tavern owner stood silently in the background, his hands balled into fists. Ansie waited for him to speak, to break their cover and tell the truth but he remained silent. She wondered what frightened him more, the threat of *vox prima* in his tavern or the Gallians discovering he knew the truth.

In an odd moment, Ansie met his eye and they stared at one another as the words swirled around them. The Gallian captain began to berate Larn and Willem with questions, asking about the two men in the room next door. Willem's cover was given, the words filling the room and still, she couldn't look away from the owner. They remained transfixed, one looking to the other, knowing all their lives depended on the lies being told. Quite suddenly, Ansie realized why he remained silent. He was as afraid as she was.

"Is this true?" the soldier turned to the tavern keeper, the blonde mustache continuing to quiver.

"Of course it's true." The gruff man looked away from Ansie to stare at the dead Nexen. "He was badgering them down near the bar, asking all sorts of questions and wanting to see papers. But he wasn't dressed like that. I told these three they could stay the night, this one proved he was married to the girl." He nodded in Larn's direction.

"And how did he prove it, exactly?" the Gallian asked, cutting directly to the quick. "Do you have your papers?"

"No," Larn said, "but—"

The soldier cut him off. "If they don't have a license, then by the law they aren't married."

"Not with those markings of his."

Larn tensed against her.

"What markings?" Every eye turned to look down at them.

Larn's voice rumbled in his chest. "As you may have guessed, I'm not from around here. By the law of the Regent, I'm allowed to keep to my customs as marked by the Maereo tribes of *Excelsis Bestia*. Upon marriage, we're given a mark to show our bondage to one another," he drew back from her and Ansie felt suddenly alone.

He fumbled with the strings near the top of his shirt. As he let the coat drop to the ground, it made an odd wet sound, one she hoped the soldiers wouldn't hear.

He rose to his feet before her, whipping his shirt over his head, baring his cream-tanned skin and strong shoulders. Turning to the left, he showed the soldier something on his skin, pointing to it.

"This is the mark received of any man married in my tribe."

Willem caught her eye, but she refused to understand what Larn was saying. He was married? Or at least he had been. Why did it seem so shocking to her? And how had the tavern owner known?

"I see," the Gallian captain replied, his voice going softer now that he had some form of proof. He hesitated. "And I assume she has one as well."

"Not yet," Larn shook his head, throwing his shirt back over his body. "We are newlyweds after all and she won't be properly marked until we reach my tribe—that's where were headed."

There was an awkward pause, one in which Larn seemed to challenge the Gallian, daring him to question the ways of his tribe. Though the Maereo were free of the Regent's laws for having helped them overthrow Anglas, they were seen as less-than citizens. But there were enough stories about the tribes from the north to strike fear in the hearts of the men. Ansie somehow knew Larn was smart enough to use what people thought about him to his own advantage.

"I see," the mustache puffed, as the man exhaled. "But that doesn't clear up the matter of three dead Nexen."

"No, it doesn't," Larn agreed. "All we can say is the men came after us first, and we did what needed to be done to protect ourselves. I don't even understand how you know they are Nexen, I thought they were Anglans, dressed like that." With one simple phrase, Larn had the Gallian soldier trapped. Either the captain had to admit he knew of the plan, or let them go.

"All of this will be reported to the Regent," he threatened, and Ansie swallowed.

"I would expect nothing less," Larn gave him a slight bow.

The Gallian and his soldiers moved toward the door, retreating slowly. "And you're registered?"

"Yes, sir." The lie about their marriage registration rolled right off of Larn's tongue.

"Good, good." The mustache hanging over the man's lips had a way of making his words seem as though they came from nowhere. "Golt, Jern, retrieve the bodies and bury them outside."

Two men split from the group and grabbed the arms of the dead soldier. Ansie turned away, not wanting to see the blank eyes again. She could still remember the feeling of his clammy hand against her mouth.

The scuffed dragging of the body from the room sent shivers down her spine. There would be no sense in trying to sleep for the rest of the night.

"Ahem," the mustache fluffed. "We will be conducting a full investigation tomorrow, you will, of course, stay the night. If for some reason I find your marriage to be faulty," he looked between the two of them, "then I see no reason why you shouldn't be arrested."

"Of course," Larn gave another half bow.

"Thank you, sir," Willem added, his throat bobbing.

"If you would be so kind?" The Gallian addressed the tavern owner, waving his hand at the door. "We'll take our leave."

The owner nodded and filed out of the room behind the soldiers, but not before looking at each of them in turn. With a simple gesture hidden by his body, he held up one finger, telling them to wait.

The door creaked to a close.

Willem exhaled and Larn ran his fingers through his hair.

"Wha—?"

Larn silenced Willem with a look and beckoned him toward the window. When Ansie didn't move to stand, he offered a hand to her. She ignored it and came up beside him, her head reaching the middle of his chest. She remembered with all too much clarity how it felt to be in his arms and turned away.

Huddled beside the shattered window, she stood closer to Willem.

"What now?" Willem asked, finishing his earlier question.

"I don't know," Larn said and ran a hand through his hair again. "Give me a minute to figure it out."

"You got us through the first bit, now what do you think is coming for us?"

"Most likely, they'll discover the truth," Ansie said. They both turned to her and she shrugged.

It didn't take a genius to realize the many holes in their story, most blatantly a marriage that never happened.

"She's right," Larn admitted, running both hands through his hair this time.

Through the broken window a slit of light suddenly appeared on the ground outside. Ansie watched with an odd sense of foreboding, as the Gallian soldiers carried the dead Nexen from the tavern. What had once been simple was growing more complicated by the minute. Larn had bought them time, but they needed more than that.

Voices drifted up to them as the Gallian captain gave a swift bow to the tavern owner. Ansie felt as though she could see his mustache quivering even from above.

It seemed only mere moments before the tavern owner was entering their room once more, closing the door softly behind him. He crossed to where they stood, his steps silent on the wooden planks. Ansie inched closer to Willem, and he wrapped his arm around her.

Larn opened his mouth to speak, but the man held up a hand. "First things first, there's no reason to lie to me. I thought I knew who you were earlier, but after that display, I know it's true." Ansie swallowed heavily. "The rumors started trickling in last week, the boy and girl who speak to animals, and the Maereo who travels with them." He looked between all three of them.

She wondered how she hadn't noticed the deep crescents beneath his eyes, they dipped as though accentuating his pupils, the skin showing his age and wisdom. Though his skin was wrinkled, he had a muscular chest and thick, knobby fingers.

"What else do you know?" Larn asked.

"Most of the truth. The Renegades arrived in Mirtain and the rebellion has begun." When none of them challenged his claims, he nodded. "It shouldn't be too long before the Regent sends more soldiers there—if he hasn't already heard."

"We have time on our side," Willem offered.

"And time is all you need to ignite the rumors running rampant in these lands." A tight smile pulled at the corner of his mouth before he cleared his throat. "But that doesn't matter here. Word has already spread about you three. Two men and a lady traveling alone are suspicious these days."

"We'll disguise her," Larn waved a hand.

"As well as she might be able to pass off as a young boy, soldiers are trained to see past disguises. I would think you know that by now." He stared each of them down. "They won't take kindly to this, but we might be able to give you more time."

"What do you suggest?" Willem's arm tightened around her shoulders.

"Give them exactly what they're looking for."

Both Larn and Willem looked blankly at the tavern owner, but Ansie already knew what he was suggesting. Somehow in the short moment, she had stared at the tavern owner, and him back at her, while Larn and the Gallian soldier argued, she had already seen the answer in his eyes. Her future was written as soon as the word had left Larn's mouth.

"Can you do it?" she asked, only looking to the older man. His allegiance was something they couldn't have hoped to gain.

"I can have it done before you leave."

"Will you be harmed?" The last thing she wanted was for his help to cost him anything.

"I don't know," he said, a gleam entering his eye as he leaned in closer. "But I can tell you this one thing, I believe in the Animle, I believe in you— both of you."

She swallowed around the lump in her throat, uncertain of what to make of the words.

"What do you mean? What are you going to do?" Willem looked between them.

The older man straightened. "The only thing we can do to give you time. These two will be married, we'll fudge the date, and that should satisfy the captain. You can be on your way before he's any wiser."

"What about her age?" Willem asked, a soft denial. It was true, she hardly looked her own age, let alone old enough to marry.

"That doesn't matter when you have him," the man pointed to Larn. "By the laws of his tribe, they can marry at whatever age they wish."

The words were freeing, and yet ridiculous to her. In all her years, she had wondered what it might be like to live in a world where a person could decide for themselves whom to marry and when.

"Are you able to marry her?" Willem turned to Larn. "I won't give her to you if you have another wife somewhere." Something deep was stirring in Willem's voice, reminding her of the way he had spoken when he caught her with Skurn.

Skurn.

She froze, holding onto his name. She had thought she was ready to give him up, and she had, but not like this. This blotted out all hope, all intent for anything with him. She wasn't sure if she was ready for that, not with freedom from Gallia in the very air they breathed.

Once again, she had no choice.

She thought back to the last time she'd seen him. She had told him not to call her Ans, but what wouldn't she give to hear him call her that now? Her heart and mind were still turned toward him, her dreams often including him.

In a flash of panic, she remembered the way it felt to be in his arms, to feel her heart thundering as he spun her around the cobblestones on Festis Luna. Her face flushed as she recalled the way he had kissed her, the forbidden passion making her dream of a life with him.

It had been foolishness, all of it, and still, she yearned for it. Yearned for a future with him, yearned for his presence in her life.

"My mark isn't from marriage." Larn grumbled, bringing Ansie back to the present and dashing her hopes into a million pieces. He waved his hand toward his left shoulder, then turned to the tavern owner. "How do you know so much about my people?"

"You aren't the only Maereo to have wandered into my tavern." The man shrugged, holding back his secrets. "I figured you were a warrior from the moment I saw you, I knew you'd have a mark somewhere."

He was a Maereo warrior? They were the men of legends, their skills in battle renowned, and the horrors of what they did to their victims enough to make her tremble. She suddenly knew nothing about him.

Larn shook his head and ran his hand through his nearly dried hair. "I may have been once," he sighed. "Well, then." He raised his eyes to hers and her stomach dropped. "Shall we?"

Shall we? Was that all it was going to take to seal her fate? Were those the only words she would hear before it all began?

Her every thought was captivated, taken in an instant until she was moving as though watching a different body reach out and place her hand in Larn's. She felt Willem embrace her and whisper something in her ear, but all she could think of was the one she'd left behind in Mirtain.

It wasn't supposed to happen like this. She wasn't ready, she couldn't do it.

As if from a distance, she heard the tavern owner claiming there was no ordained elder in Alesmann, and he was registered as the law-bearer of the lordless village.

She stepped out of Willem's embrace and placed her other hand in Larn's, staring directly at his chest. She couldn't look him in the eye, she didn't want to think about what she would see there.

At one time she'd wondered if Skurn wasn't the one for her, maybe it was someone else, but she had never expected this. She swallowed as Larn recited the vows, the words falling from his mouth with a distant delicacy.

"I, Larn Punan, take thee Ansie to be my wife. For all the days I shall see, and for all the nights I sleep beneath the moons, you shall be mine and I shall be yours. I promise to protect you, to provide for you, care for you, and lo— love you." He paused. "I say this now and every day until death has taken the last of my breath. I render myself yours, completely."

The words chilled her bones and yet set a fire and kindling flame within her heart. They were pure and beautiful, yet filled with no meaning. She didn't even know the man standing before her. She didn't know the hands she held. Skurn had a freckle on the knuckle of his left ring finger. She blinked back the tears threatening to pour.

"All right," the tavern owner turned her way. "It's your turn."

Ansie nodded and Larn squeezed her hands. "I, Ansie Fermell, take thee Larn to be my husband." She stopped for a breath. "For all the days I shall see, and for—for all the nights I sleep beneath the moons, you shall be mine," a shaky breath, "and I shall be yours."

Another squeeze on her hands urged her on as she pulled the recited words from memory. All of Autre Gallia knew the vows, but she'd never known how words could seemingly place shackles around her wrists.

"I promise to protect you, provide for you, care for you, and love you," she blinked quickly. "I say this now and every day until death has taken the last of my breath. I render myself yours, completely."

"Good, then I bid both of you wed." The owner smiled, though it didn't reach his eyes. "You can kiss your bride." He waved a hand between them.

Her heart thundered wildly in her chest as Larn stepped closer. Was it just her imagination or had he grown taller in the last few minutes?

He leaned down and placed a kiss on her cheek. As he drew away, the smell of hay and rain lingered. She dropped her hands to her sides.

"Right," the tavern owner cleared his throat, "I have these," he pulled some papers out from beneath his shirt, "I need them signed."

Only a few moments more and Ansie saw her name next to Larn's, his simple scrawl nearly running into hers. According to the document, they had been married for three days. His last name, Punan, stood out. *Her last name, now.*

The tavern owner blew on the parchment, helping the ink to dry faster. "That should do it." He tore off the bottom sheet to give them proof. Larn tucked it away quickly, as though he could erase what had just happened.

"Shall we?" Larn asked again, gesturing toward the door.

"Don't go that way," the tavern owner said. "As much as I believe in the rebellion, I want to keep this village from being burned down. It would be better if you snuck off into the night."

"Understood," Willem said, fingering the dagger at his hip. He turned to them, "I'll grab my things."

He left the room, the tavern owner eyeing her and Larn. She had yet to look at her new husband.

"What can we call you, sir?" She asked the only words she could think to say. When he didn't answer for a moment, she glanced up.

"Oslo," he said and the kind smile was back, this time reaching his eyes. The skin around them crinkled. "It might be the only time you ever see me, but my name is Oslo."

"Thank you, Oslo," she said softly.

He patted her on the shoulder and her eyes welled, knowing how much he'd sacrificed to help them. Willem reentered the room and in a blur, they were out the already broken window and moving across the slanted wooden planks. Larn was a hunched shadow before them as the clouds parted, the moons creating glowing slivers of hinted red and white light across the muddied ground below.

Before her, Larn gathered up his cloak, which was already on the roof. She idly wondered why it was there as they edged closer to the end of the wood. The distance was no greater than she had jumped before, but her limbs were resistant.

Larn swept like carrion toward the ground, landing and turning to help her, but she was already moving. She landed beside him with hardly a sound, only allowing him to help steady her in the mud before she fell on her face. Her still damp coat and cloak stuck to her skin as they darted over the ground and toward the horses, Willem running behind them.

They were in the saddles and riding through the night before an alarm could be raised. As they left, she cast up a prayer to the stars for Alesmann's safety, it wasn't lost upon her the importance of the horses already being saddled.

Oslo and Alesmann were as much a part of the Renegades as the rest of them.

As they rode on into the night, her eyes followed Larn's back, watching him as he settled into the pounding of Tympmor's pace when they hit flat ground. Ansie eyed him, wondering just who he really was. She knew his smile and that he could be kind, but the rest of him was a mystery. Too many times she felt as though he hid his thoughts from the world. Too many times it felt as though he knew all about her, but she knew nothing of him.

And more than anything, she had sensed the longing in him. A longing to be left alone.

Willem pulled up beside her, his breaths coming heavy over the thundering of the horses' hooves. "I'm sorry," he said simply. She knew the admission pained him.

"Don't be," Ansie shook her head and knew the words would take a long time for her to feel them in her heart. As far as any part of her future was concerned, Larn would be a part of it.

For the next few hours she didn't speak, she didn't allow herself to wonder what might have been. But even as she turned away from it all, Skurn's name thrummed through her with every beat of her heart.

CHAPTER 34

She awoke to strange arms holding her, the gentle rocking of a carriage swaying back and forth. For one horrible moment, Umbris thought she was back in the cage with the other prisoners, her wrists shackled together as the clouds of dust swirling into their lungs.

But she was much too comfortable for that to be true.

It took a moment, more than she cared to admit, for her to come back to her senses, and when she did she struggled to comprehend just who those arms belonged to.

The Regent.

She nearly passed out again at the thought—her fear overcoming all logic and feeling. In a desperate attempt to get away from the arms, which had kept her from falling forward, she leaned into the cushions and stared out the pristine glass window.

Commander Jolson was still speaking to the Regent, his words rolling over her ears without thought or feeling. She remained focused on the windows, the black expanse seeming to blur and deepen before her eyes, her own reflection flickering in and out with each torch-lit post they passed. She refused to be reminded of her appearance.

Fingering the scars on her wrists, she knew all too well what the Regent and Commander Jolson saw when they looked at her. A tear escaped, but was lost to her as a new sight forced all the breath from her body.

Gates, golden bars with intricate twists and swirling curves created lines in the darkness. Their gilded glow shined even in the dark of night, catching any fraction of light and reflecting it with brilliant strength. But it was what rested behind the bars which stole her breath.

Chateau de Plaisance.

There on a low sloping hill was the palace itself, the size of it incomprehensible. A wide, circular pathway led to the front of the palace, gravel lining the road and torches stretching like beacons along either side. At the front of the gilded palace what seemed like hundreds of stairs led toward a break between two wings, the small courtyard serving as an outdoor throne room pointing in the direction of the entryway. The palace itself stretched to a length which was beyond belief. It was inlaid with gold and marble, thousands of windows created a sheen of glass along the sides, their panes glowing with an ethereal light.

Umbris stared, her mouth hanging open, as she tried to take it all in. She wanted to remember every detail, every small flicker of gold to tell someone, someday. The stories she had heard from childhood of the immaculate expanse of *Chateau de Plaisance* were mere falsehoods in light of what she now saw. Nothing in her imagination could have conjured something so beautiful. She was lost in the wonder of it, roving her eyes over the palace in much the way she liked to scour the night sky and stars stretching across its expanse.

"It seems you have an admirer," Jolson's voice reached her and though she wanted to turn, she couldn't look away from the sight.

The carriage ran along the gravel road directly in front of the palace, passing through the open gates where Gallian soldiers stood at attention. Umbris sat confused for a moment, as the carriage traveled past the circular drive which led to the front of the palace, moving for nearly half a mile along the front of the left wing, to then suddenly make a sharp turn to the right.

This time she gasped, the sound audible in the carriage but she hardly cared. The palace was grander and larger than she ever could have expected. Not only did the front of the palace seem to stretch for half of a mile, but it also seemed to reach just as deep. The side revealed depths of a few hundred more windows, and fountains decorating the grand expanse of a perfectly carved garden stretching to the horizon. The windows only hinted at the hundreds of rooms encased within. The flickering glow of the glass reflected off a long pool which rested near a powerful fountain at the front of the gardens.

There were no words to describe what she was seeing. No one could comprehend elegance of this magnitude unless they had seen it for themselves. Thinking back to her village, she knew the palace itself was larger than all the cottages and buildings put together, five times over.

The carriage turned again, this time taking a dimly lit, tree-lined, path leading toward the back of the palace. She felt as though she moved in a dream, waiting, as the carriage came to a rocking stop. The door opened and the Regent stepped out first, followed by Jolson who turned to extend his hand to her. She was all too aware of the marking on her wrist as she carefully placed her hand in his, his palm was surprisingly soft and warm.

Stepping down on the gravel, she was given no time to stare in wonder at the shadowed backside of the palace. Both men had left her behind, moving where the gravel turned to cobblestones and toward a small black door hidden in the shadows. Only when Jolson turned to beckon her, did she follow and step into the palace.

She hurried with hardly a sound, her bare feet seeming to cling to the polished floors. It surprised her, the little decoration of the maze-like paths they traipsed, the walls lacking in any ornate detail. The simplicity didn't match the extravagance she had witnessed outside.

Umbris held the folds of her shift as close to her legs as possible. She wondered if she was leaving a trail of dirt behind her as she followed both men deeper and deeper into the palace. They moved with the confidence and security that came with knowing a place. Their solid footsteps thumping along the halls with ringing finality. Every now and then, a male or female servant rounded a corner and stopped in their tracks, dipping into bows or curtsies. Their eyes had bored into Umbris's back as she passed by them and into the shadows beyond.

Her hands began to sweat and she clung more desperately to the folds of her shift, hoping her appearance wasn't as truly horrific as she feared. But she had glimpsed herself in one of the dented mirrors at *Le Jupon Rouge*, she knew exactly what the others saw, even if it wasn't true.

They ascended a winding staircase where at the top the Regent opened a door and strode into the gleaming room beyond. Nearly out of breath, she stared in wonder.

"The Fantique Coloir," Jolson whispered, and she nodded. "Corridor of Fantasy."

It was a fantasy indeed. Impressive arching windows lined one side, twelve panes making up the entirety of one window. She was nearly certain each pane was as tall as her. Candles glowed, the gold hints in the molding and around the canvas paintings glimmering in the darkness. Caramel-brown hues from the wood shined beneath her dusty feet and her bare toes could tell the planks had been polished not long ago. There was a slickness to them that encouraged one to dance. The chamber seemed to stretch the entire length of the palace, a seemingly impossible notion. How could one room be so large?

And it only appeared all the more expansive with the mirrors and windows casting each candle with numerous reflections. The space was overwhelming. An entity and palace of its own. In this space, even the twisting gold flowers which climbed up a sideboard table leg were more intricately adorned than her own reflection in the long windows.

"Come along," the Regent's voice echoed along the corridor. He was nearly halfway down, a speck in the distance.

She hurried to follow, trying not to get distracted by the paintings of ornate courtiers on the ceiling, garbed in clothing of extreme finery, the tight corsets and wide skirts of the women seemed to only make the space all the greater. The men in each painting were in motion, the former and current Regent depicted riding on charging horses and pointing at the fleeing Anglans. Umbris swallowed, knowing that this was how her people were seen.

At the direct center of the hall was a red line, painted across the floor, cutting the room in half. She stepped over the plank of wood, the red reminding her of blood. She wondered about its significance. This very palace was a realm of its own, a shrine to those who had conquered Anglas.

"Try not to be too overwhelmed," Jolson murmured beside her, his heavy boots beating against the carefully polished floor. Her own feet sounded like a child's, pattering and slapping along the perfect wood.

The warning came much too late.

At the end of the hall, they ducked into what seemed to be another servant's passageway. The smell inside was musty, not filled with the light airiness of the Fantique Coloir. Down passageways and halls, they crept, seeing no one. Umbris had the sudden wondering if this was a normal occurrence for the Regent, he seemed to know his way around.

And why wouldn't he? she wondered, knowing he had grown up in this place.

How many times had he searched these floors and halls, this endless world of perfect immaculate richness? Did he even know how the children of his own realm lived? If she had grown up in such a place, she would have never wanted to leave.

They rounded a corner and faced a dead end, the wall before them seemingly solid until the Regent pressed his hand to a particular spot. The wall swung inward, a door hidden from prying eyes.

She followed the Regent out of the dank hall and into a fire lit chamber beyond. All her eye could see was made of dark, polished wood—accented by brushed hues of azure and cushioned furnishings. The flames in the deep fireplace flickered, casting long shadows from the table, chairs, and an impressive desk perfectly arranged within the room. A plush rug of deepest blue spread over the floor caressing her feet with an almost sinful comfort, the clicking of a wound clock echoed. Two domineering windows graced the left side of the room, sky blue curtains dripping along their sides and a door on the opposing end, which Umbris presumed would lead to more rooms.

There was an intimacy in this room which she hadn't expected. In the Fantique Coloir, everything was perfect and untouched as though a person couldn't breathe without fear of dirtying the surface of the fine glass or polished wood. But in here, there were papers and documents scattered across the desk. More than one coat lay over the back of a chair, fine gloves cast aside.

There was even a riding crop resting on the table where a place setting for one remained untouched. It was to this table the Regent now walked.

After passing through the palace, Umbris had had a moment to gather some of her thoughts, to realize where she really was. But here and now in his presence, she felt her throat constrict once more. He could order her death in an instant, could wipe out all of those she'd left behind with the mere swipe of his hand, and yet he stood there holding the chair at the table open for her.

"Please," he motioned for her to take the seat. She eyed him as she moved closer, well aware he was probably used to more refined manners. Obliging, she sat on the plush cushion, hoping her shift wouldn't dirty the gentle blue that reminded her of clear waters.

Moving to the edge of the room, the Regent pulled on a rope before taking off his tri-pointed hat and coat, revealing a cream vest inlaid with stitched blue vines spanning across his chest—white sleeves billowing around his arms. Umbris averted her gaze, unsure if she should be looking as he so casually disrobed.

The door near one of the windows opened, a servant ducking inside. Like Commander Jolson, he had his hair parted down the middle, though fine golden curls curved at the bottom of the ribbon holding it in place.

"My Sire," the servant gave a slight bow, holding the door open for two maids, who scurried in to place trays on the table. Silver gleamed like a sword being pulled from its scabbard as the lids were lifted, revealing steaming meat beneath. A wonderfully delicious scent of roasted bird made Umbris's mouth water and as she watched the gravy slide over the offered crisp skin, she could feel herself leaning forward. It had been so long since she'd had anything other than simple gruel or scraps to eat.

"Garval," the Regent's elegant voice filled the room. "Please bring one more plate for my guest."

As he said the word, one of the servant girls shot Umbris a sharp glare, before averting her eyes. In that one glance, Umbris knew what the woman thought of her. She might be sitting at the Regent's table, as unbelievable as that may be, but her scars told the servant girl enough of the story.

Umbris kept her eyes fixed in her lap as the Regent's valet served them, filling her plate with more food than she'd seen at one table in over a year. Her eyes welled, the uncertainties of what was to come, nearly overpowering her. As much as she wanted to, she couldn't make herself eat.

"Is something wrong?"

She looked up, the valet had long since left, and Jolson was already digging into his plate of food; as expected, he ate with perfect precision, not a crumb out of place.

At the opposite end of the short table, the Regent was leaning back in his chair, his eyes taking in all of her. She wondered what he saw, and then presumed she would rather not know.

"No," she cast around for the right title, "my Sire," she said, recalling what the valet had said.

An amused gleam entered the deep blue of his eyes. He crossed his legs, grasping a glass before him, swirling the crimson liquid around before taking a sip. With his hair free of his hat, the light brown locks reached just below his ears, something about it made her stomach tighten.

"Then why not eat?"

She looked at her plate again, taking in the smell of what appeared to be roasted duck. As much as she wanted to take a bite, she couldn't, knowing all the while her stomach was clenched and her heart hammering in fear. Something Jolson had said back in *Le Jupon Rouge*, was haunting her.

"Why did you bring me here?" her voice was timid, hardly audible over the cracking of the flames to the left of the table.

The Regent paused, assessing her. "I've need of information and I think you might be able to help."

Jolson nodded, his head bobbing as he cut and then placed another bite of the roasted meat in his mouth. He was eating as though starved.

"You mentioned a name," Umbris began, not wanting to say it, not wanting to remember her.

"Yes," another swirl of the glass, another sip, "Kata plays a very important part in all of this."

She swallowed, her mind still whirling around how they knew so much of what she'd been through at Fort Jontru. How did they know about Kata? Somehow they knew what had gone on in the cells of that fort, how a rebellion had begun to build within the walls itself until it had ended abruptly. Kata's death had been the end to it all.

"Now," the Regent leaned forward, his eyes coming clearer as a strand of his hair fell down over his forehead. He brushed it away quickly. "First, you must eat," he motioned to the plate, "and I will talk."

Umbris nodded and did as asked. The saliva in her mouth was nearly overwhelming as she cut into the tender meat, juices overflowing, and raised it to her lips. She chewed carefully, lost in the taste, allowing the warm grease to slide down her throat with a satisfying heaviness. Oh, how long it had been since she had had anything that tasted half as good and had enough weight that she could feel it in her belly.

"Have you ever heard of a small village called Mirtain?" the Regent asked, his mouth forming each word perfectly. When she nodded, he gave her an odd look.

"Kata was from there," she explained quietly, knowing the village was of little to no significance to the realm. Perhaps they knew about the attempted rebellion within Fort Jontru, and her involvement. She was going to have to play her hand carefully. When time seemed immense and death imminent, they had all shared their pasts in those dank cells.

Jolson nodded at her words. "How did you meet Kata?" he asked, dabbing at the edges of his lips with a white, cloth napkin.

She swallowed another bite, keeping her head down. "She was in my cell. She cried for days without stopping." Her hands trembled in her lap, her heart thundering as the past stared at her. "Once the crying was done, she started to talk. She told me where she was from and about her family."

"Perfect," Jolson nodded again.

Both men were looking at her with such expectation she could hardly understand what it was they were searching for. None of the women in Fort Jontru were of any importance. After seeing this place, she wondered if the women here could ever comprehend what enslaved women went through. What she had been through.

"If you don't mind me asking," she said timidly, not sure if she should speak in the Regent's presence. They hadn't silenced her yet. The Regent waved a hand for her to continue, "Why does she matter? What does she have to do with anything?"

The Regent leaned forward looking down at his interlocked fingers. "She's the means to an end." He stood quite suddenly, grabbing his glass and letting it swing with each step he took around the room. If not for the fine plush rug, she was certain his boots would echo through the chamber.

"The realm," he said softly, placing his glass on the mantle of the fireplace, "is no longer at peace. There are those in Autre Gallia who believe in legends, in the myths of the Animle."

She froze. Of course, she'd heard the stories, she'd believed them, wanted them to be true, had looked to the stars in wonder and hope—and she'd never received an answer until Larn. He had told her the truth, she had given up, her belief having crumbled to dust.

"I told you they whisper about it," Jolson said, leaning back in his chair and crossing his legs. "Look at that face, she's well aware of the legends."

Umbris blanched, the color draining from her cheeks. To even speak of such things was treason. To desire for their return was a most certain death.

"In this case," she heard the Regent say, "I'm thankful she already knows."

She dared to glance up and found him watching her, his eyebrows dipped in curiosity. He was judging her character, as much as she was his.

"They're only stories," she said, her voice coming out higher than before.

He gave a half smile, weariness appearing for one split second before it passed by like a flickering flame. "Some may think so, but the truth is coming out." He picked up his glass again and stared into the flames. "I've received word that there was a sighting of a creature, unlike other animals, a *simian*," the word rolled off his tongue like a dangerous poison. "The beast was looking for a man from Mirtain before it fled captivity."

Umbris's heart was fluttering in her chest, though she'd heard the same words from Larn, hearing them from the Regent, himself, made them all the more true.

"I issued a missive which disbanded all animal fighting, and would provide a handsome reward to any Gallian who found the creature, but it never was." He sighed, "There was a battle in Mirtain. The Renegades charged into the village, overthrowing the lord in residence and took Mirtain into their own hands. A rebellion has begun, and rumors of the creatures of old are spreading across Autre Gallia." He spoke with cool conviction, but his eyes were kindled with a fire that made her shiver. Shadows from the flickering flames cast the lines of his face into sharper focus, making him appear all the more mysterious—dangerous.

"I need to find the *simian*, but more importantly, I need to find the man who called the creature into being." He turned to her then, all signs of his carefree manner gone. Her fear, which had subsided slowly in his presence, pulsed back to life. There was a gleam in his eyes she couldn't ignore.

"I—I don't understand."

Jolson sighed, leaning over the table. "I told His Sire of your canny ability to read people, to have others trust you." The Regent nodded as he paced back to the table, taking his seat across from her. "We need to know everything Kata told you, more particularly, who she knew in Mirtain."

"She didn't say," Umbris swallowed.

"Did she tell you how she was taken?" The Regent cast his eyes over his interlaced fingers, his elbows resting on the table.

"She did," she swallowed, not wanting to give any further information. "Hers was different than most."

"How so?" the Regent asked, cocking his head to the side. "There has been unrest in Mirtain since that day, and I want to know why."

Umbris stared back at him, unsure of what to say. Should she tell him? Or was he testing her? It seemed impossible he wouldn't already know, but maybe those details had been lost. Who could really care about another girl who had fallen victim to *vox prima*?

But it wasn't the girl the Regent was interested in, it was the man in the story, the one who had fought to try and save Kata.

"She was found embraced with a man, and they took her." The words came forth, the memory of the story filling her. As always, any memory brought back the wails of the prison, the crack of a whip, the stench of the dying, she swallowed. "But he wasn't the one who tried to free Kata. She said they dragged her to the ruling lord's house, but as they took her away she spotted her childhood friend running to save her. He tried to reach her, to save her, but they shut the doors. She was sent to Fort Jontru the next day."

"A name?" the Regent asked, his eyes solely focused on her. He seemed wiser somehow, more dangerous this way. She was suddenly reminded of the panther Larn had told her about. She wondered if the eyes had gleamed the way the Regent's did now.

She shook her head, "She never told me his name."

Jolson cursed, making her flinch. He strode over to the fire. "It has to be the same man." He addressed the Regent.

Umbris took a short breath through her tight lips, her chest seeming to heave beneath her shift. Something inside her stirred. Did they think the man who tried to save Kata was the same one who found the *simian*?

"One man," the Regent held up a finger, the shadows around his mouth seeming to flicker in the firelight, "one man stood up to my orders and tried to save that girl, and now we have lost the entire village." Umbris swallowed heavily, her heart racing. "One man is all it took for a rebellion to begin. One." He shook his head and turned back to her.

"Did she ever speak of him?" Jolson inquired.

"Only the one time."

"Did she talk of rebellion?" the Regent asked.

Again she shook her head. "No."

She had never felt so small in all her life. Her appearance must be one which disgusted him, one which reminded him of the underside of Autre Gallia.

"What did she talk about?"

"She didn't say much."

This time the Regent cursed, and she flinched. "I need a name, I need to find him."

"She never said one," Umbris whispered, her hands trembling again in her lap. Tears sprung to her eyes as they always did when someone yelled at her.

He sighed heavily and took another swig of his wine. "What are the rumors?"

Jolson pulled back from the fireplace. "Same as before. Mirtain is under the Renegades control, we haven't been able to get anyone in."

The Regent stared out one of the long windows in the room, his eyes seeming unfocused. He pursed his lips, his brow furrowing.

"Tell me," the Regent said, turning back to look at her again, "where are you from?"

"L—Locknett," she offered, wanting to disappear.

"That's in the lower east."

"I suppose, my Sire." She refused to look up.

"You suppose?"

She lifted her eyes, wondering how he didn't understand. "I've never seen a map."

"Hmm," was the only acknowledgment he gave. Bracing his hand on the table he leaned forward, watching her face. "And what did you do in Locknett?"

"I was a seamstress, my mo-mother trained me."

"Now, how is it you came to be in Fort Jontru with the other women?" His question was like a knife through her heart and he knew it. They were tearing her apart, the past ripping her from the inside out. She couldn't say what had happened to her, it was too much.

Remembering Neen's story, she felt the words passing through her lips, knowing they weren't true and she was lying to the Regent, himself. But she wouldn't go back to what had really happened, she couldn't. Not even the Regent could make her.

"I—I was walking with my friend, he was keeping me safe. It was nearly curfew. I stumbled and he caught me, helping me back to my feet. That's when they saw us." She raised her eyes to the ruler of the realm. Neen wasn't here to tell her story, but Umbris could tell it for her. "They killed him, and took me away right then."

He didn't blanch, didn't flinch, but simply stared back at her before taking another swig of his wine. She watched his throat bob before settling, and he leaned back in his chair.

"Has the Liege heard from his Captain yet?" the question was directed to Commander Jolson, though the Regent still watched her.

Jolson shook his head. "No, my Sire."

"What was his name again? Fergin?"

"Yes, my Sire." Jolson turned back to them. "He was supposed to report back here yesterday morning, but he's not returned. It's possible he was killed in the battle."

"Skirmish," the Regent pursed his lips. "That's all it was, nothing more. A real battle would have torn the village apart." There was a sense of foreboding in the words.

"If I may speak plainly, my Sire," Jolson stepped closer, straightening his coat. Umbris wondered if he was aware of the way his boots snapped together nearly every time he addressed the Regent. His caution to not be too casual in the presence of the Regent made her all the more wary. She found herself studying the Regent's profile, out of the corner of her eye, as he rose to stand.

He was a tall man, broad in the shoulders, trim around the waist. His hair hung past his chin, but it was the sharp lines of his jaw and the point of his nose which drew her attention. He had a rather large nose, not anything which made his appearance awkward, but it was noticeable and helped to cast his eyes more in shadow. He was watching Jolson, preparing for the commander's address. Not having his eyes on her for a moment, brought Umbris some relief.

"You may," the Regent said.

"Why not attack Mirtain?" Jolson's throat bobbed. "Extinguish this rebellion with one quick swipe of your hand. We've already wasted three days since hearing the news."

The Regent sighed and watched the licking tongues of fire flicker in the hearth. "I've thought of it," he folded his hands behind his back as he moved closer to the fire, closer to Jolson. "But it's something I cannot do until I have that man. He's the key. The key to the legends, the future, everything. Without him, I have no idea what other rebellion he might stir up, without him, I cannot be certain this is all finished." He straightened and turned to Jolson. "We know there is to be a Rising, we simply have to eliminate it before it gets out of hand. But I need that man."

"Yes, my Sire." Jolson gave a slight bow.

"You're certain the girl is dead?"

"Kata?" Jolson asked. "Yes, my Sire. I was too late arriving to Fort Jontru, but I saw her body."

The words tore at her heart.

The Regent nodded and turned back to face Umbris. For a moment, she had felt invisible. Now, more than ever before she knew she was at their mercy. Her part in their story was over, and a new one was about to begin.

"Did Kata die while you were there?"

The backs of her eyes stung, but she refused to let them see her pain, to hear the sounds echoing in her mind. "Yes," she said softly, the word coming out in a croak.

The Regent sighed and walked to the rope along the wall again. When he pulled, it took mere moments for the valet to appear once more.

"Take Umbris, to the maids' quarters," again the Regent rolled the name over his tongue with a certain foreignness. "Be sure she is given proper treatment."

Garval nodded, his golden head bobbing as he beckoned her to come with him. She rose from the chair with shaking legs, uncertain of what exactly the Regent meant by sending her to the maids' quarters. As they reached the door, she turned and did her best to curtsy in his direction, when she raised her eyes, she found him watching her.

"Sleep well, Umbris." He nodded and held up a finger. "Don't speak of what was said here, it would be a shame for you to be taken away again."

The threat lingered in the air and she curtsied once more, Garval giving her arm a nudge in the direction of the hallway beyond.

She walked as though within a fog, ducking back into the servant halls and down the stairwells. It was only when they reached an empty bedroom with a tub and a small cot along one wall that her eyes welled over.

Garval left her to tend to herself. The lavender in the soap slowly washed away the dirt and grime from *Le Jupon Rouge*. The scars on her wrists remained, but it was the ones in her heart which she carried with the most pain.

She'd tried so hard to keep the memories at bay, to keep them locked where no one could touch them and no one could hear her agony. But they had forced her to remember. Hugging her knees in the tub, she cried, letting the tears join the steaming water surrounding her.

How had she ended up here?

She shook her head, wondering, always wondering where those were she had left behind. She cried with all her heart, letting it pour out of her, as the dirt in her hair was washed away.

When she rose from the tub, clean for the first time in what felt like ages, she vowed to be done with the past.

CHAPTER 35

The sun covered them in a warm blanket, despite the cool air swirling beneath the naked branches, where the remains of maroon and golden leaves clung to the last of their life. It was an uncomfortable sensation, one which had Larn sweating beneath his cloak though his nose felt frozen. He was growing soft in this warmer weather. In the north, they were lucky to have summer days this warm.

"What do you think they're doing?" Ansie asked, her question directed at Willem who rode beside her. For the entire day, they had been riding three-abreast, the winding dirt-laden path affording them a brief respite from the thin trails along rocky mountainsides surrounding Alesmann. They were now entering the softer terrain of the grasslands, or at least on the outskirts of it. Though the road was less perilous, Larn knew that the creatures hiding in the woods became all the more dangerous the further north they traveled.

"Who?"

"Everyone back home."

Willem sighed. "Don't know. Most likely preparing for what's to come. If I had to guess, that Girshon fellow has everything in hand."

Larn smiled to himself. Only Willem would dare to refer to the leader of the Renegades in such a way. He liked Willem all the more for it.

Three days had passed since leaving the Caw's Nest, three days and Larn was no more certain about what had happened there.

Wife. He cursed the word inside his head. Of course, he would be the one to be shackled with a wife, just as the rebellion ignited and freedom was on the horizon. He had spent the last three days cursing the stars and his ill-timed luck—he would sacrifice his freedom again to save their skins, but it didn't mean he had to be happy about it.

"Do you think they're still working in the fields?" As had become her custom ever since their hasty wedding, Ansie avoided looking at him and instead only addressed Willem. Of course, she had spoken to him, but only about their travels, questions on direction, nothing like the way she had been before. A spark seemed to have gone out of her. More than once Larn had caught her with tears in her eyes, as she gazed upward at the sky.

Just last night he had asked her a question that she didn't hear, or chose not to. Her mind seemed elsewhere, but on what he didn't know.

"Most likely," Larn interrupted, making her turn.

As always, her warm, knowing gaze shocked him. Until yesterday, he hadn't noticed the way the six freckles surrounding her right eye formed a near perfect crescent moon. In the light of the midday sun, her eyes had a copper glow that neared the buttery-warm caramel he had once tasted at Sicarmman.

He cleared his throat now that he had her attention. "Girshon's plan was to allow the fields to be worked and to train the men in battle tactics."

"Not the women?" Ansie asked.

He quirked a smile, "The women too."

"Do you think the Regent will attack?" Willem wondered aloud, as always, he sat with his back straight in the saddle.

Larn had a hard time believing Willem had trained himself to track and hunt. Ever since Ansie had told him about the three grinspurs Willem had killed, Larn couldn't quite look at him the same way.

"It won't be a full division," Larn admitted, remembering his conversation with Girshon. "But the Regent will send soldiers to test the strength of the village, to see what he's really up against."

"Do you think they're already there?" Ansie's voice was hushed, a calm inside it which had become normal over the past three days. Larn was surprised to find he missed the way she used to talk, as though she was always waiting for something to make her smile, for a joke to laugh at. But that glimmer of humor seemed to have died.

"If I had to guess, the Regent's going to deal with this as quietly as possible. He doesn't want rumors spreading. The shift of allegiance we saw in Alesmann would only be the beginning."

"True," Ansie nodded.

Willem gave a rare short laugh. "His hesitation is only going to allow Mirtain to get stronger."

Larn smiled, the sunlight streaming through the breaks in the trees making him squint. "Exactly, he's stuck. Either admit the rebellion is happening and overcome it quickly, or try to subdue it without rumors spreading." What Willem and Ansie didn't know was the years of careful planning which had gone into choosing a southern village to begin the rebellion. Call it fate, but who would have known that an Animle creature would have shown up there as well.

"The second option affords him the most control over Anglan allegiance," he continued. "The first would extinguish all threat in Mirtain, but he's afraid of more villages, and hidden Renegades beginning to rebel. My guess, which is practically my job," he winked at Ansie, she didn't smile, "is that the Regent fears just how many would rebel against him if given the chance."

"Fear can only keep Autre Gallia in check for so long," Willem added. "Eventually, cracks will open and those brave enough to jump will rebel."

Larn nodded, the words were almost uncharacteristic for the hunter. There was unbelief in Willem, something in his eyes which resisted any hint of rebellion and the return of the Animle.

"It won't be long before everyone will have to choose a side," Willem continued.

"Those brave enough will side with us. To rebel against something which has long been accepted, is not easily done," Larn said.

"There's more to it than that," Ansie's hood fell back, the auburn strands of her hair gleaming in the sunlight with flecks of gold.

"What do you mean?"

"If it was a question of one person being brave, each individual deciding for themselves, then there would be many more who would join. But that's not the case." She shook her head, her vibrant hair shimmering. "People have responsibilities, families, loved ones. When they make the decision to join the Renegades, they're deciding for their families too."

Willem scowled and Larn knew he was thinking of Ansie. If there had been a way to keep Ansie out of the rebellion, out of any threat, he knew Willem would have taken it, no matter the consequences to himself.

"It's a sacrifice," Larn shrugged. "It comes down to the belief that there has to be something better. If you believe it, then nothing can hold you back from striving for something more."

"Still," Ansie countered, "if all you have is family, then losing them will cost everything."

Family. He hardly understood the notion. From birth, he'd been labeled an outsider, and even those closest had kept him at a distance. For years he had struggled to be accepted by them, by his own people, but it was to no avail. And it hadn't ended there. All his life he had been the different one, the outsider. *Outcast*, his mother had called him that once. He ran a hand through his hair refusing to travel down that worn road.

He glanced to the side as Ansie straightened, cracking her back. Following their flight from Alesmann, Willem had spoken to him the next morning. Spoken was a rather gentle word, as he had threatened Larn to within an inch of his life if he touched Ansie before she was ready. Larn couldn't have agreed more and hastened to set that unnecessary worry aside.

But Willem's concern had haunted him. Within an instant, he had seemed to change, his true worry coming forth. The hunter had whispered, "She's all I have." In that one simple phrase, Larn realized the sacrifice Willem was making, and how hard it had been for him to hold his tongue when Oslo married them. To not be the one to protect Ansie after so many years hurt him.

Through the threats, a realization had come to Larn which he still didn't understand. He would do what was necessary to keep her safe, though she hardly needed it. She'd proven herself capable more than once. Yet, he still felt the need to protect her.

Casting his thoughts aside, he addressed Ansie. "This rebellion isn't asking anything more than what you've sacrificed all along." He adjusted Tympmor's reins. Finally, she looked at him, met his gaze for the first time in what felt like weeks.

"When you worked in those fields, was it for yourself?" he asked. "No, it was because you were ordered to do so. You didn't fight back because you wanted to keep yourself and those you care for safe. If you stood up to it, you would have been the outsider. That's how all this works, you see?" he leaned a little closer to her. "All it takes is one person to start a rebellion, but it's what comes after that gives it life. One person can be killed quickly, dealt with and forgotten in an instant. But when others join, when they become part of something larger than themselves, the safety in numbers begins to thrive, and even those who fear for their families will join."

The hint of a spark gleamed in her warm eyes before she turned away, seeming to ponder his words.

"I see your point," she said, as they followed the flat winding dirt path before them, "but I'm not ready to concede just yet."

"But I have you considering it, that has to count for something."

"A small victory," the corner of her mouth lifted. He smiled to himself.

Minutes passed and with it, Ansie's lips fell, the lightness in her eyes disappearing, until nothing remained. Somehow, Larn couldn't help feeling responsible for the mood she was in. He'd been the one to pose as her husband—it had saved all their necks, but no one had forced him to threaten those Nexen soldiers.

To threaten them, and then fall asleep on that damned roof. He sighed, knowing there was nothing he could do about it now.

Glancing to his left, he let his gaze wander over the slump in Ansie's shoulders. He wasn't fool enough to think their hasty marriage was the only thing bothering her, there was something else. Or rather someone else who captured her thoughts.

An unbidden image of a blonde man from Mirtain entered his mind. *Skurn*, that's what she'd called him. With him, she had spoken with familiarity—not distance like she did now. Her future had been forever altered, but then again, so had Larn's. He was married. The word was like poison in his mind.

Married. He shook his head in frustration. Pike would laugh when he heard the news. Girshon would be less than pleased.

"Keep your hood up," he said softly, the words gruffer than he intended. Ansie glanced at him in question, but pulled the dark fabric over her head without a word. She had no idea how bright her hair was in a forest this bare.

Like a damned target.

Tympmor gave an agitated snort beneath him, the heavy head rearing up and shaking side to side. Larn leaned forward to give him a pat along the side of his neck.

"So," Willem began, stretching his back. "How far north do you think we'll have to go before we find one of the Animle?"

"No telling," Larn nudged Tympmor along. The gentle lope of the hooves on packed dirt and dried leaves settled around them.

"So we have no idea?" Ansie asked.

"Exactly, it's just guesswork, occupational hazard." A yawn passed through his lips.

"They could be anywhere."

"Well, yes, but we have a pretty good idea."

"Oh, you have a good idea," Ansie shook her head, the hood falling off once more. Maybe she needed to pin it up. "I'm not worried as long as you have a good idea." Larn could almost feel her rolling her eyes.

"I have some places in mind."

"Yes," Willem grumbled, "ancient forests and abandoned ruins."

Larn straightened, glancing around them. It was true, most of where he was taking them had yet to be seen. He'd heard tales of the fog surrounding Initium, the mystical ruins where the Animle had taken their final stand, but he'd never seen it with his own eyes. When he'd first heard a trader speaking of the place, he'd expected to hear about how men and women had disappeared into the fog, but he was wrong. According to the trader, there was nothing special about it. Just an old ruin.

There was a very real chance his guesswork was wrong. They might reach Initium and find nothing, but some gut feeling told him to keep going.

"We will stop in Initium, and if we don't find anything there, we'll move on to *Excelsis Bestia*." He refused to let the seriousness of their questions keep him from his goal.

"And if we don't find anything there?" Ansie's question lingered.

"Now where's your belief in me?" he asked, winking. He was about to say more when a branch snapped in the distance.

"What?"

"Shhh," he put a finger to his lips, pulling back on Tympmor's reins.

Ansie and Willem stopped, their eyes searching the forest. The trees were set wide apart, their trunks and branches nearly bare, the golden and maroon dried leaves only made the pathway all the brighter. To either side were small slopes, nothing of drastic concern, but enough to give Larn pause.

"Hold still," Willem whispered, his voice hardly carrying anything behind it. Larn glanced his way.

He sensed it too. Something was out there.

Ansie squinted through the sunlight, cupping a hand around her eyes. She gave Larn a questioning look and leaned closer to the neck of her horse, her hand now moving to the dagger at her waist.

Brushing his finger across the hilt of his sword, a habit, he nudged Tympmor forward, motioning for the others to do the same. Willem's mount skittered to the side, the tense atmosphere making the ears fall back. Even Tympmor was twitching more than usual.

Larn muttered under his breath, his heart beating all the heavier by the moment. He shifted in the saddle, pulling the reins to his left until his leg was brushing against Ansie's. She hardly seemed to notice as her knuckles whitened on the hilt of her dagger.

A curse ran through his mind when another crunch sounded in the distance. This time, it came from the right. He peered through the trees, ears trying to pick up something that would give the culprit away.

Nothing was out of place. No leaf, no branch gave way to anything unnatural, and yet, he knew something was following them.

"We're being watched," he muttered under his breath.

"No," Willem said, sitting straighter when another branch snapped behind them, "we're being hunted."

A snarling growl echoed through the sloping valley, and Tympmor launched forward into a sprint, the other mounts following his lead. Willem's words made the hairs on the back of Larn's neck stand to attention, as the slither of skittering paws came at them from all sides.

They shot across the rough worn path, the horses' hooves thundering beneath them. Ansie was leaning lower in her saddle, her face coming within inches of her mount's neck.

Ahead, two dark shadows loomed, blocking their path. The skittering of four others bounded behind them.

Verrals. Larn cursed.

They were vile creatures. Moving like cats, paws clawing at the dirt, but their heads twitching side to side in the same manner as a bird's—the dark grey scales along their necks bending and twisting. Their pointed snouts revealed rows of needle-sharp teeth and bright blue eyes pierced out of their bony skulls. Curved spikes rose from their shoulder blades to protect their thick scaled-bodies from any blow from above. Larn knew the tips were sharp enough to slice through a man's hand—and had seen it done.

Though they stood no higher than Tympmor's knee, they were creatures of death—and when they launched forward charging at them, Larn's eyes focused on the center, a six-inch claw protruding from each paw.

He cursed each verral to the pits below as he pulled two daggers from his belt. His aim was better from the ground, but there was no time. If they stalled the verrals would all attack at the same moment. These creatures were known for hunting in packs, trapping a kill until it was too late for escape.

Beside him, Ansie's blade flashed in her hand, Willem's long sword still sheathed behind his back.

"Aim for the underbelly," Willem yelled.

Larn fingered the dagger in his hand, the blade shining for a moment before he threw it toward an approaching verral. It fell, having been hit directly in the chest.

A high-pitched growl resounded from behind and the rustling of the leaves left him no time to think. He'd been told verrals were intelligent. They always aimed for the weakest member of a group, and Larn had no doubts they would close in on Ansie immediately if given the chance.

With nothing but instinct to guide him, he pushed Ansie to the side, his knowing ears hearing one of the feral creatures launch into the air, ready to strip her from her saddle. The air stirred by his head, and he grasped Ansie's wrist, having to let go of one of his daggers to keep her steady on her horse.

Willem stabbed the creature as it launched above them, one of the front claws came close to clipping Willem's arm. Larn didn't have time to think about the gash it would have left. Stories of the way verrals jabbed their claws into the hearts of their victims, twisting until the claw snapped off and the victim was left to bleed to death, flashed through Larn's mind.

He let go of Ansie's arm and unsheathed his sword.

A verral leapt into the air and Tympmor danced to the side, allowing Larn to lop off a leg of the creature. A piercing shrill cracked the air, making the hairs on the back of his neck prickle.

Upon a moment's notice, he beckoned for Tympmor to charge toward the remaining verrals, knowing his only chance was to meet them head-on. They were much too clever and knew how to hunt man.

One of the verrals drew back, stuttering as if turning to run and he nearly charged directly for it when he heard Willem yell. "Go for the others!"

Larn changed course with a slight flick of Tympmor's reins and the horse swung to the side at the exact moment the verral leapt into the air, jaws snapping. Larn knocked it to the ground with his sword, but the blade only glanced off the spikes of the shoulder blade. The verral turned, and this time charged forward skittering side to side, leaves scattering beneath its claws, before launching directly at Tympmor's legs.

A split second was all the time it took for Larn to see the clear decision in the creature's eyes and he rolled off the saddle and onto the leaf-covered ground before the beast could slice its claw through Tympmor's flesh. He darted to the side and drove the sword into the verrals mouth, the blade going all the way through the rather fragile skull.

He pulled back, the sword removing easily. Another verral was coming for him, but he was already on the move. To the side, Ansie was turning her mount back in Willem's direction. The hunter was holding off three verrals at once, each one snapping and moving closer, but he kept them at bay with small feints and swings of his sword. Two verrals already lay dead upon the ground at Willem's feet, a sight the verrals kept glancing at and then twitching their heads back up to look at Willem. The piercing blue of their eyes was unsettling.

A sharp hiss echoed as three sets of eyes turned to Larn upon his approach. More hisses and they all moved in unison, communicating with one another. Standing against Willem's right, they had both sides covered. Willem holding his sword in his left and Larn holding his in his right.

"Watch him," Willem shouted just before the middle verral feigned forward and then back with a snap. Larn nearly jumped but held his ground. The verral on the far right eyed him, head twitching back and forth and from side to side so he couldn't get a clear look at the creature's intentions. From somewhere behind him, he heard Ansie gasp and wanted to turn, but knew if he did his life and Willem's would be forfeit.

As one, all three verrals took two steps back, their scaled tails twitching high in the air. They crouched low, giving them no means of a target. Then, as though some call had been given that Larn couldn't hear, they all attacked at once. Claws slashed out and he removed the front leg of the verral on the right as the center one snapped for his head. He did a backbend to move beneath the slicing claw and had to roll across the ground to recover his sword. He stabbed the already wounded verral in the belly and was about to attack the center verral when he spotted Willem already dealing a death blow—and somehow he'd already killed the verral from the left.

A deep breath passed through his lungs. And then another as he looked at the destruction all around them. Only now did he begin to understand the skill with which Willem could move.

Silence settled around them, the air suddenly still. Willem gave him a weary smile, his chest heaving. There was a streak of smeared blood along his cheek.

It all seemed to happen at once. The rustle of leaves, a hissing growl, and a gasp. Larn turned to see the three-legged verral launching in the air, heading directly for him.

He froze, seeing the creature as though from outside of his own body. The sharp blue eyes flashed at him, but it was the remaining front paw that stole his focus. The center claw was missing.

He didn't have time to even raise his sword before the verral was knocked aside, a dagger buried deep within its belly.

The verral fell at his feet, dead. Larn met Willem's confused stare.

He glanced around, only to find Ansie standing there, her eyes on the verral. Dirt smudged her face and golden leaves stuck to her hair, but it was her pale lips that drew his attention. She raised her eyes to his, blinking twice. And that's when he saw the blood dripping off her hand.

"Ansie!" Willem yelled.

She trembled and suddenly sank to her knees. Her eyes fluttered and she toppled forward onto a bed of golden leaves.

Willem was moving before Larn could even think. Her guardian had her in his arms as her face paled, her hands were trembling and Larn could see the cuts and scrapes along her skin. His eyes darted to the now-dead verral, before settling on the wound that caused her to fade out of consciousness.

In her shoulder was the missing verral claw.

CHAPTER 36

"We'll have to pull the claw out."

Larn's words made Willem's stomach flip again. He pressed a hand to his mouth as he looked down at Ansie. They were tucked away in a damp cave, hidden from sunlight and anything that might hear Ansie's groans of pain. But her pain didn't worry him as much as the slow blinking of her eyes and the paleness of her cheeks.

How long Ansie had fought with the wounded verral was beyond him. The verral had launched in for the kill, attempting to drive its claw into her heart. She must have rolled away at just the right moment.

"Get some embers going," he grumbled, as he readied to lower Ansie onto the cave floor. She gave a small gasp of pain. "All right, you have to help me, Ans."

She nodded and braced her body the best she could, as he placed her on the blanket Larn had hastily spread over the stone. With a grimace, her pale face sweating, she rolled to her stomach, exposing the wound in her left shoulder, the blood slowly ebbing around the verral claw. He didn't want to see the way her hand shook.

He internally cursed, knowing what he was going to have to do. This was what he had feared when they left Mirtain. Every moment they were gone, he knew her safety was at risk. And yet, it was her fate as much as his.

"Just pull it out," she groaned, turning her head to the side. She watched the small pile of sticks slowly jump to life with sparks, as Larn stoked the flames.

"Give me a minute," he looked to Larn, "I need water, a needle if you have it, and stick this in the flames." He handed his dagger to the northern man.

405

Larn nodded, his mouth set in a grim line. For once he didn't have anything to say.

Working quickly, Willem sliced at the fabric of her coat and shirt to get to her skin. The iron tang to the blood permeated his nose and he nearly gagged. The blood of an animal was no matter, even of man, but hers hurt him.

Larn shoved a water skin into his hand. The liquid was so simple, sloshing beneath the leather, and yet, he knew it would only heighten her pain.

"Ready?" he asked, looking at Ansie, her eyes were closed, her face calm. He knew he asked more for his own benefit than hers. Larn knelt on her other side, taking her right hand in his.

Willem poured the water as gently as he could over the wound, hearing her gasp as the liquid pooled and then drained down her side. For a simple moment, the wound was clean, revealing how the claw had dug into her flesh. It had entered at an angle and he cursed, knowing the claw would be even more difficult to pull out.

Shaking his head, he watered the wound again, ignoring her inhalation. He would have to steel himself against it all. Glancing up, he readied himself.

"It entered at an upward angle. You're going to have to hold her down. Once I remove it, hand me that blade," he pointed to his dagger sitting in the embers, "that should stop the blood flow."

"No," Ansie groaned. "Don't do...that...just stitch it...up." Her words were labored, pausing every few words.

"I don't know if that'll work," he admitted, a new kind of fear gripping him. He'd spent years working with his hands, but nothing like this. He was a hunter, his expertise gruesome at best.

"It will," Larn said, his voice steady. "Get the claw out and I'll see what I can do." He then bit his lip, the indecision clearly written in the lines of his face. He looked down at Ansie and squeezed her hand. "We may still have to burn the wound."

She took a deep breath, closing her eyes tighter. "Just do whatever needs to be done."

Willem nodded, though he knew she couldn't see him and set about as she asked. "Here we go," he nodded to Larn and grasped the tip of the claw. He pulled, watching the blood bubble from the wound, but it didn't budge. Ansie ground her teeth.

Shaking his head, he settled himself higher above her, angling his body in the direction the claw had entered her shoulder. Again, he wrapped his hand around the claw. Pulling harder than before, he felt it give way as Ansie's whole body flinched in response. Larn leaned forward, placing his hand which wasn't in hers along her back, pinning her to the ground.

Willem pulled once more, easing the claw out of her flesh, trying to maintain the angle. With one final tug, it released and he nearly fell backward, not realizing how hard he had been struggling.

Moving as fast as he could, he cast the claw aside and poured water into the wound. "It's bleeding too fast."

Larn slapped his hands away and pressed a thick cloth to the wound, pushing until she cried out in pain.

"Stop!" Willem hissed, nearly pushing him aside, but Larn wasn't listening. He was concentrating on Ansie's back, the tan skin of his hands tightening as he pushed down on her flesh. A lump formed in Willem's throat.

Larn looked up at him, "You told me to keep her safe, I will. I cauterized one of my men once. I don't want to do that to her, not if we can care for it this way."

Willem nodded. Off and on, Larn pressed against the wound, while Willem prepared a needle and thread.

"Here," he said.

Larn took the needle and began stitching up the wound without even a glance toward Ansie's face. His mouth was set in a hard line.

Willem watched the needle pass through her skin and grasped Ansie's hand. Each time the needle pricked her skin, her fingers tightened around his. "I'm so sorry, Ans," he murmured.

She was shaking, her body seeming to be overcome with the pain. Her eyes were squeezed tight, but that didn't prevent him from seeing the one tear which escaped and trailed over her nose onto the rough blanket beneath her cheek.

A burning sensation filled his eyes and he shook his head. Staring into the glow of the embers, he prevented the tears from falling. He never was able to handle her pain well.

"Here," Larn said, his hand reaching for Willem's. He gave him the bloodied needle and he let go of Ansie's hand to begin cleaning the small tool. It took him a second to clean the blood from his own hands and he watched as Larn began to bind her wound with the strips of blanket Willem had cut moments ago.

"I don't think we'll need to stitch her up again, but keep that clean." Larn took a deep breath, his eyes on Ansie.

Willem nodded. Larn poured some of the water from the skin onto his hands, the water turning to a muddied brown and draining down the gentle slope out of the cave.

"Ans?" Willem whispered. She gave a soft grunt. "It's all done now."

"Thank you," she peaked up at him, one brown eye gleaming with unshed tears. "Both of you."

He nodded. She was even tougher than he'd realized. And that was saying something—she'd always been stronger than him.

"It was high time I returned the favor," he said and brushed his hand along the top of her hair. She gave him a small smile, knowing what he referred to. How many times had she been forced to clean his wounds?

He nearly winced thinking of all she'd done to heal him the day Kata and Jethron were taken. He was no longer sure what was worse, having to tend to the wound, or go through the pain of it all. In some ways, he felt as though trying to help her was worse.

"The horses could use some feeding," Larn said softly. Willem glanced up, the words an offering he hadn't expected. The perfect excuse to step into the fresh air and clear his mind for a moment.

"Right," he swallowed heavily, making his way out of the cave, past the horses to the place where the verrals still lay dead on the ground. How they had come out of the massacre with only Ansie wounded was beyond him. By all accounts, they should be dead.

Kneeling over the carcasses, he attempted to pull the scales apart to salvage what meat was inside. Back in Mirtain, he'd killed more than one verral, but he'd never seen so large a pack before. Usually, he avoided them at all cost, only once had he nearly been trapped and killed. He'd never told Ansie that story, knowing she would have refused to let him go to the Black Market again, regardless of Hernan's orders.

As usual, the verrals had very little meat on their bones and all too soon he knew there was no point in skinning the carcasses. What he wanted to do was burn the bodies and the claws to remove the memories of their snapping jaws and piercing eyes, but the smoke would attract others. Whether patrols or more verrals, he didn't wish to find out.

Sighing, he set about cutting the claws from each paw, knowing each would fetch a fair price.

He moved back toward the cave, only glancing inside for a moment. Larn was sitting beside Ansie, his head tipped back against the cave wall as he watched her every breath. Willem knew Larn was aware of his presence, but the last thing he wanted was to see that knowing look in his dark eyes.

He remained just outside the mouth of the cave, his back braced against the slope, for the time being, he would remain awake as long as necessary. Every sound and crack in the woods had his mind turning, but the horses were well at ease, a sign this day would be coming to an end soon.

And then on to night, he thought, wondering just what they would do as darkness descended upon them.

A soft sigh sounded from in the cave and he leaned around to peek inside. Ansie's eyes were still closed, Larn sitting near her head. Larn looked his way and mouthed that she was asleep. Willem nodded, rest would do her good.

Leaning back, he gazed up at the dim light glinting through the golden leaves. The sun's descent cast leering shadows upon the ground. Unbidden, a yawn passed through his lips. He'd hardly slept since leaving the Caw's Nest, and even there he'd spent the night pacing for a few hours before attempting to fall asleep.

Rubbing his jaw, a gentle breeze stirred the branches above and rained down the last of the clinging leaves. For a moment, it was as though the sky itself was pouring the golden leaves down upon him.

He had come close to death in that tavern, they all had. Somehow out here, away from Mirtain, death was more probable. Or maybe it was his fear of the unknown which kept him from really being able to relax. Death was coming for him in forms he'd never had to face before.

His entire life had been spent in a routine which Lord Hernan had set for him. Though Ansie hadn't always been safe, he'd hardly ever feared for her life.

Deep down, Willem knew he was happier than he'd been in Mirtain. More satisfied. He was doing something, taking action, but sometimes the cost seemed too high. He wondered if he would have made it this far if Ansie hadn't come with him.

He smiled wryly to himself, already knowing the answer. He probably wouldn't have left Mirtain if she hadn't forcibly decided to go. He hadn't been given much in his life, but the one thing which had been entrusted to him was to see her safe, and so he had.

But now his role had changed. None of them had spoken of it since leaving Alesmann. Larn had said nothing about saving all their necks by marrying Ansie, and Ansie, well she had been avoiding Larn as much as possible.

Willem was indebted to this strange man of the north, and it ate at him. But more than that was the anger he felt at having ruined Ansie's dreams. There had been a time, back when Kata had chosen Jethron over him, that he had lost hope. Ansie had become the one shining glory in his life, the one glimpse of joy.

And now—he sucked in a shaky breath—he'd stood by and watched as her happiness was extinguished. She'd once spoken of a life beyond Mirtain, of freedom, seeing the mountains, raising a family, and he knew just who she'd wanted to make those dreams with. But now, it was over. She was bound to Larn, and him to her. In mere moments, Willem had watched her tie her life to a practical stranger, and she was no longer his.

A crisp golden leaf fell on his head, and opening his eyes, he pulled it off, twirling it in his fingers. What an odd thing, something so beautiful and yet so deadly when it came to blending in with the forest.

We're lucky to be alive. The thought seemed to burn in his mind and he knew it was true. They really shouldn't be alive at this point. By all accounts, the verrals should have killed them.

For a moment, all his helplessness and worry slipped away. Without knowing what he was doing, he looked up to the sky, staring at the blank expanse as though searching for answers.

Thank you. He let the words fill him, casting them from himself as though some unseen being might hear. Somehow, as the sky deepened in color, and the sun continued to dip lower, he felt as though his voice had been heard.

CHAPTER 37

Darkness met Ansie's eyes when she next opened them. A deep blanket seeming to cover the earth, though she heard the subtle clacking of bare branches stirring in the wind. Her face was pressed against something rough, and as her eyes slowly adjusted, she began to see the glow of the moons on the leaf-strewn ground.

She could just make out the dim outlines of Tympmor and the other horses, tied to a tree just outside the cave.

The cave. Ansie grimaced, remembering the reason why they were there in the first place. Images of the verrals fiercely attacking them flashed through her mind. And then there was the verral who'd nearly killed her, its claw aimed directly for her heart.

She closed her eyes, not wanting to remember turning away the hot breath of the verral on her neck as she ducked. It had been the searing pain of the claw entering her shoulder which had made her vision turn white.

She'd lain there, thinking she was dead when she came to and spotted her dagger lying nearby. Scrambling over the leaves and struggling to her feet, she spotted the verral as it readied to leap at Larn.

Ansie internally flinched, remembering the utter terror of seeing Willem and Larn recovering from their fight and not noticing the prowling verral. Her hand had risen on its own and thrown the dagger into the belly of the beast.

The pain that followed had brought her to her knees, and it was all she remembered until the cave. Like shards of glass, she had moved in and out of understanding as Willem and Larn worked to remove the claw from her shoulder. She knew it was Larn who had held her hand.

Larn. His name was like a beacon.

Her eyes searched the cave, not seeing him anywhere in the darkness. He'd certainly been there when Willem left. He'd talked to her, mumbled strange words in that language of his.

While lying on her cheek, she could only see outside the cave. As another gust of wind rattled the bare trees, a few leaves tumbled upon the stone closer to her. She glanced around, wondering if she was the only one awake. The thought chilled.

Lifting her head to turn it to the other side, pain shot across her shoulder with radiating heat. She gasped.

"Careful," Larn's soft voice reached her from further in the cave.

She made to move again, and he told her to stay put. With a soft groan, he stepped over her until she could see him, his body silhouetted against the shadows of the trees outside. Maybe it was her imagination, but it seemed the moons were shining all the brighter the more she awakened.

Distracted, she let her eyes rove over the tinges of rose light. As always, the Neho moon shone brighter than Cadna's. Only on Festis Luna would hers shine with a vibrant red, to remind the realm of their passionate love.

She sighed, closing her eyes. "Where's Willem?" She asked, wondering why her throat was so dry.

"Just outside, sleeping."

She wanted to nod but knew it would be too painful. A silly notion to think such a simple gesture could cause her pain.

A weight seemed to rest between them, an expanse which hadn't been present until the events at Caw's Nest. She'd lost track of the days since she spoke her vows, each one blending into the next and the distance growing greater by the moment.

She was a coward and knew it. Deep down, she wished she could be the kind of girl who placed her heart on the line, the one who wasn't afraid to risk opening up to someone. But that wasn't who she was. It didn't matter who she had been with Skurn, deep down she knew that she had welcomed his care because it was easy. They'd been comfortable together, but she'd never really given him all of her heart—because, in the end, she feared being alone.

Returning back to the conversation at hand, she yawned. "I'm glad he's resting, he needs it."

Larn chuckled. "So do you."

"True." She met his gaze, wondering what he was thinking. "How bad is it?"

He glanced at the bulky bandage along her shoulder. "It'll be a scar worthy of a warrior." He winked, a flippant grin parting his lips.

She fought back a smile and allowed his humor to placate her for the moment. What he wasn't telling her was the ghastly sight of the wound. It had been deep, she'd been able to feel how far it dug into her flesh. And every budge had sent a fire along her back as Willem forcibly removed the imposing claw.

"Can I see it?" she asked.

"Maybe if you turn your head, but I have a feeling that's not the best idea right now."

"Not the wound," she yawned again, "the claw."

"Oh," he said and pulled the claw out of his pocket. Somehow without the rest of the verral attached to it, the claw didn't seem so dangerous. "Rather impressive," Larn said, staring at the tip that had entered her shoulder. She swallowed, not really certain what to say.

A lingering sense of unspoken words filled the silence. She could feel the things she wanted to say creeping up her throat, hear the words in her mind, but her tongue was unable to speak what must be said. They both continued to stare at the razor edges of the claw.

"It was my fault," Larn muttered softly. Her brow furrowed, in confusion. "For what happened at the Caw's Nest. I should've been paying more attention, I shouldn't have threatened them—it's my fault we ended up in this mess."

As he spoke, she watched him carefully. He was staring at the opposite cave wall, blinking quickly in obvious discomfort. This was the Larn she had glimpsed a few times. Normally he was carefree, the calm in the storm, but here was the man whose heart had thundered beneath her ear as he tricked death in the Caw's Nest.

"Not your fault," she said, and his dark eyes moved to hers. They seemed to glow in the darkness, reflecting what little moonlight reached inside the cave. "You were exhausted, we all were."

"That's not a good enough excuse," he murmured.

"Well, if you and Willem would let me be on watch for more than two hours at a time, maybe you wouldn't be so tired."

He chuckled, the sound seeming to rumble in his chest. "True enough." The words were half-hearted.

"You saved us all from death, that has to be worth something." She licked her lips. "And I wanted to thank you, for-for giving up your freedom."

"You gave up yours too, saved my neck."

"Just make sure it's worth saving," she winked and was pleased to see the grim line of his mouth ease. It was interesting how a few simple words could overcome the expanse between two people.

"I never thought I'd be married," Larn confessed, glancing down at her and away again. She wondered if he knew his hair shimmered even in the dark of night. It looked soft, and she found herself watching as he ran his fingers through it.

"I did," she admitted.

He looked up. The regret in her voice was something she couldn't hide.

"Who would you have married?" He was watching her now with an intensity she hadn't quite seen before. It was deep, coursing through him. She had the strange notion that he was the type of person who cared deeply for those close to him. His heart wasn't easily won, but once bought, it could never be returned. In those eyes, she saw a divine spark of passion, unencumbered and pulsing through him.

Unbidden, Skurn came to mind. She knew it would've been him if she'd stayed in Mirtain. If given the chance, they would've married or run away and started a life together.

"I don't know," she said and shrugged, immediately regretting it as fire shot across her shoulder and down her arm.

"Careful," Larn chided.

Her eyes were closed, waiting for the last wave of pain to ebb away. She felt as though the skin along the back of her shoulder had been stretched and pulled until it could no longer move the way it was supposed to. It burned as though the needle was still poking her flesh and tightening over the wound, sealing it shut.

"I wish we had something to ease the pain," Larn said, she could feel his gaze on her. She would have fidgeted if it didn't hurt so much.

"It'll pass," she sighed. "Maybe if we meet up with that Gallian patrol again I can show them my scar. Then he'll think it's my mark."

She didn't mean for the words to be funny, but they had Larn laughing to himself all the same. "That's one way to think about it."

Hours in the saddle had allowed her mind to wander. She still didn't quite understand what Oslo had meant about a marking on Larn. She bit her lip, wondering if she should ask. Her timid heart wanting to draw back and leave things as they were.

"What—what is your mark?

"I thought I already told you."

Her face flushed. "You told me what it was for, not what it is. I—I couldn't see it."

"Oh," he said, and there was a distinct tightness around his eyes that she didn't understand. "It's simple really, sort of a coming of age ritual. The Maereo believe in the spirits of animals, and when a boy becomes a man, or warrior, he is marked with some animal that represents his nature."

"Like a quality?"

"Sort of," he sighed, running a hand through his hair again. This time he drew his knees up and rested his forearms along the tops. "We're marked with a gift, something innate to us. I have higher than normal levels of hearing, and I communicate with animals well."

"So you're part animal?" she asked, trying to make him laugh again. She had liked the sound.

"No," he smiled, the lines around his mouth suddenly appearing. "It's the mark of a wolf."

She hadn't intended for it to happen, but even hearing the word sent a shiver down her spine, and searing pain along her shoulder. Perhaps her eyes had widened, the horrors of that day in Mirtain forest with the *simian*, coming back to her. She squeezed her eyes shut, not wanting to relive it all.

"Hey," Larn said softly, all traces of laughter gone. She looked up. "There's no reason to be scared of me." He shifted uncomfortably.

"I'm not," she said, swallowing her memories and forcing herself to stay in the moment. If she thought about the wolves or the verrals, and how there could be more not far from their little cave, she would worry herself to tears.

"I'll do what I can to protect you, just as Willem does." He kept his steady gaze focused on her the entire time he spoke, his words running over her like a soothing balm. He seemed to be speaking as much to her as to himself.

"I know," she said softly, surprised to realize she meant it. "What did you want, before all of this?"

"Before what? Before getting dragged into a rebellion?" He snorted, "since I was a child, probably just food."

The thought warmed her. "No, really."

"Freedom," he whispered, and she recognized the longing in the word. It was a cry from his soul, one she had often felt. "My plan was to fight this war, and if I lived through it, I was going to find somewhere all to myself to simply be. To live my own life without having any rules or restrictions on my back."

The silence stretched between them and she felt as though her every breath was a gift he had given her. Only because of his quick thinking were they still alive.

"So," he began, "what were you going to do with your life before all this happened?"

"Those are two very different questions—with very different answers." She smiled, he was diverting. She wondered if he was distracting her on purpose.

"How so?"

"Well, there was reality, and then there was what I hoped for."

"Start with the first," he suggested.

She sighed, "I would've spent all my days in Mirtain, alone, until death came for either me or Willem." She glanced up. "Lord Hernan wouldn't let me marry anyone, I was his bargaining chip over Willem."

"He's a pleasant fellow." He leaned his head back against the cave wall. "And what about the other?"

Ansie swallowed, not sure if she could say the words, or if she dared to share this part of herself with him. Taking a deep breath, she felt as though she was standing on the edge of a cliff, about to plunge into a space where she had no control. "I would have married Sk-Skurn," she stumbled, "and we would've run off and lived in a place to call our own."

It was silent for a long moment and she glanced up again. His brow was furrowed, creating shadowed lines along his forehead. "I see," was all he said.

She breathed in the darkness, letting it fill the space between them as she waited for him to speak. For some reason, her heart was pounding heavily within her chest. Never before had she spoken her desire to marry Skurn. She had dreamed dreams with Skurn, hoped upon a whim, but her deepest desires had remained a mystery,even to Skurn. There was a time when she would've told him, but that was before she realized it was never to be—and now it never could.

The ground beneath her cheek grew tough, but she remained for fear of the pain that would erupt in her shoulder. Ever so slowly, she realized she was watching Larn as he stared outside the cave. Her breaths began to match his, in, and then, out. She wondered if he understood how calm he often made her feel.

Maybe it was the way he seemed to view the world, as though it could offer him nothing more than he allowed. Or maybe it was the aloofness with which he placed himself in all situations. But deep down, she knew it was the closeness they had shared in that tavern. For that one moment she had felt the beat of his heart, and knowing his own fear, somehow made him all the more real to her. All the assurance she needed was in the careful protection he had provided in that moment. He had acted, selflessly, and calmly, though his fears had rivaled hers.

"Larn?" she whispered, enjoying the way his name rolled easily off her tongue. "Can you tell me about the moons?"

He glanced her way, a softness easing around his mouth. For a moment, he turned to look outside, the glow of the moons casting the lines of his face in shadow again. He was more tired than he let on, more exhausted than he cared to let her see.

"At the fall of the Animle, some of the Praelia sought refuge in the mountains, their strength waning as they climbed through the frozen land. They told us a different story about the origin of the moons, one of a spirit and fire." Despite the passion of his words, he rubbed at his nose, sniffing. "The Praelia believe in the Espiritu, a sort of presence," he waved his hands, "like a force that governs the realm. It seeks out the hearts of men and women, and works for the good, for the light."

Looking up, he paused. The clouds shifted, bending and rippling like stalks of wheat in a field.

"The white moon was said to represent the Espiritu, the powerful force fighting for good. The red," he took a deep breath, "was said to be the blood of the Animle."

Ansie blinked, not sure if she had heard him correctly. "Blood?"

He nodded. "The blood of a promise, to fight the darkness and to never let hope die."

Tiny bumps rose along her flesh and a breeze passed by, shifting the naked branches of the trees. The rustle of the leaves across the ground left a chilling tingle in her spine. She suddenly had the feeling they weren't alone. The air around them stilled, sounds slowing, dimming, until all that was left was a low hum. It wasn't loud, nor was it soft, but it was persistent. A thrum like a steady pulse, reverberating through one's chest.

It was calling to her, she could feel it. It was warmth, light, but not the light of the moon, but the inward heat of the sun that seeped through one's skin and into their soul. A kind of warmth that brought a smile to her lips. Without thinking, she began to reach out with her good hand, sliding it along the stone floor.

And then, as fast as it had come, it was gone. She gasped, realizing she hadn't taken a breath for a time.

"Did you feel that?" She asked.

Larn was watching her, the lines around his mouth dipping. "It's just a story," he said.

"I—I've never heard it before." Had she imagined that presence, that feeling of being watched, of being known? Larn had spoken of a force, was it true?

She shied away from the thought. If it was true, then how could there be so much death and destruction? No, it couldn't be true. She couldn't believe in some force, what she believed in was right in front of her. It was life, death, hope, fear. All of it, she knew and felt, but this force, this supposedly, Espiritu, it was something foreign.

"What about Neho and Cadna?" The story had always been her favorite.

"Most likely it's a myth," he leaned closer to her. "You realize I just told you the other one to pass the time, right? That's what all of these tales are, ways to pass the time when you're so cold you can't think straight, or when you survived a verral attack and need some relief." He smirked.

"Nice," she grumbled. Deep down she wanted to believe him, and she would've if not for that odd sense of presence.

"All I can think is that some poor man made up the story to pass the time, it got swapped around campfires until it became truth."

"But you believe in the Animle," she pointed out.

"Did you see that *simian*?" He turned to face her. "That's something I can understand, it's before me, it's real, it's—" he broke off suddenly and whipped a dagger out of his belt, pointing it into the darkness behind Ansie. Her heart skipped a beat.

Crouching forward, he peered into the dark. Shifting, his feet slowly across the ground, he passed her and entered the dark, she wanted to turn her head but knew she couldn't. Silence filled the cave, and she held her breath for fear it would give them away.

Larn's sigh nearly made her scream. "Must have been a trick of the light," he mumbled. His boots scuffed the stone as he settled somewhere behind her, out of sight.

"What did you think it was?" She whispered, still afraid to breathe.

"I could've sworn I saw a hand."

"A hand!" She gasped.

"Shhh," he fretted, the hint of a laugh in his voice. The sound was enough to calm her fears, if only slightly.

"Why don't you get some sleep Ansie," he said. Her face warmed, it was the first time he had said her name since the Caw's Nest.

"I'll try, although I can't promise my dreams will be any good. Not after all these stories of strange spirits and magical hands."

"And the verrals, don't forget them."

"Thank you," she rolled her eyes even though he couldn't see them. "I wouldn't want to forget them."

"I wouldn't think so," there was a smile in his voice, a gentleness to the way he spoke. It was how she knew it was genuine. Too often he smiled, but there was an edge to it, the hidden Larn residing deep within.

"Goodnight," she yawned.

"You can call me Larn, you know?"

She bit her lip. Had he noticed how she had been avoiding calling him by name too? How she had been holding him at a distance?

For the first time since leaving Mirtain, Ansie felt a growing affection bud in her chest. It was soft, with the subtle glow of a fading summer sun. For just a moment it warmed her, and she found herself wanting to offer him something in return. She could offer him friendship, couldn't she? She would have to move now, if she ever did. Once the light of the moons disappeared with the dawning of morn, the closeness they shared would fade away.

"Well then, goodnight, Larn."

"I'm guessing you still won't let me call you Ans?"

The name hung in the air between them. Daring, she licked her lips. "No, but if you ever want to, you could call me Anserietta. That's my full name."

Silence met her words, and she felt as though she could hear his thoughts churning. Did he understand that only Willem had known her by that name? Not even Kata had known what Ansie stood for.

Her heart thundered as she waited, and then it came, so softly if she hadn't been listening, she might have missed it. "Goodnight, Anserietta."

Her mouth lifted and her eyes closed. Somewhere in the night, the memory of it all faded, and with the morning light came the rising of a new challenge. And that was to see if she could move. Anserietta was once again tucked away.

CHAPTER 38

Umbris was quite certain her fingers were going to fall off, either her fingers or her eyes would give out. It was simply a matter of which would happen first.

A hissing gasp escaped her lips when she pricked her thumb. She hastened to suck the drop of blood away from the wound. It was the fourth time she had stabbed herself with the offensive little weapon that evening alone. There had been a point of time in her life in which she had thought she was rather skilled with a needle, but it seemed the many hours and lack of significant lighting were getting to her.

It had been nearly a week since Umbris had been brought to the palace, and still, she had no further idea as to what she was doing. Every day she awoke with the sense today would be the moment she was sent back to *Le Jupon Rouge*. Her fears were well-founded, her uncertainty of what the Regent meant to do with her was a mystery.

Six days and she had yet to see or hear anything from the Regent or Commander Jolson, or even the valet, Garval. She shivered, as always, thinking of the night the men had questioned her about Fort Jontru.

Though it hadn't taken her long to fall asleep the first night, her world had been entirely different when she awoke the following morning. The chatter and gentle movements, of the maids hurrying to prepare for the day, along the hall had left her wondering what to do when the head maid, Charlise, had opened her door.

Umbris was given a new set of clothes to change into, a faded blue bodice and dull striped skirt which was nearly too long. It swept along the floor and most likely would have tripped her if she was ever given the chance to leave her room. She would need to hem it if she could ever find the time. Over the dress was a dark brown apron which was more than likely a scrap of an old blanket tucked into the waistline of her skirt.

More than anything, Umbris had found the corset to be uncomfortable. It seemed all the women in the palace wore a corset, something Anglans never did, at least not on a daily basis. A few of the Anglan women would hasten to wear one at special events, but wearing one daily was a way of subtly showing one's wealth. The garment made it difficult to move and breathe, thus giving others the impression of a higher status of living.

After only a day of wearing the accursed corset, she had cast it aside. As it was, she was still thin enough from her imprisonment that others wouldn't know the difference if she was wearing it or not.

Upon that first morning, Charlise had returned with two maids in tow. One carried a tray of warmed bread and the other had a pile of mending in her arms. They were the same two maids who had seen her in the Regent's chambers.

Even thinking of their narrowed stares had Umbris wondering what she could have done to make them hate her so much.

Sighing, she leaned in closer to the quickly melting candle, the only light in the room. Her eyes strained to see the stitches in the worn fabric. After her first assignment of mending the stable hand's aprons and rags, Charlise had seen her abilities and given her more important work. Umbris now found herself mending the hems and seams of the maids' dresses.

The familiar clatter and scuffs of tired feet sounded along the hall, the day was coming to an end. She always kept her door open, hoping in some way she would be able to pick up a scrap of information, but it seemed she was going to waste away, sequestered in the small chamber. Not that she minded, at least, not entirely.

Another prick of her thumb had her sucking away at the blood again. If her mother was here, she would chide her for being too distracted. Tears sprung to her eyes, the wetness making it nearly impossible to see. It wasn't the first time she'd thought of her mother as she worked. It came as no surprise, with every stroke of the needle, she could hear her mother giving her little bits of advice and guidance.

Sometimes it was all too much.

A soft knock sounded on her door and she wiped at her eyes. Charlise was standing in the doorway, her dark blue dress with a gold braided bodice was as pristine as always.

"The mending?" she asked, raising one of her dark eyebrows. She always spoke in clipped, short words. Very different from the gentle cadence most Gallians spoke with. Charlise had ink-black hair, the kind that when it was pulled back, made her look as though she had no hair at all. Although, the few graying strands helped to diminish the shadow of her sleek hair. Only at the end of the day were a few strands out of place, creating soft, fuzzy ringlets around her ears.

"I'm nearly finished," Umbris replied, keeping her head low.

"With all of it?"

"Yes, Madame." Umbris nodded and looked up. It wasn't the first time the woman seemed surprised by her ability to mend quickly. What Charlise didn't understand was how idleness accompanied memories, and memories brought pain and worry into her heart. She would do anything to keep it at bay.

Charlise stepped into the room, picking up a few of the items before folding them on the cot. "Well done. It seems you'll be in need of more work tomorrow." Umbris nodded, her questions resting on her tongue, as they had for the last few days. "I will send Magetta to give you more mending."

"Yes, Madame."

"You need not call me that," Charlise sighed, and when Umbris looked up she found the older woman peering at her in a way which made her draw back into herself. It was a gaze that saw her, not just what she appeared to be. It put her on edge, reminding her of how the Regent had watched her that first night. "Everyone here calls me Charlise."

"Yes, Mad—Charlise." The name sounded odd and informal on her tongue.

Charlise gave her a tight smile, her lips seeming to stretch. "That's better."

Umbris was left to herself all too soon, the silence of the night pulling at her. As she leaned in to look closer at her stitches, she found her mind wandering as it so often did to the Regent. For some reason, as night fell she couldn't stop thinking of the way he had looked at her as she left his chambers.

Sleep well, Umbris. He'd said. *Don't speak of what was said here, it would be a shame for you to be taken away again.*

The warning in his words had sent her reeling backward, and yet, he had actually seen her. Through all the dirt and the grime of her life, she knew he had actually seen the person beneath it all.

As always, the thought got her heart racing and she didn't even notice the woman who had entered her room.

"Keeping your door open now?" It was a high voice which spoke, refined with sultry perfection and dripping with pride.

Umbris looked up from her work, finding one of the maids who had served her while she was in the Regent's chambers, the blonde one. Umbris assumed her name was Magetta. By the looks of the stack of mending in the maid's arms, Umbris knew she was in for a long day tomorrow. Her back protested all the more simply thinking about the hours she would spend sitting in the hard chair. Maybe the corset would help to keep her back straight, but it would probably make things worse.

"What?" Umbris asked.

Magetta shrugged. She had a delicate frame, curved in all the right places. Her hair was perfectly golden and soft, but there was nothing about her gaze which was light. She glared at Umbris, dropping the new pile of mending onto the floor at her feet.

"That should satisfy you for tomorrow," it was a statement, not a question. Magetta placed her hands on her hips, seeming to establish her presence in the room. Umbris wondered if the maid was aware of how low her bodice was. It seemed she must be, so much skin showing must make her cold.

"Thank you," Umbris said simply, turning back to her work. She had spent enough time around spiteful females to know how to handle a girl like Magetta. She'd been in places this woman could hardly imagine and for some reason, the thought nearly had her smiling. For all the fire Magetta had, she was nothing compared to some of the women Umbris dealt with in Fort Jontru.

"Don't thank me," Magetta spit. "You're nothing to me. The Regent should send you back to whatever gutter you came from. Seems odd he's even kept you for so long."

She was digging for information, Umbris gave her a once over and returned to her work. "It is odd."

"Where did you come from anyway?"

"That's not really your concern."

"It is actually," Magetta's voice turned sickeningly sweet. "I'd prefer to know if I'm living under the same roof as a whore, although by the looks of it I already have my answer."

How the girl was so easily able to disarm her, Umbris didn't know. With one glance at her wrists, her shame was borne.

Umbris swallowed heavily around the lump in her throat. She'd had practice hiding her true self, she knew how to keep all of it as far away as needed, forcing her reality to be something entirely different than who she really was. She had built her walls high.

They couldn't touch her, not really. So why did it still hurt?

"Why are you here?" Magetta asked, crossing her arms, blocking the only way out of the room as though Umbris might run. But Magetta didn't know how she felt comfortable in closed walls. It was outside where she was afraid.

"Doesn't matter."

"I need an answer, now."

"Charlise doesn't need one." Umbris threw the head maid's name in the girl's face, hoping to scare her off.

"There have been lots of rumors about you." Magetta took a step further into the room. Umbris wondered if the maid could see the way her pulse thrummed in her neck. "I have my theories," she pursed her round lips. "I saw you in the Regent's chambers, but what he would be doing with rubbish like you, I have no idea."

She's jealous. The thought struck Umbris quite suddenly.

As soon as the words came out of the girl's mouth, Umbris heard them for what they truly were. The woman was jealous of finding her in the Regent's private chambers, the thought was so ridiculous it nearly had her laughing.

As far as she was concerned, Magetta could have him.

"Perhaps you should ask the Regent," Umbris suggested and watched with pleasure as shock and then anger passed over Magetta's face. For a moment, they glared at one another until Umbris broke the silence. "If you would excuse me, it seems I have a lot of mending to do."

Magetta clenched her jaw, the threat evident. Only now did Umbris realize why the girl's bodice was so low. As Magetta turned and left the room, Umbris shook her head. If the maid only knew how much she wished to trade lives, she wouldn't be jealous at all.

The following morning brought a sharp rap on the door. Umbris had fallen asleep in the chair by her bed, a crick had formed in her neck from sleeping at an odd angle, her mending in her lap.

"Yes?" she asked, her voice raspier than usual.

The door opened quickly, Charlise stepping inside. "Get up."

Umbris hurried to stand, straightening her skirt and the worn, mud-colored apron bulging around her hips. She kept her eyes on the floor, suddenly very aware of how her hair was sticking out at all angles.

"I'm s-sorry, Mada—Charlise."

"None of that," Charlise waved a hand, her breaths coming in huffs. "These need to be fixed and right away."

Looking up, Umbris now noticed the black breeches in the woman's hand. Charlise tossed them to her and upon immediate touch, Umbris knew it was finer fabric than she had ever handled before.

"I'll get started." She sat in her chair once more and began to pull out black thread as she examined the long tear along the outward seam in the breeches. As it was split along the seam, no patchwork would be necessary. She could fix the breeches without a trace of her hand having touched them.

"Good, finish it as soon as you can, and then deliver them to His Sire's chambers."

She froze. "The Regent?"

"Of course," Charlise disposed her question quickly. "See to it you get those to His Sire before he readies for his daily ride. You have less than an hour."

Charlise disappeared in an instant leaving Umbris staring at the empty doorway, her thoughts seemingly paused, and yet running frantically through her mind all at once. Only touching the fabric brought her back to her senses.

She hurried through the stitches, making sure they matched the original thread. Only once was she given pause as the smell of fresh pine wafted up to her. Her hands froze, making her realize just what she was doing. The sheer incredibility of it all had her shaking from the inside out.

Tying off the last of the thread, she quickly examined her work, making sure it was unnoticeable. If there was one thing her mother had taught her, it was to make sure no one knew where her needle had been.

She raced out of her room and down the hall for the first time in days. It seemed all of the maids walked to the right, so she hurried along hoping she was going the correct way. It hadn't occurred to her to ask Charlise where she was supposed to go.

Down some stairs, and into a dimly lit hallway, she hurried. There was nothing on the walls to mark it different from any other. No one was in sight and as she rounded a few more corners, she suddenly knew she wouldn't be able to find her way back to her own room. The thought gave her panic as she began to try every door she saw.

Closets seemed to line the entire hall, bed sheets and linens, tools and extra uniforms layered on shelves. One closet was even filled with silver candlesticks, more silver than she had ever seen in her life.

Pushing on another door, she suddenly found herself outside the servants' quarters and in the palace itself. As though being awakened quite suddenly by a loud noise, she realized how inappropriate her clothes were when surrounded by such finery. Even if she had been wearing the light blue maid's uniform, she would have felt dingy compared to it all.

There was no time to waste as she paced down one of the halls, hoping to find someone who could point her in the right direction. She highly doubted she would recognize anything after her whirlwind through the palace in the dark.

Swallowing heavily, she began to walk faster than before, each room seeming to outdo the next with finery and dripping in gold. She paced back and forth between doors, torn from one side to the next, uncertain of just what to do. Room after room, she chose one door, or a hall over the other, having no idea if she was even heading in the same direction she had come.

All the while, a ticking clock in her mind warned her of each passing second. She burst through another door, the room inside larger than any she had seen thus far, books upon books were stacked on shelves, their golden titles gleaming at her. Large windows tracked from the floor to the ceiling, revealing a breathtaking view of the gardens which seemed to stretch for miles.

A fumbling clatter and a string of curses caught her attention.

"Hello?" she asked.

A light-brown head shot up from the other side of a couch, the curls creating a near halo. He flicked his head to the side to clear a long curl from his eyes.

"I didn't know anyone was here." His eyes were wide, his cheeks rosy with embarrassment. If the boy only knew what horrible things she'd heard in fort Jontru, he wouldn't be so concerned.

"I need to find His Sire's chambers." She held up the pants in her hand, suddenly wondering if she should have folded them. "I'm in quite a hurry."

"His Sire's chambers?" the boy's eyebrows shot up beneath the curls hiding his forehead.

"Yes, I think I'm lost."

"I would say so," he nodded. "You're on the wrong side of the palace. This is the Livre Wing."

She bit her lip, it was as though he was speaking a different language. "Oh," she mouthed and turned to look in the direction she had come.

"Not that way," he smiled, a dimple forming on his right cheek, and then pointed to the other door.

She hurried toward the side of the room, then paused. "I have no idea where I'm going, even if this is the right direction." She only now saw the many books stacked in piles at his feet. A dirty rag lay on the ornate rug and a few of the books had fallen over in shambles. "I'm sorry, you have work to finish."

"As do you," he said and stepped out from behind the couch. He wore the uniform of the male servants, deep blue vest, white shirt perfectly cleaned, and black boots reaching to his knees. "Would you like my assistance?"

"Please," she said and dashed to the door. "I'm supposed to give this to him as soon as possible."

"Those are His Sire's?" his eyes widened slightly again, as he pointed at the clothing.

"Yes," she threw open the door, trying to make him realize how much she needed to get moving. Only now did he seem to understand the direness of her situation. He hurried along the halls, waving her along behind him, his nervousness only making the pit in her stomach gape wider.

Down halls and through chambers they moved, their feet not making a sound over the plush rugs. It was a subtle change, but one she noticed when the walls began to shift from light shades of cream to the slightly darker tones of pastel blues and polished wood. Somehow, she knew they were getting close and she gripped the breeches all the tighter.

"Here we are," the servant boy pulled up next to a door. It was polished to perfection, the shiny wood smelling of cedar and it glinted, reflecting the light from the enormous windows at the end of the hall. In the center of the door was a crest inlaid with gold—a twisting 'R' that curved and dipped, the end of the letter blending in with golden flowers decorating the frame. She stared, it was the same swirling letter that marked the inside of her wrists.

"Should I knock?" she asked, her voice shaking.

His eyes widened, "You should probably wait for Garval." He was already edging away from the door.

She nodded. It seemed odd Charlise hadn't told her to deliver the pants to the valet, even odder was her giving the task to Umbris.

"I leave you here," the young servant's voice reached her and though she wanted to take her eyes away from the door, she couldn't. She didn't even remember being in this hall the night the Regent had brought her here. Perhaps they had taken some other passage directly to his rooms—the whole night was a blur.

"Where do I go after?" she said softly, her voice nearly hoarse.

"Take that door," she looked away to see him point to the wall at the end of the long, blue-carpeted hall. "It's a servant's passage, try and head to the left whenever you can, that should get you back to the maid's quarters, in the East Wing."

Umbris nodded and turned back to the door. All too soon, she realized she was alone—the young boy had left her to return to his own work.

An uneasiness lumped in her stomach, and her hands shook as she reached up to knock. The sound seemed to echo in the hall but nothing happened. She expected the valet to answer the door and scold her for her boldness.

After a moment longer of waiting, she pushed on the golden handle, the door swinging open to reveal the blue room she had been in the first night. In the light of day, the alternating deep and pastel blues draping the walls and cushions seemed to have a calming effect on her nerves. In here, a gentle essence of pine reached her nostrils.

The hearth stood empty, the private table where she had dined was scattered with the remains of a meal. She couldn't help noticing how the room seemed dirtier than it had before. After the immaculate halls she had passed through, she wondered why the Regent's own chambers were so neglected.

"Hello?" she asked, her voice barely above a whisper. "Garval?"

No answer, no sound except for the ticking of the clock on the mantle. She paced across the room, all too aware of the bright light from the glorious sun outside, which poured into the room. The beams awakened the entire space, the soft streams revealing the floating specs of dust clinging to the air.

Standing before the bedroom door, she hesitated, uncertain. Once more she raised her hand, pausing as her heart hammered in her chest, it didn't seem right.

Maybe he already left, the thought gave her hope and she lowered her hand, only to raise it once more.

Taking a deep breath, she prepared to knock when a muffled voice sounded just behind the door. She scurried away, heart in her throat, only to hear the door open. She froze, pants still in hand.

Succumbing to her fate, she turned and faced the doorway, hoping her cheeks weren't as red as they felt. Meeting her gaze was a woman, a nightgown covering her slim frame, dark golden ringlets hanging down around her shoulders in disarray.

"Yes?" the woman asked, a lilt in her voice. She was certainly of the upper class. Umbris shifted beneath her curious stare.

"I brought these for His Sire," she held out the breeches as though they were an offering. She wasn't sure if she should curtsy or not.

"Hmm," the woman made an odd sound in the back of her throat, when Umbris looked up she noticed where the woman's focus was. Her wrists, the marks of her shame flashed between them. It took Umbris only a moment to notice the nakedness of the other woman's wrists. She bared no marks.

"I'm sure you did," she gave her a look up and down, then seemed to focus on Umbris' hair.

"Here," Umbris held them out, knowing what the woman must be thinking. The very thought of it set her heart pounding, the past was closing in.

The deep timbre of a mumbled voice from inside the room made her stomach clench. The woman turned back, a smirk still gracing her lips.

"It isn't Garval," she called into the room, her speech dripping with playful elegance. There was a response, but again, Umbris couldn't make out the words.

She was still standing with her arm awkwardly extended, the pants in hand when the Regent stepped out of the room, his chest bare and pants hanging low off his hips. The riding breeches fell from her hand to the floor, and Umbris cast her eyes to her feet.

"Garval isn't feeling well," the Regent crooned, "I told you as much last night."

"I must have forgotten," the woman said and then giggled.

If it was possible, Umbris' cheeks flamed all the brighter as he kissed the woman. If she could shrink into the wall and disappear, she would have.

"What do you have for me?" The Regent asked her, his bare feet suddenly coming into her line of sight on the floor.

"These, my Sire," she bent over to grab the breeches which lay in a pool of black fabric near their feet. She cursed herself for not having folded them beforehand.

She held them out again and when he didn't take them, she raised her gaze. He stood before her, arms by his sides, chest bared and hair hanging down below his ears. For only a moment did he show a glimpse of surprise before he smiled, the creases around one side of his mouth creating perfect little half circles. His dimple deepened.

"Thank you," he drawled, turning back to the woman in the nightgown. "You're dismissed, I must speak to this maid alone."

The woman's eyes flashed back and forth between them, her gaze landing on Umbris's wrists before she sauntered forward with a pout. Her intent was clear until the Regent held up his hand—the motion enough to stop the woman in her tracks. She soon disappeared back into the bedroom, only to reappear moments later, her dress and shoes in hand.

Umbris shifted on her feet as the door closed behind them, well aware she was in the presence of the ruler of the realm, and very much alone.

"What can I do for you, Umbris?"

Her head flashed back up, surprised at his remembering her name. He turned to the table where some fruit rested in a bowl. He popped two grapes into his mouth while she watched him, her heart pounding in her chest.

He looked back at her expectantly, his deep blue gaze pulling her in. She nearly trembled where she stood.

"I was only told to bring these to you," she still held the pants in her hand.

"Ah, yes," he waved the words away. "I do believe they were torn on my ride yesterday morning, and I have need of them today."

She nodded as though it was a perfectly logical explanation, though the idea of him having worn something only yesterday, which she was now touching, made her heart pound all the harder. She felt again as though she was seeing some part of him he didn't let others see—something forbidden.

"Wh—where would you like me to put them—my—my—Sire?" she stammered through the question, uncertain whether or not she was even allowed to speak in his presence. If she had any bit of authority in this place, she would go to Charlise and demand an answer for not being forewarned.

"In there is fine," he waved a hand toward the door to the bedroom.

She nodded and hurried through the doorway. Inside was an expansive room, the shades of blue even more evident and profound. Deep blue curtains draped from the windows, blocking out some of the light, though one had been pulled back, bathing the rather large bed in streams of sunlight. The blankets and sheets on the bed were matted and rumpled, the pillows strewn on the floor.

Umbris hurried to one of the chairs in the corner, folding the pants and draping them across the arm as quickly as she could. Only when she turned around, did she notice his presence. He had thrown a shirt over his bare chest, but with the sunlight streaming in behind him, she could still see the outline of his body.

Her face flamed as she ducked her head and moved toward the doorway.

"A maid must be dismissed before she can leave my presence."

She froze and turned back to him. Digging her hands into the worn striped skirt, she hoped the apron hid her trembling.

"I'm s-s-orry, my Sire." She kept her head down and heard him chuckle.

"I'm only teasing," there was a smile in his voice and across his lips when she looked up. "Of course," he turned toward the window, "you do have to wait until I excuse you, but I'm willing to let that slide, given your recent employment."

"Thank you, my Sire."

"What do they have you doing?" he asked, turning back toward her, his hands braced on his hips.

"Mending," she nearly whispered.

"I see, it seems you've done well then." He spoke as though it was obvious, not a question. She nodded, uncertain as to what he wanted with her. "Are they treating you well?"

"Yes, my Sire."

"Good," he nodded and then looked around the room, lips pursed. "It would seem my valet is ill this morning and has forgotten to send someone to set out my clothes. I dress myself most mornings." He spoke as though he was proud of the fact.

He began to rummage through a wardrobe and then pulled on a door near the back end of the room, inside were more shelves than she could fathom. It seemed ridiculous she had been told to mend the riding breeches when he had so many more clothes.

Ripping off his shirt once more, he bared his back to her, the muscles moving seamlessly beneath pristine skin. She found herself looking to the window and the morning light streaming through it.

"My Sire?" she asked, her voice more timid than before.

"Yes?"

"May I leave?"

"You may," he said and from the corner of her eye, she saw him wave a hand toward the door. Without further encouragement, she moved away when her questions from earlier came back to her. She wondered if she could ever be so bold.

"My Sire?" This time, she looked directly back at him. He'd been watching her leave, a new crisp shirt covering his chest.

"Yes?" Somehow when he said the word this time, his voice was deeper, softer in a way that eased her nerves.

"Why am I still here?" She couldn't hold his gaze, her eyes drifting to the laces at the top of his shirt.

"In my chambers? Or my palace?" The smirk was back in his voice and when she met his gaze, she knew he was teasing her again. She didn't smile.

He grew serious in an instant, one blink of his eyes transforming him into a ruler. "Out that window is a realm filled with people trying to fight for what they believe is right. There are spies in my cities, spies in my villages, and my forests. They work for the Renegades and will seek any means to gather information. You heard too much. I need you here, to keep you quiet."

She swallowed, her thoughts turning to Pike and Larn, the Regent had no idea how close he was to the truth. He had no way of understanding her position before she had come to his palace.

"So I won't be going back?" she asked, her voice a little stronger than before.

"No," he pursed his lips, "this is your home now. I suggest you get to know it. And the servant's exit is that way." He pointed to a door on the side of the room without windows. She located the subtle line that revealed a crack along the light blue wall—another nearly hidden door.

She nodded and he waved his hand once more in dismissal.

Heart hammering, she fled from the room and pushed on the hidden door. Beyond the doorway was a small pathway, no larger than for two people to stand abreast. It split, one part leading to the left and what looked like more hallways, and on the right, there was a door which she assumed led to the antechamber of the Regent's rooms.

Cursing herself for having come through the front door, she hastened along the servant passageways. Remembering the servant boy's words from earlier, she kept to the left and followed the many halls and staircases behind the elegant walls of the palace. Her steps seemed to beat beneath her, timing with her heart in a rhythm she couldn't ignore. She had seen the Regent twice and an idea slowly began to form in the back of her mind. She was closer to him than any in the Renegades. Could she dare to help?

There was a chance she would hear something others would never know. She swallowed and let the thoughts swirl around her. If she was going to do it, then she couldn't write anything down. There would be no evidence to convict her.

The Regent himself had told her to get to know the palace, and it seemed he was right. This was her new home, might as well make the most of it.

For who would suspect the girl with the scarred wrists—the very product of the Regent's own making.

CHAPTER 39

"He should have been back by now."

Willem smirked. Hearing Ansie grumble was a welcome sound after the two days of near silence. She had suffered enough, for the time being, the wound on the back of her left shoulder seemed to slowly ease its throbbing.

He had worried after the first night that she would be in undue pain, but she had borne it all with the strength he knew she had. Even now, she sat near the entrance of the cave, her eyes searching the forest though they could hardly make out anything in the early gray of dawn. The temperature had continued to drop over the last two days and combined with the rainfall from the previous evening, there was a thick fog rolling past the cave. At times it remained frozen, unmoving and unchanging, but when the wind stirred it rustled by like water passing over rock.

"Relax, he'll be back," Willem said gently, having already been snapped at twice in the last hour. The grating of his whetting stone on the sword seemed to further Ansie's agitation.

"He said he would be back by sunrise, it's way past that." She tugged on the blanket lying across her shoulders, underneath she wore a crudely fashioned sling from a belt and some cloth.

"You can hardly tell," he muttered and she shot him a fierce look that had him retreating back to his work at hand.

"Will you stop laughing at me?" she stared at the fog as though she could part it with a glare. Two of the horses were visible as blurred shadows, still tied to one of the nearest trees. Somewhere out there, Larn was riding on Tympmor, trying to find some form of game. As it turned out, the little verral meat Willem had salvaged had been too tacky to really eat.

"It's really not funny, Willem." Ansie continued and turned to look at him, wincing as her shoulder shifted.

"I didn't say anything," he held his hands up in surrender, making her roll her eyes. He had to bite back another laugh. She was hardly ever like this, her spirits usually so high he had trouble keeping up. "You don't have to worry about him, he can take care of himself."

"I know that."

"Okay," he smiled, looking back at his sword. He'd struck a nerve.

"What's that supposed to mean?"

"What?"

"That," she was glaring at him now, her amber eyes narrowing, "your ridiculous smile. What does that mean?"

He shrugged, knowing he was getting on her nerves, anything to keep her from wanting to trudge into the fog and find Larn. He'd already had that conversation twice and both times had to persuade her that she wasn't ready to move so much yet. Stars help him, he would tie her to a tree if he had to.

It was easier to laugh at her agitation than confront the realities of why she worried so much. She hated being left behind, and he knew it well. Her father had left her once, and told her he would return. But he never did.

"All I said was you don't have to worry about Larn." Willem sighed, speaking the same way he had the night he found her all alone in the forest. They had never really spoken about it. Sometimes he wondered if she even remembered where he found her. She had been shivering, lost and alone.

As though in response to his thoughts, she shivered again. "Well, I'm not worried," she mumbled. "I know he can take care of himself, but he said he was going to be back and he isn't."

"If only I had a serc for every time you've done that to me."

If there had been something she could throw within reach, he knew she would have done it. Instead, she fixed him with another glare and began muttering under her breath as she turned away. A part of Willem didn't blame Larn for being gone so long. For being in such constant discomfort that she could hardly sleep, Ansie was proving rather irritable.

Willem focused on his sword, scraping the stone along the edge of the blade until it shined, the gleam of it hardly noticeable with so little light to reflect. Lost in the sound of the long grind and concluding zing, he fell into a rhythm. Scrape, zing. Scrape, zing. Scrape, zing.

"You know, after all the times I nursed you back to health, I was never this annoying."Ansie shot the words in his direction, pulling him out of his thoughts.

"I don't know if that's entirely true," he said, without looking up. He could feel her challenge, daring him to make another sound. He was all too willing to accept.

Scrape, zing.

"Do you remember when that stag gored me, flipping me over its antlers and into the tree?" He asked. She grunted in disapproval, clearly recalling his wounds. "You forced me to eat your warm mush for five days straight and prattled on about the gossip in Mirtain every night for hours."

"That was years ago."

"Doesn't matter, I still remember the torture."

"That was for your own good," she muttered, though the beginnings of a small smile tugged at the corner of her mouth. "Besides, I was only following Kata's orders."

A familiar pang tightened his chest, the lightness of the moment disappearing in an instant. He turned back to his sword, letting the stone fill the silence between them.

He often wondered when it would stop, the never-ending ache and longing for Kata. Somedays he thought he was better and then there would be some small reminder of her, and it would all come crashing back. The way it had felt when she smiled at him, when she laughed at one of his jokes.

It reminded him of the fields in Mirtain when the grain stalks reached the height of his hand. There, standing in the middle of a field he liked to watch the ripple of the wind as it rolled across the tops of the grain. He'd often stood there wondering just what had brought the wind, and why did it pass so quickly.

Like the gentle nudging of wind, a thought of Kata would come to him every now and then. Slipping across his mind and touching the parts of his heart he thought were dead. Memories of days when he'd been able to see how the sunlight danced upon her skin, the glimmer of her hair warming as she laughed. She'd had a way of reaching people who often thought they were worthless, a way of letting them know that even if no one else would listen, she would.

He had loved her then. Loved her from afar. And now, he loved her for who she was.

Scrape zing.

His thoughts swirled, going over every detail of what would be their final conversations. How had he not seen? How had she kept so much of herself hidden from him? He couldn't understand it, yet he knew it was true. Jethron's confession had been enough to taint the memories of their shared closeness. He'd thought they knew he was ready to rebel against Lord Hernan. But deep down, he knew that if they had asked him to risk everything to join the Renegades, he wouldn't have been able to. He would have said no, and that's what hurt him the most. His own weakness was part of Kata's downfall.

The day he'd asked her to be his, he'd thought his heart was broken. But even the news of her death didn't hurt him as much as the words Jethron had spoken in Mirtain. The truth was Kata hadn't been able to fully trust him, and it was the worst thing he had ever done to her. For when she'd chosen Jethron, he had promised to love and protect her from afar. But he hadn't, he'd been the cause of her downfall.

"Really, Willem," Ansie turned to him, "would you please stop?" He blinked looking up. His palm was sweating on the stone. "If that isn't sharp enough to cut clean through a man's body with one swing by now, then it's never going to be."

A shadow suddenly loomed out of the fog, and Willem nodded his head in its direction. "There he is."

Ansie's attention was distracted, as Larn dropped from Tympmor's back, two rabbit carcasses hanging from one hand. The cold seemed to swirl around him, stirring his cloak as he cast off his hood and threw the rabbits onto the ground near the pitiful pile of twigs that served as a fire. With a gentle smack to Tympmor's rump, he let the horse roam free. It was odd how the creature never ran off.

"Took you long enough," Ansie grumbled, her face pinched, whether with pain or annoyance, Willem couldn't tell.

"Ahh, I see the charming princess is awake." Larn grinned. "And just how is her highness this morning?"

Willem coughed back a laugh. He had to give it to Larn, the man was undeterred by Ansie's prickled temper. If he had to guess, he would think Larn rather enjoyed it and egged her on to see what she might say.

Instead of answering, Ansie mumbled something under her breath. Whatever she said was too low for Willem to hear, but made Larn smile all the brighter as he took off his swords. One look in Willem's direction nearly made him laugh out loud. He pressed his lips together, all too aware of the sorts of words Ansie tended to say when frustrated.

Larn sighed, and straightened, arms folded across his chest. "Her royal highness is right, I'm late. I can repeat the other words, but I think we've heard enough curses from you." He smirked and Ansie glowered at him, her mouth in a hard line.

"Any sign of a patrol?"

Larn shrugged, "Possibly, but I only spotted three soldiers. About a mile off. Most likely they're looking for those Chroniclers, otherwise, there'd be no reason for them to patrol this road."

The road Larn referred to was hardly a road at all. It was more of a pathway picked across by animals and the occasional traveler, though the spacing between the trees allowed for easy passage.

Larn ran a hand through his hair. "We can remain here for a bit longer."

"I know what you're doing," Ansie huffed.

"What?"

"You're trying to act like this is all part of the plan." She gestured to her shoulder. "Let's call a turd a turd, we're stuck here until I can move."

Larn stared down at her as though she'd just grown another head. "What did you just say?"

"It's an expression," she lifted her nose into the air and glared outside. Her cheeks warmed with color. Willem knew she often hated how the warmth of her face gave away her true feelings.

"Can't believe that hasn't caught on," Larn rolled his eyes and began to skin the rabbit carcasses. "These are going to take forever to cook."

Willem nodded. It would take time to roast the meat, but in the end, it would be worth it. His stomach was already grumbling as it was. To have something more substantial than helark, a sort of moss which often grew in damp areas that had a bitter cotton texture, would be a nice change. Helark was rather disgusting, but it filled an empty belly. Just thinking of rabbit meat was enough to set Willem's mouth to watering.

"Since we're on the subject," Larn began, his words interspersed as he blew on the sparks to coax them to life, "when do you think you can ride?"

His question was directed at Ansie, and she remained with her back straight, staring out into the billowing fog. Willem knew that look all too well, the furrow of her brow told him she was in pain, but she would never admit it.

"I'm at your will, your highness," she shot Larn a glance, her lips turned up in a mocking grin.

"Well if that's the case," he winked and she turned away again, this time her cheeks deepened in color. Willem cleared his throat, not quite sure what to say.

"Can we leave tomorrow?" Willem proposed. Ever since Larn had left to find game, something had been nagging him. He had a distinct feeling that they were being watched. It was a sort of prickling of the hairs on the back of his neck, the weighted silence of bated breath.

"Well?" Larn asked, waiting for Ansie to answer.

"Yes," she admitted. "But I won't be able to ride alone."

"Really?" Larn challenged.

"Oh shut it," she huffed. "If you would just—"

Suddenly, Larn shot to his feet, sword in hand. "Shh!"

Willem hastened beside him. All day the fog had seemed like a blessing, a curtain hiding them from sight, but now it hid whatever Larn was listening too.

"Move her further back," Larn muttered, "quietly."

Ansie eased to her feet with the help of Willem's hand, as she moved toward the shadows, one of the horses outside nickered. Willem cursed the creature, his ears straining for something, but what he didn't know.

"Should I put out the fire?" He asked, Larn nodded.

As he knelt to the ground and dribbled water over the sparks, he heard a gasp from behind them.

"Shhh," a voice said, a man's voice.

Willem whipped around as eyes two men stepped out of the shadows, one holding Ansie before him, his hand clamped over her mouth. Willem's hand tightened on his sword.

Both men had dark hair hanging to their shoulders, dirt clinging to their bearded faces, and the cracks in their skin dried and bony. They resembled one another, not in their way of dress, but rather the similarities in their high cheekbones, pointed chins, and dark eyes. It was only as Willem's eyes flicked back and forth between them that he began to realize neither man was in uniform. They weren't soldiers.

Larn shifted beside Willem, his sword raised at the men. He was about to say something when the man on the right, the younger one held up both his hands.

"Don't," he whispered, "we're on your side."

The man holding Ansie nodded, and he loosened his arms from around her. Only now did Willem realize he hadn't touched her injured shoulder. She stepped away from the men and behind Willem.

"Who are you?" Larn demanded, his voice a sharp whisper.

"Later," the older stranger said, as he shifted forward, nearing the edge of the cave. "What did you hear?"

"Horses," Larn stepped aside, eyeing the man.

"They're coming," the younger one said.

"Yes," the older grumbled, rubbing his beard.

"Make a run for it?"

"We won't make it."

"He led them right back here."

"Give in?"

"Perhaps," the older one rested his hand on the hilt of his sword. The dark brown shirt he wore was smeared with dirt and appeared damp with sweat.

"Who are you?" Larn demanded again, looking between the men, his frustration rolling off of him.

"You're the Chroniclers, aren't you?" Ansie guessed.

The younger man smiled, "Brother, we're famous."

"Chroniclers," they all stared and Willem felt his lips part, his jaw dropping. For some reason when Larn had told them about the missing Chroniclers, he'd pictured men bent with age, their days of youth long behind. But that was not what stood before them.

Though their youth had faded, they both stood with poise. Their backs were straight, and their shoulders rounded with muscle, though the sharp edges of their cheekbones hinted at a lack of sustenance. By the way, the older brother stood with his knees slightly bent, leaning forward on the balls of his feet,

Willem presumed the sword hanging off his hips wasn't simply for show. The younger was a little shorter than his brother, but there was a calm peace around him which intrigued Willem. A sort of careful presence as though he carried a secret.

"You're the missing Chroniclers," Larn whispered, his sword slowly lowering toward the ground.

"Yes," the older grumbled. "Now you have some information on the Animle?"

They all glanced at one another, Ansie biting her lip in debate. "Perhaps," Larn straightened.

The younger one chuckled. "We've heard everything you said for the last two days."

The looming darkness of the cave behind the men took on its own presence. A chill ran down Willem's spine.

"The soldiers you saw," the older stranger focused all of his attention on Larn, green eyes piercing, "were they Nexen or Gallian?"

"Gallian," Larn shifted, looking back and forth between the two men.

"How far?"

"A mile."

The younger man shook his head and clicked his tongue. "Not far enough."

"I can make it," the older said.

"Dur—"

"I can make it," the older brother, Dur, cut off the younger one. It was only then that Willem realized Dur's weight was mostly shifted to his right foot and there was a tear along his pant leg. He noticed Willem's glance. "The verrals had a go at us before you arrived."

The younger one crossed his arms over his chest. "No doubt they would have killed us if you hadn't come along when you did."

"Did it—get you?" Ansie motioned toward Dur's leg. He nodded. A small shiver shook her shoulders and she winced.

"Come on Fer," Dur said and limped toward the cave opening.

"Wait," Larn turned, "how have you remained hidden? We've been searching for you. All this time."

"For over a year," Fer grinned, a twinkle in his eyes that Willem didn't understand.

"Yes, why hide?"

"That," Dur huffed, "is a question for another time. We have to get out of here before those soldiers find this cave."

"Where will you go?" Ansie stepped forward.

"Somewhere they can't find us until it's time."

"What time?" Willem shook his head, the men were making no sense.

"You'll know when it happens."

"When what happens?"

"When the spark of the Animle burns once more." Fer spoke with such conviction that Willem felt a warmth spread in his chest. It was a calling from within. An awakening deep within his soul. It felt as though a part of him had been crying out for years, a part he had snuffed out with every intention of never letting it speak again. Yet, here, in this damp cave, he felt it stir once more.

"Too late." Larn held his hands up in warning and placed a finger to his lips. Moments later the crunch of hooves over the fallen leaves and clanking of metal filled the forest. "The horses," he cursed under his breath. Just beyond the edge of the slope, two of the horses they had brought from Mirtain were tied to a tree. Tympmor was nowhere in sight.

Fer turned to Willem, "Can you tell me the Animle will return?"

"What?"

The man stared at him, intensity burning in his eyes. He stepped closer, whispering. "Have they returned?"

"Y-yes?" Willem hated the way his eyes flickered to Ansie and Larn, as though needing them to corroborate his words. This was what he had been wrestling with since leaving Mirtain. The enormity of what the *simian* had meant, to him, to Mirtain, to the realm. It was the return of a power long held back.

"A simian looked to him," Larn whispered, leaning away from the mouth of the cave. Both brothers smiled, tears reaching their eyes.

A saddle creaked as a soldier dismounted. Willem tightened his hand around the hilt of his sword.

They all froze, waiting. A few commands were given, and more soldiers dismounted. There were more than three soldiers outside. Dur seemed to have come to the same conclusion as he glanced at their weapons. He locked eyes on his brother and Willem watched as a silent conversation took place. If he hadn't been paying attention, he never would have seen it. With a short nod, Dur set his sword silently on the stone floor of the cave. Fer followed suit and they removed daggers from their belts.

Willem shifted uncertain what they were doing, until they put their hands in the air. He moved to say something but was silenced by Dur's glare. It was at once a plea and a command, and something else lingered deep within his eyes.

Side by side the brothers placed their hands on their heads and stepped out of the mouth of the cave. The soldiers shouted and the leaves rustled as the Chroniclers disappeared from sight down the slope, enveloped in the shrouded fog. They listened as the men were bound faster than Willem thought possible, and they left with the two horses in tow. Silence reigned once more.

He swallowed around the lump in his throat, pushing down the rising fear in his gut. "We have to go after them."

Larn stared at the discarded weapons lying next to the twigs of their meager fire. He gave a short nod. "I don't know how."

"We'll just figure it out when we get there," Ansie said.

"We can't follow without horses," Willem muttered. They were stranded.

"Horses no, but one horse, maybe." Larn clicked his tongue softly and stared out of the cave. Not a few seconds later Tympmor's bobbing head appeared. "He doesn't like other horses, at least when I'm not around."

The horse had the ability to look self-satisfied as he shook his mane.

Within minutes they had Ansie situated on top of Tympmor, her sling tightened across her back to hold her shoulder more firmly in its place. Willem had to look away when he noticed the furrow between her eyebrows. She was already in pain and he knew it.

For the next few hours, they trudged slowly through the forest. Ansie held onto the pommel of the saddle with one hand as Larn led Tympmor behind him. Willem worked as quickly as he could tracking the soldiers. But it was slow going, and he knew they were now hours behind the soldiers and their captives. He gritted his teeth in frustration as the sky began to darken and the fog swirled around them once more.

"Ride with her," Larn said when they reached an open valley. Willem glanced up at Ansie. Her eyes were closed and she gripped the pommel of the saddle with whitened knuckles. Beads of sweat glistened on her upper lip, her cheeks lost of all color. "We need to catch up."

Larn took off his sword and fastened it to the saddle as Willem hopped onto Tympmor's back. "Keep on and I'll try to stay with you." He clicked his tongue and Tympmor began to trot, the jolts making Ansie whimper in pain until their bodies settled into the gentle rhythm of the creature carrying them across the land.

Beside them Larn ran, his arms and legs pumping gracefully as he kept stride with the jogging horse. All through the night, he ran beside them. More than once, Willem had pulled up on Tympmor's reins when Larn fell too far behind. Each time, he asked him to switch, Larn merely shook his head, sucking in air through his nose before taking off once more.

Into the night they ran, until the sun crested over the mountains and the trail beneath their feet was fresher than before. They were catching up.

Willem smiled to himself. Nudging Ansie's sleeping head back onto his chest, they pressed on.

CHAPTER 40

The night passed in a blur of pain and sweat, mixed with the chill of darkness sweeping across her face. More than once, Ansie knew she had passed out—her head banging against Willem's chest until he held it in place. She had refused to say anything, determined to keep going.

With each mile, she cried out to the stars above for the pain to cease, but it seemed to only increase. Though her sling held her arm tight against her body, she could feel the stitches stretching along her flesh and feared the wound had reopened. Though with the way she was sweating, she would never be able to tell if blood or sweat covered her back.

All through the night she dipped and swayed in the saddle. At times she opened her eyes and watched the ground pass beneath Tympmor's hooves, and at other times following the long gentle glide of Larn striding beside them. More than once he had glanced up, his brow furrowed as he looked at her.

She couldn't be certain she had really even seen him, watched him as he had stripped off his shirt, his chest gleaming with sweat as he ran through the valley, his breaths deep in the foggy night air.

When they finally dismounted along the sloping mound of a hill, Willem told her to rest. She had nearly collapsed in his arms from exhaustion and curled into a ball, making the moss-strewn ground her bed.

She awakened hours later—or at least she thought she was awake—to Larn resting beside her, his arm covering his face and his lips gently parted.

She stared at him, her eyes wandering over him as he rested. Each breath filled his chest, and she could just hear the soft exhale through his lips. It was a comforting, reliable sound. She swallowed.

When he stirred, she shut her eyes tight, heart thundering. She cursed her cheeks as they warmed, having suddenly felt as though she had been caught spying. Was she truly awake?

"Ans?" Willem whispered and she stirred. When she opened her eyes, she found Willem kneeling beside her his hand on her forehead, checking her temperature. She blinked quickly, realizing Larn was still beside her, it hadn't been a dream. Only this time, he was watching her, his gaze resting on her face. Her cheeks warmed again.

"I'm fine," her voice came out in a croak. She needed water.

Larn pushed himself up beside her and reached for a water skin. After taking some himself, he offered it to her. "Where are we?" He asked, glancing around at the trees, their golden canopy of leaves dripping with dew.

Willem shrugged, "Don't know, but I found a fort." He sounded like a child who had found a hidden treasure. "Just on the other side of this mountain is an old fort, there are guards posted around what looks like a makeshift prison."

"The Chroniclers?" Larn asked, taking another swig of the water before passing it back to Ansie.

"Our horses are outside."

"Perfect," was all Larn said. Leaning forward he began to clear away the moss covering the ground until there was just dirt between them. He drew a small mark on the ground. "That's us, and here's the mountain, now where would you say is the fort?"

Willem leaned forward and Ansie watched as the plan began to unfold.

The fort was decrepit at best. The original stones of the structure having fallen away in chipped pieces, moss coating its sides, and the vines crawling between the cracks. A leaning tower of great girth seemed to rest against the rotting structure beside it. Standing along the edge of a short cliff, a river ran past the right side of the fort. What had most likely been an easy place for soldiers to fish, had eroded over time to the cliff that now left the fort standing precariously close to the edge.

The roar of the water had been enough to cover the sounds of their approach. For two days they had rested and waited in hiding on the other side of the mountain, taking turns to observe the transitions of the guards. Over and over again they recited the plan, the waterfall that dipped off about fifty yards from the fort shrouding their voices.

"Put your hood back on," Larn whispered close to Ansie's ear, and she obliged.

Ansie found it odd that he asked it of her so often, but wrote it off as concern for her well-being. It was rather chilly waiting on the sloped hill with the cusp-of-winter breeze cutting through their clothes. She had yet to really bring her hands outside of her cloak all day.

Together they laid low to the ground, their chests pressed into the moss as they watched the soldiers sitting before the fort, a fire crackling as they passed around a drink. Every now and then their voices drifted toward them. Ansie wondered if Larn could hear what they were saying.

"How much longer?" she asked.

"Give it about twenty more minutes," he said beside her, his breath creating a small cloud before dissipating. "Do we need to go over the plan again?"

"No, I've got it." The timing was nearly perfect. Once the sun dipped behind the mountain, shadows would stretch across the fort. But they had to break in before night descended upon the realm, before the guard was switched. At this time, only four soldiers stood on duty, the rest were in the hall beside the tower, most likely resting or having their dinner.

"Right," Larn said and sniffed. Though he hadn't admitted it, Ansie was quite certain Larn was getting a cold. She had asked him about it the day before and he had firmly denied it. If she had a chance to guess, she would say his throat was feeling dry and scratchy.

A northern man catching a cold. The thought brought a small smile to her lips.

Heaving a breath, she waited. She shifted on the ground, always careful to keep her shoulder as still as possible. It was healing, and the two days of rest had done wonders, but it still throbbed from time to time and she often woke up in pain, the muscles beneath the wound clenched as though they were under attack.

"What if he isn't in the tower?" She had worried over the thought for a long time.

"They let him in the same door as the Chroniclers, I highly doubt they would have moved him."

"But we aren't certain."

"Nothing is ever certain," Larn muttered and she nodded, still worrying over Willem.

Last night, before dusk fell, Willem had approached the ruins, his hands in the air, and worked his way into the Gallian soldiers' midst. She had watched with Larn as they took him in hand, growing suspicious of the story he told. Though Willem had practiced for hours, he was horrible when it came to acting, and being a simpleton was not a guise he could easily pull off. But whatever he had said was enough to get him thrown into the tower where they knew the Chroniclers were—much to Larn's surprise.

His exact words were, "Not too bad for ole' stiff britches." Ansie still had to choke back a laugh at that observation.

But the comment had done little to still the worries swirling through her mind. Willem had logically explained that they needed someone inside the tower to work through the escape plan with Dur and Fer—and the other captives.

She sucked in a deep breath, still hesitant to believe any of this would work. "I'll look more like a child than a threat."

"True enough, play it either way." Larn breathed. "How's your shoulder?"

"Same as it was five minutes ago when you asked." A passing gust of wind sent a shiver along her spine.

Larn smirked at her frustration. "Use that fire," he winked, "you're going to need it."

She nodded and turned away before her cheeks warmed beneath his gaze. Every now and then her stomach seemed to flip when he winked at her like that. She forced the thought away, refusing to even allow her mind to go in that direction.

She turned from him, refusing to let herself notice the way his shoulder touched hers. She had yet to figure out if she liked the feeling.

Thinking back on their conversation about the moons in the cave, her heart began to beat faster. The words he had spoken that night still ran through her mind, and she itched to know more.

"Do you really think they'll know about the Animle?" she asked quietly, her voice so soft she hardly heard it herself.

"I suppose so," he shifted, his shoulder bumping her good one. "There has to be a reason for the Regent holding—dammit!" He swore quite suddenly, making her jump.

Pain radiated down her shoulder and she grimaced. "What?"

He held still, listening, and then cursed again. "Wolves."

"Wolves," she mouthed, hardly putting a voice to the word—fear shooting through her like a knife. How could they be here? "You can hear them?"

"How else would I know they're coming?" he snapped and ran a hand through his hair. He swore again. "they'll be the death of me. Right," he breathed. "We have to go now, before sunset. I have to get them out before the Nexen arrive."

"Okay," her breath clouded, her mind jumping ahead to what was to come.

"Follow the plan as usual, all we have to do is work faster." He sounded as though trying to convince himself.

"Okay," she said again. "How long until they get here?"

"Let's not think about that."

Too soon. She pushed to her feet, making sure to stay in a crouch. "Be careful," she said as she passed by him, meaning to pat him on the back, but missed, and instead ended up patting the side of his neck and ear.

That wasn't awkward at all Ans, good one.

"Stay safe," his voice was tight, but eyes far off as he listened to things she didn't want to contemplate.

Ansie knew he was watching from above as she picked her way down the slope, still hidden behind the bushes and trees. Slipping the sling off her shoulder, pain seared through her arm. If she was going to do this, then she needed to do it right.

Reaching the bottom of the slope, she edged her way along the path. The sun was dipping somewhere behind the clouds, the cold gray shadows of the trees stretching across the path. One moment she was in darkness, the next visible.

Breathe, Ans. She told herself as her boots brought her closer to the ruins. Somewhere inside was Willem and the Chroniclers. They were counting on her.

She stepped around the last of the trees, making sure to strut as Larn had taught her. Hoping against hope, she called to the stars above to make these soldiers see only what was right before them. After two days of their coarse talk, she knew they would take the bait if she convinced them.

"Hello?" she called, dropping her voice an octave. With her hair tucked back into the hood around her head, she prayed she looked like the young boy Larn had assigned her to play.

Four heads shot up. The two on the right side of the fire pit jumped to attention, their hands braced on swords. Their slight hesitation gave her all the information she needed, Larn had told her what to expect.

"I'm sorry," she said sounding as simple as possible. Willem had told her to think of Jep's sons and mimic their movements. She stuffed her hands in her pockets. "I seem to have lost my way. Do you know where Succto is?" She dropped the name of the village as though she had been there before.

"We do," one of the soldiers on the right replied. He had a pinched sort of face, young, but flat, his nose hardly poking out and his eyes seemingly close together. "Are you from there?"

A sharp wind gust passed by, and those still sitting, hunkered down in their deep blue cloaks, shiny gold buttons winking at her. Ansie's heart thundered as she continued to move closer. One step at a time. Breathe.

"No, I'm not." She waved a hand, keeping her voice low. "You see, I got lost on my way there, I was traveling with my family but we came across some travelers. They-they tried to fight us."

"How many?"

"Three."

"Three travelers?" The man with the pinched face took the bait. "What did they look like?"

"Well, there were two men and a girl, I didn't get to see their faces. My horse spooked, you see. One of them was mutterin' in some strange language and my horse just took off runnin' like a heathen. I had to throw myself to the ground in order to save my life."

The other standing soldier had a narrow face, high cheekbones, and eyes which seemed to pop out from his skull, making him appear eternally surprised.

"What did that one look like?" he prodded.

All too quickly, she noticed he had the annoying habit of exhaling through his nose when he finished speaking. His nose was so thin it seemed to allow very little air to pass through it, and thus had the ability to make him sound as though he was whistling with each breath.

"I don't really know. I didn't get a good look at him." She shivered and the pinched-face soldier motioned toward the fire. She stepped closer. "Thank you, sir."

He nodded, watching her as she stepped closer. She prayed her feigned voice was enough to fool them. It wouldn't be long before Larn made his move toward the fort. The slope on the left side was just close enough he could make the jump onto the building and walk the ridge to enter the tower. What awaited him inside was a mystery.

Thinking of the wolves, she shivered again. Time was ticking.

"So which way am I supposed to go?" she asked, her voice sounding foolish even to her own ears. She prayed they weren't able to see through her disguise. The dirt she had smeared on her face did little to hide the fact she was a woman, Larn had been very clear to point that out.

"You're actually a long ways off," the soldier with the whistling nose said. "You'll have to head back in the direction you came. Once you get to the road, take a left."

"The road?" she faked all innocence.

Somehow, instinct told her Larn was on the move. He wouldn't make the leap quite yet, that would come later, but her chance to get the men interested in a story was over. There was no way for her to get them entirely distracted until darkness overcame the ruins, it was simply impossible.

"Yeah," the whistler said, "the road takes you to Succto. Just keep walking straight that way, following the river and then you'll reach it." He motioned directly behind her and she turned to glance at the makeshift pathway, careful to keep her cloak as wide of her hips as possible.

"How long do you think it might take me?" she stalled, glancing back at the men. Out of the corner of her eye, she saw Larn picking his way across the top of the building to the left, she didn't dare look up.

"I don't know," the pinch-faced soldier said, "probably a couple of hours."

"Oh," she let her voice fall, hoping they could see her disappointment. Heart thundering, she shifted, unsure of how to stall them further.

"You'd best get going, we have duties here." The nose-whistler turned slightly to the side, warming his hands by the fire. Larn was clearly visible along the top of the building with nowhere to hide. He had paused, frozen on the roof. She internally cursed as her heart seemed to leap into her throat.

"I—I," she fumbled for words, "I was hoping I might stay here for the night. I won't bother you, I just, I'm afraid to travel alone."

All four men laughed, waving away her concerns. She was simply a young boy in their eyes.

"We've got more important stuff to do than watch children, boy."

Larn's shadow lingered, waiting for the right moment to make the final dash across the roof and into the tower. If he moved now, the whistler would certainly see him.

"I can tell you more about the travelers I saw," she offered, and the pinched face soldier laughed.

"What are you going to say this time? That they were traveling with some animals?"

"They had horses."

The whistler shook his head. "Sounds like you got run into by some bandits or gypsies. Now move along."

She hesitated. With no way of knowing how soon the Nexen would arrive, she was desperate.

"I said, go." The whistler pointed, Larn was still within his line of sight if he dared to turn his head slightly to the right.

"I can't," she whined, letting her voice return to normal. Her hands shook as she wrapped them around her body, it was time to look as small as possible—her shoulder protested.

"You can't, or you won't?" the pinch face soldier threatened.

"Both," she murmured, and before she could talk herself out of it, she pulled off her hood and loosened the tie around her hair. The simple movement stung her left shoulder, the fire burning along the stitches.

The other Gallians jumped to their feet.

"I know," she held up her hands in surrender, "I'm a woman, I lost my family, that part was true, but I don't have anywhere to go and I can't be seen traveling alone."

"True enough," the whistler said and took a step closer, eyeing her. One more step and he wouldn't be able to see Larn. "But how do we know you're not lying now? For all we know, you could be an escaped prisoner or a slave of some sort." He ran his gaze up and down her body.

"That's why I dressed as a boy, I didn't think anyone would believe me. I didn't want them to think I was something *else*." She put emphasis on the word.

"Show me your wrists." The whistler commanded. She shook her head, hoping she looked terrified. "Show me!"

Succumbing to fate, she thanked the stars above she had thought ahead. Pulling back her sleeves, the cool air chilled her fingers, making them feel as though they were merely bone.

She pushed up her sleeves and shoved her wrists forward.

The resounding gasps had the desired effect she needed. As the pinch-faced soldier took another step closer to look at the fake markings on her wrists, she only hoped they looked real in the dim light of looming dusk. During their ride through the night, her wound had reopened. While Larn and Willem slept she had struggled to reach behind her neck and gather the blood with her fingers. It was then a simple matter of painting the ring and encircled 'R' on her wrist.

If they looked close enough, they would see that it was fake, none of her flesh was burned, but just maybe they wouldn't notice.

"You're—you're a…" he drifted off.

"Yes?" she raised an eyebrow, challenging them. "So what if I am?" She placed her hands on her hips, out of sight.

The nose-whistler took a step forward, unaware of the shadow of Larn's cloak disappearing into the tower.

"Now," she cocked her head to the side, hip jutting out, "will you let me sit by your fire? I would hate to be all alone on a cold night like tonight."

They beckoned her forward and she tugged the sleeves of her shirt down. One part of the deception was over—her only hope was for Larn and Willem to hurry.

CHAPTER 41

Anise flashed what Larn hoped were fake scars.

He heard the inhalations of the soldiers and it took most of his self-control to keep from calling out to her. Why she thought to do such a thing was ridiculous, a risk he didn't think she would ever take. But she was always surprising him.

He hurried into the tower, a winding staircase meeting him just beyond the window he crawled through. Drawing two swords, one from his back, the other from his waist, he began to silently move down the stairs. Both swords preceded him on each curve, his own held higher than Willem's, which he carried. The weight of the sword was foreign.

"Oh, it's so much warmer here." Ansie's voice reached him from outside, still stalling. Some of the soldiers chuckled.

He kicked himself for not having planned better, but he would have to take it one problem at a time. The path Ansie had chosen was a little reckless, something he had begun to realize about her. She moved first and thought later. He only now realized how much of a fault it could be, how many times had Girshon chastised him for the same thing?

He sprinted down the stairs, his boots whispering on the stones as years of training took over. He was nearing the bottom when a yell rang out, and he counted the shadows of soldiers on the opposing wall.

He rounded the corner, knowing surprise was his only chance. Ducking beneath two daggers, he cut down the first and second soldiers as the last two ran for him. He blocked a blow from one with both swords above his head, the other soldier getting into position with a dagger. Looking past his opponent, he waited for the right moment.

One breath, one lunge and the dagger from the final soldier was flying toward them. He shifted to the side, the blade hitting his attacker in the back.

The soldier's body fell to the floor and the last man drew his sword. He was on the ground before it was fully drawn.

Larn didn't pause for breath as he searched for the keys, sheathing both swords.

"No, not at all!" Ansie laughed outside, the high trill fake to his ears. "That's not how it happened, I wear these scars proudly. It beats working in the fields." Her words brought on a ring of laughter from the men. Larn shook his head, his hands fumbling.

The keys! He found them on the waist of the last man and hurried to the door. It was only a short matter of time before the soldiers realized what was happening and alerted the others. They had counted the numbers over and over again. At least twenty-two soldiers.

He'd already taken down four. Two against eighteen wasn't something he wanted to think about, not to mention the howling he had heard. If the Nexen were moving fast, it wouldn't be long before they arrived. If he had time to curse, he would have.

The door to the dungeon swung wide, revealing the Chroniclers, Willem, and five other prisoners.

"Let's go," he nodded to Willem, the older men shifting forward.

"He's a—" one of the prisoners pointed upon seeing his face.

"Yes, I'm *maeri*, but seeing as how you're already damned, you can come with me. Now, let's move." Larn whipped Willem's sword and harness off his back and tossed it to him. The practiced hunter had it on and was out the door before another word was spoken.

"Grab any weapons you can find," Larn heard Willem say. And the dirtied men hurried to do as told. Their ages all varied, but they stood in groups of two, just as Willem had instructed them. Dur and Fer rolled their shoulders, preparing for what was to come. Dur gave him a curt nod, signaling they were ready.

Of all the prisoners in the tower, these two were their main concern. Get them out and save the others if they could, if they couldn't that was their loss. They had all been told the risks.

"Willem," Larn grabbed his arm before he could run up the stairs. "Ansie's keeping them distracted, but her cover will be blown the moment we get out there. I'm faster, let me go for her."

Willem nodded, adjusting his sword in his hand, all the more ready.

"And there's one more thing."

"What?"

"Nexen. They could be here any minute."

"Sounds about right." Willem nearly smiled.

"I'll take that as concern?" Larn nearly laughed, never having seen Willem show so much humor.

Willem rolled his eyes, "You'll take it as whatever the hell gets us out of here."

Larn grinned. Willem had a tendency to curse when he was nervous. His ward cursed when she was mad. The thought almost made Larn smile. Without another word, Larn ran up the stairs toward the main door, the prisoners following behind him.

Bracing his shoulder against the wood, he paused, Willem facing him.

"Well it's all simple really, I just lean in like this," Ansie's voice was different, soft and whispery in a way Larn had never heard before. The image those words conjured wasn't one he wanted to dwell on. At least not right now. "Do you see?" She asked, and the soldier with the musical nose responded in breathless agreement.

"What the—" Larn almost finished mumbling to himself when Willem nodded and shoved the door open without his confirmation. He fell forward, whacking his head on the wood.

For one split second, he saw the scene as though it was a painting, something he could look upon, touch with his fingers, and walk away from.

Ansie was on the whistler's lap, her arms wrapped around his neck, the other soldiers all watching her with wonder. The man's arms were secured around her waist and when he turned to look at them, the air brushed her hair back from her neck, the skin there perfectly clean and smooth. Larn wondered how it would feel to brush his fingers across her throat, to feel the thrum of her pulse.

With startling clarity, he spotted her cloak on the ground and all he could think about was getting her out of that man's arms.

Willem's yell snapped him back to reality, as the hunter ran forward to meet the oncoming swords. The soldier with the pinched face sprinted forward, his blade flashing as he collided with Willem.

Larn ignored them both, his only intent to reach Ansie. She screamed as he ran forward, playing her part as she tried to break free of the soldier's arms. The man threw her to the ground as he readied to move forward, but Ansie's boot caught his foot and he tripped, nearly falling.

Unsettled, he attempted to block the blows of Larn's sword. It only took a few moves to unhand him.

More shouts rose from behind and before him. The prisoners brandished their stolen daggers and swords, somehow managing to bring down one of the soldiers. A blow to one of the older men told Larn they had already lost one.

More soldiers poured out of the fort, shouts echoing over the roaring river. Larn grabbed for Ansie's hand, pulling her to her feet and hearing her cry of pain as it was her bad arm.

"Run for the water!" he yelled and she took off, only to be stopped by a soldier heading her way. Larn caught the near-blow as it was coming down toward her, using his other arm to push her behind him. The swords came down, a blade clipping him on his chin.

A grunt passed through his lips. She tugged on his belt, once and then twice, as he blocked another blow.

"Will you stop?" he yelled.

"Let go, dammit!" she cried, and he had the oddest notion to almost laugh. Something pulled loose from his belt and when the gleam caught his eye, he spotted his long dagger in her hands.

"The river!" he yelled, but she was already running toward the prisoners attempting to help them, he hated the way she was holding her left arm close to her body.

He focused on the oncoming soldiers. He knew there were only eighteen of them, but it seemed like a hoard sweeping out of the fort. Willem somehow made his way beside him and they fought together, blocking one another's sides from attack. With all he could, Larn attempted to keep the Gallians from making it to the prisoners.

"The river!" Willem yelled over his shoulder, and a few of the prisoners took off running for the small cliff to plunge into the water below. Larn heard Ansie's yell as he took down another Gallian and nearly cursed her to the depths of the realm, of all who needed to jump into the water, it was her.

"Got him!" Willem exhaled, just before taking down the last soldier and giving them a moment to breathe.

Larn turned toward the river. Dur and Fer stood near Ansie, both wielding Gallian swords. They breathed heavily, Dur hardly placing any weight on his injured leg.

Larn was just about to thank them for helping Ansie when a howl split the air. He whipped around facing the ruins. They were coming from the other side, just as he'd predicted.

"Run," he breathed to Willem and they only had a split second to move before the wolves tore through the last of the trees.

Willem was before him, sprinting for the water when Larn spotted Dur and Fer. He hadn't noticed the way Dur was clutching his waist, a red pool of blood spanning over his shirt. Ansie shuffled near them, indecision making her shift on her feet, her eyes wide in panic.

Larn could see it all happening, as though it had already taken place. He watched as the wolves bore down upon them, one taking him, the next taking Willem. And then there was only Ansie and the Chroniclers left.

The jaws and growls snapped behind him, moving faster than was fathomable. They would all die. He had to stall them, he had to do something. His trembling subsided as a sudden calm came over him, a peace that stilled the thundering of his heart.

He took a breath, and another. A pulsing ache awakened within his chest.

Stopping in his tracks, a deep beckoning gripped him and he turned to the leader of the pack. He had heard the commands given to the wolves in Mirtain, why couldn't it work now?

A howl of a wolf erupted from his throat. The wolves faltered.

"*Confu!*" he shouted, making eye contact with the leader, and holding out his hand. There were five of them, all seemingly larger than other wolves he had faced. The command had come from a memory of Captain Fergin shouting at his wolves in Mirtain forest.

Two of the wolves faltered and he heard Ansie scream his name, her desperation reaching high above the growls. He blocked out the sound, focusing solely on the leader, the red eyes flaming.

"*Confu!*" he shouted with more force, and this time the leader faltered, slowing to a stop. The wolves stumbled to a halt only a stone's throw from him. "*Confu! Confu!*" He nodded, and took a step backward.

Willem yelled for him to run—but he knew they wouldn't make it in time.

Thundering hooves sounded on the other side of the ruins, the black shadows of the Nexen appearing.

Larn remained fixated on the red gleaming eyes before him. The alpha wolf's lips trembled, hackles raised and back arched—the claws digging into the dirt, as though restrained by an invisible leash.

Instinct told Larn if he broke eye contact, the wolves would reach him in an instant.

"*Imcaedo!*" one of the Nexen soldiers shouted and the wolf took a clawing step forward. The forces at will warring within.

"*Confu!*" Larn yelled again and took two steps back, his hold was slipping—he could feel it.

"Come on! Go!" Willem called from behind, and he heard two splashes.

All five wolves were now digging into the dirt, their claws itching to run forward, but Larn kept his focus solely on the leader. The beast was larger than any he had ever encountered. The head higher than the others and he knew the jaws could snap off his arm in one quick bite.

"*Confu!*" he shouted, desperate.

"*Imcaedo!*" The Nexen soldier yelled again.

The leash snapped.

"LARN!" Ansie screamed in panic, but he was already sprinting their way.

The ground seemed to slow him down, the wolves chasing him. He pumped his legs, watching Ansie and then Willem disappear over the edge. The white frothing foam of the river was a welcoming beacon, but every step seemed to take an eternity.

He knew the commands would be of no more use as the jaws snapped behind him, barks turning into the cries of hunters. They were nearly upon him, when with one final leap he sprang for the open air, arms circling, floundering for balance.

A claw caught his ankle, but he was already plunging for the depths, the water hitting him like an icy wall.

───────────────

His body was racking in shivers, the icy water still clinging to his clothes, his fingers numb. The musty smell of mildew clung to the cave walls around them, a steady mist filling the air and licking their skin.

They were hidden behind a thundering curtain of water cascading over the rocks and into the river beyond. He had found the hidden cave as they laid plans to break into the fort. It was by sheer luck Tympmor was unafraid of water. As though hearing his thoughts, Tympmor gave a soft nicker and nudged Larn with his nose.

Rubbing a hand along the smooth side of the horse's back, he tried to forget the searing pain radiating from his ankle. He had cut it a little close near the fort, one misstep and he could have been taken captive or fed to the Nexen wolves. He shivered.

Something about those creatures always set him on edge. He knew it had to do with his past, that they haunted him, but he refused to go further down that road. Even now, if he strained to listen, he could catch a howl of one of the wolves. So far their scent had been washed away with the river. They were being hunted and the Nexen wouldn't give up easily.

"Thank you again," murmurs from one of the prisoners rang off the walls. Larn winced and signaled for them to be quieter. Even with the constant rush of the water at the mouth of the cave, he didn't trust the wolves not to hear.

Willem was standing with two of the prisoners, they were much older than the others, their clothes clinging to their frail bodies. They left through the water, shielding their heads from the onslaught above—if they were careful, they would find the trail leading toward the forest.

Larn grumbled to himself, not liking to see them leave. He didn't trust them, any of them, to not give away their hiding spot if they were caught by the Nexen. It was for that very reason he wanted to move, and soon.

He motioned Willem over. "Give it about two hours, and we'll go."

Willem nodded, only glancing over his shoulder to where Dur and Fer rested against the cave wall. Dur leaned heavily against the wall, Ansie having done the best she could with what little supplies they had. For the time being, the shallow slice along his abdomen had stopped bleeding.

How the man had had enough strength to keep his head above the surging rapids and climb out of the water, Larn would never know. But just one look at the men told him there was something about them that was different.

He turned away, not wanting to contemplate just what that different thing might be. For so many years the Renegades had been searching for a way to know more about the Animle, about the Praelia—those who had first believed in a higher power.

Larn shivered, his flesh raising into little bumps. Why was it so cold?

Willem leaned in closer. "Any idea how we get out of here without getting caught?"

Larn shook his head, he didn't want to think about it. Though he knew he needed to. His mind hardly moved, lethargic as it shifted from one possibility to the next. For years he had worked as a spy, his training allowing him to adapt to his surroundings, to move with the rhythms of the situation, but for the time being, he didn't want to move at all. Everything became blurry— exhausting.

All he wanted was to sit down. He almost said as much.

He blinked slowly and mumbled, "I'll think of something." Another shiver ran down his spine, one he couldn't hide.

"That's the third time you've done that." He hadn't heard Ansie approach. He turned to find her standing behind him, one eyebrow quirked in disapproval. "Will you let me help you now?" Her tone didn't allow for rebuttal.

He limped his way over to the cave wall, opposing Willem and the two elders. For the moment, he simply wanted some peace and quiet. If he knew anything, Ansie wasn't going to give him any.

Sinking down to the ground, he grimaced as he leaned back and extended his injured leg. He had felt the claws dig into his ankle as he launched into the air, they had dug straight through his boot and into his flesh. He was lucky to not have left more of himself with the wolves. Having reached the cave, he'd removed the boot as soon as he could, before the swelling could set in.

Ansie knelt before him, her hair a deeper red than usual, almost a ruddy brown as it still clung to her brow, one strand sticking to her cheek. She leaned over his foot, examining the wound—a cloud of mist swirled around her head.

"Well, I don't know much, but it looks clean," she tapped a finger on her thigh in indecision. He found himself tracing the lines of her forehead as they furrowed in concentration. Did she realize how the half-moon of freckles around her eye stood out all the more in the dark? Her pale cheeks giving birth to their color.

"Imagine that," he said wryly, and she flashed him a steel-ice look. She had seemed frustrated with him ever since reaching the cave.

"I'm going to wrap it and then we can check it in the morning." She spoke simply, not giving him any room to argue with her assessment.

Normally, he would have told her they were leaving soon. He would've let her know the plans, but he simply didn't want to make the effort. Another shiver coursed down his spine and he gave into a cough.

"I knew it," Ansie said.

All too soon, she was leaning in close to him as she pressed her hand to his forehead. Her fingers were cool against his skin which suddenly felt flushed. He fought the urge to not lean into her hand and instead settled for closing his eyes. As long as he felt awful, he might as well enjoy something.

"You're sick," she muttered.

He almost chuckled at that. "It's nothing serious." He'd felt the illness coming on for days.

"Nothing serious?"

Her face was much too close when he reopened his eyes. The soft brown of her irises was enough to take his breath away. Even in the shadows of the cave, they seemed to glow—the outer edges were a darkened brown, reminding him of the warmed chocolate he'd had once, their center lightened, the deep brown turning to melted caramel. He wondered how he had never noticed their color so acutely before.

"You do realize you've been getting sick for the last few days?" she gave him a solid stare. "Your voice has been changing for days. Not to mention the way you can't stop shaking now."

He gave her a small smile. "It seems I'm at your mercy."

"If we were in a different situation, I'd swaddle you up in blankets next to a fire."

"There's an idea," he lifted an eyebrow. An image coming to his mind that she would find completely repulsive. He grinned and was rewarded with another glare.

"You know what I mean," she said. "Now, as we don't have any extra clothes, I suppose one of the blankets will have to do. It's mostly dry, which is better than I can say for you right now. Take off your shirt."

He nearly laughed, looking at her beneath hooded eyes, his head tipped back against the cave wall. When had it become so hard to hold it up?

"I don't think you're supposed to say that," he said, all of the sudden aware of how tired he was. As soon as he had sat down, the idea of lifting any part of his body was too much.

He was suddenly aware of other voices murmuring in the cave. Distracted, he searched for the source and spotted Willem conversing with Dur and Fer. Normally, he would have tried to discern what they were saying, but as it was, he no longer cared.

"Larn," Ansie scolded, and he realized she was pulling on the clasps of his jacket. The garment was soaked through and heavy, making it difficult to breathe. "You have to sit up," she chided him.

It took more concentration than it should to sit up. When she began to tug on the bottom of his shirt, he let a laugh pass through his lips, which soon turned into a cough.

"Never thought I'd see you do this," he muttered, leaning into her as she wrapped her arms around his back to peel the wet garment from his skin.

She muttered something about men under her breath and pulled the shirt over his head a little rougher than necessary. He would have berated her, but the moment she had wrapped the nearly dry blanket around his shoulders, his words were lost.

He closed his eyes and slumped back against the cave wall—all resistance lost. The murmurs of Willem and the Chroniclers seemed to swirl around him, try as he might, he couldn't focus on one word alone. He let the voices rise and fall, allowing his own breath to settle into the rhythm of the words.

Frozen fingertips touched his arm and his eyes shot open.

"Sorry," Ansie muttered, her hands held halfway between them uncertainty. He looked at the culprit fingers, knowing they were like shards of ice. "I—I— wanted to make sure you were comfortable." She stumbled over the words.

His brow furrowed. Something wasn't right, his senses might be dulled, but even in the dark, he could tell she was blushing. He wondered at the action, thinking it odd for her to feel ashamed of something so simple. When he shifted, his left shoulder slipped out of the blanket.

Her eyes drifted, staring at his arm, and he suddenly realized what she had been doing.

There on his skin lay the mark his people had given him when he returned to his village. It disgusted him every-time he looked at it, reminding him how he'd failed. What a fool he'd been, earning his freedom and returning home to the Maereo. His own mother had welcomed him with open arms, but it had all been a lie.

She was the one who'd sold him to a traveling caravan as a child, and in the end, it didn't matter how strong he'd become, he never could satisfy her visions.

Visions. He nearly cursed. It was the supposed visions, the foresight gifted to the Maereo that had started this whole mess. His own mother believed she had seen a vision before having him. A half-breed child, part white man, part Maereo, but he'd never lived up to her expectations. And the white blood that ran through him made him hated among his own people.

Most didn't see it. His eyes were angled, tilting on the edges, his dark hair reaching his neck, and his skin easily tanned in the sun, but underneath he was different. He didn't fit with the white men of the southern lands, but he wasn't seen as pure in the eyes of the Maereo. He was an anomaly, an outcast among his own people.

For one brief moment he had thought they wanted him, but in the end, it was all a ruse. They welcomed him back as a young man as one of their own, but their good humor had only lasted the night. As they feasted, they drugged him and instead, when he awakened they had marked him with a reminder to never trust anyone.

"A wolf," Ansie whispered, her voice breathless and pulling him from his thoughts.

"The mark of the wolf," he flashed an ironic smile at her. "Odd isn't it?" She didn't say anything but continued to stare at the four lines etched into his skin, the perfect representation of a wolf's claws

"My people, worship animals. They gave me the wolf, because of my hearing, and sight," the lie he had told for years rolled off his tongue. "When I returned to my tribe, they felt the need to give me something. Loyalty and all that." He gave a wry laugh, the false words sour in his mouth. At another time, he would have run his hand through his hair, but it seemed too difficult a task now.

"Returned?" she asked, her gaze settling on the mark they had given him. The four claw-shaped slices stretched across the top of his arm, around the ball of his shoulder.

"Yes," he sighed. "When I was quite young, my mother realized I wasn't able to predict the future, something my people pride themselves on. She sent me away and I ended up at Sicarmman." Surprise lit Ansie's face as she stared at him. Even in the most southern lands of Autre Gallia, Sicarmman's fame was known. "I trained for years, not knowing Girshon paid for it. He was one of the trainers at the school. When I turned eighteen he trusted me with his secret. Not long after, I joined the Renegades." One side of his mouth lifted. He idly wondered why he was telling her all of this.

She sat in the silence, her eyes drifting first to the mark on his shoulder and then to his hands still grasping the blanket around him. He wondered what she was thinking, just what she thought about him. Did she realize how jealous he

473

was of her and how she had grown up with Willem? He knew there was more to her story, but in Willem, she had a place to call home. He'd never had that.

"Perhaps," Ansie cleared her throat, the silence between them having stretched for a few minutes, "you should get some sleep." He'd almost forgotten she was still looking at his hands. She readjusted the blanket over his shoulder.

"Maybe I don't want to," he murmured.

She shook her head, her lips gently lifting at the corners. "I knew it, you're going to be the worst patient I've ever had."

He coughed around a laugh. "Then you must've had a lot of patients."

"Not really," she shrugged and settled herself along the wall beside him. Odd, he'd expected her to leave him. Most people did when they realized just how different he was.

"Willem is pretty much the only patient I've ever had, and he is absolutely dreadful." Her smile brightened, the creases along her brow easing.

"So all I have to do is be better than him." He pursed his lips in mock perusal, liking the ease and comfort she seemed to bring him. "I will warn you, I can be like a child when I'm sick."

"So you've shown me," she agreed.

Still leaning his head back against the wall, he gave her a side-long glance. "How's your shoulder?"

She grimaced. "It hurts more than I want to admit, but I'll survive." He'd noticed the way she was refusing to move it. It was possible he would have to fix her stiches—he preferred to not think about doing that again.

"It's only been a few days."

"True," she said and then turned to him. "Do you think it will always hurt to lift my arm?" There was something so innocent about her question.

"No," he gave her a smile, "it will ease. Don't worry about it, and just give it time."

She settled back against the wall. "I'm not worried, only wondering."

"Essentially the same thing," he mumbled around a yawn. "The hardest part of healing is up here." He tapped his temple. "Pain can thrive on memories."

She nodded, eyes wide. She remembered every single bit of the torment she had been through, he was certain of it. He'd been impressed with her strength when the claw was removed from her shoulder. She'd only passed out once, and when she'd come to, she hadn't cried.

"Do you still have the claw?" she asked, her voice betraying her fear. He knew all too well the tentative curiosity and disgust of that first wound. While at Sicarmman, he'd been dealt a blow to his upper thigh by a girl. He nearly smiled thinking of it now, but it had come as quite a shock and reminder as a young boy. He still carried the scar with him, a dark purple line tracing the thick muscle along his upper leg.

Thinking of the verral claw, he motioned toward his pocket—idly wondering why he had held onto it for so long. By all accounts he should have thrown it into the saddle bag with the others Willem had gathered. Eventually, they would trade for them.

"Do you want it?" he asked, drifting, the roar of the waterfall lulling him.

"No," her voice was small again. "At least not right now." He smiled at her admission and felt as though he was seeing the girl from Mirtain again. That first night they had spoken in the hallway of Lord Hernan's manor had shown him the worrisome girl who hid behind the fiery-spirit. Ansie was both scared and courageous—he liked her all the more for it.

"I should let you sleep," she said and patted his arm; the kind gesture warmed him.

Moments of the day flashed through his mind, images of what they had gone through at the fort becoming as real as if they had happened only a moment ago. One stood out from the rest, and his curiosity got the best of him. He opened his eyes and lifted his head, searching for his answer on her flesh.

She was unaware of his search, until he reached out and grasped for her wrist. The blanket fell away, a shiver wracking his spine.

"What?" she asked as his fingers encircled her wrist with ease. He turned her hand back and forth, searching. Nothing was there but the cream alabaster of her skin.

His brow furrowed, he was certain he had seen the marks. "Where?"

She looked down to where his hand grasped hers. "It was only dried blood. My wound reopened, and I painted the marks on myself. It didn't look as real as it should have, but it worked." She spoke in a whisper, the sound caressing the stillness between them.

He ran his thumb over the inside of her wrist, as though needing to reassure himself that she hadn't been branded. Memories of Umbris and her scars were flooding his mind. He hadn't realized until now how much those marks meant, how they completely transformed the way a woman was seen in the eyes of Gallians.

"At least we made it," she said, looking up through her eye lashes. There was something in her warm gaze which made him want to draw her closer and push her away at the same time.

He was suddenly very aware he was still rubbing his thumb over her wrist, and when she shivered, he drew back, pulling the blanket tighter around his shoulders. Closing his eyes, he leaned into the cave wall, hoping it would drown out all thought and drifted asleep.

It seemed only moments later when something nudged his foot. He opened his eyes to find the grey light of dawn glistening on the other side of the waterfall, Willem squatting before him.

"Dur and Fer, they want to tell us something."

Larn nodded, latching onto the idea to avoid the pain burning his ankle and along his forearm where a sword had clipped him during the skirmish. He shifted against the wall and focused on the two men across the cave, only with a tinge of disappointment did he realize Ansie had left to sit closer to Willem.

His spot along the wall suddenly seemed very cold.

"We know a secret way out," Fer was the first to speak.

Willem glanced between both men, and then over at Larn.

"How?" Ansie asked, leaning toward them, her voice hopeful. Larn wondered if the others heard it.

"Secrets," Fer winked at her.

Dur grumbled and rose to stand. The older man seemed to hardly notice the wounds along his body—his hand pressed to his gut. "What our Regent doesn't know is that there are caves and tunnels all throughout this realm."

So this was how these men had remained hidden from the Regent's clutches for so long.

Larn coughed, "And this is one of them?" He stared past the men and into the darkness beyond. For all he could tell, it might be a dead end.

Fer shifted. "We think so."

"It's better than risking open land," Willem nodded, though indecision creased the edges of his mouth.

Larn glanced at the water pouring over the entrance to the cave. It was only a matter of time before the Nexen doubled back to retrace their steps, and when they did, they would find a group of five wounded rebels and one horse.

It took more strength than he cared to admit, but as he stood with the help of Tympmor's side, he motioned toward the darkness. "Lead on."

CHAPTER 42

The cool glow of dawn matched the briskness of her steps as she crossed the great expanse from the stables. Taking another deep breath, Umbris filled her lungs with the chilled morning air as though she hadn't taken a breath in weeks.

As a prisoner, she had spent countless nights and days beneath the sky, so many she had wondered if she would ever miss it. But after the seemingly endless days cooped up in her tiny room mending, she was well aware of the need.

It was colder than she expected, each breath clouding before her. Across the grounds, she felt the bite of the wind cut through her bodice, the rough shawl she had been given doing little to stop the cold.

"Madame!" a voice called and she spun on her heels, a jolt shooting through her. Out here on the great expanse of the palace grounds, she felt as though eyes were watching her from all around. Maybe her small bedroom was more of a blessing than she realized.

A lanky figure dressed in a deep blue servant uniform was hurrying up the slope she had just climbed. It was the boy who had helped her find the Regent's chambers. She stilled, glancing toward the various gardeners and servants working on the grounds to see if they were watching.

"Hello," Umbris said, her throat tight. She secured the brown shawl tightly around her shoulders.

The servant boy was all smiles, the dimple she had remembered seeing appeared when he reached her. "I thought it was you." He stood about a head taller than her.

She nodded, uncertain. "I was just delivering some finished work to the stable hands." She spoke quickly, feeling as though she needed to explain her presence on the palace grounds. Her appreciation of the early morning air was quickly disappearing, she'd been foolish to ask Charlise if she could do the job herself, thinking it might help to clear her mind.

The boy's grin broadened, "I assumed as much." The light brown curls that framed his face stirred in the breeze.

He glanced back in the direction she'd come, where the movements of the stable hands were perfect shadows. One horse reared on its hind legs, the whinny reaching them moments later. In the dim glow of dawn, the beast's breath clouded, making him all the fiercer.

The stables rested on the outer edge of the expansive gardens, with a grove of thin trees lining the rutted cobblestone pathway. The building was slightly curved, dipping inward to match the circular courtyard where the horses were bridled to the royal carriages. Umbris had lingered for a moment as the sun began to peek over the horizon and shatter the morning fog, her eyes grazing over the intricate architecture of the stables which seemed to have the same design as the palace. Though smaller in size, she found herself wondering just how many rooms and stables it withheld.

Beside her, the servant boy stood with his hands behind his back, his shoulders straight. He was taller than she remembered, older too. Most likely close to her age. He wore the pastel blue vest of the servant's garb, but this time he had the light grey, trimmed coat covering the vest and loose-sleeved shirt she'd seen him in before. He had a gray woolen scarf tied around his neck and by the rosy blush to his cheeks, she knew he had been in the cold for some time. She idly wondered what he'd been doing so early in the morning.

When he looked back at her, she gave him a curt nod before turning to make her way along the pebbled path to the palace.

"We haven't been properly introduced," he said, matching her step for step. "I'm Pavier." When she didn't answer, he continued. "I'm a hall boy, it's mostly grunt work, but work all the same."

She didn't say anything, her only intent to get back inside before others noticed their conversation. Though Charlise had agreed to her little excursion to the stables, she'd told her to be quick about it.

"Now would be the time for you to say your name," he prodded and she hated the way her heart beat all the harder. They had turned her into a mouse, a shell of what she'd once been.

"Umbris," she said, softly. "My name is Umbris."

"Umbris," he repeated, his slight accent making it sound a little foreign, but not nearly as odd as when the Regent said it. "And how are you enjoying the morning air, Umbris?"

He spoke with all cheeriness, but she refused to let it deter her. "I'm sorry," she said quickly. "I can't be seen with you."

She glanced up at the palace, the windows were like eyes watching her. The roof gleamed, the gold squinting in the sun as the first rays smiled upon it. Some of the windows were already cast open, the shutters within pulled back to allow the sunlight to warm the coolness inside. To wake to the dawn was something she had never been afforded, but she was not of noble birth, like so many who lived within the palace.

Only last night had she realized how many nobles lived with the Regent. His court, as she heard the other maids call it, lived with him for the entire winter season. Last night was the beginning of their extended stay at the palace.

Together, the nobles would celebrate Adlemas, a Gallian festival centered around the worship of some god of fire. Umbris had never understood what it truly meant, but the festivities could go on for days in Gallia. Here at the royal palace, she heard it could be weeks.

Though she believed in no such god, she was curious to see just what this festival was all about. Last night, as the noble guests arrived, she had been tempted to leave her room to chance a glance at the revelry and refinement, but the risk was too great. The markings on her wrists made sure of that.

All across the gardens, servants were hurrying to move in portable fireplaces, logs the size of trees, furs to cover stone benches, and white rose petals to decorate the gravel walkways. Here at the palace, even if it didn't snow, the Regent could make it so.

Along the backside of the palace, which stretched before her, she could just make out the outline of noble servants scurrying from carriages with trunks and bags heaved onto their shoulders. The constant commotion was enough to make her want to watch, at the chance of catching a glimpse of these people who lived in such decadent refinement.

Odd that she didn't always think of the Regent as one. After all, this was all his.

She pursed her lips, eyes wandering over the largest fountain in the garden. It was nearly as long as the Fantique Coloir and had already begun to reflect the golden windows in the light of dawn. In the center of the fountain was a man, clad in armor, his pants ripped to reveal muscular legs and his cloak billowing in an invisible wind. He stood upon a chariot and in his hand were reins restraining twelve horses, each representing one of the ancient twelve cities of the Circle Triumphe in Gallia. His other hand held a sword, the corded muscle on his arm so real Umbris had stopped to stare at the statue for longer than she would admit.

But it wasn't just the arm that was so life-like, no, it was the face of the man. Though the artist had been careful not to carve the Regent's face directly, it was obvious there was an influence. The nose, in particular, was rather large, long and pointed on the end, just like the man who ruled within the palace.

With gold covering every minute detail of the fountain, Umbris couldn't help wondering what it must look like beneath the austere glow of sunset. She could imagine it all now.

On either end of the fountain were two concave amphitheaters carved out from the sloping earth. Both were said to serve as outdoor ballrooms. The right was dedicated to the Pure Moon, everything inside painted white, the tiles along the ground almost a mirror in their shine. On the left, the Blood Moon reigned. Red roses blossomed and rubies decorated the walls. The architect had set the stones in place to perfectly tremble with red hues when any light touched their surface. Even now a few servants worked to set up the bonfire in the middle of the ballroom, the dim light of morn casting a tinge of crimson upon their skin.

The warmth which would spread from that space alone would be tremendous in power. As though in answer to her thoughts, a brisk wind tugged on her shawl.

"I don't understand," Pavier said beside her, pulling her from her thoughts. She'd forgotten he was still walking beside her. "What do you mean you can't be seen with me?"

"The law," she said, but he only stared at her more confused. She envied his innocence and stopped before him. "I'm a woman, and you're of age, we can't be—be seen together. Alone. It's considered wrong and we—you—I— there would be punishment." She chose her words carefully, not wanting to conjure up the past.

Pavier's brow furrowed in confusion.

She bit her lip, wondering even now if others had seen them. Surely some of the servants working in the gardens had already noticed.

Just then, a group of servants walked around the corner of the palace, only glancing their way as they struggled to carry the wooden chairs and table between them. On their heels came the women with fur shawls and blankets.

They hurried down the gravel path to place the chairs at tables already placed in the lower courtyards, decorated with billowing golden clothes. A few of the men glanced their way.

Pavier waved a hand, "Don't worry about them. There's no punishment, not really." He spoke offhand and turned to walk up the path, each step crunching beneath his boots.

Giving one last look at the elaborate display, Umbris hurried to catch up with him.

"What do you mean?" she asked, sniffing, the cold air was making her nose run. She was quite certain her skin was blotched red.

He turned back to her. "They won't think anything of it."

"You don't worry about such things here?" She could hardly believe it. How could the Regent make laws for his people and not include them in his own household?

"No," Pavier said and took a step toward her, "we're not required to live by the same laws—at least those of us who are Gallian." His eyebrows pulled together as he watched her reaction. "What I meant was your presence here is well understood, no one would think anything of it."

Ever so slowly, the words sank in. They broke over her like the water she used to swim in, until she felt as though she was drowning beneath the weight of it all. Without another word, she tightened her shawl and hurried along the path.

The quick crunch of gravel scuffed behind her.

"Did I say something wrong?" He hurried beside her, but she couldn't look at him. She was too shocked to be embarrassed, too convicted to think he hadn't meant it as an insult.

"I—I didn't mean to up—upset you," he stumbled over his words, breathless. "It's just simple, really. His Sire brought you here to be his mistress. There have been many others, it's nothing to be ashamed of."

Umbris stopped suddenly, looking up at him. "Is that what you think of me?"

"Of course, you did go directly to his chambers—didn't you?"

Tears pricked her eyes. Would the sting of her scars never leave?

She had wished it all away, but the guilt and shame weighed upon her every waking moment. As much as she wanted to blame the laws of the realm for what she had become, she knew it wasn't the only truth.

She had done this, all of it, to herself. Those other women had deserved better, she didn't—and yet, by some cruel twist of fate she had been the one to survive.

"I only mended his clothes," she said through tight lips before continuing on.

Pavier held his hands up in surrender. "It's simply assumed you're his mistress. If I'd known, I would've offered to escort you back to your room, instead of leaving you there."

He sounded as though he was offering an apology, but she could hardly comprehend the reasoning. None of it seemed right.

"I'm not his," she mumbled, knowing the scars burned onto her wrists spoke differently. She wasn't what she used to be—but she certainly wasn't his mistress.

"I see," Pavier grumbled, doubt lacing his words.

"I only delivered the breeches to him," she said.

"All right."

"Really," she said, turning to Pavier. For some reason, she needed him to understand. "I'm not what you think I am, he hasn't..." she drifted off, not knowing how to say what needed to be said.

She wanted so desperately for one person to know she wasn't what she seemed. For just one person to understand.

He heaved a breath, and offered his arm, a small smile gracing his mouth. "If you say so, I believe you."

She stared at his arm, afraid to take it. He waited patiently for her to move. She was reminded of a forest, and a young man coaxing a starved dog out of a muddied hole.

The vision came so clearly that she nearly lost sight, her eyes pricking in the brisk wind around them. She hadn't thought of him in so long. Her heart thundered, pulsing in her ears, for she could hear his shouts as they came down upon him, swords swinging through the air. And then there was silence.

She blinked back tears and realized Pavier was still watching her. With trembling fingers, she wrapped her hand around his arm. She couldn't remember the last time she had willingly touched someone.

"No need to worry," Pavier said and patted her cold fingers. She wondered if he was always so cheerful, she focused on his words, dispelling the memories that haunted her. "No one can be a threat to you now."

"How so?" she doubted it was true.

"Regardless of what you say, everyone in this palace thinks you're the Regent's mistress, and with that comes power." He leaned in closer, a hint of parchment and spice clinging to him. She wondered if he always smelled that way.

"Power?"

"No one will cross you, not while you're able to seek the Regent's presence alone."

"I hardly seek his presence."

"Precisely," he squeezed her hand, "he seeks yours." The words lingered between them. "It's a coveted position. It won't be long before lords and ladies are asking for your ear."

She blinked trying to think through his words, not fully understanding their power. Was it really so incredible that she had spoken to the Regent more than once? She already knew the answer, and yet, it didn't seem true.

They continued their walk through the gardens. Two maids glanced their way, and she recognized one as Magetta. The maid glared at her, pausing in her work until Garval snapped some order in her direction. The Regent's valet gave Umbris a passing glance, his haughty air never leaving his pinched lips for a moment.

"See," Pavier said, drawing her attention away, "they all know about your meeting with the Regent."

She swallowed tightly. It didn't seem right to have them all thinking she was at the palace for the Regent's use. And yet, in some way she was.

The Regent refused to let her leave his palace, and more than once, she had felt as though he was digging for information. He had control over her, and she knew it.

It's all just a matter of power.

The idea came upon her and she wanted to shake it from her mind, but knew it was what had been haunting her for weeks. It was a thought which had followed her since Larn had noticed her inclination to watch people. He had been the one to tell her she had a purpose, different than what the realm dictated.

She wondered if Pavier could feel the way she was trembling. Inside she knew she had to take action, she had told Pike as much when she last saw him.

Taking a deep breath, she eased her way into it. After so many nights of memorizing the names she heard, and all the Regent had said and asked of her, it was time she did some searching of her own.

The next time she saw Pike, she wouldn't let him leave empty-handed.

"What does a hall boy do?" she asked, hoping he didn't hear the tremor in her voice.

"I'm assigned to the libraries; I spend my hours amongst the books."

No wonder he smelled of paper. "What is it that you do? With the books, I mean."

"I clean them, and archive them in an easier manner for His Sire."

"His Sire enjoys reading?"

"Very much," Pavier nodded. "He oftentimes asks me to look for particular volumes. He's very interested in the history of the realm, the old religions, the gods, that sort of thing. If I find anything that has to do with Autre Gallia's history I take it to him. "

She glanced at Pavier, his words reminding her of something Larn had said about the Chroniclers. Was it possible the Regent needed them for something? Perhaps something more than just silencing their voices? Thinking of the *simian* Larn had spoken of, she pressed on.

"I guess he is well-read," she said by way of comment.

"Very," Pavier agreed. "Just last week he had me search through the Livre Wing for some of the oldest texts. One nearly fell apart when I held it." He glanced down at her. "That's what I was doing when I saw you."

She made a sound of agreement. She would have to think of some way to get her hands on those books, and she would need to figure out how to return to the Livre Wing.

Old books had been outlawed throughout the realm hundreds of years ago. In the days when the Animle walked the realm, knowledge was a requirement of all Anglans, but it was thrown aside and cast away from any who wished to know. The history of the ancient practices and the people who had lived during their time, were as much a mystery to her as the tales of the Neho and Cadna moons.

At one point in time, Festis Luna had been her favorite day of the year, but she had never truly believed in the legend of the lovers. She had believed in the Animle once, at least that they could return—and Larn had told her as much, but she no longer knew what to think.

In order to believe in such a thing, she would have to confront her past. And no one could ever make her return there.

"Do you know how to read?" Pavier asked, drawing her back to the reality of the world around her. He looked down at her, the long, dark curls of his hair lifting in the breeze.

"I do," she said softly, setting her mouth in a determined line. Not all Anglans knew how to read. "Do you think? Would it be all right, if, you gave me a book of the palace grounds? Or the gardens." She wiped away at a strand of hair tickling her cheek. "I get lost easily. It would help."

Pavier smiled again, the dimple springing into existence. "I think I know just the one. Although you wouldn't be able to keep it."

"Of course," she nodded, "I would just like to see it, sometime."

"I think I might be able to manage that as long as—" he broke off when the call to attention rose throughout the garden.

Pavier pulled her to the side of the gravel walkway, dropping her arm as though it was burning, and sank into a bow. She dipped into a curtsy, following the other servants' example. Her heart jilted, knowing what all the commotion meant.

More than one voice paraded down the path, the Regent's accompaniment flushed with morning air. Not looking up, she watched their approach through her eyelashes.

Six men in riding gear strode across the ground, their boots clapping with confidence over the gravel. Yet, none were as regally garbed as the Regent. A cobalt blue coat with red trim and gilded buttons lining both sides reached just past his hips. A cream waistcoat covered a white silken shirt where a black cravat matched his knee-high riding boots—a scabbard dangling from his belt.

Returning her eyes to the ground, Umbris listened as they came closer. She cast a prayer above that he would pass by.

Ever so slowly, his boots came into her line of sight, stopping before her. She inhaled shakily, trembling as his hand extended before her, a gold ring with a sapphire resting on his smallest finger.

Heart in her throat, she placed her hand in his, the smoothness of his skin reminding her of the night he had brought her to the palace. His hand was unlike any she had ever seen, large and masculine, but refined with perfection—though callouses threaded beneath the flesh.

As he pulled her out of her curtsy, she raised her head, her gaze meeting his for the first time. His hair was pulled back, the soft brown strands secured at the nape of his neck. He carried a cloak in one arm, and a pointed hat in his hand—the azure of his eyes seeming to deepen, to match the colors around him.

"Leave us," he said, not looking away from her. The men behind the Regent dispersed, Commander Jolson among them. They exited along the path toward the palace—Pavier too had disappeared.

Alone in his presence, she tried to draw her hand away from his, but he held on tighter. Without a glance at the many servants now standing at attention near the tables, he pulled her behind him, leading her off the path and into an alcove not far from the stables.

The subtle gold of rising dawn spanned the sky, casting the immaculately trimmed shrubs with a light glow. Umbris felt each breath as though it was the first she'd taken in months, her senses heightened. The feel of his hand around her fingers and the crunch of the grass under her thin boots only made her more aware of his presence.

"How are you this morning, Umbris?" he said, his pronunciation of the name always slightly foreign. They slowed to a leisurely pace.

"Well, my Sire." She hoped her words were enough to soothe him. She was all too aware of the small crowd which had seen him lead her away—the rumors would only grow stronger. "And h-h-how are you?" She breathed, and tacked on, "my Sire?"

His hand tightened beneath her fingers and she wondered if she had said something wrong. When she glanced up, she caught him watching her. He dropped her hand, the other arm holding his discarded cloak in the crook of his arm. She hastily grasped the edges of her shawl and pulled the cloth closer to her body.

"This morning is rather cold, if I'm being honest." He quirked an eyebrow, as though wanting her to contradict him, but she said nothing. "Do you not find it chilling?"

"Yes, my Sire," she said, confused. It was obvious she was terribly cold, the air cut through her bodice as though it were made of only parchment—the shawl doing little to brace her against the chill. Maybe if she had worn the corset, like most women, it would have helped.

"I'm looking forward to a warm bath of sorts before today's festivities begin," he mused. She had the sudden notion he was trying to coax her into conversation, but about what, she had no idea. "Did you enjoy watching the festivities last night?"

"No, my Sire," she shook her head and stopped short. She recovered quickly. "What I mean is, I didn't see it. Though I'm sure it was impressive."

He cocked his head to the side. "I thought I placed you among the maids?"

"You did, my Sire."

He pursed his lips, "It seems I must be clearer in my orders."

"I don't think it was done intentionally, my Sire," she said quickly. The last thing she wanted was for Charlise to get into trouble. "My work kept me in my room."

He nodded, "Do you even know what is being celebrated?"

"I think so," she swallowed. He waved a hand before them, urging her to continue. "It's the beginning of your court, the season of Adlemas."

"Exactly," he gave a mirthless laugh, "a celebration of spending the next four months with all these men and women vying for my attention. But do you want to know my secret?"

Umbris glanced up at him, surprised to see the gleam in his eyes. Only in his bedchamber, had she seen him so jovial. Simply thinking of what he had been doing with that woman brought color to her cheeks. She nodded and he leaned in forward to whisper in her ear.

"I would prefer it if they all left." He winked before drawing away, leaving her in the middle of the alcove, the tall shrubs blocking them from all eyes. "I couldn't care less if these courtiers were here, or if they were gone. I assume you wonder why I put up with them?" He quirked an eyebrow in her direction, the ghost of his dimple nearly forming on his right cheek. "How else am I to know what they think of me?"

Umbris nodded. He'd said as much the first night. To him, knowledge was power.

To have his nobles within reach was something she'd heard he did. It was nearly impossible to match the actions of the man before her, to the many stories she'd been told as a child.

"I don't know why I'm telling you all this," he turned back to look at her, his posture straighter and more refined than she remembered. "Perhaps..." he pursed his lips, seeming to take in all of her at once, "because you're new here?" He seemed to be asking himself as much as her. His brow furrowed.

"Maybe, my Sire," A shiver ran down her spine as another gust lifted the hem of her skirt, chilling her ankles.

"It's a game, you see," he flicked one of the leaves on the shrubs that hid them from sight. "They think they are simply my guests, but I watch, I listen, I learn from them. They play their role to perfection, bowing and flattering me, all the while plotting for the moment when they can make their next move."

He stared down the pathway, and Umbris wondered if he even realized he was talking outloud. She remained frozen to her spot, watching him as his shoulders shifted beneath the cobalt blue of his coat.

"It's all a distraction, a show. I keep them busy, filling them with titles and lands, granting them favors and fripperies, when piece by piece they give themselves to me. They grow impatient and try to buy my favor, but I wait them out, and all they have becomes mine. All of it is mine."

Umbris swallowed, her spine stiffening at his words. Then the Regent shook his head and smiled to himself, only to find her watching him.

"That's why I seek your company," he admitted, his voice softer than she had ever heard it. For some odd reason, she felt drawn to it.

Their eyes met and as she watched him, she realized quite suddenly that all the stories had been wrong. There within the Regent's gaze was a depth she had never expected to see. He was a person, down to the core he was as much the same as any man, woman, or child. And there, deep in the azure of his eyes was the one thing she was afraid to see, the one thing she understood so well.

Loneliness.

He alone carried the weight of a crown. She wondered if it clung to him as much as the chains had weighed down her wrists, how the marks burned into her flesh set her apart.

She wanted to slam the door of realization firmly back in place. She didn't want to see his pain, his loneliness, but it was there all the same and she could no longer ignore it.

He blinked and looked away, his chest rising steadily with each breath.

With indecision, his mouth puckered before he spoke. "You've only asked one thing of me. A simple question, wondering why you're here." He took a step closer to her, and she fought the urge to move back. "Even those men you saw moments ago, the very soldiers I choose to accompany me, cannot keep silent about their desires when in my presence. Not one of them, not one," he held up a finger, "except for you. Why is that?"

He stood before her, looking down and searching her face as though he might find the answers there. Her throat was suddenly dry as she tried to answer him in a way which would please him.

"I have nothing to ask for," she offered, her body shivering for a brief moment. The way he looked at her made her want to run, to flee in the direction of the palace. But she had been warned before of leaving his presence without his dismissal.

"Nothing?" he cocked his head slightly to the side, the piercing blue of his eyes like ice.

His free hand reached for her cheek. She forced herself to remain still as his fingers brushed against her face. He lingered there, hardly touching, hardly reaching, and yet she felt it through her entire body—for, in his eyes, he recognized her own yearning to be known. She tried desperately to hide it, but it only took a glance to know he already understood.

He towered above her, his other hand reaching for her face. Her heart skipped a beat. He'd lowered his mask, somehow becoming simply a man before her, she found herself almost leaning into his hand—

"My Sire!" a shout pierced the air from down the alcove.

The Regent's hands fell from her cheeks. Three soldiers were running in their direction. The Regent straightened, ready to face them.

"What is it?" he asked, a mask of calm settling over his expression, all emotion drained from his voice.

"We have news," the soldiers were breathless, "the Chroniclers." Their eyes flicked to Umbris in uncertainty.

"Spit it out," the Regent barked.

"Kraven Hall," the head soldier blurted, his words filled with breath, "was attacked two nights ago. All the prisoners, including the two Chroniclers, are missing."

For a moment she thought the Regent would curse, yell, do something, but he held still, his calm all the more disconcerting. With each breath, Umbris felt her muscles tighten, ready to flee if she must.

Suddenly, with a swiftness she hardly saw, he whipped his sword from its scabbard and cut down the nearest sculpted shrubbery, the blade slicing clean through. Umbris shrank away, pressing her lips together to stifle the scream in her throat.

Screaming hadn't helped against swords before, and it wouldn't help now.

The Regent took a deep breath, his shoulders shifting as though trying to loosen the muscles. He sheathed his sword and smoothed back the loose strands of his hair. In an instant, he transformed before her eyes.

The Gallian soldier continued, visibly shaking. "The men of Captain Dondol's division only just returned. They arrived on the scene too late to help."

"You," the Regent pointed to one of the soldiers, "get Commander Jolson, he shouldn't be far, send him to me. Collect Dondol and tell him to report to my chambers. I want a full recount. And you, send for Chrish, I must have him write a letter to the Liege, now!"

Both men fled as though death were behind them, soon disappearing in the midst of the long alcove. The remaining soldier seemed to shrink in his boots.

"What else did Dondol say?" the Regent barked.

Umbris took an involuntary step backward, not wanting to be near the swing of the Regent's sword should he pull it out again.

"They broke in before Dondol and his wolves arrived, my Sire." The man trembled and Umbris had the sudden notion, the worst of the news had yet to be relayed. She retreated another step, her back pressing into the thick shrubbery lining the alcove.

"How many?" the Regent demanded.

"My Sire?"

"How many men broke into the Kraven ruins?"

"Three, my Sire." The man barely got the words past his lips.

"Three!" the Regent shouted.

"Yes, my Sire. All the men on duty are dead, Dondol doesn't know what happened. They arrived just as the prisoners and the men jumped into the river. He had the rest of his Nexen searching up and down the banks, but they found no trace of them."

"And how far did they cover?"

"Five miles, before Dondol retreated to report back here. He left his men to continue the search. Perhaps they've found them." This last statement was barely uttered with breath.

"My Sire?" Commander Jolson's voice rang through the alcove as he rounded the corner, his hand on the sword at his waist.

"You've heard?" the Regent asked, Jolson nodded.

"What are your orders, my Sire?"

"I want these men found. I need those Chroniclers, the report we received yesterday was certain it was them. I will not have a year's worth of searching go unrewarded..." he drifted off for a moment, thinking to himself, before continuing. "So help me, they know more than they're letting on. I cannot have them getting to the Renegades!" His voice was rising by the moment. "Take your men and find them, recover those brothers at all cost."

"What about the three traitors?"

"Bring them in, alive, if you can. I'm sending for the Liege as we speak, we need to put the wolves on their trail."

The soldier who had delivered the news made a small sound. The Regent fixed him with a frozen glare. The soldier opened his mouth to speak, not once, but twice.

"Spit it out!" the Regent roared.

"The wolves, one of the men," he gasped for breath, cheeks flapping, "Dondol said one of the traitors controlled them. He...he stopped the wolves from attacking."

"The man from Mirtain," the Regent grit his teeth, the words hardly passing through his lips. "Come with me!" He ordered Jolson and the soldier. "I want two parties sent out, one to find them, the other to follow their trail. Start in Mirtain and check every village they may have stopped. There has to be some tavern, some traveler, some village that's seen them. We'll need to..." his voice faded away as he moved out of sight along the alcove.

A sudden stillness settled over the garden.

Umbris could hear each of her breaths as though they were ringing in her ears—the words of the Gallian soldier playing over and over again in her mind.

The man from Mirtain.

He was a threat, but not as much as the one who had controlled the wolves. If she had to guess, she knew just who had kept them at bay. The Regent was wrong, there were two threats to Gallia. She had seen the mark on Larn's arm, had heard the stories of his people and why they were given the mark of an animal.

It only seemed right Larn would be the one to stop the wolves.

With more hope than she could have imagined, she stooped to pick up the Regent's hat and cloak from the ground. Her mind was so full of what she had heard that she hardly noticed the servants' stares as she hurried by.

Every word, every name, every place, she repeated them in her mind. Committing them to memory.

She passed along the garden greenway leading to the palace, knowing the eyes of the other servants were on her. She secured the cloak and hat on her arm, marching for the palace steps, her every move lightened by the intoxicating notion of hope.

The Renegades were on the move.

CHAPTER 43

The sporadic dripping of the cave walls made Ansie's skin crawl, each splat reminding her they hadn't seen the sun in two days.

Too many times she tried to look up, as though the sun was merely hidden behind clouds, but there was nothing to be seen—nothing but the ghostly glow of a blue line along the cave wall. Dur and Fer called the line the filumen, it curved and dipped with the swells of the cave, glowing with an ethereal blue light. They claimed filumen meant "line of light," and supposedly, there was some connection to Initium, but when Larn had asked, Fer had just smiled and told him to carry-on.

Of course, the only way to actually get Larn moving had been to grab his hand and pull him along behind her. Every now and then, Ansie could see the lines of his face as he continued to glance at the azure glow on the cave wall. It reminded her of blue flames, pulsing with its own strength.

Dur inhaled deeply behind her. He had been riding on Tympmor's back for the past few hours. Though he was far from healed, he had been sitting a little straighter—though at times he'd had to press his body flat against Tympmor's back to fit through some of the chamber openings. Both Chroniclers swore the caves were large enough for a horse, and so far they'd been right, but each time Ansie held her breath, knowing Larn wouldn't go one step further without his horse.

She stumbled a bit in her boots, a soft scraping, and grasped onto Willem's arm. He steadied her and continued on, though not before giving her hand a squeeze. He knew how much she hated being trapped in the dark.

As the glow of the blue line dimmed, she squinted toward her feet, trying to make out the narrow pathway they'd been walking along for two days. Quite suddenly, as it always did, the light disappeared completely and they were left in total darkness. She swallowed, the rhythmic clop of Tympmor's hooves silenced on the stone.

A deep exhale filled the chamber, and she watched in awe as the light began to grow.

Fer stood with his mouth near the cave wall, his face illuminated by the blue throbbing light. He breathed again and the light ran along the wall, extending forward and into the dark. She trembled.

How many times had they done this? Waited as Fer used his own breath to light their way.

The first time the line appeared, Willem reached out to touch it. In shock, he'd turned to her.

"There's nothing there," he said.

She also reached out and ran her hand over the line, the light disappeared beneath her fingertips for a moment. All that met her flesh was stone.

Fer chuckled. "Soon, you'll understand," he said and they began their journey deep into the caves.

For another hour they traipsed along the path until she was quite certain she heard the rushing of water once more. Though this was different, not the thundering roar of a waterfall, but instead the soft lapping of a creek. Glancing behind her, she shot Larn a curious look. He nodded—she'd heard right.

Deep breaths, Ans.

"Take a left," Dur's grumbling baritone startled all of them, her boots scuffed across the ground again. This time Larn caught her by the back of her cloak.

"Thanks," she mumbled awkwardly, the front of her shirt cutting into her chin. Once righted she followed Fer and Willem to the left, only slightly concerned at the sudden break in the blue line.

"Umm," Willem mumbled as the darkness covered them in a shroud.

"Wait a moment," Fer said and shifted about, "I just have to find the right spot."

"Move to your left, no further," Dur directed and then mumbled something under his breath that made Larn chuckle. The older brother dismounted and hobbled toward a cave wall. His exhale filled the space, but nothing could have prepared Ansie for what happened next.

At the touch of his breath, a light began to travel along the wall until it spilt and then split again. Over and over, lines broke away from each other, curving around the walls until they created a web above their heads. Ansie blinked, the light hurting her eyes after spending so long hidden in the dark.

"Right," Dur straightened and limped toward his brother to settle himself on the ground.

"We'll rest here before moving forward, we're nearly there." Fer turned and dropped to the ground next to his brother.

Ansie wondered if she had dark circles underneath her eyes too. They had only slept for a few hours at a time since leaving the waterfall, and though they'd been shrouded in darkness, she had a difficult time falling asleep. The only good thing that had come from their long trek through the caves was the healing it brought her shoulder. She had kept it pinned by her side as they walked, stretching it each time the light dimmed and she had to wait for Fer to relight their way.

They all settled into the makings of a camp, a blanket here, boots cast off over there, foot rubs and groans as hard biscuits were passed around. All was silent, lost in the gentle lapping of the creek just outside the chamber. When the web of light above their heads began to dim, Larn leaned to the side and breathed on the line, it glowed with new life above them.

"Don't look so surprised," Fer chuckled, seeing her expression, "anyone can beckon the filumen to life. It's not magic."

She nearly blushed, for she had been wondering if that was exactly what it was.

"How does it work," Willem asked, breaking off a piece of his biscuit, crumbs fell on his chest.

"It's water painted on the rock, waters taken from one of the pools of Initium."

Though Fer spoke with conviction, Ansie had a distinct feeling he wasn't telling them everything. After being in the dark for so long, she hardly cared anymore.

Leaning back against the cave wall, she watched as Larn removed Tympmor's saddle. Though he limped on his injured leg, the movements were smooth and effortless. She focused on his hands, watching as he patted down the black steed's coat, his fingers long and graceful. There was something almost intimate in watching him move with such practiced ease—as though she was catching a glimpse of his life, something he had done so many times he no longer had to think about it.

Breathing in the stale air around them, she continued to follow the brush strokes of his hand, her thoughts whirling around what he'd told her. His childhood had hardly been one at all. Sold by his own mother, she shook her head.

In some ways, she wished she hadn't known about his past. And she had tried, tried to tuck away those thoughts, but they collided in her head with increasing clarity the more she attempted to forget them. For what she saw in Larn was a man who had walked through fire and still held onto hope. Though his own mother hadn't cared for him, he cared for others.

He probably wouldn't admit it if she asked him, but she didn't need to. The truth was in his actions, and she saw so much goodness in him that it broke her heart to see his unsettled nature. She could feel it in his gaze when he looked at her, the uncertainty and desperation lingering in their depths.

"How much further?" Willem asked, breaking the silence again.

"About an hour's walk and we will be within a few days of Initium."

Larn looked over his shoulder, catching her eye before asking Fer, "Near the grasslands?"

"Exactly." Fer nodded slowly, his weariness seeming to settle in his shoulders. "Dur and I were headed for Initium ourselves before you found us."

Larn hobbled to the cave wall beside Tympmor and sat, his face just out of reach of the blue light illuminating most of the chamber.

"We felt the Rising," Dur placed a hand over his chest, "and we knew Initium was where we needed to return."

"You've been there before?" Ansie asked.

"Many times. It's where the Animle's story was supposed to end, in what better place could it begin again?"

"So it ended?" Larn mused.

"No," Dur objected, "it was merely frozen for a time."

Larn shook his head and looked away. Ansie thought she heard him mumble something about hundreds of years.

"What's in Initium?" Ansie wondered aloud, Larn having told her of the place where the Animle had taken their final stand.

"Ruins," Fer smiled, and her heart dropped a little—notions of magical places disappearing. "Nothing more than a pile of rocks formed into a building."

She rolled her eyes. "But it's where the Animle took their final stand?"

"You mean, their last stand until now?"

The words hung between them and she wondered if what he really said could be true. The roar of the *simian* echoed in her ears. It was true.

"Though the Animle have long been forgotten, the Espiritu is alive."

Was it just her imagination, or did the light along the chamber walls shimmer with vibrancy at the word?

"Espiritu?" Willem was no longer leaning against the cave wall, but watching the brothers intently.

Fer closed his eyes for a moment. "It's a spirit, a sense of presence that lives in those who believe. In this world, there is both good and bad, the light and the dark always in conflict. But the dark cannot win—it will not win."

At a different time, Ansie would've thought Fer was speaking out of determination, but he wasn't. It was with deep-seated conviction that he spoke—something inside of her thrummed to life.

"The Espiritu is the living breathing spirit of light, the good thrives in it, breathes in it, and through it you experience freedom." Again the room shimmered for a moment. Ansie looked up, waiting for it to move again.

"It has nothing to do with the Animle, though," Larn's grumble reached them all.

"It has everything to do with them." Fer shot the words at Larn with calm ferocity. "Do you think it is by mere chance that you found these two?" He waved a hand toward Willem and Ansie. "Do you think it was chance that brought the *simian* to them? Was it chance that brought you to the very cave we sought refuge in? Was it chance that you left the Maereo to fight for the freedom of others?"

Ansie's eyes widened and she looked at her hands resting in her lap. The silence that followed was heavy, poignant and laced with some sort of inkling she felt Fer had. Was it possible he knew some of Larn's past?

From the glower on Larn's face, she guessed he might know something.

"So, it wasn't by chance," Willem said.

"No, it was by design. The Espiritu willed it, and it is so."

Larn was already shaking his head, though he remained silent.

"Others thought like you," Dur said, watching Larn. His voice was deeper, rougher. "They were warriors, Animle, bonded with their *anima reflecta*, yet they began to seek power for themselves. They doubted the Espiritu, and look what it brought to the realm? An army of former-defenders who decided to seek their own glory."

Fer shook his head in disgust as Dur continued on. "These fallen Animle, betrayers of light, swarmed over the border of Gallia to conquer their lands, but the dark followed them there. They were eliminated, beaten and broken when they returned without their beasts—their bond of *simul ad mortem* broken for all eternity."

The desperation in the *simian*'s gaze flickered before Ansie's eyes, a lump forming in her throat.

"When they returned to Initium, they were disowned, cast from the light of the Espiritu. Darkness rushed in and some turned to Gallia for help. There in the midst of those lands they had seen the beginnings of a new power. A rise of wolves swarming across the realm. For those who had lost their animal bond, they sought the glory of before and sold themselves to darkness."

Pressure built within Ansie's chest, the very light around them softening as though it too mourned those who had turned away.

"But for all their trying, they never could harness the power of *simul ad mortem* with the wolves. And in anger they led their revenge on Initium, searching for the answers they could only find in the Espiritu."

"Then why not listen to it?" Willem asked, his voice strained. Ansie watched him, wondering what it was that pained him so.

"Because to believe is to give all of yourself. There is no turning back," Fer took a deep breath, "no holding back. And your future is no longer your own, that's what they couldn't let go of."

"What happened?" Ansie asked.

"The faithful Animle died," Fer smiled, though the words were mournful. "They fought to keep the secrets of the Espiritu from those who would use it to destroy, and they won. Even in death, they won."

"Brother, he doubts," Dur nodded in Larn's direction.

Sure enough, Larn was brooding, all traces of his easy-grins and carefree manner had disappeared. In its place was a man Ansie had never seen before.

"If all this ended hundreds of years ago, how can you claim it's alive?" She had never heard Larn's voice so devoid of emotion.

"We feel it, hear it, see it moving in this realm." Fer closed his eyes for a moment. Ansie shifted, glancing around the room as though expecting a wispy spirit to take form. "It lives in here." Fer pointed to his chest.

"But if you want to know the facts, a man by the name of Rolin rescued an ancient text from the fires of Initium," Dur said, his gaze locked on Larn.

"Though the remaining faithful Animle lay dead upon the ground, there beneath the marked stone was the Tetel—the book of light. The Praelia have that book and have been studying it for years in secret."

Willem let out a breath and stood to his feet. By the set of his shoulders, Ansie could tell he was angry, though at what she didn't understand.

"What is it?" she asked, but he shook his head.

"So this spirit has been living in secret for hundreds of years," Larn mused, "but you said yourself that the Animle haven't existed since the fall of Initium."

"The Animle are not light itself, the Espiritu is. The Animle protect the light, defend the light, use the light for the good of others."

"So it has been dormant all these years?"

Dur glanced at his brother, "One doesn't have to be a called warrior of the Animle to wield the power of the Espiritu. There are those who are called Wielders."

"What—?" It sounded as though Larn was going to ask more when Dur rose to his feet.

"Attack me," he commanded.

"No." Larn shook his head, taking in the way Dur stood with most of his weight on one leg. Though now that Ansie thought about it, Larn's stance wasn't much better.

"Do it, or are you afraid?" Dur challenged.

Larn rose to his feet, his hand unclasping his cloak. It fell to the stone floor and silenced the fall of his sword a moment later. Shaking his hands slightly, he shrugged and leaned onto the balls of his feet.

"I don't have all day." The words were barely out of Dur's mouth before Larn charged at the older man. At just the moment when he would leap onto the Chronicler, a shield of blue light shot from Dur's palm knocking Larn aside. His body slammed into the opposing cave wall and he fell to the floor.

The web of light above their heads seemed to throb with power as all held still. Larn stared at Dur, his arms bracing his body, chest heaving. Ansie bit her lip, uncertain of just what to do.

Dur sucked in a breath. "Here, in this haven, it is easier to summon the power, but to try use it for my own gain out there," he pointed above their heads, "and it will not come. The Espiritu has a will of its own."

Fer was now standing. "The Praelia hold this power close and have hidden it in secret, but now, now it is time for the Rising long foretold."

As one, they all seemed to look at Willem. He hadn't spoken or made a sound during the entire display, yet before he said a word, Ansie knew it wouldn't be good. She could see it in the tightness of his shoulders, the lack of emotion in his eyes. Oh, so many times she had wanted to slap that look off his face. It was the face of a man long-tormented and lost.

"You want me to bring light to the darkness," he said, his voice tight as he stared at the brothers, "but I have seen how dark the night is, and the day isn't coming."

Without another word, he stepped over Larn and out of the chamber.

It turned out the grasslands were exactly as they sounded. Valleys of golden stalks tucked between patches of mountains, their naturally dull color almost brilliant after spending so long in the caves. Ansie took another deep breath, reveling in the fresh scent of dirt. She never thought she'd live to see a day when dirt was the best thing she smelled.

Stepping carefully through the waist-high grass, she glanced behind. They were a motley crew, each more haggard than the last. Dur and Fer's bloodstained clothes did little to hide the hollow dips where fat was supposed to protect bone. Though their faces betrayed their hunger, neither had ever complained.

Beside them was Larn, his eyes on the ground. Though his limp was less-pronounced than the days prior, she knew his ankle was still bothering him. By the creases along the sides of his mouth, she knew he was still pondering Dur's words.

And then came Willem, bringing up the rear of their group. She sighed watching him, she hadn't seen that look on his face since leaving Mirtain. Her heart ached to see it now.

Slowing, she waited for Larn to catch up, Tympmor walked with Dur on his back, his head bobbing over the grass and cutting a wide trail for the rest of them to follow. Glancing up at Larn, she watched as the gentle breeze lifted the strands of hair near his ears.

"What?" he asked, noticing her perusal.

"You need to get off your ankle," even as she said the words she watched him grimace. Whether in annoyance or pain, she didn't know.

"I'm fine."

"Your limp says otherwise," she pointed at his feet. He glanced around at the others, but their words were hidden beneath the constant rustle of the grass, sometimes the stalks snapped completely, though most of them bent and remained crushed on the ground as they passed.

Another crisp breeze whipped across the land, the dip in the grass beginning near the end of the valley and surging like a wave closer to them. By the time it reached them, Ansie had wrapped her arms around her body, hugging her cloak to her middle.

"I'm not weak," Larn grumbled.

She blinked, not sure if she had heard him correctly. "I didn't say you were."

"You implied it." The lines around his mouth creased downward.

"I did not."

"You did."

She shook her head and glanced at the clouds moving quickly above them. Breaks of sunlight appeared for a moment before disappearing completely, only to be revealed once more. A chunk of her hair blew across her mouth, she spit out the stray stands and tucked them behind her ear.

"All I meant was you might need to take a turn on Tympmor, or at least we need to think about getting another horse."

"Oh, yes, that will be so easy." He limped forward, seeming to try and move faster.

"Larn," she chided, trying to keep herself calm at his stubbornness, "Dur said he would trade."

"I'm not injured."

Shaking her head in annoyance, she looked over the dipping swells of the stalks, their constant rustle reminding her of rain. "Of course you aren't, and I have two good shoulders." She rolled her eyes, hoping he realized how foolish he was.

He mumbled something under his breath.

"What?" She asked. When he didn't answer, it was her turn to grumble. "You know, I hate it when you do that."

He finally turned to her, "Do what?"

"Mumble under your breath like that." Were his eyes always so clear this early in the morning? She wondered how she had never noticed the way a glower from him seemed to pierce the very air around her. "If you have something to say, just say it."

"Fine," he obliged. "I said, 'If you have two good shoulders, then Tympmor's a stubborn ass.'"

She stared at him for a moment and then snorted. "I don't think that proves your point. He's pretty stubborn."

"That's why I said it under my breath."

A smile rose to her lips and she glanced at him. He sighed and stared toward the end of the valley. Something dark lingered around him, weighed on him. She thought back to that mark on his shoulder—there was more than he was saying.

"Everything is going to change when we get to Initium, you know that right?"

"What do you mean?" She didn't like the sound of trepidation in his voice, and something else, some hint of longing she didn't understand.

"You'll see," he said, closing his mouth in a firm line. She could tell he'd said enough on the matter.

"Well, all right, then," she shrugged her shoulders, a twinge of pain shooting through her arm. She grimaced.

"And I'm the one who's injured," Larn rolled his eyes.

She hadn't realized he was watching. "You know what?" she turned to him, her nose in the air, but the words suddenly disappeared as she met his gaze. Some wound festered in his chest that made him lash out at her now.

The fight in her died. "Never mind," she said and turned to walk toward Willem.

She felt his eyes on her the entire way. Keeping her back straight, she forced herself not to think about what was bothering him. Instead, she focused on the conundrum he made. He was gentle, yet strong, flippant, and yet often humorless. At times she wondered if he distrusted all of them, his manner of keeping each of them at a distance was all the more apparent after their moments in the filumen chamber.

A part of her wanted to glance back at him, to see if he was still watching. After so long in the dark, she'd nearly forgotten the way his eyes could catch the light, sparking something inside her. She shook the thought away and pushed back strands of her hair.

When she reached Willem, she fell into stride beside him.

"Larn looks pleased."

She scoffed, "Ticked off is more like it."

"He can probably hear you."

"I know."

Let him hear, she thought and finally looked his way. Somehow she knew he had heard what she said, though he gave away nothing. It was the steadiness that seemed to surround him which told her all she needed to know. She had watched him on numerous occasions as he listened to everything around him, his breath would still, his body go stiff, as though he could stop the rushing of his blood through his veins.

It was in those moments that he became like a statue. *Ridiculous.*

But it hadn't been ridiculous in Alesmann. She'd felt him still as he held her close, but the thundering of his heart was enough to belay her fears. Somehow, the thrum of his heart beneath her ear had told her he was as scared as she was. And it was in that fear that she found the man she could understand. For though his heart had trembled, he'd moved forward with calm assurance, rescuing them all from certain death.

A beam of sunlight broke through the swiftly moving clouds and swept over him. For just a moment his dark hair had a shimmer of auburn to it. She wondered if Dur's words were eating at him still, the dark mask he fixed in place a sign to the inner turmoil of his heart.

"He's been quiet," Willem observed. "Or quieter than usual." She only nodded. "Whereas you say too much."

She could hear the slight smile in his voice. "That's why I'm not saying anything."

"Right," he bumped her good shoulder, making her sidestep. When she matched his stride once more, a rumble of thunder rolled in the skies above. He glanced up, "Hopefully it will hold until we make it to the trees."

She nodded, secretly welcoming the oncoming rain. It was one of her favorite sounds, the gentle patter and splat rhythm hitting the cottage roof, often a plink sounding on the floor where the buckets caught the leaking remains of runoff.

For the first time since leaving Mirtain, she realized she truly missed it. Not the work in the fields or even the people there, but the cottage itself. Ever since she'd been brought out of the forest and Willem had asked to care for her, she'd called the cottage home. Now, she didn't know what to think. She no longer had a home.

"Do you miss home?" she asked and watched as Willem's head dipped slightly—anguish creasing his eyes.

What had she said wrong now? It seemed everything coming out of her mouth lately only caused pain.

CHAPTER 44

Why was she bringing this up now? Willem wondered.

Of course, he missed home, but didn't Ansie realize that she was his home? And now she was tied to whatever fate aligned with Larn.

He'd never told her, but the day he brought her out of the forest and back to the cottage was when he found his strength again. It seemed like a lifetime since his mother had been killed.

There was so much about his past he kept hidden, even from Ansie. Fer's words ran through him again, the task ahead looming with an insistent force. He knew that it was coming for him, the moment when he would have to decide his fate. He pondered the words for hours, turning them inside out and all around, all that remained was the truth.

The Rising would cost him everything.

A sour taste filled his mouth and he peered at the dark clouds beginning to form on the horizon. It wouldn't be long now.

"Sometimes I miss it," he finally said. Ansie had waited patiently for him to speak. It was one thing he always appreciated about her, she understood his need to gather his thoughts.

"But you're glad we left Mirtain," she said matter of factly and gave a short nod to herself.

"True enough." She had no idea how much he preferred being gone. To be away from the eyes of those who had judged him all his life, to not wonder what Lord Hernan was up to locked away in his rooms. The shard of anger dug deeper into his heart—the cost never forgotten.

"Are you happy we left?" he asked.

"I thought I was, but now I don't know."

"What do you mean?"

She sighed. "All of this, the realm, Fer and Dur, what they told us, all of it just seems like too much."

"I know," he said, his voice turning darker. "And who knows what will happen when we reach Initium." Ansie glanced toward Larn, and then stuck her chin in the air. He didn't know what had been said between the two of them, but if it made her do that with her chin, it couldn't be good. He'd received that look one too many times.

She shivered in the breeze. "I still believe them, though."

Willem remained silent for a long time. "I do too," he admitted. "But what they're asking of us is too much."

"How so?"

He took a deep breath. "I've known about the Praelia since I was a boy." Trying not to notice her surprise, he carried on. "My mother told me about them, about their power—but I just can't put my trust in it."

"Why not?"

"I'm nothing," he admitted, "why should I be chosen to carry on what others could also do? Why would some powerful spirit use any of us?"

"But that isn't what really worries you." She observed, as always cutting to the heart of the matter. It was a skill she'd always had, a way of reading him that no other person had acquired. He sucked in a breath.

Surely she, above all others, had understood what he meant in the filumen chamber. He had seen darkness and the light wasn't coming.

"I can't justify what happened to Kata," he whispered, tucking his heart behind a wall made of stone. He wouldn't be broken.

She sighed, hugging her cloak to her body. A gust of wind swirled her hair around her head, and for a moment she was in a struggle to keep it under control.

"I don't know if there was a purpose," she whispered. "It just, it happened. It was the law and Hernan took advantage."

From the hidden places of his soul, a roaring anger gripped him as it always did. It wasn't right, it wasn't fair. It shook him to his core to think that what had happened to her had been the vile darkness of a heart—a leering grasp of a disgusting, greedy man. His lips began to tremble as he held back his anger, barely maintaining control.

"That's what bothers me the most."

Ansie remained silent and he wondered if she agreed with him. It was all so strange. One minute Jethron and Kata had been with them, and the next they were gone. Kata was gone.

As always, the tear lanced his heart. Reaching out with his hand, he brushed it over the tops of the grass beside him. The rustle of their stalks as he passed by at once comforting and annoying.

"Why didn't you tell me about the Espiritu?" Ansie kept her eyes focused straight ahead, her chin tilted slightly. It was his turn to wonder about what he'd done to deserve that look.

"I didn't trust it," he finally said. It was part of the truth, but not all of it. It had been easier to ignore his mother's final words than to confront them day after day. He'd only been a boy, but even then he'd been able to sense the power in her words before they dragged her away.

"All our talks, our planning," she waved a hand as though Shirnway Castle stood before them, "and you never said anything."

He reeled back from the accusation, silence falling between them. He'd said nearly the same thing to Jethron. What excuse could he give?

"I forced myself not to believe," his admission gave him pause. Testing the words for truth, he continued. "When they killed my mother," Ansie looked up, he'd never truly admitted the Gallians had killed her, "I didn't want to listen to her final words. I didn't understand why other kids got to have their families, and I had nothing. I didn't want to understand why I was alone."

"But we spent hours talking about the Animle."

"I know, I just," he searched for the right words, "I didn't want you to feel the unending sense of loss I did."

Did she notice the way she began to walk faster? Was it intentional? He knew it wasn't, she often did that when she was angry, pace and move until her energy wore out.

"I was afraid," he said softly, she slowed. "I still am. I don't understand why I should be chosen for this. My mother believed I would become a warrior," he gave a low chuckle, "if she could only see me now. What a loss I've turned out to be."

It wasn't a loss, it was failure. Failure to see things for how they truly were. Failure to protect those he loved.

Every day since Kata was taken he had awakened to the pain of knowing that he had failed her. It didn't matter that Jethron and Kata had planned the whole thing. What mattered was what Hernan had done to her. He went against the law, taking her for himself, and there was nothing Willem could have done to stop it. He'd tried, but he'd failed.

Too many nights he'd awakened to her screams ringing in his head.

Lost in thought, they pressed on. Larn called them forward, motioning to a cottage not far from the edges of the valley. After a quick check of the area, they ducked inside just as the clouds released their anger upon the land.

Shaking the water from his head, he watched Ansie as she moved to a back corner. With a huff, she sat down on the floor, tucking her legs close to her body. He moved closer, kneeling before her.

"I should've told you," he apologized, "but I didn't want to give you false hope. You'd already lost as much as I had, I couldn't have it ripped away from you too."

Her eyes held the remnants of tears when she finally looked up.

"Indeed," Fer said, drawing closer. "You became exactly what the Regent wanted you to be."

They both stared at the man. It didn't seem possible the Regent could even be aware of the ways of the past. Having blotted out history, he refused to let others know about the Animle, the Praelia, the Espiritu, all of it. But it made sense that he would know. What better way to prevent his own downfall than to study the power that had held Anglas together for so many years?

"What did the Regent do to you?" The question rose to Willem's lips.

"We were summoned to Wollmorn to meet with the Regent," Fer said. "He interviewed each of us personally, asking about the fall of Anglas and what we knew of the Animle." Fer smiled to himself, as though enjoying a private joke. "Most Chroniclers spent no more than a few minutes with him, but Dur's," he glanced back at his brother, "his lasted well over an hour."

Ansie stared at Fer in wonder. "You met with him personally?"

Fer turned to her, the dark scruff along his chin only interrupted by a thin scar. Willem wondered how he'd received the mark. It appeared aged and faded with time.

"I did, and I spoke with him for nearly an hour as well. It seems our Regent didn't believe I would be able to confirm what my brother had told him." His eyes sparkled in amusement. "Dur has never been one to back away from telling others about the Espiritu. Even to the Regent."

To think of doing such a thing was certain death, and yet, Dur had risked it. Their every action went against logic.

"Did His Sire believe either of you?" Willem asked.

"Why do you think he commanded all animal fighting to cease? He had all those animals slaughtered." Fer smiled, the mischief in his eyes was unlike anything Willem had ever seen. "He believed all right, but he refused to understand what set the Animle apart."

"And what is that?"

"Selflessness, it's something the Regent cannot understand."

"As if he needs anything else," Ansie muttered, but Fer heard her.

"You should pity him," he corrected. "He has heard the truth and won't believe it because of the world he lives in. All his life he has been given the right to power and nothing has ever been denied him. He thinks he has no reason to hope for more, and it makes him blind."

"Didn't he have you beaten?"

"Ansie," Willem chided.

"Yes," Fer confirmed without flinching, "he did."

"How then can you pity him?"

"Well," Fer crossed his arms, seeming to brace himself against the draft which swirled through the open door, "when you see death in a man's eyes, you can't help but feel pity for him."

"But you were whipped," Ansie said, her brow furrowed.

"I was, and so were many others, and thousands throughout the realm have endured far worse. He had ten of the other Chroniclers killed before us." Fer's words were strong, without a hint of regret. "But in trying to prove his power, he revealed his greatest weakness."

The feeling that had overcome Willem in the filumen chamber rose once more. It was a deep stirring in his chest, it ignited and burned within him, a spark of something he didn't fully understand. All he knew was that if he turned to it, power awaited.

"The Regent is a man of deep emotion," Fer continued. "He fears what he cannot control. He wants nothing more than absolute power, and those who remain outside his reach are considered threats."

"And how is that a weakness?" Willem asked, attempting to hide the growing surge inside him. They could not make him hope.

"Every time we were beaten, the Regent was nowhere to be seen. And his every act of violence against his people takes place away from himself. He controls with a blind eye."

"So we shouldn't fear him?" Ansie asked.

"Fear him? No. But of what he can do? Yes." Fer nodded and eyed Ansie. "He will do whatever it takes to maintain his hold over Autre Gallia. He sees the realm as his, given to him by the gods the Gallians cling so tightly to—the gods of the stars." He waved a bony hand dismissing the thought. "The Animle are a threat to everything he believes in, to everything he is."

Willem turned away and looked toward the open door. The grass outside was cringing beneath the pelting drops of rain.

"Why won't you believe?" Fer asked suddenly.

"Why should I?" He glared, hating the way this man's words conjured up images he had turned away from long ago.

Fer met his stare head on. "Your enemy is afraid of the Espiritu, and the Rising. He fears what you might become if you find your Animle. Perhaps, then, it's time you started wondering why."

Without another word, the older man left him, returning to his brother. Willem could have cursed him from the rooftops, but it no longer seemed to matter.

Confusion and doubt roiled within. He could no more believe, than he could forget the past. It was impossible, and there was nothing he could do to change it.

Cursing, he moved toward the door. "I'll take first watch."

The matter wasn't up for debate.

CHAPTER 45

Ansie seemed aware of Larn's movements before he even stepped outside the cottage. Her hair seemed to glow in the cloud covered night. He almost told her to put her hood up, but the last thing he needed was for her to think he cared.

"How did you sleep?" she asked. She'd offered to take the second watch, a few hours after Willem had left the cottage.

"Well enough," he said, allowing a yawn.

He stretched his back, the familiar pinch of the hard ground had made his muscles tight. If anything, he had awakened more bitter than before. Glancing down at her, he grit his teeth. She stirred something in him he didn't want to understand. He knew his words had frustrated her earlier, but she didn't understand why.

Old wounds dug deep.

It had first happened in the cave, the filumen web glowing above their heads. He'd listened to Dur's words and believed them, but they weren't intended for him. They were meant for Willem and Ansie. Once again he was an outsider.

"Willem's been out for hours," Ansie whispered, glancing up at him from her spot on the ground. An amused grin lifted the edges of her lips. Sure enough, Willem's head had fallen to the side to rest on his shoulder, his arms and legs limp.

"Have you slept any?" he asked, rubbing at his eyes.

"No," she yawned and looked back inside the cottage. "Are you taking watch?"

He shook his head, a part of him wishing he could help her, but he already knew where that would lead. Before it had been easier to think what they had might turn into something, that this sham of a marriage could form into a friendship of sorts, but he knew now it was over. She was destined for greatness and he would be lost in the wake of her flight.

He rubbed a hand across his chin, making a note to control his face. The last thing he needed was for her to ask him what was wrong. She'd tried hard enough to help him earlier. It was high time he began to build the wall between them, it would only make things easier down the road.

"I have to leave," he said, fastening his sword around his waist.

"Leave?"

Was that a bit of sadness? He cast the thought aside—it no longer mattered.

"I'll be back. There's someone I must speak to."

"A contact? How? Where?"

He nodded, pulling his coat tighter. It really was cold, the chill of the wind biting into his bones. He was still not over his illness and the weather was not helping, but he refused to give it acknowledgment. As far as he was concerned, it was a little uncomfortable.

"I realized we're close to Flocorna, a secret trading hub," he explained. "I have to check on one of the traders, he often has information for me."

"Should I tell Fer you're leaving?"

"No, why?"

"He's been up all night muttering and talking to someone I can't see."

"Probably talking to the supposed spirit that lives in him," Larn grumbled and passed her, heading in the direction of Tympmor. She rose to follow him.

"That's what I thought too, only, it's different," she said, her voice drifting off for a moment as though she was trying to gather her thoughts. "He talks as though he's talking to his brother."

"Who knows," Larn said, bending over to grab at the saddle lying on the ground. Tympmor turned to him, his large brown eyes seeming to tell him he wanted to sleep longer. At another time, Larn would have talked to the horse, telling him he was sorry to have to leave so soon. But he'd spent too many moments letting Ansie into his world, only to be reminded she didn't belong there.

And even if she did, she wouldn't stay if she knew everything about him.

Dur had cut him to the quick, his words sharpening the wounds in his chest. It was true, the Maereo didn't leave a member of their tribe behind unless they were cast out. He could kick himself for having told Ansie about his mother.

She'd listened so intently, allowing him to share a bit of his past. At that moment, he'd stood on the edge, ready to plunge forward and show her more of himself, but he'd held back in fear.

Seeing her now only made Larn grateful for having held onto his past. She was much too pretty for her own good. If he let himself, he could fall for her smiles.

He had fooled himself into thinking he belonged with her and Willem, but the truth now stared him in the face. They were chosen, both of them selected to carry out the work of the Animle. His role was to simply help them find their *anima reflecta* and then he could drift away into obscurity.

That's what you've always wanted.

He paused in his movements, lost in his own thoughts when her hand touched his. He jumped a little, forcing himself not to pull away.

"What is it?" she asked, her voice filled with an innocence that was the product of a sheltered life. What did she know of emptiness? Of feeling lost?

"Nothing," he said, busying himself with fastening the saddle around Tympmor's back.

"Something's bothering you."

"How observant."

"Larn," she chided and when he turned, she had her arms crossed over her chest, her hip cocked to the side.

"Don't start," he said.

"I wouldn't have to if you would just tell me what's bothering you. You've been acting weird ever since Dur and Fer told us what they know."

He turned back to Tympmor, focusing on the straps. Why were his hands not working as quickly as usual?

"Is it something they said?" she asked, watching him. Her lips were pressed together in concentration. "It has to do with that wolf mark on your shoulder, doesn't it?"

She was observant, he would give her that. He shook his head in denial, yet another lie.

How could he tell her that the wolves haunted his every step? It hadn't begun when he joined the Renegades, or even when his mother sold him to the caravan. No, the wolves had loomed over his life, over his people, since the night he was born.

"Forget it," he mumbled, but her hand reached for his once more.

Her fingers were so petite and soft, though there were calluses on her palms which only revealed the depths of her strength. She was fiercer than she appeared and more than he would ever deserve.

"You can tell me," she said, and he finally turned to look at her.

As always, the warmth of her brown eyes drew him in, like the welcoming of a warm fire on a cold night. He wanted to tell her, but knew he couldn't. There had already been too many things said between them. He would continue to offer his protection, but that was as far as it could go.

"Don't worry about it," he said, his carefree mask sliding into place. He forced his lips to turn upward in a grin. "You were right before, I'm getting sick."

She raised an eyebrow, seeming to see straight through him. "That's it?"

A stiff wind whipped past and he shivered. "Yes," he said and moved closer to Tympmor, preparing to hop into the saddle.

"Why won't you tell me?" He hated the sudden meekness in her voice, knowing he was the cause of it.

He grit his teeth. "Leave it alone, Ansie."

"I just want to help."

Help. It was the very word that pushed him over the edge. As a child, he'd turned to so many for help, but in the end, it had come down to him to make things happen. He was the only one he could trust, the only one he knew wouldn't betray him.

His anger frothed like a raging river deep inside his gut. He was never enough for anyone. Well, maybe if he showed her what everyone else saw, then she wouldn't be so keen to understand him.

"Quit badgering me," he grumbled under his breath, knowing she hated it. When she opened her mouth to say something in reply, he cut her off. "No, you've said enough. You don't have to be like Kata and try and keep the peace."

He regretted the words immediately when she flinched.

She took a deep breath. Whether to calm herself or to collect her thoughts, he didn't know. Staring at the ground between them, she asked, "Can I come with you?"

"What? Why?"

"Because I can't stay here, not with them," she waved at the cottage. "If a patrol found us it would be like the Caw's Nest all over again."

He nearly laughed. "That'll be the least of your worries." She looked up, confused. "You're traveling with two men the Regent has placed a rather handsome reward on. By now there have to be rumors of you and Willem spreading, not to mention who you are traveling with," he motioned to himself, "you'd be dead within minutes of their arrival."

"A sunny picture," she mumbled.

"It's reality. The sooner you learn that the better." He wanted so desperately for her to understand that all of this was a matter of life and death. He didn't know what she'd been through, but he knew enough to realize that she didn't see things the way he often did. If only she could grasp how the world worked, how others were unkind and only out for themselves, just maybe she wouldn't be so hopeful.

His blood began to pound furiously in his ears. "Not all of us have the privilege of living in your dream world."

Her mouth dropped open, the soft lines of her face disappearing almost instantly. He reveled in it.

For one single moment, he wanted her to feel as worthless as he did. Their shared moments of friendship were only that, moments with the need to speak to one another, nothing more. He had to tell himself that.

She had wanted to see the real him, well, this was it.

"Fine, go ahead and leave," she said, her voice hollow. She turned away, but stopped, only to whip back around. Her eyes shimmered with a fiery anger he'd never seen before. "Even if you don't believe, what Dur and Fer are offering is hope. How can you throw that away?"

He stepped closer to her, rising to the challenge in her eyes.

"Don't act like you want everything they told us," he retorted, bitterness lacing his words. "They aren't offering hope, they're offering years of war and bloodshed, years of sacrifice and fighting. Are you ready for that? Are you ready to become the most hunted woman in the realm? Are you prepared to give all of yourself and never get what you want?"

"How would you know what I want?" she shot back at him. There was a gleaming fire in her that reminded him of the filumen. He tried to ignore it.

"You told me about the life you dreamed of—marrying Skurn and having a place of your own," she took a step back from him as he shot the words at her. Her eyes grew wide as he continued, "Some place the rest of the realm couldn't find you. Well, if you haven't noticed you're living the exact opposite right now," he spread his arms out wide, "and that's going to continue if you follow what they teach. You'll never get what you desire. Ever. End of story."

Ansie lifted her chin, the bottoms of her eyes swelling with unshed tears. Her chin began to tremble, but she fixed him with a steady gaze. "You're right," she admitted. "I did want something different. But who are you to tell me I could never be happy?"

They glared at one another, neither backing down. Only now did he realize how close he was to her, nearly towering over her. He took a deep breath, waiting for the thrum of his heart to still.

"Just some nomad who married you to save your life," he waved a hand.

"Is that what this is all about?" she asked. "Are you mad because you saved me?"

"This has nothing to do with that."

"Then why bring it up?" she spit. Their voices were barely raised above a whisper, and yet, Larn felt as though they were yelling—as though the swish of the grasslands behind them was drowned out by their voices. Ansie was fuming, the shimmer of her red hair making her cheeks seem all the brighter.

"I didn't."

"You did. You think I'm angry because you saved my life and now I have no chance with Skurn." Her words were pointed and sharp, they darted beneath the wall he'd tried to build. He prepared to counterattack.

"Well, you listen," she pushed his arm, "I ended things with Skurn way before you came along."

He launched forward on the assault. "But he was the protector you were looking for." She flinched again and this time he knew he'd hit his mark. "Skurn was the one who was supposed to keep you safe when the rest of the realm forgot."

This time, one of the tears pooled over and ran down her cheek. She didn't wipe it away.

His shame covered him almost immediately. Just another badge to carry with him—like the mark on his shoulder.

"I never said that," she finally uttered, her breath clouding between them. Her face had gone pale, the alabaster skin seeming to shimmer in the dark.

"You didn't have to."

"You're wrong," she whispered.

He shook his head and leaned in closer. "There's a reason I was promoted to Head of Intelligence. I see things when no one's looking. I've watched you stare at the stars in longing, I've heard you whisper his name when you sleep. Ever since Oslo deemed us married, you've been ignoring the fact as though it never happened."

Somehow he'd cornered her. Her back bumped into Tympmor's side, but she kept her chin raised glaring back at him.

"If you don't want me, then say it now," he said, edging closer their bodies almost touching.

He wanted her to say the words, to confirm the piercing ache in his chest. He wanted to hear her disappointment, to feel the drowning depths of his own self-loathing.

She said nothing, refusing to back down. Her bottom lip trembled again and for a moment he was focused on it solely, their gazes no longer locked.

"Tell me how much you hate having to be stuck with me," he murmured. He placed his hands on Tympmor, his arms on either side of her body. "Say how you wish none of this had ever happened." He leaned in, lifting his gaze to hers.

This close, he was suddenly aware of how large her eyes were, how the deep brown flickered with flecks of gold. She stared back at him, unflinching, her kindness having fled. What was left was something he didn't want to see. She wasn't as innocent to the evil of the world as he thought.

"And if I don't?" she asked, her words lingering between them.

"Then maybe I'll have to convince you," he whispered, nearly breathless.

A faint hint of grass and wildflowers seemed to cling to her skin, the smell at once fresh and sweet. It made him think of sunshine. Funny, he'd never noticed it before.

Tympmor shifted behind her back, but her gaze never left his. For a moment, her eyes fell to his lips. A soft blush began to flush over her cheeks and along her neck, but when she met his gaze once more, the spark in those golden flecks had dimmed.

She looked away from him—strands of her hair blowing across her face. He watched mesmerized and had the sudden urge to push them away from her cheeks, but forced his hands to remain on Tympmor.

"Perhaps you should go," she said, her voice flat. The words hit him in the gut.

He stepped back, suddenly realizing just how close they'd been. For some reason, the increased space did nothing to calm the erratic beat in his chest.

She began to walk away from him and stopped to speak over her shoulder. "I hope you find what you're looking for."

"I'm coming back," he admitted.

"Fine," was all she said, continuing to walk away. A sudden crisp wind picked at her hair, lifting it from her shoulders.

"Put your hood up," he called after her, nearly cursing himself for caring. She turned back to him, confused. "You're like a damned target."

Her hand lifted to her hair, her eyes wide, but he turned away and mounted Tympmor. Only as he trotted away did he glance back and see her retreating to the cottage. For a moment her presence was obvious, her hair seeming to glow, until it suddenly disappeared.

He shook his head, knowing he'd shown exactly what he wanted to keep hidden. He cared for her. He'd known it for a long time now, and the realization did nothing but grip him in fear. For he knew what would happen. Once she realized how much he cared for her, she would use it against him.

Someone always had.

Not wanting to think on it any longer, he nudged Tympmor into a run and lost himself in the beat of the hooves and the wind whipping against his skin.

Here in the darkness, he was home.

Larn stepped beneath the final archway and into the grand center of Flocorna, a network of caves and the hub trading center for the Black Market. Marked above ground by a rounded hill decorated with a semicircle band of wildflowers, the market was rumored to have been a hiding place for nomads at the fall of Anglas.

Larn now wondered if the rumors were all a lie. The Praelia having used the caves to survive in secret. Even now, he glanced at the cave walls, wondering if the filumen would glow here if he dared to bring it to life.

Standing upon a ledge, a winding pathway worked down to the great room where tents and poorly constructed stands scattered along the great expanse. Legend said the caves had once held horse races, though how a hoofed creature would ever be able to maneuver the dips and swells of the water-carved walls and floors, Larn had never understood. Yet he believed their worth, for crude paintings illuminated the walls, long-since faded depictions of the riders and their chariots—horses breathing hot breaths of fire.

Hiding his face in the shadow of his hood, Larn made his way along the path and into the fray of the pressing crowd. Hundreds of villagers milled around him, traders displaying their goods and guards stood as silent watchers over all who passed. It was to these silent people he looked.

Torches lit the chamber, or at least what could be seen of it. Larn had once heard there were so many chambers inside Flocorna that it had never been fully explored. He had heard such tales as a small boy when Girshon had begun his training, but it wasn't until he was ten years old and visited Flocorna that he truly believed the stories.

Above his head, flickering in the torchlight, were the stalactites proclaiming the eeriness of all around him—ghosts of the past looking down upon them all. A herder bumped into Larn's shoulder, his field-hands following in his wake. No doubt their cattle were located somewhere nearby above ground.

Larn shifted uncomfortably. After so many days spent with only Willem and Ansie for company, and the Chroniclers, the thrum of voices seemed to pulse in his chest. He embraced it, casting Ansie from his mind. He wasn't here for her.

"For you, sir!" A woman called, swinging beads in her hands, with the clear intent of getting him to move closer to her stand of spices. He refused and kept his gaze sweeping from side to side, searching for the one mark he knew so well.

Over the crush of many heads, he spotted the silver moon and stars with the thistle branch embossed across a deep crimson banner. He pushed his way through the crowd, keeping his hand secured around the dagger at his waist.

"No, that is a fair price, and I won't go any lower." Sarnon, the Black Market trader he'd known for many years, was haggling with a customer at the front of his stand. Larn inched forward, making sure to hide in the shadows where the trader often looked.

The grey, wizened eyes shifted from the customer holding a vial of herbs for a mere moment. The aged head jerked toward the back of his tent. Without further acknowledgment, Larn stepped inside, passing by the stand and ducking beneath the hanging herbs and bottles, to move behind a partition in the tent. He knew from experience, the back room was where Sarnon kept all of his priceless goods.

But goods Larn had little use for, information was all he needed.

A masked figure stood beside Sarnon's chest, her dark clothes making her seem a shadow along the back wall of the caves.

"Larn," her voice reached him from behind her mask, "it's been too long."

He smiled, it had been longer than planned since he last saw her. It was hard to think of how simple things had been when they first met.

"Gabrella," he acknowledged.

"What can I do for you?" she asked and reached up to pull off the hood and mask, revealing the angled tilt of her eyes and tanned skin which nearly matched his own.

"That depends on what you can tell me," he whispered, and one side of her mouth twitched. Only on rare occasions would she smile, he found the notion comforting. After spending so much time with Ansie he needed to remember the way the realm worked.

Cursing himself for thinking of Ansie again, he cast her from his mind.

"Should I tell you what happened in Mirtain?" Gabrella cocked her head to the side. He rolled his eyes. "I thought not. Seems as though you already know."

"Why would you ever doubt me?" he smirked, turning to look at the fresh herbs hanging from the tent.

He always found it interesting for a trader who dealt in grinspur horns, gold, and verral claws to spend his time drying herbs. Gabrella had once tried to convince Larn of their worth, but he was unconvinced of their purpose.

He reached up to touch one, a sweet fragrance filling the air for a moment. He breathed in, the summery essence reminding him of days he'd spent in the Plenus Mountains. He glanced to see if there was a label, but it remained unmarked.

Gabrella was still watching him. "I have my reasons to doubt you." She pulled her braid over her shoulder so it dipped down to her waist. As long as he'd known her, she'd never had it cut. Even as children when they trained at Sicarmman, she'd kept her black hair in immaculate condition, always tightly wound.

She folded her arms before her, the motion somehow innocent, but he knew the strength she could muster. Her skill in Sicarmman had not gone unnoticed, though the realm had been unkind to a female without knowledge of anything but the movements of battle. There had been a time—when they were much too young to think of such things—when they had dreamed of fleeing the school. But by then, Girshon had convinced Larn to join the Renegades—to make something of himself.

What lightness had been in Gabrella's eyes disappeared as suddenly as it had arrived. Larn noticed how the creases around her mouth turned down.

"You've started a chain reaction across Autre Gallia, villages are rising up against their ruling lords."

Larn nodded, Pike had told him as much. "And what of the Regent?"

She cocked her head to the side, "Seems a fort was broken into, and two very important Chroniclers have gone missing again." She quirked an eyebrow. "Word is, he's sending soldiers to Mirtain to quell any resistance there. And the Master of the Legion of Nex has been summoned to Bastion Nocta. Rumors say there are three miscreants he's searching for."

Larn nodded keeping his expression blank, though a strike of fear coursed through him. The Liege was coming to Autre Gallia. He rubbed a hand along his jaw. "And what does the Liege know of these miscreants?"

"Supposedly there's a man, the one from Mirtain who can speak to animals." She tacked Willem off with a finger. "And the other man, the *maeri*, who accompanies him," a knowing look was shot his way as another finger came up—the slur applying to herself as well. "And then a girl. Flaming red hair, I've heard." A third finger joined the first two.

"I see," was all he said. The rumors were much too close to the truth.

He hated the way his heart flipped at the thought of others knowing Ansie's hair color. She was already a target in the midst of fighting, or even in the night, but having others know would only make her more recognizable.

Gabrella stepped closer. "He's sending the Nexen after you."

He stilled his breath, controlling his expression. She would never know what had happened at Kraven Hall. He still didn't understand it himself. He'd turned to stop the wolves out of desperation and it had worked, if only for a moment. But he had seen the soldiers' surprise, they would come for him, hunt him, kill him, if they could.

He could almost feel those jaws snapping at his heels. His injured ankle protested, but he hid his limp well in Gabrella's presence—he wouldn't give her the satisfaction of seeing him hurt.

"There's more," Gabrella said, taking another step forward. She was nearer to him than she would ever let any other person. "I've heard of what happened at the Caw's Nest, it seems you have responsibilities now."

Again, a shot of alarm passed through him. He stilled, forcing a laugh from his lips. He wouldn't let Gabrella get to him, not her, not Ansie, not anyone.

"You've grown soft since our days at Sicarmman," she said, retreating a step, the lingering scent of the lavender oil she used in her long braid, filled the space between them. "I remember a time when you weren't so easily swayed."

He stiffened. "That was different."

"How so?" She asked, and the crack in her hard, worn exterior widened. "Because I was too much like you?" She swallowed, her throat bobbing. He hated seeing her like this, it brought back too many memories.

"Don't," he whispered, "it's not worth bringing up again. You know we never could have run away."

"We could've at least tried."

"And died in the process," he whispered, knowing he'd said the words before. They were as true now as they were then. He'd known they would be caught, a whipping would have been the least of their punishment—being hunted by assassins would have been their fate.

Not so different from now.

He ran a hand through his hair, watching Gabrella return to her spot next to Sarnon's chest of valuables. "He treats you well enough?" he asked.

"Yes," she admitted, crossing her arms again, the mask she normally wore in her hand. "He treats me better than any Maereo guard deserves."

There had been a time when he met with her and she would throw her rank at him, but no more. He'd seen the way she had risen, moving from Sarnon's servant to his most trusted guard. But there was still a part of him which wondered what would have happened if they had left Sicarmman together. Maybe they would have made it, maybe not. But he knew one thing was certain, he would have failed her. It was better he had turned her away while she still had a chance.

"I'm glad to hear it," he said. He paused then, his eyes roaming, taking in her life. "You deserve more than this."

"And yet," she motioned around her, "here I am."

"Girshon will be pleased to know you're still alive."

She gave a hoarse laugh. "Of course he will. Tell him my answer is the same as it was last time."

"But you still gather information for me."

"What else would I have to keep me busy?" she gave a small, mournful smile.

"I do appreciate it, we all do." He nodded her way, knowing she would understand him.

Girshon had extended a position for her to join the Renegades more than once, but she had turned his offer down each time. As much as she hated being a guard, Gabrella enjoyed the comforts Sarnon offered. The hard labor and constant riding of the Renegades was something she said she could never grow used to. But Larn knew it had more to do with her need to feel safe.

There were few she ever spoke to, and even fewer still whom she trusted. It was only to Larn who she gave information, her responses to Girshon's requests were only directed to him, never to the leader himself. Larn had often wondered what she truly thought of Sarnon.

"There's one more thing, one of Lord Duggard's men traded with Sarnon a week ago. There's to be a festival of sorts next month at his stately manor, it might be the right place to pick up information about the Regent's plans for battle," she suggested with a shrug. "You know who Lord Duggard is, don't you?"

"I might," he feigned innocence. She didn't need to know how often he visited Kirath, Lord Duggard's village. The thriving Gallian society in his lands was brimming with information.

"A festival?" He asked, edging forward—eyeing her reaction. She made none.

"A *masked* festival, celebrating Joute Deliverance," she pointed out.

Joute Deliverance—the festival the Gallians celebrated for liberating Anglas. That's how they viewed history.

"Take whatever clothes you need for a disguise," Gabrella said. "Sarnon will not miss a thing. He's made more money off the grinspur horns than that farmer boy could ever imagine."

Larn nodded, her reports of the goings on in Mirtain were the main reason he'd been willing to trust Jethron when his messages first reached the Renegades.

"Thank you, Gabrella."

"Of course," she said. "And you might want to take your girl with you."

"What?" he hated the way her words struck him, his worry for Ansie seeming to now be a part of him.

"Too many people know you work alone, take her and no one will suspect anything amiss. Be sure to use one of Sarnon's wigs. From what I hear, her hair is redder than flame." Her lips parted, a small curve lifting one side. Larn refused to respond.

The aching realization of how much he cared for Ansie stirred in his chest. She hadn't deserved the words he'd shot at her. She deserved the world, and he couldn't give her any of it. Cursing himself, he remained silent.

"Just remember," Gabrella smiled gently, pulling him from his thoughts, "as long as you hide in plain sight, they'll never see you for what you truly are."

He chuckled. He'd told her the same thing the day he left with Girshon. Outside of his tribe, he had never met another like him, except for her. She had a special place in his heart.

"I'll never let them," he said, recalling her words from so many years ago.

She nodded and pulled her hood back over her head. As soon as the mask was in place, she became a shadow once more. "And take some of those herbs for your illness, you sound terrible."

He nearly chuckled but ducked his head in thanks before passing the partition. He dealt quickly with Sarnon, trading for the verral claws. He wasn't foolish enough to not notice the sharp glances of the trader in his direction. So many claws were a novelty.

Larn bit the inside of his cheek, not wanting to think about what Sarnon must know. Only someone like Willem would be able to survive an attack from so many verrals. The result of the valuable claws was enough supplies to load down Tympmor, exquisite clothes for the masque, and two, albeit rather sad, horses.

After paying one more visit to a trader in jewels, Larn left Flocorna behind.

He tied the supplies, which included the healing herbs for his cold, onto Tympmor's back before swinging into the saddle. His thoughts soon turned to Gabrella's request from so many years ago.

He had left her then and he would do it again if given the chance. He was good at leaving.

As Flocorna disappeared behind him, he could only wish there was some way to make Ansie understand—leaving was all he knew how to do.

CHAPTER 46

Ansie would be lying if she said Larn's words hadn't cut her to the core. For what seemed like hours she had watched the grasslands wave and bow beneath the breeze—a part of her wishing she could somehow leap upon the wind and disappear.

Sleep eluded her in the cottage. Dur and Fer remained on watch, their conversation lost to her. She had tried to listen, but the wind stole their words before reaching her ears. She shivered, securing her cloak more firmly around her body. Due to her size, she could tuck all of herself beneath the cloak if she cured into a ball.

She was no more than a lump on the floor.

A soft nicker of a horse sounded outside. Willem gathered to his feet and left the worn cottage. Her heart hammered in her chest, knowing just what awaited her.

Larn had returned, and though it eased her worries about his safety, it did nothing to quell the heat flooding through her veins. She'd been all too aware of her reaction to him. As they argued, his arms on either side of her body, she'd nearly leaned into his chest. Never before had they been so close, and now it felt as though they'd never been farther apart.

"Larn's back," Willem said, his head peeking around the cottage doorway.

"Okay," she said softly, moving outside. If Larn wanted to push her away, then perhaps he would get his wish. She steeled herself against the wind and seeing him. The last thing she needed was to meet his gaze.

Outside, already munching on tall stalks of grass were two new horses. Though new was not quite the right word. One had a sagging back and was working desperately to try and pull a stalk of grass from the ground, his head turned sideways, puffy lips grasping. The other merely stood with its eyes closed.

Valiant steeds indeed.

Throwing her hood over her head, she strode into the dark and toward the new horses. As the drooped-back steed finally got purchase of the grass, his head flew back. She watched, with mirth as he then tried to lip the entire stalk into his mouth.

Behind her, the men began to talk as this new horse eyed her, his lips still quivering. "I think I'll call you Muncher." She patted the horse's neck and he seemed to approve. As she leaned into his side, he reached for another stalk of grass. "And your buddy will be Sleeper. Does he always do that?" She ran a hand through Muncher's wiry mane, wondering just why she was talking to this horse.

Maybe because he couldn't talk back. The last person she'd spoken to had certainly had plenty to say.

Seeing him out of the corner of her eye, she decided to keep her attention fixated on Muncher.

"Let's go, Ans." Willem was walking toward her.

"I think I'm going to ride Muncher here," she said.

"You'll have to ride with Larn," Willem said. She whipped around to face him.

"No," she nearly stomped her boot.

Behind Willem, Larn was already approaching. Color rose to her cheeks, making her all the more frustrated. She hated herself for it.

"This one can only hold one rider," Willem motioned toward Muncher's sloped back, "and that one," *Sleeper,* she thought, "can hold two of us, but Larn thinks it should be Dur and Fer. They weigh less than me."

"So, I can't ride with you on Tympmor?"

"No," it was only one word from Larn as he approached. His bitterness seemed to not have left him in his absence. The mere sound of his voice made her spine straighten.

When it came to Tympmor, Larn was territorial. Ansie glanced between Willem and Larn. "Fine," was all she said, realizing she was going to lose the battle. She pushed past them both, only to hear Larn following her.

"Did you get the information you needed?" She asked, her words coming out sharper than she'd planned.

"I did," he said. He was a shadow walking by her side. There was a strength in him she had only just begun to realize. When he had towered above her, she knew he could overpower her in an instant, and yet, she knew he never would. But those very same thoughts did little to comfort her now. Instead, they made her stomach clench, her gut seeming to flip on itself.

A rather large lump sat on Tympmor's back, attached to the saddle. "What is that?"

"You'll see," he said, offering nothing further.

Biting her tongue at his stubbornness, she remained silent. Tympmor's enormous head turned to her, the large orb of his eye sending her a distorted reflection of herself. She swallowed around the lump in her throat. What she wouldn't give to talk to Safron or Kata.

You'll never get what you desire. Ever. End of story. Larn's words haunted her. Tears threatened, but she forced them back.

There was a time for crying, but this wasn't it.

"Come on," Larn nudged her arm, the gesture familiar and annoying at the same time. If only he could understand how much he frustrated her.

The reality of what was happening sank in. She thought to try her hand one more time. "I'm not riding with you," she said under her breath, knowing full well he would be able to hear her.

"You are," he confirmed and laced his fingers together to make a step for her to climb into the saddle.

She stared at him. "I'm going to ride with Willem."

He straightened. "As much as you want to be rid of me right now, Tympmor has had enough exercise carrying my weight alone. I won't burden him with two men, and those other horses can hardly manage it either. Now," he reached out suddenly and grasped her waist, his large hands strong and sure, "let's get moving."

He tossed her into the saddle, as easily as lifting a child, giving her only a moment to adjust her position before he swung up behind her. His arms reached around to grab the reins, his cloak blocking her from the stirring air.

Straight-backed, she did everything in her power to keep his body from touching hers. A rather hard task when sitting in the same saddle, but she managed, if only slightly. All her willpower focused on keeping some distance between their bodies.

Willem drew his mount up beside them, riding a little lower on Muncher's sloped back. Behind him, Dur and Fer waited.

Sleeper shook his mane, looking rested and ready to take off into the night. Ansie looked away from the beast, feeling as though it had somehow betrayed her. She wanted to curse Larn under her breath, but knowing her luck, he would hear.

"Where to?" Willem asked.

"Initium," Larn said, his voice stirring near her ear.

"Best turn in the other direction," Fer said, a hint of amusement playing around his mouth. "Time to move North." Dur nodded before him.

Larn adjusted Tympmor's reins to the left, the giant head turning. With a swift word in a language Ansie couldn't understand, he urged the beast into a sprint straight into the darkness of the woods. Her only hope was the horse's eyesight was better than her own.

"Relax," Larn murmured in her ear nearly an hour later as the trees passed them in a blur. Though her back ached to do as he asked, she refused to give him the pleasure of being right. His words still stinging her heart.

By the time dawn was creeping over the mountains, her will to fight waned—exhaustion from a sleepless night taking hold. Suddenly, she found herself leaning backward into his chest, and she wondered why she had fought him for so long.

They were no longer moving quickly, but picking their way across the dips and swells of the mountain range when she felt herself drifting forward. In her dreary state, a hand pressed to her forehead, pushing her back against Larn's shoulder.

Her eyes fluttered. "Sleep now," he mumbled in her ear, "you're safe."

She wondered if he knew she'd heard. The words were those of the kind friend she knew. Not the man who'd dared her to cast him aside. To say he was nothing.

Leaning into Larn, she remembered no more.

CHAPTER 47

The soft rap on Umbris's door came just after she had finished mentally running through her list of names and information for the fifth time. Each word was carefully memorized, and she often found herself repeating the list as she worked.

Someday, it would be of use.

Slipping out of bed, she reached for the robe she had only recently discarded. Another rap on the door sounded and she fingered the chilled handle, the tang of metal clinging to her fingers.

Sliding the door open a crack, the face of Commander Jolson awaited her in the poorly lit hall. She stared, her mouth dropping open.

Even during their long days on the prison caravan—through the rain, the sweat, and the dust—he'd never looked so unkempt. Whiskers shadowed his jaw and there were darkened half-circles beneath his eyes.

Umbris found herself wondering when he had last slept. By the worn creases and wrinkles in his coat, it seemed to have been quite some time. Even his dark hair, which was always carefully parted down the middle, was lumped and frayed. Her hand tightened on the door handle.

"Come with me," he whispered.

"Where?"

"The Regent has need of you."

Her throat went dry in an instant, her lips parting more than once, but no words passed through them.

"Come quickly," he said and pushed the door open wider as though it was the only thing holding her back.

"I—I—have to change."

"No time for that," he said and pushed the door open further, grabbing her hand and pulling her out into the hall.

"Wait," she said, looking back to her room. She was shaking. "I c-c-can't."

He gave her a curious look, but only tightened his grip. "Come, the others will need a respite."

Blinking quickly, she followed him, keeping a hand on the top of her robe.

They hurried along the halls, dipping through the servant passages as messengers of the night. Down a long staircase and into an unlit hallway, he led her, his hand never tightening, but his grip strong and secure on her arm. At a split in the hall, they passed to the left and up a staircase which split again. She thought she knew where they were, but when the door at the end of the passage opened it revealed a golden room, gleaming in the night.

Her stockinged feet nearly slipped on the polished floor, squares of bronzed marble separated by strips of burnished blue. Jolson's footsteps echoed as they moved beneath a golden archway, both sides held by columns decorated with twisting gilded vines and flowers climbing along the edges. Before Umbris could take her eyes away from the arch, she was suddenly pulled to the center of the chamber and her breath left her.

She had certainly never seen this room before. Though one could hardly call it a room.

Jolson paused, glancing back at her as she stared above. She couldn't have spoken even if she wanted to.

High over their heads was a vaulted ceiling, lines of gold weaving like spider webs across a dome in an intricate display of craftsmanship. The vines and flowers were nearly distinguishable even from her lowly place in the middle of the long hall. To either side were more archways like the one she had just passed through—the flowers and vines blooming in a life of their own, each arch different than the next.

Spinning on her heel, she looked to the end of the decadent hall where a light blue velvet curtain draped from the ceiling, dipping back to the edge of the wall and cascading to the floor behind a rather large chair. The gold winked at her, the seat at the end of the hall seeming to glow, though the only light came through nearly hidden windows along the walls.

The throne.

"Come on," Jolson said again. This time his voice was only a whisper, though the sound seemed to echo at her from all directions. Umbris could only wonder at the power of the Regent's voice in a place like this.

She swallowed heavily, her eyes still wandering over the ceiling as Jolson took her wrist once more. As they neared the throne, he moved to the left where a white door, inlaid with golden trim rested.

He placed his hand along the door handle but turned to her first, giving her a look of caution. Letting go of her wrist, he placed a finger over his lips, beckoning her to silence. She couldn't have spoken, even if she'd wanted to.

The door slid forward without objection, revealing a dimly lit wooden chamber beyond. Numerous strangers, well-dressed men, stood along the walls. Three of the men were leaning over a table, but it was the straight back of the Regent which drew Umbris's attention as she slid through the crack of the parted door.

He stood behind an expansive table which depicted an enormous map of what she could only assume was Autre Gallia, and possibly Gallia as well. She had always wondered what it looked like, but from her vantage point, she could hardly make out the different colors on the worn tabletop, all the letters upside down.

One man was speaking, but she hardly heard the words as she watched this courtier point and wave with his hands at various places on the map. Her eyes were solely focused on the Regent, and his attention was on the man before him. She found it odd that he never once looked at the map, but kept his eyes on the lord who was now gesturing with his hands in a grand sweep of his arm.

The Regent seemed to be looking for something, though what, she didn't know.

Most of the men in the room were dressed in their night clothes, robes hanging across their shoulders. One of the courtiers clutched a pipe in his teeth, hints of tobacco floating on the air. As the lord continued to speak, some mumbled in agreement while others shook their heads.

Eyeing the room, Umbris suddenly realized who these men must be—advisors. Glancing back at the Regent, she noted the downturn of his mouth, the way his eyes slightly narrowed at certain words. Did anyone else realize that his anger thrived when all grew still?

Jolson at least understood.

The courtier pressed on, unaware. He was urging the Regent to move cautiously, though about what, she couldn't say. All she could see was the Regent's chilled stare which followed the courtier. It had been over a week since he'd taken her aside in the garden and given her a glimpse into the pressures of his world.

His thoughts had felt like confessions as he worried away the cares of his court. He'd revealed his frustrations of the falseness, the games which enveloped him—the edge of betrayal always lurking. Umbris trembled, recalling his anger when he'd whipped his sword out of its scabbard.

Dropping her gaze, she continued to follow Jolson's steps along the outer edge of the room, behind the courtiers. They were nearly halfway around when the room fell silent; Jolson stopped. Her eyes fell on the Regent once more.

He was ill-dressed, his clothes rumpled as though he had been resting. He wore no jacket but instead was garbed with an open bedchamber robe, made with golden and blue inlay, its length brushing the floor. Beneath the robe, he wore a loose white shirt that was tucked on his right hip, in the waistband of his pants, but hung loosely on the other side. He wore nothing on his feet and she suddenly wondered if his feet were cold on the wooden floor.

The silence between all the men stretched to the point of awkwardness and she wanted to shift simply to have something to do. She refrained and waited, it seemed she wasn't the only one who found the sudden quiet daunting. One of the lords cleared his throat.

"It seems my mind has been made for me," one side of the Regent's mouth twitched—each word spoken with careful precision.

The room itself seemed to hold its breath.

"I apologize, my Sire," the courtier who'd droned on hastened to bow. "I don't mean to offend. You asked for our next course of action, this is the route we highly suggest you take."

"Suggest?" the Regent cocked his head to the side, the steadiness of his face was duped by the fire in the icy glare of his eyes. He turned and looked at the other men in the room, eyeing each one in turn until the silence was almost too much to bear. "I did not ask whether you thought this should be done. I asked if it could be done. Now, give me your answer.'

Another moment of bated breath stretched throughout the room. From somewhere on the wall, a clock ticked, its incessant click asking to be noticed.

Some of the courtiers shifted beneath his gaze, but Umbris remained frozen, a hand hovering over her heart. She'd seen the flash of anger in his eyes. Like lightning across a darkened sky, his silence was the stilling moment of held breath between the illuminating flash and crack of thunder.

"Now!" he barked and she jumped as did a few of the other men.

"My Sire," a younger lord stepped forward. "Perhaps we should wait for the Liege to arrive, he can't be far, and he will know what—"

"No! I will have my answers, and now. I am ruler. Tell me, can it be done?"

One of the men leaning over the table nodded, his bald head shining against the candles gathered around the room. "It can, My Sire. But what you're planning is something which has never been done before."

"Which is exactly why it must be done."

"There will be more rebellion."

"We run that risk either way," his thin lips lifted in a humorless smile as he pointed at the table. "If we take these villages," his hand waved over some part of the southern region of the realm, "and split half the people and send them North, and in turn send half of the northern Anglans to the southern lands, we might be able to separate the rebels for the time being. We will have to take a census and create a border somewhere along here." He drew a line with his finger. "The grasslands might provide a natural separation."

More than one throat was cleared and a few of the men shuffled closer with guarded interest. Umbris swallowed, her thoughts on those she had left behind.

What he was proposing was a partial exodus. Sending half of the southern people to the north, and the same way around. She could only imagine the turmoil, angst, and bloodshed it would cause.

"If I may?" A younger courtier stepped forward, his hands hidden beneath his too big sleeves. Blond hair hung into his eyes and an unnaturally high voice came out of his mouth. "This move will cause rebellion, however, it just might be what takes the focus off you. Those in the north will not go easily, but their disapproval of the southernlands will keep them busy."

"Precisely," the Regent slammed a hand down on the table.

"But there will be bloodshed," one lord pointed out.

"Lord Havroe, I am well aware of that fact." The Regent turned to the man who had been speaking when Umbris and Jolson first entered the room. "These people want to govern themselves; we have tried pushing their rebellion back with small forces, but word of their strength is rising by the day. I have called each of you together because I want to enact this division without resistance from my own lords! I thought I asked a simple thing, but it seems my own men are against the very idea of maintaining control throughout the realm. Lord Havroe, there will be bloodshed, but it will not be Gallian blood."

Umbris's breath caught for the second time that night. The Regent's words having declared the truth of what he thought of his own subjects.

"But my Sire—"

"No!" he yelled, slamming his hand onto the table again, the man who had dared to step forward moved back once more, trembling. "Can I count on my lords to assist me in this?" The Regent eyed his advisors, his gaze passing over each of them until they fidgeted, when before Umbris could hide, his eyes were on her.

Deep blue washed over her and the anger which roiled inside him seemed to still for an instant. He blinked, and she held his gaze. The rise and fall of each breath matched her own. Somehow the rest of the room fell away, though she knew Jolson stood beside her, she no longer felt him near. All she saw was the Regent's eyes, their depth trapping her like they had in the gardens.

She pondered what he saw when he looked at her. What she even saw when she looked at him. He was a Regent, a powerful ruler—but there was more to him than sheer supremacy. She felt it in his gaze, in the way he watched her.

"Leave us!" he barked, making her jump again.

The courtiers hurried from the room, but she never looked away. Only as the chamber grew quiet did she realize why Jolson had brought her to the Regent. Her breath stilled.

Stepping out of the shadows, Garval offered his master a chair. The Regent seated himself, bracing his elbows against the armrests where his knuckles were white. "Why are you here?" he asked her.

Jolson stepped forward, "I brought her."

The gaze flashed away from her and found Jolson. "You did?"

As he stared at Jolson, Umbris realized his eyes weren't quite as dark blue as she had always thought. It reminded her of a time when a cold wind had whipped through the lands and the water in the creeks and small rivers had frozen over. It was the first time she had ever seen snow or frozen water. She had remembered staring at it, seeing that not far beneath, the water still flowed and crinkled past.

The Regent's eyes seemed to harden, the deep blue reminding her of an upset sky, but the flecks of light crystal in his irises hinted at the intelligence underneath. She had the distinct feeling there was more beneath him than he showed—more coursing through his veins than anyone dared to realize.

"I thought she might have more to say on this matter than the rest of us. She is from one of the southern villages after all." Jolson's voice seemed to be lodged in his throat.

One dark eyebrow rose in clear disapproval, and once again his eyes were on her. "Well then, what do you think, Umbris?"

"My Sire?" she asked. She had only gathered enough information to grasp what he was planning to do—an act she knew would cause many to lose their lives on the journey from their homes. Her thoughts turned to innocent children.

"I'm planning a full-scale attack on all Anglans." The Regent voiced the words without a hint of regret. "They need to understand they answer to me. They might be able to overthrow the lords of their villages, but those same men are my own and I will not have Gallians treated in such a manner."

"I see, my Sire," she said, her voice sounding smaller than a child's.

And she did see. In the villages, Anglans and Gallians were set against one another, a separation which only furthered tension and angst.

"But you don't agree?" he cocked his head to the side, seeing through her easily.

"I don't," she dared to admit.

When she didn't say anything more, he waved a hand before him. "Please." The word was a command.

"I don't know my Sire," she swallowed. "Many will die."

He pursed his lips, "It's true, the north and the south will not tolerate one another long. But their own feuds will overtake the land and their anger toward the throne will dissipate."

"Perhaps," Umbris said and bit her lip.

"But you don't think that will be the case?"

She didn't answer. Jolson stepped forward.

"It's what I told you, my Sire. These people aren't going to give up. We have to wait for the regiment to reach Mirtain, once order is restored and Lord Hernan freed, then we can speak of what might become of the other villages. You said yesterday you wanted to stamp out the flames where all of this began. Deal with Mirtain first, then worry about the rest."

Umbris held her breath at his words. *The rest? How many had rebelled?*

The Regent clicked his tongue and turned to look at the map once more. Each movement was stilted, his knuckles white. For the first time, she saw the dark circles beneath his eyes. He hid his exhaustion well—all of it cloaked in anger.

The quiet stretched and though her eyes never left the Regent, she could feel Jolson looking toward her. Suddenly, she remembered the way he had cautioned her outside the door to this chamber. He had beckoned her to remain quiet while the men were speaking, but a new idea formed—a memory from the alcove.

How many thrust their ideas upon this man daily? How many asked and requested for his ear? Day after day, he listened to them.

He had revealed his need to be heard in the garden. She hadn't forgotten the gentle relief in his voice.

Only now did she truly understand why Jolson had brought her to the Regent. He had said once, she was able to see people. With new eyes, she looked at the Regent now. His light-brown hair falling in waves past his ears, the collar of his shirt open, revealing part of a strong chest beneath. But it was his eyes that pulled her to him.

In one instant, the façade fell away and she saw into the waters lingering beneath the dark ice in his eyes. He was a man. Simply, a man.

Her mother had always known what to do in these instances. Without thinking, she found herself moving for him.

Stepping forward, her heart thundered in her chest as she approached the Regent. His attention remained on the map as she reached out and touched his arm. Her fingers trembled when she slid the sleeve of his robe and shirt up his forearm, the gentle curve of corded muscle holding back the garments. Kneeling beside his chair, she brushed the tips of her fingers along his arm, running from wrist to elbow and back again.

In the stillness, time seemed to drift away, the only change was the rise and fall of his chest with each passing of her fingers over his arm. She tried to ignore the way her skin seemed to prickle as she touched him—the spark bringing back something she had felt once before.

Her eyes remained focused on the whites of his knuckles, waiting for them to release. He needed to relax, something her mother had always told Umbris to do. In those quiet moments, when the world seemed too heavy, her mother had given her a hug and brushed her fingers over Umbris's arm until she could breathe once more.

How many times had her mother done this for her? Tears pricked her eyes as she thought of her, wondering what shame had been brought upon her family. She hadn't even seen them the day she was taken, there was only one face she remembered above all others.

The knuckles before her blurred and she drew her hand back into her lap, no longer feeling the spark between them as the past taunted her. She would never outrun the look she had seen in his eyes. She could never overcome what she'd done to him. The long-buried ache raged in her chest—it was her fault he was dead. And so many others after him.

A finger curled beneath her chin, lifting her face. Past forgotten, she allowed him to draw her closer.

The depths of his eyes, now released, washed over her like the cool spring she used to swim in. Refreshing and free, she was captivated by their glow. His hand moved from beneath her chin until it cupped her cheek, his thumb passing over her skin, leaving an icy trail behind.

When his head moved closer, she stiffened and drew back.

She shook her head. "Please, don't." The words were hardly a whisper passing over her lips.

"Why?" he asked.

Tears threatened her eyes. She wouldn't think of it, she couldn't. Reality hit and the spell was broken.

Pulling on the wrists of her robe, she covered the marks that were there because of his decree. She was foolish. To even think she was something more than what he had made her, was a fault which couldn't be understood.

"Umbris?" He said the name gently, all signs of his earlier frustrations gone.

She shook her head again and hastened to stand, ready to leave his presence. His fingers wrapped around her wrist keeping her from walking away.

"Tell me," he commanded.

She turned to him, his presence suddenly overwhelming as he stood. He towered above her, standing much too close to keep her fears at bay.

"I can't."

When he said nothing, she raised her eyes to his. The anger tightening his jaw was enough to make her flinch back and away from him, he let her go, his hand falling to his side.

Staring at the other side of the room, he murmured something to himself which she couldn't make out. A part of her wanted to run in fear, but she knew she would have to face this. She had always known she would have to face it.

"I'm not a patient man." His voice rumbled. "I'm your ruler, I own you."

"Yes, my Sire." She nodded, holding her chin high even as a tear escaped one eye. His mark was on her wrists, of course she knew. "But you also said I never asked you for anything."

One eyebrow rose, a spark of recognition for the words he'd spoken in the alcove.

"I'm asking now. Please, will you let me go?"

He eyed her carefully. In a moment, she saw what she had been missing before. She had thought he was simply a man, but he was a man with power. A man who thrived on control.

Stay calm, she told herself.

He clicked his tongue and turned to the massive table in the room. He braced his hands along the edge.

"It's not often I grant requests." His shoulders tightened as though the very idea of not getting what he desired was enough to make him overthrow the realm. She trembled beneath her too-thin nightgown, knowing he was on the brink of a decision.

"Do you fear me?" he turned to her.

She nodded.

Everything about him exuded strength and overwhelming confidence, his very presence made her breath grow short. She bore the scars on her wrists which proclaimed her very being to be his, and though she had denied him, he remained at a distance.

Who was she to deny the Regent?

"You fear me, and yet, you will not do as I wish." He didn't ask her. His simple words spoken in confusion.

"I cannot, my Sire," she repeated, the weakness in her voice appearing once more. It was true. She couldn't do what he asked.

For all the times she had been in his presence, she couldn't understand his view of her. The many stories she had heard of his great power and strength were true, but she had never expected him to speak to her, to see her, to look directly at her. Sometimes, she felt as though he could see into the depths of her soul.

"What do you want from me?" he asked, still turned away.

A myriad of ideas came to mind.

She wanted to be kept safe. She desired to be as far away from him and his court as possible. She wanted to go home. But none of those answers would satisfy him. She had seen enough of him in action to know he didn't take being thwarted easily.

She needed to be here, in his presence. There were many in the Renegades counting on her, and Larn wanted her to work from the inside. She had agreed to the task and would do what was needed to remain as she was, but to do more was unthinkable. She could not become what they had made her.

"To forget what happened to me."

He turned then, his back slowly straightening as he watched at her. "I cannot control your memories."

"I know, my Sire," she admitted. "I am marked, but I wish to remain here, untouched."

His eyes drifted to where her wrists lay hidden. "I see," he said, his eyes never leaving her. Something dark flickered in his gaze, but it was gone before she had a chance to decipher it. "I will make you a deal." She waited. "You will work in my chambers with Garval, a position above the other maids, and in return, I will see you safe."

"My Sire?" she asked, her mouth hanging open.

"It's what you want, isn't it?"

She nodded, not entirely sure how he'd so clearly understood. "Thank you," she whispered.

"You are dismissed," he said and turned away from her once more, facing the map.

She didn't know if any of her words had stilled his threats to the realm, but she had done what little she could. As she walked from the room, she suddenly realized Jolson had disappeared at some point, leaving her alone with the Regent. Garval stood just outside the door and nodded in her direction as she exited. It was the first time he'd truly looked at her.

Turning away, she passed through the throne room and paused to look down the hall at the now darkened throne. The glimmer from the moons was tucked behind the clouds and all the former glory of the glittering gold had disappeared. What had once dazzled her, now thrust her into a world of shadows and intrigue.

She stepped as close to the throne as she dared, not even halfway across the room. If she was spotted, she was certain there would be repercussions.

Allowing her thundering heart to settle, Umbris hastened her way to the servants' halls. The process of trying to unwind the web of the palace became a more difficult task than she expected. The darkness in the hall cast yawns upon her and after hours of searching with no way of knowing if she was walking down the same hall, or in circles, she finally found her bedroom.

As she closed her eyes, the Regent's promise ran through her mind. And she wondered when she saw him tomorrow who he would be. Would it be the man? Or the Regent?

She understood the man to an extent, but the Regent was a force she could never withstand.

"Come along dear."

A hand wrapped around Umbris's ankle and shook her foot.

"What?" she mumbled and peeked one eye open. The cream walls of her meager room met her eyes. Disappointment fled through her as she realized her wishes had not come true. Her dreams were where she wished to stay—her old world.

"Come, come." Charlise leaned over the bed and shook her shoulder. "It seems you had an interesting night."

Night? Umbris tried to put her thoughts in order. What had she done last night? And why was she so tired?

Her dreams swirled around her, the small cottage in the village—the smell of mulled wine wafting in through the rafters, and her siblings tangled in the blankets on the long pallet mattress in the loft. She wished so desperately for it to be true.

She wanted to hear her mother calling up the half-rotted stairs for them to get ready, and to hear her own father kiss her mother goodbye before leaving for the day. It all seemed to be a dream, or a dream of a dream.

But it was the one face she knew so well which had come to her in the night. He had walked with her, as he so often had, his arm brushing against hers every now and again. His lips mingling with hers. If only she had known what she was doing at the time. If only she had been smart enough to heed the warnings in her heart.

"I'm sorry," she ran a hand over her face. "What am I late for?"

In the hall, the windows were free of shutters, only the deep grey of a dreary end to night was visible. It seemed Charlise had woken her before the morning sun had a chance to break across the horizon.

"You aren't late yet," Charlise stood above her, hands on her hips. "But if you don't move, you will be."

Her dream fog was dissipating quicker than she wished, falling away like a warm blanket on a cold night to reveal the harshness of the chilled room around her.

"And what," she asked, as she slipped from the bed and hastened into her dress, "am I late for?"

"It seems you're to have new quarters in a different wing of the palace."

Curious, Umbris watched the older woman raise one eyebrow as though it would give her a clue as to what was happening. If only Umbris could remember what orders she had been given, most likely last night…

She gasped, suddenly remembering. The Regent.

You will work in my chambers with Garval, a position above the other maids, and in return, I will see you safe.

His words came back to her in startling clarity. It seemed as though they were a dream of their own. "Where are you taking me?" She asked, her fingers stilling on the corset which tied in the front.

"The Regent has requested you be placed in the servants' quarters in the Aurore Wing."

Umbris blinked. She had never heard of such a thing.

Charlise smoothed a hand along her dark hair, making the few silver streaks she had all the brighter for a moment. The other hand rested near her waist where a key ring hung over the dark blue of her skirts.

"Aurore Wing?" she asked.

"The royal wing."

Umbris nodded, as though this was all to be expected and forced herself to focus on the task at hand. She finished dressing and looked around the room, her gaze settling on her mending box. It had been given to her by Charlise.

"Take that with you," Charlise nodded and when Umbris grabbed it, the head maid also handed her the discarded nightgown. "Is that everything?"

Umbris nodded, in some way feeling foolish, her life attached to so few objects that weren't even her own. But she had arrived with only the worn dress on her back, and she was not thoughtless enough to forget the weight of the chains around her wrists. Sometimes, she felt as though she could still hear the clanging and the moans of the other women in the cells of Fort Jontru.

Casting those thoughts aside, she followed Charlise out the door and into the hall where they wound through the palace on much the same route she had traipsed during the night. She idly wondered where Commander Jolson had wandered off to.

All too soon, they stepped into a hallway and Charlise pointed to a little plaque on the wall labeled: Aurore Wing.

How Umbris had never noticed the markers before was beyond her. Somehow, someway, she was going to have to figure out how to make her way around the palace. Her poor sense of direction would have to be overcome.

Charlise rounded a corner, a side hall opening before them. "Your room is at the end of this hall."

"And where does that door lead?" Umbris asked, pointing to the white door directly before them.

"It will take you to the hallway just outside the Regent's chambers," the head maid gave her a sidelong look filled with meaning, which Umbris chose to ignore. They walked down the hall passing a series of empty rooms and unlocked doors. It seemed this hallway would be even quieter than the last.

Charlise stopped at a door and pushed it open, gesturing for Umbris to enter. Where her previous bedroom had been complete with cream walls and simple floors, this one was resplendent with polished wood floors. The walls were a soft yellow, the color of them magnified by the cream bedding standing in the center of the room. Never in her life had she ever slept in something so large. It was made for two people, but back at home, it would have fit five of her siblings. She swallowed heavily, wondering at the expense of it all.

Above the bed was a small shelf with a flowering plant and a little window. She could only wonder as to which way the window faced.

"You can put your things here." Charlise showed her a little armoire tucked against the wall. "Most likely you will have new clothes."

"I don't need any," she whispered.

"That is for His Sire to decide."

Again, the woman gave her an odd look and Umbris tried to squelch the feeling twisting her gut. It wasn't the first time she'd experienced unwarranted words. Ever since she had arrived, it seemed as though everyone spoke in words which had more than one meaning.

"Where is the mending?" she asked.

"I don't believe you will be doing much mending. Garval will be here shortly to see you understand your duties."

"And what might those be?" she asked. For some reason, she needed to confirm the Regent's promise. He had told her he would keep her safe. Stars above, she hoped he wouldn't go back on his word.

"Attending to the Regent, of course." Charlise gave her a curt nod and moved to step out of the room. "One more thing, I know some of the other maids were giving you trouble. Put them in their place, you're above them now."

"I am?" she asked.

Charlise nodded again. "You are. They are only scullery maids amongst the outer wings, but you are now a chambermaid in the Aurore Wing. You attend to His Sire, none of them can say that."

Was that a smile lurking in the corners of the headmistress's mouth?

Umbris blinked. All too soon she was alone in her new room without a clue of what to do. The silence was something she had grown used to in the servants' quarters she had previously occupied. She hadn't even thought to ask Charlise which wing those resided in.

It was quiet, almost too quiet, especially at this time of day. According to the lightening grey from the window, dawn was breaking across the horizon.

Normally, the hallway outside her room was filled with the subtle bumps and scuffs of tired maids rising for the day's work—the scuttle of hurried feet rushing down the hall and about the palace.

But here, everything was different. Not a sound occupied the hallway, reminding her of the daytime hours when she sat alone in her room mending.

What to do? she wondered and paced to the armoire. Hanging her nightdress on a hook, she placed her mending box beneath it and shut the door. Without either object in sight, she was a complete stranger in the room.

Suddenly, the clipped steps of heeled shoes sounded down the hall. She waited, hoping they would pass by for her to catch a glimpse. The golden head of Garval appeared around the door and he moved into her room without a word.

She gave him a quick curtsy, uncertain of what was expected of her.

"You will address me as 'sir.' I run a tight wing, very different from Madame Charlise. If you are in need of anything, you can speak with her."

She nodded.

"Your duties will begin each morning. You will help with the presentation of His Sire's meals and the transfer of his clothes to the launderer."

Again she nodded.

"You are also to be discreet. What happens within the Regent's chambers, who he sees, who he speaks to, is not shared with the other staff. Is that understood?"

"Yes, sir." Umbris swallowed heavily, still uncertain of what to do with her hands.

He continued. "Per His Sire's request, you will be working directly with me. I will not tolerate any dallying or mindless chatter. You will obey my instructions without question."

"Yes, sir."

"Now, let's get to it." With a flamboyance she had not seen him reveal before, he spun on his heel and walked from the room with a complete state of arrogance—his nose high in the air. This man had seen her when she arrived from the *Le Jupon Rouge,* she could only imagine what he must think of her.

She hurried after him, trying to keep her footsteps in rhythm with his own. He walked as though he was the only man in the room, perhaps something he had learned from his master.

They came to a small door in the wall and Garval pulled it toward him, revealing a world entirely of its own on the other side.

"Tomorrow," Garval said, turning to her, "do take care to pin up your hair. You look a mess."

Her eyes widened and she followed him into the room assuming this would be a day she would never forget, and she couldn't have been more right. The first two hours were filled with preparations for the Regent's 'rising', as Garval called it. His clothes were laid out in the chamber connected to his bedroom. As they moved about, she had the innate feeling she was trespassing into some area of his life she had never wished to see. It was as though she could feel the Regent's presence behind the blue wall.

After laying out his clothes, they had set the table in the chamber with more food than one man could ever eat. Her mouth had watered, not having eaten anything herself, but she would never dream of touching any of it. Garval himself seemed unaffected by the delicacies.

After the food came the stacks of various documents and letters, each inscribed with an address to the Regent. She kept her eyes away from the words beneath the address, not wanting Garval to find her snooping on her first day. She wasn't even allowed to handle the papers, Garval making sure to keep her as far from them as possible.

Just before the Regent exited his chamber, Garval sent her into a small hallway which connected the chamber to the bedroom. He explained, in his clipped way, that she would therefore go unseen and could remake the bed before His Sire was done with his meal. It was the same hallway she'd taken the first time she'd entered the Regent's bedchamber so many mornings ago.

Umbris set about her work, trying not to let her heart hammer too heavily in her chest as she listened to the Regent speak with Garval on the other side of the door. His voice was doing something to her. The deep timbre of his refined words reminding her of the way he had looked at her the night before.

It took more concentration than she realized to not be affected by the gentle warmth of the bed covers beneath her fingers.

She disappeared back into the hallway, long before he was done eating. Uncertain of what to do, she froze there, listening to him speak.

"…I'm uncertain whether or not the plan will work, but Commander Jolson seems to think it a foolish idea. He believes we should stamp out the rebellion through military feats."

"But you do not agree, my Sire?" Garval asked.

"On the contrary, I do." He confirmed. "But it's the three miscreants romping through the realm who have my attention. I have already sent soldiers to Initium to see if they can be found."

"You do not sound confidant, my Sire."

"I'm not." The Regent clicked his tongue and Umbris remained surprised at how frank he was with his valet. It seemed the two men shared a deeper bond than she had realized.

"Enough for now, my Sire?"

"Yes," a chair scraped against the floor. "I will dress for my ride."

"Yes, My Sire. I will be in in a moment." Garval said, and only when she heard the transfer of the Regent's footsteps into his bedroom did she dare to enter the sitting chamber.

"Well done," Garval said in a hushed tone. He motioned to the table. "Place all of this on the tray, Pavier will be by to take it. Then return to your room. I will be there shortly for your next task."

She nodded, surprised the hall boy worked so close to the Regent—he hadn't mentioned that before. Garval disappeared into the Regent's bedchamber, closing the door behind him. Hurrying to do as requested, she placed all the food onto the tray. She had just finished with the last dish when Pavier entered the room.

He stopped mid-step and then smiled. "I see you've had a change of work."

"Perhaps," she said, feeling a smile tug at the corners of her own lips.

"Garval has been needing an extra hand for a while now."

"And you couldn't fill in for him?"

"What offense," he placed a hand over his heart. "I told you, I'm a hall boy. I work in the libraries, why else would I be bringing these with me?"

He held up two bound books, ancient by the looks of them, she hadn't noticed before and placed them on the mantle above the fireplace. The efficiency of the Aurore Wing was becoming more apparent by the moment.

"Then you won't be helping Garval all day?" the hope was evident in her voice, but it was simply nice to see a friendly face.

"Only to clear the dishes when His Sire eats."

"I see," she said, playing with the folds in her skirt. "So my job is more difficult than yours?"

"Perhaps," he winked. "Well, I had best get going."

"Any advice?"

"Learn to know your way around this wing, you're going to need it, especially in the evenings. But Garval will fill you in on that later."

"I wish I had a map," she muttered, attempting to remind him of her earlier request.

His mouth puckered. "Maybe I can find one. I'll be on the lookout."

"Thank you," she whispered. A map would do wonders. If she was going to be of use, she needed to know her way around. Thoughts of Larn and Pike entered her mind, but she pushed them back not wanting her motivations to become apparent.

Slipping through the door across from the table, she stepped into the tiny servant's hallway which branched off and led toward her room. Sitting on her bed, she waited—her mind running through the words the Regent had spoken.

She had her guesses that Larn was among the three traitors heading to Initium. If only there was some way to warn him and his companions.

For by the sounds of it, if they dared to traipse through the ancient ruins of Initium, they wouldn't be alone when they arrived.

CHAPTER 48

As soon as they entered Timtus Forest, Willem could feel the lurking presence of eyes watching them. No matter how many stops they made, or shifts in direction, he felt as though something was breathing down his neck.

Maybe it was the stories that had filled his head as a child—rumors of strange beasts and leering predators that could kill you in an instant. But there was something in the air, as though the very forest itself was breathing. It clung to his skin, like the sweat dripping along his spine.

Not for the first time, Willem glanced to either side, wondering if the others felt it too. Dur and Fer only grew quieter the further they moved in the forest. The older brother's mouth was set in a grim line, but Fer's eyes were kindled with a sense of anticipation.

To his other side, Larn and Ansie seemed more unaware than the Chroniclers. They'd hardly spoken a word to one another since leaving the grasslands behind—Ansie's jaw closed tight as she clung to the pommel of the saddle. Above her, Larn kept his gaze locked on the trail ahead. From experience, Willem knew his passive expression was only a ruse to what was taking place in his mind. He was more than acutely aware.

A strange warble sounded in the distance, echoing between the tree trunks. Willem fought down the shiver running along his spine and pushed onward, hoping it was only his imagination that made his heart thud so heavily in his chest. Trepidation gripping his gut.

"How much further?" Larn asked, his eyes never leaving the trail. Tympmor picked his way carefully through the bracken.

"It shouldn't be much further," Fer's voice drifted. Dur clucked his tongue at the horse. At least their horse had a chance of making it out of the forest alive. Muncher, as Ansie called him, lopped along, slightly behind the others, his hooves heavily hitting the packed earth, his sloped back swaying from side to side. Willem knew he must have made quite a sight astride the strange creature.

"Not much further? You said that nearly an hour ago," Larn pointed out, Ansie elbowed him in the ribs. Larn didn't look at her and instead remained focused ahead. Something was eating away at him, but Willem didn't know what.

"As I told you before, be patient," Fer said, making Dur grumble and Larn shook his head, though at what, Willem didn't know.

Winding along the root-covered trail, Muncher stumbled more than once and Willem wanted to curse him to the depths of eternity. If the horse would just show some provocation toward eagerness, he might be able to forgive him. But it wasn't to be.

For another hour they picked along the path, the trees slowly thinning around them. What had once been a forest filled with deep golden and brown leaves was now a dank and musty fortress of aged trunks. Low dripping moss hung in wispy curtains, the thick bodies of the trees obstructing most of their view. The sunlight hidden behind the clouds was quickly waning, shadows stretching across the ground. More than once Willem had been startled by his own shadow. Muncher's legs seeming to stretch for eternity.

They wove along a self-made path—the trees shifting and morphing their forms. What were originally aged, thick trunks, turned into thin and sparse trees poking from the ground like knives across the forest floor.

"We're very close," Fer confirmed as they wove through the sparse trees, their bent and twisted trunks making the shadows dance upon the ground as the wind pushed them aside.

"Should we be on the lookout for anything in particular?" Larn whispered. Ansie was merely a small lump in front of him, with her hood pulled over her head and her face cast in shadow, Willem could hardly make her out in the darkness.

Off to his left, a loud cracking shook the forest. They froze.

Numerous trees bent forward only to snap back once more. Willem waited, but nothing else moved. He told himself it must have been a tree branch from one of the rare thicker and taller trees, falling on the smaller ones below.

Amazing what the mind would make up, just to have a practical understanding to assuage fears.

You're out of your element. The thought was one he'd had numerous times before. In Mirtain Forest he had moved with the land, knowing it as well as his home. But here he was a stranger.

Yet, there was a distant thrumming in his soul that told him he belonged here. Shaking his head, he tried not to think of the filumen in the cave, or the way Dur's hand had glowed.

Here, instinct was his sole companion.

Another snap sounded in the distance, this time followed by a looming quiet—as though the forest was listening too.

"Hey," Willem whispered and Tympmor came to a halt.

Larn shot him a glance that told Willem he'd heard it too. Dur edged a hand toward his dagger. Somehow seeing the Chronicler move in precaution, made Willem all the more wary.

"What is it?" Ansie whispered.

Larn shifted, readjusting the reins into one hand, a hint of worry lining his voice. "I don't know."

Was Larn feeling it now? That looming presence.

"Should we keep moving forward?" Larn asked, looking towards Dur.

Willem debated. Here in Timtus Forest there were legends of creatures— long serpent-like monsters with six legs and heads lined with dagger-sharp teeth. Rumor said that they hid against tree trunks, their course-skinned bodies making them nearly invisible. Only when a person passed directly by would they reveal themselves, launching in a backward dive, taking off your head as they hurtled toward the forest floor.

Willem had no way of knowing if the stories he'd heard at the Black Market years ago were true. He cast a prayer up above that he would never find out.

Ansie fidgeted. "Something's watching us."

Muncher edged to the side to grab a weed growing along a root. Willem reigned him in, the horse's lips still grasping for the miscreant plant.

"Keep going," Fer said, peaceful confidence hovering over him. "It's not far now. Less than a few minutes."

Larn gave a dismissive grunt, but pushed Tympmor on, each step seeming to crunch louder than the last. They picked their way down the winding path, the trees growing thicker as they went. A short glimpse of a shrouded hill appeared for a brief moment through the trees. Fer sat straighter in the saddle behind his brother.

Willem suddenly knew this was it.

He wanted to kick Muncher into a run, wishing to move faster than the clipped pace which allowed his thoughts to wander and overtake him. He needed to move, and now.

Larn pulled back on Tympmor's reins quite suddenly, his lips moving fast as he muttered in that strange language to his horse. The northern man then let his voice drift in the direction of the other two horses, both standing at alert. Even Muncher was ready to bolt.

The horses appeased for the moment, Larn pointed in the direction of the enormous hill Willem had glimpsed through the trees. Something was out there.

Bringing Tympmor closer, Larn leaned in to whisper, "Initium is surrounded."

Willem's hand twitched, ready to swing the sword off of his back upon a moment's notice.

A low shout rang through the night air, where before them, in the direction of the ruins, mist shrouded the ground. It was a rallying cry.

To press on or retreat? Willem licked his lips, Muncher swaying beneath him.

Another shout sliced the fog, and it seemed as though his mind was made up for him. "Let's get out of here while we still can," he muttered.

For one instant, Larn's eyes tightened and he glanced down at Ansie, but it was gone in an instant. A smirk in its place. He nodded and they turned, to leave.

A shimmer of muted light broke through the fog. *Torches.*

They froze once more, Willem only now realizing that Dur and Fer hadn't moved to retreat.

They watched as the fuzzy orbs of light came together through the gaps of the trees. The soldiers, whether Gallian or Nexen, Willem didn't know, were standing around the bottom of the sloping hill where the ruins could hardly be glimpsed at the top.

"They're standing guard," Dur mumbled. "They knew we would come here."

"Not to worry," Fer said, never taking his eyes from the line. "We have to break through the main line, make it through and we can reach the hall."

Dur nodded before him, drawing a line in the air with his finger. "The barrack ruins will provide us some cover," he glanced their way, "it'll be up to you to fight your way through."

Muncher pulled on a vine, rattling a tree branch. Willem would kill the beast and run to Initium himself if the horse didn't cooperate.

Glancing up at the ruins shrouded on the hill, Willem felt a stirring inside that he couldn't ignore. It was a call, a beacon pulling him toward some unknown. A flash of blue illuminated the ruins for a blink of an eye. He stared, wondering if it was a trick of the light.

"This is a fool's errand," Larn was shaking his head. His arms tightened around Ansie and he leaned back in the saddle.

Dur turned on Larn then. "This is no errand."

"It doesn't matter where we are, the *anima reflecta* will find us," Fer inhaled deeply, the encroaching trees and mist seeming to have no effect upon his mood.

The whites around Larn's eyes suddenly became visible. "What are you saying, old man? We could have stayed away from this cursed forest?"

"Perhaps. Rumors of Animle are in the Beastly Mountains, that's true, but I think we might just find one here. Call it intuition." The man tapped his temple and smiled. "This place is sacred after all."

Larn stared at Fer as though he now had two heads. Willem's own heart was thundering in his chest.

"Larn," Ansie's small voice was a whisper, her pale hand touching one of Larn's arms.

They turned and watched in horror as the torchlights began to move toward them. Shouts and cries were suddenly ringing through the forest. They would be surrounded if they remained much longer.

"We fight our way through," Ansie said, leaning forward.

Willem thought he saw Dur smile in the dark, he pulled the dagger from his belt.

Larn ignored them all and drew Tympmor back. Attempting to gather Muncher, Willem turned the horse around ready to urge him into a run. Larn was muttering to Tympmor, and Muncher seemed to be listening to the words as shouts rose behind them.

Dur and Fer remained behind, until it happened.

A roar, unlike any Willem had ever heard, shattered through the forest, the deafening sound rumbling with unrestrained power. Lost in the sound, the rumbling turned to a long moan and then split through the air once more with tremendous force.

Both horses shot away from the roar, their muscles quivering and Larn's mutterings long forgotten. They bolted toward the ruins of Initium—for the torches looming ahead. It was all Willem could do to reamin seated.

Dur and Fer charged beside them, both men leaning forward in the wind.

Swiping his sword off of his back, the silver of the blade gleamed as he sliced it through the fog.

Again, a roar came from behind them, and a smile split across Willem's lips for some odd reason. The shapes of the men beneath the torches were visible through the mist, the glow of them turning to fuzzy balls of light like the setting sun.

Shouts echoed, reminding him of the battle on Mirtain's fields. Gritting his teeth, he readied himself. After endless days of inaction, his mind and body were more than ready for what lay ahead.

The closer they got, the stronger the mist became, hanging like a shroud over the ruins. With a final awkward leap that landed all too short, Muncher ran beneath a tree and into the fray. A low hanging branch caught him across the face. He swore.

One of the torches charged, he sliced at the soldier. The sharp contact vibrated up his arm, the shudder a feeling he remembered all too well.

He knocked the man aside, with no time to stay and exchange blows, his only intent to remain astride Muncher. Tympmor was leading the way up the slope, his thundering hooves making the other torches turn in their direction, but the roar of a looming beast prolonged their advance.

Up the slope they charged, running down soldiers and casting aside advances. They darted past broken walls and turned over stones, their once majestic structures overrun by the forest. Willem's sword was slick with blood, though he hardly remembered making contact with anything other than metal.

Before him, Tympmor reared on his hind legs and smashed his hooves into the wooden door of the forlorn ruins at the top of the slope. An echoing crash resounded as the door slammed into the wall, but Tympmor paid it no mind as he charged down the hallway, his hooves clattering on the stones. Willem's mount followed.

Tucking himself into a ball, Willem rolled off of Muncher in one simple move and ran to the door. He was certain there were hundreds of holes the soldiers could crawl through, but best not to give them an open door to charge in all at once. Dur and Fer passed him in a fury.

He threw all of his weight against the wooden door, slamming it shut. A set of age-spotted hands worked beside his. Together they grappled with a fallen beam, jamming it into the creases of the wall and sealing off the entrance.

Glancing up, he noticed the light blue shimmer hovering around Dur's hand, it disappeared almost as soon as he saw it. Outside the roar rattled the ground again, and soldiers cried out in agony. Willem shivered, whether from fear, or awe, he didn't know.

"Willem?!" Ansie's panicked cry shattered the silence in the hall. He sprinted toward the sound, his palm sweating on the hilt of his sword as he broke into a nearly circular room.

Ansie stood in the middle of the space, Larn beside her, both with swords drawn and looking his way. He stopped quickly, seeing she was fine and looked behind him wondering why she had yelled.

Her sword clattered to the ground and she ran for him then, hugging him around his waist. He held her tight, looking to Larn, uncertain of what had her so terrified. For the moment, it seemed they were safe.

Larn pointed to where Tympmor and Muncher stood, their sides heaving and eyes wide. It was only then that Willem saw the saddle he had been sitting on. A dark red stain was smeared along the side where his leg had recently been, and he suddenly realized what it must have looked like when the horse came into the room rider-less. The blood wasn't his own.

He held Ansie tighter. "I'm fine—really."

She nodded, her hair shining in the dark and her breaths coming in short gasps.

A shuffling behind him had them all turning, poised for battle. But Dur stepped into the room, his thin frame hardly more than a shadow. Fer walked beside him, leading Sleeper. If the younger brother could look any more carefree, he would have been whistling to himself. "I knew we could make it," he said.

Glancing up at the once-domed ceiling above, Fer nodded to himself. His eyes searching the empty shelves lining the room.

If Willem had to guess, this had once been a grand meeting place but was now nothing more than a dusted, discarded room. Fer seemed to be searching for something along the floor, but what, Willem had no idea. There was too much dust, dirt and dried remnants of leaves to see anything but ruin.

Turning away from the man, he looked to Larn. He was certain Larn could hear the shouts still ringing outside, and the subtle roar from the mysterious creature every now and again. Willem's only comfort was the fading of the shouts, as though they were drifting away—or being silenced.

Around the room, rotted bookcases stretched to the ceiling, where he assumed a dome of glass used to cover it. Along the outside of the room were windows facing out over the forest, their glass long since shattered. But one look from Larn told him they wouldn't have to worry about an attack from there—the walls too steep for any man to climb.

It seemed the Chroniclers were right. With only one entrance, they could hold their ground for some time. Looking at the man now, he watched Fer slowly walk around the room, a sorrowful smile on his creased face. Dur remained next to the horse, his eyes closed, breathing deeply—humming to himself.

Larn noticed them both as well and gave Willem a look, his eyebrows raised high. "Well," he said, eyes wide, "they've lost it."

Willem chuckled and gave Ansie a final squeeze as he turned away. He paced the room, looking to the shadows, wondering just what had caused that glowing light earlier.

What was left of his curiosity turned into a prodding. Watching Fer stare at a stone upon the floor, the man knelt to wipe his hand in the dirt. He smiled brightly and called Dur over to him. Willem could have sworn he saw a tear slide down Dur's cheek, but such a thing seemed impossible.

"So," Ansie said, breaking the silence, "now what?"

"You can't do that."

"And why not?"

"Because I said so." Ansie was glaring at him, hands on her hips.

"She has a point," Larn joined in.

"You stay out of this," Willem pointed, knowing Larn was only trying to tip the scales.

Larn waved a hand, his sword still hanging at his hip. "You brought this on yourself."

Ansie raised her chin in the way she always did when she knew she was right. "See."

"I only said I would get close enough to count them, they won't even know I'm there." Willem stated his case yet again.

It was an excuse and he knew it. What he really wanted was to find that creature. A stirring lingered in him, a sort of beckoning to what awaited outside.

"And I'm sure whatever's out there knows you aren't with the Gallians," Ansie rolled her eyes for the third time.

"Again, an excellent point," Larn smiled, seeming to enjoy himself.

"Well, one of us has to go and see, and I have the most experience tracking animals."

"A creature of the night," Larn said, mock-seriousness in his tone. Ansie bit her lip, trying to hide the slight lift on the side of her mouth. Willem was ready to punch Larn.

"Leave it for now," Fer's voice suddenly broke through the room—he'd been silent since entering the chamber, lost in his thoughts.

Larn turned, eyebrows raised. "Look who's back." He hooked a thumb in Fer's direction. "I thought we lost you to your mutterings. Tell me, did you have a good chat with the unseen?"

"Why yes, I was talking about you," Fer shot back, a mysterious gleam in his eye. "Seems the Espiritu is aware of your misdeeds—it's quite a long list."

The humor in Larn's smile faded. Dur winked at Ansie from behind his brother's back, she grinned.

"Enough of this," Willem grumbled. "I'm going to take a look—shouldn't take me very long."

"Nonsense," Dur waved a hand. "We can remain in this room for as long as we need. It's sacred." Larn rolled his eyes. "Have some respect," the older man grumbled, his tone far from teasing. "Or do I need to remind you about the force of the filumen?"

"There are those who sacrificed their lives in this room. A sacrifice for the sake of the realm," Fer said.

Willem cast his eyes about the chamber. It seemed as though Fer was telling the truth, but nothing remained. The many branches and leaves, which had fallen through the broken ceiling and blown in through the shattered windows, gave the space a feeling of never having been anything more than what it was now. A ruin.

"Were they Animle?" Ansie wondered aloud.

A breeze stirred, scattering the leaves across the floor, brushing them over Willem's boots. The lingering grip of the roar from outside still preying upon his mind.

"They were," Fer confirmed, a hint of a smile playing around his lips. "They took their final stand in this very room. And it was beneath this stone, Rolin found the Tetel."

He pointed toward the center of the floor the broken pieces of a stone tablet remained. It looked like there was some marking upon it, but from where Willem stood, he couldn't make out what it was.

"It is from that book, we know of the filumen, that, and word of mouth."
Fer crossed to the edge of the chamber, his eyes scanning the mountains in the
distance. "When the Animle traitors led the newly formed Nexen to Initium,
they found it already in flames."

Willem turned to one of the windows, the shrouded shadows of ruined
buildings were scattered along the bottom of the hill.

"Three Animle were left defending this keep," Fer turned back to them,
something burning in his eyes. "Three. The leader of the keep, Mysta Hosta,
and his two faithful warriors remained as the final defenders of Initium. They
killed those who had turned away from the Espiritu and retreated to this
chamber."

From across the room, Dur looked toward the ruined ceiling, as though he
could see the smoke clouding the very air of Initium. "The bodies of the
traitors, both man and beast, were burned as the Nexen charged the keep."

Willem leaned into the words, waiting, knowing there was more. There had
to be. Something in his gut was gripping him. A thought that became more
than a premonition. It was a feeling. A stirring. A knowing. A calling. He
breathed it in, waiting, wondering, and dreading the words to come. For deep
down, he knew how it would all end.

He was hardly aware of anything around him as he stepped closer to the
glassless window. He felt as though he could see it all before him. The
buildings rising in flames, the bright tongues licking toward the sky and the
thick smoke creating a pyre for those who had lost the fight in the end.

"The two warriors returned here, where Mysta Hosta and his *anima reflecta*
burned all the records of the Animle—to keep the realm safe from the Nexen.
They severed the bond of *simul ad mortum*, killing their Animle beasts."

Willem heard Ansie gasp, but before him lingered the eyes of the *simian*.
That final breath haunting him.

Dur continued for his brother. "They fought, and died—giving Rolin a
chance to find the Tetel, allowing the Praelia to survive."

The weight of what had happened here settled between them. The course of history altered within these very walls.

"What were their names?" Ansie asked, her voice thick with emotion.

"Hosta's creature was Tegnus, a *simian*. The warriors were Festra and her *cheeterah*, Risus, and Sindro and his *panthier*, Aurea. Neither was much older than any of you."

An unbidden image came to Willem. The bodies of two large cats and warriors lying near one another, their blood spilled across the dirt-covered stones.

"For generations the Praelia have passed down this knowledge, waiting for the Rising and the return of the Animle." Fer didn't so much as look Willem's way, but he could feel it in his soul. Something was watching him.

The Rising.

It was what they had talked about, dreamed about as children. Oh, the many hours they had fantasized what a warrior might be like. Jethron had always said he wished to fly on the back of a *dravir*—a sharp-toothed beast with wings spanning the length of a cottage. Ansie had chosen a *buffulus*—though he'd never known why.

But it was Kata who had always surprised him. She'd dreamed of an *aquilum*—a water spirit that flew along the surfaces of the oceans far from Mirtain. He'd always wondered why she chose to be so far from Mirtain, he'd never asked.

And he never could. Pain struck his chest like it had so many times before. He sucked in a breath, the feeling one he knew well.

He would have thought after so much time of missing her, he would be passed this. He had known when they took her that it was his fault, and he would never see her again.

In some way, Willem was thankful she had died because her misery had ended. But he selfishly wanted her back for himself, he wanted to hold her and tell her how much he still loved her. He wanted to give her all of himself.

But she was forever lost to him.

Unbidden, the image of her smiling came to mind, her bright eyes shining as her hair rippled in the glow of the setting sun.

Tears filled his eyes. It was the first time he'd had a peaceful memory of her. A memory not accompanied by the pain of what came later.

"Why haven't the Praelia brought back the Animle before now?" Larn asked, doubt lacing his every word.

"There is a time for everything." Fer paced, stopping near the broken stone in the middle of the chamber. "The Espiritu moves of its own will—no one can grasp it completely, but the power it holds, you cannot deny."

"So the Animle have the Espiritu?"

Dur nodded, "And others. Not all are warriors of flesh and blood, some are warriors of the spiritual realms."

Was it just a trick of the light, or did the ethereal glow of the filumen pulse around Dur's fingers when he spoke? Willem blinked.

"Those who believe in the Espiritu, the Praelia as we have been called, have the filumen as a guiding light, a force to shatter the darkness of Nex."

A chill ran down Willem's spine. "Nex?"

"The dark spirit—a spirit of death. It was born out of pride and from it came the fall, but that is a story for another time." He waved a hand, a breeze passing them and forcing the loose fabric of his shirt against his thin frame. Yet he stood as a man commanding power—he bowed to no one. "In order to fight—an Animle warrior must understand the power of steel, yes, but the ultimate might of the filumen will cast out darkness."

Another roar shattered the air outside, making them all jump. Willem drew away from the broken window.

Spirits, darkness and light, filled his mind—but he would deal with what he knew. Strapping his sword on his back he left the chamber without a word. He knew how to count soldiers, how to kill them if needed.

As he left the chamber, a prodding darkness lurked around the edges of his mind. He shoved it back, ignoring it all.

"This isn't my battle," he muttered to no one, hoping someone would here.

Even if he wanted to believe in the Espiritu, he couldn't. The Animle were meant to defend, to save, to fight the dark. But the dark had always won.

Willem woke to the chilling calm of an eerie night.

Ansie lay near him, curled on her side in a little ball beneath her cloak. Larn was somewhere on the other side of her, far enough he couldn't touch her—his hand holding a dagger.

Willem didn't know how long he had been asleep, but it was enough for Fer to have fallen off duty, unconscious beside his brother. The older man hardly stirred when Willem got to his feet, his body protesting to each move of his stiff joints.

A soft thump grabbed his attention from out in the hall, and his hand moved to the dagger at his waist. Sidling carefully to the edge of the room, he peeked into the hallway, the soft glow of ethereal blue light met his eyes.

He swallowed. It was quiet.

Too quiet.

He stepped into the hall, the dagger hilt clammy beneath his sweating palm. Reason told him to retreat and wake Larn, with two his chances were better. But something kept him from calling out.

The pulsing beat of the filumen called to him.

Moving carefully, he passed down the hall and into another pathway. The darkness shrouded him, the light of the moons snuffed out by the clouded night sky.

His heart began to pound heavily in his throat as the filumen grew, the power of it throbbing, the glow nearly blinding him. He stepped into a chamber, the walls were barren, overturned tables littered with dust and bracken, but he hardly noticed as the light collected—the pulsing lost as a steady glow focused on the creature at the end of the room.

A lion.

The creature was massive, gold-tarnished fur covering its sides and legs, paws the size of a man's head and claws as long as fingers held its weight. Flecked brown eyes remained solely focused on him. The jaw was open, revealing teeth which could crush through flesh and bone.

The muscles quivered, the large shoulders trembling with restrained power. Willem shifted a step back, holding his dagger before him.

He looked for blood on the beast, certain this was the creature who had been terrorizing the Gallian soldiers outside the Initium ruins. He stilled his breath, waiting, muscles twitching.

He watched the creature, and it watched him back.

Each breath became a moment, a frame of time he could remember clearly. Somewhere in the back of his mind, he knew he should cry for help, or try and recall something Fer and Dur had told him, but nothing came forth.

The filumen glowed, rippling over the lion, only to retreat against the wall. A pounding began in Willem's chest that had nothing to do with his heart. Something unknown, something long forgotten was stirring inside him—ready to break free.

He took a step to the right, and the beast followed. A massive paw plodded onto the stones, the tail behind its maned-head twitching and flicking into existence.

The beast crouched down, shoulders hunched, ready to launch across the room. Willem leaned forward, readying the dagger in his hand. The lips of the lion curled back, each tooth flashing like a blade in the dark chamber. A low rumble issued from its bared mouth.

The gathered light of the filumen pulsed on the wall, the beat matching the throbbing in Willem's chest. He swallowed, taking another step to the side.

Who do you think you are? A voice echoed inside his head, startling him— he nearly dropped the dagger.

He blinked. The lion's body curved, the tail snapping back and forth.

Are you prepared for what's to come? The voice spoke again, a cool, chilling sound. It gripped his heart, a shadow of darkness spilling inside.

He suddenly realized there was a battle going on inside his mind. A storm raging, and only now did he hear the cries of war echoing within. The darkness inside smiled, the grin vile with pleasure.

It was all a lie, a distraction—the war had always been going on inside.

Blinking it back, Willem crouched forward, the muscles in his thighs nearly trembling in anticipation. The head of the lion swayed slightly, the lips curling back in a grin like the darkness within Willem's heart. The beast was pleased. Willem didn't know how he knew, he simply knew.

On the wall behind the lion, the filumen glowed—the light beckoning him. One glance and Willem's lungs were filled—the darkness faltering for a moment.

The lion licked his lips as though taunting him.

You don't have what it takes to be a warrior. The voice was smooth, elegant—cold.

Willem crouched further, ready for the attack which was surely coming. With a beast of such strength, he didn't stand much of a chance.

You have failed everyone.

A shadow loomed before him—born from the lion's mouth. It fell upon the floor between them, the shape twisting, gyrating in grotesque turns until suddenly it rose and there was his mother. He saw her, her cheek bleeding, her lips pleading for the Gallian soldier to spare Willem's life and take her instead.

He tried to close his eyes, but he couldn't. Fear clenched his heart—throbbing to the point of pain. The soldier grabbed his mother, forcing her to drink from the chalice. She collapsed on the stone floor.

The body morphed, a man taking her place. His hair was parted down the center, his polished hands tucked beneath his robe. The sneer he always wore lingered on his lips, those eyes darting with malice. He smiled at a smaller shadow, a young Willem—the boy Willem, telling him he would be protected, telling him he would be the hunter of Mirtain. If only he did as he was told.

The shadow shuddered—Lord Hernan disappearing.

The mass of darkness twisted, grotesquely morphing once more. A laugh echoed throughout the chamber—and then she was before him. Searing pain shot through his chest. It took all of his concentration not to drop the dagger.

Kata and Jethron stood before him, locked in an embrace. They pulled apart, eyes widening with terror at something behind him. He didn't have to turn to know what would happen next. Her eyes found him then, that gaze he knew so well shuttering in horror.

Then the screams began. He felt the blows upon his back, the shattered remembrance of justified pain, but it was the cries within the shadow that tormented him. They were her screams, the last he had ever heard from her.

The darkness shifted again, pleased with itself—her cries still ringing in his ears. He fought against the tears, against the darkness within.

You've never fought back. You failed.

He shook his head, the gaping hole in his chest aching—throbbing with heat. Each rebuttal he conjured bowed to the darkness. Every doubt flying through him.

He'd never been enough. He'd failed—over and over again, he'd failed. But most of all he'd failed her. Lost her.

Yes. The beast echoed inside his head, feeding off Willem's memories of her. Kata was laughing, smiling up at him—the shadow smeared it all away.

You weren't enough to save her.

He knew it was true. The shadow loomed, darkness spreading in his veins. He shuddered.

From behind the lion's head, the filumen trembled—not with fear, but with pulsing power.

He was drawn to it, a lightness hollowed out a tiny spot in his chest. He focused on it, grasped it in desperation—forcing the echoing screams away.

He inhaled, watching the filumen, letting it spread further within.

A warmth began to melt through his chest, reaching for his arms, for his legs. The shadow retreated in surprise at first, then halted, ready for battle.

Gritting his teeth, Willem gathered the light, the fire that seemed to be burning him from the inside out. He held it close to his heart, the chill of the shadow forgotten as he stared into the eyes of the lion. The beast licked its lips.

War.

Willem launched across the room with a guttural cry, slicing through the shadows. The lion pounced with a roar of its own.

Their bodies collided, the weight of the creature knocking him to the ground. He scrambled to his feet, a giant paw hitting him in the side making him roll across the floor, dagger still in hand. A swipe of the claws shot out of the dark and sliced over his chest, ripping through his shirt and tearing the flesh beneath.

He gasped, the pain stinging him as he darted forward once more trying to get to the back of the creature. Each step forward was forced back with a swing of those paws. He retreated. The beast pounced again.

This time he was prepared. He slid beneath the belly of the animal, ready to plunge his dagger into the soft flesh beneath when one of the paws knocked the blade aside.

The beast landed on top of him. The weight collapsing the air from his lungs, his head snapped back against the stone floor.

The shadow rejoiced above them. From somewhere behind, Willem could feel the pulse of the filumen.

Hot breath clouded around his face and he did all he could to protect himself. As the jaws came closer, he grasped onto the top and bottom, pushing them back with a cry of strength and power he didn't know he had.

Blue light poured forth, the darkness trembling.

The beast lifted its head and Willem rose with it, waiting for the right moment. One of the front paws shot forward, knocking his side, cutting into his flesh, but he had already released the jaws and made his move. His arms could hardly wrap around the neck of the beast, his face pressed into the mane—the soft fur nearly suffocating him.

He struggled to lock one hand around his other wrist, the connection his sole focus. The voice began again, taunting him with the doubts of his past. Showing him his failures—one by one.

Over and over again. He saw his mother. He saw Lord Hernan. He saw Kata.

Let go. The voice said in his head, but he didn't. He saw Lord Hernan. He watched as they dragged Kata into the manor.

He held on as tight as he could as the lion reared back struggling for breath. The claws dug into his chest and stomach, scraping down his entire body, digging into his flesh, and he cried out in agony.

Help me! He shouted into the void.

Let go.

The voice had changed—the chill gone, and inside it was warmth, light, life.

He wouldn't. He couldn't.

He was losing air, hardly able to breathe even as he tightened his hold on the lion's neck.

His failures all passed before him, each one standing out as though the world had been lost. He was nothing like what he was meant to be.

Let go. The darkness shifted, the pulsing warmth inside him growing stronger. The shadows retreated—their scars remained. *Let go.*

The voice held power, life. He was drawn to it, but to step closer, he suddenly realized what he could not do.

It told him to let go. But he couldn't. He couldn't let her go.

Fighting was all he knew.

A tear rolled down his cheek and into the mane of the lion. He was clinging to the beast now, his legs crumpled on the ground. Above him, the creature held still.

Let go. This isn't yours to bear.

He shook, knowing when his arms released she would be gone from him. He would have no claim on her.

But he never had.

A sob tore through his throat as the pain of her loss overwhelmed him. He couldn't do anything to protect her anymore, she was gone.

This time, he was the one to send his thoughts to the light—to the protector he clung to. For the filumen glowed around the lion, the warmth of the creature searing through him and into the pulsing light within.

This time, it was Willem's words that pierced the darkness—speaking to the Espiritu.

Take her—keep her safe.

He collapsed.

The stone floor shattered through his wounded body, blood oozing from the clawed stripes down his chest. The wounds should have been enough to kill him, but instead, he felt peace. A breath, a release of a weight he hadn't known he'd been carrying.

He wasn't alone.

He dared not open his eyes. Even with them closed, he knew the filumen was shining all around him.

"Willem?" The voice called forth memories, called forth love.

The light was blinding as he opened his eyes, trying to find the face of the one who had always believed in him. His mother stood before him, her arms outstretched as she called to him. One look at her and he knew all of it was true. Every word of it. The Animle, the Espiritu, all of it.

He sucked in a gasping breath, a smile stretching across his face. He finally saw her the way she had been before the illness spread, before they poisoned her and left him to fend for himself.

"Make me proud," she said and turned away from him, her golden hair blowing in a soft breeze he couldn't feel. He reached out, wanting to call to her. She looked back once more, "I will see you again, my son."

Tears rolled down his cheeks as he stared into the blinding light. His mother stepped further and further away from him, her silhouette soon disappearing.

The light continued to shine, the heat of it filling him with a peace he had never known. Though his lungs should be harmed, he felt well, he felt whole…

Willem jolted awake with a near cry of pain. The darkness of night disorienting him.

He searched frantically.

He was back in the circular chamber with the others—Ansie sleeping by his side. His hands shook as he sat up, passing them along his body to where the deep cuts and gashes had torn through his chest.

It was impossible.

What he had seen, what he had felt. It had to be real.

He struggled to his feet, looking around the room as though expecting to see the lion waiting in the darkness. He had never been more certain of what creature loomed outside the ruins than he was at that moment.

There was a lion within their midst, and it was meant to be his.

He heaved a breath and ran a hand through his hair. Each moment that passed seemed an eternity, yet the stars still glowed through the open ceiling above.

"Willem?" At the sound of Fer's voice, he nearly stumbled. He spun toward the hallway he thought he had walked down not long ago. Fer's brow creased. "Are you all right?"

Was he? He blinked quickly, for the first time in ages, he wasn't sure what he was.

He heaved a breath and looked around the room, only to return his eyes to the Chronicler. Fer had a curious, knowing look about him.

Willem didn't answer, a sudden knowing filling him—a light from within guiding.

Leaving his sword and dagger behind, he walked from the room and down the hall to where the door of Initium was barred. Pulling down the barricade, he stepped out into the midst of the night.

His steps seemed to echo as he strode across the ground, the heavy footfalls shattering through the force of the light throbbing in his veins. But the padded steps weren't his own.

Out of the mist came a shadow. The heavy mane shook with power and grace as the deep golden-brown eyes reached his.

It was immediate, one moment he was Willem and the next he was of another calling. There was a knowing, a simplicity which overwhelmed him. He suddenly knew this was what he had been waiting for.

He knew the creature and it knew him.

He smiled and the beast licked its jaw with a long pink tongue.

Hello, Mitus. Willem thought, sending the words to the creature, somehow knowing it was his name.

The creature gave a slight bow of its head, stepping closer until Willem reached out and placed his hand along the thick mane. Looking into the golden eyes, he saw himself, an odd reflection, and suddenly, he was whole.

Blue light shined in the forest.

Without a command, Willem leapt onto the creature's back, digging his hands into the fur. They took off through the forest, their minds working together as they soared over the ground and through the night.

The Rising of the Animle had come.

CHAPTER 49

"When do you think he'll be back?" Ansie asked.

Larn sighed, forcing back a grin, amused by her frustration. "Any minute now." He'd been in trouble twice already for not taking her seriously.

"Really?"

He quirked an eyebrow in her direction, unable to resist temptation. "Yes, I do believe I'm picking up something," he paused, putting a finger behind his ear. "Oh wait, no, that's just a bird flapping its wings."

She punched his shoulder with deserved force. He chuckled.

Cool morning air filled the chamber of Initium, a draft winding through the broken windows whenever the treetops outside stirred. Though the sun had risen, the day was forged in clouds, shrouded veils covering what they could make of the forest.

"I don't know why I even bother," Ansie grimaced.

"Hey," he held his hands up in surrender. "You asked the same question three times in the last ten minutes. You didn't like my first answers, so I had no choice but to change things up a bit."

"You're ridiculous."

He watched her as she moved close to one of the windows. It was true, she was nervous about Willem. Upon waking a few hours ago, Fer had told them of Willem's departure, leaving them wondering what had happened. Larn had the distinct feeling Dur and Fer weren't telling them everything, but he was past asking questions. All they would give him were cryptic responses.

He'd spent the first hours of dawn debating on going after Willem. Something didn't fit, but it was the look in Fer's eyes that kept him back.

Outside the trees stirred as though in response to his thoughts. Larn shook the thought aside—this place was eating away at his logic.

"Ansie," Fer said, gently. She glanced his way, her hair dipping below her shoulder blades. Had it always been so long? And so careful to catch the breeze and drift past her cheeks?

He supposed it had. Though why he was noticing now, he couldn't say. He pushed all rebuttals down. He wouldn't think about the way she'd looked the night he almost kissed her. The night they had argued.

"What?" she asked. Her voice was soft again, vulnerable.

It was a wonder Larn had only just begun to notice, the way she could so quickly flip from anger to timidity. In the absence of Willem, her worry was creased across her brow. He wanted to do something to make it disappear, to watch those lines ease and her lips lift in the smile he knew so well.

She was afraid. That much was certain.

If it had been anything other than fear, he would have been able to walk away and not look back. But it was her worry that rooted him, that called on something inside of him to reach for her, hold her if she needed.

He nearly cursed himself for thinking such things—wondering why now, of all times he was noticing this about her.

You've never seen her left behind. The thought was as interesting to him as it was true.

"He's fine," he said softly, and she turned to him—the freckles around her eye standing out against her pale cheeks. He wondered if she was tired. He'd heard her muttering in her sleep all through the night—not something she normally did. More than once he'd had to force himself not to wake her, comfort her—he pushed the thought away. "I'm sure he'll be back."

"There are other things out there," she waved a hand toward the window. Her eyes had widened in terror earlier when she saw the destruction on the hill.

Though she'd been brave during their charge through the line of Gallian soldiers, her fears had been evident when he'd shoved a sword into her hand.

But she had done her duty, and more than that. She'd kept his right side clear as he attempted to protect her left and keep them both seated on Tympmor. In all his years with the horse, Larn had never seen the creature so frightened.

"True enough," Dur said, his words rolling over one another. "Willem can handle himself."

Ansie gave a disappointed grumble and returned to looking out the window, her back straight. She was annoyed, that much was certain.

Stubborn is more like it, Larn thought, trying and failing to keep his anger toward her.

Their argument in the grasslands passed through him, his own words haunting. She'd not been pleased to share Tympmor's back with him, and her true stubbornness had flaunted its colors. For hours, she fought off sleep, leaning back ever so slightly in exhaustion until she touched him, and then she would straighten once more.

The inches between their bodies had become a battleground. A truce was met when they collided in the midst of night, her head lolling to sleep on his chest.

He shook away the thought, not wanting to remember the smell of her, the fresh scent of the grasslands clinging to her skin, making him think of sunshine. He wondered if in this dank place she still smelled of warmth.

"Why don't you find something to entertain yourself?" he suggested and was rewarded with a sharp glare.

"If you're suggesting we play your dumb game again, no thank you."

This time, he let his chuckle escape. He'd taught her how to play Pikspee, a game which consisted of tossing small stones into a drawn grid he'd made by dragging his finger through the thick dust and dirt on the floor. From an assigned distance, a player's goal was to toss stones into the squares—if a player was any good, shots which banked off their opponent's stones, or blocked them out of squares, were the best. It was a simple game really, one he had played for years. No matter where he was, stones and dirt always seemed readily available. He was one of the best in the Renegades. Pike was the only one who had beaten him a few times, but Ansie didn't need to know that.

"We don't have to play if you don't want to." He shrugged. "I would only win again, and—"

"Leave her alone," Fer chided, a chuckle following his words. Ansie turned his way.

"Not you too?" She sighed, placing her hands on her hips. "Of all people to be converted to Larn's ridiculousness, I would have thought you could avoid it."

"It's just the general effect I have on people," Larn winked at her and she rolled her eyes, much to his pleasure. The way he saw it, the more she was picking at him, the less she was worrying about Willem. He wasn't foolish enough to not realize she was scared. But of what he wasn't sure. A part of Larn desperately hoped it wasn't the thought of being left behind with him.

There was an innate sense of responsibility he felt for her. Perhaps it was their vows, sham of a marriage though it was, and he was committed to keeping them. At least, that's how he convinced himself on his way back from Flocorna. Over and over again he'd told himself that all he felt toward her was his duty, it was his job to take care of her, protect her.

Yet, there was that other part he refused to recognize. He wouldn't even let it reside in his mind for fear it would take root.

More than anything, he blamed the cold which he had been fighting. Surprisingly, the herbs Gabrella had given him cleared his head and throat almost instantly. Now if his ankle would allow him to move without a slight limp, he would be back to his usual pleasant self.

"While we wait," Larn said, and Ansie shot him a look, "I say we lay out plans for our next move." Thoughts of Gabrella brought back the information she'd given him. A new adventure awaited them in the north.

"Enlighten me," Ansie said, droll with excitement. She held her head high, shoulders back and arms crossed over her chest. Her discomfort became all the more evident. Was it possible all of her anger was from a fear of being left behind?

The thought prodded something, a remembrance of her fury in the grasslands. Her body close to his. He shook away the thought. She couldn't have been worried about him—there was no reason for her to be.

"When I was in Flocorna, my contact there told me about a festival given by a particular lord. It's in one week's time. We're not far from his land, and the village is quite a sight to see."

"Cut through the dung and get to the point."

He bit back a smile. "The village is much larger than Mirtain, called Kirath. I was there not too long ago in search of information about the missing Chroniclers." He shot a look in Fer's direction, the man smiled back, giving him a nod.

"Is this that Lord Duggard's place?" she asked. "You mentioned him at the Caw's Nest."

He nodded, surprised she remembered anything from that tavern other than the attack and their hasty marriage. "Yes," he said. "It's a place I frequent, in different disguises of course, but it's usually plentiful with information about the Regent's moves."

"Why?" She asked, her shoulders beginning to loosen, if only a little.

"My guess is the Regent is in close correspondence with him." He shrugged, often times he'd wondered about it too.

It seemed odd that so many of the Renegades moves, which had proved fruitful, had come from interactions with Lord Duggard, his servants, or the Gallians within Kirath. Even the villagers were teeming with secrets. Thinking of the icemen who had given himself, Pike, and Heben a lead from his last visit, was enough to make Larn smile.

"I normally have a man stationed there, but due to the rebellion in Mirtain, I pulled him out for safety. He should be in the southern lands by now." He placed his hands on his hips. "Regardless, we may be able to find out some of the Regent's plans if we're careful."

"We?" She asked.

"Yes," he nodded, leaning the side of his right arm against the wall. He kept his eyes focused solely on her as she seemingly pondered his words.

"But…" her voice trailed off.

"I have everything we need. I traded for it all with the verral claws." He pointed to the rather large bundle strapped to Tympmor's back.

"Won't you be recognized?"

"It's a masked ball, or festival," he said and pushed away from the wall to snatch the bundle from his still uneasy steed. If there was one thing he knew about Tympmor, it was his need for open spaces and flat ground, only then was the mount completely satisfied. Otherwise, he simply dealt with the discomfort by ignoring most of Larn's instructions or attempts to placate him.

Larn opened the bag and fingered through the contents until he found the midnight blue gown at the bottom. Handing it to Ansie, she let the dress unfurl to the floor with obvious awe. He couldn't be certain, but from what he had seen of Mirtain, it was most likely the most expensive fabric she had ever touched.

"So it's a festival?" she asked.

He nodded. "Joute Deliverance. It's a festival for—"

"I know what it is."

He nodded. It was a lively celebration for Gallians, an annual remembrance of overthrowing Anglas. Ansie grimaced, but at what memory he wasn't sure. From what he'd heard of these celebrations, most Anglans were forced to participate—though the celebration wasn't on their side.

"I had forgotten," she said, her fingers still passing over the fabric. Her brown eyes were brighter, the churning darkness having disappeared. Or maybe it was the blue in the dress she held that brought out the gold flecks in her gaze.

"So had I," he said softly and she nearly smiled. It was the first time in so long that he had almost made her smile—he wondered why he didn't try it more often.

"Well then," she whispered back. "What are the rest of your plans?"

He dug deeper into the bag and pulled out two masks. One, a blue and gold eye mask with feathers adorning the left side, was hers, the other, a full-face mask would be his. No one would guess he was Maereo with his entire face hidden. The lips of the mask turned upward in an eerie toothless grin, half of the face painted black, the other lined in gold.

"Isn't this a bit too fancy for a festival?" she asked.

"Not at all. Lord Duggard is not one to forego finery, no matter what the purpose of the celebration."

Ansie leaned over to look more fully at his mask and smiled. "No one will suspect who you are beneath that thing."

"Exactly," he said. "Which brings me to this."

He pulled the dark wig out of the bag and handed it to her. Gabrella was right, Ansie's hair was far too noticeable.

"A wig?" she cocked an eyebrow up at him.

He shrugged. "You can't be seen otherwise."

"And why not?"

"Enough people are hunting for you, the last thing we need is to stand out in a crowd."

"Right," she nodded, "we need to blend in, good idea."

As she looked down at the mask, a strand of her hair fell across her cheek. Again he had the sudden urge to swipe it away from her face. He resisted the temptation.

"Do you know how to dance?"

"Yes, quite well, actually, but I haven't danced since..." she broke off, clearing her throat before beginning again, "it's been a while."

Now, what had that aversion been about? He searched her expression for more clues—none were forthcoming, though a slight blush colored her cheeks.

"Most likely we'll have to dance some," he said and she nodded, a solemnness entering her eyes that he didn't understand. He nearly asked her what was wrong, when she reached further into the bag.

"What will Willem wear?"

"He won't be going." He waited, watching as the realization of what he was proposing swept over her.

"Oh," she swallowed. "Why?"

"We need to lay low," he explained. "I usually work alone. Having you with me will turn curious eyes away, but three of us," he shook his head, "it would be a trap."

She nodded, agreeing much too quickly. She had no idea what she was really getting herself into. Something she often did.

"Will it be dangerous?"

"Most likely."

"Okay."

She was so trusting. "We'll be safe. No one will know." He watched her throat bob. Stepping closer to her, their gazes locked—he leaned in. "I live my life by a motto. If I hide in plain sight, they'll never catch me."

She bit her lip and his eyes were drawn downward. An unsteady breath parted her mouth and color crept across her skin, spreading down her neck. When he lifted his eyes to hers once more, all worry had disappeared—in its place was a hardness he'd never seen before.

He suddenly felt as though something had just altered between them—some shift, some change, but he didn't know what it was. She moved back, only an inch, but the space felt like a mile between them. Whatever barrier she'd let him through, he was being forced out of again.

"It's a good thing you have the mask then," she said, dropping the dress on the bag at his feet. "No one would ever accuse you of smiling that much."

Without another word, she turned on her heel and left him standing beside the window completely confused. Suddenly the draft outside seemed all the colder.

CHAPTER 50

Idiot. Ansie cursed herself.

How many times did she have to say things she didn't mean before she'd learn her lesson? Shaking her head, she kicked at a worn table that was tipped on its side. The wood was cracked, deep gashes covering its surface.

It was all her fault that she felt this way. She'd known it ever since the fort, ever since hiding behind that waterfall—ever since seeing the mark on Larn's shoulder. Somehow, he'd begun to mean something to her, something more than a stranger.

Kicking at the table again, she cursed as the pain reverberated through her foot. She knew better than to let someone in. It was because of Skurn that she knew what it meant to relax the hold on the restraints around her heart. At one time, she'd thought it was a wall—or a fortress no one could touch. But Skurn had climbed over those barriers and into her heart.

Somehow she'd been able to keep going with him gone, but now everything had changed. She blinked back a tear of frustration.

It was there, the feeling staring at her with wide eyes, the attraction to Larn. She'd felt it before, but just now she knew it went deeper than attraction. When he'd leaned in, her breath had caught, her heart skipping a beat as she traced the lines of his face with her eyes.

In that moment she knew he would never be just Larn. And she hated him for it.

After all her careful planning to protect the walls around her heart, all her vigilance to watch and see if he climbed over like Skurn, she hadn't noticed the way his very essence had begun to crumble the fortress she'd built.

So she had struck back—pushing him away in the only way she knew how. Sucking in a breath, she began to pace the room.

She hated when she got like this, it always happened when Willem was away from her. When she felt alone. There were countless nights she'd spent in their cottage, waiting for him to return. Sometimes spending the entire night worrying over him—listening for some sound, some footfall to tell her he was home.

Blinking back tears, she wrapped her arms around her body. Her father had left her. He had said he would come for her, but he never had. The familiar lump in her throat threatened to choke her. She cleared her throat and pushed the memories aside—burying them back where they belonged.

This was exactly why she had to hold up the barrier. She couldn't keep going like this if her carefully laid walls crumbled to dust at her feet.

Her memories were her own to hold and she wasn't ready for Larn to see them. The horrors of her childhood belonged to the deepest parts of her, and she wouldn't pull them out for anyone. Even Willem didn't know everything, and he never would.

Once, not long after he'd found her in the woods, he'd brought home a dead elk. The creature seemed to take up most of the cottage and he told her to close her eyes, not wanting her to see all of the blood. She had watched from her cot as he cleaned the animal, the blood not bothering her one bit. She had seen more blood than he ever had.

And yet, even though he only knew a piece of her story, he knew her best. She dug her fingers into her sides, wondering for the thousandth time where he was.

"Don't leave me," she whispered.

Standing in the musty room, she cast her thoughts to whatever the Espiritu was. Dur and Fer had spoken of it with such conviction, and she'd seen the power of the filumen when it shot from Dur's hand. She shook the thought away, not wanting to think about the journey ahead.

Somehow it was easier to feel as though there was nothing great in this world, as though there wasn't some grand plan or purpose for all that was taking place. It was simpler to think there was life and death, but no hope. She sighed, turning away from it all.

For just the moment, she simply wanted to be. She wanted to forget.

Gliding over the stone floor, she hummed to herself—a song she had often sung in the fields with Safron. Mirtain seemed so far away.

As though a distant memory, music began to fill her mind. The twirling of pipes and vibrations of fiddles warming her lonely heart. It had been so long since she'd danced.

She smiled solemnly at the thought. Festis Luna seemed a lifetime ago. Had it really been so long since she'd last been in Skurn's arms?

Simply thinking his name conjured Larn's haunting words in the grasslands.

"You told me about the life you dreamed of—marrying Skurn and having a place of your own...You'll never get what you desire. Ever. End of story."

She shuddered, just as she had when he dealt the acute blow. He'd seen through her. All her smiles, all her dreams, shattered and he saw what was left. Pushing down on the mingled sorrow and fear rising in her chest, she made a half turn, listening to the music in her head.

Moving over the stones with a grace she had practiced from childhood, she dipped and swayed, the melody of her own heart thrumming to life, filling her with a sense of being. When she closed her eyes she could see the bonfire in Mirtain, feel the cobblestones beneath her feet, the beat of the music in her chest.

Just maybe she could get through Joute Deliverance with her heart intact. Larn wanted his freedom, and she could give it to him if she only held him at a distance. She couldn't let him in. She wouldn't. Maybe they could simply work for the good of the realm—never leaning closer to one another. A standoff in friendship—amiability.

It might work...her face twisted in doubt.

She was lost in a world of her own, dancing along the center of the room in a sedated spin, her muscles slow to remember the movements. Flicking her hair over her shoulder, she spun once more, this time a little faster, until she saw the door leading to the hallway. A shadow lingered.

She came to an abrupt stop.

"Don't mind me," Larn held his hands up in surrender.

She gritted her teeth as heat began to flood her cheeks. Of course, he would be there to see her. She could already imagine the cracks he would make at her foolishness and she drew herself up, ready to go to battle.

"I was just practicing, for the festival," she explained, absently wrapping a strand of her hair around a finger.

He made a face, cocking his head to the side. "Looks like a difficult task all by yourself." Was he offering? She stared back blankly. "Shall we?" he asked, the corner of his mouth pulling up, the lines there beginning to curve around his mouth.

The smile eased some of her worries. She had often realized how he swung into this carefree manner when he had nothing of great importance to say. It was only when the smile faded that he spoke true.

That's what made his words in the grasslands hurt so much. He'd meant them. Every single one of them.

Recalling them now, she took a deep breath, bracing her hands on her hips. "You can dance?" If he could be friendly, so could she. "I guess I shouldn't be surprised by now."

"What do you mean?" he asked, stepping further into the room. He was nearly an arm's length away when she replied.

"You seem to have many skills."

"True," he pursed his lips, a playful glint in his eyes, "but each one is only mediocre. I only pretend to know what I'm doing."

"I see," she cocked her head to the side. "I would never have suspected anything else."

His smile tightened, if only slightly. She wouldn't have noticed if she hadn't been watching him so carefully. "Always failing," he murmured, stepping past her.

"I didn't mean—"

"Shall we?" he asked, extending his hand in her direction.

His palm faced upward, an open invitation.

"We probably shouldn't, we don't have enough healthy limbs between the two of us to make a whole person." It was an excuse and he knew it.

He clicked his tongue. "My arm still burns and my ankle will take some time to fully heal from that cursed wolf, but I do believe you have two good legs and an arm." He left the statement hanging in the air, raising an eyebrow in question.

"Well, I also fell off Tympmor pretty hard," she offered, trying to establish the ease with which they usually spoke. She could forget the grasslands if she tried.

A lightness entered his gaze that hadn't been there in some time. She untwisted the hair from around her finger, knowing all the while it was an excuse to not touch him. It had been one thing to ride before him, to feel his chest against her back, and to have his arms wrapped around her to grab the reins, but this was different. Unnecessary.

"If you had simply waited, you wouldn't have fallen out of the saddle." The edges of his mouth lifted slightly, the creases forming.

"How was I supposed to know that?"

When they had charged down the hall and into the circular chamber of Initium, Larn had rolled out of the saddle as easily as jumping off a cot. He swung back to help Willem, sword in hand, only to see Muncher arrive riderless. It was terror which had made her try and jump from Tympmor, slip on her feet, and fall on her backside. She had forgotten about it until now.

"I assume you have a bruise as proof?" he asked, the lines around his mouth growing more pronounced. Odd how she had never noticed how much the right side pulled above the other.

"Perhaps," she waved a hand, "I haven't had time to check."

"Might be your turn to be the patient." He gave a sly smile that made the bottom of her stomach plummet.

"As if you would know anything about healing a bruise," she opted for teasing. "Most likely you'll say something like 'toughen up' or 'it's nothing much.'"

"That does sound a bit like me," he admitted.

"I've been around you for far too long it seems."

He stepped closer. "It would appear so. Somehow you seem to know about all my skills, and now even what I say."

"I'm observant," she shrugged, the familiar pang running across her shoulder. They were playing on dangerous ground, the battle lines wavering.

His smile turned to a soft chuckle and she joined in, the awkwardness slowly fading. He extended his hand again, this time she placed her own within his grasp. With a firmness she had come to expect in his movements, he drew her closer until his hand was on her waist. She was suddenly very aware of her breath. Each one she held, only exhaling as quietly as possible when necessary.

She could feel each of his fingers through her shirt, the press of his hand warm against her skin. She swallowed, looking up at him through her eyelashes.

"We have to at least practice," he said, grabbing her stilled hand to put it on his shoulder. He was tall, taller than she often realized. Standing before him she was suddenly very aware of how wide his shoulders were, how his chest rose and fell with each breath. "We can't have Lord Duggard and his men seeing through our disguise."

Ansie shook her head. "We wouldn't want that."

Without another word, he began to gently lead her through the movements of the dance. A slow step, sliding side to side then swinging around. Her boots scuffed along the floor, following him as he led her around the room, each move patient and precise. More than once she stumbled, but he held her fast, not letting go. She'd never stumbled through a dance in her entire life—what was wrong with her?

She held her breath as she moved with him. It was as though he was touching her for the first time. She was all too aware of the way her fingers felt inside his, the way his muscles shifted beneath the hand on his shoulder.

Maybe it was the sudden closeness after the distance they had recently shared, but she suddenly felt as though she was back in the cave with him, her back splayed to her pain and him telling her the legends of his people.

And calling you by name, she thought and tried to pull away from the memory. *Anserietta*. Only her father had called her that.

She had been down this road before, the small moments of simple touch turning to memories which would haunt her for the rest of her days. Memories of Skurn.

His name caused her to falter, to stumble against Larn's chest. "I'm—I'm sorry," she murmured, stepping away from him. Her hands felt empty.

She cleared her throat, ready to say more when he moved before her again. "You're thinking too much." His voice was like a caress, she couldn't meet his gaze.

Thankful she was short enough to hide her face, she let the heat flame her cheeks. He was right, she was thinking too much. All of it, with him, it was too confusing, too much.

"Here," he extended his hand again, waiting patiently.

She debated turning away and leaving him standing alone. It would be better that way—easier.

Slowly, entirely uncertain, her hand reached out and he wrapped it in his own, the calluses rubbing against her flesh. When he placed her hand on his shoulder once more, he waited. If she had been aware of each breath before, she was even more aware now.

Looking up, her eyes met his. The shine of his obsidian gaze lightened, reminding her of a clear night's sky—the gleam beckoning like long-forgotten stars. His throat bobbed when he swallowed, and he slowly began to move them across the room, each step firm but in so many ways uncertain.

Somehow, feeling his unease gave her strength. She breathed easier, until his hand tightened on her hip and he drew her closer.

"When I was training at Sicarmman," he hardly spoke, the words only for her, "they taught us a tactic to become more aware of our own bodies, how they moved, how they faltered."

"Oh," was all the reply she mustered.

"It was thought by ridding ourselves of sight, our bodies could act on instinct. We became better in tune with our surroundings."

All she could do was nod, her focus was on their feet, her boots matching his stride.

"Close your eyes," he said softly, still pulling her around to a silent melody.

"What?" she blinked.

"Close your eyes." His smile was gone, replaced with a look she wasn't ready to understand.

"I know how to dance," she said before her cursed feet scuffed across the floor, making her stumble into him.

He didn't let her retreat but held her closer. "Close them." His voice was a soft whisper in her ear.

Slowly, the tips of her lashes made everything go blurred, and then all sight was lost. In the darkness, she became muscle and breath, her mind falling away.

He moved with a firm step and her body shifted with his, passing more gracefully than before. She felt everything around her. The scuffed floor beneath her feet, the subtle change in the muscles beneath her hand, the firm grip of his fingers pressing into her waist, each breath in her chest, each movement of her hair swinging along the nape of her neck.

They glided faster now across the floor, but how quick, she could not tell. She became one with the silent melody they danced to, giving herself into the feeling of grace surrounding her. All she was fell away, giving freedom to the motions of her limbs.

He released his hand from her waist for a moment, still holding tight to the other as he spun her around before him, then grasped her with both arms again. She knew they were covering the entirety of the room, and a part of her wished she was wearing a dress, something to billow about her legs. In her mind's eye, she felt as though she danced before the Regent himself, her gown twirling upon a cloud and the marble floors of the *Chateau de Plaisance* gracing her feet.

They moved faster and faster now. He swung her wide, spinning her around him, she never faltered. He followed her, guided her, caught her hand once more and they swung around the room, over and over, until he suddenly stopped.

Her world tilted, his arms holding her in place. His breath was as loud as her own, each one deep and poignant.

She kept her eyes shut tight, aware of him, the feeling of the corded muscle beneath her hands, the touch of his fingers along her back. The marble floors and golden windows of her mind fell away, the sweet melody drifting on the breeze and the rich dress disappearing as she opened her eyes. The room seemed all the darker in light of where she had seen herself, but it was Larn's chest which heaved before her.

Lifting her eyes, she met his gaze. The obsidian was no longer a starlight sky, but a rising dawn, burning with a glow she had never seen before, a brightness which made her want to run away and draw closer at the same time.

Her eyes shifted lower to his lips, but before she could pull them back up again, he fidgeted. He had noticed, she was certain of it.

He cleared his throat, the sound shattering the stillness around them.

"Well then," he said, and took a step back. The short distance making her realize how close they had been. The lines near his eyes darkened and something like disappointment warred in him.

"Right," he said, nodding to himself, and left the room without another word.

Placing a hand on her heart to still its beat, she pondered the look he'd given her. He didn't understand this thing between them any more than she did—and he was pulling away.

She nodded, though to what she didn't know. Her only recompense was the still intact walls around her heart. She hadn't let him through.

Back in the grasslands, he'd tried to push her toward saying she hated him, that she didn't want him. Now, after seeing what he could do to her, how easily he could shake her defenses, he just might get the answer he was looking for.

Hours later, Ansie stood quickly, the padding of heavy footsteps falling on the stone floors of Initium.

Shadows dominated the hallway, what little light broke through the windows above brushed the floor. But she hardly noticed, her eyes focused solely upon the creature walking past the door and toward the circular chamber. Its body was massive, the golden sides longer than her entire body, the head as high as Tympmor's where a thick mane pronounced its power. Another step and then another, took the creature past the door, the long tail curved into the air behind its body.

Half a breath escaped through her lips as her heart thundered when a hand curved around her arm.

She startled. "Willem?"

He smiled, his gaze following the creature with a look of peace she had never seen in him before. When he finally glanced down at her, she saw the change in him. He stood taller, as though he had been carrying a weight for far too long.

Tears filled her eyes—and at that moment she knew it was true. Raising a hand to her mouth she stared at him. Here was the boy who had protected her all those years, the man who had sacrificed so much for her. Her friend. The one she called brother.

Ever since Kata had been taken, there was a piece of him missing, but now he stood before her whole. Somehow, he'd found his way home. Blinking through the tears, she stepped into his arms.

"It's true," he whispered, pulling back, "all of it." He grabbed her hand and stepped toward the circular chamber. "Come on, I want you to meet him."

Ansie swallowed, the heaviness in her heart beginning to thud with each step she took. And there he was—a giant lion, his coat gleaming golden in the darkened room.

Fer was kneeling on the floor, unashamed tears rolling down his cheeks. A smile cracked the worn face of Dur, a sight she had never seen before. But it was the lion who stole her attention, the power radiating off of him was enough to still the thrum in her heart.

"This is Mitus," Willem said, dropping Ansie's hand and moving to stand beside the great beast.

The name fit, strong and assured. The creature shifted as Willem came to stand beside him, the movement was so similar to the man she called a brother, that she stared in incredulity. It was impossible, and yet before her was the proof she had been waiting for.

The *simian* had been a creature far beyond her understanding when he first appeared in Mirtain, but there was no denying the way the beast had looked to Willem, and to her. Larn had explained how the creature had been wanting to connect with either one of them, to find his *anima reflecta*. Now before her was Willem's.

"I never thought I would live to see this day," Fer gasped. He shook his head back and forth.

She smiled, unable to move from the doorway, a part of her too afraid of what she might see if she looked in the lion's eyes.

Willem placed a hand on the lion's head, his fingers soon disappearing into the copious inches of mane. Larn cleared his throat, only now did Ansie notice him standing there. Along the back wall, Larn leaned his shoulder against Tympmor, ever the picture of ease. The horse, to his credit, was unfettered, which was more than could be said of Muncher and Sleeper. Both horses skittered, wide-eyed in fear.

"Should we all bow?" Larn asked, one side of his mouth lifting in a grin. Only Larn could disperse a momentous occasion so easily.

"That won't be necessary," Willem folded his arms over his chest. "But we do need to plan our next move. Mitus has taken care of any resistance."

"Thank you," Larn gave a mock bow. Ansie rolled her eyes.

"Only a *lioneth* could have done as much," Dur grumbled, his eyes never leaving Mitus. Ansie wondered at the odd term.

"Correction," Larn held up a finger, "there's no resistance because all the soldiers are dead. Or running scared in Timtus forest, which certainly means they're dead."

The *lioneth* gave a small grumbling moan making Sleeper skitter further back along the wall. To Ansie, it sounded as though the *lioneth* was well aware of what he had done; his duty, no doubt. For a moment the creature and Willem looked at one another.

"Exactly," Willem nodded, answering something none of them heard. He turned to them. "It's time we head for Mirtain." Could they silently communicate?

Fer, who had risen to his feet, stared at Willem. "But we have not found the other."

Ansie leaned in, forgetting so many of the things she had been told. Somehow in all the time they'd spent together, she'd forgotten her role in all of this. It had been easier to think of Willem as a warrior—he always had been to her. But she was no warrior.

Mitus's golden eyes met hers, a small black pupil dotting his focus solely upon her. His large forehead commanded strength, but something in his gaze drew her to him. A sort of longing from deep within.

A pulsing beat settled into her chest. She shuddered away from it, not wanting to know what it would mean. Her *anima reflecta* was still to be found.

"Mitus was the only Animle in Timtus forest. He's been waiting," Willem glanced at the *lioneth*, "longer than he should have, but no longer." He straightened and looked at each of them in turn. "We need to leave. Ansie won't find hers here."

Ansie swallowed, the strength of his words weighing on her. It was true then, she would be one of them.

"Mirtain is a long trip," Larn said, his words as calm as ever.

"All the better to start now."

"What about the festival?" She asked.

"What festival?" Willem asked.

"Joute Deliverance," Larn waved a hand. "A lord is throwing a masked festival in his village, Kirath, not all that far from here. Duggard has a tendency to let information slip when he's in his cups."

"And you're going?"

"We both are," Ansie said, the weight of her words settling between them. "Larn needs to further his disguise. He normally works alone, if I'm there, we won't be noticed."

"Exactly," Larn said, waving a hand in her direction.

Willem watched her carefully, but she stood her ground. She knew if she showed him how afraid she was he would stay, he always had.

"You're both fine with this?" Willem asked, glancing at Dur and Fer.

"I have always found it best to get as much information as possible," Fer agreed.

Willem returned his attention to Larn. "You're certain the information you received about this is from a trusted source?"

"Have I ever been wrong before?"

"Let's not go down that road."

Larn had the decency to look offended.

"It'll be fine, Willem," Ansie said. "Really."

He didn't look so certain when he glanced between them. For a moment his attention became unfocused and he glanced at Mitus. She wondered if he was somehow communicating with him. The *lioneth* gave a mighty huff and yawned, the massive jaws opening and revealing teeth as long as fingers. Though he remained docile, Ansie could only imagine how he would look if moved to attack.

"We have clothes, masks, and the capable ability to blend into any social gathering, well at least, that's my skill," Larn flattered himself.

Mitus stared at him, as though trying to figure out what kind of creature Larn was. Ansie nearly laughed, often times wondering the same thing.

"We could pick up information on the way back to Mirtain," Willem offered.

"Tell him what you presume about this lord," Dur countered.

Larn hurried through his explanations of the connection he believed existed between Lord Duggard and the Regent. "He has a long reach. There have simply been too many times when my men have discovered details which come straight from Bastion Nocta itself."

"I have a hard time believing the Regent would send detailed reports so far out of his reach." Willem retorted and looked to Fer. "Weren't you the one who said the Regent holds his power close?"

Fer shook his head. "No, I said he has others carry out his will—but his power remains, which in fact upholds Larn's theory. Even in the north, the Regent rules supreme."

"Not when he believes he has a divine right to the throne."

"Willem," Ansie chipped in, "he has to have loyal subjects to uphold his power. Why not this Lord Duggard?"

He turned to her. "It's just, something about it doesn't seem quite right."

"We need all the information we can get," Dur pushed.

"Not to mention, I need something to give myself some credit." Larn smiled. "I'm not turning up empty-handed in the wake of a *lioneth*."

Willem sighed and shook his head, but Ansie could tell logic had won out. "You're sure you're all right to go?"

So many times she had chaffed beneath his protective nature, now at the moment of separation, she knew she would miss it.

"I'll be fine," she said and gave him a small smile. "I don't want to show up empty-handed either."

Before anyone could say anything else, Mitus swung his large head, moving back through the hallway of the keep.

"I guess he's done talking then," Larn said and hurried to finish buckling Tympmor's saddle. Willem strapped on his swords, the familiar sight making Ansie think of all the times she watched him prepare for a hunt. A wave of sadness rolled over her, and she chastised herself. This was silly. She would see him soon.

"I'll see you when we get back," she offered, having stepped closer to him.

He nodded. "Be smart and whatever happens, stay with Larn. He'll keep you safe."

"I know," she nodded, and the words were true. She had never doubted Larn's protection, even after everything.

"I'll see you in Mirtain," he said, as though needing to hear her confirm it.

"Where else would I go?" she asked, and he smiled back.

Wrapping her arms around him, she pressed her face to his chest. He held her a moment longer and then let go, chucking her under the chin.

The ringing clop of horse hooves echoed off the walls. Larn, Dur, and Fer were seated on the horses, ready for the journey ahead. Ansie pushed down the fluttering in her gut and took Larn's proffered hand. Hoisted into the saddle, she found Willem looking up at them.

"I'll get her to Mirtain," Larn said from behind her. Willem nodded and turned to walk down the hall.

Along the stone pathways, they ducked beneath the many branches of overgrown trees and vines, coming to the doors they had so quickly rushed through only the previous night. At the edge of the stone ground was Mitus, his ears lifted, listening to sounds far off.

"He was the only Animle in Timtus Forest," Willem said again, "this land is his. He'll see you safe to the border, then you're on your own."

Ansie's throat tightened and Larn shifted a little behind her. The creak of leather from the saddles sounded as the horses waited for the *lioneth* to make the first move.

Willem placed a hand along Mitus's back, looking at both Chroniclers.

"We head south, try and keep up."

Dur nodded, Muncher skittering beneath him, Sleeper's muscles trembling in anticipation. Fer beamed—sunlight streaming around them.

Ansie was just about to ask how they were to be escorted to the border of the forest if they were headed to the northern lands, when Mitus's back straightened his head rising higher than before. Willem leapt onto the creature's back with ease, a new side of him showing as the *lioneth* raised to his full height, legs braced and tail poised.

A shattering roar exploded from the creature and Ansie flung her hands over her ears, leaning back into Larn.

Over the treetops the roar echoed, birds rising and fleeing as though death were upon them. All the horses skittered to the sides in panic, Tympmor for once misbehaving. Larn whispered to him, his voice soothing.

Without another sound, the *lioneth* and Willem sprung from Initium and disappeared into the depths of the forest, Fer and Dur not far behind, their horses running for their lives. After a moment of complete silence, Ansie slowly lowered her hands from her ears.

"Well," Larn clicked his tongue, "that ought to do it. Onward we go to Echo Valley."

She nearly laughed. "I thought they were going to take us to the edge of the forest."

"So did I," he admitted. "I guess we'll have to make do without the pompous escort."

She bit back a smile. "Maybe his roar worked."

"All the same, hold onto this," he handed her a sheathed dagger. "We might have need of it."

His fingers brushed against hers and a spark seemed to ignite beneath her hand. She ignored the feeling and stuffed the dagger into the waistband of her pants, along with the other dagger she always carried. She could grab both in an instant if needed.

Larn made a sound to clear his throat and then muttered some of the language he often used to communicate with Tympmor. The horse started moving at a walk, and then to a trot. As they bounced and jostled through the forest, she kept alert, her eyes searching everything around them. Only when they were within sight of the edge of the dense forest and the plains leading to Echo Valley, did she begin to breathe easier.

"It would be a shame to get this close and get attacked by some creature, wouldn't it?" Larn mused.

She turned to glance up at him, and he smiled, shrugging his shoulders. "Thank you for that wonderful thought."

"Any time," he said as they broke through the last of the trees and into the midst of the plains.

Snow and ice lay before them and Ansie knew she was about to grow colder than she had ever been. There was a tinge to the air that scourged all the way down her throat and into her lungs.

Larn muttered something under his breath and Tympmor took off like a bolt of lightning across the frozen earth.

A few days later in the midst of Echo Valley, the rush of water reached their ears and Larn gave a curse so loud it echoed off the mountains towering above them. She covered his mouth with her hand and he raised an eyebrow, pulling away.

"Don't worry, you can say whatever you want here. Our chances of going unnoticed were ruined by Mitus. Half the realm probably heard him." The look of complete hopelessness on his face for some odd reason made her smile until she snorted with a laugh.

A moment later the unpleasant sound was echoed back to them.

"I know you're already shivering, but I hope you don't mind freezing." He nodded his head in the direction of the river waiting for them as they rounded the next curve—chunks of ice drifted along on the surface of the water.

An expletive she hadn't used in years passed through her lips with all the dread she had in her. Tympmor's ears folded back as her voice bounced off the mountains on either side. The vulgar word sounded all the more ridiculous in the echo of the pass.

Larn threw back his head and laughed. "That's my girl."

Urging Tympmor forward, the obedient steed stepped further and further into the water until it hit Ansie's feet and she gasped. Deeper still, the water crept up until it flooded around her legs, making all breath flee her lungs. The icy air only made her teeth chatter all the more. When it reached their waists, she could think of nothing but the cold—her thoughts frozen.

"Bloody marvelous," Larn said behind her, his voice higher than she'd ever heard it. She couldn't hold back a laugh at the sheer ridiculousness of it all.

Tympmor hurried to the other side and they came out a sopping mess as Larn urged Tympmor into a canter, the wind chilling them even further. She leaned back into him for warmth, but there was none to be had. They would be lucky to arrive in Kirath as little more than frozen limbs.

CHAPTER 51

The winding stairs of the Enchante Wing nearly mirrored those of the royal Aurore Wing, and Umbris focused on each turn, following the map in her head.

Pavier had been too afraid to give her one of the royal books from the library, and instead, had sketched a map of the wings and hallways for her. Every night she studied it before going to bed, memorizing the rooms and servant closets, the hallways, and the wings. She was only just beginning to grasp the enormity of the palace.

Over the past few days, Garval had sent her on more errands than she could count. Just yesterday she only got lost twice before finding her way back to the Aurore Wing.

Given her new position in the Regent's chambers, she was now bedecked in the light blue dress of a maid. The corseted bodice of the gown was plain enough, but the quality of the fabric was finer than any she'd ever worn. It was soft and compliant, and so smooth she had run her fingers over continuously that first day until Garval had snapped at her.

The skirt of the dress, aided by the bum roll that rested beneath the fabric, fell wider than the simple gown she'd been given when first arriving at the palace. At her hips, the pale blue fabric arched out to the side just enough to give her the impression of having an even more petite waist than she already had. She had been surprised that first day when she took in her reflection in the small mirror in her bedroom. The girl in the glass nearly a stranger.

It hadn't taken long for Garval to tell her she needed to be more presentable. Each morning, she rose and washed her face in a basin of freezing water, before pinning her hair back in a low swoop along the nape of her neck.

An apron covered the front of the dress, and the most recent additions were the two leather cuffs which wrapped around her wrists.

Garval was not one to slack on propriety and had given her the cuffs without a word. Though they irritated her burned skin by the end of a long day, she didn't complain.

Stifling a yawn, Umbris stepped into the Fantique Coloir, the many candles which earlier had stood to attention, now melted to near exhaustion. The immense hall glowed with romantic light.

Long tables laden with food were being bustled away by the many skirts and working hands in the room. It was a hustle of activity, a sight she did not often see in the Aurore Wing.

If she had learned anything, it was Garval's affection for precision. He did not like to be rushed, nor did he respect those who were late. He simply allotted the specific amount of time for each task and expected it to be done on time.

"There you are," Pavier approached, his gangly legs bringing him to her side. "Come this way."

She followed him down the expansive hall, ducking beneath reaching arms and ladders as servants extinguished the thousands of candles along the walls and amongst the chandeliers. Nearly getting trampled by two men carrying a rather large, half-eaten cake, she hurried closer to Pavier.

"Where are they taking all of this?" Umbris asked, not believing the excess around her.

It was said that nearly four thousand courtiers were staying in *Chateau de Plaisance*, though she had never been near any of them, only seeing their movements from above while looking through the windows of the Aurore Wing. The courtiers were their own breed, moving about the gardens in exquisite clothes, dressed for perfection and every motion and action perfectly calculated. She'd only needed to watch them for a moment before shaking her head at the carefully constructed façades they all withheld.

She wondered if they knew what it was like to run through a field or to dance only to the beat of a drum. Or better yet, to dip their bare toes into a refreshing creek. She supposed not. Their lives were controlled by wealth and leisure.

"I'm not sure where all of it goes," Pavier shrugged and moved directly to the center of the hall.

Umbris tried not to think of the first time she'd seen the long stretch of glass and gold-paneled windows on the night of her arrival. It all seemed too long ago.

"Here we are," Pavier said and hastened to a now empty table. All that remained were the table dressings, long silken swaths of cloth stretching over the polished wood. More than one had a splash of red, and small dribbles of what looked like grease along the tops of the fabric.

Umbris hurried to follow Pavier's movements, gathering one of the table dressings in her arms, the bundle nearly too big for her to lift. She followed him down the rest of the hall where a cart with a basket the size of a small wagon rested. Pavier threw in the table dressing and she followed suit.

Over and over again, they practiced the same movements, each time having to walk farther to the end of the hall to collect the recently cleared tables. More than once she caught some of the other maids looking her way, their eyes lingering on her leather cuffs. If Garval only knew her leather-bound wrists made the matter worse.

"Pavier?" she asked, attempting to see around her latest load—she could only hope there was nothing to make her feet stumble.

"Hmm?"

"How many rooms are in the palace?"

He gave her a quick look, "You don't know?" She shook her head, the rough sketch he had given her mainly focused on the different wings and pathways.

"Eight-hundred and twelve," he said.

She blinked, pausing for a moment before catching up. She had been thinking somewhere closer to five hundred.

"Really?"

He nodded, the dimple on his cheek appearing. "Certain of it. And each room has a name, but I only know half of them."

Only half, she thought to herself. No wonder she was able to get lost so easily in this place. Her sense of direction was poor at best, but she wondered if others got lost as well. She couldn't be the only one. Over eight-hundred rooms and each one was named.

"But they also have numbers," Pavier said, having placed the latest table dressing in the basket. The laundress waiting for them to finish seemed none too pleased to hear them talking. "Each one was given a number upon its completion."

Umbris nodded as though she had heard it all before, but she hadn't. Back in her village, they had heard stories of the grand wealth in Bastion Nocta, tall-tales about the elegance of the Regent's home, but none came close to a palace this big.

"What number is this one?" she asked.

"I forget," he shrugged, sauntering over to the final two tables in the hall. "I think the numbers are even harder to remember, but I would guess it's somewhere in the seven-hundreds."

"That narrows it down," she mumbled.

"I only know that because the Aurore Wing was drawn up when His Sire was born. It was first completed when he was declared Regent, after his father's death." Pavier whisked around a table being carried out through the doors of the Fantique Coloir.

Umbris tried to calculate how many years had passed since then. The Regent was only eight years old when he had succeeded his father. It was no wonder the Aurore Wing spoke so much of the Regent's personality. Sometimes she felt as though the various shades of blue in his room were drawing her in.

In the light of day, they were calming and peaceful, but at night when the candles glowed, everything around her seemed too dark and alluring to give comfort. It clawed at her like water licking around her ankles until she was given leave to retreat into her room for the night.

Tossing the final table dressing into the laundress's cart, Umbris watched the woman pull it away. But Pavier soon directed her over to a window where rags and suds awaited them. Only given the simplest of instructions, she soon began the painstaking process of cleaning the windows, working to make all the smears and smudges invisible.

Each swipe seemed only to create more, and Pavier laughed as she tried three times to get the same spot clean. He was having no difficulty wiping away at the top corners of the lowest panes.

Looking at her own reflection, she watched herself clean the glass and could hardly believe the girl in the window was her own reflection. How had she come to be here?

Behind her bustled too many servants to count. Their voices creating a constant thrum, the activity never ceasing for a moment—they were in more of a hurry than she'd ever seen.

A splash of soap landed on top of her head.

"Hey, watch it!" Pavier called up to the man on the ladder above. A grumbled reply was all he received, but the man gave Umbris a knowing smile as he returned to his work. Heat flooded her cheeks and she kept her eyes down, all of the sudden aware of how his eyes had lingered on the bodice of her dress. From above, it was far too revealing.

"Don't let it bother you," Pavier said. "Remember, they all know you're in a powerful position, higher than the rest of the maids."

"Which is why they're enjoying watching me clean windows," she said.

It was true, the work didn't bother her all that much, but the raised noses and turned faces from many of the maids had begun to affect her more than she cared to admit. In the Aurore Wing, she had begun to live a secluded little life that suited her just fine. Most of her interactions were with Pavier, Garval, or the Regent—though he'd hardly looked at her since bringing her to his wing.

"Possibly," Pavier agreed, and they moved onto the next overly large window, a different man on the ladder above, taking charge of the topmost panes.

"You didn't see the looks Magetta was sending my way?"

"I think everyone saw," he smiled, the crooked grin which made his dimple appear. "But she always looks like that if she doesn't get what she wants. She's just jealous."

Umbris shook her head, a few more drops from the wet rag above fell down on her. Much more of this and Garval would think she had dunked her head in one of the soap buckets.

"Where did you say you were from?" Pavier asked.

If there was one thing she had learned about the boy, it was his knack for changing a subject, usually to something which made her reveal a bit more of herself. Maybe it was all the time he spent in the libraries, but he seemed too often to be lost in thought.

"I don't think I ever did."

"Well," he said, looking down at her. "Now would be a good time. We'll be here long enough." He pointed down the hall and she had to admit he was right. Her arm was already aching and it would only continue to get worse.

"I'm from Locknett," she said.

Pavier's head whipped in her direction. "Isn't that in the lower east?"

She shrugged, not wanting to admit the Regent had said as much. "All I know is it's a long way from here."

"But it's near Abattron?" He stared down at her with wide, excited eyes, his curly hair making a halo around his head.

"I suppose, I only heard the stories," she admitted, but that was as far as she would go. In truth, she wasn't positive how close Locknett was to Abattron. She would have to look at the Regent's map to determine the distance.

"Do you remember when it happened?" he asked her, the complete awe in his voice making her want to turn away.

Did she? Of course, she remembered, but then again everyone had heard about the terrors of Abattron. But she wasn't one to dwell on horrors.

If she had learned anything during her time in Bastion Nocta, it was the way its inhabitants thought of the hardships of those outside the capital. The stories of starvation, children whose parents were murdered before them, the elderly dying of disease, all of it became stories—tales to evoke emotion, but for nothing to be done. The Gallians would gasp in horror, but turn to their games of gambling and ask for another glass of wine to soothe the blow. Before long, all was forgotten.

"Yes," she whispered, trying not to notice how pale her reflection had grown.

"They all died. Well, they were slaughtered, is more like it." Pavier shivered and wiped away at a smudge on the glass above her head. "I still remember when the messenger reached the palace. The Regent was angrier than I've ever seen him. I was only a boy then."

Umbris nodded as though she had known all along, but she didn't. All she knew were the rumors which had spread across the realm. The threats and dangers hanging in the air when she was only a child. Her own father had stayed awake in a chair during the night for months, following the news. She still remembered the old sword he held in his hand all night, taking turns with mother to keep their family safe.

In the midst of peace, the Regent had sent an emissary family to Abattron. There, within the village, the courtier and his wife had dined with the Pleni— the inhabitants of the Plenus Mountains. Then, in the dark of night, the village was massacred. No man, woman, or child had been spared.

Umbris shivered now, remembering the fear which had worried her village that day and lingered for months to come. The Regent sought retribution, and the Pleni rose to challenge him, but in the end, it was determined neither side had committed the crime. Nothing more was ever found, and those who died were long ago buried.

The story of that mysterious night became nearly a myth, but she knew it was all true.

"Do you ever wonder what happened? Who they were and who was responsible for the massacre?" he asked, his thoughts seeming to follow the same track as hers.

"I used to," she said, and then moved to the next window.

"And now?" he came up beside her. He was watching her in the reflection of the window. Looking at the gilded glass, the extreme glory and resplendent glow of candles behind her, she had never felt more detached from the creaking loft of her family's house.

She kept her eyes on her hands. "And now," she paused, "I don't like to think about it. You don't know what it was like to worry about the same things happening in my village. We all feared for our lives, for months."

The silence stretched between them and he didn't say another word. Her thoughts were consumed with memories of sleepless nights, of feeling so tangled beneath the bed sheets she awoke to a patched roof, afraid someone was strangling her. Shivering, she turned away, dunking her hand into the comforting suds.

Hours later, after all the candles had been extinguished and the rest of the staff was nearly non-existent, she turned to look down the Fantique Coloir. Every last window had been cleaned, the panes shining like morning dew. She rubbed at the muscles along her neck, knowing she would hardly be able to move upon waking the next morning.

Or this morning, she thought, casting a look outside the windows.

Dawn had already broken across the horizon, smears of blood-tinted maroon streaming beneath angry clouds. A different thrum of activity sprung to life in the palace, the morning duties taking hold.

Wearied from the job, she yawned as she wound her way back up the stairs and along the main hallway to the Aurore Wing. Pavier followed behind her, his demeanor quieter than she had ever seen.

"Get some sleep, Umbris," he said when they stopped outside her door. "Garval will be by in two hours."

She nodded, another yawn passing through her lips. Normally after a party, she had the privilege of a longer morning due to the Regent's sleeping habits. After the unexpected length of the first night of Joute Deliverance, typically a seven-night affair, she could be thankful that her duties would not begin until later. It would be a long string of nightly balls leading up to the final celebration of the Regent's day of birth. Only at *Chateau de Plaisance* would Joute Deliverance be celebrated for two weeks.

"You too, Pavier," she whispered and stepped into her room.

Without changing, she fell onto her bed and was asleep within minutes—only to be wakened by her own small scream as her nightmares were filled with masked men and brandished swords.

The palace was alive with snippets of gossip, teeming rumors which tantalized the mind. The rumors traveled from one mouth to an anxious ear and onto the next.

The Regent had dispatched a Gallian brigade to Mirtain with the orders to quell any and all resistance. The words spread like wildfire through the palace, for the small regiment already sent to Mirtain had been defeated.

And now three-thousand soldiers were headed for the tiny band of rebels. Only Umbris knew it would take place on the fortieth day of winter—she'd heard it from his own mouth.

Never before had Umbris so badly wanted to send a message to Mirtain. She had spent hours trying to figure out a way to get a message out of the palace, but she didn't even know where to begin, who to trust, and how to even give directions to Mirtain.

All she could do was continue to memorize her list of names and places. It seemed much too small a help when she could clearly hear the Regent's most intimate plans. Just yesterday morning, he had spoken to his advisors as she changed the sheets on his bed. The Gallian division was not only to eliminate resistance, but they had another, secret mission. The Regent wanted his men to recapture the lord of the village—to question him. What the Regent would do to him was a mystery.

Umbris's heart had pounded heavily as she went about her duties and listened to the way his voice turned to ice, reminding her of the night he threatened to split the realm. She was shaking inside, terrified others could hear her shouting thoughts and her fears for Larn and his companions.

The realm was on the brink of war, she could feel it. And the Regent felt it too.

Stooping to pick up the discarded nightshirt, a subtle hint of pine enveloped her. She had long noticed the way the Regent's bedroom had a different scent than the rest of the palace—a smell of the outdoors that suited his restlessness and desperate need for open fields to kick his stallion into a thundering sprint.

Just the other day, she happened to see him pounding across the gravel of the gardens, his back straight and broad shoulders tight as he held his seat. There was something about the sight which radiated power, every shift of his eyes, even the curling of his hand over the reins commanded attention.

She'd watched him much longer than she should have. Long enough that he had glanced up toward the window where she stood. Whether he saw her before she ducked away, she never knew.

"Any news?" The Regent's voice traveled into the bedroom from the antechamber, pulling her from her thoughts. It would not bode well for a messenger if he was already agitated.

Umbris swallowed as she picked up one of the blankets which had been tossed onto the floor near the fireplace. She would have some laundry to do.

Moving about the room, she listened to the drawled response, nothing new to report. The Gallian division wouldn't reach Mirtain for another week if they traveled fast. Being calvary, they meant to move swiftly. Umbris could only hope the Renegades had the forethought to be prepared.

Leaning across the bed, she flattened the new bedding with a swish of her hand, tucking the sheets as tightly as possible along the edge. She had just finished when the door of the antechamber slammed open, and barking orders were given. The scrape of a chair being pushed aside scuffed the floor. She froze where she stood, halfway to the exit of the servant's hallway which connected both rooms.

"What is this?" The Regent bellowed.

A man sniffed, and when he spoke it was with a nasal sound. "My Sire, we have proof that these men have seen the man from Mirtain."

Her heart skipped a beat. Tip-toeing, she stepped into the small passageway connecting the rooms, making sure to avoid the one board which always creaked. In the darkened space, she could hear them all the more clearly. Oh, how she wanted to open the door a crack and get a peek at the men.

A scuffle and then a curse sounded in the room just beyond the door before a heavy thud hit the floor. "On your knees!" The nasal voice shouted.

More movements and then silence. There was something moving around the room—soft rhythmic clacking set her teeth on edge. The hairs on the back of her neck stood to attention.

"Speak!" The Regent commanded.

A small whimper came from some creature beyond the door, a short little bark which was hushed quickly. Umbris pressed her back up against the wall beside the door. There was only one type of creature which could make that noise and be allowed in the Regent's chambers.

Wolves.

As though the beast could hear her thoughts, a snarl rose in the antechamber.

"We split from Kraven Hall, I sent my men north and south as you directed, searching the river for them." The soldier sniffed again. "We found nothing until we ran into Captain Pugh's company. When he was told of your decree, he sent us to a mountain village, Alesmann, where he had run into three travelers. He showed us the graves of three Nexen, and the rooms where the travelers killed the soldiers. Two men, and a girl with red hair."

Umbris sucked in a breath. Had they captured them? She thought Larn and his companions were traveling north? Rumors pointed toward Initium, but maybe they had changed course—or the information was old. Her fingers dug into the sheets in her arms, their smooth texture giving little comfort.

"And?" the Regent asked, growing more impatient.

"We found this." There was a pause.

"A dagger?"

"Yes, my Sire, but look at the handle. That's no ordinary weapon, it's a Nexen dagger. We found it under one of the beds. Perhaps from one of the Nexen who went missing in Mirtain?" The sniffling man left the statement hanging in the air.

"I see," the Regent said. "And where is Captain Pugh?"

There was an awkward pause. "Seems the man knew he would be in trouble when we reached Bastion Nocta, my Sire." A deep breath. "He ran off nearly a week ago. We searched and found his remains at the bottom of a ravine. Whether he tripped or jumped, I don't know."

"And who are these prisoners, Captain Dondol?" The Regent asked. There was a small scuffle.

"We have here the tavern owner of the Caw's Nest in Alesmann. Says his name's Oslo."

"I see," the Regent said. Two soft footfalls passed near the door, she could picture him standing above the prisoners, his royal blue jacket contrasted by the gleam of his gold buttons, back straight, and feet set apart. A soldier at attention.

"Who were these travelers?" The Regent asked, each word pronounced with perfect clarity and precision. There was a forced calm in his voice, but Umbris knew what coursing anger lingered underneath.

"I don't know, my Sire." The prisoner, supposedly Oslo, spoke with a distinct, rough rolling of his tongue—the sound coming from the back of his throat. She was suddenly reminded of a few of the nomads who had shouted at the prisoner caravan—their calls ringing in her ears.

"You didn't take their names when they arrived?"

"No, my Sire." Oslo gasped. A heavy thud sucked the air from the last word. Tears sprung to her eyes, a sense of dread filling her stomach. She knew these actions, knew these sounds. Staring at the opposite wall, the white paint turned to stone, the putrid scent of the illness and death of Fort Jontru reached her nose. She nearly gagged and covered her mouth with a shaking hand.

After the failed rebellion in the fort, many of the women had been beaten. She'd watched helplessly as they succumbed to illness from their wounds.

In the antechamber, the prisoner tried to explain, his words hurried. "Business has been bad, I accept any who wish to stay in my tavern."

"I see." Two footsteps marked the Regent's movements. "And what of these?"

The man with the nasal voice, Dondol, spoke, "They were at the tavern when we arrived. This one here is a bookkeeper, the other is a barmaid."

"What do you have to say about these travelers?" The Regent asked, ice in his voice.

"I didn't notice anything, my Sire," a female answered first.

"And you?" The Regent snapped. "No, don't look at them, look at me."

"I—I, we don't know their names." The voice was young, a boy who was only just becoming a man—a low break in his voice.

"But you noticed something about them?" The Regent prodded.

"They were on edge," the boy admitted, his voice growing higher by the moment, nearly hysterical. "Nervous—"

"Hold her still!" The Regent seethed and a wolf growled. A curse from one of the soldiers and a heavy-handed slap rang through the room. Umbris thought she heard a choking sob, whether it came from the boy or the girl, she didn't know.

Silence threaded through the antechamber, though her own heart trumpeted its existence with each passing second.

"Why were they nervous?"

"I don't know, my Sire."

"What happened to the Nexen they killed?" Dondol asked.

"I—I." The boy's voice nearly cracked, and it grew silent.

A sharp slap resounded in the room again. Umbris's eyes welled with tears, one rolling down her cheek. She couldn't listen to this, she didn't want to, but her feet wouldn't move.

"Again," he commanded, "again."

The boy choked on a sob, "Stop!"

"Your father," the Regent said, "has committed treason. Harboring three outlaws is a crime punishable by death. Do you wish to watch your father die?"

"No, my Sire," the boy nearly whimpered.

"Then tell me who these rebels were! I want every detail, down to the number of drinks they had."

Silence met the Regent's words and another thud resounded. A man grumbled under his breath, but another punch silenced him. The girl shouted something that was quickly cut off. When another slap cracked the room just outside the door, Umbris bit one of the fingers over her mouth, the pain bringing back the memories, the screams, the agony, the dead.

Tears coursed down her cheeks, running off her chin.

"I'll not tell you their names." It was the tavern owner. "Do what you want with me, with my children, but know this, your time is coming to an end. My trust is in the Animle and the power of the Espiritu."

Umbris squeezed her eyes tight, the tears spilling over. The man had sealed his fate.

"Very well, then." The frozen calm in the Regent's voice was unlike anything she had ever heard before. It sent chills along her spine, making her fear her own breath. "Hang them," he said as casually as if he was requesting his nighttime meal, something in her stomach clenched and she nearly lost her breakfast.

"But leave the boy," he added, "I want him silenced, but he must go back to his village as a warning to all Renegades. One way or another, the fires of rebellion will be quenched."

The girl gave a strangled cry, as the pounding of boots wrestled the prisoners from the room. Silence hung in the absence.

Umbris counted her heartbeats, focusing on each one, breathing slowly, in short gasps around her hand. It was only then that she once again felt the pain along her finger. Dragging her hand from her lips, she saw the swollen marks of her own teeth, she'd nearly broken the skin.

"Chrish?" The sound of the Regent's voice sent a trembling shock through her. He was power, she had known that, but to hear what he could do…she nearly shook her head, but refrained for fear of being heard.

"Yes, my Sire," the man named Chrish said. She had never heard the man speak, or seen him, but if she remembered correctly, he was the Regent's scribe.

"I want a letter placed upon the boy's person, a warning to all who harbor Renegades. Any found keeping rebels safe will be punished with death to themselves and their entire family."

"Yes, my Sire." The man scurried from the room.

Silence like a blanket descending upon a bed, it hovered, then drifted downward until all was extinguished beneath it. A soft ding of a clock sprung to life, then fell to sleep once more. With each breath Umbris waited, afraid to move for fear he'd hear her.

A boot scuffed across the floor, then another. He stepped further from the doorway, each footfall lingering, one step, two, then three.

Without warning, glass shattered across the floor. She pressed her back against the wall. She was just gathering her courage to walk away, when a strangled roar of frustration awoke the room and something heavy slammed to the floor.

She ran.

Nearly tripping over her own feet, she rounded a corner and ran headlong into a body. She gasped and pulled back, the stranger's hands wrapping around the tops of her arms.

"Umbris?" Pavier asked, ducking to look down at her.

She shook her head and tried to hurry around him, but his grip tightened. Blinking back the tears, she saw him clearly and the fear in his own eyes.

"Were—were—you—" she broke off unable to say the words. His trembling told her all she needed to know. He knew what had gone on in the Regent's chamber.

"I was there," he nodded, his hands still gripping her arms. He looked away, his eyes far off, jaw set.

She opened her mouth to say something when footsteps clipped down the servant hallway. They looked at each other, eyes wide.

"Go," he whispered, freeing her from his grasp. She nodded and scurried away, heading in the direction of her bedroom.

Nearly tripping on the rumpled sheets, she ducked into her room only to hear her name called behind her. It took more control than she would have thought to step back into the hall. Hastily wiping at the tears, she turned and watched Garval approach, his blonde hair parted down the middle as always.

"Umbris," he said, "you're needed in the Regent's chambers." She shook her head in refusal without thinking. His gaze narrowed in a hardened glare. "That's an order."

"Ye—yes, sir," she said, still unmoving.

"Leave them," he eyed the sheets in her arms and she dropped them on the floor at his feet. "Go." He pointed down the hall in the direction she had just come, for some reason it looked smaller as though it could swallow her whole.

She didn't dare to challenge Garval's orders again. The meaning of her employment in the Aurore Wing wasn't lost upon her, she knew there were much worse positions. Wrapping that thought around her, she swallowed heavily. She had been through worse. She could do this.

For some reason, these men, Jolson and Garval, thought she had an effect on the Regent. Taking courage from what she had done to waylay his anger before, she hoped her own fears weren't written all over her face.

Waiting outside the door in the small corridor, she took a deep breath hoping it would keep her from quaking. The door was like ice beneath her hand as she pushed it open into the antechamber.

Her eyes alighted first on the overturned table and the papers scattered all around the room. The shattered remains of a porcelain vase decorated the floor in a grotesque manner, but it was the Regent that ultimately drew her attention. He was pacing back and forth along the length of the chamber, muttering to himself. Some of his hair had come loose from the ribbon which rested at the nape of his neck, as though he had wrung his hands through it.

She slipped into the room, her pulse jumping in her throat. For a moment she stood uncertain, not knowing if she should go to him or clean up the mess of papers and food on the floor. Moving around the shattered glass, she reached for the broken pieces and began collecting them in her apron as quietly as possible.

"What are you doing?" His voice rumbled, the pieces she'd been holding clattered to the floor.

Steeling herself, she raised her chin. "Cleaning," she said, her voice coming out higher than usual.

"Leave it," he muttered and turned to pace the floor once more.

She bit her lip, uncertain of what to do, stuck as she was kneeling on the floor. Her thoughts were on the tavern owner and his children, but the tears had stopped, and in their place was a need to do something with her hands—to fix the brokenness before her.

He stopped pacing and she knew he was watching her, his gaze almost weighted. Lifting her chin, she braced herself for what she might see, but nothing could have prepared her for the anger radiating off of him. There in the depths of his frozen gaze was fury, curling and waiting to be released.

The accusation in his eyes was directed at her. She quaked beneath it, waiting.

"Did Garval send you?" he snapped, his voice as harsh as when he had dealt with the prisoners.

"Yes, my Sire."

He gave a short exasperated laugh, the sound anything but comforting.

"Would you like me to send for him, my Sire?" The timid question made its way past her lips.

"No," he ground out the word. "I sent him away."

She nodded as though it was a perfectly reasonable response. He stepped toward one of the enormous windows facing the expansive gardens.

"Can I get you something, my Sire?" she asked.

"No," he said over his shoulder and then turned to look at her directly. "If you were Garval, you would be suggesting I take a warm bath, or go riding to distract my thoughts. 'Perhaps a bit of whiskey will calm your nerves, or shall I send for a wench.'" He gave a perfect impression of Garval's pitch, though a hint of distaste lingered in the words.

"But I'm not Garval," she said, thinking of the garden and his need to be heard. Casting the prisoners from her mind, she focused on him. A short huff of breath was the only response she received as he turned back to the window—shoulders tight.

Lingering between them was some understanding, some acquiescence that eased the horror of what had been. Here, alone with him, she knew she was safe. She didn't know how she knew, but she felt it, deep within her.

Maybe it was the promise he'd given to not to touch her. But it felt like something more. At any moment he had the power to go back on his word, use her if he wanted, no one in the realm could refuse him, and yet, she had.

"No," he shook his head slowly, "you're not Garval." He continued to look out the window. She watched as his shoulders rose and fell with each steadying breath. "Send for a hall boy to clean that up."

Without a word, she rose to her feet and tugged on the bell pull to signal for help. It would only be a moment or more before they were no longer alone.

Standing on the other side of the mess, she remained in her place and watched as two hall boys, one of which was Pavier, cleared the broken glass and scattered food onto a tray.

Pavier never glanced her way, keeping his eyes on the work. Did he mean to keep their meager friendship a secret?

All too soon, the mess was cleared and she was alone again, the Regent still gazing out the pristine glass and across the early light of morn. When he brought a hand up to pinch the bridge of his nose, she found herself moving toward him on instinct. She stepped to his side, the morning grounds opening before her. Gold glinted off the fountains, winking back at the palace with a dancing light.

If only the sun could not shine for a moment.

Looking up at him, the sun cast him in light—the ice of his gaze having eased, reminding her of clear, flowing waters. Here, near the window, she could see him in clear detail, see the dark hairs which shaped his brows, the slight hump along his long nose.

As though he could feel her watching him, he turned. She held her breath, uncertain, waiting.

She idly wondered if anyone had ever told him his lashes were beautiful? The thought scoured her soul as his gaze dropped to her mouth. Her gut clenched and she turned away.

"Go," he said, softly.

She needed no further encouragement and fled the room as quietly as she had entered, her chest still pounding out an erratic beat.

For the rest of the day, her thoughts whirled around her. Unease settling in her stomach as rumors passed in the halls. There were prisoners and one would be released.

As darkness swept across the palace, Umbris gathered what little courage she had left and began her descent into the lower levels of the palace. Passing through the servant's hallways, she moved deeper into the quieter halls of the palace, desperately trying to stay on course with the map she'd memorized.

In a basket, she carried the ruined plates from the Regent's room, her only excuse for walking so far from the Aurore Wing. If there was one benefit to the markings on her wrists, it was the lack of questions from the other servants.

Reaching the bottom floor, she moved down a hall in the direction of the courtyard. She had heard what time he was to be let go. Only when the celebration was in full-swing would the gates of the palace prison be opened.

Umbris stepped outside with her basket, the fresh air filling her lungs like pricks of ice. It was glorious and painful at the same time. Tightening her shawl around her shoulders, she moved slowly not wanting to appear as though she was lingering. Around the corner, the grinding of a gate was opened and she stashed her basket along the wall hidden in the shadows.

Gallian soldiers exited, the deep blues of their coats almost black in the dark of night. One carried a torch, the other two soldiers holding onto the prisoner between them—the young boy. Sandy hair hung over the boy's eyes, but it was the swollen bandage hanging from his mouth that made her steel herself as she walked forward.

Approaching the soldiers, they stopped, watching her.

"Please, I would like to inspect him," she said, her voice soft, and accented in a perfect imitation of how Pavier spoke—Gallian refinement rolling off her tongue.

"Stand aside." The Gallian soldier pushed the boy forward. He stumbled, the chains clanking.

"But he will not make it back to Alesmann in that condition," she waved a hand, making sure to keep her leather cuffs hidden within her shawl. "The Regent particularly requested he makes it to his village alive." She held up a little bottle which contained nothing more than water, but the label said otherwise.

Sorrowful, green eyes reached hers. The pain searing in those depths reminded her of the haunting stares she'd seen every day in Fort Jontru. It was a pain that struck deeper than the heart.

He's just a boy, she thought. Her own brother wouldn't be much older now.

The Gallian soldier looked around the empty courtyard. "Be quick about it."

She nodded and stepped forward as the soldiers moved away from the boy. He was nearly her height, but the face was much too young. "Where are you hurt?" she asked.

He blinked, the bandage in his mouth preventing any speech. His eyes welled with tears, but there in the depths was the strength she had heard. Though the Regent had threatened the lives of his father and sister, he had refused to break again. It was to that hardened courage she now appealed.

He would never speak a word again, but just maybe he could be her mouth to the Renegades.

The boy pointed to his stomach, then his shoulder, then his mouth. She nodded and began moving her hands delicately over his body, hardly pressing, her fingers too busy trying to get the slip of paper out of the cuff on her wrist.

Sliding up to his shoulders, she had him hold the small vial in his hands as she then moved onto inspecting his face. He looked her directly in the eye as she popped the cork of the bottle and leaned in to help cradle his face, as he poured a small gulp of the water around the bandage in his mouth.

When she paused to let him breathe, he gave her a curious look knowing the vial contained nothing to help him. She stared into his eyes a moment more, hoping to get her meaning across.

On the next tip of his head, as he poured the contents into his mouth, she leaned close to his ear, "Get this to the Renegades—to Larn, in Mirtain."

She straightened and as she ran her hands down his arms as though checking for any other signs of injury, she traded the vial for the small piece of paper into his ready hands. Squeezing his fingers, she made one final inspection and noticed the difference in his eyes, a glimmer of something she had not seen in him a moment ago.

Umbris stepped back. "That should keep him alive long enough to reach Alesmann," she said to the soldiers. She left without a backward glance until she blended with the shadows.

As she hurriedly climbed the stairs to the Aurore Wing she realized what it was she had seen in the boy's eyes. It was what Larn must have seen in her—a small glimpse of something beyond the darkness of the world.

Hope.

The boy had lost everything, but she had just given him a reason to keep going. She sent a silent prayer above for him to reach Mirtain, her thoughts swirling around that one thought—hope.

Oh, how much she needed it too.

CHAPTER 52

Days of hard riding in the sharp air across the northernlands and into Excelsis Bestia had left Larn's skin stinging and chapped. His days in the southern lands had made him weak, and he told Anise just as much. She hadn't responded, aside from a slight chuckle before him.

In the days of travel, conversation had been limited, all of their energy focused on gaining distance. Though words were short, something had changed between them. He wasn't sure if it was the dance, though what had made him do such a thing he couldn't say.

Well he could, he just wouldn't give voice to the thoughts.

As they moved across the frozen valley, he'd pieced together their plans, but all too often his thoughts had wandered to the small woman before him. Larn never could have imagined how much warmer it was to ride with her, how much more he enjoyed the journey.

Shaking his head, he scanned the crimson horizon, strips of deep red melding with the frozen land like blood on wool.

"Is that it?" Ansie asked, her first words in hours.

Kirath lingered in the distance. From their vantage point along one of the mountains, he scanned the outskirts of the teeming village. Well, village was probably the wrong word, for it was more of a town with thriving markets, inns, and stables for travelers, a healer's wing, and of course the main focal point, Lord Duggard's manor, and workshop. The man was an inventor, a maker of all things new. Larn had spent many nights listening to Duggard brag of his latest ventures.

It was rumored that the locoven was his invention—a line of multiple wagons that were joined together and armed with sails, where beneath their wheels were tracks and slaves would pull on levers to make the cart shoot across the land, faster than any horse. The first track to ever be laid was between Kirath and Bastion Nocta, yet another tie between the Regent and Lord Duggard.

Larn clicked at Tympmor and nudged him forward. They would spend the night in one of the rundown stables on the outskirts of Kirath. Many a time he'd sought refuge there, tucked away in the shadows. In the cold, they would easily be forgotten.

The wind whipped by, stirring the loose tendrils of Ansie's hair as they dismounted and snuck into the stall. Off in the distance, merriment and music echoed from the hub of Kirath. As much as Duggard bragged about his inventions, he bragged about his parties more. As though hearing Larn's thoughts, a light-cracker exploded across the sky—a burst of bright green spanning beneath the stars until it disappeared. Another shot into the air, a short whistle in the wind, before it cracked with a boom and lit with blue sparks.

"That should help me sleep," Ansie muttered under her breath as she settled into the back of a stall. Larn smiled to himself, knowing she'd said the words under her breath. She did that a lot, forgetting he heard every bit of it.

As he hurried to ready Tympmor for the night, he glanced in the other stalls. Two other horses were already sleeping, their heads dipping low. If anyone happened to enter the stable, they would hardly be able to make out Tympmor's sleek back in the shadows, and if they did, payment for their stay was already resting in the tin outside.

Tossing Ansie an extra blanket, she shivered, trying to wrap it around her as quickly as possible. Though the journey had been long, she hadn't complained once about the cold. Her patched, red cheeks and runny nose spoke enough for her.

Looking up, she caught him staring. He smirked.

She opened one side of the blanket to him, and he settled next to her, their shoulders touching. It only took a moment of adjusting before he leaned his head back against the worn stonewall. After constantly moving in the saddle, it felt wonderful to remain still. Each breath a blessing.

A shiver ran through Ansie's body, he peeked at her, wondering if she had any idea how her hair stuck out in all sorts of angles, as though the air had frozen it in place. A breath clouded around her lips, to only dissipate a moment later.

A boom from a light-cracker trembled behind the creaking stable walls.

"I don't know if I'm ready for tomorrow," Ansie spoke softly, leaning into him slightly. He wondered if she noticed how she often did that, lean closer to someone when speaking, as though she wanted to communicate more than her words. So many times she had pressed her back against his chest as they rode across the frozen land, her warmth seeping into him.

Shifting beneath the blanket, he wrapped his arm around her shoulders and drew her close. She shivered and pulled the blanket tight around them both.

"Those masks do look uncomfortable," he finally said.

She giggled and nodded, though her mask was much smaller, with feathers and beading lining the top of the half-mask. It looked ridiculously uncomfortable to him. He wondered what she thought of their disguise.

More than once he'd let his mind wander, wondering just what she would look like in the deep blue gown, and tight corset. In all their time together he'd never seen her in anything but the dingy pants and shirt she now wore. When they'd danced together in Initium, for a moment he'd had a glimpse of the woman she was. Spinning in his arms, twirling as he released her, and caught her once more.

Iarn still wasn't quite sure what had come over him that night. He'd been frustrated with her, ready to continue their argument when he'd seen her dancing. She was unaware of how long he'd watched her, that soft mournful smile on her face. In that moment he'd known he would do whatever it took for her to lose the longing in those warm eyes.

"Shouldn't be too difficult to stay in disguise," she breathed, bringing him back to the stable.

"We'll only have to wear them for a few hours," he offered.

"True enough." she sighed and he ran through their plans once more. Getting into the festival wouldn't be too difficult, but passing for Gallians would prove challenging. Larn knew Lord Duggard well enough to know he graciously hosted a festival for all of Kirath, but only the elite would be allowed near his manor. And that was precisely where they needed to be.

"I think my toes are frozen," Ansie whispered, digging her boots beneath the straw.

He smiled. "Mine too."

"Aren't you used to this?"

"I think 'enduring it' would be a better way of saying it."

"Oh," she said.

He glanced down, not used to seeing her face after so many days in the saddle. Her nose was nearly the color of her hair, and her cheeks were parched from windburn. She looked cold, if such a thing were possible. He was certain if she dared to touch him with her fingers, they would be as chilled as the frozen ground outside.

"So tell me," she said, shifting in the straw to wrap the blanket more fully around them, "have you been here before?"

"This stall?" He shook his head. "No, normally I take up lodgings in the one next door. Very cozy, actually. It had fine, fresh straw, and this wonderful smell of horse manure along with rotten oats in a barrel."

"That sounds lovely," she said around a yawn. She raised her hands before her, rubbing them together and breathing on them—something she had done numerous times on their journey. He watched as she worked them back and forth.

"I've actually been here many times. I've visited most of the taverns, that's where you can sometimes pick up the best bits of gossip, and I've been inside Lord Duggard's manor multiple times. Although he only thinks I've been there once." He winked when she looked up. "I'm good at picking a lock." She laughed. "I've also been allowed a peek into his workshop where he supposedly invents things, but no one is ever allowed in."

"That's tempting," she grinned.

"Exactly. Oh, and I've mingled with some local Gallian families, they find me quite exotic, but I'm only able to pull that ruse off if I go as the servant of one of my men."

"Which one?"

"Heben, I think you met him."

She nodded.

"He's quick on his feet and can adapt to most situations. Some of my other men don't do so well." He smiled to himself thinking of Pike. Though he trusted Pike with his life, he was less than skilled when it came to improvisation.

After a moment of silence, Ansie looked up at him—her brown eyes warming him. "Do you miss this?"

"Miss what?"

"The cold, working alone."

"I actually never worked entirely alone—I always had partners," he corrected. "And as for the cold, I always know I can come back and feel it whenever I want."

"So you don't miss it?" she asked.

"Not entirely." He shifted, the movement jostling both of them a bit. "I never thought I'd say this, but I actually enjoyed the warmer climate in Mirtain."

"That's because you haven't been there in the hot seasons," she countered. "It sounds wonderful now, but there are some days when the heat is so bad all you want to do is to take off all your clothes just to feel some bit of breeze on your skin."

"A pleasing thought," he said, unable to stop himself as the image danced in his mind. She nudged his side. "I'm guessing the southern lands are littered with fields full of naked people?" A smile split over her rosy cheeks and she bit her chapped lip to keep from laughing. "I'll have to plan a visit then, and make sure it's quite hot when I arrive."

She sighed. "You really should. We discussed working naked once, and I was all for it," he was already laughing, "but then I realized the sunburn would be too much. I mean, just thinking of having to bend over so many times, the sun would have scorched my—shhh," she chastised him.

He tried to stop, truly he did, but the image she conjured was too hilarious. She joined in, her little snorts of laughter behind her hand making it all the harder to stop. Tears leaked from her eyes when she looked back up at him. He sucked in a breath, his sides hurting.

How was it that there was so much warmth in laughter? He could hardly feel the cold whistling between the poorly constructed planks.

"Shhh," she chided again and began to whisper. "After work, we used to go down to this small riverbed, well, more of a large creek, but there was a little pool at the end where you could walk all the way into the water until you couldn't touch the bottom. Or at least I couldn't." She made a disgruntled face as if the world was to blame for her lack of height.

"It was tucked into this little corner of the forest, almost like a secret from the village." She pushed a stray chunk of hair from her face. "Sometimes, we would go there after a long hot day of work, but only in the middle of the night when Hernan's soldiers were less likely to spot us."

"Risk-taker," he said matter of factly, recognizing that part of himself in her.

She nodded, growing solemn. He wondered what he'd said to cause her smile to fall.

"I was."

There was something regretful in those words. She turned toward him, the six freckles caressing her right eye making a perfect crescent-like sliver of moonlight in the dark.

"I was always the one to push the laws, to see how far I could go before getting caught. And I never really did, get caught, I mean. Kata was the rule follower. Or, I thought she was."

He waited for her to say more, but she didn't.

What was this hold Kata had on both Willem and Ansie? They seemed unable to forget her. In the few times he had heard the dead girl's name, he'd begun to get an idea of her character. Somehow both Ansie and Willem seemed to remember the smallest things about her—the little details which only came with knowing someone intimately. It wasn't simply hearing a person's thoughts or dreams, but rather watching the way a person moved, the way they lived, the way they breathed.

Willem and Ansie knew the myriad faces of Kata, and Larn had no doubt that if he asked how she would have responded to a question, they would know. There was a sense of comfort when they spoke of her, almost as though with her, they'd felt peace. A part of Larn wished he'd met her, while the other part often wondered if they'd truly known the real Kata.

From Jethron's report, he and Kata had been making their secret plans for over a year before Lord Hernan found out. Was everything about Kata a lie?

"You know, Kata was the first girl in the village to talk to me." Ansie pulled him from his thoughts, leaning her head back against the wall. Her thick braid was a mess, long wisps having fallen out from their ride. She looked completely windswept, like she'd been caught in a blizzard.

"When?" he asked.

"When I first arrived," she explained.

He waited for her to continue, a part of him knowing they should let their words fall away and drift off to sleep, the other part wide-eyed and waiting. She'd never told him anything of her past before Mirtain. "You never did tell me how you became Willem's ward."

She stared at the stall dooe, the brown in her eyes reminding him of mulled cider. "I didn't?" she swallowed, her throat bobbing.

He shook his head. "You only said it was a long story."

In some way, he felt as though they were back in that hallway of Lord Hernan's manor. He'd surprised even himself that night, inviting Ansie to sit with him. It all seemed so long ago—so much had changed.

"It is a long story," she mused.

"And?"

"I don't really like to talk about it," she let the words hang in the air between them and he said nothing, hoping she would continue. With a deep breath, a small cloud of air puffed before her. "Willem found me in the woods."

Her voice was softer now, vulnerable, reminding him how young she was. He often forgot that in light of her courage when faced with danger.

"I was only seven at the time," she paused. "I can still remember it as if it happened yesterday." Her voice faded, and he wondered what she was really seeing before her. "It was foggy, a cold morning, but nothing like this." She blinked. "I was lying in the dirt, it got stuck under my nails. I remember thinking I would have to wash them. I was there for a long time before Willem found me. He was hunting, and didn't say a word as he wrapped his jacket over my ruined dress and carried me out of the forest to the cottage. He didn't even tell me his name until Lord Hernan came demanding Willem give me to him."

A spike of trepidation shot through Larn. He'd only seen the man once, but after hearing from both Jethron and Willem, he knew the vile things that ran through that man's mind.

"Willem refused and instead Lord Hernan bargained with him." She glanced up, "Willem traded his freedom to keep me safe. For years he endured Hernan's near constant threats and demands, anything that would gain him wealth." She shook her head. "One time I asked Willem why he did it, and he said 'Because I can.'"

That sounded like Willem. Always practical.

"It took Willem nearly a year to tell me that he'd lost his mother, and he knew I had no family, they were all gone, and in that, we understood one another." Her face pinched in a pained sort of way on the last word. "We found each other when we needed it most, and I guess—made a family of sorts."

She'd had a family? Larn nodded at her words, his mind churning through the possibilities of it all. How had she ended up in the woods? His arm tightened around her and she didn't seem to object.

He'd heard the story of Willem finding her and taking her to the cottage. While in Mirtain he'd asked more than a few of the villagers to confirm the stories, but no one knew anything more about her. He idly wondered if she remembered. But that downturn of her mouth spoke volumes.

She remembered all of it. The girl beside him who sometimes seemed to share all of herself was suddenly a mystery to him.

What happened to you? he wondered, looking down at her.

She glanced up again, and this time pasted a smile on her face. It didn't reach her eyes.

"I don't think that's the entire story," he said.

"It isn't."

"You won't tell me the rest?"

Her eyes searched his gaze, watching him. He held perfectly still, hoping the shadows that traced across her gaze were more from the dark of night than memory. But he knew the answer to that question already.

"Not right now," she turned away. A light-cracker boomed outside. "Besides, no one knows the whole story."

Her words carried enough weight. Not even Willem knew everything that had happened. And so, he wouldn't either. She had gently put him in his place.

He reached into his pocket and pulled out the gift he'd been carrying for so long. Why he hadn't given it to her until now, he didn't know. He offered it to her, the blanket breaking apart.

"How?" she asked, staring at the verral claw in his hand. It was the same claw that had dug into her shoulder and left the scar she would carry for the rest of her days.

"When I went to Flocorna, I had it cut and a hole driven through it. I thought you might like it."

She took the claw from his hand and held it up to what little light was in the stable. She bit her lip as she stared at it, and he wondered if she was remembering the pain when it had dug into her shoulder.

He'd had it cut to make more manageable. It now had less of a curve and instead of being the size of her entire palm; it was the length of her longest finger. She would be able to wear it around her neck by the leather string now attached to it.

Shifting beneath the blanket, she passed the necklace over her head and let the claw hang down on her chest. The string was a bit long, long enough to reach into the neckline of her shirt, but she didn't seem to mind.

"Now I can surprise my enemies," she said, a smile in her voice, still fingering the claw.

He swallowed watching her. "I thought it might remind you of how brave you are."

She looked up at him then, searching. He wondered what ran through her mind and turned away, not wanting her to know what he was thinking. He didn't want to her to know that with her tucked up against his side, he was more comfortable than he'd been in ages. For once he felt at home.

It grew quiet between them, and she leaned more heavily against his side He would be lying if he said he wasn't tired. The many hours in the saddle and remaining alert had worn him down, more than he cared to admit.

As though hearing his thoughts, she yawned making him pull in a deep breath of his own.

"Larn?" she asked, groggy.

"Hmm?" he asked, his eyes closed as he listened to the wind whipping by outside.

"How come you got so upset when Dur and Fer talked about the wolves?"

"I wasn't upset," he said.

"Hmm," she made a disapproving sound. She shivered, and he linked his arms together around her body. There beneath the blanket, the warmth of their bodies began to permeate the frigid existence they now endured.

Before them, Ansie's hands tightened on the blanket, and she settled her head onto his chest. He felt his own heartbeat in his throat.

"You were angry," she said, around another yawn. Stubborn as always.

"Not angry," he muttered, "just worried." Worried she would find out the truth.

She said nothing more and he didn't budge. It wasn't long before he felt her head grow heavier on his chest, and she unconsciously tucked herself closer to him.

He wondered if she would say anything in her sleep tonight, her little habit of muttering nonsensical words that were almost impossible to hear, even for him, made him all the more curious about what went on behind those enticing eyes of hers.

For a moment he contemplated staying awake. He knew the magic of this night would disappear with the rising of the sun. Holding her close, he closed his eyes.

"Well?" Ansie asked, holding her arms out to her sides for approval.

Larn nodded. "That should do the trick."

She smiled and looked back down at the midnight-blue dress, her hands smoothing over the front. It was wrinkled in some places, he would admit, but there was nothing to be done considering they had spent the night in the stables. She had dropped the verral necklace down within the bodice of her gown, the sight accentuating her curves which he'd noticed before—but not like this. He quickly looked away, at least she was playing her part, no one from Mirtain would even recognize her.

She was suddenly a mystery to him, the ebony curls of the wig framing her face. The gilded mask hid her eyes, though the feathers arched beautifully over her head. Larn gave a small whistle and she blushed—a pleasing sight to remind him she was still Ansie.

"Do you have your mask?" she asked.

He nodded. The smiling face looked up at him from his hands.

Half of the mask was lined with gold, deep ebony surrounded the eyes and covered the other half of the face. The lips which arched at an impossible angle into a gleaming smile were painted in deep gold. If he was being honest, the mask was just odd enough to be a bit frightening.

Suddenly, Ansie was before him, looking down at the mask in his hands. "It really is terrifying, isn't it? Lucky for you, you don't have to look at it all night."

The side of his mouth lifted. "True enough."

They awakened to the relief of warm sunlight spilling through the wooden slats of the stables, and with its arrival, the closeness of night disappeared. Ansie moved away from him and spent the rest of the day out of reach. Without the excuse for bodily warmth, it didn't make sense for Larn to keep holding her, but that didn't mean he had to like it.

More than once he'd had to stop his thoughts—he was becoming a fool when it came to her.

He reminded himself more than once he wasn't the sort of man to get attached to anyone. And he would keep on reminding himself for as long as it took.

"Are you ready?" Ansie asked, looking nothing like the girl he had come to know. He couldn't help wondering what she would look like if her red hair was free, the thick auburn waves settled against the golden lace and deep blue of the dress would be enough to set his heart to racing. He was already struggling as it was.

Cursing himself, he turned away from her to strap on the mask. "Yes," he said, tucking the last dagger into his boots.

"You look rather smashing, my lord," Ansie gave a mock curtsy. She seemed to be unaffected by their embrace last night. The thought set him back a bit.

He quirked a grin she couldn't see, "Don't I always?"

Far in the distance, he could hear the beginnings of merriment. Villagers calling to one another, more than one voice already slurred. He had been to more than a few Joute Deliverance celebrations before, and often times festival-goers would forgo the privilege of changing and would remain in the same clothes for a week—regardless of spilled drink.

"Shall we?" he asked, offering her his arm.

She nodded and looped her hand around his elbow as they stepped out of the stable and onto the patched, worn road. If anyone had been watching, they would have only seen an amorous couple exit a stable and think nothing more of it.

Torches lit their path, the closer they got to the village square. Ansie's breaths began to come in short gasps and her head turned in every direction to take in the sights around her. Though Larn knew she was playing her part as an eccentric lady, the way she stared into shop windows as they passed by nearly made him laugh. She was enjoying this more than she would care to admit later.

A bubble of warmth reached them as they stepped into the main square of Kirath. Guests began to shed their cloaks and sigh in warmth and delirious excitement as they purchased mugs of fermented cider and wine. Giant poles lined the square, their sides dotted with holes where heat poured into the open air.

Larn had seen these innovations in use once before. Lord Duggard had invented them by digging a tunnel of furnaces underneath the square. Beneath the feet of the festivities were servants working to heat the near fifty furnaces, each one coinciding with a pole. The result was an outdoor town square, heated like that of a ballroom.

Ansie's fingers on his arm relaxed in the warmth. All through the night while holding her, her body had remained stiff, often shivering. At least now, some bit of warmth was enough to awaken her senses.

Dresses of every color imaginable passed before them. Some more exquisite than others, the Gallian women decorated in jewels and so much finery their necks seemed to droop beneath the weight of necklaces. One lady passed them, her earrings reaching to her elbows, Ansie stared as she walked by.

"Try to remember who you are," he whispered in her ear, caressing her cheek—only playing his part of course. "You're used to these sorts of things."

She nodded and tipped her chin up in the perfect imitation of a Gallian who smelled something rather horrible beneath her feet. "Yes, darling."

Larn gave her hand a pat in approval. Guiding her through the rest of the crushing crowd, they passed by men in flamboyant colored jackets, high stockings, and heeled shoes. It was said to be the fashion in Bastion Nocta, though Larn was pleased some men still wore boots like his own.

Gabrella knew better than to give him heeled shoes. He had enough to deal with when it came to the incredible number of buttons lining his jacket. Why Gallians always had so many buttons, he never could understand.

"Up there," he said, pulling Ansie off to the side, his head angled in the direction of Lord Duggard's manor.

At the end of the square was a raised patio, Gallian soldiers standing guard at the bottom of the staircase. Gallian men and women passed by the guards, some holding masks to their faces, while others hardly looked human their costumes were so exquisite. Ansie gasped as a man wearing a pig mask passed by, his teeth tearing into what appeared to be mutton, juice running down his fingers and chest—the rest of him hardly dressed.

"Lovely," Larn muttered, the tangy spice of charred meat lifting in the air.

Passing over the bricks and through the crowd, they neared the raised patio where Larn thought he heard Lord Duggard's booming voice. Glancing to the right and left, he spotted Gallian soldiers lining the outer edges of the square.

"Remember," Larn leaned forward to whisper in her ear. "Hide in plain sight."

Ansie smiled prettily, already playing the part of the doting wife and highborn lady. Only just this morning Larn had wondered how the girl who had ridden on the back of a *simian* was going to transform into a Gallian lady. It seemed he had no reason to worry.

Four Gallian soldiers stood at the bottom of the pale-stone staircase, their eyes continually scanning the crowd. He felt Ansie's hand tighten even more on his arm—no doubt her thoughts on their last run-in with Gallian soldiers. The ruins of Initium seemed so long ago.

They passed up the stairs and onto the platform where two empty fountains stood on either side, both decorated with the scantily draped forms of a man and woman wrapped in an intimate embrace. Beneath the fountain, some couples were demonstrating their amorous attentions for one another. Beside him, Ansie kept her eyes carefully averted—what he could see of her cheeks flamed in a blush.

In the midst of the manor, they were embraced into a higher class of society. The dresses more elegant, the men wearing longer coats and buttons shining in the torchlight. Large pits were lit with flames before the manor, the tongues of fire licking at the butchered pigs twisting on a spit. The smoke billowed up to the sky, at times turning one direction and then another.

Maneuvering through the crowd, Larn stopped every now and again as though something drew his attention until he spotted Lord Duggard not far from where they stood.

"Do you see the cake over there along the main table," he said, turning to face Ansie completely. Again, seeing the dark wig took him off guard.

"Yes, darling," she said and swayed a bit to the music playing softly in the air. "Would you mind fetching me another drink?" she asked, for the benefit of anyone listening.

He smiled beneath his mask, she was playing her part remarkably well. "Yes, but only one more, my dear."

"Oh," she gave him a playful swat, but allowed him to lead her closer to Lord Duggard and his posy of groveling listeners.

"I do believe you're mistaken!" Lord Duggard exclaimed, and though he didn't look, Larn could imagine the way the man's hands fluttered across his hulking form. "I've heard no such thing!"

Larn shifted closer, allowing Ansie to sway to the music as though she was slightly intoxicated and enjoying herself.

"It's all that is heard!" Another man declared in clear annoyance. Often logic did nothing to persuade the Gallian lord. "In every village from here all the way to Bastion Nocta itself, the rumor is they're on the move. The Renegades are moving North."

"Ridiculous," Lord Duggard said, and Larn chanced a glance. If it was possible, the girth of the lord's belly had enlargened in the months since he last saw him. A golden sash accentuated the portents of his stomach, where spindly legs thrust toward the ground. In one hand Duggard held a clear glass, the deep crimson liquid inside sloshing as he gestured. In his other portly palm was his mask, the image of a laughing jester held upon a stick.

"Whether it is ridiculous or not, doesn't matter," Lord Duggard continued and whacked his companion on the arm.

Larn waited for the right moment, carefully anticipating when he could join the men in their dalliance of conversation. His heart thrummed in his chest, the thrill of hidden words making him come alive. Stepping carefully to his right, he drew back a moment—always securing his borders. He glanced toward the stairs they had only recently ascended. All four Gallian soldiers had left their positions.

Something was wrong. He didn't know if it was instinct, or something greater—some force of nature—or perhaps the Espiritu that Dur and Fer claimed to believe in, but whatever it was he knew they were in danger.

Ansie was still swaying to the music when he grasped her arm and eased her close to him, a lover's embrace others would ignore. "Listen to me," he whispered and she giggled, though the sound was off. "They're looking for us."

He cursed himself, realizing all too suddenly how much danger they might be in. Shaking the thought from his mind, he forced himself to remain calm, though every sense was on alert.

Ansie ran her fingers into his hair and leaned back to look up at him, her smile tight. "But what about dancing?" she asked, the faint hint of the wine on her breath reaching him. She pointed in the direction of a large group of dancing couples on a makeshift floor, the perfect excuse to watch the soldiers moving farther into the crowd. She was clever.

"We might not have the chance tonight."

"You won't leave me alone?" she asked, "To dance?"

"Of course not, my dear," he said and leaned in to give her a small chuck beneath her chin. His heart was hammering madly now. The soldiers were moving closer, searching each masked face. He drew her into the dance. "I'm going to hold you, tight," he whispered, "after they pass by, we'll leave."

She smiled, but he could see the fear lining her eyes beneath the shadows of her mask. Her cold fingers trembled against his chest.

He held her steady gazing into her eyes, no longer listening to his own unsteady breaths, but hearing the words of those around him.

The soldiers passed, still scanning the crowd. He moved. "Walk to the stairs, feigning a headache, I'll follow. If they see both of us move now, they'll know. Leave the square. I'll find you."

She patted the cheek of his mask and made a playful gesture. "Don't worry," she leaned in, placing a kiss beneath his chin, "I'll keep my hood up." Slipping into the crowd, she moved away from him and his arms felt suddenly empty.

Her words rang in his mind. She would keep herself safe at all costs, the guise would never slip. He sucked in another breath, the sound odd beneath his mask.

Glancing to the side, he no longer saw the soldiers, and afforded himself the chance to grab a glass of wine off a passing tray. It was only by a matter of sheer force that he didn't watch Ansie retreat.

They should never have come here. Every instinct that had kept him alive told him this was wrong. Why hadn't he noticed it before?

"You see," Lord Duggard's voice reached him, "I don't need to worry about these rumors of the Renegades. Nor the threats the Regent has sent about my allegiance. It's all just a matter of leverage, and I have exactly what he needs, right here."

Larn chanced a glance to his left, finding Lord Duggard looking directly at him. The man gave him a nod, the large head bobbing and making the two extra chins he had wrinkle for a moment.

A small scream rang out, and then another, different from the first.

Ansie!

He spun, looking for her in the crowd, his eyes immediately finding two women holding their heads where the soldiers nearby were pulling at hair in search of a wig. His heart leapt in his throat and he cursed himself to the underworld below as his mind screamed for him to do something.

He took a step and suddenly two soldiers were before him, swords drawn. Some of the crowd shouted, women screaming as they were shoved out of the way and into the arms of Gallian men.

Whipping out his two daggers, he approached the swordsmen. He saw their movements as if from outside his body, his every thought solely focused on Ansie.

He moved like a shadow passing over rock, darting beneath the swings of the Gallian swords with practiced ease. He was water passing through them, his every move determined to reach her.

Knocking one of the swords into the crowd, he threw the first soldier down to the ground, keeping the other at bay with a kick to the man's chest. It only took a swift slice to the gut and then a stab to the shoulder of the other to get them to back down.

He charged into the quickly parting crowd, frantically searching. It had only been a few seconds, she couldn't be far.

Then he spotted her.

Red hair declaring her betrayal to the realm, a soldier had her wrapped in his arms, a knife at her throat. He stopped. All thought, all feeling shuttering to a halt.

Never before had he felt so uncertain. So lost as to what to do. He wanted to run to her, save her, wrap her in his arms, but he couldn't move. Everything inside him screamed for him to do something, anything, to get her away from that blade.

His eyes found hers, her mask had fallen off in her struggle with the soldier. They were kindled with the same fire he had seen the day she had come charging into the battle on the back of a *simian*.

"Go," she breathed, knowing he would hear. "You'll find me."

One instant was all it took, but he knew he had no choice.

Swinging back around, he took down two soldiers who had been charging at him from behind. Knocking them aside, he ran for the manor, knowing his way through the hallways and rooms. He broke through a door, the Gallians sprinting after him. Arrows flew past his head, but they seemed to not want to hit him, only frighten him into surrender.

But he was Larn, marked by the wolf. Surrender wasn't an option.

Sprinting down halls, he kicked out a window and scaled the outer wall to the roof. He had made these moves numerous times before and it was only a simple matter of weeding his way down the window ledges to the ground before he took off along the outside of the square, darting behind buildings and hiding in the shadows until the shouts were far behind.

He sprinted to the small outcrop where Tympmor waited. He was already saddled and seemed to sense Larn's need. The black steed shot through the trees only to be pulled in as Larn watched the soldiers span out of Kirath and into the surrounding mountains.

Though the thought nearly made him sick, he would have to lay low for the time being.

Through the night the shouts and calls of the soldiers grew more frustrated as they failed to find him. At any other time, Larn would have gloated, but without Ansie by his side, the action had lost all meaning.

Over and over again he ran through plans and tactics, trying to figure out some way to rescue her. But alone he wouldn't be able to. Where was Pike when he needed him?

He cursed as he waited. And cursed again when they brought her out of Kirath.

There she was, chained in a cart upon the locoven.

It was immediate. That one glimpse of her and he knew his heart was no longer his own. Perhaps she had stolen it long before and he simply hadn't noticed.

Fighting down the panic, he counted twelve soldiers surrounding her cage, and when the shout from the leader rang through the air, Larn almost cried out. They were taking her from him.

A drum sounded and the slaves along the tracks pushed backward with their legs moving in synchronization, their arms pulling on the levers. The wheels of the locoven turned, grinding at first, until the sails above opened.

The brisk wind of the north snapped the sails to their full expanse, and the wheels turned faster. Larn cast a prayer to the skies above. Somehow, someway, he would try and keep up—it would be nearly impossible.

Lord Duggard's final words had given him hope. The Regent wanted Ansie alive, so he had until Bastion Nocta to break her free.

As if sensing the challenge, Tympmor's legs trembled in anticipation beneath him. The locoven was already thundering across the frozen tundra, and Tympmor took the chase.

Together they would see Ansie safe—or die trying.

CHAPTER 53

Mitus's ears perked forward, hearing things beyond Willem. For a while now Willem had known they were getting close, the familiar dank mist of Mirtain Forest filling his nostrils long before they dipped beneath the trees. Memories drifted.

When they'd passed the abandoned stands of the Black Market, he'd told Mitus about the *simian*. It all seemed like a lifetime ago.

They had traveled as far and as fast as they could each day since leaving Initium, taking a path near the border of the Plenus Mountains so as to avoid detection from any Gallian patrols. In the end, they arrived in Mirtain Forest hungry and weary. Somehow Dur had been able to push through the hours of hard riding, his leg still healing. They were all eager to join the Renegades.

At least Sleeper and Muncher seemed to now accept Mitus. Of course, when they finally realized the *lioneth* wasn't going to eat them, and instead killed three wild cats that thought to make them an easy meal—their allegiance swayed.

They wasted no time on words, pushing toward Mirtain, and only stopping when absolutely necessary. More than once Mitus had grown uneasy at their lack of speed, his urgency setting Willem on edge.

It had taken time for Willem to grow used to the way Mitus's body shifted beneath him. Instead of the gentle rocking backward and forward of horse riding, he learned to maintain his seat as the flesh beneath him shifted from side to side—the heavy paws padding over the land.

With the thudding of those paws, his mind wandered. Wondering what was ahead, and fearing what he had left behind. As always, the thought of Ansie sent a tug of pain through his chest. Leaving her had been harder than he expected. Too often he drifted back to the first days when he found her and she slowly began to integrate herself into his life.

But he was learning to let go. In all things, let go.

A small rumble rippled beneath the golden fur of Mitus. The distant murmur of male voices drifted through the trees.

Easy now, Willem directed his thoughts and Mitus responded with a deep rumble in his chest. The Espiritu mingled between them, sparks ready to ignite when the battle finally arrived.

Standing at the same height as a horse, Willem felt anything but dwarfed by Dur and Fer. In fact, he was eye level with the Chroniclers, and with Mitus's large head and mane, he knew they were a terrifying sight to behold.

Hold, Mitus. He sent the words to him mentally and the heavy mane shook before him in annoyance. Willem grinned. Mitus was itching for a fight—for something other than this endless travel.

Far in the distance a row of men suddenly formed, their voices fading into the morning air as Mitus padded closer, each step a thud, his head bobbing. The men stared, their eyes wide, terrified, more than one clutching his chest. Willem wondered if they even saw him astride Mitus's back, or if their eyes could only behold the Animle creature.

One of the men, who Willem immediately recognized, dropped to his knees in reverence.

"No need for that, Chet," Willem beckoned his friend with a grin, "I'm not the Regent."

A few chortles broke the silence as the men huddled together, their eyes never leaving Mitus. Willem remembered all too well the first time he had looked upon the golden face, those eyes perfectly outlined with black fur, to make his majesty appear all the brighter.

Swinging off of Mitus's back, Willem stood with the *lioneth's* head nearly resting on his shoulder. He reached beneath his chin, scratching the spot he knew Mitus loved.

"Take us to Girshon," he said nodding in the direction of Dur and Fer, who the men were just now beginning to notice.

They emerged from the forest and crossed over the ground where the wire fence had always marked the boundary. But it was no more. Only deep holes in the ground remained as evidence of what had once stood there.

They crossed by the field where the first battle had taken place, but Willem hardly recognized it. Tents and makeshift lean-tos were erected all over the field—hundreds upon hundreds of men, women and young boys watching him as he walked by with Mitus.

He stared. Their numbers far exceeded his hopes.

A part of him wanted to cower, to pull away and walk to his abandoned cottage, to leave all of this behind. After so many weeks of trying to remain hidden, he felt naked in the sight of so many.

Mitus swung his enormous head into Willem's shoulder making him stumble. The golden eyes were on him, somehow knowing what he had been thinking. A thrum strung between them, a sort of anxious pulsing that told Willem the Espiritu was at work.

It had surprised Willem more than once after waking from what he'd thought was a dream in Initium. Now he wasn't so sure if it was. Even thinking of his mother tightened his throat, but not with the pain he used to feel, but instead with longing for what was to come.

Stay close, he spoke silently to Mitus, their connection growing stronger each day. Mitus couldn't hear all of his thoughts, only the ones Willem chose to direct to him. But more and more Willem got the sense Mitus felt the same things he did, the urgency, the anticipation. In some way, they were bonded by a sixth sense.

Simul ad mortem, Larn had called it. Connected until death.

"So it's true!" A voice called out and the hulking form of Girshon, no longer wrapped in a fur cloak, walked toward them.

It seemed as though years had passed since Willem last walked by the town square—so many memories drifting in the wind, ghosts of a thought.

The Renegade leader stopped before them, his eyes shifting between their entire group. Fer waved a hand and smiled.

"Brother, I think we've come to the right place."

Dur grumbled something under his breath that no one understood. A small crowd had gathered around them, word spreading quickly throughout the village.

Girshon looked Willem up and down, then to Dur and Fer and back again. "And these men are?"

"The missing Chroniclers," Willem confirmed. Girshon stared at them in wonder.

"The ones Larn was searching for," it was more statement than question. Willem wondered if Larn had ever heard that hint of pride in Girshon's voice.

"Your rescuers happened to stumble across us, or we stumbled across them." Fer shrugged. "Call it a divine meeting set by the Espiritu."

That made the Renegade leaders eyebrows raise. He glanced at Willem who only nodded.

"Where are Larn and Ansie?" he asked.

"We split up in Initium, they headed north."

"North? What for?"

Willem quickly explained the tip Larn had received in Flocorna, a hunch that Lord Duggard might be hiding something.

Girshon gave a sharp laugh and shook his head. "Duggard is too loose with his tongue. Larn always gets something of use." He ran a dark hand over his shaved head. "And Ansie, has she...?" He let the question hang in the air.

"Not yet," Fer said with all due confidence. Willem's chest rose with pride. To think his Ansie would be chosen as an Animle as well was enough to make him prouder than ever. Maybe, just maybe, when she returned to Mirtain, she wouldn't be alone—a fierce Animle warrior at her side.

"Well," the Renegade leader waved an arm behind him, "come with me. I'm sure you're tired after your journey."

Willem nodded and allowed the man to lead them further along the square until they were walking up the steps outside Lord Hernan's manor. Never before had he entered the doors on his own terms.

"We set up headquarters in here," Girshon explained after they had walked up a staircase and down a carpeted hallway, Willem knew all too well. To his great relief, the room they entered was not Lord Hernan's study.

They entered a room Willem had never visited before, the brown floors were patched, revealing a dark rectangle of wood where a rug had at one time rested. The outer edges of the original wood were worn and lightened with time.

A long table stood in the center of the room littered with papers and maps, the heavy curtains cast open for the sunlight to pour in through giant windows, an empty hearth standing at the back of the room. Aside from the table, all other furniture had been removed.

"You chose not to use Hernan's study," Willem mused. It was lighter in here, fresher, as though the windows had been open recently. Girshon was not a man to be trapped inside, it only made sense he would choose a room not littered with the pungent sweet scent of Hernan's perfume.

"I prefer to keep away from the places he frequented. I wanted to set up my headquarters in the fields, but my men insisted I keep this room for my personal use, more for their annoyance in chasing down maps in the fields than anything else. As far as I'm concerned, I would rather burn this manor to the ground."

The problem seemed to have continued in the open room, various rocks laying on maps and scattered around the table. Willem glanced to the windows; it was the first time he'd been inside, completely surrounded by walls and glass since leaving Alesmann.

"What can you tell me about the state of the realm?" Girshon asked, leaning over the table.

"We don't know much," he admitted. "We ran into a couple of patrols, and Nexen, but our contact with them was short. We've hardly heard anything since leaving."

"And where were these patrols?" the leader looked over the map, his dark hand hovering over Mirtain.

"The first was in Alesmann. Larn seemed to know it." Girshon marked the village, where they had killed three Nexen, with a small rock and continued to lay down pebbles as Willem ran through the details of Kraven Hall, rescuing Dur and Fer, and reaching Initium. He didn't, however, relate their travels through the caves, following the filumen. He'd let Larn decide if the leader needed to know.

Off to the side, Dur and Fer didn't say a word, their arms crossed over their thin chests in concentration. With one glance from Dur, Willem knew he was right not to relay everything. There would be time later.

When he finished, Girshon glanced up. "We've reached word the Regent is on the lookout for the three of you."

"We assumed as much."

"But he's missing names, at least we think he is. Further intelligence has been lacking of late."

"We assumed as much." Willem took a deep breath. "The numbers out there," he pointed toward the windows and the Anglan rebels, "where did they come from."

"News of the *simian* traveled fast."

"Have you had any casualties?"

"A few." The leader straightened. "Each man, woman, and boy is undergoing rigorous training. The younger girls are learning to mend wounds, a woman named Arta is teaching them." He sighed. "We are weak in skill, but they make up for it in heart. Freedom has a way of strengthening a person."

Willem nodded.

Mitus settled on the wooden floor with a huff. His weight shifted for a moment, a yawn revealing his overly large teeth that could snap through a man's torso. Willem smiled to himself, knowing Mitus was only trying to attract attention.

"We did have a small battle, more of a skirmish, really. It seems the Regent has finally accepted the fact that we're a threat. After news of Kraven Hall spread, he sent a regiment here to disband our forces. They were quickly defeated."

Willem glanced at the Chroniclers and Mitus. "Must have been the soldiers we saw three days ago."

Girshon nodded. "They left much too quickly for my liking. More of a scouting party than anything else."

Testing Mirtain's strength. Willem crossed his arms and stared at the table, the only sound the soft pants of Mitus. *Do you think they will be back?* He projected his thoughts toward him. Mitus turned to face him, the same conclusion forming in the *lioneth*.

"Will we be able to withstand an attack?" Willem asked.

"We have a chance," Girshon heaved. "But the next time he sends forces, it won't be to determine our strength. It will be to break it."

"Agreed," Dur said, stepping closer to the table, his limp more pronounced after so much travel. "The Regent has lost his chance to quell this rebellion without rumors spreading. We've backed him into a corner and the full force will hit soon."

Girshon's eyes narrowed, calculating. "Rumor says you both met him."

A fact, not a question. Dur stared back, unblinking.

Fer crossed to the window and gazed over the fields littered with tents. How many times had Lord Hernan stood in this very room, watching as his fields were worked? How many times had he leered over Willem, holding all Willem held close as a threat?

A familiar shard of fury shoved its way into his gut, eating away at any peace he'd found. Leaning over the map, Willem hardly saw the worn lines of the creased parchment. Mitus snorted, the huff making all the men in the room jump.

Willem curbed his thoughts, somehow Mitus had known where his mind had turned.

Fer glanced between the two of them, the hint of a smile on his lips. Sometimes that knowing look of the younger Chronicler chilled Willem to the bones. It was the look of another world, of confidence founded in hope, and hope instilled in a power greater than all the realm had to offer.

Still looking at Mitus, Fer spoke, "The Regent is not one to take a challenge lightly. He will strive to end this rebellion by any means necessary."

Girshon stared at Fer, pondering. "Then it's a good thing we plan on meeting the challenge with all we have."

A rumble rose in Mitus's chest as his paws pushed against the creaking floorboards. The giant head turned back toward the open door of the room, Willem smiled to himself, needing to be free of the manor, of this prison.

"Your cottage is still empty if you have need," Girshon said as he left.

"Thank you, sir. But I'll be staying in camp." Willem said. He'd made up his mind long ago that it wouldn't be home if Ansie wasn't there. He could wait for her return, Larn would see her safe.

"Very well."

Willem nodded and left the room as a few men and women entered the space, their hands filled with papers of business. Their voices began to address Girshon before the door was even shut.

By the time they reached the square, a gathering of villagers spread out before them. Word of his return with a *lioneth* had spread. Every face was turned to him, their eyes wide as they took in Mitus walking by his side— those in the back craning their necks to get a glimpse they walked by.

He wanted to leave it all. To hop on Mitus's back and flee the village. But he couldn't because he had never seen such smiles on the faces of those he'd known for years. Their eyes gleaming with pride, with hope.

He glanced to his right where Mitus walked beside him and the big head dipped as though he understood. The weight of what was before him settled. The Animle of old were warriors, protectors, bearers of hope.

It was time he stopped hiding in the shadows.

A man parted from the crowd, stepping into their path. He chuckled, his voice and smile all too familiar. "Never thought I'd live to see this day."

"Hello, Jep," Willem said, grinning. "It's been some time."

"Aye," the man said and closed the distance between them, hugging him in greeting. "Come on, the children will want to see ya'." Willem nodded and followed Jep through the parting villagers. From somewhere behind, he heard Fer asking for assistance, and a woman came to help Dur.

Willem didn't dare look at the woman helping the Chroniclers into her home, she would see him healed, he knew it. But he couldn't look her in the eye, not yet.

The familiar clinging pull of the past threatened to grab hold of him. He fought it off. Maybe someday he would be able to see her again.

This used to be my home, he said to Mitus, distracting himself as they followed Jep across the land. *It feels different somehow.*

The *lioneth* rumbled a purr and nudged his shoulder gently.

Not just because you're here. He rolled his eyes.

How could he explain that he felt as though a piece of himself was missing? Or maybe it was the final returning home.

Ever since Kata and Jethron had been taken, he'd felt lost in this place. Now, suddenly, after so much time, he could breathe. It hadn't been the air in Initium, it'd been a change from within.

He filled his lungs and remained focused on the ground, even as Fer caught up to them.

"That woman said food was this way," Fer grumbled, pointing down the road. "Her food was only for the ailing. I guess starvation wasn't a good enough excuse. I should have attempted to faint."

Mitus huffed a sort of laugh.

They continued on, Willem smiling to himself. He didn't have to imagine Arta saying something like that. She had slapped his hand away from the table more than once as a child, a kind smile on her lips.

That smile had faded with time. Guilt cinched his stomach.

Somehow, he would manage to look her in the eye. They were Kata's eyes.

Soon, he would visit Kata's mother.

Jep's cabin was filled with more warmth than Willem remembered. There was a lightness to the atmosphere in the cottage, where a hearth breathed comforting flames, and wooden chairs rested, open and waiting. A large table sat in the center of the room dividing the cottage in half. Most of the family now gathered around it, and near the back of the cottage was an open doorframe leading to the flattened mattresses the family shared.

Upon entering a few hours earlier, Mitus had found a comfortable spot before the fire, lying down on the braided rug which was made from the children's old clothes—too tattered to give to others. Willem remembered when Nelna, Jep's wife, had first made it, so many years ago. Mitus seemed to be thoroughly enjoying himself as the two youngest of Jep's children, Emos and Ema, climbed on his back.

The table had been cleared of the meal, the best one Willem had eaten since leaving Mirtain. Each bite had settled pleasantly in his stomach, and for the first time in a long time, he felt himself relax. An answering rumble came from Mitus on the rug as he rested his head upon the floor and huffed. Ema giggled.

"We still work the fields," Jep was saying, "but it's different now. We work for our own. I've been given a plot of land and reap the benefits." He grinned. "We each give some to the Renegades, but it isn't even required. Makes me want to give more."

Willem nodded. If he had been here working the fields and had the option to give of his own free will, he would give and gladly.

It was just another change in many that Girshon had made since liberating Mirtain. After the first battle, he had set up camp in the fields and then reached out to the villagers to select men as representatives. Jep's eyes had teared up as he spoke of the twelve men who now worked to maintain order, thus allowing Girshon to focus on what was to come. It was a bold strategy, but one that made Willem like Girshon all the more. These people needed guidance, not dominion.

It was no wonder Mirtain was booming with volunteers, word of their liberation having spread throughout Autre Gallia. It seemed hundreds of volunteers were moving in daily.

"I've never owned any land in my life. Even this cottage was Hernan's and he could have kicked me out whenever he saw fit, but it's ours now." Jep looked up a Nelna, and she smiled. "We never thought we'd see this day—or could even hope for it."

"I'm happy for you," Willem said, leaning back in his chair. For the first time in months, he had a roof over his head and a full stomach. Never would he have thought to have both in Jep's house. Even the children looked healthier than he remembered—better fed.

A low rumble came from the floor, where Ema played on Mitus's back. She was fearless, running her hands through his thick mane and playing with the fur there. When she touched the spot Mitus loved to have scratched behind the ears, he gave another low rumble.

I have competition now, don't I? He directed his words to Mitus.

One eye opened, the gold burning right through him. With his head as high as the table, even when lying down, Mitus had a look of complete contentment—like a drunkard deep into his cups, a smile dancing on the lips. Willem laughed.

Emos then charged at Mitus, only to be engulfed by the fluffy mane around the *lioneth's* neck. The young boy cackled gleefully and backed up to do it again, but this time Mitus was ready and gently knocked him to the ground with a heavy paw. A giant tongue licked Emos's face before he began the attack again.

"He really is something," Jep murmured, watching his children play with Mitus. Willem only nodded.

"Long awaited," Fer confirmed with that strange confidence which always cloaked him. Since their arrival, Fer had hardly spoken. He remained silent, listening to Jep and eating the food Nelna provided with many thanks.

"You and your brother are the Chroniclers who went missing, aren't you?" Jep asked.

"We weren't so much missing as we were avoiding detection." Fer grinned.

"But you met the Regent?"

The lines along the sides of Fer's face eased. "I did."

Jep nodded. "Then you know what we're up against."

"I do," Fer said, "but the time has come for the Animle to rise."

A stillness settled over the cabin as though the very ground beneath their feet was listening. There was a thrum, a humming of some power in Willem's veins. He had felt it in Initium, had ridden upon its calling and power within those dank ruins. But here now, it came from within.

The Espiritu. Alive, pulsing. Mitus felt it too.

Fer glanced toward the window as a breeze drifted past. "My brother will be fine," he said softly. Willem stared, not quite sure if he had received some hidden message in the wind. Jep's older sons, Bishawn and Issak gawked at the man. They'd hardly taken a bite of food in their barely contained excitement.

"Who are the representatives?" Fer asked, settling back in his chair. Was he deliberately distilling the silence?

Jep began naming off the villagers, most of which Willem knew, and one he was much too aware of. "There's another group too, the women. They help with caring for children whose parents have—"

"Skurn?" Willem said, cutting him off.

Jep shrugged, as though he'd hoped Willem wouldn't have heard Skurn's name. "He's really taken on a role as leader, especially to the younger men."

A sour taste filled Willem's mouth. He didn't care how helpful Skurn had been in those days while training the villagers, all he saw when he looked at him was the man willing to risk Ansie's safety. It had never sat well with him and never would.

But he'd tried to prepare himself for this on their journey. He'd known Skurn and Jethron would still be here, that they would be fighting for their own freedom. Deep down he knew they were fighting for the same things, but it was hard to see it when personal pain got in the way. So many factions within one goal.

"Good for him," he managed to say, his face blank. Jep nodded and cleared his throat.

Mitus's head rose and he looked toward the door just before a shout rang outside. Glancing at Mitus, a sense of calm surrounded the *lioneth* and settled on Willem. No danger. He breathed, waiting.

The door opened without a knock and three members of the Renegades walked in, looking over the scene before them, their eyes remaining on Mitus a bit longer than anything else. One turned back and called through the open door.

"He's here, bring him in!"

Willem remained seated, eyes on the door as a boy, no older than fourteen, walked into the cottage. His sandy-brown hair hung in lank strips along his sweaty forehead, and bright green eyes settled on him, a sense of urgency wrestling in those depths. Something about him was familiar, the broad shoulders on such a young frame held with confidence.

"Well?" Willem asked when no one said anything.

"We don't know who he is, sir." One of the Renegade soldiers gestured, his eyes flicking between Willem and Mitus. "But he made known his need to see you, sir."

"Drop the 'sir,'" Willem said, rising to his feet, the boy watching him the whole time. "What's your name?"

The boy shook his head and searched the room, as though looking for something other than Willem and Mitus. The young brow furrowed and he held up three fingers, first pointing at Willem and then holding up two more fingers.

"He can't talk," the soldier said.

There was an urgency in the boy's eyes, desperation exuding from him.

"Do you know how to write?" Willem asked. The boy nodded quickly. "Fetch some parchment and ink." One of the Renegades disappeared through the doorway.

Again the boy held up three fingers.

"I have no idea what that means."

The boy sighed and ran a hand through his hair, then taking a step into the room, he patted Jep's shoulder and then Nelna's and then pointed at Willem. Again three fingers.

When Willem didn't say anything, the boy moved closer to the fire and pointed, then pointed to Ema's head which was only just visible outside of Mitus's mane. Again he pointed at Ema, making a motion for hair and then pointed back to the fire.

The boy sighed in frustration, and pointed at Nelna, Jep, and Willem, holding up three fingers.

"Three people?" Willem guessed and the boy nodded quickly, pointing sharply at him. "Three people...three people..." suddenly the boy stood straight, waiting for him to figure it out and Willem realized where he had seen that look before. It was a younger face, but familiar all the same. "Alesmann?" The boy nodded excitedly. "The Caw's Nest!"

Three people...the fire...the hair...Ansie!

"Ansie?" he asked, the boy shook his head, no. "Larn?" he asked, "Are you looking for him?" The man had spies everywhere.

The boy nodded emphatically, a small grin spreading over his face to finally be understood. He waited, looking around as though Larn would make his appearance by having heard his name. Willem wouldn't have been surprised to see him saunter in.

"He isn't here. We had to split up."

The boy's smile fell a little and he pointed to his mouth and made a slashing motion, then wrote invisible words in the air, ending by pointing at Nelna. As far as Willem could tell, pointing to Nelna meant woman, and the slashing motion meant he couldn't speak, but the rest was indecipherable.

"I'm sorry," Willem shook his head. "I don't know what you're trying to say." The boy nodded, a look of frustration in his eyes.

Jep stood. "We'll know it all soon enough. Have you eaten?" A shake of the head. "Nelna, get him some food." The boy made a face, worry lingering around his mouth. "Something soft."

As they waited for the parchment, the boy ate and Willem noticed the way his left hand stayed near his pocket, as though protecting whatever it contained.

"You needed parchment?" a familiar voice said, pushing into the room.

Willem straightened immediately at the sound, no longer looking at the boy eating, and fixing his eyes on Skurn. Mitus gave a low rumble behind him, not a warning for Skurn, but for Willem.

Skurn seemed taller than he remembered, the worn lines on his face giving way to the exhaustion, and the dirt clinging to his clothes revealing his tireless work. He hardly looked at Willem and instead stared at Mitus. "It's true," he said, his mouth hanging open, the parchment flopping in his hand.

Willem grumbled something unintelligible, feeling his old anger rise with a fury he hadn't felt in a long time. He snatched the parchment and ink from Skurn's hands and placed them on the table before the boy, who started scribbling madly.

Glancing away from the words, Willem found Skurn eyeing the entire cottage. Searching.

"She isn't here," Willem said.

He turned, unashamed to be caught looking for Ansie. "Where is she?"

"Not here," Willem turned back to the boy, and read the words. Once, twice.

A shadow of darkness spread through his chest. The thrum of the Espiritu answered, pulsing through him. Mitus stirred on the floor.

"Oslo was your father?" he asked, and the boy nodded. "You were there that night?"

Another nod and then the boy tapped lower on the parchment at some other words, barely legible in their slanted hand. Willem had to squint to read them.

"A message?" his hands stilled. "For Larn?" The boy nodded. "He isn't here, could you give it to me?" The boy shrugged.

"What's your name?" Fer asked, speaking for the first time since the boy's arrival. Willem wondered why he hadn't thought to ask the boy himself.

The quill scratched on the parchment and then he tapped his finger on the paper.

"Orin?" The boy nodded. "Orin," Willem smiled.

Orin leaned over to write more on the parchment, the only sound in the room was his quill scratching across the tabletop. When the scratching stopped and Orin leaned back, seemingly pleased with himself, though the downturn of his mouth didn't lift. Willem read the words twice through before he looked up.

"What does it say?" Jep asked.

"He—he was taken to the *Chateau de Plaisance*." More than one person gasped. "He and his father and sister were brought before the Regent. He questioned them about our stay in his father's tavern." Willem swallowed, trying to comprehend the enormity of the words on the page. "When they didn't reveal our identities, his father and sister were taken away to be...to be...hanged...and they cut out Orin's tongue."

A weight hung in the balance. The entire room drawing breath together. A simple boy sitting before them—his family the first martyrs of a new rebellion.

The sudden closeness to the Regent's iron fist stirred something deep within Willem. What was coming, loomed closer. War, lying in wait. Here before him was the reality. The cost of war.

Looking into those green eyes, he wondered how he hadn't noticed the hardness there—a hardness which was only developed with great loss.

"Thank you," Willem said, the words sticking in his throat. The boy's family had died to hide his identity, and Ansie and Larn's.

An unbidden image of Orin's father marrying Larn and Ansie entered his mind. It was Dur and Fer who had told him the Praelia often times lived in secret. Did Orin already know of the Espiritu? Or was he simply fighting for a better world?

"You have no idea the enormity of what you've given us," he continued.

One side of Orin's mouth quirked up at the corner, and he looked pointedly at Mitus and then back at Willem. *Well, maybe he does.*

Leaning back over the parchment, Orin wrote a short phrase—asking when Larn would arrive.

"He won't be back for at least a week." *If not more.* He hoped that wasn't the case. He preferred to think Ansie was already on her way here, back to where he knew she was safe.

Mitus grumbled behind them and rose to his feet, Ema sliding off his back and onto the makeshift rug. More than one person took a step back as the *lioneth* strode closer to the table, the cottage suddenly feeling quite small.

Orin eyed him, and with a confident hand reached out to rub the nose of the large creature. Mitus shook his mane, making the boy smile. The small gap in his teeth revealed an empty black hole in his mouth. Seeming to realize his wound was exposed, he clamped his lips shut again, and returned to the parchment.

The Regent gave me a letter, the words read. Willem stared. *Anyone found hiding Renegades will be executed, along with their family.*

The price of rebellion was set. Fer glanced up at Willem, his faith unwavering, but a battle raging within.

Orin scribbled a few more lines, Willem read them more than once and then nodded. Jep asked what it said, but Orin snatched the parchment away and threw it in the fire.

Fer cleared his throat. "It seems there is more to be said, perhaps in private?" Orin nodded.

Without another word, the room emptied and Willem itched to get his hands on the piece of paper Orin had mentioned.

A source from inside the palace. His gut tightened.

When the door to the cottage closed, Mitus paced around the table in a loping walk to stand guard. Orin dug into his left pocket and pulled out the small note he'd guarded with his life.

So simple, the piece of parchment fell on the table. Willem glanced at Mitus before leaning forward to read, his eyes flying over the hastily written scribbles.

> *Stay away from Initium—the Regent sent troops there. A trap. Be ready by the 40th day of winter. War will reach Mirtain. He knows there are three of you. But he has no names. Those closest to him: Commander Jolson, Chrish, his scribe, and Captain Dondol. If captured, can get information. He has sent for the Liege. I am inside, don't try to contact. I will find a way. Stay safe.*

The message was short, deliberate, scratched upon the slip of paper as though life itself depended on it. Willem reread the words, each sentence poignant with meaning.

He looked up, his mouth dry. "A servant gave this to you?" Orin nodded.

How Larn had managed to get a spy inside the palace and so closeto the Regent was beyond him. It was impossible, yet he held the paper.

"How did the spy get this to you?" He had no idea what sorts of questions Larn might ask, or what he considered a full debriefing, but Willem assumed the line of contact would need to be duplicated. Given the fact that Gallian soldiers had been waiting in Initium, what the spy predicted about the fortieth day of winter could be taken with confidence.

Rubbing a hand over his chin, he counted ahead. They didn't have much time to prepare.

Orin leaned down over a fresh bit of parchment, the scratch of the quill the only sound in the now silent room. Willem eyed the words as they came into being. "A woman?" he asked, even more surprised than before.

Orin wrote out the rest of the story, how the unnamed servant had slipped the note into his hand while pretending to inspect his mouth. *Clever*, Willem mused. No wonder Larn had her in his employ.

"Right," Willem nodded. "Can I keep this? Give it to Larn when he gets here?" Orin nodded. "Thank you, for everything."

The boy nodded, the solemnness entering his eyes once more.

"Come on," Willem said and opened the door to the cottage, allowing Mitus to walk through first. Outside, a small gathering awaited them.

"I need to speak with Girshon," he said, looking to Skurn in request. Skurn nodded and led the way.

"Orin?" Jep asked from behind Willem, "Stay with us, son. You've had a long day. What's mine is your's and ..." his voice faded away.

Willem smiled to himself. At least one problem was taken care of.

In three days it would be the fortieth day of winter. Three days and the strength of Mirtain would be tested against the power of the Regent. Mitus nudged his shoulder with a gentle touch of his nose.

I know, I know, Willem said to him. *We'll get ready in time.* They just had to.

Walking along the path to the village square, Willem found his thoughts jumping ahead the next three days. The plans forming as he looked ahead to what the future would bring. Blood would fall upon the fields.

He shook his head, it wasn't right. Cowering in wait for them to arrive.

Mitus nudged him in the shoulder, as though he knew what direction Willem's thoughts had taken.

What? He asked, waiting for some feeling to come over him. It did, the sudden thought striking him. Mitus could not speak to him in words, but he could communicate shared feelings—emotions. Determination and resistance collided.

We need to pick the place, Willem said in understanding. Mitus nodded, his strides growing longer.

New plans formed, the taste of them daunting and hopeful. Willem glanced at Mitus more than once, wondering just what they could dare to accomplish together. A thought pricked the back of his mind. It could possibly work. Just maybe.

A thrum built—the Espiritu awakening.

"Where is she?" Skurn interjected his thoughts.

The battle lines he'd been seeing in his mind disappeared, replaced by an image of Ansie astride Tympmor, Larn with his arms around her. The man who had once been a stranger now protected the one person Willem still held close in this world.

Stay safe, Ans, he whispered to the wind.

Mitus gave an agreeing rumble in his chest. He eyed the *lioneth*, knowing the beast was in some way aching for her too.

"She's fine," Willem said.

Skurn wrapped his hand around Willem's arm and pulled him back forcefully. "Where is she? Don't make me ask again." There it was, the part of Skurn that Willem had always feared. It wasn't the recklessness—but the concern, the protectiveness of her.

Skurn loved Ansie, and the very thought had nearly torn Willem apart more than once. For in Skurn, Willem had always feared he would lose her.

Fer reached where they stood, his eyes shifting between the two of them. Willem pulled his arm from Skurn's grasp. "Don't worry about it, she's safe."

"She can't be alone. Who's she with?"

Willem stared back—letting him put the pieces together.

"She's not your concern anymore."

Confusion filled Skurn's eyes, and then slowly it drifted away with understanding. "Is she with him?" Willem didn't answer. "Did he marry her?"

Again, he let the silence be an answer. He took a few steps forward when Skurn grabbed his arm once more.

"Please," Skurn nearly begged.

"Larn married her to save her life—to save all of us." He swallowed. Ansie had claimed the bond between her and Skurn was broken, but by the pain lingering in the man's eyes, Willem knew it hadn't been over. At least, not for Skurn.

Skurn sniffed, and cleared his throat, the sound of it wet. "No longer my concern," he mumbled, nodded, and then continued up the road without a word.

Willem stared after him—wondering if Ansie knew how much Skurn still cared. But it no longer mattered.

Glancing behind, he spotted Fer in the road. He was about to smile and wave him forward when he noticed the look of shock on the older man's face. In even Initium, Willem hadn't seen the Chronicler falter, but now all color had drained from his face.

"Fer? Are you all right?"

The man blinked, his eyes slowly focusing on Willem. "Quite." He didn't smile. "I must visit with my brother."

Without another word, he left Willem beside Mitus in the road.

CHAPTER 54

They were getting close now. Ansie could tell by the way the Gallian soldiers paced eagerly alongside her caged cart. Their bodies were weary, but hers was aching after the days of travel, her wrists chained together.

They had soared across the realm, the sails of the locoven speeding them over the ground in a blur. Somehow she had kept the tears back, refusing to believe she was truly alone. The slaves pulled in sync, the drumbeat to keep them in time still pounding in her head even hours after leaving the locoven behind.

They had stopped nearly fifty miles outside of Bastion Nocta, the soldiers throwing her into the caged wagon where she now sat against the bars. Looking up, she watched as the clouds passed over the stars, giving her small glimpses of the lightening deep blue sky above. Rolling her head to the side, she watched one of the soldiers, named Thrit, caution his horse. He glanced her way more than once and then set his gaze straight ahead.

He was her main target.

A shrill cackle passed through her lips as she laughed at him, sticking her hand through the bars. All the soldiers sighed and one slapped her hand back, she laughed again, though the sting of the man's slap bit against her hand.

She was tired of these theatrics, but they were the only thing keeping her from falling apart.

Alone, she had devised a plan to survive. She was the presumed traitor of the realm and wanted by the Regent—and there was power in their need to keep her alive.

That first night had been one of the worst of her life. Her fear mounting with each passing second as she worried away the hours. Slowly, ever so slowly devising a plan, knowing they wouldn't touch her. She had until Bastion Nocta to break free.

But then they'd thrown her into the locoven and whatever time she thought she'd have dwindled.

That first night, she had tried to claw and bite her way free. A well-earned kick to her gut had her sucking for air and they called her crazed. In the darkness of that cell, she became what they feared.

For days, as the locoven surged out of the Beastly Mountains and across the realm, she prattled on, little nonsense things, just enough to keep the men on edge. As they broke out of the nothernlands, she had gazed behind her, hoping she would see a black horse and a rider chasing after the tracks, but none was to be found.

Tears pricked her eyes, but the cold wind whipped them away before any of the soldiers could notice. Chin nearly trembling, she had leaned back and let out another maniacal laugh—hoping Larn was somewhere following her, coming after her.

Stay safe, her heart had cried out.

For hours, she'd trembled in the cold, her face blank, a silly smile gracing her lips, but her gut tightening with each passing second. She knew Larn wouldn't be able to catch up, no horse could keep up with the locoven, and it was enough to break her. She struggled to hang on, hoping he was there— somehow, someway that he was coming for her.

A stiff breeze pushed by, she shivered and caught Thrit's disgusted eye. She wagged her fingers at him and he turned away.

He wasn't the only one annoyed by her prattling and nonsense. As soon as she realized her voice hindered their concentration, disrupted some of their movements, she had been all too happy to oblige them with entertainment.

"Ahhh!" she suddenly screamed, making Thrit and his horse startle. "Look there!" She held back a laugh. Pointing to the sky, she used the bars to help her climb to her feet. "Oh, the stars! How pretty!" She cried and cackled with a crazed sound she knew annoyed them. One of the other soldiers at the front of the wagon grumbled curses under his breath.

She smiled and began to sing.

"Once there was a great big star,
My mama caught and put in a jar."

She giggled and more than one of the soldiers' heads hung forward. She kept going, knowing she was running out of time.

"I tried to use the light all night,
But mama said don't hold too tight.
She tried to drink it from the cup."
But from her stomach, it burned her up."

She cried out a whooping laugh and let it linger in the midnight air, clapping her hands together. The ditty had more than one purpose. It annoyed the soldiers and made them want to be rid of her. If only they knew how ready she was to leave them.

And if they thought her insane, perhaps they would think they grabbed the wrong woman. A slim chance at best, but the only weapon she could claim.

Ansie sang it again, this time pointing at one of the soldiers, staring at him for a long moment. He cursed as his horse skittered to the side. She was pleased to see the shiver he tried to suppress.

"Did you like my rhyme?" she asked, in a much too high voice. "My mama didn't." She gave a sigh and plopped down onto the bottom of the cage as though standing was too difficult a task. She began to pout.

A spear clattered against the bars, and she jerked her attention upward, smiling at Thrit who had dared to stab his spear into her cage. The leader, who only went by Captain, grasped the handle.

"Leave her alone," he grumbled at Thrit.

"I can't take her songs anymore," the soldier said. He glared down at her, his eyes lit with the madness she had been feigning this entire trip. She was getting close.

Captain pulled Thrit's attention back to him. "Ignore her. That's an order." He left them to resume his position at the front of the small caravan.

Ansie bit her lip and winked at Thrit, before suddenly letting out a scream, which startled him again. If not for the stirrups, he'd have fallen off his horse. His curses rained down upon her head, but she blotted them out with another round of her song.

Before too long, it was only her voice she heard. A call from the front made her heart jump into her throat. The two words he had spoken were enough to set every fear she had held at bay over their entire journey into a frenzy.

Bastion Nocta.

Ansie swallowed around the fear as they clattered over the bridge spanning the Partivo River. Time was running out.

Where are you, Larn? She pushed down the tears, refusing to let them win.

"Nearly there," Thrit grumbled.

Dawn was fast approaching as they moved closer to the capital city. The outer gates were swarming with people—torches lining the walls and heavily guarded turrets stretching toward the sky. At another time she would have stared in wonder, she would've wanted to see every inch of such a place.

But the shadow of death loomed in those streets.

She began to count the soldiers, loudly for Thrit's benefit, rhyming the numbers with all sorts of nonsense. By the time she got to twenty, Thrit was muttering to himself—something about cursing her to the depths of the realm.

And I am ready to be rid of you, she thought, laughing when he looked her way.

Before reaching the gate, they closed in around her, their numbers appearing stronger when closer together. A dark blanket was thrown over the cage, hiding her from prying eyes, and she held back the sigh of relief. It was the first time since they had taken hold of her that she was able to let her guard down—that she was free of their stares.

Her face crumpled and the tears she had long held at bay dripped along her cheeks. She wiped them back, struggling to hold all the scattered pieces together. There in the dark, fear fed off her.

All around the wagon voices drifted, groggy men and women, lugging their wares for the market. But over the clatter, came a sound, small at first, but growing with power.

It was the howl of a wolf. But she knew that voice—she'd heard his howl at Kraven Hall.

She pressed a hand over her mouth, the tears leaking over. Larn was here. He had followed her. Somehow, someway he had made it. She swallowed around the lump in her throat. But he was too late.

Wrapping her arms around her body, she held the last bit of her courage together. A sharp prick nicked between her breasts and she gasped, forgetting about the verral claw hidden in her corset. At least she'd had the sense to drop the necklace down her bodice when they'd first caught her.

The incessant rattle of the wagon changed, turning to the clatter of wheels on cobblestones, and the hooves of the horses clopped in a disjointed rhythm. Her heart tightened, and she took a deep breath.

Keep it together, Ans.

She began to sing another babbling song about the horses going stomp-stomp. The mutterings of the soldiers and Thrit's curses were like music to her ears.

Remembering the final look Larn had given her in Kirath, she steeled herself for what was to come. In that moment, Larn had debated, stood on the precipice of fighting until death for her or following when they took her. Even now she knew there had been nothing else he could have done.

He would find her. Deep down, she hoped to the powers of the realm, prayed to whatever the Espiritu was, that they would make it out alive.

After what seemed like an hour of clattering over cobblestones, the wagon finally came to a halt. Ansie was certain she heard the sound of gates opening and the voices of crowds pressing around the wagon, then gravel crunching beneath the wheels.

It grew quieter. The wagon halted once more, nearly sending her over.

"For His Sire," she heard Captain say and imagined the salute he would knock off, knuckle pressed to his forehead. For a moment she remained quiet, before letting out a cackle.

"What was that?" A male voice said, in a tone which immediately garnered authority.

"She—uh—we don't really know what to do with her," Captain admitted.

She began to mutter a song to herself, preparing for when they would reveal her. Whatever fears she had, it was idle to dwell on them.

Larn's eyes danced before her. He wanted her to survive, needed her to survive. Somehow in all this time together, she hadn't realized the bond that was growing between them. A sort of shift which had changed her—altering the course of her life.

Though, if she didn't live through this she never would know what it meant. Grimacing at that thought, she took a deep breath and clapped her hands together in a disjointed rhythm.

"*Once there was a great big star*..." she began again.

"Bring her around back," the new voice commanded, each word clipped and precise. "Follow me."

The wagon started again, only to stop a few moments later and the covering to her cage was thrust aside. After being hidden in the dark while dawn cracked across the horizon, she found herself squinting in the haze of a gray-blue tinted morning.

Before her stood a Gallian soldier, tall, strong, his shoulders thrust back. A commander by the looks of the sword strapped to his waist and the sash hanging from his hips. She continued to sing to herself as she watched him.

His gold buttons seemed to gleam in the cold morning, his dark hair was parted directly down the center.

"Red hair," he clicked his tongue, standing straight. "It has to be her."

As if I'm the only redheaded woman in the realm, she thought, wanting to roll her eyes.

She smiled at the commander, knowing she looked as crazed as she sounded, strands of her dirty hair hanging in her face. She started to laugh, looking up at the sky and tried not to be astonished by the immense building beside the wagon. Gold seemed to wink at her in the light of dawn from every corner and crevice. It was all she could do to keep her dazed smile in place. It was enough to take her breath away if the commander hadn't grabbed her attention, calling her captors to get her out.

With pleasure, she watched them hesitate.

She gave a high pitched girly laugh and saw the commander quirk an eyebrow at Captain, who only shook his head. As far as they were convinced, she'd lost her mind, or never had one.

"Take her," the commander repeated.

"Yes, Commander Jolson," Captain knocked off a salute and motioned to his men.

Thrit reached in to grab her and she flashed an evil grin and hissed. When he drew back, she knew her work with him was nearly complete. If she had any chance of escaping, it would be with him.

They pulled her out by her arms and yanked her across pristine cobblestones and into a building with a gated door. The fresh smell of hay and pungent manure reached her nostrils, and a black stallion poked its head out of its stable to watch as they walked by.

The span of wood before them was simple enough, though gold gleamed along the stable locks. She swallowed when they reached the staircase leading beneath the stables. Thrit ushered her down the stairs and along a wood-paneled hallway. The doors down here simple, crude, and somehow she knew hardly anyone ever looked here.

Heart thundering she glanced to her left, Thrit was watching her. Though her hands trembled, she managed to smile at him, the crazed smile that always made him shiver in fear.

Breathe, she reminded herself.

Kicking open a door at the end of the hall, they threw her inside and she caught herself on the dark wooden floor. A loud rattling and clopping shuddered the ceiling above, and she looked up as the commander stepped into the darkened space. The odd jaunt and just offbeat thundering above was muffled.

"Welcome to His Sire's stables." His expression remained blank.

She glanced up at him, the pieces slowly fitting together. A true prisoner would be kept in a royal garrison. But she was not some simple prisoner. She was a rebel, hidden from prying eyes.

Words spoken long ago came back to her. Dur and Fer had told them of the Regent's power, of his complete annihilation of anything that questioned his authority. Mainly the Animle and those who believed in the Espiritu—the Praelia.

Refusing to let her mask slip, she swallowed the lump in her throat. Hooves clattered above—the perfect cover for any sound.

Her stomach flipped, threatening to overturn what little it held.

"Now," the commander said, each word spoken with the due diligence of a man who observed details, "you will wait here. His Sire would like to speak with you."

Without another word, he turned to leave. Maybe it was fear or the ridiculousness of meeting the Regent, or perhaps it was the past days spent perfecting her ruse, but whatever it was, she did the only thing she could think to do. She laughed—a mad cackle, and laid back upon the wood floor.

"Speak to me, speak to me," she sang to herself, loud enough for the men to hear, "His Sire is going to speak to me."

The commander's footsteps paused, but she didn't look at him, instead, she slid her hands along the floor, back and forth, reciting the words to herself over and over again. The door slammed, and for the first time in what felt like years, she was left completely alone. With no windows, the darkness was nearly all-consuming.

I need help, she thought and recalled the cave where the light of the filumen had led them. Dur had conjured the power of the filumen, his hand glowing. Power had shot out of him, knocking Larn aside. She stared at her palms, wanting desperately to believe in the power of the Espiritu.

Nothing happened. Closing her eyes, she reached deep and tried to believe. She knew the power was there, stirring, pulsing in the air, but it hid behind a veil, shrouded. Untouchable to her.

Please, help me. The words poured from her heart, straining toward that power that had come from Dur's hand. Tears leaked from the corners of her eyes and ran into her hair. *Please.*

Silence was her only answer.

Sucking in a deep breath, she summoned what strength she had left. A thrum built in her chest, a sort of stirring that had nothing to do with her heart. Somehow, someway, a peace settled over her—calming the roiling in her stomach.

Letting out another cackle for the benefit of whoever stood guard outside her door, she waited.

***

He was younger than she expected.

Somehow after all the stories and rumors, the person Ansie had imagined was a distant likeness to Lord Hernan. Even thinking of the Mirtain lord brought an odd squeamish feeling to her stomach.

But he was nothing like Lord Hernan.

The Regent, himself, stepped into the room beneath the stables, his eyes on her. He was dressed elegantly—dark pants and boots, leading to a russet-gold jacket, and a light golden vest buttoned over a loose, white shirt, clasped with a golden broach at the base of his throat. The outfit nearly pulled her out of her crazed state, the costume so ridiculous in light of the other soldiers' simpler uniforms.

Commander Jolson stepped into the room behind the Regent, both of them watching her as she tried to still the erratic beating of her heart. In the hours which had passed since she was left alone, she had tried to find a means of escaping, something to give her a chance, but nothing proved helpful. Over and over again, she had wondered about Larn—if he even knew where they had taken her. For all he knew, she could be somewhere in the city.

"Her name?" the Regent asked. He had the voice of a ruler, a refined way of speaking which commanded authority even though he spoke softly. It was a voice that was used to being obeyed.

"We don't know." Commander Jolson said. "In the letter, Lord Duggard sent along with Captain Vicro, he said she didn't give his men a name— though he always makes a great deal out of Festis Luna, I'm not sure how hard he tried." The commander certainly disapproved of Lord Duggard, if not for his tone the downturn of his mouth was enough of a hint.

"Festis Luna, Festis Luna," Ansie muttered to herself, uncertain of how long her charade would last.

"Has she been like this the entire time?" The Regent asked.

"According to Captain Vicro."

The Regent made a sound in the back of his throat and stepped further into the room.

"We know the man is still out there, her companion."

"But is she worth coming after? Or a decoy?" The Regent mused.

"My thoughts exactly."

It grew silent. From her spot on the floor, she stared at his boots—the polish nearly reflecting the wood floor. Letting her eyes crawl up his body, she found him staring at her. She cocked her head to the side in silent speculation, a dazed smile on her lips.

"Hello," the Regent said, looking directly down at her. She would not shrink away from him. "What is your name?" he asked. There was something brooding beneath his voice, the calm centered on the edge of a knife.

"Festis Luna, Festis Luna," she muttered in a sing-song voice again.

"Your name."

She met his gaze, the blue like shards of ice. She could feel the anger coursing through him, the water raging beneath the frozen ice. In the north, she had crossed those rivers, stepping carefully, faltering but never failing. But Larn had been there to guide her. She would have to do this alone.

She laughed then, the loud crackle she had perfected over the past two weeks. Pounding her fist on the floor, she nodded and muttered under her breath.

"Captain Vicro says she is…unpredictable."

Unpredictable? She nearly smiled at the thought. Her work had given her a title it seemed. She could only hope it would give her enough credit to be thought insane.

"Do we have any witnesses from Kraven Hall?" the Regent asked, and she worked to keep her eyes focused on her hands, twisting them in her lap.

If she had been looking at him when he said those words, the mask may have cracked—he might have seen her secrets. The pounding of her heart thundered in her ears, to the point she feared they might hear it.

"No," the commander said. "All of our soldiers were killed. Captain Dondol and his Nexen are moving toward Mirtain as we speak."

She glanced up to find the Regent pursing his lips, indecision lingering. There were ways to make her talk, she knew they could, or at least would try. Her gut tightened, not knowing what all it would mean, but she refused to contemplate what he might be able to do to her.

He nodded to himself and her blood chilled.

"We will have to wait until they get back."

"Yes, my Sire." The commander said, the words sounding more like a question.

"Tomorrow morning, we'll have more answers."

She nearly sighed in relief. He'd given her the small gift of time. The ice was thin, but not ready to crack just yet.

Quite suddenly his boots were before her and when he knelt down in front of her, she heard the commander caution the Regent. A cool and rather large hand curled beneath her chin, forcing her to look up.

She refused to look away, refused to give in and stared at him lazily. Something he saw made him smile and his hand slipped away as he moved to stand.

"She won't give us answers now, Jolson, but she will."

"Yes, my Sire." Again, it sounded like a question. It seemed this Commander Jolson was as uncertain as she was about the Regent's next move.

Her worry began to mount and as she had over the past weeks, she fought them back by humming a dazed, disjointed tune to herself. Both the Regent and Commander Jolson watching her.

"You said Captain Dondol is on his way to Mirtain?"

Her ears perked at the name of her home. Hopefully, Willem and Mitus were already there.

"Yes, my Sire."

Her throat tightened.

"I only wish there was some way to find out if her companion is the 'man from Mirtain,'" the Regent spoke wistfully.

"Until Captain Dondol is back, hopefully with Lord Hernan, we won't be able to know."

"Perhaps, if we take some rebel prisoners they can also identify her."

"True enough, My Sire."

There was a long pause and Ansie knew they were watching, their gaze lingering like a finger on a cheek. She breathed evenly, controlling the fear stirring within. The ice seemed to be cracking.

But they didn't know it all. They had nuggets of truth, not the whole story, and she wouldn't be the one to tell them.

"Send a messenger to Captain Dondol, tell him to look for a girl in Mirtain."

"Just any girl?"

"No," the Regent paused. "Tell him to look for a girl named Kata."

The ice shattered. Her head shot up.

She immediately drew back, realizing her mistake. The damage was already done.

The Regent smiled, watching her with a look of triumph. "Well, hello," he said. The coursing rivers beneath his gaze flooded with urgency. "I must say I'm impressed."

He squatted down before her and she tried to maintain his gaze. Her heart was thundering in her ears, or maybe it was the pounding of the horses above. She stayed silent, refusing to answer—fear locking every muscle.

"Now that I have your attention, what is your name?" he asked, his tone allowing no chance to disregard his question.

She swallowed, meeting his gaze head-on. "Festis Luna," she challenged.

He glared.

"Keep your secrets, for now. But I will tell you what is happening at this very moment. I have sent three-thousand of my soldiers to Mirtain, accompanied by Captain Dondol and his wolves. You know as well as I, that a simple village cannot withstand the might of my hand." He paused as though waiting for her to comment. When she didn't, he continued. "They will attack, tomorrow morning at dawn, and your home will be destroyed."

She blinked, once, twice, and glared back at him.

"Then there's no reason to know my name," she said.

He smiled, the lines around his mouth arching in smooth curves, a dimple appearing on his right cheek. He pushed back and headed toward Commander Jolson who seemed uncertain of what to do.

"By this time tomorrow, Mirtain will cease to exist. And upon tomorrow afternoon, a hunt for the Animle will begin throughout the entire realm."

Mitus. She held her breath. The Regent still didn't know Willem had found his *anima reflecta.* There was power in the knowledge.

"You will give me your name and the names of your companions when the rebellion is destroyed. Your only chance of survival is to give them up."

He turned and prepared to step out the door, but halted when she spoke.

"With all due respect," she said, her voice dripping with sarcasm, "the Animle don't surrender. Perhaps you should study what really happened in Initium when the Animle first disappeared. Or is that why you were so desperately searching for Dur and Fer?"

The Regent turned back to her, his eyes narrowed. He was measuring her up, and she was reaching higher along the mark than he had at first anticipated, she could see it in the way he paused.

"Commander Jolson," he said. The man in question snapped to attention. "It looks as though this rebel made her trip from Kirath unscathed. Be quick about it."

Without another word, he left the room and Commander Jolson approached. She had wanted to cry out in fear, but the first blow sent her head ringing. The second and third pounded her back and the next few brought tears to her eyes. When the commander left, she could feel each place he had hit. It wasn't enough to cripple her, but enough to stem the courage she had wrapped so tightly around her.

The icy water was pulling her under.

Where are you, Larn? she pleaded. *Help me.*

Her tears stung as they rolled over the swollen bruise on her cheek.

CHAPTER 55

She brushed her fingers along the spines of the books, knowing she shouldn't touch them. Umbris stilled her breath, waiting in the Regent's chambers, the extravagant mask she had just finished held in her other hand.

Running her thumb along the edge, she carefully opened up the cover of one of the old books Pavier brought for the Regent to read. She scanned the words, the handwritten slant taking a moment for her eyes to decipher. The words made hardly any sense, and she was about to backtrack to the previous page when a bump sounded behind her. Dropping the cover back in place, she busied herself with fixing the dark feathers along the outer edges of the mask.

"Umbris," Garval said, entering the room, Pavier following his shadow.

"Sir," she gave a quick curtsy.

"Ahh," the valet came closer, "you've finished."

"Yes, sir," she held out the mask, the weight of it pulling at the muscles in her arm.

Tonight was a grand celebration—a feast to honor the Regent. His birthday was a holiday recognized by all of the realm, but at a quarter of a century old, the palace had outdone itself in commemorating the occasion.

Out in the gardens, the servants worked tirelessly to set the magic for the evening. It wasn't every day the Regent called for a masque.

Garval did not take the mask from her hands but merely inspected it. "This is very well done."

"Thank you, sir."

"You may place it in His Sire's bedroom. I will dress him later."

"Yes, sir." She gave another quick curtsy and hurried into the Regent's bedchamber.

The room was just as she had left it earlier that morning. The only thing missing was the golden brocade jacket and vest, which she had set upon the bed. She had expected him to debut the pieces that night for the grand masque, but she had been wrong. Commander Jolson had sent an urgent message to his chambers. No sooner had the Regent read the note, then he stormed from the room.

A door opened in the antechamber and the Regent's voice was immediately discernable. Her stomach flipped, as it had every time she'd seen him since that young boy left the palace.

Whenever he was near, she trembled in his presence; afraid to meet his gaze for fear he would see the secrets hidden there. Each day was a gong, a warning for the soldiers soon to arrive in Mirtain. At night she squeezed her eyes tight, as though willing that rebel boy along, hoping he somehow made it to Mirtain in time.

The fortieth day of winter was tomorrow. She worried away at her lip, steadying her hands until the feathers along the mask no longer trembled.

There was something different in the way the Regent now talked to Garval, there was a confidence in his voice which hadn't been there this morning. It brimmed with excitement—anticipation lingering beneath the surface.

"My Sire, it's finished," Garval said, his voice dripping with propriety.

"And where is it?"

Umbris didn't hear a response. His heavy boots crossed the floor. She was just about to flee to the servant's passageway when he appeared on the other side of the door.

"Umbris," he acknowledged, his eyes dropping to the mask in her hands. Moving closer, his presence made her heart accelerate. "I see you have completed my costume for the evening."

She kept her eyes on the floor, looking at the shine on the toes of his boots. "Yes, my Sire."

"It's perfect."

There was something in his voice which drew her eyes to him. He was still looking at the mask, but the way he spoke was with a sense of urgency, a threat of power ready to unfurl. The knot in her stomach tightened further.

Something had changed. She didn't know what, but if he was pleased it didn't bode well for the Renegades. Biting down on the fear gripping her stomach, her hands began to tremble.

"I am pleased you like it, my Sire," she said softly and returned her eyes to the floor.

"Allow me to change," he said and she nodded, turning to leave through the servant's corridor. "Wait in the antechamber," he commanded.

She froze, turning back to him. He was watching her, his deep blue eyes kindled with a lightness she hadn't seen in a long time.

"Garval!" he called. She spun around after a quick curtsy and fled into the adjacent chamber where Pavier was picking up his books.

"Hey," he winked. She eased closer, watching his hands as they gathered up the volumes she so desperately wanted to search through. He followed her attention. "So many at once, I don't know why he asked all of them." His voice was hardly above a whisper. "Walk with me?"

She shook her head. "He asked me to stay."

His mouth dipped at the corners. "I see."

"I think it has something to do with the mask."

"Ahh," he nodded, still serious, "probably wants to show it off. What you did is incredible."

"Thank you," she said, feeling her cheeks warm. She had tried her best to create something befitting a Regent. Never had her fingers been able to express what flowed within, the stirring passion to create. All her life, her skills had been used for practicality; sewing was a means of clothing those she cared for. But for just this once, she had been given the materials and leave to transform a simple mask into a creation of wonder.

"Do you know why he chose a lion?"

689

Pavier leaned in, "I actually think I do." His voice was so low she could hardly hear him.

He glanced toward the doorway leading to the Regent's bedchamber. From where they stood, they could hear the subtle comments and wonderings of the Regent and Garval's dignified responses.

"There's a rumor one of the Animle has surfaced. A *lioneth*."

Her mouth fell open, her heart thundering. A pulse which wasn't her own began to thrum in her ears. A strange feeling of light, or warmth, rushing through her veins. She bit down, refusing to let Pavier see the hope in her eyes.

"Really?"

He nodded.

She glanced back toward the Regent's bedroom, his voice was a soft murmur. He had specifically requested she make him a mask of a lion—a golden mane befitting of a ruler. She had complied, poured her heart into the creation to make a crowned helm of golden and brown feathers, arching from the mask in a glorious display of power.

"He means to dispel the rumors," she whispered and Pavier nodded.

"It wouldn't do to have his court worrying about a *lioneth*, especially on the eve of the great battle tomorrow."

She nodded. Her worries were mounting by the moment. Mirtain would be attacked in the morning, nothing could stop the onslaught that was coming.

"Is that why he's in such good spirits?" she asked.

Pavier nodded, his brown curls bouncing. "Gallia will annihilate all rebellion tomorrow." The confidence with which he spoke was enough to quell the warming hope in her veins. She worried her lip, glancing toward the windows and the expansive gardens beyond.

A *lioneth*. She shook her head. Had Larn and his companions actually accomplished their task? Had the Rising truly begun?

"I heard something else," Pavier leaned in, always the conspirator.

"What?"

"One of my friends in the stables told me a patrol from Kirath arrived early this morning. They caught the red-haired girl, the one we've heard so many rumors about," he whispered. Her eyes popped open wide—she'd heard plenty about Larn's companions. "Now we know why he left in such a hurry."

Fear constricted her throat, all of it running together. The Renegades. The *lioneth*. The Regent. The Rising. The battle. The girl.

She breathed, trying to calm the shaking of her heart. There were choices that would have to be made.

"I should think an hour would be sufficient time to get ready," the Regent's voice came closer to the doorway and she stepped back from Pavier. With his books in hand, he exited just as the Regent stepped inside his antechamber.

Garval moved behind him. "Very good, my Sire."

"Bring in the package," the Regent said to Garval and the man disappeared. The ensuing silence was loaded with questions Umbris knew she could never ask. Fear coursed through her like a river, rushing into her fingers, down to her toes and back to her heart.

Before her was a man of power, a man of means, and yet his iron fist had always dealt gently with her. She swallowed, knowing what it was that conflicted within her.

Somehow, someway, her heart had allowed a small piece of him to rest within its chambers. There a warm glow steadied, waiting for her to plunge forward. But she couldn't, she would have to deny all feeling. For he was the power which quelled hope.

Steeling herself, she built a wall around that small piece in her heart. It would not break.

She felt his gaze upon her and wondered if he saw the indecision within. Did he sense the change in her?

Glancing up, she met his eyes. He watched her with unrestrained appraisal.

Garval reappeared, and the regent turned, releasing her from his gaze. The valet placed a rather large box on the table and then exited without a further glance in Umbris's direction.

She waited, uncertain of whether or not she should say something. The Regent stepped closer, no longer dressed in the golden costume for the masque and instead in his normal finery of blue.

"Open it, please," he said softly, waving a hand toward the box on the table. She stared, uncertain.

Moving carefully, she lifted the lid, finding pale pink fabric and lace inside. It was a gown, befitting of a lady.

"I—I don't understand, my Sire." She looked up then, and he had moved beside her, his arm nearly touching her own.

"I seem to remember you telling me you had never seen one of my parties," he quirked an eyebrow. She swallowed. "As it's quite a grand celebration of my twenty-fifth year, I want you to see it."

She looked down at the dress, letting the smooth fabric slide between her fingers. It was beyond her comprehension, the elegance of the gown and the soft hues just plain enough to make her realize he had selected this just for her.

The piece of her heart hidden behind the wall trembled. She shoved it aside. "Me?"

"Yes," he said without blinking. He reached for her then, running his hand along her arm, her breath caught in her throat and she wanted to pull away.

She shook the thought away and focused on the dress as his hand dropped back to his side.

"You will attend as a servant of course, but Garval has been given instructions to not give you too much work to do." He smiled, the curves around his mouth deepening. "I want you to enjoy the spectacle."

What could she do but obey him? Anything she thought she might be able to do to help the new prisoner fled. Since coming to the palace, she had stood behind this glass world of finery—the dance of the elite. But now, he was asking her to step forward, to move away from the shadows and enter into this realm of influence and power.

Indecision reigned. She wondered what Larn would have her do. If only she could somehow know what had happened to that boy. If he had reached Mirtain in time.

For now, there was nothing she could do for the red-haired girl, but she would do as the Regent asked. She would watch. She would wait. For tomorrow the dawn would bring about the war for the realm.

"Yes, my Sire," she whispered, still eyeing the gown.

"What do you think?" he asked, his voice passing over her like water over rock, cool and comforting.

Would it be possible to draw closer to him? To learn secrets from him— secrets that would save the Renegades? She quelled the erratic beating of her heart.

You can do this, she told herself.

Bracing for the deep blue gaze that reminded her so much of water, she looked into his face. He was much closer now, towering above her.

I can't. She blinked.

"It's beautiful," she said, her fingers still tracing the gown.

He nodded. His gaze was like a caress she wanted to pull away from even as her cheeks flushed. Looking back down at the gown, her eye alighted on two strips of lace which were not attached to the dress. She fingered them, turning them over to see the pastel pink buttons in a row along the lace edge.

His hand slid along the leather cuffs she now wore. The weight of his touch made her wonder what it would feel like to be held in his arms. The thought had her reeling—treading in dangerous waters.

"There is a mask as well. Wear it tonight."

She nodded, his tone broaching no argument. "It is a *masque* after all."

"Indeed," he said. "Tonight will mark the beginning of a new era."

She looked up then and found him still beside her, though his attention was focused out the window.

There was a gleam of anticipation threaded into his eyes, a tightness around his jaw where the muscles clenched. Pavier's words came back to her. Change had come.

He walked toward the window and drew in a deep breath. "Have Garval bring in some wine. You are dismissed."

"Yes, my Sire," she hurried to grab the box with the beautiful dress he had given her.

"Enjoy yourself tonight," he said.

"Yes, my Sire. Th-thank you." He gave no recognition to having heard her.

Hours later, she was ready. Prepared for whatever lay ahead.

The dress became her armor, the mask her shield. She ran her fingers over the pale, pink gown and straightened the bodice that cinched her waist. With a gentle hand, she swept her fingers along her hair, which was curled into a loose twist at the nape of her neck. Plucking a few strands from the clasp, she let them fall to gently frame her face.

Stepping out of her tiny room, Umbris walked along the empty hallways, glancing at the darkened sky through the windows. Voices were ringing in the corridors up ahead, but for the first time since arriving at the palace, she was looked at without undue attention. She blended with the other masked servants, her own pink mask decorated with light feathers on one side, hiding her identity better than ever before.

She hardly recognized herself as she caught a glimpse of her reflection in the windows while following the other servants down the halls toward the gardens. A world of refinement and fantasy awaited on the palace grounds, gilded gold and shining silver dancing in the night. The task set before her was to enjoy the evening.

But how could she when she knew what the dawn would bring?

Glancing toward the stables hidden along the outskirts of the gardens, the knot in her stomach tightened. Was the girl still there?

The makings of the new era was about to begin.

CHAPTER 56

The pitch of night covered the land like a blanket, hiding their hordes along the Glaive riverbank. The sound of rushing water overcame the breath of the nearly fifteen hundred men waiting in the darkness. Willem desperately tried not to think of their lack of skill.

He had watched them ready for battle, too many were there to look at Mitus, their own abilities lacking in every way imaginable. But Skurn had done his best by them, attempting to train them into fighters. The Renegade reinforcements had yet to arrive. They would have to do this alone.

Mitus turned his large head from where he lay upon the ground. Slowly, as though waking from a nap, he rose to his feet. Willem inhaled.

Are they here? He directed his question to Mitus. The returning feeling was a resounding yes and Willem looked down the line. It wouldn't be long now.

Moving forward, all eyes were on him and Mitus as they stepped out of the trees and into the twenty yards of open bank along the river. He waited, the water glowing before them with an eerie light from the moons, casting the waters with various shades of white and blood-red.

Willem took another deep breath, keeping his focus on the Glaive bridge. If only he knew for certain his plan would work, that they would catch the Gallian division by surprise.

Thanks to the spy in the palace, they were warned of the oncoming forces. The fortieth day of winter was tomorrow. But tonight, the night of the thirty-ninth, would be the start of a war long held back.

They'd chosen well. Skurn and Heben prepared the men while Willem rode with Girshon to stake out the battleground. Mirtain was too open, too easily susceptible to attack from an oncoming force. But here on the banks of the Glaive River, a half day's ride from Mirtain, they might stand a chance. Here, they stood on the high ground.

Mitus's ears perked forward and Willem glanced behind him. Skurn was in command of a small regiment on the right, Girshon on the left. They had given the center to Willem and the Renegades who'd been fighting with Girshon for years. Their goal was to hold the bridge and block any advances from the Gallian division.

The minutes ticked by, each one making him strain to hear something beyond the roaring foam of the river, but Mitus was able to hear them. The *lioneth's* confidence was growing. He stilled his breath, thankful for Mitus's strength.

Together they were stronger. A thrum, which Willem had come to recognize as the Espiritu, began to beat in his chest.

The clinking of metal and steady thump of marching troops spanned across the water. Hidden beneath the shadows of the trees, they waited.

He held his fist into the air. *Hold.*

A low horn sounded on the other side of the river, regiments shifting, the torches giving way to their movements.

Hold.

A man coughed behind him.

Pulling his sword out from the harness along his back, the other men followed his lead. To his right, Skurn stepped forward and waved a gloved hand in the air.

The archers would be readying their arrows. Skurn glanced at Willem and nodded.

With his fist still in the air, they waited. Breaths clouding before them.

Hold.

They turned to the approaching Gallians, the forces converging as they drew closer to the river. The Glaive Bridge stood as their only gateway to cross.

Whenever you're ready, Willem directed and Mitus shot him a sardonic look which almost made him laugh. A slight dip of the chin and Willem dropped his fist.

It was time.

Mitus took a step forward. His back and shoulders covered in armor, the corded muscle of his legs protected by curved metal. The mere weight of the armor had been enough that three men had to lift each piece. He was magnificent as the gleam of the white moon stretched over him, making him glow when he stepped out of the shadows.

Digging his claws into the loose dirt, a head above the men, Mitus let an earth-shattering roar split the night air. The sound echoed off the water, reverberating across the land until silence held.

It broke.

Gallian captains shouted to their men, but not before the fiery arrows of Skurn's archers lit the night. The line of archers was only one man deep in the hopes of making the Gallians believe their numbers were greater.

They hit their targets, the cries of wounded and the angered piercing the air. They had trapped them. Fight or flee.

Ready? Willem looked at Mitus. The large head swung his way, his teeth bared in a grin which soon turned into a vicious snarl.

"To me!" Willem yelled and the Renegades behind him roared, brandishing their swords, the moonlight flashing. The cry shot them through the dark and toward the bridge, Mitus leading the way.

Another volley of arrows rained across the sky, this time unlit to kill those unsuspecting. The other bank was disorganized but a few regiments had gathered their men. The howl of a wolf rose above the confusion, and Mitus roared back, his anticipation igniting Willem.

Gallians charged and Willem prepared himself. His last clear thought was a cry for strength. *Help me, Espiritu!*

Two wolves charged at Mitus and he swatted them down, his paws knocking one into the water and another he held at his feet, dead from the blow. The rebels cheered, as more Gallian soldiers ran for the bridge.

One Nexen reached Willem, dodging around Mitus who busied himself with the wolves, jaws snapping, as growls and rumbles erupted. Willem's sword clashed with the oncoming soldier and as he took him down he became of one mind with Mitus. They would not lose their ground.

The thrum in his chest grew, a tingling in his hands. When he glanced at Mitus, he could have sworn he saw a blue light glowing in his eyes.

He flashed a grin. Mitus roared and swatted a wolf into the waters below. The Animle had awakened.

CHAPTER 57

Come on, come on, Larn cursed.

The lady who climbed into the carriage above him took her time settling. He would curse her again if anyone noticed him clinging to the bars beneath the carriage, his feet and hands securely hooked, his chest heaving with the effort to hold his body as flat as possible. Sweat beaded across his brow.

He held his breath as soldiers outside the gates of the *Chateau de Plaisance* inspected the interior of the carriage at the gates. Only when they rattled through did he let the breath go.

Patches of light broke the darkness along the gravel pathway. Larn pictured the torches lining the drive to the palace. Since Kirath, his every waking hour had been in an attempt to reach Ansie. The surging panic in his chest rising with each moment she was gone from him.

There was a time when he'd said the phrase, "I never worry," but those days were long behind him. All he did now was worry.

He knew the days, the hours, the minutes she'd been missing. Tympmor had given him everything he had to follow that locoven—and still, they had been too late. His only hope had been to free her where the locoven tracks ended, but by the time he reached Locoven Base, they had already thrown her into a caged wagon.

Tears had lept into his eyes, exhaustion taking over. He'd nearly wept to see her chained, but still, she carried on, fighting in the only way she knew how.

Hold on, Ans. He thought for the thousandth time.

He'd howled then, watching as the wagon rattled over the Partivo River and through the gates of Bastion nocta. He hoped somehow she had known it was his howl, that he was coming for her. Somehow, he would reach her. He'd cried out to the stars above, to that blue light that had shot from Dur's hand. If there was some greater power, he would need all the help he could get.

Espiritu, filumen. Whatever it all was—he needed it. He was ill acquipped for what lay ahead.

Failure threatened, but he refused to consider it. He would die before he let her come to harm. Tympmor's saddle was too spacious without her, his heart darker without her near.

Tensing the muscles of his stomach, he held tighter to the underbelly of the carriage as they rattled closer to the palace.

The couple above shifted as the carriage came to a stop. He inhaled a fortifying breath.

Keep it together.

As the carriage bounced, he slid carefully out of the bars. More than one carriage was unloading near the entrance to the palace, and as he dropped onto the ground, he glanced both ways, sliding the mask in place over his face.

It took only a moment or so more for another group of party-goers to pass by, the large skirts of the women providing the perfect cover.

He rolled out in one swift move, stumbling and grabbing onto a woman. "Excuse me," he slurred, from behind the smiling mask, perfecting the posh accent of those arriving.

The woman waved her overly large fan and laughed at him, patting his chest. He only hoped she didn't feel the daggers he wore in the harness beneath coat and vest.

Sliding through the crowd, he kept his walk to a gentle lope as he scanned the crowd, his spy's eye noting the number of guards, exits, and people in a matter of seconds. Shifting around the corner of the palace he voiced his own pleasure along with the crowd—a world of enchantment and refinery welcoming them to the palace gardens.

It was like a dream and yet a nightmare as he spotted the hundreds upon hundreds of masked men and women dancing and mingling upon the grounds. He hadn't counted on this many eyes, this many servants and guards.

How was he going to sneak away and find where they were keeping Ansie? He cursed his Maereo heritage to the depths and back. If it weren't for appearance, he could have passed for a servant—unmasked and in the shadows.

Snatching a drink off of a tray, he eased around the outskirts of the dancers, the revelry for the Regent's birthday lingering in the air with excitement. He'd heard more than one lady gossip about the announcement the Regent was rumored to make later in the evening.

Glancing toward the gilded dais at the end of the gardens he spotted the Regent for the first time. He was the opponent Larn's every tactic was pitted against. Curious, he watched him, wondering just what kind of man the Regent was.

He was a tall man, broad in the shoulders and dressed in a golden costume, which seemed to shimmer in the light of the thousands of candles illuminating the celebration. But it was his mask that radiated the power he held. The feathers creating a wide arc around his head—like that of a lion's mane.

Somehow, the Regent already knew about Mitus.

Larn shook his head. He could only manage so much at once.

For a moment, he stared, watching as the men and women in attendance bowed to the Regent in the receiving line which stretched across the gardens. He grimaced, watching them grovel, knowing that he was being bested—but from which angle he didn't know.

It had overcome him for hours at a time while racing across the realm in pursuit of Ansie. Someone had tipped Lord Duggard off of their presence. Someone had known they would be there, or had recognized him.

And he had played right into their hands.

The still smile Lord Duggard had flashed in his direction haunted him. He had no doubt the Regent was fully informed of just who had been in Kirath. Cursing the man to the depths, he stared.

What have you done with her?

Panic threatened, but he fought it off with logic. It was logic that kept him going. Logic was all he had to try and keep Ansie safe. But it had failed him, and now, he was running on instinct alone.

Glancing toward the alcoves lining the garden celebration, he itched to dart into their shadows, knowing that once hidden he would be able to think, to plot, to plan. But a guard stood at each alcove lining the gardens, their eyes never leaving the crowd, their stance that of a well-trained soldier. He wouldn't be able to slip away without drawing attention.

"Please! Please!" A lord yelled from the golden dais over the enormous crowd. The soft whisper of the violins came to an end and all turned to the gilded platform draped with silver curtains and those in the most exquisite costumes.

"A toast! To His Sire, the magnificent Regent Trinian the First—the Grand Lion!" The crowd cheered. "This great day in history is the beginning of the end! To the depths with the Renegades and long live His Sire!"

Crystal shimmered as every glass rose and a great cheer rang out over the crowd. The sound echoed, rising to the clear night sky above.

"Hey-hey!" they yelled together and the laughter in the voices nearly made Larn sick. Over and over again the cheer rang out, nearly too late, he remembered to join in.

A settling calm took over the crowd as soon as the Regent extended his hand for silence.

The gilded head turned, the mask establishing his dominance. His lips curled into a smile, arms spread wide. "Enjoy my bounty!"

Another cheer followed his words, and the violins struck up a lively melody. Dancers began to twirl around the fountains, glasses still in hand and their laughter ringing through the night.

He delayed, waiting for when he would be able to slip away into the shadows—Ansie always on his mind.

Quite suddenly, the distinct feeling of being watched crept over him. He slid his eyes to both sides, checking the faces nearest, then moving to those farther out. Scanning the soldiers, none were looking his way. He passed over the servants, then shifted back.

A servant girl was staring directly at him.

She stood with her back straight, a light pink mask aligned with feathers on one side hiding her true features. Bedecked in pastel pink and a tight corset cinching her waist, he was quite certain he had never seen her before, and yet, she stared.

Seeming to sense he was looking back beneath his full-faced mask, she moved away, weaving in and out of the crowd. He followed. The last thing he needed was another scene like Kirath.

Passing by a table, she grabbed an empty platter and casually meandered through the crowd. There was something about her that was familiar, but nothing seemed to add up.

Her dark hair was swept back into a low twist along the nape of her neck, simple, yet beautiful, revealing a curved birthmark just barely peeking out from beneath the brown waves. It was no larger than his fingernail.

She passed another servant carrying a tray laden with exquisite little delicacies. It was then he noticed the lace cuffs around her wrists. His heart jolted. It couldn't be.

Following her lead, he assumed the stance of a servant and walked with directness behind her—a tent erected at the end of the alcove. A flap opened and another woman passed by, her mask of light blue setting off her golden hair.

Just before the tent, the mysterious woman fled into the shadows and out of sight. He glanced behind and seeing no one, followed. A flash of pink rounded a corner of shrubbery and he moved faster than before. Out of the darkness, delicate hands reached for him. The woman placed a finger to her lips in silence.

Now that he saw her up close, it all fit. She gestured to her wrists and gave a weak smile.

He grinned, even though she couldn't see it. *Umbris!*

"Larn?" she whispered, her voice so soft if anyone had been standing near, they wouldn't have been able to hear.

He nodded quickly, hundreds of questions rising to his tongue. He wrapped his arms around her in a quick hug—she stiffened. "How—when—how?" he breathed in her ear, drawing back to look at her.

She was completely transformed from the girl he had met on the road so many months ago. As a prisoner, she had been deathly pale, her frame so thin when the wind blew her shift against her body, she had merely been bones. Even then, she had been pretty, her face somehow soft.

But now, she was breathtakingly beautiful. Standing before him healthy, she was curved and feminine in a way he had not noticed before. Her hair and skin glowed and there was a soft blush on her cheeks that drew one's gaze to the bright blue of her eyes. She was the face of loveliness.

"No time," Umbris whispered quickly, waving a hand. "I spotted you when you didn't raise your glass." He smiled then, she had been overly observant when he had first met her. "Did you get my note?"

"What note?"

She worried her hands before her. "I sent a note, to the Renegades, to you. Gallian soldiers are attacking Mirtain at dawn. This is his birthday celebration, but you heard that speech."

He looked back in the direction of the party, the glow from the candles lit the grass not far from where they stood, though they were hidden from sight. The stringed instruments switched from one song to another, the tune growing rowdier. The celebration thriving.

"Maybe it reached them in time," he said, hoping he wasn't speaking foolishly. "I can't worry about that now, I need your help, I need to find—"

"She's here," Umbris cut across him.

"Where?" his fingers dug into the soft flesh of her arms.

"The stables," she breathed. "They took her there in secret."

And yet you know, he wondered. "I have to get her out of here." Did he sound as desperate as he felt?

Umbris nodded, and he was about to pull away when she grabbed his arm. "I can only do so much. My situation, it's delicate. We can't risk it."

He nodded, allowing her to let him go. She then wrapped her arm through his and walked at a quick but calm pace. "In case anyone sees," she said, "I have these scars, but they will only protect us for a time. If they recognize me, you must run."

He didn't respond but took her words to heart. His mind was still reeling, wondering how she had managed to make it inside the palace gates and to be dressed so elegantly. That was no ordinary gown she was wearing, it was as fine as some of the ladies in attendance—slightly more plain, but just as fashionable.

"The stables are on the other side of the palace grounds," she breathed and tightened her grip on his arm. "We don't have much time. I will be missed."

Questions lingered, but there was no chance to ask them. His heart leapt into his throat, thinking of Ansie—he couldn't let her down, not now, not ever.

Not again.

CHAPTER 58

Ansie was pacing, the sound of her own footsteps nearly driving her mad.

Sliding her fingers along the wood-paneled walls, she continued her trail around the room. She had received a splinter earlier, the offensive prick of wood sticking out of her finger.

Pacing the room was her only action of defiance. A small step to take back some of her strength. She felt broken, but not just physically. The beating had taken its toll, but the way the Regent had shattered her courage had left her cracked.

All hope felt useless—but she refused to entirely let go.

She had heard Larn's howl at the bridge. He was near or at least trying to get to her, she had to believe that.

Something was happening at the palace. The pounding of hooves had nearly shaken the room which had become her prison cell. For a long time, she had watched the wood shudder beneath those great beasts and she'd wondered what would happen if one fell through.

She passed around the room, listening at the door once more. Again nothing.

Gritting her teeth, she began walking, the movement helping to ease the sore muscles Commander Jolson had so kindly gifted to her. She knew her lip was split and there was dried blood on her dress from the wound, but she was more concerned about the blow he had landed on her thigh. It throbbed with each step she took, she was a little afraid to see the bruise she could feel nearly bone deep.

They would come for her tomorrow. She knew it.

Her final words to the Regent about the Animle had sealed her fate. He knew she had more information, and her stomach flipped as she thought of what might happen. Pressing a hand to her gut, she stilled the nerves gripping there. It wouldn't do to throw up again.

Another round of rattling pounded above her head, the muffled shatter of hooves against wood. Glancing up, she ran her eyes over the rafters, wondering just what was happening above. It didn't seem as though the soldiers posted outside her door were concerned.

Help me out of here! She internally screamed to no one in particular, frustration reigning.

Resisting the Regent's question was one of the hardest things she had ever had to do. Tomorrow would prove to be too much, and she was running out of time. What Commander Jolson had done was a small taste of what was surely coming.

Leaning against the wall, she stopped her walking and looked up as the hooves of the horses skittered across the ceiling, the wooden planks rattling. It was then, an idea struck.

She had done it once before, perhaps she could do it again.

Her fingers fumbled with the ties of her dress, but when they broke free she let the dark fabric, smelling of sweat, dust, and blood, fall to the floor. Standing in corset and under-breeches that reached her knees, she shivered. Digging deep into her corset, she carefully removed the verral claw, which had been lodged against her ribs for so many days.

Wedging the tips of her toes into a small lip in the wooden planks, Ansie thanked her small appendages as she raised herself off the floor and edged closer to the rafters. Her wounded shoulder and newly bruised leg protested, but gritting her teeth she was able to reach the rafter running closest to the door.

She clung to it, hanging nearly upside down—her toes and fingers lodged into the small crack between beam and ceiling.

She had no time. Each breath was a decision—a moment—a chance to change her mind. But she no longer had that luxury.

Gulping down as much air as she could, she waited and then let loose a blood-curling scream. They had checked on her before, to make sure she didn't harm herself.

The door opened a crack until the Gallian soldier spotted her dress lying on the floor exactly where she had left it for him. He cursed and as he began to look around the room in panic, she thanked her lucky stars. It was Thrit.

She leapt without a sound and he collapsed beneath her. Without letting him gain his bearings, she dug the verral claw into his arm and pulled back. He cried out in pain, but she was already struggling for his sword. Holding the claw in her left hand she snapped the string from around her neck and wielded it before her. She slashed at him again but missed her mark.

He rolled away from another slash, an elbow launched in her direction. The blow landed in her stomach and she reeled backward, but not before her fingers wrapped around the hilt of his sword. The shiny steel gleamed in a way she had never known possible, a sense of power overcoming her as she stood, holding the sword at him.

He rose to his feet, sharp eyes watching her. He brandished a dagger from the harness at his waist and she suddenly knew she hadn't thought this through. The door was partially open and others would come.

Her small glimpse of freedom was disappearing all the faster.

"I've been waiting for this," Thrit smiled, a rather terrifying sight. He stepped forward but there was a telltale twitch in his hand which gave away his nerves—he had always twitched on the road when she waved at him.

He was scared of her. She straightened, holding the sword a little higher.

"What? No songs, now?" He grumbled, his foot sliding to the right, closer to the door. Blood was oozing from his arm where the claw had dug into his flesh.

She took confidence in the woman he was afraid of—that creature she had created on the journey from Kirath. She smiled.

"What would you like me to sing?" she whispered and licked her lips.

He didn't answer, but took another step as she raised the sword a little higher. "Not now, girl. You have no power here."

She smiled then, and the cackle she had perfected passed through her lips. One small flinch was all she needed, and he gave it to her.

She charged, sword swinging—her mind on the torment that surely awaited her at dawn. She would rather die now than later.

Thrit tried to counter the blow, but the blade cut into his wrist and his scream filled the room. As though from far off, she heard the thundering of hooves above.

Dodging to the side, Thrit steadied himself and she waited for the attack that was surely coming. Outside the room, there was a loud call that was cut off, but she didn't pause to think. She was running out of time.

Thrit ran straight for her and she dodged out of the way. He made the same move with a similar result, and upon the third time, he caught her in his trap and his dagger met the blade of the sword.

The zing of the metal clanked, and he pushed, beating her back. Her toes dug into the floor losing inches, then feet. He was pushing her farther and farther away from the door, away from freedom. She dropped the claw to hold onto the sword with both hands.

Swinging with all her strength, and in complete desperation, she whacked at the dagger in his hand. A sharp hiss and the clatter of steel told her she had hit her target. There was only a brief moment of success when Thrit suddenly launched himself at her.

The sword clattered to the ground as he knocked her to the floor.

She struggled, a scream building in her throat, but his hand was on her mouth. When she bit him, he cursed her with crueler words than she had ever heard, but her every thought was on her movements. She braced her feet in his chest and kicked with all her might, he hardly budged and hung onto her, his nails digging into her shoulders. Kneeing him in the groin, she rolled out from under him when his grip loosened, but his hand tightened around her ankle and she fell to the floor.

It was then the door to her makeshift prison slammed open, a man standing in her path. He was dressed for an elaborate celebration—a lord of some sort.

One blink and she saw the mask—the same mask from Kirath. The only difference in his appearance was the two long daggers he held in both hands.

"Larn," she nearly wept his name.

It was the one name that had kept her sane all these days. The one hope that had kept her going. Tears threatened.

A flash of steel caught her eye and the hand on her ankle tugged her back. Thrit was leering above her, sword in hand, ready to swing. Her eyes widened and she tried to kick away, when Larn slammed into Thrit, having dropped his daggers as they were no match for the soldier's sword.

Together the men fell to the floor and Larn soon had the sword arrested from Thrit's grip. Ansie looked away before the Gallian soldier was silenced. The struggle ended.

A gentle hand touched her arm and she jumped, feeling the motion reverberate through every sore wound along her body. A young woman, clad in a delicate pink dress knelt beside her. Ansie blinked, not understanding.

Larn moved toward them, breathing heavily. When he removed the mask, she didn't know what she had expected to see, but the fear in his wide eyes was her undoing. She crumpled into tears.

His arms wrapped around her, pulling her to him as he ran a hand over her tangled hair. "Shhh," he crooned in her ear.

Tears leaked from her eyes, and onto his chest. She hid her face from the world, never wanting to see it again.

"Come ve must go," the woman's voice was heavily laced with a Gallian accent.

Larn's arms disappeared from around her. She shivered and grasped his hand.

Moving to the center of the room, he placed the smiling mask directly in the center. The laughing face had blood near the lips, its smile facing the door.

"A little present, for His Sire," he mumbled.

Maybe it was hearing his voice, or maybe it was the release of the tension, which had held her together for so many days, but she nearly collapsed. Her hands began to tremble and she stared at her feet unsure if she could make them move.

She wanted to walk, tried to, but it seemed as though her body wouldn't respond. She watched as the strange woman moved down the hall, sliding past the four soldiers' bodies lying upon the ground.

"Ansie?" Larn curled a hand under her chin. She watched as his eyes roved over her, taking in everything they had done to her. She couldn't imagine how she must look, standing in the corset and undergarments, her crusted, split lip protruding, and the bruises along her arms discolored against her pale skin.

The corners of his mouth dipped, but when he spoke it was so gentle it felt like a caress. "We have to go, now. Can you do that for me? Help us get out of here, and I'll see you safe. Okay? I will see you safe?" He repeated, seeming to want to believe it himself.

"Come now, no time," again the woman spoke from down the hall, her voice sharp and laced with a posh cadence. Larn gave her a curious frown, and then squeezed Ansie's hand.

She nodded, signaling she was ready. The death and fear hadn't left, but with Larn's hand holding her own, she felt steady once more. Somewhere in her brain, she focused on what lay ahead. She could do this, she could break free.

Now that he was with her, she could endure.

Reaching the end of the hall, the masked woman paused, placing her hand along the door. Larn bent over and picked up a discarded silver platter from the floor. She took it in one hand and nodded to both of them.

"Ve run for the shadovs."

Just before the lady opened the door, Larn slid his coat over Ansie's shoulders—she hastened to slip her arms into the too-big sleeves and button up the front. The corset and under breeches would do little to stave the cold.

Bracing herself for the wind which would knock the breath from her, she inhaled deeply. Together, the pink lady and Larn ran through their plans, their voices swirling in her ears.

She heard nothing. Felt nothing, but her hand in his.

It became her anchor. She was with him.

It will all be over soon, she promised herself, knowing it might be a lie, for in many ways it felt as though their fight for freedom had only just begun.

CHAPTER 59

It was mayhem. Total and complete mayhem.

Willem was finding himself lost from those fighting behind him, the Renegades rallying around Mitus and driving back the forces attempting to move across Glaive Bridge.

Mitus swatted a man aside, his scream of agony matching the hundreds of cries splitting through the night. Swinging his sword, Willem clashed blades with another soldier—not seeing the man's face. He became another in the long line of Gallian soldiers he had accosted and overcome. Though his shoulders ached, he had never lasted this long fighting before—his strength was that of a lion.

Mitus tore into another soldier who had dared to creep too close. An arrow was wedged between two pieces of the armor Mitus wore, but the *lioneth* had hardly moaned when the weapon pierced his flesh. Much to Willem's surprise, the sharp sting had seemed to pierce him as well.

"Take cover!" Girshon shouted from behind them on the bank. Willem dispatched another Gallian soldier and snatched up the shield the man no longer needed. He ducked beneath it as another volley of arrows came down upon them on the bridge. A few of the men behind him groaned, but one man, who he believed was named Pike, charged forward with a laugh that soon turned to a curse.

"Come on then!" the man bellowed, his challenge rising as more curses poured from his lips.

Shouts rose as another volley of Gallian soldiers ran toward them, aiming for the bridge. Willem shoved the shield aside and looked toward Pike, who stood to his left. The man was grimacing, the arrows having finally stopped.

"We need more space," Willem heaved, the thrum in his chest pounded in time with his heart. He had long since given up wondering if the filumen would appear, a blue light shooting from his hands.

"Not enough room for my feet!" Pike shouted back and then cursed some words Willem had never heard before, but he could guess their meaning. In light of the battle, he nearly laughed.

In a rallying cry, Pike turned to the Renegades behind them. "Let's clear this bridge, you good for nothin' pieces of—"

Willem tuned out the rest and charged forward into the onslaught. They were winning, holding their ground, as they had hoped.

More space became available as the dead were thrown into the river. A great lurch pulled on Willem's stomach, but he couldn't think about it now. Never before had the sight of death bothered him, but he had been a hunter of animals, not a fighter of men.

He glanced at Mitus. There behind the snarling, bloodied jaws was sadness in the eyes of the *lioneth*. As one they eyed one another—pain reflected in the creature's gaze.

For all the power Mitus possessed, the killing made him sick. Willem nodded at Mitus, they would bear the burden together.

The great head turned away, almost ashamed of his weakness and let forth a powerful roar, which served to terrify the Gallian soldiers. A swipe of a paw, and blood splattered.

Keep it down, Mitus, Willem encouraged, the wave of nausea hitting him as well. He needed all of his wits about him to keep going. *There's time for that later.*

As though in answer to his plea, Mitus took a bounding leap toward the three soldiers sprinting across the bridge. He swiped at them with his large paws, catching one in his jaws and throwing him into the river. Willem was right behind him swinging his sword to protect the *lioneth's* blindside.

"That's it!" Pike shouted near them. The man raised his voice to those behind. "Drive them back boys! Drive them back to their Regent's frilly-laced skirts!" The men cheered and charged forward.

Taking a deep breath, Willem along with Mitus led the way into the fray, their goal the other side of the bridge. Then the next part of the plan could begin.

They moved like a wave, overcoming the first lines of Gallian soldiers and Nexen on the opposing bank. Behind them, the archers cheered as he reached the edge of the bridge and stepped onto the other side. The Gallians swarmed toward them, but the villagers were flying over the bridge and pouring onto the northern bank.

Mitus bumped into his shoulder, telling him it was time. Without a word spoken between them, Willem swung onto Mitus's back as the battle continued. They would need more than mere steel to win this battle.

Pike had it right, they wanted the Gallians running back to Bastion Nocta with terror in their eyes. It was high time Anglans fought back.

Mitus gave a small roar of approval and whipped around to sprint over the bridge, back in the direction they had come. Willem kept his sword clear of the plated metal guarding his flanks as they passed the Renegades along the bridge.

When he reached the bank dominated by the rebels, a cheer rang through the night and he scanned the dark for Skurn in the mayhem. Pointing his sword toward the Gallians, he yelled to him.

"Move your men! We have to sweep forward all at once!"

Skurn's eyes were hidden, but the flash of teeth told Willem he'd heard. Turning to his archers, Skurn whipped his sword off his back. "Swords!" was the rallying cry.

Steel flashed and Skurn began to shout the charge, but Willem was no longer near the bank. Mitus was bounding through the trees, heavy paws soon becoming the only sound, the clamor of battle disappearing beyond the trees.

A deep guttural moan ahead gave away their location. Willem smiled.

It had taken hours of tracking and cunning to entrap three grinspurs, and securing them had been no easy task. But as Mitus launched down the low crest where the beasts stood, Willem readied his sword.

There, staked to the ground with great ropes were the incredible beasts, their golden horns shining in the darkened forest. A quick ring around the stakes and solid swings of his sword, unleashed the beasts—they stumbled to gain their footing, suddenly realizing they were free once more.

Now, Willem commanded and Mitus unleashed a roar which shook the ground. All three grinspurs reared back and Mitus dodged to the side of the hooves which crashed to the earth like thunder. With ear-splitting moans they whipped around, charging into the darkness and directly toward the battle.

They followed in the wake of the massive beasts, trees falling in splinters before them, but Mitus was quick and dodged each deadly trunk. The grinspurs broke free of the trees and spilled onto the bank, launching into the water without so much as a pause. The shouts of terror from the Gallian soldiers lifted on the other shore, and a command from Skurn to his men rose above the roaring water.

As one, the Renegades retreated, diving onto the riverbank or in the water, to escape the pounding hooves. The grispurs cleared the retreating forces with a leap and charged into the now fleeing Gallian division—wolves and Nexen soldiers smashed underfoot.

A rallying yell from Girshon had the men back on their feet. As one, they swept toward the Gallians—Mitus leading the way.

Willem gripped his sword tighter as the faces flashed before him. Life became about his sword and the swing of it against the opposing blade.

He was the breath of the *lioneth*, and the *lioneth* was his own.

CHAPTER 60

Umbris moved as fast as she dared, sweeping along the grounds, the silver platter clutched in her hands. It was all becoming too real, seeing Larn with the girl, Ansie.

The tenderness in Larn's voice when he'd said her name told Umbris all she needed to know.

Hurrying across the grounds, she stuck to the shadows, thankful for the mask which covered most of her face. It was a risk to let Ansie see her. That boy the Regent had released already knew what she looked like, and now this girl too.

It was quick thinking that had made Umbris disguise her voice with a Gallian accent. Let Larn tell her otherwise if the time ever came, but for the time being Ansie would think she was a Gallian turncoat.

Her heart was racing, thrumming in her chest—in her veins.

"Hurry, zis vay," she said, layering the accent on thick—thicker than most Gallians at the palace. Larn shot her another curious glance as he ducked into an alcove of the garden. Their breath clouded before them and though Larn had his arms wrapped tightly around Ansie, she was shivering.

They rounded two more turns and Umbris hoped against hope, they would not be found. With Ansie dressed in nothing more than undergarments and Larn's coat, she would be spotted immediately—not to mention her hair.

Umbris shook her head. There was not a more blatant pair than the two following her. With Ansie's short stature and red hair, and Larn's height and Maereo heritage, they could not have been more conspicuous.

Umbris had suggested they take the soldier uniforms off the men Larn had killed at the stables, but one look at the bloodied mess was enough to destroy such a ploy. They would simply have to get off the palace grounds and out of Bastion Nocta by some stroke of luck—or power above her comprehension.

She bit her lip and then stopped—worrying would gain nothing.

Taking a deep breath, she paused as they rounded a corner and Larn halted beside her, his eyes roving over the high shrubs on either side. There was a fountain spraying a steady stream of water not far off—some goddess of the stars robed in nothing but a shrouded veil.

"Zey vill be after you soon," she said, hoping her voice didn't betray the fear coursing through her. For the first time, her eyes shifted from Larn to Ansie, the pale face was staring back at her with blurred eyes, no doubt tears.

She held back the words of comfort clinging to her tongue. Words were of little use right now. "Zey may have already found ze bodies."

Larn nodded. "The way out?"

"I—I don't know," she hated the way her voice cracked, fearing for them.

It was true she wasn't entirely sure how they were going to make it out alive. She had been trying so desperately to remember the pictures from the book Pavier had let her see, but it had all grown muddled somehow.

She cursed her sense of direction.

"Zis is as far as I 'ave gone."

"We'll improvise," Larn nodded, the lines around his mouth hardened into a frown. Determination kindled.

"Hide until ze light-crackers. Zey will—" she broke off when Larn suddenly snatched the platter from her hands.

With a giant swing, he collided the gilded dish with the face of a Gallian guard rounding the corner. The clang seemed to echo for a moment and they all held their breath staring at the unconscious man on the ground.

"That should do it," Larn breathed.

Umbris held a hand to her chest, the lace of her cuffs sticking to the sweat clinging to the flesh above her bodice. They waited, phantoms taunting her ears with the approach of soldiers. Beside her, the tension in Larn eased, if only slightly. Remembering his keen hearing, she let go of the breath she had been holding.

"So light-crackers, then leave," he asked, and she nodded.

"Go az far az you can through ze gardens without being noticed, try ze back wall, anything, but just get out." Her breath clouded before her.

He nodded again, his arms once more around Ansie, pulling her to his chest. Ansie seemed unaware of the action, shivering with her bare feet in the frozen grass.

"I wish I could do more," she said, only realizing too late she had forgotten to use her faux accent.

"You've done enough, thank you." Larn took a step back, blending into the shadows. "Oh," he said looking down at the hand which wasn't wrapped around Ansie, "here."

He held the silver platter out to her, the large dent in the middle was all too convicting. She shook her head. He shrugged and stuffed it in one of the shrubs for a gardener to find.

"Stay safe," he mouthed.

She nodded. "And you both." She turned and fled without another look.

All too soon it seemed the gleam of the party was shining before her. To think Larn and Ansie were so close to the Regent made her heart thunder in her ears. They were in more danger than they realized. She could only hope, she had done enough.

Pausing in the shadows, she ran her hands over her hair, smoothing away any loose strands. There in the darkness, she was the girl who had been taken away from her family and those she loved. Something had opened inside her that she didn't want to explore yet, something she knew would tear her from the inside out.

She could feel the looming shadow of Fort Jontru—the demons of that cell where everything had changed. Forcing it all back, she shut it away.

Standing straighter, she refused to back down.

Smoothing any wrinkles from the pink gown, her hands fumbled. She was no longer in that cell. She was Umbris, a maid to the Regent. They could not take away everything from her.

A deep breath, and then she stepped into the light of the alcove as though she had never left. Skirting the outer edges of the celebration, she took up a discarded platter, this one heavy and inlaid with gold. She forced her hands to still upon the cool glass as she glanced toward the dais where the Regent clapped a hand on a man clad entirely in green.

She found herself watching their revelry. For the moment, the Regent was unaware of who fled in his gardens. Feeling the sting of eyes upon her, she found Magetta watching her from across the gathering of guests.

Turning away, she held out her tray for another courtier to place their empty glass upon it and began to flit through the crowd as though she was nothing but a shadow.

CHAPTER 61

A hundred options flew through Larn's mind at once as he watched Umbris disappear. The cracks of laughter and tinkling of glasses were enough to set his teeth on edge. There wasn't enough space between Ansie and the Regent, not nearly enough.

He'd had to force himself to walk without drawing attention from the stables as they drew closer, her scream reaching his ears. His blood had gone cold, knowing those guards were well aware she was in pain.

He gritted his teeth, wishing he had been able to reach her sooner. Had reached her before they harmed her.

Her scream would live on in his nightmares, and he'd expected to find her writhing in pain. But he'd reached her just in time. Though, by the looks of the cut on her lip and the other bruises on her arms, she had been hit, and hard. His hands tightened just thinking about it—he would never be able to forgive himself for leaving her in Kirath.

He was far beyond the indecision of letting her into his heart. That scream had stolen the last piece of him.

Working quickly, he stripped the unconscious soldier at their feet of his clothes—the silver platter having done its job.

"Come on," he whispered, bundling the soldier's clothes beneath one arm and grabbing Ansie's hand. He didn't like how cold her fingers were. He could only imagine what state her toes were in. It was a wonder she hadn't caught a chill traveling from Kirath.

Reaching the edge of the alcove, he headed in what he assumed was the quickest way to the palace walls. Umbris told them to try the back wall. From his studying of the palace, the back wall of the gardens was a few miles from the palace and firmly planted outside the city. If the Regent caught wind of their escape from the stables, he would think twice before sending soldiers to the back wall, thus allowing them time to escape. Bastion Nocta would eventually be the goal—he had to return for Tympmor, but they he had to get out of the gardens first.

Think, he cursed himself.

"Here," Larn said, in a hushed voice.

He held out the clothes for Ansie and she took them with trembling hands. Her fingers struggled to undo the buttons of the coat he had given her, each one seeming to take an eternity. Quickly shoving her hands aside, he let the coat drop to the carefully manicured grass without ceremony, her body hardly covered by the little clothing she wore.

"This will help you get warm," he said in a rush. Her useless fingers fumbled with tying knots to hold the clothing in place. In the end, the boots were too big and she slipped on the socks, bundling them around her ankles. The shirt was knotted at her waist and the cloak dropped over her shoulders, hanging past her feet and grazing the ground.

He looped the cloak up under her arm to wrap over her body and back over her shoulder again. Shaking his head, he took her in one quick glance. "You've got to be the shortest Gallian soldier I've ever seen."

"Then they won't see me coming." There was the courageous girl he knew so well.

He pulled her to him, placing a kiss on her forehead. To have her here now, within reach, safe for the moment—it was enough for him to thank whatever power had kept her alive.

Not giving himself time to think further, he ducked closer to the shrubs, pulling her with him. She winced and he tried to curb the anger building inside him.

"What's the plan?" she whispered.

He shook his head, the words Umbris had spoken to him, though odd with her fake accent, were running through his mind. It was clear now a long run to the back wall would prove disastrous.

"We get as close to the perimeter wall as we can, and then wait for the light-crackers." The plan sounded feeble even to his ears.

Ansie nodded and he shrugged into the jacket she had previously worn, it was surprisingly chilled for having been on her so recently. He wondered again about her health.

"Here," he said, sliding one of his daggers into her hand. "Use it only if necessary."

She nodded and he strapped the sword from the knocked out soldier along his waist. He had spent too long without his own sword, it still being attached to Tympmor's saddle.

They ran through the gardens and he found himself more thankful than ever before that he had a sense of direction. He was on high alert, but as far as he could tell, the Gallians were both unaware of his presence, and the lack of Ansie's in the stables.

Running a bit faster than before, he kept a firm grip on Ansie's hand, pulling her along behind him. She grimaced more than once and when they stopped, rubbed her leg. With a quick silencing look, he knew better than to ask. For the time being, she was right, wounds would heal, but being found would lead to certain death.

The back wall was definitely out.

"There it is," he breathed in her ear and she nodded. He nearly smiled as her hand slid up to the cloak around her shoulders and she dipped the hood over her head. The glow of her hair immediately extinguished.

"We wait," she said softly, her mouth so close to his ear, she hardly had to give the words breath.

He nodded, a lump in his throat, and held her closer. If only there was some way for him to warm her, she was so cold, shivering in his arms. Even with their run through the expansive gardens, she was still freezing.

Larn cursed himself as he turned to watch the guards walking along the outer wall. It was going to take more cunning than he would like to get over the wall without being noticed. Even the gilded gate was firmly secured, its height towering as high as the trees lining the gardens.

"There's a gap," Ansie said, pointing toward the gate he had been eyeing. "I can get through that."

"Where?" he searched.

"The top."

He nearly gaped. There in the shadows, at the height above the trees, was an opening small enough for a child.

He was shaking his head before he had even let the entire plan formulate, watching her fall on the other side in his mind. It wasn't worth it. He hadn't come this far to watch her fall to her death.

"We wait, then I'm going to climb. There should be a lever at the top, which can unlock the gate." Her breath tickled his ear. "I bet that chain wheel at the bottom is where it's usually unlocked," she pointed, "but I think I can do it manually from the top."

He tensed, his mind scrambling for some way to talk her out of this nonsense.

"I'm doing it, whether you're going to let me or not," she gritted her teeth. How had she known he would be against it?

"Fine," he said and prayed—to that power Dur and Fer had wielded—that he wasn't making another huge mistake.

CHAPTER 62

Come on Ansie, breathe. She told herself. It was time to focus.

As much as she wanted to keep the socks on, they wouldn't help her climb the iron gate. Though she was enjoying the warmth emanating from Larn, she would have to forgo it. Sliding out of the socks, she once more felt the cold grass pressing against her feet and shivered.

"Ansie," Larn whispered, a soft scold on his lips.

She glanced up. "You're starting to sound like Willem." His eyes widened and she smiled, a lightness she hadn't felt in a long time returning. Though they were on the brink of disaster, having him here made all the difference.

"It's too cold for—"

Whatever else Larn was going to say was cut off by the red glare and enormous boom of a light-cracker exploding across the dark sky. Before he could say anything else, or talk her out of her ridiculousness, she slipped from his grasp.

"Duty calls," she whispered, glancing up at the domineering wall where the soldiers stared as the light-crackers lit the night. Without another word, she darted forward, running faster than she would have thought her stiff limbs could move.

Blues and greens illuminated the ground with a soft, brief glow which too soon disappeared. She measured out her short, but efficient strides and lept for the shadow beneath the wall. Staring at the bottom of the gate, she began to climb.

Her toes clung to the nearly frozen metal. After everything she'd been through, the hope of freedom was beginning to pump in her veins.

The booms thundered above, covering the soft clang of the gate as she climbed. A passing soldier on the ground made her freeze. Larn was on him before he could raise alarm.

Fingering up to the gap at the top of the gate, she used the last of her strength to pull her body into the small space. Below, Larn ducked into the shadows beneath the gate—she could just make out the whites of his eyes as he watched her. She stilled the fear gripping her, the gate higher than she'd anticipated.

Sliding across the top pole, the iron dug into her chest and stomach, her toes clinging to the metal. She didn't want to think about the painful drop if she happened to slip.

Turning her head to the side, she squeezed her way through the gap, muscles straining. One of the small spikes grazed her cheek, and another pricked her hip. It was nothing compared to the split skin, which now opened on the creases of some of her fingers.

Sucking in a breath, it took more than a little maneuvering to get her backside through the gap—at another time she would have laughed. She grimaced as the pricker on her hip adjusted, digging into flesh.

With numb fingers, she reached out for the lever. The heavy, metal bar was wedged high against the wall, a chain draped around it. If she moved it the entire chain was going to drop to the ground. No amount of light-crackers would hide that racket.

"Get ready to run," she whispered, knowing Larn would hear.

Not sparing him a glance, she shoved as hard as she could against the lever, it barely budged. Again, she pressed against it, and still nothing.

Sliding closer to the wall, she raised herself as far off the single iron bar holding her weight, her toes and legs the only thing keeping her in place. With a huff, she pushed the lever down and it gave way as a light-cracker exploded above.

As the chain slid down the side of the metal lever, she felt herself slipping and struggled to grab hold of something that would keep her from falling to her death.

The chain was about to drop when she caught it with her hand and grasped the metal lever. The gate swung and she lost her footing, her hands clinging to the metal lever, the heavy weight of the chain pulling down on her. Inch by inch, she slid, her body protesting.

Not like this, she thought in panic.

Her toes struggled for something, anything, when the gate swung closer, and she hoped Larn had made his way through. Swinging her body, she made the leap to the bars, letting the chain fall. The iron cut her palms and she landed fifteen feet below where she had been before, but there was no time to think.

The chain rattled with a tremendous cacophony.

Scurrying down the poles, she hissed at the blood leaking from her hands. Beneath her Larn was waiting—shouts and curses ringing from above.

"Jump!" Larn yelled, desperate.

She was already in the air. He hardly set her feet on the chilling stones when he took off onto the streets of Bastion Nocta, weaving through the darkness, the rattling of soldiers' feet pounding behind them.

Everything passed in a blur, and she tried to keep up. Her fingers clinging to his, the slickness of the blood wetting their joined hands.

"Come on, come on," Larn urged her forward and it was all she could do to maintain her footing.

Rounding a corner, someone shouted and Larn retreated—she snapped backward as he pulled her to him. She could feel the erratic beat of his heart in his chest beneath her hand. The soldiers passed by and Larn pressed forward.

"Not much farther," he said, his eyes continually sweeping the streets and shadows. Turning down an alleyway, she wondered how he knew where he was going when he stopped again. He turned back and forth to both ends of the street.

"We're surrounded," he said, hearing more than she could ever hope to. His chest rose and fell heavily beneath her hand and she began to panic.

"You're sure?"

He didn't answer. He didn't have to.

"Up you go," he said pointing to a window above their heads. She nodded and climbed up him and through the slightly open window. She noticed a sign above them creaking in the wind, some red garment painted across a wooden sign.

Rolling through the window, she clattered into a table and fell onto a plush rug along the floor. Larn wasn't far behind and slid into the room with hardly a sound. His shoulder bumped into an unlit candlestick and as he tried to grasp the ridiculous object, it slipped and fell to the floor.

She reached to right it, but he stilled her hands. "Your wounds," he explained. She nodded, seeing the blood on his shirt from her palms.

A knock sounded on the front door, and Larn let out a soft curse.

He pulled her after him, sticking his head out into the hallway. A loud banging reverberated on the door down the hall, not far from where they had entered. Stairs were before them and they ran faster than before. Reaching the second floor, Larn listened at three doors, the sounds inside distinct and making Ansie realize just what sort of place this was.

Finally, he shoved one of the doors open, pulling her with him.

"Hurry," he said, fumbling with her clothes. She caught on all too quickly, her hands ridding herself of the soldier's garb. "Leave the cloak," he said.

She covered her hair and he slipped out of his jacket, tossing it onto the floor. He then pulled her to him, the boning of the corset digging into her flesh. His heaving breaths grazed her neck.

She gasped when his cold palm brushed her shoulder. "Hopefully they'll pass," he muttered and then grasped her hand between their bodies, placing a dagger in her bloodied fingers.

All thought fled as they listened as each door was kicked in, soldiers shouting at the inhabitants. She trembled.

Larn backed her up to the wall and left her there for a moment. He returned shirtless, his body somehow warm. Adjusting the cloak across her head, he pressed his cheek against hers, waiting.

When a loud thumping began on their door, he ducked his head against her neck, and she hooked one leg around his hip—waiting.

The door burst open with a shattering crack. She screamed, partly in terror and partly to play her role. The soldiers took one glance at Larn's discarded clothes and her exposed leg, before slamming the door behind them as curses and shouts rang down the hall.

Larn's hand slipped from the secure place it had been residing along her face to keep the cloak in place, and he moved back an inch, deeply exhaling. Her leg fell to the floor, his chest was heaving, rising and falling beneath her hands.

"Get us out of here," she pleaded, her terror finally catching up with her.

She leaned into the warmth of him and he seemed to hesitate before wrapping his arms around her. She felt his lips press gently on her head again before he tucked her closer.

"I will." The words sounded like more of a promise to himself. "Tympmor's not far from here." As he spoke, he ran his hands along her back. "As soon as they leave this corner of the city, we'll go find him."

She nodded, her breath beginning to slow.

There would be time later to think about what they'd been through. Having heard Tympmor's name, there was nothing she wanted more than to be on the black mount's back, Larn behind her and riding home to Mirtain.

"Hold on, just a bit longer," he whispered and she closed her eyes, the banging and smashing beginning to fade into the night. "Just a bit longer."

Nearly an hour later, they snuck out of the brothel where women were laughing with men as though nothing had happened—the sounds hollow and lost. They walked the streets, clad in nearly matching black pants and white shirts, with leather jackets they had stolen from the house. Ansie found hers a bit large, but it was nothing she couldn't handle. Keeping the cloak over her head, they reached the makeshift barn in a dodgy part of the city where Tympmor was secured to a wall. He was covered in mud and dirt, hiding his true nature from those who didn't take the time to look at his strength.

Without a word, Larn tossed her into the saddle and swung up behind her. "Are you ready to see Gallia?"

"What? Why?"

"The east gates will be swarming with soldiers, I say we try our luck to the west."

She nodded—if he was with her, she was ready. She had survived the trip to Bastion Nocta on her own, now with Tympmor and Larn, she could do this. With him, she could do it.

"Then let's," Larn said and urged Tympmor out of the ramshackle barn.

Holding onto the pommel of the saddle, they made their way through the city and by dawn entered into the open lands of Gallia.

As though they needed a reason to celebrate, as soon as the gates were out of sight, Tympmor launched into a sprint, leaving behind what had nearly been their end. After an hour of running due west, Larn turned Tympmor to the left in a sweeping arc.

"Let's go home," he said and Ansie smiled.

She reached up to kiss him on the cheek. He blinked.

Leaning forward to adjust her weight to Tympmor's powerful stride, she felt Larn's arms tighten around her. For now, it was enough.

CHAPTER 63

The battle was long since over, and the Gallian soldiers, who were still drawing breath, were retreating to Bastion Nocta. Willem and Mitus had departed from the rebels, moving to a secluded area where he was able to remove the arrow from the *lioneth's* powerful shoulder.

Mitus was the first to give into the retching, and Willem had followed not long after. Passing a hand over his mouth, his stomach finally stilled. The bile left a bitter taste, but at least he could breathe without the threat of losing his stomach.

Thanks for sharing that, he said, looking at Mitus who finished with one final gag.

The large eyes rolled and he shook his mane. There was a distinct feeling of annoyance between them, and Willem ran his dirtied hands through the thick mane.

We need to get cleaned up.

A huff of agreement was the response. Moving back toward the makeshift camp between Mirtain and the Glaive River, Willem had taken two steps before realizing Mitus was not following.

Looking back, the *lioneth* was walking toward the battlefield. They shared their emotions now, a connection Willem was still learning and trying to understand. He was stronger than he ever was before, and he knew the power was not his own. In much the same way, their emotions were now shared, as were their bodies.

His strength was Mitus's, and Mitus's was his.

Catching up to Mitus, the *lioneth's* ears flicked back and laid low on his head. In the way Mitus communicated to Willem, a feeling of regret and thankfulness came over him. Willem glanced at him wondering just what he wanted.

Stepping out of the trees and onto the riverbank, Mitus eyed the desolation before him. The Renegades had already gathered the dead, placing them in graves, and the wounded had been brought back to camp—even the Gallian wounded. But all of it didn't seem to faze Mitus.

The heavy head dropped, bowing a sort of reverence, a stillness descending on the land. Willem waited, expectation wandering. Then it came.

The pulse started somewhere in his chest, a soft and gentle stirring of a power that was not his own, that was not Mitus's—but a being, a spirit.

The Espiritu.

As though beckoned, an ethereal glow rippled upon the water, waving in the current. Mitus stepped closer to the river's edge, the water lapping over his paws, the blood washed away.

Willem kneeled beside him, placing his hands in the water. The dried blood eased away in a cloud, never to be seen again. His breath puffed before him as he glanced up at Mitus.

What?

The giant paws eased into the water, the current surging around the golden fur. Each step took him deeper. The ethereal light—the filumen trembled, pulsed, calling to Willem. Removing nothing, he inched into the water, the liquid easing around his body, sinking deep into his skin with frozen tongues.

Willem sucked in a breath, following Mitus. When the water reached his chest they stopped, watching as the light drew near. Placing a hand on Mitus, he waited.

All around him the filumen swirled, and he was suddenly warm. The lapping river settled into his bones, into his very soul. Looking down, his hands glowed as a peace, unlike any he had felt before, overcame him.

This was it, the power that had been held back during the battle. It was violent and peaceful, raging and gentle. A surging force of will, of goodness, of light.

Mitus dipped his head beneath the water, the river cresting over him before he came up shaking, the streams draining from his jowls. The filumen seemed to fill him, to glow in his brown eyes.

A heavy paw was laid upon Willem's shoulder, the weight of it nearly knocking him over. He bowed his head, somehow knowing that it had all led to this.

The weight pushed him under. What light had glowed above was darkness compared to what flowed around him beneath the surface. It was blinding, like fire and stars burning in a dawning sky. It consumed him, his entire body pulsing with the thrum of the Espiritu.

It was familiar, and suddenly he knew it had been there all along. It was the pulsing thrum which had called him into the forest after his mother was killed. The light of Jep's family which had kept him sane during those times of sadness. It was the guidance which had led him to find Ansie, the beating of her heart as he carried her from the forest.

There in those moments, the good and the bad, it had been there. That coursing, raging spirit. Powerful and strong, standing beside him in Hernan's chambers. Helping him to put his heart back together after Kata's death.

It was life, it was everything.

When his head broke the surface once more, he looked up to the stars, to the two moons.

There in the middle of the Glaive River, they had become what was foretold. The Animle had returned—the light shined through the dark, and its beating heart could not be overcome.

It was the understanding of the Praelia that coursed through him now. Those people who had long believed in the light.

The battle had only just begun, Willem knew it with every part of his being. What had been done this night was only a piece of what lay ahead.

Mitus looked to the stars, his neck straining. Together they would join the Praelia and fight against the dark.

Willem smiled and leaned back in the water, his arms spread wide in open surrender.

As they later approached the rebel camp, shouts of jubilation and singing reached their ears. Willem hadn't heard anything like it in all his life.

The sounds of freedom. Willem glanced at Mitus and the *lioneth* shook his head in a smiling pant.

They passed groups of men and women cheering, the torches casting long shadows across the chilled ground. What had felt frozen and covered in the shadows of death at the Glaive riverbanks, had all but disappeared here. The villagers danced and sang together—nothing to enhance their joy but their own sense of freedom.

Willem raised a hand in greeting and thanks each time the rebels cheered him and Mitus as they passed, chanting their names. The attention was something he would have to get used to. Mitus, too.

He stepped into the largest tent where Girshon had, not so long ago, given his final orders before the battle. It all seemed like a dream of some kind, as though he had just awakened from a long night of tossing and turning in sleep.

"Willem! Mitus!" Some of the leaders in the tent called their names and Willem nodded. Mitus seemed a bit more pleased and shook his mane proudly.

So much for humility, Willem said to him and Mitus bumped his shoulder. The large cat plopped down near the entrance of the tent as Girshon walked over to them.

"Well, done," the Renegade leader said, extending his hand in Willem's direction. No one commented on his clothes which were still dripping from the river.

"And you, sir," Willem said, shaking his hand and taking comfort in the strong grasp. The Renegades had a leader of both strength and intelligence, who had proved his discernment in the last few days.

"I wasn't so certain of victory, but it seems we have the chance to keep breathing. At least for now," Girshon grumbled.

"Yes, sir," Willem allowed.

His thoughts had been much the same before battle. He moved to leave the leader and find some water to wash away the bile still lingering in his mouth, when Girshon stilled him with a hand on his arm.

"Before you move on to celebrate, I must warn you I just received word from Mirtain. A band of soldiers went undetected around Glaive Lake. They infiltrated Hernan's manor." Girshon spoke with the direct assurance of a leader. "They took him. My men followed their tracks but were too late to catch up. They are headed for Bastion Nocta."

Willem could only nod. The familiar weight of his past guilt pushed down on him. But the strength of it seemed somewhat diminished. Mitus gave a huff from across the tent and Willem forced a smile as he glanced back at the large creature. Those golden, amber eyes were all too seeing.

It seemed like a dream, that light which had flowed around them in the river. The Espiritu's essence, the filumen. Only now Willem could feel it coursing through his veins, drawing him closer as the past threatened to lead him into darkness.

"Thank you, sir."

Girshon nodded and moved away, blending into the many leaders and dirtied soldiers standing in the tent. Lost in his thoughts, the pain of the past pressed on him once more. Being so close to the places and people who had witnessed the worst of him, was more difficult than he had expected.

His hand shook as he reached for a glass of mulled wine, no doubt provided by the wonderful Mrs. Cobert. It had always been a favorite around Festis Luna.

"Well done, Willem." A voice said behind him and he turned.

Skurn stood, glass in hand, his face dirtied and hair clinging with sweat to his forehead. He quickly noticed Skurn was leaning a bit more heavily on his right foot than his left.

"And you," Willem admitted. He knew the outcome would not have been possible without the efforts of the man beside him. They stood in silence, side-by-side, watching the others talk and drink with one another.

"He's really something," Skurn nodded, watching Mitus, who was yawning as though he had just awakened from a long nap.

"He is," Willem agreed.

Skurn heaved a breath. "What you did tonight, it was—"

"It all worked out," Willem cut across him. "And thanks to you the men were trained."

Skurn looked down at the rusted cup and took a rather large breath. "Thank you, for that."

Willem shrugged. He had never been one to say more than was necessary. "Did you hear about Hernan?"

"Yes," Skurn nodded. "He shouldn't have gotten away so freely."

Willem nodded. "Only time will tell." He took another sip of the wine, enjoying the tang it left in its wake.

"You know," Skurn paused to swallow, "I mean, I know Jethron wants to speak with you."

Willem hated the way his gut lurched at the sound of Jethron's name. It still stung, the betrayal both Jethron and Kata had laid at his feet. He had known he would have to face Jethron when he returned, he knew he could only wait for so long.

"Not tonight," he said, softly.

"Of course," Skurn waited, opening his mouth more than once before something finally came out. "I think—I think he is afraid of what they did. His role in what happened to her. At least, he has overcome his fear of fighting, he did his part tonight." Skurn waved a hand in the direction of the Glaive.

"I saw," Willem nodded. He had noticed Jethron doing his part in the midst of the battle. More than a few Gallian soldiers had met their end by Jethron's sword—such a change from the friend he used to know.

Skurn nodded and took a sip of Mrs. Cobert's wine. "Have you heard anything from Ansie?" he asked, the question weighted with meaning. "I haven't seen her…since, well…before all of you left…" His voice drifted off.

"I thought she might be here by now," Willem admitted. They couldn't have been that far behind. He knew Larn liked to travel fast, but it could still be some time yet.

"I guess we should hope she's safe."

Willem nodded and moved to leave. "I'm certain she is. Larn will do whatever it takes to keep her safe."

He hadn't meant the words to sound accusing, but they came off that way all the same. He stepped aside, excusing himself when he suddenly noticed Fer step out of the shadows. The Chronicler had insisted on being near the battle, his prayers being offered up throughout the night.

"Fer," Willem acknowledged.

"Might I have a word?"

"Of course." He motioned outside the tent and sent a look at Mitus telling him he could stay, before exiting. "What is it?"

Fer took a deep breath. "It's something to do with Ansie," he wrung his hands and Willem was immediately on alert.

"What about her? Have you heard something?"

"No, no," Fer reassured him. "It's about her and Larn. You mentioned something to that boy, Skurn."

"Yes?" Willem asked thoroughly confused.

"You said she wasn't, his concern anymore. Do you mean to tell me she's married to Larn?" Fer looked at him intently, his eyes searching Willem's.

"Yes," Willem said, almost hesitating as he watched the man's face crumble. "Larn married her to protect her—to protect all of us—at the tavern in Alesmann."

"It's as I feared," Fer shook his head and then looked up to the sky, "How long must we wait, how long?"

Willem stared at the man, waiting for an explanation. When Fer finally returned his eyes to him, there was pain there which Willem hadn't expected to see.

"There's a prophecy," Fer said, running a hand over his face, "that two Animle would marry and become the strongest of all warriors. The bond you forged with Mitus is called *simul ad mortem*. You are connected with him until death. You share each other's emotions, weaknesses, and strengths. You were more than likely stronger and faster during that battle weren't you?" Fer let the question dangle but left no time for Willem to answer. "But this prophecy spoke of two Animle who had already forged their bond with their *anima reflecta* and were then joined together by love, in marriage, to be the first of *unum ad mortem*—a connection of two souls, in which the strength of one matched the other. Their abilities would be enhanced and where one was weak, the other would be strong. A perfect balance." Fer sighed. "It's supposed to be the time when peace overcomes the realm and the Espiritu returns in full glory."

Willem stared at the Chronicler and waited calmly for him to say something more. Fer merely stared at his own hands, deep breaths released with a shaky sound.

Slowly, the words sank in.

"You thought Ansie and I—"

Fer waved a hand, stopping him from speaking further. "I knew there was a connection. For some reason, I hadn't realized she was your ward. I spoke with your friend, Jep, he told me how you found her. It would seem you're more brother and sister."

Willem gave a half smile. "We are."

"And Skurn, they cannot be together now, can they?"

Alarm rattled Willem, he glanced back at the tent. "Is Skurn?"

"We all have a piece of warrior inside us. It's what we choose to do with it that makes the difference." Fer smiled mournfully. "Forget I said anything. It was a fool's hope. I only wished after all this time, the rise of peace would overcome all the bloodshed."

"It's not a bad thing to hope for," Willem offered.

"I suppose not." The man smiled. "The Animle came close once before, but it ended in their deaths. They both died in Initium."

Willem's thoughts returned to the ruins of the once great building which had been the sanctuary for the Animle.

"Well, a man can dream," Fer said, and patted Willem's arm before walking away. For the first time, Willem realized he looked older than he usually behaved, and he pondered the man's words until Mitus stepped out of the tent.

Together they walked to a secluded place and Willem knew upon the morning he would have more concerns than he wanted. There were Skurn, Jethron, Girshon, Jep and his family, the many rebel soldiers who looked to him, the villagers, and Fer's worries over an uncertain future.

He was surprised by the weight of his own heart. A tenderness at the wounds from those who knew him so well. They wanted him to be their leader and move against the Regent. He would do what he could and try to do his best by them all.

But for the moment, he needed sleep, and he needed Ansie to be safe, where he could see her.

There was only one task he could accomplish directly, and sleep soon overtook him as he laid with his head to rest along Mitus's back.

CHAPTER 64

Long into the night, the celebration of the festival continued. Umbris was nearly dead on her feet, nerves stretched to the point of breaking when the light-crackers had lit the night sky.

An hour had passed since the revelry of the tremendous explosions. She waited, nearly flinching each time one of the guards moved, expecting the alarm to sound. It took everything she had to not drop the platters she carried back and forth between the serving tent and the masque.

Glancing up at the covered dais where the Regent rested in a plush chair, his shoulders wrapped in an expensive fur, he was more animal than man. She swallowed, knowing what she had done would send him into a fury beyond what he had shown before. If he ever found out her role in allowing Larn and Ansie to escape, her life would be forfeit.

But you've already given up that life.

He must have felt her eyes on him, for the lion mask turned in her direction. She knew he was staring back at her, watching as she stood amongst the other servants, shivering in the too thin gown for a winter's evening.

He raised his hand and beckoned her from across the party. The music had changed, the upbeat melodies drifting to the slower sway which led the dancers to hold one another closer. She passed around them, her heart seeming to beat in her throat, walking toward the dais while he watched.

Keeping her eyes on him, she lifted her skirts and rose up the stairs, moving into the cloud of warmth stretching from the dais, where his most trusted men resided. Some had foregone their masks, but many remained dressed for the occasion, their laughter and words a little slurred. She recognized one of the men as Commander Jolson, the deep blues of his coat covered in what appeared to be some sort of shimmering fabric—he was dressed like a god of water.

Sitting beside the Regent was the man she had spotted earlier. His green coat covered his broad shoulders, matching his eyes. His clothing was simpler, like that of a soldier. She eyed him carefully from behind her mask and noticed he was doing the same—his round jaw tight, as though he was gritting his teeth.

Stopping before the Regent, she dropped into a curtsy, before meeting his eyes as she stood. There was an easiness to his manner she had not seen in a long time, the excitement from earlier in the day having burned away to embers.

"Please send word to have Garval prepare my chambers, I will be retiring soon." He held up a finger before she left. "Come back after you send word."

"Yes, my Sire." She dipped a quick bob and did as he requested, returning to stand near his side, waiting.

"They will be here soon, my Sire," the man in green said. He had blonde hair that flopped down along either side of his tanned face. By the small brown spots along his forehead, Umbris knew he spent many hours in the sun. She didn't like the sound of his voice. There was no warmth in it, but instead, an odd lilt which sounded as though he had a bubble in his throat.

It makes him sound like he is holding something back, she thought.

"Then the dawn of a new age can begin," the Regent said swirling the red drink in his crystal glass. "I will hunt down every last one of the Animle until their very existence is forgotten. This is my reign." The Regent's words were slightly slurred and Umbris stiffened when his companion only nodded.

"To a new age," the man said and clinked his glass with the Regent's.

She didn't like the way the man eyed the mask on the Regent's face. Something in her wanted to pull the Regent away from him.

Garval soon appeared and the Regent stood, the others on the pavilion rising with him. They all bowed and she swooped into a curtsy, only standing with the others after the Regent passed by.

741

When she rose to her full height again, she found the stranger's gaze on her. She turned away waiting for the Regent to exit the celebration. He stooped to the nearest servant and muttered something before striding off along the pathway with Garval heading toward the palace.

Once more, she found the stranger's eyes on her. She swallowed, staring back at him, afraid to look away. A smirk curled one side of his mouth, an arrogant puckering of his lips.

"Madame?" a voice said at her shoulder. She blinked but didn't turn to the young male servant, her eyes still focused on the man in green. "His Sire requests your presence."

The smirk grew as her heart skipped a beat. The man in green lifted his glass in her direction, the grin growing but never reaching his eyes.

She suppressed the shiver that threatened to course along her spine.

"Thank you," she managed to breathe. She forced herself to walk calmly from the dais, feeling the gaze of the stranger on her the entire way. Whether she was shaking from the cold or from that man, she didn't know.

She found the Regent in his antechamber, a lone candle resting on the table. Garval was just ducking out the door when she entered, the lion mask in his hands.

"You asked for me, my Sire." She hoped she didn't sound as weak as she felt.

"Yes," he said, turning to her. He had removed the golden coat, the vest and white shirt making him look all the taller, the dark boots stretching to his knees. He was handsome, and he knew it. His figure illuminated by the golden window behind him.

She took a step forward, sensing the change in the room, the calm which didn't always exist. Hadn't she told herself she could do this? Draw close to him to help the Renegades?

But she hadn't expected it to feel like this, that she would be drawn to him. She was ready to force herself to move closer, but force had nothing to do with it. Here, now, she wanted to be closer to him. She could feel the pull of him—the energy he exuded.

There was something about him which she was drawn to, and deep down, she knew he felt the same. It was why she was here—why he had pulled her from that hole at *Le Jupon Rouge*.

Unable to look him in the eyes, she stared at the floor, when his boots suddenly appeared. His hand curled beneath her chin and lifted her face so he could look at her. She closed her eyes at his touch, not wanting him to see what she hid there.

His hand slipped along her cheek, his thumb sliding across her bottom lip. She was quaking—afraid of what she felt for him. This was what she had truly feared in his presence, what she had been suppressing all along.

He reached around the back of her head and loosened the strings of the pink mask until she was free. A fresh coldness stung her face after having worn the mask for so long. She met his eyes then, and before his hands returned to her cheeks, he released her hair from its soft twist.

"You're shaking," he said, his voice husky.

"I'm cold."

He squinted at her and she knew what he was about to do. She placed her hand on his chest, disbelieving she was actually touching him, halting him from moving closer. He looked down at her then, a question burning in his eyes. The candlelight flickered across his face.

She knew he could do to her whatever he wanted. He had the power to do whatever he wished to anyone in the realm. It was his will against others, and no one could go against it.

But you already have, a thought prodded her and she shoved it aside, lest he see the betrayal in her eyes.

She didn't answer the question he was asking, his brow furrowed and his thumb gently passing circles over her cheek. She needed to breathe, to move away from him.

It had been there, that night in the map room when she had stroked his arm. She had felt it then, this connection to him. He wanted her, and she wanted him. But she couldn't, he didn't understand, but she couldn't.

Shaking her head, she took a step back. He held his hand in the air, as though she still stood before him.

"Your celebration was excellent, my Sire," she said, forcing herself to remain calm. His hand dropped.

He cocked half a grin and looked away for a moment. "Tomorrow will be the beginning of a new era." She nodded as though she understood, hoping her note had reached Mirtain in time. Maybe the Renegades had done something to help defend their ground. "Now that the Liege is here, Autre Gallia will be forced to bow to my rule." He took a deep breath and turned back to her, a smile lighting his face.

She bit her lip, running through his words.

The Liege? The man in green.

"May I be excused, my Sire?" she asked quite suddenly, speaking around the lump in her throat.

"I'll have no more of that."

"What, my Sire?" she asked, blinking quickly.

"That title." He waved a hand. "Call me by my name. I call you Umbris, do I not?" How did he make the name sound so poetic?

"Yes, my—" she broke off and stared at the floor.

He was before her again. This time she looked up as he ran a hand along her cheek. "Call me by my given name."

She swallowed, her breath passing into the small space between them. "Trinian."

He smiled then, and his hand paused. He cautioned her with his eyes and leaned forward, the hint of wine upon his breath. She was no longer breathing when he placed his lips on her forehead.

She suddenly remembered the feeling of a butterfly on her finger once, the soft patter of its wings against her skin as she sat beside the waters near her home. She had laughed then, back when she used to laugh, back before they had stolen it from her. There was the trickling of water in her memories, the splashes of those she loved still dancing in her mind.

Closing her eyes, she let the Regent, no, *Trinian*, hold her and breathed in the smell of him as her past flashed before her. She knew why she had opened up, why the memories swirled through her. The way his large hand rested upon her cheek, reminded her too much of another.

Tears filled her eyes as she pulled back from Trinian. He was only a man— no longer the Regent. And she was only a woman.

A Regent she could fight. A Regent she could hate. But this man was different. He had opened something inside of her tonight, something she couldn't put back.

Without asking, she placed a hand over her heart and fled his presence.

She was a spy in the midst of the palace and she would not be thwarted. No one would stop her, not even Trinian.

Within her own heart, a new battle had begun.

CHAPTER 65

"Are we close?" Ansie asked before him. They were the first words spoken between them in the past few hours.

Since they had begun their journey through Gallia, they had remained, for the most part, silent. Ansie had leaned into him, only for warmth, he told himself as they had passed through the frigid air. They had been through enough cold, as of late. He desperately wished for a fire but knew there would be no time for one in light of their travels. Tympmor was going to have to prove his worth, getting them to Mirtain as quickly as possible.

"We are," he said and wrapped his arms a bit tighter around her. She fit so perfectly before him.

He hardly wanted to admit to himself how much having her there reassured him. He needed her to be with him, he needed her to be safe.

Looking down at her hands, which were hastily tied with makeshift bandages, he knew she was not entirely unscathed. Every time he looked at her face, he had a twisting in his gut for what she had endured beneath the Regent's stables.

He shook his head even now, not fully understanding the strength of the fiery girl before him.

"How close?" she asked, and he shrugged.

Realizing she couldn't see the motion, he replied. "Less than a few miles."

She turned to him, her eyes not entirely clear, as they shifted in the saddle in perfect rhythm with Tympmor's gait. "Should we be so close?"

"I'm staying as far away as I can," he admitted to the truth. If he had his choice, he would keep her at least a day's ride away from Bastion Nocta.

"There's a bridge over the Partivo on the south side. It will bring us within a mile of Bastion Nocta."

She nodded and set her shoulders, as though preparing for what was to come.

An hour later, he slowed Tympmor to a walk and Ansie covered her head as diligently as she could manage. The clothing they had stolen from *Le Jupon Rouge* was much too big for her, but if anyone happened to see them from a distance they would see a man traveling with his son.

When he dismounted to give Tympmor a rest, she grabbed his hand. "You won't leave me?" she asked and the question stung. He had done just that in Kirath.

"Never," he promised and patted her hand.

She seemed to take comfort in his words and sat up straighter in the saddle. Every now and then, her feet swung back and forth, as he walked beside Tympmor, her too big boots brushing his shoulder. When it happened for the second time, he glanced up at her and caught her looking down at him.

Help him, those brown eyes seemed to cut right through him.

Did she know how worried he had been when she climbed that border gate at the palace? Was she aware of how desperately he had clung to her in *Le Jupon Rouge* hoping, praying his plan would work?

She hadn't known he had nearly turned around to kill the Gallian soldiers who had entered the room, knowing full well he would have died trying to save her.

Shaking his head as he walked, he felt his chest tighten. There was something about her which had gotten to him over the past months, something he didn't want to explore quite yet.

"What are you thinking about?" she asked, drawing him from his thoughts.

She had asked the question often enough on their way to Kirath. Before, he had wondered if she asked when she knew his mind was weighed down with too many concerns. He certainly could have used her help as he desperately tried to follow the locoven from Kirath.

747

"Nothing." He shrugged and knew she would see through the lie. Her boot swung by again, always too short to reach the stirrups, it was a wonder she stayed seated at all.

"I think you're thinking something," she said. There was a bit of tension in her voice that told him she was worried again.

"Actually," he said and began digging into one of Tympmor's saddlebags as they walked, "I have something for you."

Her brow furrowed, but when he dropped the little circle of silver into her bandaged palm, she stared down at it blinking.

"I thought you might want something to make answering questions easier," he cleared his throat, "for when we get to Mirtain."

Her mouth hung open as she stared at the ring. He knew it would be too big for her finger, but he could fix it once they reached the southern lands.

"You can use this to tie it around your neck if you would like," he placed a leather string in her palm, "for now."

She stared at both and merely nodded. "When did you—?" Her question lingered.

"In Flocorna," he answered. He didn't need to tell her he'd traded three of the verral claws to pay for it. Too bad the claw he'd given her on a necklace was lost. He had wondered what the guards thought when they found it in the room beneath the royal stables near his mask.

He glanced at the ring she still held in her palm, wondering what she really thought. He didn't tell her he'd almost given it to her when they danced in Initium. He hadn't been able to get her out of his mind, even when he had been angry and left for Flocorna—even then, he'd traded for the ring on a whim, merely thinking she would take pleasure in having it.

"Thank you," she said and patted his hand.

He looked up and winked at her. "Don't mention it."

She smiled then, the one that made the curved freckles around her right eye stand out all the more. It warmed him to see it.

As she fumbled with the string and the ring, Larn suddenly became aware of a sound far off. It was coming from his left. He could already see the river which lined the border between Gallia and Autre Gallia, but the movement he heard was not water.

Moving carefully, he kept his ears tuned to the sounds on the other side of the hill. Something was moving, a force of some kind.

"What is it?" Ansie whispered. She was always so aware of him.

He was no longer worried who saw them, something about the sounds on the other side of the hill were all too familiar and made the pit of his stomach clench in dread.

Swinging into the saddle, he kept Ansie before him and eased Tympmor forward until they crested a small edge of the hill. She gasped, the sight before them revealed a terror far beyond what he had imagined. He covered her mouth as quickly as he could.

There within the valley not far from Bastion Nocta was an army. The full strength and pride of the Nexen.

The snapping and snarling of hundreds upon hundreds of wolves rose into the clear brisk day. Their route would lead them directly to Bastion Nocta and then into Autre Gallia.

Moving faster than before, he grasped Tympmor's reins and urged him into a sprint, murmuring his tribe's language to him.

Ansie rested her hands over his, as he ducked into the wind, Tympmor sprinting across the border and into Autre Gallia. The fight for freedom had only just begun. War was on the horizon.

A wolf howled behind them, raising the hairs on Larn's neck.

The rest soon joined—a pack of demons on the wind calling them to battle.

END OF BOOK I

Pronunciation Guide

CHARACTERS & PEOPLES
Anserietta (ans-air-ee-ettta)
Maereo Tribes (ma-ray-o)
Magetta (ma-hetta)
Pavier (pav-ee-air)
Praelia (pray-lee-ah)
Tympmor (timp-more)
Varne (var-nay)

PLACES
Aurore Wing (ah-roar-ay wing)
Autre Gallia (ah-tray guh-lee-uh)
Brescht (berkt)
Chateau de Plaisance (sha-toe day play-saunce)
Enchante Wing (on-shon-tay wing)
Excelsis Bestia (ex-sell-sis best-ee-ah)
Fantique Couloir (fawn-teek cole-war)
Fort Jontru (fort zhon-troo)
Gallia (guh-lee-uh)
Initium (in-eet-ee-um)
Le Jupon Rouge (le zhoo-pon roo-zh)

PHRASES
anima reflecta (ah-nee-ma reflect-ah)
cheeterah (chee-tear-ah)
Joute Deliverance (zhoot de-liv-er-ance)
lioneth (leon-eth)
maeri (ma-ri)
panthier (pan-teer)
simul ad mortem (see-mul ad mor-tum)
unum ad mortem (un-um ad mor-tum)
vox prima (vawks preem-ah)

Other books by Meaghan Rauscher

To be a mermaid sounds like a dream, but when Lissie Darrow is transformed against her will she is thrown into a world of danger, palace intrigue, and mythical creatures. Upon meeting the mysterious Patrick a bond forms, but it's threatened by destruction as Lissie begins to realize that Patrick's sordid past is closely tied to the merman that haunts her every nightmare. Lissie prepares for battle. A battle for love, and against the dangerous fate looming on the horizon.

 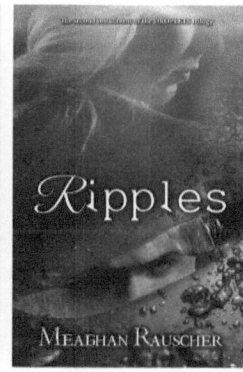 

Amazon reviews from fans and readers like you!

"Blown away and nothing like I expected (in a good way)" –Savannah
"Marvelous story!" –Brandy

"I enjoy mermaid books, but this one got me hooked." –Carmen

"From beginning to end I was drawn into the story. The characters were actually believable even being mermaids/mermen that I have already gone to [Kindle] to get books 2 and 3." –Aminuts

"I bought this book originally for the cover being so pretty. However, Meahgan Rauscher completely sucked me into the story. It was so beautifully written, I felt like I was there with Lissie and Patrick through the story." –Kari

Meaghan Rauscher's debut as an author was the *Droplets* trilogy. With the first book written while in high school, she proceeded to complete her mermaid trilogy throughout college.

Meaghan currently lives in her hometown of Augusta, GA and is beginning to work on the second installment of the *Roar of the Realm* series.

She graduated Magna Cum Laude from the University of Georgia in 2014 with a degree in English Literature.

Instagram: @MeaghanRauscher
Facebook: Meaghan Rauscher, Author

www.ingramcontent.com/pod-product-compliance
Lightning Source LLC
Chambersburg PA
CBHW030836030726
47495CB00005B/1254